Before writing full-time, Michael Robotham was an investigative journalist in Britain, Australia and the US. He is the pseudonymous author of ten best-selling non-fiction titles, involving prominent figures in the military, the arts, sport and science. He lives in Sydney with his wife and daughters.

MICHAEL ROBOTHAM OMNIBUS

The Suspect
The Night Ferry

sphere

SPHERE

This omnibus edition first published in Great Britain in 2010 by Sphere

A CIP catalogue record for this book
is available from the British Library.

ISBN 978-0-7515-4426-8

Printed and bound in Great Britain by
Clays Ltd, St Ives plc

Sphere
An imprint of
Little, Brown Book Group
100 Victoria Embankment
London EC4Y 0DY

An Hachette UK Company
www.hachette.co.uk

www.littlebrown.co.uk

THE SUSPECT

To the four women in my life:
Vivien, Alexandra, Charlotte and Isabella

Acknowledgements

For his counsel, wisdom and sanity I thank Mark Lucas and all the team at LAW. For her belief ahead of all others, I thank Ursula Mackenzie and those who took the gamble with her.

For their hospitality and friendship I thank Elspeth Rees, Jonathan Margolis and Martyn Forrester – three of many friends and family who have answered my questions, listened to my stories and shared the journey.

Finally, for her love and support I thank Vivien who had to live with all my characters and my sleepless nights. A lesser woman would have slept in the guest room.

Book One

'I did that,' says my memory.
'I could not have done that,' says my pride,
and remains inexorable.
Eventually – the memory yields.

Friedrich Nietzsche
Beyond Good and Evil

1

From the pitched slate roof of the Royal Marsden Hospital, if you look between the chimney pots and TV aerials, you see more chimney pots and TV aerials. It's like that scene from *Mary Poppins* where all the chimneysweeps dance across the rooftops twirling their brooms.

From up here I can just see the dome of the Royal Albert Hall. On a clear day I could probably see all the way to Hampstead Heath, although I doubt if the air in London ever gets that clear.

'This is some view,' I say, glancing to my right at a teenager crouched about ten feet away. His name is Malcolm and he's seventeen today. Tall and thin, with dark eyes that tremble when he looks at me, he has skin as white as polished paper. He is wearing pyjamas and a woollen hat to cover his baldness. Chemotherapy is a cruel hairdresser.

The temperature is 3°C, but the wind chill has chased it below zero. Already my fingers are numb and I can barely feel my toes through my shoes and socks. Malcolm's feet are bare.

I won't reach him if he jumps or falls. Even if I stretch out and lean along the gutter, I will still be six feet short of catching him. He realises that. He's worked out the angles. According to his oncologist, Malcolm has an exceptional IQ. He plays the violin and speaks five languages – none of which he'll speak to me.

For the last hour I've been asking him questions and telling him stories. I know he can hear me, but my voice is just background noise. He's concentrating on his own internal dialogue, debating whether he should live or die. I want to join that debate, but first I need an invitation.

The National Health Service has a whole raft of guidelines for dealing with hostage situations and threatened suicides. A critical incident team has been pulled together, including senior members of staff, police and a psychologist – me. The first priority has been to learn everything we can about Malcolm that might help us identify what has driven him to this. Doctors, nurses and patients are being interviewed, along with his friends and family.

The primary negotiator is at the apex of the operational triangle. Everything filters down to me. That's why I'm out here, freezing my extremities off, while they're inside drinking coffee, interviewing staff and studying flip charts.

What do I know about Malcolm? He has a primary brain tumour in the right posterior temporal region, dangerously close to his brain stem. The tumour has left him partially paralysed down his left side and unable to hear

4

from one ear. He is two weeks into a second course of chemotherapy.

He had a visit from his parents this morning. The oncologist had good news. Malcolm's tumour appeared to be shrinking. An hour later Malcolm wrote a two-word note that said, 'I'm sorry'. He left his room and managed to crawl on to the roof through a dormer window on the fourth floor. Someone must have left the window unlocked, or he found a way of opening it.

There you have it – the sum total of my knowledge about a teenager who has a lot more to offer than most kids his age. I don't know if he has a girlfriend, or a favourite football team, or a celluloid hero. I know more about his disease than I do about him. That's why I'm struggling.

My safety harness is uncomfortable under my sweater. It looks like one of those contraptions that parents strap on to toddlers to stop them running off. In this case it's supposed to save me if I fall, as long as someone has remembered to fix the other end. It might sound ridiculous, but that's the sort of detail that sometimes gets forgotten in a crisis. Perhaps I should shuffle back towards the window and ask someone to check. Would that be unprofessional? Yes. Sensible? Again yes.

The rooftop is speckled with pigeon droppings and the slate tiles are covered in lichen and moss. The patterns look like fossilised plants pressed into the stone, but the effect is slick and treacherous.

'This probably makes no difference, Malcolm, but I think I know a little about how you're feeling,' I say, trying once more to reach him. 'I have a disease too. I'm not saying that it's cancer. It's not. And trying to make comparisons is like mixing apples with oranges, but we're still talking about fruit, right?'

The receiver in my right ear begins to crackle. 'What in Christ's name are you doing?' says a voice. 'Stop talking about fruit salad and get him inside!'

I take the earpiece out and let it dangle on my shoulder. 'You know how people always say, "It'll be fine. Everything is going to be OK"? They say that because they can't think of anything else. I don't know what to say either, Malcolm. I don't even know what questions to ask.

'Most people don't know how to handle someone else's disease. Unfortunately, there's no book of etiquette or list of do's and don't's. You either get the watery-eyed, I-can't-bear-it-I'm-going-to-cry look or forced jokiness and buck-up speeches. The other option is complete denial.'

Malcolm hasn't responded. He's staring across the rooftops as if looking out of a tiny window high up in the grey sky. His pyjamas are thin and white with blue stitching around the cuffs and collar.

Between my knees I can see three fire engines, two ambulances and half a dozen police cars. One of the fire engines has an extension ladder on a turntable. I haven't taken much notice of it until now, but I see it slowly turning and begin to slide upwards. Why would they be doing that? At the same moment, Malcolm braces his back against the sloping roof and lifts himself. He squats on the edge, with his toes hanging over the gutter, like a bird perched on a branch.

I can hear someone screaming and then I realise that it's me. I'm yelling the place down. I'm wildly gesticulating

6

for them to get the ladder away. I look like the suicidal jumper and Malcolm looks totally calm.

I fumble for the earpiece and hear pandemonium inside. The critical incident team is shouting at the chief fire officer, who is shouting at his second-in-command, who is shouting at someone else.

'Don't do it, Malcolm! Wait!' I sound desperate. 'Look at the ladder. It's going down. See? It's going down.' Blood is pounding in my ears. He stays perched on the edge, curling and uncurling his toes. In profile I can see his long dark lashes blinking slowly. His heart is beating like a bird's within his narrow chest.

'You see that fireman down there with the red helmet?' I say, trying to break into his thoughts. 'The one with all the brass buttons on his shoulders. What do you think my chances are of gobbing on his helmet from here?'

For the briefest of moments, Malcolm glances down. It's the first time he's acknowledged anything I've said or done. The door has opened a chink.

'Some people like to spit watermelon seeds or cherry pips. In Africa they spit dung, which is pretty gross. I read somewhere that the world record for spitting Kudu dung is about thirty feet. I think Kudu is a kind of antelope but don't quote me on that. I prefer good old-fashioned saliva and it's not about distance; it's about accuracy.'

He's looking at me now. With a snap of my head I send a foaming white ball arcing downwards. It gets picked up by the breeze and drifts to the right, hitting the windscreen of a police car. In silence I contemplate the shot, trying to work out where I went wrong.

'You didn't allow for the wind,' Malcolm says.

I nod sagely, barely acknowledging him, but inside I have a warm glow in a part of me that isn't yet frozen. 'You're right. These buildings create a bit of a wind tunnel.'

'You're making excuses.'

'I haven't seen you try.'

He looks down, considering this. He's hugging his knees as if trying to stay warm. It's a good sign.

A moment later a globule of spit curves outwards and falls. Together we watch it descend, almost willing it to stay on course. It hits a TV reporter squarely between the eyes and Malcolm and I groan in harmony.

My next shot lands harmlessly on the front steps. Malcolm asks if he can change the target. He wants to hit the TV reporter again.

'Shame we don't have any water bombs,' he says, resting his chin on one knee.

'If you could drop a water bomb on anyone in the world, who would it be?'

'My parents.'

'Why?'

'I don't want to have chemo again. I've had enough.' He doesn't elaborate. It isn't necessary. There aren't many treatments with worse side effects than chemotherapy. The vomiting, nausea, constipation, anaemia and overwhelming fatigue can be intolerable.

'What does your oncologist say?'

'He says the tumour is shrinking.'

'That's good.'

He laughs wryly. 'They said that last time. The truth is they're just chasing cancer all around my body. It doesn't go away. It just finds somewhere else to hide. They never talk about a cure; they talk about remission. Sometimes they don't talk to me at all. They just whisper to my parents.'

He bites his bottom lip and a carmine mark appears where the blood rushes to the indentation.

'Mum and Dad think I'm scared of dying, but I'm not scared. You should see some of the kids in this place. At least I've had a life. Another fifty years would be nice but, like I said, I'm not scared.'

'How many more chemo sessions?'

'Six. Then we wait and see. I don't mind losing my hair. A lot of footballers shave their hair off. Look at David Beckham; he's a tosser, but he's a wicked player. Having no eyebrows is a bit of a blow.'

'I hear Beckham gets his plucked.'

'By Posh?'

'Yeah.'

It almost raises a smile. In the silence I can hear Malcolm's teeth chattering.

'If the chemo doesn't work my parents are going to tell the doctors to keep trying. They'll never let me go.'

'You're old enough to make your own decisions.'

'Try telling *them* that.'

'I will if you want me to.'

He shakes his head and I see the tears starting to form. He tries to stop them, but they squeeze out from under his long lashes in fat drops that he wipes away with his forearm.

'Is there someone you can talk to?'

'I like one of the nurses. She's been really nice to me.'

'Is she your girlfriend?'

He blushes. The paleness of his skin makes it look as though his head is filling with blood.

'Why don't you come inside and we'll talk some more? I can't raise any spit unless I get something to drink.'

He doesn't answer, but I see his shoulders sag. He's listening to that internal dialogue again.

'I have a daughter called Charlie who is eight years old,' I say, trying to hold him. 'I remember when she was about four, we were in the park and I was pushing her on a swing. She said to me, "Daddy, do you know that if you close your eyes really tightly, so you see white stars, when you open them again it's a brand new world". It's a nice thought, isn't it?'

'But it's not true.'

'It can be.'

'Only if you pretend.'

'Why not? What's stopping you? People think it's easy to be cynical and pessimistic, but it's incredibly hard work. It's much easier to be hopeful.'

'I have an inoperable brain tumour,' he says incredulously.

'Yes, I know.'

I wonder if my words sound as hollow to Malcolm as they do to me. I used to believe all this stuff. A lot can change in ten days.

Malcolm interrupts me. 'Are you a doctor?'

'A psychologist.'

'Tell me again why should I come down?'

'Because it's cold and it's dangerous and I've seen what people look like when they fall from buildings. Come inside. Let's get warm.'

He glances below at the carnival of ambulances, fire engines, police cars and media vans. 'I won the spitting contest.'

'Yes, you did.'

'You'll talk to Mum and Dad?'

'Absolutely.'

He tries to stand, but his legs are cold and stiff. The paralysis down his left side makes his arm next to useless. He needs two arms to get up.

'Just stay there. I'll get them to send up the ladder.'

'No!' he says urgently. I see the look on his face. He doesn't want to be brought down in the blaze of TV lights, with reporters asking questions.

'OK. I'll come to you.' I'm amazed at how brave that sounds. I start to slide sideways in a bum shuffle – too frightened to stand. I haven't forgotten about the safety harness, but I'm still convinced that nobody has bothered to tie it off.

As I edge along the gutter, my head fills with images of what could go wrong. If this were a Hollywood movie Malcolm will slip at the last moment and I'll dive and pluck him out of mid-air. Either that or I'll fall and he'll rescue me.

On the other hand – because this is real life – we might both perish, or Malcolm could live and I'll be the plucky rescuer who plunges to his death.

Although he hasn't moved, I can see a new emotion in Malcolm's eyes. A few minutes ago he was ready to step off the roof without a moment's hesitation. Now he wants to live and the void beneath his feet has become an abyss.

The American philosopher William James (a closet phobic) wrote an article in 1884 pondering the nature of fear. He used an example of a person encountering a bear. Does he run because he feels afraid, or does he feel afraid after he has already started running? In other words, does

11

a person have time to think something is frightening, or does the reaction precede the thought?

Ever since then scientists and psychologists have been locked in a kind of chicken-and-egg debate. What comes first – the conscious awareness of fear or the pounding heart and surging adrenalin that motivates us to fight or flee?

I know the answer now, but I'm so frightened I've forgotten the question.

I'm only a few feet away from Malcolm. His cheeks are tinged with blue and he's stopped shivering. Pressing my back against the wall, I push one leg beneath me and lever my body upwards until I'm standing.

Malcolm looks at my outstretched hand for a moment and then reaches slowly towards me. I grab him by the wrist and pull him upwards until my arm slips around his thin waist. His skin feels like ice.

The front of the safety harness unclasps and I can lengthen the straps. I pass them around his waist and back through the buckle, until the two of us are tethered together. His woollen hat feels rough against my cheek.

'What do you want me to do?' he asks in a croaky voice.

'You can pray the other end of this is tied on to something.'

2

I was probably safer on the roof of the Marsden than at home with Julianne. I can't remember exactly what she called me, but I seem to recall her using words like irresponsible, negligent, careless, immature and unfit to be a parent. This was after she hit me with a copy of *Marie Claire* and made me promise never to do anything so stupid again.

Charlie, on the other hand, won't leave me alone. She keeps bouncing on the bed in her pyjamas, asking me questions about how high up it was, whether I was scared and did the firemen have a big net ready to catch me?

'At last I have something exciting to tell for news,' she says, punching me on the arm. I'm glad Julianne doesn't hear her.

Each morning when I drag myself out of bed I go through a little ritual. When I lean down to tie my shoes I get a good idea of what sort of a day I'm going to have. If it's early in the week and I'm rested, I will have just a little trouble getting the fingers of my left hand to co-operate. Buttons will find buttonholes, belts will find belt-loops and I can even tie a Windsor knot. On my bad days, such as this one, it is a different story. The man I see in the mirror will need two hands to shave and will arrive at the breakfast table with bits of toilet paper stuck to his neck and chin. On these mornings Julianne will say to me, 'You have a brand new electric shaver in the bathroom.'

'I don't like electric shavers.'

'Why not?'

'Because I like lather.'

'What is there to *like* about lather?'

'It's a lovely sounding word, don't you think? It's quite sexy – *lather*. It's decadent.'

She's giggling now, but trying to look annoyed.

'People *lather* their bodies with soap; they *lather* their bodies with shower gel. I think we should *lather* our scones with jam and cream. And we could *lather* on suntan lotion in the summer . . . if we ever have one.'

'You are silly, Daddy,' says Charlie, looking up from her cereal.

'Thank you, my turtle dove.'

'A comic genius,' says Julianne as she picks toilet paper from my face.

Sitting down at the table, I put a spoonful of sugar in my coffee and begin to stir. Julianne is watching me. The spoon stalls in my cup. I concentrate and tell my left hand to start moving, but no amount of willpower is going to budge it. Smoothly I switch the spoon to my right hand.

'When are you seeing Jock?' she asks.

'On Friday.' *Please don't ask me anything else.*

'Is he going to have the test results?'

'He'll tell me what we already know.'

'But I thought—'

'He didn't say!' I hate the sharpness in my voice.

Julianne doesn't even blink. 'I've made you mad. I like you better silly.'

'I am silly. Everyone knows that.'

I see right through her. She thinks I'm doing the macho thing of hiding my feelings or trying to be relentlessly positive, while really I'm falling apart. My mother is the same – she's become a bloody armchair psychologist. Why don't they leave it to the experts to get it wrong?

Julianne has turned her back. She's breaking up stale bread to leave outside for the birds. Compassion is her hobby.

Dressed in a grey jogging suit, trainers and a baseball cap over her short-cropped dark hair, she looks twenty-seven, not thirty-seven. Instead of growing old gracefully together, she's discovered the secret of eternal youth whereas I need two tries to get off the couch. Monday is yoga, Tuesday is Pilates, Thursday and Saturday are circuit training. In between times she runs the house, raises a child, teaches Spanish lessons and still finds time to try to save the world. She even made childbirth look easy, although I would never tell her that unless I developed a death wish.

We have been married for sixteen years and when people ask me why I became a psychologist, I say, 'Because of Julianne. I wanted to *know* what she was really thinking.'

It didn't work. I still have no idea.

* * *

Sunday morning is normally *my* time. I bury myself under the combined weight of four newspapers and drink coffee until my tongue feels furry. After what happened yesterday I'm going to avoid the headlines, although Charlie is insisting we cut them out and make a scrapbook. I guess it's pretty cool being 'cool' for once. Up until yesterday she's regarded my job as more boring than cricket.

Charlie's rugged up in jeans, skivvy and a ski jacket because I've promised she can come with me today. After gulping down her breakfast, she watches me impatiently – convinced that I'm drinking my coffee too slowly.

When it's time to load up the car, we carry the cardboard boxes from the garden shed and put them next to my old Metro. Julianne is sitting on the front steps with a cup of coffee resting on her knees. 'You're both mad, you know that?'

'Probably.'

'And you'll get arrested.'

'And that's going to be your fault.'

'Why is it my fault?'

'Because you won't come with us. We need a getaway driver.'

Charlie pipes up. 'C'mon, Mum. Dad said you used to.'

'That's when I was young and foolish and I wasn't on the committee at your school.'

'Do you realise, Charlie, that on my second date with your mother she was arrested for scaling a flag-pole and taking down the South African flag.'

Julianne scowls. 'Don't tell her that!'

'Did you really get arrested?'

'I was cautioned. It's not the same thing.'

16

There are four boxes on the roof racks, two in the boot and two on the back seat. Fine beads of sweat, like polished glass, are decorating Charlie's top lip. She slips off her ski jacket and tucks it between the seats.

I turn back to Julianne. 'Are you sure you won't come? I know you want to.'

'Who's going to post bail for us?'

'Your mother will do that.'

Her eyes narrow, but she puts her coffee cup inside the door. 'I'm doing this under protest.'

'Duly noted.'

She holds out her hand for the car keys. 'And I'm driving.'

She grabs a jacket from the coat rack in the hallway and pulls the door shut. Charlie squeezes herself between the boxes on the back seat and leans forward excitedly. 'Tell me the story again,' she says as we swing into light traffic along Prince Albert Road, alongside Regent's Park. 'And don't leave anything out just because Mum's here.'

I can't tell her the whole story. I'm not even sure of all the details myself. At the heart of it is my great-aunt Gracie – the *real* reason I became a psychologist. She was my maternal grandmother's youngest sister and she died at the age of eighty, having not set foot outside her house in nearly sixty years.

She lived about a mile from where I grew up in West London, in a grand old detached Victorian house with mini-turrets on the roof, metal balconies and a coal cellar underneath. The front door had two rectangular panes of leadlight. I would press my nose against them and see a dozen fractured images of Aunt Gracie bustling down the

17

hallway to answer my knock. She would open the door just wide enough to let me slip inside and then close it again quickly.

Tall and almost skeletal, with clear blue eyes and fair hair gone streaky white, she always wore a long black velvet dress, with a string of pearls that seemed to glow against the black material.

'Finnegan, come! COME! Joseph's here!'

Finnegan was a Jack Russell without a bark. His voice box had been crushed in a fight with a neighbourhood Alsatian. Instead of barking, he huffed and puffed as though auditioning to play the big bad wolf in a pantomime.

Gracie talked to Finnegan as though he were a person. She read him stories from the local paper, or asked him questions about local issues. She would nod her agreement whenever he responded with a huff, or a puff, or a fart. Finnegan even had his own chair at the table and Gracie would slip him morsels of cake and admonish herself in the same breath for 'feeding an animal from the hand'.

When Gracie poured the tea she half filled my cup with milk because I was too young to have full-strength brew. My feet could barely touch the floor when I sat on the dining chairs. If I sat back, my legs stuck straight out underneath the white lace tablecloth.

Years later, when my feet could reach the floor and I had to bend down to kiss Gracie on the cheek, she continued to add half a cup of milk to my tea. Maybe she didn't want me to grow up.

If I'd come straight from school, she made me sit next to her on the chaise longue, clutching my hand in her own. She wanted to know everything about my day. What I

18

learned in class. What games I played. What fillings I had in my sandwiches. She soaked up the details as though picturing every footstep.

Gracie was a classic agoraphobic – terrified of open space. She once tried to explain it to me, having grown sick of fobbing off my questions.

'Have you ever been afraid of the dark?' she asked.

'Yes.'

'What did you fear would happen if the lights went out?'

'That a monster would get me.'

'Did you ever see this monster?'

'No. Mum says that monsters don't exist.'

'She's right. They don't. So where did your monster come from?'

'Up here.' I tapped my head.

'Exactly. I have a monster too. I know he's not supposed to exist, but he won't go away.'

'What does your monster look like?'

'He is ten feet tall and he carries a sword. If I try to leave the house he's going to cut my head off.'

'Are you making that up?'

She laughed and tried to tickle me, but I pushed her hands away. I wanted an honest answer.

Tiring of this conversation, she screwed shut her eyes and tucked loose strands of white hair into her tightly wrapped bun. 'Have you ever watched one of those horror films where the hero is trying to get away and the car won't start? He keeps turning the key and pumping the accelerator, but the engine just coughs and dies. And you can see the villain coming. He's got a gun or a knife. And you keep saying to yourself, "Get out of there! Get out! He's coming!".'

I nod, wide-eyed. 'Well, you take that fear,' she said, 'and you multiply it by a hundred and then you'll know how I feel when I think about going outside.'

She stood and walked out of the room. The discussion had ended. I never raised the subject again. I didn't want to make her sad.

I don't know how she lived. Cheques would arrive periodically from a law firm, but Gracie would place them on the mantelpiece, where she could stare at them each day until they expired. I guess they were part of her inheritance, but she wanted nothing to do with her family's money. I didn't know the reason . . . not then.

She worked as a seamstress – making wedding gowns and bridesmaids' dresses. I would often find the front room draped in silk and organza, with a bride-to-be standing on a stool and Gracie with her mouth full of pins. It was not a place for young boys – not unless they fancied modelling a dress.

The rooms upstairs were full of what Gracie called her 'collectibles'. By this she meant books, fashion magazines, reels of cloth, cotton bobbins, hatboxes, bags of wool, photograph albums, soft toys and a treasure trove of unexplored boxes and trunks.

Most of these 'collectibles' had been recycled or purchased by mail order. The catalogues were always open on the coffee table and each day the mailman brought something new.

Not surprisingly, Gracie's view of the world was rather limited. The TV news and current affairs programmes seemed to magnify conflict and pain. She saw people fighting, wilderness vanishing, bombs falling and countries starving. While these weren't the reasons she ran away from the world, they were certainly no incentive to go back.

'It scares me just seeing how small you are,' she told me. 'It's not a good time to be a child.' She glanced out the bay window and shuddered as though able to see a terrible fate awaiting me. I only saw an overgrown and unkempt garden with white butterflies flitting between the gnarled branches of the apple trees.

'Don't you ever want to go outside?' I asked her. 'Don't you want to look up at the stars or walk along a riverbank or admire the gardens?'

'I stopped thinking about it a long while ago.'

'What do you miss most?'

'Nothing.'

'There must be something.'

She thought for a moment. 'I used to love the autumn, just as the leaves turn and begin to fall. We used to go to Kew Gardens and I'd run along the thoroughfares, kicking up the leaves and trying to catch them. The curled leaves would slip from side to side, like miniature boats riding the air until they settled into my hands.'

'I could blindfold you,' I suggested.

'No.'

'What if you put a box over your head? You could pretend you were inside.'

'I don't think so.'

'I could wait until you were asleep and push your bed outside?'

'Down the stairs?'

'Mmmm. Bit tricky.'

She put her arm around my shoulders. 'Don't you worry about me. I'm quite happy here.'

From then on we had a sort of running joke. I kept suggesting new ways to get her outside and new pastimes like hang-gliding and wing-walking. Gracie would react in mock horror and tell me I was the *real* lunatic.

'So what about her birthday?' says Charlie impatiently. We're driving through St John's Wood, just passing Lord's cricket ground. The traffic lights gleam brightly against the dullness of the outer walls.

'I thought you wanted the whole story?'

'Yes, but I'm not getting any younger.'

Julianne gets a fit of the giggles. 'She gets the sarcasm from you, you know.'

'OK,' I sigh. 'I'll tell you about Gracie's birthday. She never admitted her age, but I knew she was going to be seventy-five because I found some dates by looking through her photo albums.'

'You said she was beautiful,' says Charlie.

'Yes. It's not easy to tell from old photographs because nobody ever smiled and the women looked plain scary. But Gracie was different. She had twinkling eyes and always looked as though she was about to giggle. And she used to cinch her belt a little tighter and stand so the light shone through her petticoats.'

'She was a flirt,' says Julianne.

'What's a flirt?' asks Charlie.

'Never mind.'

Charlie frowns and hugs her knees, resting her chin on the patched knees of her jeans.

'It was pretty difficult to plan a surprise for Gracie because, of course, she never left the house,' I explain. 'I had to do everything when she was asleep—'

'How old were you?'

'Sixteen. I was still at Charterhouse.'

Charlie nods and begins pinning her hair up high on her head. She looks exactly like Julianne when she does that.

'Gracie didn't use her garage. She had no need of a car. It had big wooden doors that opened outwards, as well as an internal doorway into the laundry. First I cleaned the place up, clearing away the junk and washing down the walls.'

'You must have been very quiet.'

'I was.'

'And you put up fairy lights?'

'Hundreds of them. They looked like twinkling stars.'

'And then you got the big sack.'

'That's right. It took me four days. I had to carry the hessian sack over my shoulder and ride my bike. People must have thought I was a street sweeper or a park ranger.'

'They probably thought you were crazy.'

'Absolutely.'

'Just like we're crazy?'

'Yep.' I sneak a glance at Julianne, who isn't biting.

'What happened next?' asks Charlie.

'Well, on the morning of her birthday, Gracie came downstairs and I made her close her eyes. She held my arm and I walked her through the kitchen, into the laundry and then the garage. As she opened the door an avalanche of leaves came tumbling out around her waist. "Happy Birthday," I said. You should have seen her face. She looked at the leaves and then back at me. For a moment I thought she was angry, but then she gave me this beautiful smile.'

'I know what happened next,' says Charlie.

'Yes. I've told you before.'

'She ran into all those leaves.'

'Yep. We both did. We threw them in the air and kicked up our knees. We had leaf fights and made leaf mountains. And eventually, we were both so exhausted we collapsed on to a bed of leaves and stared up at the stars.'

'But they weren't really stars, were they?'

'No, but we could pretend.'

The entrance to Kensal Green Cemetery is in Harrow Road and is easy to miss. Julianne follows the narrow road and parks in a circle of trees as far from the caretaker's cottage as possible. Glancing out the windscreen, I see neat rows of gravestones intersected by paths and beds of flowers.

'Is this against the law?' whispers Charlie.

'Yes,' says Julianne.

'Not exactly,' I counter as I start unloading boxes and handing them to Charlie.

'I can take two,' she announces.

'OK, I'll take three and we'll come back for the rest. Unless Mum wants to—'

'I'm fine just here.' She hasn't moved from behind the wheel.

We head off, keeping close to the trees at first. Long fingers of lawn stretch between the graves. I walk cautiously, not wanting to tread on any flowers or knock my shins on one of the smaller headstones. The sounds of Harrow Road disappear and are replaced by snatches of birdsong and the periodic roar of intercity express trains.

'Do you know where we're going?' asks Charlie from behind me, puffing slightly.

'It's over towards the canal. Do you want a rest?'

'I'm OK.' Then her voice takes on a doubtful tone. 'Dad?'

'Yes?'

'You know how you said that Gracie loved kicking up leaves?'

'Yes.'

'Because she's dead, she can't really kick these up, can she?'

'No.'

'I mean, she can't come back to life. Dead people don't do that, do they? Because I've seen scary cartoons about zombies and mummies that come back from the dead, but that doesn't really happen, does it?'

'No.'

'And Gracie is in heaven now, isn't she? That's where she's gone.'

'Yes.'

'So what are we doing with all these leaves?'

It's at times like these I normally direct Charlie to Julianne. She sends her straight back to me, saying, 'Your father is a psychologist. He knows these things.'

Charlie is waiting.

'What we're doing is sort of symbolic,' I say.

'What does that mean?'

'Have you ever heard people say, "It's the thought that counts"?'

'You always say that when somebody gives me a present that I don't like. You say I should be grateful, even if the present sucks.'

'That's not quite what I mean.' I try a new approach. 'Aunt Gracie can't really kick up these leaves. But wherever she is, if she's watching us now I think she'll be laughing. And she'll really appreciate what we're doing. That's what counts.'

'She'll be kicking up leaves in heaven?' adds Charlie.

'Absolutely.'

'Do you think she'll be outside or will heaven have an inside place?'

'I don't know.'

I set my boxes on the ground and unload Charlie's arms. Gracie's headstone is a simple square of granite. Someone has left a muddy shovel leaning against the brass plaque. I have visions of gravediggers taking a tea break, except nowadays they use machines instead of muscle. I toss the shovel to one side and Charlie gives the inscription a polish with the sleeve of her ski jacket. I creep up behind her and dump a box full of leaves on top of her head.

'Hey! That's not fair!' Charlie scoops a big handful and stuffs them up the back of my jumper. Soon there are leaves tumbling all over the place. Gracie's headstone disappears completely under our autumnal offering.

Behind me somebody loudly clears his throat and I hear Charlie give a little yelp of surprise.

The caretaker is silhouetted against the pale sky, with his hands on his hips and legs akimbo. He's wearing a pea-green jacket and a pair of muddy Wellingtons that appear to be too big for his feet.

'Do you mind explaining what you're doing?' he asks in a monotone. He steps closer. His face is flat and round with a wide forehead and no hair. It brings to mind Thomas the Tank Engine.

'It's a long story,' I say feebly.

'You're desecrating a grave.'

I laugh at how ridiculous he sounds. 'I hardly think so.'

'You think this is funny? This is vandalism. This is a crime. This is littering—'

'Fallen leaves aren't technically litter.'

'Don't play games with me,' he stutters.

Charlie decides to intervene. With breathless eloquence, she explains, 'It's Gracie's birthday, but we can't give her a party because she's dead. She doesn't like going outside. We brought her some leaves. She likes kicking up leaves. Don't worry; she's not a zombie or a mummy. She's not going to come back from the dead. She's in heaven. Do you think there are trees in heaven?'

The caretaker looks at her with utter dismay and takes a few moments to realise that her last question is directed at him. Rendered almost speechless, he makes several unsuccessful attempts to speak before his voice deserts him. Having been totally disarmed, he crouches to be at her eye-level.

'What is your name, Missy?'

'Charlie Louise O'Loughlin. What's yours?'

'Mr Gravesend.'

'That's pretty funny.'

'I guess so.' He smiles.

He looks at me with none of the same warmth. 'Do you know how many years I've been trying to catch the bugger who spreads leaves all over this grave?'

'Around fifteen?' I suggest.

'I was going to say thirteen, but I'll take your word for it. You see, I worked out when you come. I made a note of the date. I nearly caught you two years ago but you must have come in a different car.'

'My wife's.'

'And then last year it was my day off – a Saturday. I told young Whitey to watch out for you but he thinks I'm fixating. He says I shouldn't get so worked up over a pile of leaves.'

He nudges the offending mound with the toe of his boot. 'But I take my job very seriously. People come here and try to do all sorts of things, like planting oak trees on graves or leaving kids' toys behind. If we let 'em do what they like, where will it end?'

'It must be a hard job,' I say.

'Too bleedin' right!' He glances at Charlie. 'Pardon me language, Missy.'

She giggles.

Over his right shoulder, on the far side of the canal, I notice flashing blue police lights as two cars pull up to join another already parked on the towpath. The lights reflect off the dark water and strobe against the trunks of winter trees that stand like sentries above the gravestones.

Several policemen are staring into a ditch beside the canal. They look frozen in place until one of them begins sealing off the area, wrapping blue and white police tape around the trees and fence posts.

Mr Gravesend has fallen silent, unsure of what to do next. His planning had involved catching me, but didn't extend any further than that. Moreover, he hadn't expected Charlie to be here.

I reach into the pocket of my overcoat and produce a Thermos. In my other pocket there are two metal mugs.

'We were just about to have a hot chocolate. Would you like to join us?'

'You can use my cup,' says Charlie. 'I'll share.'

He considers this, wondering if the offer can be construed as a bribe. 'So it's come to this,' he says in a clear, soft voice. 'Either I have you arrested or I have a hot chocolate.'

'Mum said we'd get arrested,' pipes Charlie. 'She said we were mad.'

'You should have listened to your mum.'

I hand the caretaker a mug and give the other to Charlie.

'Happy birthday, Aunt Gracie,' she says. Mr Gravesend mumbles an appropriate-sounding response, still stunned by the speed of his capitulation.

At that moment I notice two boxes approaching, swaying on black leggings and sneakers.

'That's my mum. She's our look-out,' observes Charlie.

'Not her strong suit,' Mr Gravesend replies.

'No.'

Julianne drops the boxes and lets out a startled squeak, not unlike Charlie's reaction.

'Don't worry, Mum, you're not going to be arrested again.'

The caretaker raises his eyebrows and Julianne smiles feebly. Hot chocolate is shared around and we make small talk. Mr Gravesend gives us a commentary on the writers, painters and statesmen buried in the cemetery. He makes them sound like personal friends, although most have been dead a century.

Charlie is kicking through the leaves until she suddenly goes still. She gazes down the slope towards the canal. Arc lights have been turned on and a white marquee is being set up beside the water. A flashgun fires time after time.

'What's happening?' she asks, wanting to go down and see. Julianne gently reaches out and pulls her close, draping her arms around her shoulders.

Charlie looks at me and then at the caretaker. 'What are they doing?'

Nobody answers. Instead we watch in silence, weighed down by an emotion that goes beyond sorrow. The air has grown colder. It smells of dampness and decay. The shuddering screech of steel in the distant freight yard sounds like a cry of pain.

There is a boat on the canal. Men in yellow fluorescent vests peer over the sides, shining torches into the water. Others walk in a slow line along the banks with their heads down, searching inch by inch. Occasionally one of them stops and bends down. The others wait rather than break the line.

'Have they lost something?' asks Charlie.

'Shush,' I whisper.

Julianne's face is bleak and raw. She looks at me. It's time to leave.

At that moment a coroner's van pulls up next to the marquee. The back doors open and two men in boiler suits pull out a stretcher on a collapsible trolley.

Over my right shoulder a police car appears through the cemetery gates, with flashing lights but no siren. A second car follows.

Mr Gravesend is already walking back towards the car park and the caretaker's cottage.

'Come on, we better go,' I say, tipping out the cold dregs

of the chocolate. Charlie still doesn't understand but realises that it's time to be quiet.

I open the car door and she slips inside, escaping the cold. Across the bonnet, eighty yards away, the caretaker is in conversation with the police. Arms are pointed towards the canal. A notebook is produced. Details are taken.

Julianne is in the passenger seat. She wants me to drive. My left arm is trembling. I grip the gear lever to make it stop. As we pass the police cars, one of the detectives glances up. He is middle-aged with pockmarked cheeks and a punch-worn nose. He's wearing a crumpled grey overcoat and a cynical expression, as though he's done this before and it never gets any easier.

Our eyes meet and he looks straight through me. There's no light, no story, no smile in his eyes. He arches an eyebrow and cocks his head to one side. By then I'm gone, still gripping the gearshift and struggling to find second gear.

As we reach the entrance, Charlie peers through the back window and asks if we're coming back next year.

3

I walk to work every weekday morning across Regent's Park. At this time of year, when the temperature drops, I wear non-slip shoes, a woollen scarf and a permanent frown. Forget about global warming. As I get older the world gets colder. That's a fact.

The sun is like a pale yellow ball floating in the greyness and joggers slip past me with heads down and their trainers leaving patterns on the wet asphalt. The gardeners are supposed to be planting bulbs for the spring, but their wheelbarrows are filling with water. I can see them smoking cigarettes and playing cards in the toolshed.

As I cross Primrose Hill Bridge, I peer over the side at the canal. A lone narrow boat is moored against the towpath and mist curls from the water like wisps of smoke.

What were the police looking for? Who did they find?

I watched the TV news last night and listened to the

radio this morning. Nothing. I know it's just morbid curiosity, yet a part of me feels as though I've been a witness – if not to the crime then the aftermath. It's like when you watch those *Crimewatch* shows and the police ask for people to come forward if they have any information. It's always someone else. It's never someone we know.

A soft rain slips down and clings to my jacket as I start walking again. The Post Office Tower is etched against the darkening sky. It is one of those landmarks that allow people to navigate a city. Streets will disappear into dead ends or twist and turn without reason, but the tower rises above the eccentricities of urban planning.

I like this view of London. It still looks quite majestic. It's only when you get close up you see the decay. But then again, I guess you could say the same about me.

My office is in a pyramid of white boxes on Great Portland Street designed by an architect who drew inspiration from his childhood. From ground level it doesn't look finished and I'm always half expecting a crane to turn up and hoist a few more boxes into the gaps.

As I walk up the front steps I hear a car horn and turn. A bright red Ferrari pulls on to the pavement. The driver, Dr Fenwick Spindler, raises a gloved hand to wave. Fenwick looks like a lawyer but he runs the psychopharmacology unit at London University Hospital. He also has a private practice with a consulting room next to mine.

'Good morning, old boy,' he shouts, leaving the car in the middle of the pavement so that people have to step around it on to the road.

'Aren't you worried about the parking police?'

'Got one of these,' he says, pointing to the doctor's sticker on the windscreen. 'Perfect for medical emergencies.'

Joining me on the steps, he pushes open the glass door. 'Saw you on the TV the other night. Jolly good show. Wouldn't have caught me up there.'

'I'm sure you would have—'

'Must tell you about my weekend. Went shooting in Scotland. Bagged a deer.'

'Do you *bag* deer?'

'Whatever,' he waves dismissively. 'Shot the bastard right through the left eye.'

The receptionist triggers a switch to open the security door and we summon a lift. Fenwick examines himself in the internal mirrors, brushing specks of dandruff from the bunched shoulders of an expensive suit. It says something about Fenwick's body when a hand-tailored suit doesn't fit him.

'Still consorting with prostitutes?' he asks.

'I give talks.'

'Is *that* what they call it nowadays?' He guffaws and rearranges himself via a trouser pocket. 'How do you get paid?'

He won't believe me if I tell him I do it for nothing. 'They give me vouchers. I can redeem them for blowjobs later. I have a whole drawer full of them.'

He almost chokes and blushes furiously. I have to stop myself laughing.

Fenwick, for all his obvious success as a doctor, is one of those people who tries desperately hard to be somebody else. That's why he looks vaguely ridiculous behind the wheel of a sports car. It's like seeing Bill Gates in board shorts or

George W. Bush in The White House. It just doesn't look right.

'How's the you-know-what?' he asks.

'Fine.'

'I haven't noticed it at all, old boy. Come to think of it, Pfizer is trailing a new drug cocktail. Drop by and I'll give you the literature . . . '

Fenwick's contacts with drug companies are renowned. His office is a shrine to Pfizer, Novatis and Hoffmann-La Roche; almost every item donated, from the fountain pens to the espresso machine. The same is true of his social life – sailing in Cowes, salmon fishing in Scotland and grouse shooting in Northumberland.

We turn the corner and Fenwick glances inside my office. A middle-aged woman sits in the waiting room clutching an orange torpedo-shaped lifebuoy.

'I don't know how you do it, old boy,' Fenwick mutters.

'Do what?'

'*Listen* to them.'

'That's how I find out what's wrong.'

'Why bother? Dish out some antidepressants and send her home.'

Fenwick doesn't believe there are psychological or social factors in mental illness. He claims it is completely biological and therefore, by definition, treatable with drugs. It is just a matter of finding the right combination.

Every morning (he doesn't work after midday) patients march one by one into his office, answer a few perfunctory questions before Fenwick hands them a scrip and bills them £140. If they want to talk symptoms, he wants to talk drugs. If they mention side effects he changes the dosage.

35

The strange thing is that his patients love him. They come in *wanting* drugs and they don't care which ones. The more pills the better. Maybe they figure they're getting value for money.

Listening to people is considered to be old-fashioned nowadays. Patients expect me to produce a magic pill that cures everything. When I tell them that I just want to talk, they look disappointed.

'Morning, Margaret. Glad to see you made it.'

She holds up the lifebuoy.

'Which way did you come?'

'Putney Bridge.'

'It's a good solid bridge that one. Been around for years.'

She suffers from Gephyrophobia – a fear of crossing bridges. To make matters worse, she lives south of the river and has to walk her children to school across the Thames every day. She carries the lifebuoy just in case the bridge falls down or is swept away by a tidal wave. I know that sounds irrational but simple phobias are like that.

'I should have gone to live in the Sahara,' she says, only half joking.

I tell her about Eremikophobia, the fear of sand or deserts. She thinks I'm making it up.

Three months ago Margaret panicked mid-crossing while walking her kids to school. It took an hour before anybody realised. The children were crying, still clutching her hands. She was frozen by fear, unable to speak or nod. Passers-by thought she might be a 'jumper'. In reality Margaret was holding up that bridge with sheer willpower.

We've done a lot of work since then, trying to break the thought loop that accompanies her irrational fear.

'What do you believe is going to happen if you cross the bridge?'

'It's going to fall down.'

'Why would it fall down?'

'I don't know.'

'What is the bridge made of?'

'Steel and rivets and concrete.'

'How long has it been there?'

'Years and years.'

'Has it ever fallen down?'

'No.'

Each session lasts fifty minutes and I have ten minutes to write up my notes before my next patient arrives. Meena, my secretary, is like an atomic clock, accurate to the last second.

'A minute lost is a minute gone for ever, 'she says, tapping the watch pinned to her breast.

Anglo-Indian, but more English than strawberries and cream, she dresses in knee-length skirts, sensible shoes and cardigans. And she reminds me of the girls I knew at school that were addicted to Jane Austen novels and always daydreaming about meeting their Mr Darcy.

Sadly, I'm losing her soon. She and her cats are off to open a Bed & Breakfast in Bath. I can just imagine the place – lace doilies under every vase, moggy figurines and the toast soldiers in neat ranks beside every three-minute egg.

Meena is organising the interviews for a new secretary. She has narrowed them down to a shortlist but I know I'll have trouble deciding. I keep hoping that she'll change her mind. If only I could purr.

Mid-afternoon, I glance around the waiting room. 'Where's Bobby?'

'He hasn't arrived.'

'Did he call?'

'No.' She tries not to meet my eyes.

'Can you try to find him? It's been two weeks.'

I know she doesn't want to make the call. She doesn't like Bobby. At first I thought it was because he didn't turn up for appointments, but it's more than that. He makes her nervous. Maybe it's his size or the bad haircut or the chip on his shoulder. She doesn't really know him. Then again, who does?

Almost on cue, he appears in the doorway with his odd-legged shuffle and an anxious expression. Tall and overweight, with flax-brown hair and metal-framed glasses, his great pudding of a body is trying to burst out of a long overcoat made shapeless by its bulging pockets.

'Sorry I'm late. Something came up.' He glances around the waiting room, still unsure whether to step inside.

'Something came up for two weeks?'

He makes eye contact with me and then turns his face away.

I'm used to Bobby being defensive and enclosed, but this is different. Instead of keeping secrets he's telling lies. It's like closing the shutters in front of someone and then trying to deny they exist.

I take a quick inventory – his shoes are polished and his hair is combed. He shaved this morning, but the dark shadow has returned. His cheeks are red from the cold but at the same time he's perspiring. I wonder how long he spent outside, trying to get up the courage to come and see me.

'Where have you been, Bobby?'

'I got scared.'

'Why?'

He shrugs. 'I had to get away.'

'Where did you go?'

'Nowhere.'

I don't bother pointing out the contradiction. He's full of them. Restless hands look for somewhere to hide and escape into his pockets.

'Do you want to take off your coat?'

'It's OK.'

'Well, at least sit down.' I nod towards my office. He walks through the door and stands in front of my bookshelves, perusing the titles. Most of them are texts on psychology and animal behaviour. Eventually he stops and taps the spine of a book, *The Interpretation of Dreams* by Sigmund Freud.

'I thought Freud's views had been pretty much discredited these days.' He has the faintest hint of a northern accent. 'He couldn't tell the difference between hysteria and epilepsy.'

'It wasn't one of his best calls.'

I point to the chair and Bobby folds himself down into it, with his knees facing sideways towards the door.

Apart from my own notes, there is very little paperwork in his file. I have the original referral, neurological scans and a letter from a GP in north London. These mention 'disturbing nightmares' and a sense of being 'out of control'.

Bobby is twenty-two years of age, with no history of mental illness or habitual drug use. He has above average intelligence, is in good health and lives in a long-term relationship with Arky, his fiancée.

I have a basic history – born in London, educated at state schools, O-levels, night classes, odd jobs as a delivery driver and storeman. He and Arky live in a tower block in Hackney. She has a little boy and works at the candy bar in the local cinema. Apparently it was Arky who convinced him to seek help. Bobby's nightmares were getting worse. He woke screaming in the night, hurtling out of bed and crashing into walls as he tried to escape his dreams.

Before the summer we seemed to be getting somewhere. Then Bobby disappeared for three months and I thought he'd gone for good. He turned up five weeks ago, with no appointment or explanation. He seemed happier. He was sleeping better. The nightmares were less severe.

Now something is wrong. He sits motionless but his flicking eyes don't miss a thing.

'What's happened?'

'Nothing.'

'Is something wrong at home?'

He blinks. 'No.'

'What then?'

I let the silence work for me. Bobby fidgets, scratching at his hands as though something has irritated his skin. Minutes pass and he grows more and more agitated.

I give him a direct question to get him started. 'How is Arky?'

'She reads too many magazines.'

'Why do you say that?'

'She wants the modern fairytale. You know all that bull-shit they write in women's magazines – telling them how to have multiple orgasms, hold down a career and be a perfect mother. It's all crap. Real women don't look like fashion models. Real men can't be cut out of magazines. I don't know what I'm supposed to be – a new age man or a man's man. You tell me! Am I supposed to get drunk with the boys or cry at sad films? Do I talk about sports cars or this season's colours? Women think they want a man but instead they want a reflection of themselves.'

'How does that make you feel?'

'Frustrated.'

'Who with?'

'Take your pick.' His shoulders hunch and his coat collar brushes his ears. His hands are in his lap now, folding and unfolding a piece of paper, which has worn through along the creases.

'What have you written?'

'A number.'

'What number?'

'Twenty-one.'

'Can I see it?'

He blinks rapidly and slowly unfolds the page, pressing it flat against his thigh and running his fingers over the surface. The number '21' has been written hundreds of times, in tiny block figures, fanning out from the centre to form the blades of a windmill.

'Do you know that a dry square piece of paper cannot be folded in half more than seven times,' Bobby says, trying to change the subject.

'No.'

'It's true.'

'What else are you carrying in your pockets?'

41

'My lists.'

'What sort of lists?'

'Things to do. Things I'd like to change. People I like.'

'And people you don't like?'

'That too.'

Some people don't match their voices and Bobby is one of them. Although a big man, he seems smaller because his voice isn't particularly deep and his shoulders shrink when he leans forward.

'Are you in some sort of trouble, Bobby?'

He flinches so abruptly the legs of his chair leave the floor. His head is shaking firmly back and forth.

'Did you get angry with someone?'

Looking hopelessly sad, he bunches his fists.

'What made you angry?'

Whispering something, he shakes his head.

'I'm sorry, I didn't hear that.'

He mouths the words again.

'You'll have to speak up a little.'

Without a flicker of warning he explodes: 'STOP FUCKING WITH MY HEAD!'

The noise echoes in the confined space. Doors open along the corridor and the light flashes on my intercom. I press the button. 'It's OK, Meena. Everything's fine.'

A tiny vein throbs at the side of Bobby's temple, just above his right eye. He whispers in a little boy voice, 'I had to punish her.'

'Who did you have to punish?'

He gives the ring on his right index finger a half turn and then turns it back again as if he's tuning the dial on a radio, searching for the right frequency.

'We're all connected – six degrees of separation, some-times less. If something happens in Liverpool or London or Australia, it's all connected . . . '

I won't let him change the subject. 'If you're in trouble, Bobby, I can help. You have to let me know what happened.'

'Whose bed is she in now?' he whispers.

'I beg your pardon?'

'The only time she'll sleep alone is in the ground.'

'Did you punish Arky?'

More aware of me now, he laughs at me. 'Did you ever see *The Truman Show*?'

'Yes.'

'Well, sometimes I think I'm Truman. I think the whole world is watching me. My life has been created to someone else's expectations. Everything is a façade. The walls are plywood and the furniture is papier mâché. And then I think that if I could just run fast enough, I'd get around the next corner and find the back-lot of the film set. But I can never run fast enough. By the time I arrive, they've built another street . . . and another.'

4

In real estate terms we live in purgatory. I say this because we haven't quite reached the leafy nirvana of Primrose Hill; yet we've climbed out of the graffiti-stained, metal-shuttered shit-hole that is the southern end of Camden Town.

The mortgage is huge and the plumbing is dodgy but Julianne fell in love with the place. I have to admit that I did too. In the summer, if the breeze is blowing in the right direction and the windows are open, we can hear the sound of lions and hyenas at London Zoo. It's like being on safari without the mini-vans.

Julianne teaches Spanish to an adult education class on Wednesday evenings. Charlie is sleeping over at her best friend's house. I have the place to myself, which is normally OK. I reheat some soup in the microwave and tear a French loaf in half. Charlie has written a poem on the white board, next to the ingredients for banana bread. I feel a tiny flicker of loneliness. I want them both here. I miss the noise, the banter.

Wandering upstairs, I move from room to room checking on the 'work in progress'. Paint pots are lined up on the windowsill and the floors are covered in old sheets that look like Jackson Pollock canvases. One of the bedrooms has become a storeroom for boxes, rugs and bits of cat-scratched furniture. Charlie's old pram and high chair are in the corner, awaiting further instructions. And her baby clothes are sealed in plastic tubs with neat labels.

For six years we've been trying for another baby. So far the score stands at two miscarriages and innumerable tears. I don't want to go on – not now – but Julianne is still popping vitamin pills, studying urine samples and taking temperature readings. Our lovemaking is like a scientific experiment, with everything aimed at the optimum moment of ovulation.

When I point this out to her she promises to jump on my bones regularly and spontaneously as soon as we have another baby.

'You won't regret a single moment when it happens.'

'I know.'

'We owe it to Charlie.'

'Yes.'

I want to give her all the 'what ifs' but can't bring myself to do it. What if this disease accelerates? What if there is a genetic link? What if I can't hold my own child? I'm not being mawkish and self-obsessed. I'm being practical. A cup of tea and a couple of digestives aren't going to fix this problem. This disease is like a distant train, hurtling through the darkness towards us. It might seem like a long way off, but it's coming.

At six-thirty the cab arrives and we join the rush hour. Euston Road is backed up past Baker Street and there's no point trying to find a shortcut past an obstacle course of bollards, speed bumps and one-way signs.

The driver is complaining about illegal immigrants sneaking through the Channel Tunnel and making the traffic problems worse. Since none of them have cars I can't understand this, but I'm too depressed to argue.

Shortly after seven he drops me at Langton Hall in Clerkenwell – a squat red-brick building with white-trimmed windows and black down pipes. Apart from a light over the front steps, the building looks deserted. Pushing through the double doors, I cross a narrow foyer and enter the main hall. Plastic chairs are arranged in rough lines. A table to one side holds a hot-water urn beside rows of cups and saucers.

About forty women have turned up. They range in age from teens to late thirties. Most are wearing overcoats, beneath which some are doubtless dressed for work in high heels, short skirts, hotpants and stockings. The air is a technicolour stink of perfume and tobacco.

On stage Elisa Velasco is already speaking. A wisp of a thing with green eyes and fair hair, she has the sort of accent that makes northern women sound feisty and no-nonsense. Dressed in a knee-length pencil skirt and a tight cashmere sweater, she looks like a World War II pin-up girl.

Behind her, projected on to a white screen, is an image of Mary Magdalene painted by the Italian artist Artemisia

Gentileschi. The initials PAPT are printed in the bottom corner and in smaller letters: 'Prostitutes Are People Too'.

Elisa spies me and looks relieved. I try to slip along the side of the hall without interrupting her, but she taps the microphone and people turn.

'Now let me introduce the man you have *really* come to hear. Fresh from the front pages, I'd like you to welcome Professor Joseph O'Loughlin.'

There are one or two ironic handclaps. It's a tough audience. Soup gurgles in my stomach as I climb the steps at the side of the stage and walk into the circle of brightness. My left arm is trembling and I grasp the back of a chair to keep my hands steady.

I clear my throat and look at a point above their heads.

'Prostitutes account for the largest number of unsolved killings in this country. Forty-eight have been murdered in the past seven years. At least five are raped in London every day. A dozen more are bashed, robbed or abducted. They aren't attacked because they're attractive, or asking for it, but because they're accessible and vulnerable. They are easier to acquire and more anonymous than almost anyone else in society.'

Now I lower my eyes and connect with their faces, relieved to have their attention. A woman at the front has a purple satin collar on her coat and bright lemon-coloured gloves. Her legs are crossed and the coat has fallen open to reveal a creamy thigh. The thin black straps of her shoes criss-cross up her calves.

'Sadly, you can't always pick and choose your customers. They come in all shapes and sizes, some drunk, some nasty—'

'Some fat,' yells a bottle-blonde.

'And smelly,' echoes a teenager wearing dark glasses.

I let the laughter subside. Most of these women don't trust me. I don't blame them. There are risks in all their relationships, whether with pimps, punters or a psychologist. They have learned not to trust men.

I wish I could make the danger more real for them. Maybe I should have brought photographs. One recent victim was found with her womb lying on the bed beside her. On the other hand these women don't *need* to be told. The danger is ever present.

'I haven't come here tonight to lecture you. I hope to make you a little safer. When you're working the streets at night, how many friends or family know where you are? If you disappeared, how long would it take for someone to report you missing?'

I let the question drift across them like a floating cobweb from the rafters. My voice has grown hoarse and sounds too harsh. I let go of the chair and begin walking to the front of the stage. My left leg refuses to swing and I half stumble, before correcting. They glance at each other – wondering what to make of me.

'Stay off the streets and if you can't then take precautions. Operate a buddy system. Make sure someone is taking down the number plate when you get into a car. Only work in well-lit areas and organise safe houses where you can take clients rather than using their cars . . . '

Four men have entered the hall and taken up positions near the doors. They're clearly policemen in plain clothes. As the women realise I hear mutters of disbelief and resignation. Several of them glare angrily at me as though it's my doing.

'Everybody stay calm. I'll sort this out.' I carefully swing down from the stage. I want to intercept Elisa before she reaches them.

The man in charge is easy to spot. It's the detective I saw at Kensal Green Cemetery, with the lived-in face and crooked teeth. He's wearing the same rumpled overcoat, which is a culinary road map of stains and spills. His rugby club tie has a silver plate tiepin of the Tower of Pisa.

I like him. He isn't into clothes. Men who take too much care with their presentation can look ambitious but also vain. When he talks he looks into the distance as if trying to see what's coming. I've seen the same look on farmers who never seem comfortable focusing on anything too close, particularly faces. His smile is apologetic.

'Sorry to gatecrash your convention,' he says wryly, addressing Elisa

'Well fuck off then!' She says it with a sweet voice and a poisonous smile.

'It's lovely to make your acquaintance, Miss, or should I say *Madam*?'

I step between them. 'How can we help you?'

'Who are you?' He looks me up and down.

'Professor Joseph O'Loughlin.'

'No shit! Hey, fellas, it's that guy from the ledge. The one who talked down that kid.' His voice rumbles hoarsely. 'I never seen anyone more terrified.' His laugh is like a marble dropped down a drain. Another thought occurs to him. 'You're that expert on hookers, aren't you? You wrote a book or something.'

'A research paper.'

He shrugs ambivalently and motions to his men, who separate and move down the aisles.

Clearing his throat, he addresses the room. 'My name is Detective Inspector Vincent Ruiz of the Metropolitan Police. Three days ago the body of a young woman was found in Kensal Green, West London. She died about ten days earlier. At this stage we have been unable to identify her, but we have reason to believe that she may have been a prostitute. You are all going to be shown an artist's impression of the young woman. If any of you recognise her, I would appreciate it if you could make yourself known to us. We're after a name, an address, an associate, a friend – anyone who might have known her.'

Blinking rapidly, I hear myself ask, 'Where was she found?'

'Buried in a shallow grave beside the Grand Union Canal.'

The images are like snapshot memories. I can still see the white marquee and the arc lights: the scene-of-crime tape and the strobing of the flashguns. A woman's body fresh from the earth. I had been there. I had watched her being uncovered.

The hall seems cavernous and echoing. Drawings are passed from hand to hand. The noise level rises. A languid wrist is thrust towards me. The sketch looks like one of those charcoal drawings you see tourists posing for in Covent Garden. She's young with short hair and large eyes. That describes a dozen women in the hall.

Five minutes later the detectives return, shaking their heads at Ruiz. The Detective Inspector grunts and wipes his misshapen nose on a handkerchief.

'You know this is an illegal gathering,' he says, glancing at the tea urn. 'It's an offence to allow prostitutes to assemble and consume refreshments.'

'The tea is for me,' I say.

He laughs dismissively. 'You must drink a lot of tea. Either that or you take me for an idiot.' He's challenging me.

'I know what you are,' I bristle.

'Well? Don't keep me in suspense.'

'You're a country boy who found himself in the big city. You grew up on a farm, milking cows and collecting eggs. You played rugby until some sort of injury ended your career, but you still wonder if you could have gone all the way. Since then it's been a struggle to keep the weight off. You're divorced or widowed, which explains why your shirts need a decent iron and your suit needs dry-cleaning. You like a beer after work and a curry after that. You're trying to give up smoking, which is why you keep fumbling in your pockets for chewing gum. You think gyms are for wankers, unless they have a boxing ring and punch bags. And the last time you took a holiday you went to Italy because someone told you it was wonderful, but you ended up hating the food, the people and the wine.'

I'm surprised by how cold and indifferent I sound. It's as though I've been infected by the prejudices swirling around me.

'Very impressive. Is that your party trick?'

'No,' I mumble, suddenly embarrassed. I want to apologise but don't know where to start.

Ruiz fumbles in his pockets and then stops himself. 'Tell me something, Professor. If you can work out all that just by looking at me, how much can a dead body tell you?'

'What do you mean?'

'My murder victim. How much could you tell me about her if I showed you her body?'

I'm not sure if he's being serious. In theory it might be possible, but I deal in people's minds: I read their mannerisms and body language; I look at the clothes they wear and the way they interact; I listen for changes in their voices and their eye movements. A dead body can't tell me any of this. A dead body turns my stomach.

'Don't worry, she won't bite. I'll see you at Westminster Mortuary at nine o'clock tomorrow morning.' He roughly tucks the address into the inside pocket of my jacket. 'We can have breakfast afterwards,' he adds, chuckling to himself.

Before I can respond he turns to leave, flanked by detectives. At the last possible moment, just before he reaches the door, he spins back towards me.

'You were wrong about one thing.'

'What's that?'

'Italy. I fell in love with it.'

5

Outside on the pavement, Elisa kisses me on the cheek. 'I'm sorry about that.'

The last of the police cars are disappearing, along with my audience.

'It's not your fault.'

'I know. I just like kissing you.' She tousles my hair, then makes a fuss about getting a brush from her bag and fixing it up again. She stands in front of me and pushes my head down slightly. From here I can see down her sweater to the swoop of her lace-covered breasts and the dark valley in between.

'People are going to start talking,' she teases.

'There's nothing to talk about.' The statement is too abrupt. Her eyebrows lift almost imperceptibly.

She lights a cigarette and then guillotines the flame with the lid of her lighter. For a fleeting moment I see the light reflect off the golden specks in her green eyes. No matter how Elisa styles her hair it always appears sleep-tousled and wild. She cocks her head to one side and looks at me intently.

'I saw you on the news. You were very brave.'

'I was terrified.'

'Is he going to be OK – the boy on the roof?'

'Yes.'

'Are you going to be OK?'

The question surprises me, but I don't know how to respond. I follow her back into the hall and help her stack the chairs. She unplugs the overhead projector and hands me a box of pamphlets. The same painting of Mary Magdalene is printed on the front fold.

Elisa puts her chin on my shoulder. 'Mary Magdalene is the patron saint of prostitutes.'

'I thought she was a redeemed sinner.'

Annoyed, she corrects me. 'The Gnostic Gospels call her a visionary. She's also been called the Apostle of Apostles because she brought them the news of the Resurrection.'

'And you believe all that?'

'Jesus disappears for three days and the first person to see him alive is a whore. I'd say that was pretty typical!' She doesn't laugh. It isn't meant to be funny.

I follow her back on to the front steps, where she turns and locks the door.

'I have my car. I can give you a lift home,' she says, fumbling for her keys. We turn the corner and I see her red Volkswagen Beetle on a parking meter.

'There is another reason I chose that painting,' she explains.

'Because it was painted by a woman.'

'Yes, but that's not all. It's because of what happened to the artist. Artemisia Gentileschi was raped when she was nineteen by her instructor, Tassi, although he denied touching her. During his trial he said Artemisia was a lousy painter, who invented the rape story because she was jealous. He accused her of being "an insatiable whore" and called all his friends to give evidence against her. They even had her examined by midwives to find out if she was still a virgin.' Elisa sighs dolefully. 'Not much has changed in four centuries. The only difference now is that we don't torture our rape victims with thumbscrews to find out if they're telling the truth.'

Turning on the car radio, she signals that she doesn't want to talk. I lean back in the passenger seat and listen to Phil Collins singing 'Another Day in Paradise'.

I first set eyes on Elisa in a grotty interview room at a children's home in Brentford in the mid-eighties. I had just been accepted as a trainee clinical psychologist with the West London Health Authority.

She walked in, sat down and lit a cigarette without acknowledging I was there. She was only fifteen years old, yet had a fluid grace and certainty of movement that caught the eye and held it for too long.

With one elbow propped on the table and the cigarette held a few inches from her mouth, she stared past me to a window high on the wall. Smoke curled into her unruly fringe of hair. Her nose had been broken at some point and a front tooth was chipped. Periodically she ran her tongue across the jagged edge.

Elisa had been rescued from a 'trick pad' – a temporary

brothel set up in the basement of a derelict house. The doors had been rigged so they couldn't be opened from the inside. She and another adolescent prostitute had been imprisoned for three days and raped by dozens of men who were offered sex with underage girls. A judge had placed her into care, but Elisa spent most of her time trying to escape from the children's home. She was too old to be placed with a foster family and too young to live on her own.

In that first meeting she looked at me with a mixture of curiosity and contempt. She was accustomed to dealing with men. Men could be manipulated.

'How old are you now, Elisa?'

'You know that already,' she said, motioning to the file in my hands. 'I can wait while you read it, if you like.' She was teasing me.

'Where are your parents?'

'Dead, hopefully.'

According to the file notes Elisa had been living with her mother and stepfather in Leeds when she ran away from home just after her fourteenth birthday.

Most of her answers were the bare minimum – why use two words when one will do? She sounded cocky and indifferent but I knew she was hurting. Eventually I managed to get under her skin. 'How the hell can you know so little?' she yelled, her eyes glistening with emotion.

It was time to take a risk.

'You think you're a woman, don't you? You think you know how to manipulate men like me. Well, you're wrong! I'm not a walking fifty-quid note looking for a blowjob or a quick fuck in a back lane. Don't waste my time. I've got more important places to be.'

Anger flared in her eyes and then disappeared as they misted over. She started crying. For the first time she looked and acted her age. The story came tumbling out, in between her sobs.

Her stepfather, a successful businessman in Leeds, had made a lot of money buying flats and doing them up. He was a real catch for a single mum like Elisa's. It meant they could move out of their council flat and into a proper house with a garden. Elisa had her own room. She went to grammar school.

One night, when she was twelve, her stepfather came to her room. 'This is what grown-ups do,' he said, putting her legs over his shoulders and his hand over her mouth.

'He was nice to me after that,' she said. 'He used to buy me clothes and make-up.'

This went on for two years until Elisa fell pregnant. Her mother called her a 'slut' and demanded to know the name of the father. She stood over her, waiting for an answer, and Elisa glimpsed her stepfather in the doorway. He ran his forefinger across his throat.

She ran away. In the pocket of her school blazer she had the name of an abortion clinic in south London. At the clinic she met a nurse in her mid-forties with a kind face. Her name was Shirley and she offered Elisa a place to stay while she recuperated.

'Hold on to your school uniform.'

'Why?'

'It might come in handy.'

Shirley was a mother figure to half a dozen teenage girls and they all loved her. She made them feel safe.

'Her son was a real dickhead,' said Elisa. 'He slept with

a shotgun under his bed and he thought he could have sex with any of us. Wanker! The first time Shirley took me out to work, she was saying, "Go on, you can do it." I was standing on Bayswater Road wearing my school uniform. "It's OK, just ask them if they want a girl," she said. I didn't want to disappoint Shirley. I knew she'd be angry.

'Next time she took me out, I did some hand jobs but I couldn't do the sex. I don't know why. It took me three months. I was getting too tall for my school uniform but Shirley said I had the legs to get away with it. I was her "Little Pot of Gold".'

Elisa didn't call the men she slept with 'punters'. She didn't like any suggestion that they were gambling with their money. She was a sure thing. And she didn't treat them with contempt, even if many were cheating on their wives, fiancées and girlfriends. This was purely business, a simple commercial transaction; she had something to sell and they wanted to buy it.

As the months went by she became desensitised. She had a new family now. Then one day a rival pimp snatched her off the street. He wanted her for a one-off engagement, he said. He locked her in the basement of a house and collected money at the door from the men who queued up. A river of skin, of all different colours, flowed across her body and leaked inside her. 'I was their "Little White Fucktoy",' she said as she stubbed out another cigarette.

'And now you're here.'

'Where nobody knows what to do with me.'

'What do you want to do?'

'I want to be left alone.'

6

The first law of the National Health Service is that dead wood floats. It is part of the culture. If somebody is incompetent or hard to get along with, promotion is an easier option than sacking.

The duty supervisor at Westminster Mortuary is bald and thickset with pouchy jowls. He takes an instant dislike to me. 'Who told you to come here?'

'I'm meeting Detective Inspector Ruiz.'

'I haven't been told. Nobody made an appointment.'

'Can I wait for him?'

'No. Only family of the deceased are allowed in the waiting room.'

'Where can I wait?'

'Outside.'

I catch his sour smell and notice the sweat stains under his arms. He has probably worked all night and is doing overtime. He's tired and he's cranky. I normally have sympathy for shift-workers – in the same way that I feel sorry for loners and fat girls who never get asked to dance. It must be a lousy job, looking after dead people.

I'm just about to say something when Ruiz arrives. The supervisor begins his spiel all over again. Ruiz leans across the desk and picks up the phone. 'Listen, you jumped up little shit! I see a dozen cars parked on expired meters outside. You're going to be really popular with all your workmates when they get clamped.'

A few minutes later I'm following Ruiz along narrow corridors with strip lights on the ceiling and painted cement floors. Occasionally we pass doors with frosted glass windows. One of them is open. I glance inside and see a stainless steel table in the middle of the room with a central channel leading to a drain. Halogen lights are suspended from the ceiling, alongside microphone leads.

Further along the corridor, we come across three lab technicians in green medical scrubs standing around a coffee machine. None of them looks up.

Ruiz walks fast and talks slowly. 'The body was found at 11.00 on Sunday morning, buried in a shallow ditch. Fifteen minutes earlier an anonymous call was made from a pay phone a quarter of a mile away. The caller claimed his dog had dug up a hand.'

We push through double plexiglass doors and dodge a trolley being wheeled by an orderly. A white calico sheet covers what I imagine to be a body. A box of test tubes full of blood and urine is balanced on top of the torso.

We reach an anteroom with a large glass door. Ruiz taps on the window and is buzzed in by an operator sitting at a desk. She has blonde hair, dark roots and eyebrows plucked to the thinness of dental floss. Around the walls are filing cabinets and white boards. On the far side is a large stainless steel door marked 'STAFF ONLY'.

I suddenly get a flashback to my medical training when I fainted during our first practical lesson working with a corpse. I came round with smelling salts waved under my nose. The lecturer then chose me to demonstrate to the class how to direct a 150mm needle through the abdomen to the liver to take a biopsy sample. Afterwards he congratulated me on a new university record for the most organs hit with one needle in a single procedure.

Ruiz hands the operator a letter.

'Do you want me to set up a proper viewing?' she asks.

'The fridge will be fine,' he replies, 'but I'll need an SB.' She hands him a large brown paper bag.

The heavy door unlocks with a hiss like a pressure seal and Ruiz steps aside to let me go first. I expect to smell formaldehyde – something I came to associate with every body I saw in medical school. Instead there's the faint odour of antiseptic and industrial soap.

The walls are polished steel. A dozen trolleys are parked in neat rows. Metal crypts take up three walls and look like oversized filing cabinets, with large square handles that can accommodate two hands.

I realise Ruiz is still talking. 'According to the pathologist she'd been in the ground for nine or ten days. She was naked except for a shoe and a gold chain around her neck with a St Christopher's medallion. We haven't found the rest of her clothes. There is no evidence of a sexual assault . . .' He checks the label on a drawer and grips the handle.

'I think you'll see why we've narrowed down the cause of death.'

The drawer slides open smoothly on rollers. My head snaps back and I lurch away. Ruiz hands me the brown paper bag as I double over and heave. It's difficult to throw up and gasp for breath at the same time.

Ruiz hasn't moved. 'As you can see, the left side of her face is badly bruised and the eye is completely closed. Someone gave her a real working over. That's why we released the drawing instead of a photograph. There are more than twenty stab wounds – not one of them more than an inch deep. But here's the real kicker – every last one was self-inflicted. The pathologist found hesitation marks. She had to work up the nerve to force the blade through.'

Raising my head, I glimpse his face reflected in the polished steel. That's when I see it: fear. He must have investigated dozens of crimes, but this one is different because he can't understand it.

My stomach is empty. Perspiring and shivering in the cold, I straighten up and look at the body. Nothing has been done to restore the poor woman's dignity. She is naked, stretched out with her arms against her sides and her legs together.

The dull whiteness of her skin makes her look almost like a marble statue, only this 'statue' has been vandalised. Her chest, arms and thighs are covered in slashes of crimson and pink. Where the skin is pulled taut the wounds gape like empty eye sockets. At other places they naturally close and weep slightly.

I have seen post-mortems in medical school. I know the

process. She has been photographed, scraped, swabbed and cut open from her neck to her crotch. Her organs have been weighed and her stomach contents analysed. Bodily fluids, flakes of dead skin and dirt from beneath her finger-nails have been sealed within plastic or beneath glass slides. A once bright, energetic, vibrant human being has become exhibit A.

'How old was she?'

'Somewhere between twenty-five and thirty-five.'

'What makes you think she was a prostitute?'

'It's been nearly two weeks and nobody has reported her missing. You know better than I do how prostitutes move around. They take off for days or weeks at a time and then turn up at a totally different red-light area. Some of them follow the conference trade; others work the truck stops. If this girl had a strong network of family or friends, some-body would have reported her missing by now. She could be foreign but we have nothing from Interpol.'

'I'm not sure how I can help?'

'What can *you* tell me about her?'

Although I can't bear to look at her swollen face I'm already collecting details. Her fair hair is cut short in a practical style that's easy to wash, quick to dry and doesn't need constant brushing. Her ears aren't pierced. Her fingernails are trimmed and well cared for. She has no rings on her fingers, or any sign that she normally wore them. She's slim and fair-skinned, with larger hips than bust. Her eyebrows have been tidily shaped and her bikini line has been waxed recently, leaving a neat triangle of pubic hair.

'Was she wearing make-up?'

'A little lipstick and eye-liner.'

'I need to sit down for a while and read the post-mortem report.'

'I'll find you an empty office.'

Ten minutes later, alone at a desk, I stare at a stack of ring-bound photograph albums and folders bulging with statements. Among the pile is the post-mortem report and results from blood and toxicology analysis.

I glance at the summary page.

CITY OF WESTMINSTER CORONER
Post-Mortem Report

Name: Unknown   Post-Mortem No: DX-34 468
DOB: Unknown   Death D/T: Unknown
Age: Unknown   Post-Mortem D/T: 10/12/2000 0915
Sex: Female

Anatomical Summary:

1. Fourteen lacerations and incised wounds to the chest, abdomen and thighs, penetrating to a depth of 1.2 inches. They range in width from 3 inches to half an inch.

2. Four lacerations to the upper left arm.

3. Three lacerations to the left side of the neck and shoulders.

4. The direction of the sharp force injuries tends to be downward and they are a mixture of stabbing and incised wounds.

5. The hesitation marks are generally straight and accompany the deeper incisions.

6. Heavy bruising and swelling to the left cheekbone and left eye-socket.

7. Slight bruising to the right forearm and abrasions to the right tibia and right heel.

8. Oral, vaginal and rectal swabs are clear.

Preliminary Toxicology Study:
    Blood ethanol – none detected
    Blood drug screen – no drugs detected

Cause of Death:
    Post-mortem X-rays reveal air in the right ventricular chamber of the heart, indicating a massive and fatal air embolism.

I scan the report quickly, looking for particular details. I'm not interested in the minutiae of *how* she died. Instead I look for clues that relate to her life. Did she have any old fractures? Was there any evidence of drug use or sexually transmitted diseases? What did she have for her last meal? How long since she'd eaten?

Ruiz doesn't bother to knock.

'I figured you were milk, no sugar.'

He puts a plastic cup of coffee on the desk and then pats his pockets, searching for cigarettes that exist only in his imagination. He grinds his teeth instead. 'So what can you tell me?'

'She wasn't a prostitute.'

'Because?'

'The median age of girls becoming prostitutes is only sixteen. This woman was in her mid-twenties, possibly older. There are no signs of long-standing sexual activity or

65

evidence of sexually transmitted diseases. Abortions are common among prostitutes, particularly as they're often coerced into not using condoms, but this girl had never been pregnant.'

Ruiz taps the table three times as though typing three ellipsis dots. He wants me to go on.

'Prostitutes at the high-class end of the scale sell a fantasy. They take great care with their appearance and presentation. This woman had short fingernails, a boyish hairstyle and minimal make-up. She wore sensible shoes and very little jewellery. She didn't use expensive moisturisers or paint her nails. She had her bikini line waxed modestly . . . '

Ruiz is moving around the room again, with his mouth slightly open and a puckered brow.

'. . . she took care of herself. She exercised regularly and ate healthy food. She was probably concerned about putting on weight. I'd say she was of average or slightly above average intelligence. Her schooling would have been solid; her background most likely middle class.

'I don't think she's from London. Someone would have reported her missing by now. This sort of girl doesn't go missing. She has friends and family. But if she came to London for a job interview, or for a holiday, people might not have expected to hear from her for a while. They'll start to get worried soon.'

Pushing back my chair a little, I lack the conviction to stand. What else can I tell him?

'The medallion – it's not St Christopher. I think it's probably St Camillus. If you look closely, the figure is holding a pitcher and towel.'

'And who was he?'

'The patron saint of nurses.'

The statement concentrates his attention. He cocks his head to one side and I can almost see him cataloguing the information. In his right hand he flicks open a book of matches and closes it again. Open and then closed.

I shuffle the papers and glance at the full post-mortem report. A paragraph catches my attention.

There is evidence of old lacerations running the length of her right and left forearms and inside her upper thighs. The degree of scarring suggests an attempt at self-suturing. These wounds were most likely self-inflicted and point towards past attempts at self-harm or self-mutilation.

'I need to see the photographs.'

Ruiz pushes the ring-bound folders towards me and in the same breath announces, 'I have to make a phone call. We might have a lead on a missing woman. An X-ray technician in Liverpool hasn't heard from her flatmate in a fortnight. She matches the age, height and hair colour of our Jane Doe. And how's this for a coincidence, Sherlock? She's a nurse.'

After he's gone I open the first folder of photographs and turn the pages quickly. Her arms had been along her sides when I viewed her body. I couldn't see her wrists or inner thighs. A self-mutilator with multiple stab wounds, all self-inflicted . . . Surely it's only a coincidence.

The first photographs are wide-angle shots of open ground, littered with rusting forty-four-gallon drums, rolls of wire and scaffolding poles. The Grand Union Canal forms an immediate backdrop but on the far side I see a smattering of well-established trees and the headstones in between.

The photographs begin to focus down on to the banks of the canal. Blue and white police tape has been threaded around metal posts to mark out the area.

The second set of photographs shows the ditch and a splash of white that looks like a discarded milk container. As the camera zooms closer it reveals it to be a hand, with fingers outstretched, reaching upwards from the earth. Soil is scraped away slowly, sifted and bagged. The corpse is finally exposed, lying with one leg twisted awkwardly beneath her and her left arm draped over her eyes as though shielding them from the arc lights.

Moving quickly, I skim over the pages until I reach the post-mortem pictures. The camera records every smear, scratch and bruise. I'm looking for one photograph.

Here it is. Her forearms are turned outwards and lying flat against the dull silver of the bench top. Awkwardly, I stand and retrace my steps along the corridors. My left leg locks up and I have to swing it in an arc from back to front.

The operator buzzes me into the secure room and I stare for a few seconds at the same bank of metal crypts. Four across. Three down. I check the label, grasp the handle and slide the drawer open. This time I force myself to look at her ruined face. Recognition is like a tiny spark that fires a bigger machine. Memories roar in my head. Her hair is shorter. She has put on weight, but only a little.

Reaching for her right arm, I turn it over and brush my fingertips along the milky white scars. Against the paleness of her skin they look like embossed creases that merge and crisscross before fading into nothing. She opened these wounds repeatedly, picking apart the stitches or slicing them afresh. She kept this hidden, but once upon a time I shared the secret.

'Need a second look?' Ruiz is standing at the door.

'Yes.' I can't stop my voice from shaking. Ruiz steps in front of me and slides the drawer shut.

'You shouldn't be in here by yourself. Should have waited for me.' The words are weighted.

I mumble an apology and wash my hands at the sink, feeling his eyes upon me. I need to say something.

'What about Liverpool? Did you find out who . . . ?'

'The flatmate is being brought to London by the local CID. We should have a positive ID by this afternoon.'

'So you have a name?'

He doesn't answer. Instead I'm hustled along the corridor and made to wait as he collects the post-mortem notes and photographs. Then I follow him through the subterranean maze until we emerge, via double doors, into a parking garage.

All the while I'm thinking, I should say something now. I should tell him. Yet a separate track in my brain is urging, It doesn't matter any more. He knows her name. What's past is past. It's ancient history.

'I promised you breakfast.'

'I'm not hungry.'

'Well I am.'

We walk under blackened railway arches and down a narrow alley. Ruiz seems to know all the back streets. He is remarkably light on his feet for a big man, dodging puddles and dog faeces.

The large front windows of the café are steamed up with condensation, or it could be a film of fat from the chip-fryer. A bell jangles above our heads as we enter. The fug of cigarette smoke and warm air is overpowering.

The place is pretty much empty except for two sunken-cheeked old men in cardigans playing chess in the corner and an Indian cook with a yolk-stained apron. It's late morning but the café serves breakfast all day. Baked beans, chips, eggs, bacon and mushrooms – in any combination. Ruiz takes a table near the window.

'What do you want?'

'Just coffee.'

'The coffee is crap.'

'Then I'll have tea.'

He orders a full English with a side order of toast and two pots of tea. Then he fumbles for a cigarette in his jacket pocket before mumbling something about forgetting his phone.

'I didn't take any pleasure from dragging you into this,' he says.

'Yes, you did.'

'Well, just a little.' His eyes seem to smile but there is no sense of self-congratulation. The impatience I noticed the previous night has gone. He's more relaxed and philosophical.

'Do you know how you become a Detective Inspector, Professor O'Loughlin?'

'No.'

'It used to be based on how many crimes you solved and people you banged up. Nowadays it depends on how few complaints you generate and whether you can stick to a

70

budget. I'm a dinosaur to these people. Ever since the Police and Criminal Evidence Act came into force *my* sort of policeman has been living on borrowed time.

'Nowadays they talk about pro-active policing. Do you know what that means? It means the number of detectives they put on a case depends on how big the tabloid headlines are. The media run these investigations now – not the police.'

'I haven't read anything about this case,' I say.

'That's because everyone thinks the victim is a prostitute. If she turns out to be Florence bloody Nightingale or the daughter of a duke I'll have forty detectives instead of twelve. The Assistant Chief Constable will take personal charge because of the "complex nature of the case". Every public statement will have to be vetted by his office and every line of inquiry approved.'

'Why did they give it to you?'

'Like I said, they thought we were dealing with a dead prostitute. "Give it to Ruiz," they said. "He'll bang heads together and put the fear of God into the pimps." So *what* if any of them object? My file is so full of complaint letters that Internal Affairs have given me my own filing cabinet.'

A handful of Japanese tourists pass the window and pause. They look at the blackboard menu and then at Ruiz, before deciding to keep going. Breakfast arrives, with a knife and fork wrapped in a paper napkin. Ruiz squeezes brown sauce over his eggs and begins cutting them up. I try not to watch as he eats.

'You look like you got a question,' he says between mouthfuls.

71

'It's about her name.'

'You know the drill. I'm not supposed to release details until we get a positive ID and inform the next of kin.'

'I just thought . . . ' I don't finish the sentence.

Ruiz takes a sip of tea and butters his toast. 'Catherine Mary McBride. She turned twenty-seven a month ago. A community nurse, but you knew that already. According to her flatmate she was in London for a job interview.'

Even knowing the answer doesn't lessen the shock. Poor Catherine. This is when I should tell him. I should have done it straight away. Why do I have to rationalise everything? Why can't I just say things when they enter my head?

Leaning over his plate, Ruiz scoops baked beans on to a corner of toast. His fork stops in mid-air in front of his open mouth. 'Why did you say, "Poor Catherine"?'

I must have been speaking out loud. My eyes tell the rest of the story. Ruiz lets the fork clatter on to his plate. Anger and suspicion snake through his thoughts. 'You knew her.'

It's an accusation rather than a statement. He's angry.

'I didn't recognise her at first. That drawing last night could have been almost anyone. I thought you were looking for a prostitute.'

'And today?'

'Her face was so swollen. She seemed so . . . so . . . vandalised. It wasn't until I saw the scars that I was certain. She used to be a patient.'

Not satisfied. 'You lie to me again, Professor, and I'll put my boot so far up your arse your breath will smell of shoe polish.'

'I didn't lie to you. I just wanted to be sure.'

His eyes haven't left mine. 'And when were you thinking of telling me all this?'

'I would have told you.'

'Yeah. Sure.' He pushes his plate to the centre of the table. 'Start talking – why was Catherine a patient?'

'The scars on her wrists and thighs – she deliberately cut herself.'

'A suicide attempt?'

'No.'

I can see Ruiz struggling with this. Leaning closer, I try to explain how people react when overwhelmed by confusion and negative emotions. Some drink too much. Others over-eat or beat their wives or kick the cat. And a surprising number hold their hands against a hotplate or slice open their skin with a razor blade.

It's an extreme coping mechanism. They talk about their inner pain being turned outwards. By giving it a physical manifestation they find it easier to deal with.

'What was Catherine trying to cope with?'

'Mainly low self-esteem.'

'Where did you meet her?'

'She worked as a nurse at the Royal Marsden Hospital. I was a consultant there.'

Ruiz swirls the tea in his cup, staring at it as though it might tell him something. Suddenly he pushes back his chair, hitches his trousers and stands.

'You're an odd fucker, you know that?' A five-pound note flutters on to the table and I follow him outside. A dozen paces along the footpath, he turns to confront me. 'OK, tell me this. Am I investigating a murder or did this girl kill herself?'

'She was murdered.'

'So she was *made* to do this – to cut herself all those times? Apart from her face there are no signs that she was bound, gagged, restrained or compelled to cut herself. Can you explain that?'

I shake my head.

'Well, you're the psychologist! You're supposed to understand the world we live in. I'm a detective and it's beyond my fucking comprehension.'

7

As far as I can recall I haven't been drunk since Charlie was born and Jock took it upon himself to get me absolutely hammered because apparently that is what intelligent, sensible and conscientious fathers do when blessed with a child.

With a new car you avoid alcohol completely and with a new house you can't afford to drink, but with a new baby you must 'wet the head' or, in my case, throw up in a cab going around Marble Arch.

I didn't even get drunk when Jock told me about my Parkinson's Disease. Instead I went out and slept with a woman who wasn't my wife. The hangover didn't last. The guilt won't go away.

Today I had two double vodkas at lunchtime – a first for me. I felt like getting drunk because I can't get the image of Catherine McBride out of my mind. It's not her face I see but her naked body, stripped of all dignity; denied even a modest pair of panties or a strategically placed sheet. I want to protect her. I want to shield her from public gaze.

Now I understand Ruiz – not his words but the look on his face. This wasn't the terrible conclusion to some great passion. Nor was it an ordinary, kitchen sink killing, motivated by greed or jealousy. Catherine McBride suffered terribly. Each cut had sapped her strength like a banderillero's barbs in the neck of a bull.

An American psychologist called Daniel Wegner conducted a famous experiment on thought suppression in 1987. In a test that might have been created by Dostoevsky, he asked a group of people *not* to think about a white bear. Each time the white bear entered their thoughts they had to ring a bell. No matter how hard they tried, no person could avoid the forbidden thought for more than a few minutes.

Wegner spoke of two different thought processes counteracting each other. One is trying to think of anything except the white bear, while the other is subtly pushing forward the very thing that we wish to suppress.

Catherine Mary McBride is my white bear. I can't get her out of my head.

I should have gone home at lunchtime and cancelled my afternoon appointments. Instead I wait for Bobby Moran who turns up late again. Meena gives him the curt, cold treatment. It's six o'clock and she wants to go home.

'I would hate to be married to your secretary,' he says, before checking himself, 'she's not your wife, is she?'

'No.'

I motion for him to sit down. His buttocks spread out

to fill the chair. Tugging at the cuffs of his coat, he seems distracted and anxious.

'How have you been?'

'No thanks, I've just had one.'

I pause to see if he realises that his answer makes no sense. He doesn't react.

'Do you know what I just asked you, Bobby?'

'Whether I want a tea or coffee.'

'No.'

A brief flicker of doubt crosses his face. 'But you were going to ask me about the tea or coffee next.'

'So you were reading my mind?'

He smiles nervously and shakes his head. 'Do you believe in God?' he asks.

'Do you?'

'I used to.'

'What happened?'

'I couldn't find him. He's supposed to be everywhere. I mean, he's not supposed to be playing hide and seek.' He glances at his reflection in the darkened window.

'What sort of God would you like, Bobby – a vengeful God or a forgiving one?'

'A vengeful God.'

'Why?'

'People should pay for their sins. They shouldn't suddenly get forgiven because they plead they're sorry or repent on their deathbed. When we do wrong we should be punished.'

The last statement rattles in the air like a copper penny dropped on a table.

'What are you sorry for, Bobby?'

'Nothing.' He answers too quickly. Everything about his body language is screaming denial.

'How does it feel when you lose your temper?'

'Like my brain is boiling.'

'When was the last time you felt like this?'

'A few weeks ago.'

'What happened?'

'Nothing.'

'Who made you angry?'

'Nobody.'

Asking him direct questions is useless, because he simply blocks them. Instead I take him back to an earlier point and let him build up momentum like a boulder rolling down a hill. I know the day – 11 November – because he missed his appointment that afternoon. I ask him what time did he wake? What did he have for breakfast? When did he leave home? Slowly I move him closer to the moment when he lost control. He had taken the Tube to the West End and visited a jeweller in Hatton Garden. He and Arky are getting married in the spring. Bobby had arranged to pick up their wedding rings. He argued with the jeweller and stormed out. It was raining. He was running late. He stood on Holborn Circus trying to hail a cab.

Having got this far, Bobby pulls away again and changes the subject. 'Who do you think would win in a fight between a tiger and a lion?' he asks in a matter-of-fact voice.

'Why?'

'I'd like to know your opinion.'

'Tigers and lions don't fight each other. They live in different parts of the world.'

'Yes, but if they *did* fight each other, who would win?'

'The question is pointless. Inane.'

'Isn't that what psychologists do – ask pointless questions?' His entire demeanour has changed in the space of a single question. Suddenly, cocky and aggressive, he jabs his finger at me. 'You ask people what they'd do in hypothetical situations. Why don't you try me? Go on. "What would I do if I was the first person to discover a small fire in a movie theatre?" Isn't that the sort of question you ask? Would I put the fire out? Or go for the manager? Or evacuate the building? I know what you people do. You take a harmless answer and you try to make a sane person seem crazy.'

'Is that what you think?'

'That's what I *know*.'

He's talking about a Mental Status Examination. Clearly Bobby has been evaluated before, yet there's no mention of it in his medical history. Each time I put pressure on him, he reacts with hostility. It's time to crank it up a notch.

'Let me tell you what I *know*, Bobby. Something happened that day. You were pissed off. You were having a bad day. Was it the jeweller? What did he do?'

My voice is sharp and unforgiving. Bobby flinches. His hackles rise. 'He's a lying bastard! He got the engraving wrong on the wedding bands. He misspelt Arky's name but he said it was my mistake. He said I gave him the wrong spelling. The bastard wanted to charge me extra.'

'What did you do?'

'I smashed the glass on his counter.'

'How?'

'With my fist.'

He holds up his hand to show me. Faint yellow and purple bruising discolours the underside.

'What happened then?'

He shrugs and shakes his head. That can't be all. There has to be something more. In our last session he had talked of punishing 'her' – a woman. It must have happened after he left the shop. He was on the street, angry, his brain boiling.

'Where did you first see her?'

He blinks at me rapidly. 'Coming out of a music store.'

'What were you doing?'

'Queuing for a taxi. It was raining. She took my cab.'

'What did she look like?'

'I don't remember her.'

'How old was she?'

'I don't know.'

'You say that she *took* your cab – did you say anything to her?'

'I don't think so.'

'What did you do?'

He flinches.

'Was she with anyone else?'

He glances at me and hesitates. 'What do you mean?'

'Who was she with?'

'A boy.'

'How old was he?'

'Maybe five or six.'

'Where was the boy?'

'She was dragging him by the hand. He was screaming. I mean, really screaming. She was trying to ignore him. He dropped like a dead weight and she had to drag him along. And this kid just kept screaming. And I started wondering, why isn't she talking to him? How can she let him scream?

He's in pain or he's frightened. Nobody else was doing anything. It made me angry. How could they just stand there?'

'Who were you angry at?'

'All of them. I was angry at their indifference. I was angry at this woman's neglect. I was angry with myself for hating the little boy. I just wanted him to stop screaming . . . '

'So what did you do?'

His voice drops to a whisper. 'I wanted her to make him stop. I wanted her to listen to him.' He stops himself.

'Did you say anything to her?'

'No.'

'What then?'

'The door of the cab was open. She pushed him inside. The kid was thrashing his legs. She gets in after him and turns back to get the door. Her face is like a mask . . . blank, you know. She swings her arm back and, *bang!*, she elbows him right in the face. He crumples backwards . . . '

Bobby pauses and then seems about to continue. He stops himself. The silence grows. I let it fill his head – working its way into the corners.

'I dragged her out of the cab. I had hold of her hair. I drove her face into the side window. She fell down and tried to roll away, but I kept kicking her.'

'Did you think you were punishing her?'

'Yes.'

'Did she deserve it?'

'Yes!'

He's staring directly at me – his face as white as wax. At that moment I have an image of a child in a lonely corner of a playground, overweight, freakishly tall, the owner

81

of nicknames like Jellyarse and Lardbucket; a child for whom the world is a vast and empty place. A child seeking to be invisible, but who is condemned to stand out.

'I found a dead bird today,' Bobby says absent-mindedly. 'Its neck was broken. Maybe it was hit by a car.'

'It's possible.'

'I moved it off the path. Its body was still warm. Do you ever think about dying?'

'I think everyone does.'

'Some people deserve to die.'

'And who should be the judge of that?'

He laughs bitterly. 'Not people like you.'

The session overruns but Meena has already gone home to her cats. Most of the nearby offices are locked up and in darkness. Cleaners are moving through the corridors, emptying bins and chipping paint off the skirting boards with their trolleys.

Bobby has also gone. Even so, when I stare at the dark-ened square of the window, I can picture his face, soaked in sweat and spotted with the blood of that poor woman.

I should have seen this coming. He is *my* patient, *my* responsibility. I know I can't hold his hand and make him come to see me, but that's no consolation. Bobby was close to crying when he described being charged, but he felt more sorry for himself than the woman he attacked.

I struggle to care about some of my patients. They spend ninety quid and gaze at their navels or whinge about things they should be telling their partners instead of me. Bobby is different. I don't know why. At times he seems totally incapacitated by awkwardness, yet he can startle me with his confidence and intellect. He laughs at the wrong places, explodes unexpectedly, and has eyes as pale and cold as blue glass.

Sometimes I think he's waiting for something – as though mountains are going to move or all the planets will line up. And once everything is in place he'll finally let me know what's really going on.

I can't wait for that. I have to understand him now.

8

Muhammad Ali has a lot to answer for. When he lit the flame at the Atlanta Olympics there wasn't a dry eye on the planet.

Why were we crying? Because a great sportsman had been reduced to this – a shuffling, mumbling, twitching cripple. A man who once danced like a butterfly now shook like a blancmange.

We always remember the sportsmen. When the body deserts a scientist like Stephen Hawking we figure that he'll be able to live in his mind, but a crippled athlete is like a bird with a broken wing. When you soar to the heights the landing is harder.

It's Friday and I'm sitting in Jock's office. His real name is Dr Emlyn Robert Owens – a Scotsman with a Welsh name – but I've only ever known him by his nickname.

A solid, almost square man, with powerful shoulders and

a bull neck, he looks more like a former boxer than a brain surgeon. His office has Salvador Dali prints on the walls, along with an autographed photograph of John McEnroe holding the Wimbledon trophy. McEnroe has signed it, 'You cannot be serious!'

Jock motions for me to sit on the examination table and then rolls up his sleeves. His forearms are tanned and thick. That's how he manages to hit a tennis ball like an Exocet missile. Playing tennis with Jock is eighty per cent pain. Everything comes rocketing back aimed directly at your body. Even with a completely open court he still tries to drill the ball straight through you.

My regular Friday matches with Jock have nothing to do with a love of tennis – they're about the past. They're about a tall, slender college girl who chose me instead of him. That was nearly twenty years ago and now she's my wife. It still pisses him off.

'How is Julianne?' he asks, shining a pencil torch into my eyes.

'Good.'

'What did she think about the business on the ledge?'

'She's still talking to me.'

'Did you tell anyone about your condition?'

'No. You told me I should carry on normally.'

'Yes. *Normally!*' He opens a folder and scribbles a note. 'Any tremors?'

'Not really. Sometimes, when I try to get out of a chair or out of bed, my mind says get up but nothing happens.'

He makes another note. 'That's called starting hesitancy. I get it all the time – particularly if the rugby's on TV.'

He makes a point of walking from side to side, watching my eyes follow him. 'How are you sleeping?'

'Not so well.'

'You should get one of those relaxation tapes. You know the sort of thing. Some guy talks in a really boring voice and puts you to sleep.'

'That's why I keep coming here.'

Jock hits me extra hard on my knee with his rubber hammer, making me flinch.

'That must have been your funny bone,' he says sarcastically. He steps back. 'Right, you know the routine.'

I close my eyes and bring my hands together – index finger to index finger, middle finger to middle finger, and so on. I almost manage to pull it off, but my ring fingers slide past each other. I try again and this time my middle fingers don't meet in the middle.

Jock plants his elbow on the desk and invites me to arm-wrestle.

'I'm amazed at how high-tech you guys are,' I say, squaring up to him. His fist crushes my fingers. 'I'm sure you only do this for personal satisfaction. It probably has nothing to do with examining me.'

'How did you guess?' says Jock as I push against his arm. I can feel my face going red. He's toying with me. Just once I'd like to pin the bastard.

Conceding defeat, I slump back and flex my fingers. There's no sign of triumph on Jock's face. Without having to be told I stand and start walking around the room, trying to swing my arms as though marching. My left arm seems to hang there.

Jock takes the cellophane wrapper from a cigar and snips

off the end. He rolls his tongue around the tip and licks his lips before lighting up. Then he closes his eyes and lets the smoke leak through his smile.

'God, I look forward to my first one of the day,' he says. He watches the smoke curl towards the ceiling, letting it fill the silence as it fills the empty space.

'So what's the story?' I ask, getting agitated.

'You have Parkinson's Disease.'

'I already know that.'

'So what else do you want me to say?'

'Tell me something I don't know.'

He chomps the cigar between his teeth. 'You've done the reading. I'll bet you can tell me the entire history of Parkinson's – every theory, research programme and celebrity sufferer. Come on, you tell me. What drugs should I be prescribing? What diet?'

I hate the fact that he's right. I can give him chapter and verse. In the past month I have spent hours searching the Internet and reading medical journals. I know all about Dr James Parkinson, the English physician who in 1817 described a condition he called 'shaking palsy'. I can tell him that 120,000 people are affected by Parkinson's in Britain. It's more common in people over sixty, but one in seven patients show symptoms before they turn forty. About three-quarters of sufferers will develop a tremor at the onset, while the others may never have one.

Of course I've gone looking for answers. What did he expect? Except there aren't any to find. All the experts say the same thing – that Parkinson's is one of the most baffling and complex neurological disorders.

'What about the tests you ran?'

'The results aren't back yet. I should get them by next week. Then we'll discuss a drug regime.'

'What drugs?'

'A cocktail.'

He's starting to sound like Fenwick.

Jock ashes his cigar and leans forward. He looks more like a CEO every time I see him. Soon he'll be wearing coloured braces and golfing socks. 'How's Bobby Moran doing?'

'Not so good.'

'What happened?'

'He kicked a woman unconscious for stealing his cab.'

Jock forgets and inhales suddenly, coughing violently. 'Charming! Another happy outcome.'

It had been Jock who'd originally sent Bobby to me. A local GP had referred him for neurological tests but Jock could find nothing physically wrong, so he'd passed him on. His exact words to me were: 'Don't worry, he's insured. You might actually get paid.'

Jock thinks I should have stuck to 'real medicine' when I had the chance instead of having a social conscience more expensive than my mortgage. Ironically, he used to be just like me at university. When I remind him of the fact he claims all the best-looking girls were left wing in those days. He was a summer-of-love socialist – anything to get his leg over.

Nobody ever dies of Parkinson's Disease. You die with it. That's one of Jock's trite aphorisms. I can just see it on a bumper sticker because it's only half as ridiculous as 'Guns don't kill people, people do'.

My reaction to this disease normally comes under the heading, 'Why me?' but after meeting Malcolm on the roof of the Marsden I feel rather chastened. His disease is bigger than mine. His conker wins.

I began to realise something was wrong about fifteen months ago. The main thing was the tiredness. Some days it was like walking through mud. I still played tennis twice a week and coached Charlie's soccer team. During our training games I managed to keep up with a dozen eight-year-olds and picture myself as Zinedine Zidane, the play-maker, dispatching through balls and doing intricate one-twos.

But then I started to find that the ball didn't go where I'd intended it to any more, and if I took off suddenly I tripped over my own feet. Charlie thought I was clowning around. Julianne thought I was getting lazy. I blamed turning forty-two.

In hindsight I can see that the signs were there. My handwriting had become even more cramped and button-holes had become obstacles. Sometimes I had difficulty getting out of a chair and when I walked down stairs I held on to the handrails.

Then came our annual pilgrimage to Wales for my father's seventieth birthday. I took Charlie walking on Great Ormes Head, overlooking Penrhyn Bay. At first we could see Puffin Island in the distance, until an Atlantic storm rolled in, swallowing it like a gigantic white whale. Bent against the wind, we watched the waves crashing over rocks and felt the sting of the spray. Charlie said to me, 'Dad, why aren't you swinging your left arm?'

'What do you mean?'

'Your arm. It's just sort of hanging there.'

Sure enough, it was flopping uselessly by my side.

By next morning my arm seemed to be OK. I didn't say anything to Julianne and certainly not to my parents. My father – a man awaiting the summons to be God's personal physician – would have castigated me for being a hypochondriac and made fun of me in front of Charlie. He has never forgiven me for giving up medicine to study behavioural science and psychology.

Privately, my imagination was running wild. I had visions of brain tumours and blood clots. What if I'd had a minor stroke? Was a major one coming? I almost convinced myself that I had pains in my chest.

It was another year before I went to see Jock. By then, he too had noticed something was wrong. We were walking into the locker room at the tennis club and I started drifting towards the right, forcing him to stop in mid-stride. He had also noticed my left arm hanging limply by my side. Jock made a joke about it but I sensed that he was watching me closely.

There are no diagnostic tests for Parkinson's. An experienced neurologist like Jock relies on observation. There are four primary symptoms – tremors or trembling hands, arms, legs, jaw and face; rigidity or stiffness of the limbs and trunk; slowness of movement; and postural instability or impaired balance and coordination.

The disease is chronic and progressive. It is not contagious, nor is it usually inherited. There are lots of theories. Some scientists blame free radicals reacting with neighbouring molecules and causing damage to tissue. Others blame pesticides or some other pollutant in the food chain. Genetic factors haven't been entirely ruled out because there seems to be a slight genetic predisposition in families, and it may be that it's somehow age-related.

The truth is, it could be a combination of all – or none – of these things.

Perhaps I should be grateful. In my experience of doctors (and I grew up with one), the only time they give you a clear, unequivocal diagnosis is if you're standing in the surgery with, say, a glue-gun stuck to your head.

At four-thirty I'm outside trying to push against the early tide of people walking to underground stations and bus stops. I head towards Cavendish Square and hail a cab as it starts to rain again.

The desk sergeant at Holborn Police Station is pink-faced and freshly shaven, with his hair slicked down over his bald crown. Leaning on the counter, he dunks biscuits into a mug of tea, spilling crumbs on to the breasts of a page three girl. As I push through the glass door, he licks his fingers, wipes them down his shirt and slides the news-paper under the counter. He smiles and his cheeks jiggle.

I show him a business card and ask if I could possibly see the charge sheet for Bobby Moran. His good humour disappears.

'We're very busy at the moment – you'll have to bear with me.'

I look over my shoulder. The charge room is deserted except for a wasted teenage boy in torn jeans, trainers and an AC/DC T-shirt, who has fallen asleep on a wooden bench. There are cigarette burns on the floor and plastic cups copulating beside a metal bin.

With deliberate slowness, the sergeant saunters towards a bank of filing cabinets on the rear wall. A biscuit is stuck to the backside of his trousers and the pink icing is melting into his rump. I allow myself a smile.

According to the charge sheet, Bobby was arrested in central London eighteen days ago. He pleaded guilty at Bow Street Magistrates' Court and was bailed to appear again on 24 December at the Old Bailey. Malicious wounding is a Section 20 offence – assault causing grievous bodily harm. It carries a maximum penalty of five years' jail.

Bobby's statement is typed over three pages, double-spaced, with the corrections initialled in the margins. He makes no mention of the little boy or his argument with the jeweller. The woman had jumped the queue. For her troubles, she suffered a fractured jaw, depressed cheekbone, broken nose and three busted fingers.

'Where do I find out about the bail conditions?'

The sergeant leafs through the file and runs his finger down a court document.

'Eddie Barrett has the brief.' He grunts in disgust. 'He'll have this downgraded to ABH quicker than you can say ring-a-ding-ding.'

How did Bobby get a lawyer like Eddie Barrett? He's the best-known defence solicitor in the country, with a genius for self-promotion and the ability to produce the perfect soundbite.

'How much was the bail?'

'Five grand.'

Considering Bobby's circumstances, it seems an impossible sum.

I glance at my watch. It's still only five-thirty. Eddie's secretary answers the phone and I can hear Eddie shouting in the background. She apologises and asks me to wait. The two of them shout at each other. It's like listening to a Punch and Judy show. Eventually, she comes back to me. Eddie can give me twenty minutes.

It's quicker to walk than to take a taxi to Chancery Lane. Buzzed through the main door, I climb the narrow stairs to the third floor, weaving past the boxes of court documents and files that have been stacked in every available space.

Eddie is talking on the phone as he ushers me into his office and points to a chair. I have to move two files to sit down. Eddie looks to be in his late fifties but is probably ten years younger. Whenever I've seen him interviewed on TV he's put me in mind of a bulldog. He has the same swagger, with his shoulders barely moving and his arse swinging back and forth. He even has large incisor teeth which must come in handy when ripping strips off people.

When I mention Bobby's name Eddie looks disappointed. I think he was hoping for a medical malpractice case. He spins his chair and begins searching the drawer of a filing cabinet.

'What did Bobby tell you about the attack?'

'You saw his statement.'

'Did he mention seeing a young boy?'

'No.' Eddie interrupts tiredly. 'Look, I don't want to get off on the wrong foot here, Roseanne, but just explain to me why the fuck I'm talking to you? No offence.'

'None taken.' He's a lot less pleasant up close. I start again. 'Did Bobby mention he was seeing a psychologist?'

Eddie's mood improves. 'Shit, no! Tell me more.'

'I've been seeing him for about six months. I also think he's been evaluated before but I don't have the records.'

'A history of mental illness – better and better.' He picks up a ringing telephone and motions for me to carry on. He's trying to conduct two conversations at once.

'Did Bobby tell you why he lost his temper?'

'She took his cab.'

'It's hardly a reason.'

'You ever tried to get a cab in Holborn on a wet Friday afternoon?' he chuckles.

'I think there's more to it than that.'

Eddie sighs. 'Listen, Pollyanna, I don't ask my clients to tell me the truth. I just keep them out of jail so they can go and make the same mistakes all over again.'

'The woman – what did she look like?'

'A fucking mess in the photographs.'

'How old?'

'Mid-forties. Dark hair.'

'What was she wearing?'

'Just a second.' He hangs up the phone and yells to his secretary to get him Bobby's file. Then he riffles through the pages, humming to himself. 'Mid-thigh skirt, high heels, a short jacket . . . mutton dressed as lamb if you ask me. Why do you want to know?'

I can't tell him. It's only half an idea. 'What's going to happen to Bobby?'

'Right now he faces prison time. The CPS won't down-grade the charges.'

'Jail isn't going to help him. I can do you a psych report. Maybe I can get him into an anger management programme.'

'What do you want from me?'

'A written request.'

Eddie's pen is already moving. I can't remember the last time I could write that fluidly. He slides it across the desk.

'Thanks for this.'

He grunts, 'It's a letter, not a kidney.'

If ever a man had issues. Maybe it's a Napoleon complex, or he's trying to compensate for being ugly. He's bored with me now. The subject no longer interests him. I ask my questions quickly.

'Who put up the bail?'

'No idea.'

'And who phoned you?'

'He did.'

Before I can say anything else, he interrupts. 'Listen, Oprah, I'm due in court and I need a pee. This kid is *your* nutcase; I just defend the sorry fuck. Why don't you take a peek inside his head, see if anything rattles and come back to me? Have a terrific day.'

9

Julianne and Charlie are watching television downstairs. I'm sitting on the floor of the attic room, going through boxes of my old case notes looking for my files on Catherine McBride. I don't know why exactly. Maybe I'm hoping to bring her to life in my mind so I can ask her questions.

Ruiz doesn't trust me. He thinks I'm trying to hide something. I should have told him sooner and I should have told him everything. It won't make any difference. Nothing can bring Catherine back.

The notebooks are all labelled with a month and year, which makes them easy to find. There are two of them, with dark green covers and mottled spines where silverfish have been feasting.

Downstairs in the study, I turn on the light and begin reading the notes. The A4 pages are neatly ruled, with a wide margin showing the date and time of each appointment.

Assessment details, medical notes and observations are all here.

How do I remember Catherine? I see her walking down the corridor of the Marsden dressed in a light blue uniform with dark blue trim on the collar and sleeves. She waves to me and smiles. She has a key chain on her belt. Most nurses have short-sleeved tunics but Catherine wore hers long.

In the beginning she was just another face in the corridor or in the cafeteria. She was pretty in a genderless way, with her boyish haircut, high forehead and full lips. She nervously cocked her head from one side to the other, never looking at me with both eyes at once. I seemed to bump into her a lot – often just as I was leaving the hospital. Only later did I suspect that she was orchestrating this.

Eventually she asked if she could talk to me. It took me a few minutes to realise that she meant professionally. I made an appointment for her and she arrived the next day.

From then on she came to see me once a week. She would put a bar of chocolate on my desk and break up the pieces on the silver foil, like a child divvying up sweets. And in between smoking menthol cigarettes, she would let the chocolate melt under her tongue.

'Do you know this is the only office in the entire hospital where you can smoke?' she told me.

'I guess that's why I get so many visitors.'

She was twenty, materialistic, sensible and having an affair with someone on staff. I don't know who it was but I suspect he was married. Occasionally she would say 'we' and then, realising her mistake, change to the singular.

Very rarely did she smile. She would cock her head and look at me with one eye or the other.

I also suspected she had seen someone like me before. Her questions were so precise. She knew about history-taking and cognitive therapy. She was too young to have studied psychology so she must have been a patient.

She talked of feeling worthless and insignificant. Estranged from her family, she had tried to mend fences but feared that she would 'poison their perfect lives'.

As she spoke and sucked pieces of chocolate, she sometimes rubbed her forearms through her buttoned-down sleeves. I thought that she was hiding something but waited for her to find the confidence to tell me.

During our fourth session she slowly wound up her sleeves. Part of her was embarrassed to show me the scars, but I also sensed defiance and a hint of self-satisfaction. She wanted me to be impressed by the severity of her wounds. They were like a life-map that I could read.

Catherine had first cut herself aged twelve. Her parents were going through a hate-filled divorce. She felt caught in the middle, like a rag doll being pulled apart by two warring children.

She wrapped a hand-mirror inside a towel and smashed it against the corner of her desk. She used a shard to open up her wrist. The blood gave her a sense of wellbeing. She was no longer helpless.

Her parents bundled her into the car and drove her to hospital. Throughout the entire journey they argued over who was to blame. Catherine felt peaceful and calm. She was admitted to hospital overnight. Her cuts had stopped bleeding. She fingered her wrist lovingly and kissed her cuts goodnight.

'I had found something I could control,' she told me. 'I

could decide how many times I cut, how deep I would go. I liked the pain. I craved the pain. I deserved it. I know I must have masochistic tendencies. You should see the men I end up with. You should hear about some of my dreams . . . '

She never admitted spending time in a psychiatric hospital or in group therapy. Much of her past she kept hidden, particularly if it involved her family. For long periods she managed to stop herself cutting. But with each relapse she punished herself by cutting even deeper. She concentrated on her arms and thighs, where she could hide the wounds under her clothing. She also discovered which creams and bandages helped minimise scarring.

When she needed stitches she chose Accident & Emergency centres away from the Marsden. She couldn't risk losing her job. She would give a false name to the triage nurse and sometimes pretend to be foreign and unable to speak English.

She knew from past experience how nurses and doctors regard self-mutilators – as attention-seekers and time-wasters. Often they get stitched without anaesthetic. 'If you enjoy pain so much, have a little more,' is the attitude.

None of this changed Catherine's behaviour. When she bled she escaped the numbness. My notebooks repeat her words, 'I feel alive. Soothed. In control.'

Dark brown flecks of chocolate are stuck between the pages. She would break off pieces and drop them on the page. She didn't like me writing. She wanted me to listen.

To break the cycle of blood, I gave her alternative strategies. Instead of reaching for a blade I told her to squeeze a piece of ice in her hand, bite down on a hot chilli or rub liniment on her genitals. This was pain without the scarring or the guilt. Once we broke into her thought loop, it was possible to find new coping mechanisms, less physical and violent.

A few days later, on 15 July, Catherine found me in the oncology ward. She had a bundle of sheets in her arms and was looking anxiously from side to side. I saw something in her eyes that I couldn't recognise.

She motioned me to follow her into an alcove and then dropped the sheets. It took me a few moments to notice the sleeves of her cardigan. They were stuffed with paper towels and tissues. Blood leaked through the layers of paper and fabric.

'Please don't let them find out,' she said. 'I'm so sorry.'

'You have to go to A and E.'

'No! Please! I need this job.'

A thousand voices inside my head were telling me what I should do. I ignored every one of them. I sent Catherine ahead to my office while I collected sutures, needles and butterfly clips, bandages and antibiotic ointment. Behind drawn blinds and a locked door I stitched up her forearms.

'You're good at this,' she said.

'I've had some practice.' I applied the antiseptic. 'What happened?'

'I tried to feed the bears.'

I didn't smile. She looked chastened. 'I had a fight with someone. I don't know who I wanted to punish.'

'Your boyfriend?'

She blinked back tears.

'What did you use?'

'A razor blade.'

'Was it clean?'

She shook her head.

'OK. From now on, if you insist on cutting yourself, you should use these.' I handed her a packet of disposable scalpels in a sterilised container. I also gave her bandages, steri-strips and sutures.

'These are my rules,' I told her. 'If you insist on doing this, you must cut in one place . . . on the inside of your thigh.'

She nodded.

'I'm going to teach you how to suture yourself. If you find that you can't do this, then you must go to a hospital.'

Her eyes were wide.

'I am not going to take the cutting option away from you, Catherine. Nor am I going to tell your superiors. But you must do everything in your power to control this. I am placing my trust in you. You can repay my faith by not harming yourself. If you weaken you *must* call me. If you fail to do this and cut yourself then I am not going to blame you or think any less of you. At the same time, I will not run to you. If you harm yourself I will not see you for a week. This is not a punishment – it is a test.'

I could see her thinking hard about the ramifications. Her face still showed fear but her shoulders betrayed her relief.

'From now on we set limits for your self-harm and you take responsibility for it,' I continued. 'At the same time we're going to find new ways for you to cope.'

I gave Catherine a quick sewing lesson using a pillow. She made a joke about me making someone a fine wife. As she rose to leave she put her arms around me. 'Thank you.' Her body sank into mine and she clung to me so tightly I could feel her heart beating.

After she had gone I sat staring at the blood-soaked bandages in the wastepaper bin. I was trying to work out if I was completely insane. I could see the coroner, rigid with indignation, asking me why I had given scalpels to a young woman who enjoyed slicing herself open. He would ask me if I also favoured handing matches to arsonists and heroin to junkies.

Yet I could see no other way to help Catherine. A zero-tolerance approach would simply reinforce her belief that other people controlled her life and decided things for her. That she was worthless and couldn't be trusted.

I had given her the choice. Hopefully, before she took up the blade, she would think closely about her reasons and weigh the consequences. And she would also consider other ways that she might cope.

In the months that followed Catherine slipped up only once. Her forearms healed. My stitching job was remarkably neat for someone so out of practice.

The notes end there but there's more to the story. I still cringe in embarrassment when I remember the details because I should have seen it coming.

Catherine started taking a little extra care with her appearance. She made appointments to see me at the end of her shift and would have changed into civvies. She wore make-up and a splash of perfume. An extra button was undone on her blouse. Nothing too obvious – it was all very subtle. She asked what I did in my spare time. A friend had given her two tickets to the theatre. Did I want to go with her?

There is an old joke about psychologists being the experts you pay to ask questions your spouse asks you for nothing.

We listen to problems, read the subtexts and build up self-esteem, teaching people to like who they really are.

For someone like Catherine, having a man really listen and care about her problems was enormously attractive, but sometimes it can be mistaken for something more intimate.

Her kiss came as a total surprise. We were in my office at the Marsden. I pushed her away too suddenly. She stumbled backwards and tripped, landing on the floor. She thought it was part of a game. 'You can hurt me if you want to,' she said.

'I don't want to hurt you.'

'I've been a bad, bad girl.'

'You don't understand.'

'Yes, I do.' She was unzipping her skirt.

'Catherine, you're making a mistake. You've misread the signs.'

The harshness in my voice finally brought her round. She stood beside my desk with her skirt at her ankles and her blouse undone. Pantyhose hid the scars on her thighs. It was embarrassing for both of us – but more so for her. She ran out with mascara leaking down her cheeks and her skirt clutched around her waist.

She quit her job and left the Marsden but the ramifications of that day have plagued me for the rest of my career. Hell hath no fury like a woman scorned.

10

Julianne is doing her stretching exercises in the spare bedroom. She does these yoga-like poses every morning with names that sound like Indian squaws: 'Babbling Brook' meets 'Running Deer'.

A veteran early riser, she is combat-ready by 6.30 a.m. Nothing like me. I've been seeing bloody and beaten faces all night in my dreams.

Julianne pads barefoot into the bedroom wearing just a pyjama top. She bends to kiss me.

'You had a restless night.'

Pressing her head against my chest, she lets her fingers go tap-dancing up my spine until she feels me shiver. She is reminding me that she knows every square inch of me.

'I didn't tell you about Charlie singing carols with the choir.'

'Bugger! I totally forgot.' It was Thursday morning in Oxford Street. 'I was with that detective.'

'Don't worry. She'll forgive you. Apparently young Ryan Fraser kissed her on the bus on the way home.'

'Cheeky sod.'

'It wasn't easy. Three of her friends had to help her catch him and hold him down.'

We laugh and I pull her on top of me, letting her feel my erection against her thigh.

'Stay in bed.'

She laughs and slides away. 'No. I'm too busy.'

'C'mon?'

'It's not the right time. You have to save your fellas.'

My 'fellas' are my sperm. She makes them sound like paratroopers.

She's getting dressed. White bikini pants slide along her legs and snap into place. Then she raises the shirt over her head and shrugs her shoulders into the straps of a bra. She won't risk giving me another kiss. I might not let her go next time.

After she's gone I stay in bed listening to her move through the house, her feet hardly touching the floor. I hear the kettle being filled and the milk being collected from the front step. I hear the freezer door open and the toaster being pushed down.

Dragging myself upright, I take six paces to the bathroom and turn on the shower. The boiler in the basement belches and the pipes clunk and gurgle. I stand shivering on the cold tiles waiting for some sign of water. The showerhead is shaking. At any moment I expect the tiles to start coming loose from around the taps.

After two coughs and a hacking spit, a cloudy trickle emerges and then dies.

'The boiler is broken again,' yells Julianne from downstairs.

Great! Brilliant! Somewhere there is a plumber laughing at me. He's no doubt telling all his plumber mates how he pretended to fix a Jurassic boiler and charged enough to pay for a fortnight in Florida.

I shave with cold water, using a fresh razor, without cutting myself. It may seem like a small victory, but worth noting.

I emerge into the kitchen and watch Julianne make plunger coffee and put posh jam on a piece of wholemeal toast. I always feel childish eating my Rice Krispies.

I still remember the first time I saw her. She was in her first year studying languages at London University. I was doing my postgraduate degree. Not even my mother would call me handsome. I had curly brown hair, a pear-shaped nose and skin that freckled at the first hint of sunlight.

I had stayed on at university determined to sleep with every promiscuous, terminally uncommitted first-year on campus, but unlike other would-be Lotharios I tried too hard. I even failed miserably at being fashionably unkempt and seditious. No matter how many times I slept on someone's floor, using my jacket as a pillow, it refused to crumple or stain. And instead of appearing grungy and intellectually blasé, I looked like someone on his way to his first job interview.

'You had passion,' she told me later, after listening to me rail against the evils of apartheid at a rally in Trafalgar

Square, outside the South African embassy. She introduced herself in the pub and let me pour her a double from the bottle of whisky we were drinking.

Jock was there – getting all the girls to sign his T-shirt. I knew that he would find Julianne. She was a fresh face – a pretty one. He put his arm around her waist and said, 'I could grow to be a better person just being near you.'

Without a flicker of a smile, she took his hand away and said, 'Sadly, a hard-on doesn't count as personal growth.'

Everybody laughed except Jock. Then Julianne sat down at my table and I gazed at her in wonderment. I had never seen anyone put my best friend in his place so skilfully.

I tried not to blush when she said I had passion. She laughed. She had a dark freckle on her bottom lip. I wanted to kiss it.

Five doubles later she was asleep at the bar. I carried her to a cab and took her home to my bed-sit in Islington. She slept on the futon and I took the sofa. In the morning she kissed me and thanked me for being such a gentleman. Then she kissed me again. I remember the look in her eyes. It wasn't lust. It didn't say, 'Let's have some fun and see what happens.' Her eyes were telling me, 'I'm going to be your wife and have your babies.'

We were always an odd couple. I was the quiet, practical one, who hated noisy parties, pub-crawls and going home for weekends. While she was the only child of a painter father and interior designer mother, who dressed like sixties flower children and only saw the best in people. Julianne didn't go to parties – they came to her.

We married three years later. By then I was house-trained

– having learned to put my dirty washing in the basket, to leave the toilet seat down and not to drink too much at dinner parties. Julianne didn't so much 'knock off my rough edges' as fashion me out of clay.

That was sixteen years ago. Seems like yesterday.

Julianne pushes a newspaper towards me. There's a photograph of Catherine and the headline reads: 'Tortured Girl is MP's Niece'.

Junior Home Office minister Samuel McBride has been devastated by the brutal murder of his 27-year-old niece.

The Labour MP for Brighton-le-Sands was clearly upset yesterday when the Speaker of the House expressed the chamber's sincerest condolences at his loss.

Catherine McBride's naked body was found six days ago beside the Grand Union Canal in Kensal Green, West London. She had been stabbed repeatedly.

'At this moment we are concentrating on retracing Catherine's final movements and finding anyone who may have seen her in the days prior to her death,' said Detective Inspector Vincent Ruiz, who is leading the investigation.

'We know she took a train from Liverpool to London on the thirteenth of November. We believe she was coming to London for a job interview.'

Catherine, whose parents are divorced, worked as a community nurse in Liverpool and had been estranged from her family for a number of years.

'She had a difficult childhood and seemed to lose her way,' explained a family friend. 'Recently attempts had been made for a family reconciliation.'

Julianne pours another cup of coffee. 'It's quite strange, don't you think, that Catherine should turn up after all these years?'

'How do you mean, strange?'

'I don't know.' She shivers slightly. 'I mean, she caused us all those problems. You nearly lost your job. I remember how angry you were.'

'She was hurting.'

'She was spiteful.'

She glances at the photograph of Catherine. It's a shot of her graduation day as a nurse. She's smiling fit to bust and clutching a diploma in her hand.

'And now she's back again. We were there when they found her. What are the chances of that? Then the police asked you to help identify her—'

'A coincidence is just a couple of things happening simultaneously.'

She rolls her eyes. 'Spoken like a true psychologist.'

11

Bobby is on time for once. He is dressed in his work clothes – a grey shirt and trousers. The word Nevaspring is sewn into the breast pocket. Again I'm surprised at how tall he is.

I finish the last of my notes, struggling to loop each letter, and then look up to see if he's ready. That's when I realise he'll never be entirely ready. Jock is right – there is something fragile and erratic about Bobby. His mind is full of half-finished ideas, strange facts and snatches of conversation.

Years ago a café called 'Oddballs' opened in Soho, which was supposed to attract all the eccentrics who inhabit the West End of London – the wild-haired artists, drag queens, punks, hippies, gonzo journalists and dandies. It never happened. Instead, every table in the place was filled with ordinary office workers, who arrived en masse hoping to see the oddballs. They finished up looking at each other.

Bobby often talks about writing in his spare time and his stories are sometimes sprinkled with literary allusions.

'Can I see some of the things you've written?' I ask.

'You don't really mean that.'

'Yes, I do.'

He thinks about this. 'Maybe I'll bring one next time.'

'Did you always want to be a writer?'

'Ever since I read *Catcher in the Rye*.'

My heart sinks. I have visions of another ageing angst-ridden teenager who thinks Holden Caulfield is Nietzsche.

'Do you relate to Holden?'

'No. He's an idiot!'

I feel relieved. 'Why?'

'He's naïve. He wants to save the children from falling over the cliff into adulthood – to preserve their innocence. He can't. It's impossible. We all get corrupted in the end.'

'How were you corrupted?'

'Ha!'

'Tell me more about your parents, Bobby. When was the last time you saw your father?'

'I was eight years old. He went to work and didn't come home.'

'Why?'

Bobby changes the subject. 'He was in the air force. He wasn't a pilot. He kept them in the air. A mechanic. He was too young for the war but I don't think it bothered him. He was a pacifist.

'When I was growing up he used to quote Marx to me – telling me about religion being the opium of the masses.

And most Sundays we took a bus from Kilburn to Hyde Park so he could heckle the lay preachers on their packing crate pulpits.

'This one preacher looked like Captain Ahab from *Moby Dick*, with long white hair tied back in a ponytail and a big booming voice. "The Lord will repay the wages of sin with eternal death," he said, looking directly at me.

'And Dad yelled back, "Do you know the difference between a preacher and a psychotic?" He paused and then answered, "It's the sound of the voice they hear." Everybody laughed except the preacher, who puffed up like a blowfish. "Is it true that you welcome all denominations, but you prefer tens and twenties?" said Dad.

' "You, sir, will go to hell," yelled the preacher.

' "And which way is that? Do I turn right or go straight on?" '

Bobby even has their voices down pat. He looks at me self-consciously, embarrassed to be so vocal.

'How did you get on with him?'

'He was my dad.'

'Did you do things together?'

'When I was young I used to ride on the crossbars of his bike, between his arms. He used to pedal really fast and make me laugh. One day he took me to see Queen's Park Rangers play at home. I sat on his shoulders and wore a blue and white scarf. Afterwards there were running fights between rival fans on Shepherd's Bush Green. Police on horseback charged the crowd but Dad wrapped his coat around me. I should have been scared but I knew that nothing was ever going to knock him down, not even those horses.'

He lapses into silence, scratching at his hands.

Every childhood has a mythology that materialises around it. We add our own desires and dreams until the stories become like parables that are more emblematic than edifying.

'What happened to your father?'

'It wasn't his fault,' he says defensively.

'Did he abandon you?'

Bobby explodes out of his chair. 'You know nothing about my father!' He's on his feet, sucking air between clenched teeth. 'You'll never know him! People like you destroy lives. You thrive on grief and despair. First sign of trouble you're there, telling people how they should feel. What they should think. You're like vultures!'

Just as suddenly the outburst dissipates. He wipes away white flecks of spit from his mouth and looks at me apologetically. He fills a glass with water and waits, with a strange calm, for my next question.

'Tell me about your mother.'

'She wears cheap perfume and she's dying of breast cancer.'

'I'm sorry to hear that. How old is she?'

'Forty-three. She won't let them give her a mastectomy. She's always been proud of her breasts.'

'How would you describe your relationship with her?'

'I heard the news from a friend in Liverpool. That's where she lives.'

'You don't visit her.'

'Ha!'

His face twists in frustration and he stops himself. 'Let me describe my mother to you . . .' He makes it sound like

113

a challenge. 'She was a grocer's daughter. Isn't that ironic? Just like Margaret Thatcher. She grew up in a corner shop – having her nappies changed right next to the cash register. By the time she was four she could tot up a basket of groceries, take the cash and hand back the correct change.

'Every morning and afternoon, as well as Saturdays and public holidays, she worked in that shop. And she read the magazines on the rack and daydreamed about escaping and living a different life. When Dad came along – dressed in his air force uniform – he said he was a pilot. It's what all the girls wanted to hear. A quick shag behind the social club at RAF Marham and she was pregnant with me. She found out he wasn't a pilot soon enough. I don't think she cared . . . not then. Later it drove her crazy. She said she married him under false pretences.'

'But they stayed together?'

'Yeah. Dad left the air force and got a job working as a mechanic fixing buses for London Transport. Later he became a conductor on the number ninety-six to Piccadilly Circus. He said he was a "people person", but I think he also liked the uniform. He used to ride his bike to the depot and home again.'

Bobby lapses into silence, reliving the memories. Prompting him gently, he tells me his father was an amateur inventor, always coming up with ideas for timesaving devices and gadgets.

'People talk about building a better mousetrap; well, he was doing stuff like that.'

'What did your mother think?'

'She said he was wasting his time and their money. One minute she'd be calling him a dreamer and laughing at all his "stupid inventions" and the next she'd be saying he didn't dream big enough and that he lacked ambition.'

Blinking rapidly, he looks at me with his odd pale eyes, as though he's forgotten his train of thought. Suddenly he remembers.

'She was the *real* dreamer, not Dad. She saw herself as a free spirit, surrounded by boring mediocrity. And no matter how hard she tried she could never live a bohemian lifestyle in a place like Hendon. She hated the place – the flat-front houses with their pebbledash façades, the net curtains, cheap clothes, greasy spoon cafés and garden gnomes. Working-class people talk about "looking after our own", but she scoffed at that. She could see only smallness, insignificance and ugliness.'

He's settled into a dull riff, as though he's told the story too often before.

'She'd get dressed up and go out most nights. I used to sit on the bed and watch her get ready. She'd try on different outfits – modelling them for me. She let me zip up the back of her skirts and smooth her stockings. She called me her Little Big Man.

'If Dad wouldn't take her out, she went by herself – to the pub, or the club. She had the sort of wicked laugh that told everyone she was there. Men would turn their heads and look at her. They found her sexy even though she was plump. Pregnancy had added pounds that she had never managed to shed. She blamed me for that. And when she went dancing or laughed too hard she sometimes wet her pants. That was my fault, too.'

This last comment is delivered through gritted teeth. His fingers pick at the loose skin on the back of his hands, twisting it painfully, as though trying to tear it off. His body humbled, he begins again.

'She drank white sparkling wine because it looked like champagne. And the drunker she got, the louder she became. She used to start talking in Spanish because it sounded sexy. Have you heard a woman speaking Spanish?'

I nod, thinking of Julianne.

'It cramped her style if Dad took her out. Men won't flirt with a woman when her husband is standing at the same bar. By herself she had them all over her, putting arms around her waist, squeezing her arse. She stayed out all night and came home in the morning, with her knickers in her handbag and her shoes swinging from her fingertips. There was never any pretence of fidelity or loyalty. She didn't want to be the perfect wife. She wanted to *be* someone else.'

'What about your dad?'

A long minute passes before he finds the answer he wants. 'He grew smaller every day. Disappearing little by little. Death by a thousand cuts. That's how I hope she dies.'

The sentence hangs in the air but the silence isn't arbitrary. It feels as though someone has reached up and put a finger in front of the second hand on the clock.

'Why did you use that term?'

'Which one?'

'"Death by a thousand cuts".'

His smile is slight, involuntary and crooked. 'That's how I want her to die. Slowly. In pain. By her own hand.'

'You want her to kill herself?'

He doesn't answer.

116

'Do you ever imagine her dying?'

'I dream about it.'

'What do you dream?'

'That I'll be there.'

He stares at me, his pale eyes like bottomless pools.

Death by a thousand cuts. The ancient Chinese had a more literal translation: 'One thousand knives and ten thousand pieces'. The woman Bobby dragged from the cab was roughly the same age and wore the same sort of clothes as his mother. She also showed a similar coldness towards her son. Is this enough to explain his actions? I'm getting closer. The desire to understand violence has built-in brutality. Don't think of the white bear.

Another patient is waiting outside. Bobby slowly rises and turns towards the door.

'I'll see you on *Monday*,' I say, putting emphasis on the day. I want him to remember it. I want him to keep coming back.

He nods and reaches across to shake my hand. He's never done that before.

'Mr Barrett said you're going to help me.'

'I'm going to prepare a psych report.'

He nods. 'I'm not mad, you know.'

'I know.'

He taps his head. 'It was just a stupid mistake.'

Then he's gone. My next appointment, Mrs Aylmer, is already sitting down and telling me how many times she checks the locks before she goes to bed. I'm not listening. I stand at the window, watching Bobby emerge on to the street and walk towards the station. Every so often he checks his stride so as not to walk on the cracks in the pavement.

He stops when he spies a young woman walking towards him. As she passes, he turns his whole body to keep watching her. For a moment I think he's debating whether to follow her. He looks one way and then the other as though caught at a T-junction. Then, after several seconds, he skips over a crack and carries on.

I'm back in Jock's office, listening to him rattle off my results, which I don't understand. He wants to start me on medication as soon as possible.

There is no definitive test for Parkinson's. Instead they have lots of games and exercises that gauge the progression of the disease. Clicking a stopwatch, Jock makes me walk along a line of masking tape on the floor, turn and walk back again. Then I have to stand on one foot with my eyes closed.

When he brings out the coloured blocks I groan. It feels so childish – stacking blocks one on top of the other. First I use my right hand and then my left. My left hand is trembling before I start, but once I pick up a block it's OK.

Putting dots in a grid is more difficult. I aim for the centre of the square but the pen has a mind of its own. *It's a stupid test anyway.*

Afterwards Jock explains that patients like me, who present initially with tremors, have a significantly better prognosis. There are lots of new drugs becoming available to lessen the symptoms.

'You can expect to lead a full life,' he says, as though reading from a script. When he sees the look of disbelief on my face he attempts to qualify the statement. 'Well, maybe you'll lose a few years.'

He doesn't say anything about my quality of life.

'Stem-cell research is going to provide a breakthrough,' he adds, sounding upbeat. 'Within five or ten years they'll have a cure.'

'What do I do until then?'

'Take the drugs. Make love to that gorgeous wife of yours. Watch Charlie grow up.'

He gives me a prescription for Selegiline. 'Eventually you'll need to take Levodopa,' he explains, 'but hopefully we can delay that for maybe a year or more.'

'Are there any side effects?'

'You might get a little nauseous and have trouble sleeping.'

'Great!'

Jock ignores me. 'These drugs don't stop the progression of the disease. All they do is mask the symptoms.'

'So I can keep it secret for longer.'

He smiles ruefully. 'You'll face up to this sooner or later.'

'If I keep coming here maybe I'll die of passive smoking.'

'What a way to go.' He lights up a cigar and pulls the Scotch from his bottom drawer.

'It's only three o'clock.'

'I'm working on British summer time.' He doesn't ask, he simply pours me one. 'I had a visit from Julianne last week.'

I feel myself blinking rapidly. 'What did she want?'

'She wanted to know about your condition. I couldn't tell her. Doctor–patient privilege and all that bollocks.' After a pause, he says, 'She also wanted to know if I thought you were having an affair.'

'Why would she ask that?'

'She thinks you've been telling lies.'

I take a sip of Scotch and feel it burn my oesophagus. Jock watches through a stream of smoke, waiting for an answer. Instead of feeling angry or at fault, I have a bizarre sense of disappointment. How could Julianne have asked Jock a question like that? Why didn't she ask me directly?

Jock is still waiting for an answer. He sees my discomfort and begins to laugh, shaking his head like a wet dog.

I want to say, 'Don't you look at me like that – you've been divorced twice and are still chasing women half your age.'

'It's none of my business, of course,' he says, gloating. 'But if she walks out on you I'll be there to comfort her.'

He's not joking. He'd be sniffing around Julianne in a flash.

I quickly change the subject. 'Bobby Moran – how much do you know about him?'

Jock rocks his tumbler back and forth. 'No more than you do.'

'There's no mention in the medical notes about any previous psychiatric treatment.'

'What makes you think there has been any?'

'He quoted a question to me from a Mental Status Examination. I think he's been evaluated before.'

'Did you ask him?'

'He wouldn't talk about it.'

Jock's face is a study of quiet contemplation, which looks

as though it's been practised in the mirror. Just when I think he might add something constructive, he shrugs, 'He's an odd fucker, that's for sure.'

'Is that a professional opinion?'

He grunts. 'Most of my patients are unconscious when I spend time with them. I prefer it that way.'

12

A plumber's van is parked out front of the house. The sliding door is open and inside there are trays stacked one on top of the other, with silver and brass fittings, corners, S-bends and plastic couplings.

The company name is attached to the side panels on magnetised mats – D.J. Morgan Plumbers & Gas Fitters. I find him in the kitchen, having a cup of tea and trying to catch a glimpse of Julianne's breasts beneath her v-necked top. His apprentice is outside in the garden showing Charlie how to juggle a football with her knees and feet.

'This is our plumber, D.J.,' says Julianne.

Getting lazily to his feet, he nods a greeting without taking his hands from his pockets. He's in his mid-thirties, tanned and fit, with dark, wet-looking hair combed back from his forehead. He looks like one of those tradesmen you see on lifestyle shows, renovating houses or doing make-overs. I can see him asking himself what a woman like Julianne's doing with someone like me.

'Why don't you show Joe what you showed me?'

The plumber acknowledges her with the slightest dip of his head. I follow him to the basement door, which is secured with a bolt. Narrow wooden steps lead down to the concrete floor. A low-wattage bulb is fixed to the wall. Dark beams and bricks soak up the light.

I have lived in this house for four years and the plumber already knows the basement better than I do. With a genial openness, he points out various pipes above our heads, explaining the gas and water system.

I contemplate asking him a question but know from experience not to advertise my ignorance around tradesmen. I am not a handyman; I have no interest in DIY, which is why I can still count to twenty on my fingers and toes.

D.J. nudges the boiler with his work boot. The inference is clear. It's useless, junk, a joke.

'So how much is this going to cost?' I ask after getting lost halfway through his briefing.

He exhales slowly and begins listing the things that need replacing.

'How much for labour?'

'Depends how long it takes.'

'How long will it take?'

'Can't say until I check all the radiators.' He casually picks up an old bag of plaster, turned solid by the damp, and tosses it to one side. It would have taken two of me to move it. Then he glances at my feet. I am standing in a puddle of water that is soaking through the stitching of my shoes.

Mumbling something about keeping costs down, I retreat upstairs and try not to imagine him sniggering behind my back. Julianne hands me a cup of lukewarm tea – the last of the pot.

'Everything OK?'

'Fine. Where did you find him?' I whisper.

'He put a flyer through the letterbox.'

'References?'

She rolls her eyes. 'He did the Reynolds' new bathroom at number seventy-four.'

The plumbers carry their tools outside to the van and Charlie tosses her ball into the garden shed. Her hair is pulled back into a ponytail and her cheeks are flushed with the cold. Julianne scolds her for getting grass stains on her school tights.

'They'll come out in the wash,' says Charlie.

'And how would you know?'

'They always do.'

Charlie turns and gives me a hug. 'Feel my nose.'

'Brrrrrrr! Cold nose, warm heart.'

'Can Sam stay over tonight?'

'That depends. Is Sam a boy or a girl?'

'Daaaad!' Charlie screws up her face.

Julianne interrupts. 'You have football tomorrow.'

'What about next weekend?'

'Grandma and Grandpa are coming down.'

Charlie's face brightens as mine falls. I had totally forgotten. God's personal physician-in-waiting is giving a talk to an international medical conference. It will be a triumph, of course. He will be offered all sorts of honorary positions and part-time consultancies, which he will graciously refuse because travel wearies him. I will sit in silence through all of this, feeling as though I am thirteen again.

My father has a brilliant medical mind. There isn't a modern medical textbook that doesn't mention his name. He has written papers that have changed the way paramedics treat accident victims and altered the standard procedures of battlefield medics.

His father, my grandfather, was a founding member of the General Medical Council and its longest-serving chairman. He established his reputation as an administrator rather than as a surgeon, but the name is still writ large in the history of medical ethics.

This is where I come in – or don't come in. After having three daughters, I was the long-awaited son. As such, I was expected to carry on the medical dynasty, but instead I broke the chain. In modern parlance that makes me the weakest link.

Perhaps my father should have seen it coming. My failure to play rugby with any passion or aptitude should have tipped him off. All I can say for sure is that my flaws have mounted steadily since then and he's come to regard me as his own personal failure.

He couldn't understand my affection for Gracie. I didn't even try to explain. She was like a dropped stitch in our family's history – just like Uncle Rosskend, who was a conscientious objector during the war, and my cousin Brian who was done for stealing lingerie from department stores.

My parents never talked about Gracie. I had to pick up bits and pieces from cousins and distant relations who each had a tiny piece of the puzzle. Eventually I had enough to get a general picture of what had happened.

Gracie had been a nurse during World War I and fell pregnant to a childhood sweetheart who didn't return from the fighting. She was seventeen, unmarried, heartbroken and alone.

'No man wants a woman with a baby,' her mother told her as she put her on a train for London.

Gracie glimpsed her baby only once. The good sisters at Nazareth House in Hammersmith erected a sheet halfway down her body to stop her seeing the birth, but she tore it down. When she saw the mewling infant, ugly and beautiful all at once, something broke inside her that no medical doctor could ever fix.

My second cousin Angelina says there are family photographs of Gracie in mental asylums and county hospitals. All I can say for sure is that she moved into her house in Richmond in the early twenties and was still there when I went to university.

My mother called me to tell me that Gracie had died. I was mid-way through my exams in my third year of medicine – the exams I failed. According to the coroner's report, the blaze started in the kitchen and spread quickly through the ground floor. Even so, Gracie had ample opportunity to get out.

The firemen had seen her moving around upstairs before the fire had completely taken hold. They said she could have crawled out of a window on to the garage roof. But if that's the case, why couldn't the firemen have gone in the same way and saved her?

All the books, newspapers and magazines fed the flames

– along with the tins of fabric paint and bottles of dye in the laundry. The temperatures were so great that her entire rooms of 'collectibles' were reduced to a fine white ash.

Gracie had always sworn that they would have to carry her out of there in a pine box. In the end they could have swept her into a dustpan.

I had already decided that I didn't want to be a doctor. I just wasn't sure of the alternatives. I had questions instead of answers. I wanted to find out why Gracie had been so frightened of the world. Mostly, however, I wanted to discover if somebody could have helped her.

In the four years that it took me to get my degree, my father never once missed an opportunity to call me 'Mr Psychologist' or to make cracks about couches and inkblot tests. And when my thesis on agoraphobia was published in the *British Psychological Journal*, he said nothing to me or to anyone else in the family.

A comparable silence has greeted every stage of my career since then. I finished my training in London and was offered a job with Merseyside Health Authority. Julianne and I moved to Liverpool – a city of snub-nosed ferries, mill chimneys, Victorian statues and empty factories.

We lived in a gaunt, reformatory-like building with a pebbledash front and barred windows. It was opposite the Sefton Park bus terminal and we were woken each morning by the coughing and hacking of diesel engines that sounded like an ageing smoker spitting phlegm into a sink.

I lasted two years in Liverpool and still regard it as a place that I escaped from – a modern-day plague city full of sad-eyed children, long-term unemployed and mad poor people. If it hadn't been for Julianne I might have drowned in their misery.

At the same time I'm grateful because it taught me where I belong. For the first time London felt like home. I spent four years at West Hammersmith Hospital and later moved to the Royal Marsden. When I became a senior consultant my name was painted on a polished oak board in the foyer of the Marsden, opposite the front door. Ironically, my father's name was being taken off the same board as he, in his own words, 'scaled down commitments'.

I don't know if the two incidents were linked. I don't care. I long ago stopped worrying about what he thinks or why he does things. I have Julianne and Charlie. I have my own family now. One man's opinion doesn't matter – not even his.

13

Saturday mornings and soggy sports fields seem to go together like acne and adolescence. That's how I remember the winters of my childhood – standing ankle-deep in mud, freezing my bollocks off, playing for the school's Second XV. God's personal physician-in-waiting had a bellow that rose above the howling wind. 'Don't just stand there like a cold bottle of piss,' he'd shout. 'Call yourself a winger! I've seen continents drift faster than you.'

Thank goodness Charlie is a girl. She looks really cute in her soccer gear, with her hair pulled back and shorts down to her knees. I don't know how I managed to become coach. My knowledge of the round ball game could fit on the back of a coaster, which is probably why the Tigers haven't won a game all season. You're not supposed to count the score at this age, or keep a league table. It's all about having fun and getting every child involved. Tell that to the parents.

Today we're playing the Highgate Lions and each time they score the Tigers trudge back to halfway, debating who gets to kick off.

'It isn't our strongest side,' I say apologetically to the opposition coach. Under my breath I'm praying, 'Just one goal, Tigers. Just give us one goal. Then we'll show them a real celebration.'

At halftime we're down four nil. The kids are sucking on quarters of orange. I tell them how well they're playing. 'This team is undefeated,' I say, lying through my teeth, 'but you guys are holding them.'

I put Douglas, our strongest kicker, in goal for the second half. Andrew, our leading goal-scorer, is fullback.

'But I'm a striker,' he whinges.

'Dominic is playing up front.'

They all look at Dominic, who has only just worked out which direction we're running. He giggles and shoves his hand down his shorts, grabbing his scrotum.

'Forget about dribbling, or passing, or scoring goals,' I say. 'Just go out there and try to kick the ball as hard as you can.'

As the game restarts I have a posse of parents bending my ear about my positional changes. They think I've lost the plot. But there's a method to my madness. Soccer at this level is all about momentum. Once the ball is moving forward the whole game moves in that direction. That's why I want my strongest kickers at the back.

For the first few minutes nothing changes. The Tigers may as well be chasing shadows. Then the ball falls to Douglas and he hoofs it up field. Dominic tries to run out of the way, falls over and brings down both defenders. The ball rolls loose. Charlie is closest. I'm muttering under my breath, 'Nothing fancy. Just take the shot.'

Accuse me of favouritism. Call me biased. I don't care. What comes next is the most sweetly struck, curling, rising, dipping, swerving shot ever sent goal-wards by a size six football boot. Such are the scenes of celebration that any independent observer must be convinced that we've won.

Shell-shocked by our new strategy, the Lions fall apart. Even Dominic poaches a goal when the ball bounces off the back of his head and loops over the goalkeeper. The Tigers beat the Lions five goals to four.

Our finest endorsement comes from Julianne, who isn't what you'd call a dedicated football mum. I think she'd prefer Charlie to do ballet or to play tennis. Looking immaculate in a long black hooded coat and Wellingtons, she announces that she has never seen a more exciting piece of sport. The fact that she calls it a 'piece of sport' is testament to how little she watches football.

Parents are wrapping their children up warmly and putting muddy boots into plastic bags. As I gaze across the field I notice a man standing alone on the far side of the pitch with his hands in the pockets of an overcoat. I recognise the silhouette.

'What brings you out so early on a Saturday, Detective Inspector? It's not the exercise.'

Ruiz glances towards the jogging path. 'There's enough heavy breathers in this town already.'

'How did you know where to find me?'

'Your neighbours.'

He unwraps a boiled sweet and pops it into his mouth, rattling it against his teeth.

'How can I help you?'

'Do you remember what I told you at our breakfast? I said that if the victim turns out to be the daughter of someone famous I'll have forty detectives instead of twelve.'

'Yes.'

'Did you know your little nurse was the niece of a Tory MP and the granddaughter of a retired county court judge?'

'I read about her uncle in the papers.'

'I got the hyenas all over me – asking questions and shoving cameras in my face. It's a media fucking circus.'

There's nothing I can say, so I stare past him towards London Zoo and let him keep talking.

'You're one of the bright boys, right? University education, postgraduate degree, consultancy . . . I thought you might be able to help me out on this one. I mean, you knew this girl, right? You worked with her. So I figured you might have an insight into what she might be mixed up in.'

'I only knew her as a patient.'

'But she talked to you. She told you about herself. What about friends or boyfriends?'

'I think she was seeing someone at the hospital. He might have been married because she wouldn't talk about him.'

'She mention a name?'

'No.'

'Do you think she was promiscuous?'

'No.'

'Why are you so sure?'

'I don't know. It's just a feeling.'

He turns and nods at Julianne, who is suddenly beside me, slipping her arm through mine. Her hood is up and she looks like a nun.

'This is Detective Inspector Vincent Ruiz, the policeman I told you about.'

Concern creases her forehead. 'Is this about Catherine?' She pushes back her hood.

Ruiz looks at her as most men do. No make-up, no perfume, no jewellery and she still turns heads.

'Are you interested in the past, Mrs O'Loughlin?'

She hesitates. 'That depends.'

'Did you know Catherine McBride?'

'She caused us a lot of grief.'

Ruiz's eyes dart to mine and I get a sinking feeling.

Julianne looks at me and realises her mistake. Charlie is calling her. She looks over her shoulder and then turns back to Ruiz.

'Perhaps I should talk to your husband first,' he says slowly. 'I can always catch up with you later.'

Julianne nods and gives my arm a squeeze. 'I'll take Charlie for a hot chocolate.'

'OK.'

We watch her leave, stepping gracefully between muddy puddles and patches of turf. Ruiz tilts his head to one side as though trying to read something written sideways on my lapels.

'What did she mean?'

My credibility is non-existent. He's not going to believe me.

'Catherine made an allegation that I sexually assaulted her under hypnosis. She withdrew the complaint within hours but it still had to be investigated. It was all a misunderstanding.'

'How do you misunderstand something like that?'

I tell him how Catherine had confused my professional concern for something more intimate – about the kiss and her embarrassment. Her anger.

'You turned her down?'

'Yes.'

'So she made the complaint?'

'Yes. I didn't even know until after it had been withdrawn, but there still had to be an inquiry. I was suspended while the hospital board investigated. Other patients were interviewed.'

'All because of one letter?'

'Yes.'

'Did you talk to Catherine?'

'No. She avoided me. I didn't see her again until just before she left the Marsden. She apologised. She had a new boyfriend and they were going up north.'

'You weren't angry with her?'

'I was bloody furious. She could have cost me my career.' Realising how harsh that sounds, I add, 'She was very fragile emotionally.'

Ruiz gets out his notebook and begins writing something down.

'Don't make too much of it.'

'I'm not making anything out of it, Professor, it's just information. You and I both collect pieces of information until two or three of them fit together.' Turning the pages of his notebook, he smiles at me gently. 'It's amazing what you can find out these days. Married. One child. No religious affiliation. Educated at Charterhouse and London University. BA and MA in psychology. Taken into custody in 1980 for projecting the image of a swastika on South

Africa House during a 'Free Mandela' demonstration in Trafalgar Square. Twice caught speeding on the M40; one outstanding parking ticket; denied a Syrian visa in 1987 because of a previous visit to Israel. Father a well-known doctor. Three sisters. One works for the United Nations refugee programme. Your wife's father committed suicide in 1994. Your aunt died in a house fire. You have private medical insurance, an overdraft facility of ten thousand pounds and your car tax is due for renewal on Wednesday.' He looks up. 'I haven't bothered with your tax returns, but I'd say you went into private practice because that house of yours must cost a bloody fortune.'

He's getting to the point now. This whole spiel is a message to me. He wants to show me what he's capable of.

His voice grows quiet. 'If I find that you've withheld information from my murder inquiry I'll send you to jail. You can practise some of your skills first-hand when you're two-up in a cell with a Yardie who wants you to give it up for Jesus.' He closes the notebook and slips it into his pocket. Blowing on his cupped hands, he adds, 'Thank you for your patience, Professor.'

14

Bobby Moran intercepts me as I cross the lobby. He looks even more dishevelled than normal, with mud on his overcoat and papers bulging from his pockets. I wonder if he's been waiting for sleep or something bad to happen.

Blinking rapidly behind his glasses, he mumbles an apology. 'I have to see you.'

I glance over his head at the clock on the wall. 'I have another patient—'

'Please?'

I should say no. I can't have people just turning up. Meena will be furious. She could run a perfectly good office if it weren't for patients turning up unannounced or not keeping appointments. 'That's not the way to pack a suitcase,' she'll say and I'll agree with her, even if I don't completely understand what she means.

Upstairs, I tell Bobby to sit down and set about rearranging my morning. He looks embarrassed to have caused such a fuss. He is different today – more grounded, living in the here and now.

'You asked me about what I dream.' He is staring at a spot on the floor between his feet.

'Yes.'

'I think there's something wrong with me. I keep having these thoughts.'

'What thoughts?'

'I hurt people in my dreams.'

'How do you hurt them?'

He looks up at me plaintively. 'I try to stay awake . . . I don't want to fall asleep. Arky keeps telling me to come to bed. She can't understand why I'm watching TV at four in the morning, wrapped in a duvet on the sofa. It's because of the dreams.'

'What about them?'

'Bad things happen in them – that doesn't make me a bad person.' He is perched on the edge of the chair, with his eyes flicking from side to side. 'There's a girl in a red dress. She keeps turning up when I don't expect to see her.'

'In your dream?'

'Yes. She just looks at me – right through me as though I don't exist. She's laughing.'

His eyes snap wide as though spring-loaded and his tone suddenly changes. Spinning around in his chair, he presses his lips together and crosses his legs. I hear a harsh, feminine voice.

'Now, Bobby, don't tell lies.'

– 'I'm not a blabbermouth.'

'Did he touch you or not?'

– 'No.'

'That's not what Mr Erskine wants to hear.'

– 'Don't make me say it.'

'We don't want to waste Mr Erskine's time. He's come all this way—'

– 'I know why he's come.'

'Don't use that tone of voice with me, sweetie. It's not very nice.'

Bobby puts his big hands in his pockets and kicks at the floor with his shoes. He speaks in a timid whisper, with his chin pressed to his chest.

– 'Don't make me say it.'

'Just tell him and then we can have dinner.'

– 'Please don't make me say . . . '

He shakes his head and his whole body moves. Raising his eyes to me, I see a flicker of recognition.

'Do you know that a blue whale's testicles are as large as a Volkswagen Beetle?'

'No, I didn't know that.'

'I like whales. They're very easy to draw and to carve.'

'Who is Mr Erskine?'

'Should I know him?'

'You mentioned his name.'

He shakes his head and looks at me suspiciously.

'Is he someone you once met?'

'I was born in one world. Now I'm waist deep in another.'

'What does that mean?'

'I had to hold things together, hold things together.'

He's not listening to me. His mind is moving so quickly that it can't grasp any subject for more than a few seconds.

'You were telling me about your dream . . . a girl in a red dress. Who is she?'

'Just a girl.'

'Do you know her?'

'Her arms are bare. She lifts them up and brushes her fingers through her hair. I see the scars.'

'What do these scars look like?'

'It doesn't matter.'

'Yes it does!'

Tipping his head to one side, Bobby runs his finger down the inside of his shirtsleeve, from his elbow to his wrist. Then he looks back at me. Nothing registers in his eyes. Is he talking about Catherine McBride?

'How did she get these scars?'

'She cut herself.'

'How do you know that?'

'A lot of people do.' Bobby unbuttons his shirt cuffs and slowly rolls the sleeve along his left forearm. Turning his palm face-up, he holds it out towards me. The thin white scars are faint but unmistakable. 'They're like a badge of honour,' he whispers.

'Bobby, listen to me.' I lean forward. 'What happens to the girl in your dream?'

Panic fills his eyes like a growing fever. 'I don't remember.'

'Do you know this girl?'

He shakes his head.

'What colour hair does she have?'

'Brown.'

'What colour eyes?'

He shrugs.

'You said you hurt people in your dreams. Did this girl get hurt?'

The question is too direct and confrontational. He looks at me suspiciously. 'Why are you staring at me like that? Are you taping this? Are you stealing my words?' He peers from side to side.

'No.'

'Well, why are you staring at me?'

Then I realise that he's talking about the 'Parkinson's mask'. Jock had warned me of the possibility. My face can become totally unresponsive and expressionless like an Easter Island statue.

I look away and try to start again, but Bobby's mind has already moved on.

'Did you know the year 1961 can be written upside down and right-way up and appear the same?' he says.

'No, I didn't.'

'That's not going to happen again until 6009.'

'I need to know about the dream, Bobby.'

'*No comprenderas todavía lo que comprenderas en el futuro.*'

'What's that mean?'

'It's Spanish. You don't understand yet what you will understand in the end.' His forehead suddenly creases as though he's forgotten something. Then his expression changes to one of complete bafflement. He hasn't just lost his train of thought – he's forgotten what he's doing here. He looks at his watch.

'Why are you here, Bobby?'

'I keep having these thoughts.'

'What thoughts?'

'I hurt people in my dreams. That's not a crime. It's only a dream . . .'

140

We have been here before, thirty minutes ago. He has forgotten everything in between.

There is an interrogation method, sometimes used by the CIA, which is called the *Alice in Wonderland* technique. It relies upon turning the world upside down and distorting everything that is familiar and logical. The interrogators begin with what sound like very ordinary questions, but in fact are totally nonsensical. If the suspect tries to answer, the second interrogator interrupts with something unrelated and equally illogical.

They change their demeanour and patterns of speech in mid-sentence or from one moment to the next. They get angry when making pleasant comments and become charming when making threats. They laugh at the wrong places and speak in riddles.

If the suspect tries to cooperate he's ignored, and if he doesn't cooperate he's rewarded – never knowing why. At the same time, the interrogators manipulate the environment, turning clocks backwards and forwards, lights on and off, serving meals ten hours or only ten minutes apart.

Imagine this continuing day after day. Cut off from the world and everything he knows to be normal, the suspect tries to cling to what he remembers. He may keep track of time or try to picture a face or a place. Each of these threads to his sanity is gradually torn down or worn down until he no longer knows what is real and unreal.

Talking to Bobby is like this. The random connections, twisted rhymes and strange riddles make just enough sense for me to listen. At the same time, I'm being drawn deeper into the intrigue and the lines between fact and fantasy have begun to blur.

He won't talk about his dream again. Whenever I ask about the girl in the red dress, he ignores me. The silence has no effect. He is totally contained and unreachable.

Bobby is slipping away from me. When I first met him I saw a highly intelligent, articulate, compassionate young man, concerned about his life. Now I see a borderline schizophrenic, with violent dreams and a possible history of mental illness.

I thought I had a handle on him, but now he's attacked a woman in broad daylight and confessed to 'hurting' people in his dreams. What about the girl with the scars?

Take a deep breath. Review the facts. Don't force pieces to fit the puzzle. One in fifteen people harm themselves at some point in their lives: that's two children in every classroom, four people on a crowded bus, twenty on a commuter train and two thousand at an Arsenal home game.

In my sixteen years as a psychologist I have learned unequivocally not to believe in conspiracies or to listen for the same voices my patients are hearing. A doctor is no good to anyone if he dies of the disease.

15

The school is beautiful: solid, Georgian and covered with wisteria. The crushed quartz driveway begins to curve as it passes through the gates and finishes at a set of wide stone steps. The parking area looks like a salesroom for Range Rovers and Mercedes. I park my Metro around the corner on the street.

Charlie's school is having its annual fund-raising dinner and auction. The assembly hall has been decked out with black and white balloons and the caterers have set up a marquee on the tennis courts.

The invitation said 'formal casual' but most of the mothers are wearing evening gowns because they don't get out very much. They are congregated around a minor TV celebrity who is sporting a sun-bed tan and perfect teeth. That's what happens when you send your child to an expensive private school. You rub shoulders with diplomats, game-show hosts and drug barons.

This is our first night out in weeks but instead of feeling relaxed I'm on edge. I keep thinking about Julianne's visit to see Jock. Somehow she knows I lied to her. When is she going to say something? Ever since the diagnosis I have descended into dark moods and withdrawn from people. Maybe I'm feeling guilty. More likely it's regret. This is my way of disinfecting those around me.

I am losing my body bit by bit. One part of me thinks this is OK. I'll be fine as long as I have my mind. I can live in the space between my ears. But another part is already longing for what I haven't yet lost.

So here I am – not so much at a crossroads as at a cul-de-sac. I have a wife who fills me with pride and a daughter who makes me cry when I watch her sleeping. I am forty-two years old and I have just started to understand how to combine intuition with learning and do my job properly. Half my life lies ahead of me – the best half. Unfortunately, my mind is willing but my body isn't able – or soon won't be. It is deserting me by increments. That is the only certainty that remains.

The fund-raising auction takes too long. They always do. The master of ceremonies is a professional auctioneer with an actor's voice that cuts through the chatter and small talk. Each class has created two artworks – mostly brightly coloured collages of individual drawings. Charlie's class made a circus and a beachscape with coloured bathing huts, rainbow umbrellas and ice-cream stalls.

'That would look great in the kitchen,' says Julianne, putting her arm through mine.

'How much is the plumbing going to cost us?'

She ignores me. 'Charlie drew the whale.'

Looking carefully, I notice a grey lump on the horizon. Drawing isn't one of her strong suits, but I know she loves whales.

Auctions bring out the best and worst in people. And the only bidder more committed than a couple with an only child is a besotted and cashed-up grandparent.

I get to make one bid for the beach scene at £65. When the hammer comes down, to polite applause, it has made £700. The successful bid is by phone. You'd think this was bloody Sotheby's.

We arrive home after midnight. The babysitter has forgotten to turn on the front porch light. In the darkness I trip over a stack of copper pipes and fall up the steps, bruising my knee.

'D.J. asked if he could leave them there,' apologises Julianne. 'Don't worry about your trousers. I'll soak them.'

'What about my knee?'

'You'll live.'

We both check on Charlie. Soft animals surround her bed, facing outwards like sentries guarding a fort. She sleeps on her side with her thumb hovering near her lips.

As I clean my teeth, Julianne stands beside me at the vanity taking off her make-up. She is watching me in the mirror.

'Are you having an affair?'

The question is delivered so casually it catches me by surprise. I try to pretend I haven't heard her but it's too late. I've stopped brushing. The pause has betrayed me.

'Why?'

She's wiping mascara from her eyelashes. 'Lately I've had the feeling that you're not really here.'

'I've been preoccupied.'

'You still want to be here, don't you?'

'Of course I do.'

She hasn't taken her eyes off me in the mirror. I look away, rinsing my toothbrush in the sink.

'We don't talk any more,' she says.

I know what's coming. I don't want to go in this direction. This is where she gives me chapter and verse about my inability to communicate. She thinks that, because I'm a psychologist, I should be able to talk through my feelings and analyse what's going on. Why? I spend all day inside other people's heads. When I get home, the hardest thing I want to think about is helping Charlie with her times tables.

Julianne is different. She's a talker. She shares everything and works things through. It's not that I'm scared of showing my feelings. I'm scared of not being able to stop.

I try to head her off at the pass. 'When you've been married as long as we have you don't need to talk as much,' I say feebly. 'We can read each other's minds.'

'Is that so? What am I thinking now?'

I pretend I don't hear her. 'We're comfortable with each other. It's called familiarity.'

'Which breeds contempt.'

'No!'

She puts her arms around me, running her hands down

146

my chest and locking them together at my waist. 'What is the point of sharing your life with someone if you can't communicate with them about the things that matter?' Her head is resting against my back. '*That's* what married couples do. It's perfectly normal. I know you're hurting. I know you're scared. I know you're worried about what's going to happen when the disease gets worse . . . about Charlie and me . . . but you can't stand between us and the world, Joe. You can't protect us from something like this.'

My mouth is dry and I feel the beginnings of a hangover. This isn't an argument – it's a matter of perception. I know that if I don't answer, Julianne will fill the vacuum.

'What are you so frightened of? You're not dying.'

'I know.'

'Of course it's unfair. You don't deserve this. But look at what you have – a lovely home, a career, a wife who loves you and a daughter who worships the ground you walk on. If that can't outweigh any other problems then we're all in trouble.'

'I don't want anything to change.' I hate how vulnerable I sound.

'Nothing *has* to change.'

'I see you watching me. Looking for the signs. A tremor here, a twitch there.'

'Does it hurt?' she asks suddenly.

'What?'

'When your leg locks up or your arm doesn't swing.'

'No.'

'I didn't know that.' She puts her fist in my hand and curls my fingers around it. Then she makes me turn so her eyes can fix on mine. 'Does it embarrass you?'

'Sometimes.'

'Is there any special diet you should be on?'

'No.'

'What about exercise?'

'It can help, according to Jock, but it won't stop the disease.'

'I didn't know,' she whispers. 'You should have told me.' She leans even closer, pressing her lips to my ear. The droplets of water on her cheeks look like tears. I stroke her hair.

Hands brush down my chest. A zipper undone; her fingers softly caressing; the taste of her tongue; her breath inside my lungs . . .

Afterwards, as we lie in bed, I watch her breasts tremble with her heartbeat. It is the first time we've made love in six years without checking the calendar first.

The phone rings.

'Professor O'Loughlin?'

'Yes.'

'This is Charing Cross Hospital. I'm sorry to wake you.' The doctor sounds young; I can hear the tiredness in his voice. 'Do you have a patient named Bobby Moran?'

'Yes.'

'The police found him lying on the walkway across Hammersmith Bridge. He's asking for you.'

16

Julianne rolls over and nestles her face into my pillow, pulling the bedclothes around her.

'What's wrong?' she asks sleepily.

'Problem with a patient.' I pull a sweatshirt over my T-shirt and go looking for my jeans.

'You're not going in, are you?'

'Just for a little while.'

It takes me fifteen minutes to reach Fulham at that hour of the morning. Peering through the main doors of the hospital, I see a black cleaner pushing a mop and bucket around the floor in a strange waltz. A security guard sits at the reception desk. He motions me to the Accident & Emergency entrance.

Inside the plastic swinging doors, people are scattered around the waiting room, looking tired and pissed off. The triage nurse is busy. A young doctor appears in the corridor and begins arguing with a bearded man who has a bloody rag pressed to his forehead and a blanket around his shoulders.

'And you'll be waiting all night if you don't sit down,' says the doctor. He turns away and looks at me.

'I'm Professor O'Loughlin.'

It takes a moment for my name to register. The cogs slip into place. The doctor has a birthmark down one side of his neck and keeps the collar of his white coat turned up.

A few minutes later I follow this coat down empty corridors, past linen trolleys and parked stretchers.

'Is he OK?'

'Mainly cuts and bruises. He may have fallen from a car or a bike.'

'Has he been admitted?'

'No, but he won't leave until he sees you. He keeps talking about washing blood from his hands. That's why I put him in the observation room. I didn't want him upsetting the other patients.'

'Concussion?'

'No. He's very agitated. The police thought he might be a suicide risk.' The doctor turns to look over his shoulder. 'Is your father a surgeon?'

'Retired.'

'I once heard him speak. He's very impressive.'

'Yes. As a lecturer.'

The observation room has a small viewing window at head-height. I see Bobby sitting on a chair, his back straight and both feet on the floor. He's wearing muddy jeans, a flannelette shirt and an army greatcoat. He tugs at the sleeves of the coat, picking at a loose thread. His eyes are bloodshot and fixed. They are focused on the far wall, as if watching some invisible drama being played out on a stage that no one else can see. He doesn't turn as I enter.

'Bobby, it's me, Professor O'Loughlin. Do you know where you are?'

He nods.

'Can you tell me what happened?'

'I don't remember.'

'How are you feeling?'

He shrugs, still not looking at me. The wall is more interesting. I can smell his sweat and the mustiness of his clothes. There is another odour — something familiar but I can't quite place it. A medical smell.

'What were you doing on Hammersmith Bridge?'

'I don't know.' His voice is shaking. 'I fell over.'

'What can you remember?'

'Going to bed with Arky and then . . . Sometimes I can't bear to be by myself. Do you ever feel like that? It happens all the time to me. I pace around the house after Arky. I follow her, talking about myself constantly. I tell her what I'm thinking . . . '

At last his eyes focus on me. Haunted. Hollow. I have seen the look before. One of my other patients, a fireman, is condemned to listening to the screams of a five-year-old girl who died in a blazing car. He rescued her mother and baby brother but couldn't go back into the flames.

Bobby asks, 'Do you ever hear the windmills?'

'What sound do they make?'

'It's a clanking metal noise, but when the wind is really strong the blades blur and the air starts screaming in pain.'

He shudders.

'What are the windmills for?'

'They keep everything running. If you put your ear to the ground you can hear them.'

'What do you mean by everything?'

'The lights, the factories, the railways. Without the windmills it all stops.'

'Are these windmills God?'

'You know nothing,' he says dismissively.

'Have you ever seen the windmills?'

'No. Like I said, I hear them.'

'Where do you think they are?'

'In the middle of the oceans; on huge platforms like oilrigs. They pull energy from the centre of the Earth – from the core. We're using too much energy. We're wasting it. That's why we have to turn off the lights and save power. Otherwise we'll upset the balance. Take too much out from the centre and you have a vacuum. The world will implode.'

'Why are we taking too much energy?'

'Turn off the lights, left, right, left, right. Do the right thing.' He salutes. 'I used to be right-handed but I taught myself to use my left . . . The pressure is building. I can feel it.'

'Where?'

He taps the side of his head. 'I've tapped the core. The apple core. Iron ore. Did you know the Earth's atmosphere is proportionately thinner than the skin of an apple?'

He is playing with rhymes – a characteristic of psychotic language. Simple puns and wordplay help connect random ideas.

'Sometimes I have dreams about being trapped inside a windmill,' he says. 'It's full of spinning cogs, flashing blades

152

and hammers striking anvils. That's the music they play in hell.'

'Is that one of your nightmares?'

His voice drops to a conspiratorial whisper. 'Some of us know what's happening.'

'And what is that?'

He rears back, glaring at me. His eyes are alight. Then a peculiar half smile passes over his face. 'Do you know it took a manned spacecraft less time to reach the moon than it did for a stagecoach to travel the length of England?'

'No. I didn't know that.'

He sighs triumphantly.

'What were you doing on Hammersmith Bridge?'

'I was lying down, listening to the windmills.'

'When you came into the hospital, you kept saying that you wanted to wash the blood off your hands.'

He remembers, but says nothing.

'How did you get blood on your hands?'

'It's normal enough to hate. We just don't talk about it. It's normal enough to want to hurt people who hurt us . . . '

He's not making any sense.

'Did you hurt someone?'

'You take all those drops of hate and you put them in a bottle. Drop, drop, drop . . . Hate doesn't evaporate like other liquids. It's like oil. Then, one day, the bottle is full.'

'What happens then?'

'It has to be emptied.'

'Bobby, did you hurt someone?'

'How else do you get rid of the hate?' He tugs at the cuffs of his flannelette shirt, which are stained with something dark.

'Is that blood, Bobby?'

'No, it's oil. Haven't you been listening to me? It's all about the oil.' He stands and takes two steps towards the door. 'Can I go home now?'

'I think you should stay here for a while,' I say, trying to sound matter-of-fact.

He eyes me suspiciously. 'Why?'

'Last night you suffered some sort of breakdown, or memory lapse. You might have been in an accident or had a fall. I think we should run some tests and keep you under observation.'

'In a hospital?'

'Yes.'

'In a general ward?'

'A psych ward.'

He doesn't miss a beat. 'No fucking way! You're trying to lock me up.'

'You'll be a voluntary patient. You can leave any time you want to.'

'This is a trick! You think I'm crazy!' He's yelling at me. He wants to storm out but something is keeping him here. Maybe he has too much invested in me.

I can't legally hold him. Even if I had the evidence I don't have the power to section or detain Bobby. Psychiatrists, medical doctors and the courts have such a prerogative but not a humble psychologist. Bobby's free to go.

'And you'll still see me?' he asks.

'Yes.'

He buttons his coat and nods his approval. I walk with him down the corridor and we share a lift. 'Have you ever had absences like this before?' I ask.

'What do mean "absences"?'

'Gaps in your memory where time seems to disappear.'

'It happened about a month ago.'

'Do you remember which day?'

He nods. 'The hate had to be emptied.'

The main doors of the hospital are open. On the front steps Bobby turns and thanks me. There is that smell again. I know what it is now. Chloroform.

17

Chloroform is a colourless liquid, half again as dense as water, with an ether-like odour and a taste forty times sweeter than sugar cane. It is an important organic solvent, mainly used in industry.

The Scottish physician Sir James Simpson of Edinburgh was the first to use it as an anaesthetic in 1847. Six years later, the English physician John Snow gave it to Queen Victoria during the birth of Prince Leopold, her eighth child.

A few drops on a mask or a cloth are usually enough to produce surgical anaesthesia within a few minutes. The patient awakens in 10–15 minutes, groggy but with very little nausea or vomiting. It is highly dangerous and causes fatal cardiac paralysis in about one in 3000 cases . . .

Closing the encyclopaedia, I slip it back on to a shelf and scribble a note to myself. Why would Bobby Moran have chloroform on his clothes? What possible use would he have for an industrial solvent or an anaesthetic? I seem to remember that chloroform is sometimes used in cough medicines and anti-itching creams, but the quantities aren't enough to create the unique odour.

Bobby said he worked as a courier. Maybe he delivers industrial solvents. I will ask him at our next session, if Major Tom is in touch with ground control by then.

I can hear banging coming from downstairs in the basement. D.J. and his apprentice are still working on the boiler. Apparently our entire internal plumbing system was put together by a maniac with a fetish for bending pipes. The insides of our walls look like a modern sculpture. God knows how much it's going to cost.

In the kitchen, having poured a coffee, I sit next to Charlie at the breakfast bar. She props her library book against a box of cereal. My morning paper is resting against the orange juice.

Charlie is playing a game – mimicking everything I do. When I take a bite of toast, she does the same. When I sip my coffee, she sips her tea. She even cocks her head the same way I do when I'm trying to read newsprint that has disappeared into the fold of the paper.

'Are you finished with the marmalade?' she asks, waving her hand in front of my face.

'Yes. Sorry.'

'You were away with the pixies.'

'They send their regards.'

Julianne emerges from the laundry, brushing a stray strand of hair from her forehead. The tumble dryer is rumbling in the background. We used to have breakfast together – drinking plunger coffee and swapping sections of the morning paper. Now she doesn't stop for long enough.

She packs the dishwasher and puts my pill in front of me.

'What happened at the hospital?'

'One of my patients had a fall. He's OK.'

She frowns. 'You were going to do fewer emergency calls.'

'I know. Just this once.'

She takes a bite from a quarter of toast and starts packing Charlie's lunchbox. I smell her perfume and notice that she's wearing new jeans and her best jacket.

'Where are you off to?'

'I have my seminar on "Understanding Islam". You promised to be home by four o'clock for Charlie.'

'I can't. I have an appointment.'

She's annoyed at me. 'Someone has to be here.'

'I can be home by five.'

'OK, I'll see if I can find a sitter.'

I call Ruiz from the office. In the background I can hear the sound of industrial equipment and running water. He's beside a river or a stream.

The moment I announce myself I hear a telltale electronic click. I contemplate whether he's recording our conversation.

'I wanted to ask you something about Catherine McBride.'

'Yeah?'

'How many stab wounds were there?'

'Twenty-one.'

'Did the pathologist find any traces of chloroform?'

'You read the report.'

'There wasn't any mention of it.'

'Why do you want to know?'

'It's probably not important.'

He sighs. 'Let's do a deal. Stop ringing me up asking bullshit questions and I'll waive that unpaid parking fine of yours.'

Before I can apologise for troubling him, I hear someone calling his name. He grunts a thanks-for-nothing and hangs up. The man has the communication skills of a mortician.

Fenwick is lurking in my waiting room, glancing at his gold Rolex. We're going to lunch in Mayfair at his favourite restaurant. It is one of those places that gets written up in the Sunday supplements because the chef is temperamental, handsome and dates a supermodel. It is also a known hangout for celebrities, according to Fenwick, but they never seem to show up for me. I did see Peter O'Toole in there once. Fenwick referred to him as 'Peter' and sounded very chummy.

Today Fenwick is trying extra hard to be affable. On the walk to the restaurant he asks after Julianne and Charlie. Then he runs through the entire menu out loud, commenting on each dish as though I can't read. When I choose mineral water instead of wine he looks disappointed. 'I've sworn off alcohol at lunchtime,' I explain.

'How antisocial.'

'Some of us work in the afternoon.'

The waiter arrives and Fenwick delivers precise instructions as to how he wants his meal prepared, right down to suggesting oven temperatures and whether the meat should be tenderised in advance. If the waiter has any sense he'll make sure these instructions never reach the kitchen.

'Didn't anyone ever tell you not to upset the person preparing your food?' I ask.

Fenwick looks at me quizzically.

'Forget it,' I say. 'You obviously didn't work your way through university.'

'I had an allowance, old boy.'

Typical!

Fenwick glances around, looking for any familiar faces. I'm never quite sure what these lunches are about. Usually, he's trying to convince me to invest in a property deal or a start-up biotech company. He has absolutely no concept of money or, more importantly, how little most people earn and the size of their mortgages.

Fenwick is probably the last person I would normally ask for advice, but he's here and the conversation has reached a lull.

'I have a hypothetical question for you,' I say, folding and unfolding my napkin. 'If you had a patient who you suspected might have committed a serious crime, what would you do?'

Fenwick looks alarmed. He glances over his shoulder as if worried someone might have overheard. 'Do you have any evidence?' he whispers.

'Not really . . . more a gut instinct.'

'How serious a crime?'

'I don't know. Perhaps the most serious.'

Fenwick leans forward and cups a hand over his mouth. He couldn't be more conspicuous. 'You must tell the police, old boy.'

'What about doctor–patient confidentiality? It lies at the heart of everything I do. If patients don't trust me, I can't help them.'

'It doesn't apply. Remember the Tarasoff precedent.'

Tarasoff was a university student who murdered his ex-girlfriend in California in the late sixties. During a therapy session he told a psychologist that he planned to kill her. The murdered girl's parents sued the psychologist for negligence and won their case.

Fenwick is still talking, his nose twitching nervously. 'You have a duty to divulge confidential information if a client communicates a plausible intention to do serious harm to a third party.'

'Exactly, but what if he's made no threat against a specific person?'

'I don't think that matters.'

'Yes, it does. We have a duty to protect *intended* victims from harm, but only if the patient has communicated the threat of violence and actually identified someone.'

'You're splitting hairs.'

'No, I'm not.'

'So we leave a killer roaming the streets?'

'I don't know if he's a killer.'

'Shouldn't you let the police decide?'

Maybe Fenwick is right, but what if I'm jumping to the wrong conclusion? Confidentiality is an integral part of clinical psychology. If I reveal details of my sessions with Bobby without his consent, I'm breaking about a dozen regulations. I could end up being disciplined by my association or facing a lawsuit.

How confident am I that Bobby is dangerous? He

attacked the woman in the cab. Other than that I have his psychotic ramblings about windmills and a girl in a dream.

Fenwick drains his wine and orders another glass. He is actually enjoying this cloak and dagger stuff. I get the impression that people don't regularly seek his advice.

Our food arrives and the conversation ebbs and flows over familiar territory. Fenwick tells me about his latest investments and holiday plans. I sense that he's building up to something but can't find an opening in the conversation that moves us smoothly on to the subject. Finally, over coffee, he plunges in.

'There's something I'd like to ask you, Joe. I'm not the sort of chap who usually asks for favours, but I have one to ask of you.'

My mind is automatically working out how to say no. I can't think of a solitary reason why Fenwick might need my help.

Weighed down by the gravity of the request, he starts the same sentence several times. Eventually he explains that he and Geraldine, his long-time girlfriend, have become engaged.

'Good for you! Congratulations!'

He raises his hand to interrupt me. 'Yes, well, we're getting married in June in West Sussex. Her father has an estate there. I wanted to ask you . . . well . . . what I wanted to say . . . I mean . . . I would be honoured if you would acquiesce to being my best man.'

For a brief moment I'm worried I might laugh. I barely know Fenwick. We have worked in adjacent offices for two years, but apart from these occasional lunches we have never socialised or shared a round of golf or a game of tennis. I vaguely remember meeting Geraldine at an office Christmas party. Until then I had harboured suspicions that Fenwick might be a bachelor dandy of the old school.

'Surely there must be someone else . . .'

'Well, yes, of course. I just thought . . . well, I just thought . . .' Fenwick is blinking rapidly, a picture of misery.

Then it dawns on me. For all his name-dropping, social climbing and overweening pride, Fenwick hasn't any friends. Why else would he choose me to be his best man?

'Of course,' I say. 'As long as you're sure . . .'

Fenwick is so excited I think he's going to embrace me. He reaches across the table and grasps my hand, shaking it furiously. His smile is so pitiful that I want to take him home as I might a stray dog.

On the walk back to the office he suggests all sorts of things we can do together, including arranging a stag night. 'We could use some of your vouchers from your lectures,' he says sheepishly.

I am suddenly reminded of a lesson I learned on my first day at boarding school, aged eight. The very first child to introduce himself will be the one with the fewest friends. Fenwick is *that* boy.

18

Elisa opens the door wearing a Thai silk robe. Light spills from behind her, outlining her body beneath the fabric. I try to concentrate on her face but my eyes betray me.

'Why are you so late? I thought you were coming hours ago.'

'Traffic.'

She sizes me up in the doorway, as if not quite sure whether to let me inside. Then she turns and I follow her down the hall, watching her hips slide beneath her robe.

Elisa lives in a converted printing factory in Ladbroke Grove, not far from the Grand Union Canal. Unpainted beams and timber joists crisscross each other in a sort of bonsai version of a Tudor cottage.

The place is full of old rugs and antique furniture that she had sent down from Yorkshire when her mother died. Her pride and joy is an Elizabethan love seat with elaborately carved arms and legs. A dozen china dolls, with delicately painted faces, sit demurely on the seat as if waiting for someone to ask them to dance.

She pours me a drink and settles on to the sofa, patting a spot beside her. She notices me pause and pulls a face. 'I thought something was wrong. Usually I get a kiss on the cheek.'

'I'm sorry.'

She laughs and crosses her legs. I feel something shred inside me.

'Christ, you look tense. What you need is a massage.'

She pulls me down and slides behind me, driving her fingers into the knotted muscles between my shoulder blades. Her legs are stretched out around me and I can feel the soft crinkle of her pubic hair against the small of my back.

'I shouldn't have come.'

'Why did you?'

'I wanted to apologise. It was my fault. I started something that I shouldn't have started.'

'OK.'

'You don't mind?'

'You were a good fuck.'

'I don't want you to see it like that.'

'What was it then?'

I contemplate this for a moment. 'We had a brief encounter.'

She laughs. 'It wasn't that *fucking* romantic.'

My toes curl in embarrassment.

'So what happened?' she asks.

'I don't think it was fair on you.'

'Or your wife?'

'Yes.'

'You never told me why you were so upset that night.'

I shrug. 'I was just thinking about life and things.'

'Life?'

'And death.'

'Jesus, not another one.'

'What do you mean?'

'A married guy who reaches his forties and suddenly starts pondering what it all means? I used to get them all the time. Talkers! I should have charged them double. I'd be a rich woman.'

'It's not like that.'

'Well, what is it?'

'What if I told you I had an incurable disease?'

She stops massaging my neck and turns me to face her. 'Is that what you're saying?'

Suddenly I change my mind. 'No. I'm being stupid.'

Elisa is annoyed now. She thinks she's being manipulated. 'You know what your problem is?'

'What's that?'

'All your life you've been a protected species. Somebody has always looked after you. First it was your mother, then boarding school, then university, and then you got married.'

'And your point is?'

'It's been too easy. Nothing bad has ever happened to you. Bad stuff happens to other people and you pick up the pieces, but *you've* never fallen apart. Do you remember the second time we ever met?'

I nod.

'Do you remember what you told me?'

Now I'm struggling. It was in Holloway Prison. Elisa had

been charged with malicious wounding after she stabbed two teenage boys with a flick-knife. She was twenty-three years old and by then had graduated to working for an escort agency in Kensington, being flown all over Europe and the Middle East.

One night she was called out to a hotel in Knightsbridge. She didn't know the client. As soon as she walked into the room she sensed something was wrong. Normally her clients tended to be middle-aged. This one was a teenager. There were a dozen empty beer bottles on the coffee table.

Before she could react, the bathroom door opened and six youths emerged. One of them was having an eighteenth birthday party.

'I'm not fucking all of you.'

They laughed.

After the first rape she stopped fighting. She pleaded with them to let her go and at the same time concentrated on reaching her coat pocket, stretching her hand out along the bed, moving it just a fraction at a time. The boys took her two at a time. The rest waited their turn – watching Manchester United play Chelsea on *Match of the Day*.

Elisa struggled to breathe. Snot ran from her nose, mingling with tears. She finally reached her coat and in the pocket her fingers closed around the knife.

Ryan Giggs had picked up the ball near the halfway line and made a run down the left . . . Hands gripped the back of Elisa's bobbing head. Steve Clarke was trying to force Giggs to go wider, but he cut inside and then out again . . . A belt buckle dug into her chest and her forehead slapped against a stomach . . . Mark Hughes made a run to the near post, drawing the two central defenders. Giggs floated in

167

the cross. Cantona struck the volley first time. The net bulged. So did Elisa's cheeks.

Pulling her mouth free, she whispered, 'It's *over*.'

She drove the knife into the buttocks of the boy in front of her. His scream filled the room. Then she spun and stabbed the boy behind her in the thigh.

As he reared backwards, she rolled away, grabbed the neck of a beer bottle and smashed it across the corner of the bedside table. With the knife in one hand and the jagged bottle in the other, she faced them across the bed.

The blade was only two inches long so none of the wounds were deep. Elisa phoned the police from the hotel lobby. She worked out the odds and realised she had no other option. Then she went through the motions of giving a statement. The boys each had a lawyer present as they were interviewed. Their stories were identical.

Elisa was charged with malicious wounding while the youths were given a stern talking to by the station sergeant. Six young men – with money, privilege and a walk-up start in life – had raped her with absolute impunity.

While on remand in Holloway Prison she asked for me by name. Although older, she seemed just as fragile. She sat on a plastic chair with her head cocked to one side and her hair falling over one eye. Her chipped tooth had been fixed.

'Do you think that we determine how things turn out in our lives?' she asked me.

'Up to a point.'

'And when does that point end?'

'When something happens that we have no control over: a drunk driver runs a stop sign, or the lotto balls drop in the right order, or rogue cancer cells begin dividing inside us.'

'So we only have a say over the *little* things?'

'If we're lucky. You take the Greek playwright Aeschylus. He died when an eagle mistook his bald head for a rock and dropped a tortoise on it. I don't think he saw that coming.'

She laughed. A month later she pleaded guilty and was sentenced to two years in jail. She worked in the prison laundry. Whenever she became angry or bitter about what had happened, she opened a dryer door, put her head inside and screamed into the big warm silver drum, letting the sound explode into her head.

Is that what Elisa wants me to remember – my own pithy homily on why shit happens? She slips off the sofa and pads across the room, looking for her cigarettes.

'So you came here to tell me that we're not going to fuck any more.'

'Yes.'

'Did you want to tell me before or after we go to bed?'

'I'm being serious.'

'I know you are. I'm sorry.'

She lets the cigarette hang from her lips as she re-ties the sash of her robe. For a brief moment I glimpse a small, taut nipple. I can't tell if she's angry or disappointed. Maybe she doesn't care.

'Will you read my Home Office submission when I'm finished?' she asks.

'Of course.'

'And if I need you to give another talk?'

'I'll be there.'

She kisses my cheek as I leave. I don't want to go. I like this house with its faded rugs, porcelain dolls, tiny fireplace and four-poster bed. Yet already I seem to be disappearing.

My home is in darkness, except for a light downstairs leaking through the curtains of the sitting room. Inside the air is warm. The fire has been burning in the front room. I can smell the smokeless coal.

The last of the red embers are glowing in the grate. As I reach for the lamp switch my left hand trembles. I see the silhouette of a head and shoulders in the armchair by the window. Forearms are braced along the wide arms of the chair. Black shoes are flat on the polished wooden floor.

'We need to talk.' Ruiz doesn't bother to stand.

'How did you get in here?'

'Your wife said I could wait.'

'What can I do for you?'

'You can stop pissing me about.' He leans forward into the light. His face looks ashen and his voice is tired. 'I asked the pathologist about chloroform. They didn't look the first time. When someone has been stabbed that many times, you don't bother looking for much else.' He turns to stare at the fireplace. 'How did you know?'

'I can't tell you.'

'That's not the answer I want to hear.'

'It was a long shot . . . a supposition.'

'Suppose you tell me why?'

'I can't do that.'

He's angry now. His features are chiselled instead of worn down. 'I'm an old-fashioned detective, Professor O'Loughlin.

I went to a local comprehensive and straight into the force. I didn't go to university and I don't read many books. You take computers. I know bugger all about them but I appreciate how useful they can be. The same is true of psychologists.'

His voice grows quiet. 'Whenever I'm involved in an investigation, people are always telling me that I can't do things. They tell me I can't spend too much money, that I can't tap particular phones or search particular houses. There are thousands of things I *cannot* do – all of which pisses me off.

'I've warned you twice already. You deny me information that is relevant to my murder inquiry and I'll bring all of this,' he motions to the room, the house, my life, 'crashing down around your ears.'

I can't think of a sympathetic response to disarm him. What can I tell him? I have a patient called Bobby Moran who may, or may not, be a borderline schizophrenic. He kicked a woman unconscious because she looked like his mother – a woman he wants dead. He makes lists. He listens to windmills. His clothes smell of chloroform. He carries around a piece of paper with the number '21' written on it hundreds of times – the same number of stab wounds that Catherine McBride inflicted on herself . . .

What if I say all this – he'll probably laugh at me. There is nothing concrete linking Bobby to Catherine, yet I'll be responsible for a dozen detectives hammering on Bobby's door, searching through his past, terrifying his fiancée and her son.

Bobby will know I've sent them. He won't trust me again. He won't trust anyone like me. His suspicions will be vindicated. He reached out for help and I betrayed him.

I know he's dangerous. I know his fantasies are taking him somewhere terrible. But unless he keeps coming back to me I might never be able to stop him.

Bitterness and rancour hang in the air like the smell of smokeless coal. Ruiz is putting on his coat and walking towards the front door. My left arm is trembling. It's now or never. Make a decision.

'When you searched Catherine's flat – did she have a red dress?'

Ruiz reacts as though struck. He spins and takes a step towards me. 'How did you know that?'

'Is the dress missing?'

'Yes.'

'Do you think she might have been wearing it when she disappeared?'

'Possibly.'

He is framed in the open doorway. His eyes are bloodshot but his stare fixed. Fingers open and close into fists. He wants to rip me apart.

'Come to my office tomorrow afternoon. There's a file. You can't take it away. I don't even know if it will help, but I have to show it to someone.'

19

The blue manila folder is on the desk in front of me. It has a ribbon that twists around a flat circular wheel to seal it shut. I keep undoing it and doing it up again.

Meena glances nervously behind her as she enters the office. She walks all the way across to my desk before whispering, 'There is a very scary-looking man in the waiting room. He's asking for you.'

'That's OK, Meena. He's a detective.'

Her eyes widen in surprise. 'Oh! He didn't say. He just sort of—'

'Growled?'

'Yes.'

'You can show him in.' I motion her closer. 'In about five minutes, I want you to buzz me and remind me of an important meeting outside the office.'

'What meeting?'

'Just an important meeting.'

She frowns at me and nods.

With a face like an anvil, Ruiz ignores my outstretched hand and leaves it hanging in the air as though I'm directing traffic. He sits down and leans back in the chair, spreading his legs and letting his coat flare out.

'So this is where you work, Prof? Very nice.' He glances around the room in what appears to be a cursory way, but I know he's taking in the details. 'How much does it cost to rent an office like this?'

'I don't know. I'm just one of the partners.'

Ruiz scratches his chin and then fumbles in his coat pocket for a stick of chewing gum. He unwraps it slowly.

'What exactly does a psychologist *do*?'

'We help people who are damaged by events in their lives. People with personality disorders, or sexual problems, or phobias.'

'Do you know what I think? A man gets attacked and he's lying bleeding on the road. Two psychologists pass by and one says to the other, "Let's go and find the person who did this – he needs help."'

His smile doesn't reach his eyes.

'I help more victims than I do perpetrators.'

Ruiz shrugs and tosses the gum wrapper into the bin. 'Start talking. How did you know about the red dress?'

I glance down at the file and undo the ribbon. 'In a few minutes from now, I'm going to get a phone call. I will have to leave the office, but you are quite welcome to stay. I think you'll find my chair is more comfortable than yours.' I open Bobby's file.

'When you're finished, if you wish to talk about anything

I'll be over the road having a drink. I can't talk about any specific patient or case.' I tap Bobby's folder to stress the point. 'I can only talk in general terms about personality disorders and how psychotics and psychopaths function. It will be much easier if you remember this.'

Ruiz presses the palms of his hands together as if in prayer and taps his forefingers against his lips. 'I don't like playing games.'

'This isn't a game. We do it this way, or I can't help you.'

The phone rings. Meena starts her spiel but doesn't finish. I'm already on my way.

The sun is shining and the sky is blue. It feels more like May than mid-December. London does this occasionally – puts on a glorious day to remind people that it isn't such a bad place to live.

This is why the English are among the world's greatest optimists. We get one magnificent hot dry week and the memory will give us succour for an entire summer. It happens every time. Come spring we buy shorts, T-shirts, bikinis and sarongs in glorious expectation of a season that never arrives.

Ruiz finds me standing at the bar nursing a mineral water.

'It's your round,' he says. 'I'll have a pint of bitter.'

The place is busy with a lunchtime crowd. Ruiz wanders over to four men sitting in the corner by the front window. They look like office boys, but are wearing well-cut suits and silk ties.

Ruiz flashes his police badge under the level of the table.

'Sorry to trouble you, gents, but I need to commandeer

this table for a surveillance operation on that bank over there.'

He motions out the window and they all turn in unison to look.

'Try to make it a little less obvious!'

They quickly turn back.

'We have reason to believe it is being targeted for an armed hold-up. You see that guy on the corner, wearing the orange vest?'

'The street sweeper?' one of them asks.

'Yeah. Well, he's one of my best. So is the shopgirl in that lingerie shop, next door to the bank. I need this table.'

'Of course.'

'Absolutely.'

'Is there anything else we can do?'

I see a twinkle in Ruiz's eye. 'Well, I don't normally do this – use civilians undercover – but I am short of manpower. You could split up and take a corner each. Try to blend in. Look for a group of men travelling four-up in a car.'

'How do we contact you?'

'You tell the street sweeper.'

'Is there some sort of password?' one of them asks.

Ruiz rolls his eyes. 'It's a police operation, not a fucking Bond movie.'

Once they've gone, he takes the chair nearest the window and sets his glass on a coaster. I sit opposite him and leave my glass untouched.

'They would have given you the table anyway,' I say, unable to decide if he likes practical jokes or dislikes people.

'Did this Bobby Moran kill Catherine McBride?' He wipes foam from his top lip with the back of his hand.

The question has all the subtlety of a well-thrown brick.

'I can't talk about individual patients.'

'Did he admit to killing her?'

'I can't talk about what he may or may not have told me.'

Ruiz's eyes disappear into a narrow maze of wrinkles and his body tenses. Just as suddenly he exhales and gives me what I suspect is a smile. He's out of practice.

'Tell me about the man who killed Catherine McBride?'

The message seems to have reached him. Pushing Bobby out of my head, I try to reflect on Catherine's killer, based on what I know of the crime. I've had a week of sleepless nights thinking of little else.

'You are dealing with a sexual psychopath,' I begin, unable to recognise my own voice. 'Catherine's murder was a manifestation of corrupt lust.'

'But there were no signs of sexual assault.'

'You can't think in terms of normal rape or sex crime. This is a far more extreme example of deviant sexuality. This man is consumed by a desire to dominate and inflict pain. He fantasises about taking, restraining, dominating, torturing and killing. At least some of these fantasies will mirror almost exactly what happened.

'Think about what he did to her. He took her off the street or enticed her to go with him. He didn't seek a quick and violent sexual coupling in a dark alley and then silence his victim so she couldn't identify him. Instead he aimed to break her – to systematically destroy her willpower until she became a compliant, terrified plaything. Even that wasn't enough for him. He wanted the ultimate in control; to bend someone so completely to *his* will that she would torture herself . . . '

I'm watching Ruiz – waiting to lose him. 'He almost

succeeded, but in the end Catherine wasn't entirely broken. She still had a spark of defiance left. She was a nurse. Even with a short blade she knew where to cut if she wanted to die quickly. When she could take no more she cut the carotid artery in her neck. That's what caused the embolism. She was dead within minutes.'

'How do you know that?'

'Three years at medical school.'

Ruiz is staring at his pint glass, as though checking to see if it is centred properly on the coaster. The chimes of a church bell are ringing in the distance.

I continue: 'The man you're looking for is lonely, socially inept and sexually immature.'

'Sounds like your basic teenager.'

'No. He isn't a teenager. He's older. A lot of young men start out like this, but every so often one emerges who blames someone else for his loneliness and his sexual frustration. This bitterness and anger grow with each rejection. Sometimes he'll blame a particular person. Other times he will hate an entire group of people.'

'He hates all women.'

'Possibly, but I think it's more likely he hates a particular sort of woman. He wants to punish her. He fantasises about it and it gives him pleasure.'

'Why did he choose Catherine McBride?'

'I don't know. Perhaps she looked like someone he wanted to punish. He may have been driven by opportunity. Catherine was available so he changed his fantasy to incorporate her looks and the clothes she wore.'

'The red dress.'

'Perhaps.'

'Could he have known her?'

'Quite possibly.'

'Motivation?'

'Revenge. Control. Sexual gratification.'

'I take my pick?'

'No, it's all three.'

Ruiz stiffens slightly. Clearing his throat, he takes out his marbled notebook. 'So who am I looking for?'

'Someone in his thirties or forties. He lives alone, somewhere private, but surrounded by people who come and go – a boarding house, perhaps, or a caravan park.

'He may have a wife or a girlfriend. He is of above average intelligence. He is physically strong, but mentally even stronger. He hasn't been consumed by sexual desire or anger to the point of losing control. He can keep his emotions in check. He is forensically aware. He doesn't want to be caught.

'This is someone who has managed to successfully separate areas of his life and isolate them completely from each other. His friends, family and colleagues have no inkling of what goes on inside his head.

'I think he has sadomasochistic interests. It's not the sort of thing that springs out of nowhere. Someone must have introduced him to it – although probably only a mild version. His mind has taken it to a level that far outstrips any harmless fun. His self-assurance is what amazes me. There were no signs of anxiety or first-time nerves . . . '

I stop talking. My mouth has gone slack and sour. I take a sip of water. Ruiz is gazing at me dully, sitting up straighter and occasionally writing notes. My voice rises above the noise again.

'A person doesn't suddenly become a fully fledged sadist overnight – not one this skilful. Organisations like the KGB spend years training their interrogators to be this good. The degree of control and sophistication was remarkable. These things come from experience. I don't think he started here.'

Ruiz turns and stares out of the window, making up his mind. He doesn't believe me. 'This is bullshit!'

'Why?'

'None of it sounds like your Bobby Moran.'

He's right. It doesn't make sense. Bobby is too young to have this degree of familiarity with sadism. He is too erratic and changeable. I seriously doubt that he has the mental skills and malevolence to dominate and control a person like Catherine so completely. The physical size, yes; but not the psychological strength. Then again, Bobby has constantly surprised me and I have only scratched the surface of his psyche. He has held details back from me or dropped them like a trail of breadcrumbs on a fairytale journey.

Fairytales? That's what it sounds like to Ruiz. He's on his feet and threading his way to the bar. People hurriedly step out of his way. He has an aura like a flashing light that warns people to give him space.

I'm already beginning to regret this. I should have stayed out of it. Sometimes I wish I could turn my mind off instead of always looking and analysing. I wish I could just focus on a tiny square of the world, instead of watching how people communicate and the clothes they wear; what they put in their shopping trolleys; the cars they drive; the pets they choose; the magazines they read and the TV shows they watch. I wish I could stop looking.

Ruiz is back again with another pint and a whisky chaser. He rolls the liquid fire around in his mouth as if washing away a bad taste. 'You really think this guy did it?'

'I don't know.'

He wraps his fingers around the pint glass and leans back. 'You want me to look at him?'

'That's up to you.'

Ruiz exhales with a rustle of dissatisfaction. He still doesn't trust me.

'Do you know why Catherine came down to London?' I ask.

'According to her flatmate, she had a job interview. We found no correspondence – she probably had it with her.'

'What about phone records?'

'Nothing from her home number. She had a mobile, but that's missing.'

He delivers the facts without comment or embellishment. Catherine's history matches with the scant details she gave me during our sessions. Her parents had divorced when she was twelve. She hooked up with a bad crowd, sniffing aerosols and doing drugs. At fifteen she spent six weeks in a private psychiatric hospital in West Sussex. Her family kept it quiet for obvious reasons. Becoming a nurse had seemed to be the turning point. Although she still had problems, she managed to cope.

'What happened after she left the Marsden?' I ask.

'She moved back to Liverpool and got engaged to a merchant seaman. It didn't work out.'

'Is he a suspect?'

'No. He's in Bahrain.'

'Any other suspects?'

Ruiz raises an eyebrow. 'All volunteers are welcome.' He smiles wryly and polishes off his drink. 'I have to go.'

'What happens next?'

'I get my people digging up everything they can on this Bobby Moran. If I can link him to Catherine, I'll ask him very politely to help me with my inquiries.'

'And you won't mention my name?'

Ruiz looks at me contemptuously. 'Don't worry, Professor, your interests are paramount in my concerns.'

20

My mother has a pretty face, with a neat upturned nose and straight hair that she has worn in the same uniform style – pinned back with silver clips and tucked behind her ears – for as long as I can remember. Sadly, I inherited my father's tangle of hair. If it grows half an inch too long it becomes completely unruly and I look like I've been electrocuted.

Everything about my mother denotes her standing as a doctor's wife, right down to her box-pleated skirts, unpatterned blouses and low-heeled shoes. A creature of habit, she even carries a handbag when taking the dog for a walk.

She can arrange a dinner party for twelve in the time it takes to boil an egg. She also does garden parties, school fêtes, church jamborees, charity fundraisers, bridge tournaments, car boot sales, walkathons, christenings, weddings and funerals. Yet for all this ability, she has managed to get through life without balancing a chequebook, making an investment decision or proffering a political opinion in public. She leaves such matters to my father.

Every time I contemplate my mother's life, I am appalled by the waste and unfulfilled promise. At eighteen she won a mathematics scholarship to Cardiff University. At twenty-five she wrote a thesis that had American universities hammering at her door. What did she do? She married my father and settled for a life of cultivating convention and making endless compromises.

I like to imagine her doing a 'Shirley Valentine' and running off with a Greek waiter, or writing a steamy romantic novel. One day she is suddenly going to toss aside her prudence, self-discipline and correctness. She will go dancing barefoot in daisy fields and trekking through the Himalayas. These are nice thoughts. They're certainly better than imagining her growing old listening to my father rant at the TV screen or read aloud the letters he's written to newspapers.

That's what he's doing now – writing a letter. He only reads the *Guardian* when he stays with us, but 'that red rag', as he refers to it, gives him enough material for at least a dozen letters.

My mother is in the kitchen with Julianne, discussing tomorrow's menu. At some stage in the previous twenty-four hours it was decided to make Sunday lunch a family get-together. Two of my sisters are coming, with their husbands and solemn children. Only Rebecca will escape. She's in Bosnia working for the UN. Bless her.

My Saturday morning chores now involve moving a ton of plumbing equipment from the front hallway to the basement. Then I have to rake the leaves, oil the swing and get two more bags of coal from the local garage. Julianne is going to shop for the food, while Charlie and her grandparents go to look at the Christmas lights in Oxford Street.

My other chore is to buy a tree – a thankless task. The only truly well-proportioned Christmas trees are the ones they use in advertisements. If you try to find one in real life you face inevitable disappointment. Your tree will lean to the left or the right. It will be too bushy at the base, or straggly at the top. It will have bald patches, or the branches on either side will be oddly spaced. Even if you do, by some miracle, find a perfect tree, it won't fit in the car and by the time you strap it to the roof rack and drive home the branches are broken or twisted out of shape. You wrestle it through the door, gagging on pine needles and sweating profusely, only to hear the maddening question that resonates down from countless Christmases past: 'Is that really the best one you could find?'

Charlie's cheeks are pink with the cold and her arms are draped in polished paper bags full of new clothes and a pair of shoes.

'I got heels, Dad. Heels!'

'How high?'

'Only this much.' She holds her thumb and forefinger apart.

'I thought you were a tomboy,' I tease.

'They're not pink,' she says sternly. 'And I didn't get any dresses.'

God's personal physician-in-waiting is pouring himself a Scotch and getting annoyed because my mother is chatting to Julianne instead of bringing him some ice. Charlie is excitedly opening bags. Then she suddenly stops. 'The tree! It's lovely.'

'So it should be. It took me three hours to find.'

I have to stop myself telling her the whole story about my friend from the Greek deli in Chalk Farm Road, who told me about a guy who supplies trees to 'half of London' from the back of a three-ton truck.

The whole enterprise sounded pretty dodgy but for once I didn't care. I wanted to get a flawless specimen and that's what it is – a pyramid of pine-scented perfection with a straight trunk and evenly spaced branches.

Since getting home I have been wandering back and forth to the sitting room, marvelling at the tree. Julianne is getting slightly fed up with me saying, 'Isn't that a great tree?' and expecting a response.

God's personal physician-in-waiting is telling me his solution to traffic congestion in central London. I'm waiting for him to comment on the tree. I don't want to prompt him. He's talking about banning all delivery trucks in the West End except in designated hours. Then he starts complaining about shoppers who walk too slowly and suggests a fast and slow lane system.

'I found a tree today,' I interject, unable to wait. He stops abruptly and looks over his shoulder. He stands and examines it more closely, walking from side to side. Then he stands back to best appreciate the overall symmetry.

Clearing his throat, he asks, 'Is it the best one they had?'

'No! They had dozens of better ones! Hundreds! This was one of the worst; the absolute pits; the bottom of the barrel. I felt sorry for it. That's why I brought it home. I adopted a lousy Christmas tree.'

He looks surprised. 'It isn't *that* bad.'

'You're fucking unbelievable,' I mutter under my breath, unable to stay in the same room. Why do our parents have the ability to make us feel like children even when our hair is greying and we have a mortgage that feels like a Third World debt?

I retreat to the kitchen and make myself a gin and tonic, with an extra large slurp of gin that spills over the counter. My father has only been here for ten hours and already I'm hitting the bottle. At least reinforcements arrive tomorrow.

I was always running in my childhood nightmares – trying to escape a monster or a rabid dog or perhaps a Neanderthal second-rower forward with no front teeth and cauliflower ears. I would wake just before getting caught. It didn't make me feel any safer. That is the problem with nightmares. Nothing is resolved. We rouse ourselves in mid-air or just before the bomb goes off or stark naked in a public place.

I have been lying in the dark for five hours. Every time I think nice thoughts and begin drifting off to sleep, I jump awake in a panic. It's like watching a trashy horror movie that is laughably bad, but just occasionally there is a scene that frightens the bejesus out of you.

Mostly I'm trying not to think about Bobby Moran, because when I do it leads me to Catherine McBride and that's a place I don't want to go. I wonder if Bobby is in custody, or if they're watching him. I have this picture in my head of a van with blacked out windows parked outside his place.

People can't really sense when they're being watched – not without some clue or recognising something untoward. However, Bobby doesn't operate on the same wavelength as most people. He picks up different signals. A psychotic can believe the TV is talking to him and will question why workmen are repairing phone lines over the road, or why there's a van with blacked out windows parked outside.

Maybe none of this is happening. With all the new technology, perhaps Ruiz can find everything he needs by simply typing Bobby's name into a computer and accessing the private files that every conspiracy theorist is convinced the government keeps on the nation's citizens.

'Don't think about it. Just go to sleep,' Julianne whispers. She can sense when I'm worried about something. I haven't had a proper night's sleep since Charlie was born. You get out of the habit after a while. Now I have these pills which are making things worse.

Julianne is lying on her side, with the sheet tucked between her thighs and one hand resting on the pillow next to her face. Charlie does the same thing when she's sleeping. They barely make a sound or stir at all. It's as though they don't want to leave a footprint in their dreams.

On Sunday morning the house is full of cooking smells and feminine chatter. I'm expected to set the fire and sweep the front steps. Instead, I sneak to the newsagents and collect the morning papers.

Back in my study, I set aside the supplements and magazines and begin looking for stories on Catherine. I'm just about to sit down when I notice one of Charlie's bug-eyed goldfish is floating upside down in the aquarium. For a moment I think it might be some sort of neat goldfish trick, but on closer inspection it doesn't look too hale and hearty. It has grey speckles on its scales – evidence of an exotic fish fungus.

Charlie doesn't take death very well. Middle-eastern kingdoms have shorter periods of mourning. Scooping up the fish in my hand, I stare at the poor creature. I wonder if she'll believe it just disappeared. She *is* only eight. Then again, she doesn't believe in Santa or the Easter Bunny any more. How could I have bred such a cynic?

'Charlie, I have some bad news. One of your goldfish has disappeared.'

'How could it just disappear?'

'Well, actually it died. I'm sorry.'

'Where is it?'

'You don't really want to see it, do you?'

'Yes.'

The fish is still in my hand, which is in my pocket. When I open my palm it seems more like a magic trick than a solemn deed.

Being very organised, Julianne has a whole collection of shoeboxes and drawstring bags that she keeps for this sort of death in the family. With Charlie looking on, I bury the bug-eyed goldfish under the plum tree, between the late Harold Hamster, a mouse known only as 'Mouse' and a baby sparrow that flew into the French doors and broke its neck.

By midday most of the family has assembled, except for my eldest sister Lucy and her husband Eric, who have three children whose names I can never remember, but I know they end with an 'ee' sound like Debbie, Jimmy or Bobby. God's personal physician-in-waiting had wanted Lucy to name her eldest boy after him. He liked the idea of a third generation 'Joseph'. Lucy held firm and called him something else – Andy, maybe, or Gary, or Freddy.

They're always late. Eric is an air-traffic controller and the most absent-minded person I have ever met. It's frightening. He keeps forgetting where we live and has to phone up and ask for directions every time he visits. How on earth does he keep dozens of planes apart in the air? Every time I book a flight out of Heathrow I feel like ringing up Lucy in advance and asking whether Eric is working.

My middle sister Patricia is in the kitchen with her new man, Simon, a criminal lawyer who works for one of those TV series that exposes miscarriages of justice. Patricia's divorce has come through and she's celebrating with champagne.

'I hardly think it warrants Bollinger,' says my father.

'Why ever not?' she says, taking a quick slurp before it bubbles over.

I decide to rescue Simon. Nobody deserves this sort of introduction to our family. We take our drinks into the sitting room and make small talk. Simon has a jolly round face and keeps slapping his stomach like a department store Santa.

'Sorry to hear about the old Parkinson's,' he says. 'Terrible business.'

My heart sinks. 'Who told you?'

'Patricia.'

'How did she know?'

Suddenly realising his mistake, Simon starts apologising. There have been some depressing moments in the past month, but none quite so depressing as standing in front of a complete stranger who is drinking my Scotch and feeling sorry for me.

Who else knows?

The doorbell rings. Eric, Lucy and the 'ee' children come bustling in, with lots of vigorous handshakes and cheek kisses. Lucy takes one look at me and her bottom lip starts to tremble. She throws her arms around me and I feel her body shaking against my chest.

'I'm really sorry, Joe. So, so sorry.'

My chin is resting on the top of her head. Eric puts his outstretched hand on my shoulder as if giving me a Papal blessing. I don't think I have ever been so embarrassed.

The rest of the afternoon stretches out before me like a four-hour sociology lecture. When I get tired of answering questions about my health, I retreat to the garden where Charlie is playing with the 'ee' children. She is showing them where we buried the goldfish. I finally remember their names, Harry, Perry and Jenny.

Harry is only a toddler and looks like a miniature Michelin man in his padded jacket and woollen hat. I toss him in the air, making him giggle. The other children are grabbing my legs, pretending I'm a monster. I spy Julianne looking wistfully out the French doors. I know what she's thinking.

After lunch we retire to the sitting room and everyone says nice things about the tree and my mother's fruitcake.

'Let's play "Who Am I?"' says Charlie, whose mouth is

speckled with crumbs. She doesn't hear the collective groan. Instead, she hands out pens and paper, while breathlessly explaining the rules.

'You all have to think of someone famous. They don't have to be real. It can be a cartoon character, or a movie star. It could even be Lassie . . . '

'That's my choice gone.'

She scowls at me. 'Don't let anyone see the name you write. Then you stick the paper on someone else's forehead. They have to guess who they are.'

The game turns out to be a scream. God's personal physician-in-waiting can't understand why everybody laughs so uproariously at the name on his forehead: 'Grumpy' from *Snow White and the Seven Dwarfs*.

I'm actually starting to enjoy myself when the doorbell rings and Charlie dashes out to answer it. Lucy and Patricia start clearing the cups and plates.

'You don't look like a policeman,' says Charlie.

'I'm a detective.'

'Does that mean you have a badge?'

'Do you want to see it?'

'Maybe I should.'

Ruiz is reaching into his inside jacket pocket when I rescue him.

'We've taught her to be careful,' I say apologetically.

'That's very wise.' He smiles at Charlie and looks fifteen years younger. For a brief moment I think he might ruffle her hair, but people don't do that so much nowadays.

Ruiz looks past me into the hall and apologises for disturbing me.

'Is there something I can do for you?'

'Yes,' he mumbles, and then pats at his pockets as though he's written a note to remind himself.

'Would you like to come in?'

'If that's OK.'

I lead him to my study and offer to take his coat. Catherine's notes are still open on my desk where I left them.

'Doing a little homework?'

'I just wanted to make sure I hadn't forgotten anything.'

'And had you?'

'No.'

'You could let me be the judge of that.'

'Not this time.' I close the notebooks and put them away.

Walking around my desk, he glances at my bookcases, studying the various photographs and my souvenir water pipe from Syria.

'Where has he been?'

'I beg your pardon?'

'You said that my murderer didn't start with Catherine, so where has he been?'

'Practising.'

'On whom?'

'I don't know.'

Ruiz is now at the window, looking across the garden. He rolls his shoulders and the starched collar of his shirt presses under his ears. I want to ask him what he's learned about Bobby but he interrupts me. 'Is he going to kill again?'

I don't want to answer. Hypothetical situations are perilous. He senses me pulling back and won't let me escape. I have to say *something*.

'At the moment he is still thinking about Catherine and how she died. When those memories begin to fade, he may go looking for new experiences to feed his fantasies.'

'How can you be so sure?'

'His actions were relaxed and deliberate. He wasn't out of control or consumed by anger or desire. He was calm, considered, almost euphoric in his planning.'

'Where are these other victims? Why haven't we found them?'

'Maybe you haven't established a link.'

Ruiz flinches and squares his shoulders. He resents the inference that he's missed something important. At the same time he's not going to jeopardise the investigation because of overweening pride. He *wants* to understand.

'You're looking for clues in the method and symbolism, but these can only come from comparing crimes. Find another victim and you may find a pattern.'

Ruiz grinds his teeth as though wearing them down. What else can I give him?

'He knows the area. It took time to bury Catherine. He knew there were no houses overlooking that part of the canal. And he knew what time of night the towpath was deserted.'

'So he lives locally.'

'Or used to.'

Ruiz is seeing how the facts support the theory, trying them on for size. People are moving downstairs. A toilet flushes. A child cries in anger.

'But why would he choose such a public place? He could have hidden her in the middle of nowhere.'

'He wasn't hiding her. He *let* you have Catherine.'

'Why?'

'Maybe he's proud of his handiwork, or he's giving you a sneak preview.'

Ruiz grimaces. 'I don't know how you do your job. How can you walk around knowing sick fucks like that are on the loose? How can you live inside their heads?' He crosses his arms and jams his hands under his armpits. 'Then again, maybe you enjoy that sort of shit.'

'What do you mean?'

'You tell me. Is it a game for you, playing detective? Showing me one patient's file and not another's. Phoning up and asking me questions. Are you enjoying this?'

'I . . . I didn't ask to be brought into this.'

He enjoys my anger. In the silence I hear laughter downstairs.

'I think you had better leave.'

He regards me with satisfaction and physical superiority, before taking his coat and descending the stairs. Exhausted, I can visualise my energy draining away.

At the front door, Ruiz turns down the collar of his jacket and looks back at me. 'In the hunt, Professor, there are foxes and there are hounds and there are hunt saboteurs. Which one are you?'

'I don't believe in fox hunting.'

'Is that right? Neither does the fox.'

When all our guests have gone, Julianne sends me upstairs to have a bath. Some time later, I'm aware of her sliding into bed beside me. She turns and nestles backwards until her body moulds into mine. Her hair smells of apple and cinnamon.

'I'm tired,' I whisper.

'It's been a long day.'

'That's not what I'm getting at. I've been thinking about making a few changes.'

'Like what?

'Just changes.'

'Do you think that's wise?'

'We could go on a holiday. We could go to California. We've always talked of doing that.'

'What about your job . . . and Charlie's schooling?'

'She's young. She'll learn a lot more if we go travelling for six months than she will at school . . .'

Julianne turns around and props herself up on her elbow so she can look at me. 'What's brought this on?'

'Nothing.'

'When this all started, you said you didn't want things to change. You said the future didn't have to change.'

'I know.'

'And then you stopped talking to me. You give me no idea of what you're going through and then you spring this!'

'I'm sorry. I'm just tired.'

'No, it's more than that. Tell me.'

'I have this rackety idea in my head that I should be doing more. You read about people whose lives are packed with incident and adventure and you think, wow, I should do more. That's when I thought about going away.'

'While there's still time?'

'Yes.'

'So this *is* about the Parkinson's?'

'No . . . I can't explain . . . just forget it.'

'I don't want to forget it. I want you to be happy. But we don't have any money – not with the mortgage and the plumbing. You said so yourself. Maybe in the summer we can go to Cornwall . . .'

'Yeah. You're right. Cornwall would be nice.' As hard as I try to sound enthusiastic, I know I don't succeed. Julianne slips an arm around my waist and pulls herself closer. I feel her warm breath on my throat.

'With any luck I might be pregnant by then,' she whispers. 'We don't want to be too far away.'

21

My head aches and my throat is scratchy. It could be a hangover. It might be the flu. According to the papers half the country has succumbed to some exotic bug from Beijing or Bogotá – one of those places that nobody ever leaves without carrying a virulent germ.

The good news is that I have had no detectable side effects from taking Selegiline except for the insomnia, a pre-existing condition. The bad news is that the drug has had absolutely no effect on my symptoms.

I telephone Jock at seven a.m.

'How do you know it isn't working?' he says, annoyed at being woken.

'I don't feel any different.'

'That's the whole point. It doesn't make the symptoms go away – it stops them getting worse.'

'OK.'

'Just be patient and relax.'

That's easy for him to say.

'Are you doing your exercises?' he asks.

'Yes,' I lie.

'I know it's Monday but do you fancy a game of tennis? I'll go easy on you.'

'When?'

'I'll meet you at the club at six.'

Julianne will see right through this, but at least I'll be out of the house. I'm owed some leeway after yesterday.

My first patient of the day is a young ballet dancer with the grace of a gazelle and the yellowing teeth and receding gums of a devoted bulimic. Then Margaret arrives clutching her orange lifebuoy. She shows me a newspaper clipping about a bridge collapse in Israel. The look on her face says, 'I told you so!' I spend the next fifty minutes getting her to think about how many bridges there are in the world and how often they fall down.

By three o'clock I'm standing at the window, looking for Bobby among the pedestrians. I wonder if he's going to turn up. I jump when I hear his voice. He's standing in the doorway, rubbing his hands up and down his sides as if wiping something from them.

'It wasn't my fault,' he says.

'What?'

'Whatever it is you think I've done.'

'You kicked a woman unconscious.'

'Yes. That's all. Nothing else.' Light flares off the gold frames of his glasses.

'Hostility like that has to come from somewhere.'

'What do you mean?'

'You're an intelligent young man. You get the idea.'

It's time to confront Bobby, to see how he reacts under pressure.

'How long have you been my patient? Six months. You disappeared for half that time. You've been late for appointments, you've turned up unannounced and you've dragged me out of bed at four in the morning . . . '

He blinks rapidly. My tone of voice is so polite that he isn't sure whether I'm criticising him or not.

' . . . even when you *are* here, you change the subject and prevaricate. What are you trying to hide? What are you so frightened of?'

I pull my chair closer. Our knees are almost touching. It's like looking into the eyes of a beaten dog that doesn't know enough to turn away. Some aspects of his functioning I see so clearly – particularly his past – but I still can't see his present. What has he become?

'Let me tell you what I think, Bobby. I think you are desperate for affection, yet unable to engage people. This started a long while ago. I see a boy who is bright and sensitive, who waits each evening to hear the sound of his father's bicycle being wheeled through the front gate. And when his father comes through the door in his conductor's uniform, the boy can't wait to hear his stories and help him in the workshop.

'His father is funny, kind, quick-witted and inventive. He has grand plans for weird and wonderful inventions that will change the world. He draws pictures of them on scraps of paper and builds prototypes in the garage. The boy watches him working and sometimes at night he curls up to sleep among the wood shavings, listening to the sound of the lathe.

'But his father disappears. The most important figure in his life – the only one he truly cares about – abandons him. His mother, sadly, doesn't recognise or excuse his grief. She regards him as being weak and full of dreams, just like his father. He is never good enough.'

I keep a close eye on Bobby, looking for signs of protest or dissent. His eyes flit back and forth as though dreaming, but somehow he stays focused on me.

' . . . this boy is particularly perceptive and intelligent. His senses are heightened and his emotions are intense. He begins to escape from his mother. He's not old enough or brave enough to run away from home. Instead, he escapes into his mind. He creates a world that others never see or know exists. A world where he is popular and powerful: where he can punish and reward. A world where nobody laughs at him or belittles him, not even his mother. She falls at his feet – just like all the others. He is Clint Eastwood, Charles Bronson and Sylvester Stallone all rolled into one. Redeemer. Revenger. Judge. Jury. Executioner. He can dispense his own brand of justice. He can machine-gun the entire school rugby team or have the school bully nailed to a tree in the playground . . . '

Bobby's eyes glitter with connected memories and associated sounds – the light and dark that shade his past. The corners of his mouth are twitching.

'So what does he grow into, this boy? An insomniac. He suffers bouts of sleeplessness that jangle his nerves and have him seeing things out of the corner of his eye. He imagines conspiracies and people watching him. He lies awake and makes lists and secret codes for his lists.

'He wants to escape to his other world but something is

wrong. He can't go back there because someone has shown him something even better, more exciting – real!'

Bobby blinks and pinches the skin on the back of his hand.

'Have you ever heard the expression, "One man's meat is another man's poison"?' I ask him.

He acknowledges the question almost without realising it.

'It could be a description for human sexuality and how each of us has different interests and tastes. This boy grows up and as a young man he tastes something that excites and disturbs him in equal measure. It is a guilty secret. A forbidden pleasure. He worries that it makes him a pervert – this sexual thrill from inflicting pain.'

Bobby shakes his head; his eyes magnified by each lens.

'But you needed a point of reference – an introduction. This is what you haven't told me, Bobby. Who was the special girlfriend who opened your eyes? What did it feel like when you hurt her?'

'You're sick!'

'And you're lying.' Don't let him change the subject. 'What was it like that first time? You wanted nothing to do with these games but she goaded you. What did she say? Did she make fun of you? Did she laugh?'

'Don't talk to me. Shut up! SHUT UP!'

He clutches the cuffs of his coat in his fists and covers his ears. I know he's still listening. My words are leaking through and expanding in the crevices of his mind like water turned to ice.

'Someone planted the seed. Someone taught you to love the feeling of being in control . . . of inflicting pain. At first you wanted to stop, but she wanted more. Then you noticed that you weren't holding back. You were enjoying it! You didn't want to stop.'

'SHUT UP! SHUT UP!'

Bobby rocks back and forth on the edge of the chair. His mouth has gone slack and he's no longer focused on me. I'm almost there. My fingers are in the cracks of his psyche. A single affirmation, no matter how small, will be enough for me to lever his defences open. But I'm running out of story. I don't have all the pieces. I risk losing him if I overreach.

'Who was she, Bobby? Was her name Catherine McBride? I know that you knew her. Where did you meet? Was it in hospital? There's no shame in seeking help, Bobby. I know you've been evaluated before. Was Catherine a patient or a nurse? I think she was a patient.'

Bobby pinches the bridge of his nose, rubbing the spot where his glasses perch. He reaches slowly into his trouser pocket and I suddenly feel a twinge of doubt. His fingers are searching for something. He has eighty pounds and twenty years on me. The door is on the far side of the room. I won't reach it before he does.

His hand emerges. I'm staring at it, transfixed. He is holding a white handkerchief, which he unfolds and lays in his lap. Then he takes off his glasses and slowly cleans each lens, rubbing the cloth between his thumb and forefinger. Maybe this slow-motion ritual is buying him time.

He raises the glasses to the light, checking for any smudges. Then he looks past them and stares directly at me. 'Do you make up this crap as you go along, or did you spend all weekend coming up with it?'

The pressure is dispelled like air leaking from a punctured

raft. I have overplayed my hand. I want to ask Bobby where I went wrong, but he's not going to tell me. A poker player doesn't explain why he calls a bluff. I must have been near the mark, but that's a lot like NASA saying its Mars Polar Lander achieved its target because it crashed and went missing on the right planet.

Bobby's faith in me has been shaken. He also knows that I'm frightened of him, which is not a good basis for a clinical relationship. What in God's name was I thinking? I've wound him up like a clockwork toy and now I have to let him loose.

22

The white Audi cruises along Elgin Avenue, slowing as it passes me. I continue limping along the pavement, my tennis racket under one arm and a bruise the size of a grapefruit on my right thigh. Ruiz is behind the wheel. He looks like a man who is willing to follow me all the way home at four miles an hour.

I stop and turn towards him. He leans over to open the front passenger door. 'What happened to you?'

'A sporting injury.'

'I didn't think tennis was that dangerous.'

'You haven't played against my mate.'

I get in beside him. The car smells of stale tobacco and apple-scented air freshener. Ruiz does a U-turn and heads west.

'Where are we going?'

'The scene of the crime.'

I don't ask why. Everything about his demeanour says I don't have a choice. The temperature has fallen to just above freezing and a mist blurs the streetlights. Coloured lights are blinking in windows and plastic wreaths of holly decorate front doors.

We drive along Harrow Road and turn into Scrubs Lane. After less than half a mile the lane rises and falls over Mitre Bridge, where it crosses the Grand Union Canal and the Paddington rail lines. Ruiz pulls over and the engine dies. He gets out of the car and waits for me to do the same. The doors centrally lock as he walks away, expecting me to follow. My thigh is still stiff from Jock's well-aimed smash. I rub it gingerly and limp along the road towards the bridge.

Ruiz has stopped at a wire cyclone fence. Grabbing hold of a metal post, he swings himself upwards on to a stone wall flanking the bridge. Using the same post, he lets himself down the other side. He turns and waits for me.

The towpath is deserted and the nearby buildings are dark and empty. It feels a lot later than it is – like the early hours of the morning, when the world always seems much lonelier and beds much warmer.

Ruiz is walking ahead of me with his hands buried in his coat pockets and his head down. He seems full of pent-up rage. After about five hundred yards the railway tracks appear to our right. Maintenance sheds are silhouetted against the residual light. Rolling stock sits idle in a freight yard.

With barely any warning a train roars past. The sound bounces off the tin sheds and the stone walls of the canal, until it seems as though we're standing in a tunnel.

Ruiz has stopped suddenly on the path. I almost run into him.

'Recognise anything?'

I know exactly where we are. Instead of feeling horror or sadness, my only emotion is anger. It's late; I'm cold; and more than anything else I'm tired of Ruiz's snide glances and raised eyebrows. If he has something to say, get it over with and let me go home.

'You saw the photographs.'

'Yes.'

Ruiz raises his arm and for a moment I think he's going to strike me. 'Look over there. Follow the edge of the building down.'

I trace the path of his outstretched hand and see the wall. A darker strip in the foreground must be the ditch where they found her body. Looking over his left shoulder, I see the silhouettes of the trees and the headstones of Kensal Green Cemetery. I remember standing on the ridge, watching the police uncover Catherine.

'Why am I here?' I ask, feeling empty inside.

'Use your imagination – you're good at that.'

He's angry, and for some reason I'm to blame. I don't often meet someone with his intensity – apart from obsessive-compulsives. I used to know guys like him at school; kids who were so ferociously determined to prove they were tough that they never stopped fighting. They had too much to prove and not enough time to prove it.

'Why am I here?'

'Because I have some questions for you.' He doesn't look at me. 'And I want to tell you some things about Bobby Moran.'

'I can't talk about my patients.'

'You just have to listen.' He rocks from foot to foot. 'Take my word for it, you'll find it fascinating.' He walks two paces towards the canal and spits into the water. 'Bobby Moran has no girlfriend or fiancée called Arky. He lives in a boarding house in north London with a bunch of asylum seekers waiting for council housing. He's unemployed and hasn't worked for nearly two years. There is no such company as Nevaspring – not a registered one at any rate.

'His father was never in the air force – as a mechanic, a pilot, or anything else. Bobby grew up in Liverpool, not London. He dropped out of school at fifteen. He did stints at night school and for a while worked as a volunteer at a sheltered workshop in Lancashire. We found no history of psychiatric illness or hospitalisation.'

Ruiz is pacing back and forth as he talks. His breath condenses in the air and trails after him like he's a steam engine. 'A lot of people had nice things to say about Bobby. He is very neat and tidy according to his landlady. She does his washing and doesn't remember smelling chloroform on any of his clothes. His old bosses at the shelter called him a "big softie".

'That's what I find really strange, Professor. Nothing you said about him is true. I can understand you getting one or two details wrong. We all make mistakes. But it's as though we're talking about a completely different person.'

My voice is hoarse. 'It can't be him.'

'That's what I thought. So I checked. Big guy, six-two, overweight, John Lennon glasses – that's our boy. Then I wondered why he'd tell all these lies to a shrink who was trying to help him. Doesn't make sense, does it?'

'He's hiding something.'

'Maybe. But he didn't kill Catherine McBride.'

'How can you be so sure?'

'A dozen people at an evening class can verify his whereabouts on the night she disappeared.'

I don't have any strength left in my legs.

'Sometimes I'm pretty slow on the uptake, Prof. My old mum used to say that I was born a day late and never caught up. Truth is, I normally get there in the end. It just takes me a little longer than clever people.' He says it with bitterness rather than triumph.

'You see, I asked myself why Bobby Moran would make up all these lies. And then I thought, what if he didn't? What if *you* were telling the lies? You could be making this whole thing up to divert my attention.'

'You can't be serious?'

'How did you know that Catherine McBride cut her carotid artery to hasten her death? It wasn't mentioned in the post-mortem.'

'I studied to be a doctor.'

'What about the chloroform?'

'I told you.'

'Yes, you did. I did some reading. Do you know that it takes a few drops of chloroform on a mask or a cloth to render a person unconscious? You have to know what you're doing when you play around with that stuff. A few drops too many and the victim's breathing is shut off. They suffocate.'

'The killer most likely had some medical knowledge.'

'I came up with that too.' Ruiz stamps his shoes on the bitumen, trying to stay warm. A stray cat, wandering along inside the wire fence, suddenly flattens itself at the sound of our voices. Both of us wait and watch, but the cat is in no hurry to move on.

'How did you know she was a nurse?' says Ruiz.

'She had the medallion.'

'I think you recognised her straight away. I think all the rest was a pretence.'

'No.'

His tone is colder. 'You also knew her grandfather – Justice McBride.'

'Yes.'

'Why didn't you say so?'

'I didn't think it was important. It was years ago. Psychologists often give evidence in the family division. We do evaluations on children and parents. We make recommendations to the court.'

'What did you make of him?'

'He had his faults but he was an honest judge. I respected him.'

Ruiz is trying hard to be cordial, but polite restraint doesn't come naturally to him.

'Do you know what I find really hard to explain?' he says. 'Why it took you so long to tell me about knowing Catherine McBride and her grandfather, yet you give me a crock of shit about somebody called Bobby Moran. No, sorry, that isn't right – you *don't* talk about your patients, do you? You just play little schoolboy games of show and tell. Well, two can play that game . . . ' He grins at me – all white teeth and dark eyes. 'Shall I tell you what I've been doing these last two weeks? I've been searching this canal. We brought in dredging equipment and emptied the locks. It was a lousy job. There was three feet of putrid sludge and slime. We found stolen bicycles, shopping trolleys, car chassis, hubcaps, two washing machines, car tyres, condoms and over four thousand used syringes. Do you know what else we found?'

I shake my head.

'Catherine McBride's handbag and her mobile phone. It took us a while to dry everything out. Then we had to check the phone records. That's when we discovered that the very last call she made was to your office. At 6.37 p.m. on the thirteenth of November. She was calling from a pub not far from here. Whoever had arranged to meet her hadn't turned up. My guess is that she called to find out why.'

'How can you be sure?'

Ruiz smiles. 'We also found her diary. It had been in the water for so long the pages were stuck together and the ink had washed away. The scene of crime boys had to dry it very carefully and pull the pages apart. Then they used an electron microscope to find the faint traces of ink. It's amazing what they can do nowadays.'

Ruiz has squared up to me, his eyes just inches from mine. This is his Agatha Christie moment: his drawing room soliloquy.

'Catherine had a note in her diary under November thirteenth. She wrote down the name of the Grand Union Hotel. Do you know it?'

I nod.

'It's only about a mile along the canal, near that tennis club of yours.' Ruiz motions with a sway of his head. 'At the bottom of the same page she wrote a name. I think she planned to meet that person. Do you know whose name it was?'

I shake my head.

'Care to hazard a guess?'

I feel a tightness in my chest. 'Mine.'

Ruiz doesn't allow himself a final flourish or triumphant gesture. This is just the beginning. I see the glint of handcuffs as they emerge from his pocket. My first impulse is to laugh, but then the coldness reaches inside me and I want to vomit.

'I am arresting you on suspicion of murder. You have the right to remain silent, but it is my duty to warn you that anything you do say will be taken down and may be used in evidence against you . . .'

The steel bracelets close around my wrists. Ruiz forces my legs apart and searches me, starting at my ankles and working his way up.

'Have you anything to say?'

It's strange the things that occur to you at times like this. I suddenly remember a line my father used to quote to me whenever I was in trouble: 'Don't say anything unless you can improve on the silence.'

Book Two

We are often criminals in the eyes of the earth, not only for having committed crimes, but because we know what crimes have been committed.

Hombre de la Máscara de Hierro
(The Man in the Iron Mask)

1

I have been staring at the same square of light for so long that when I close my eyes it's still there, shining inside my eyelids. The window is high up on the wall, above the door. Occasionally I hear footsteps in the corridor. The hinged observation flap opens and eyes peer at me. After several seconds, the hatch shuts and I go back to staring at the window.

I don't know what time it is. I was forced to trade my wristwatch, belt and shoelaces for a grey blanket that feels more like sandpaper than wool. The only sound I can hear is the leaking cistern in the adjacent cell.

It has been quiet since the last of the drunks arrived. That must have been after closing time – just long enough for someone to fall asleep on the night bus, get into a fight with a taxi driver and finish up in the back of a police van. I can still hear him kicking at the cell door and shouting, 'I didn't fucking touch him.'

My cell is six paces long and four paces wide. It has a lavatory, a sink and a bunk bed. Graffiti have been drawn, scratched, gouged and smeared on every wall, although valiant attempts have been made to paint over them.

I don't know where Ruiz has gone. He's probably tucked up in bed, dreaming of making the world a safer place. Our first interview session lasted a few minutes. When I told him that I wanted a lawyer, he advised me, 'Get a bloody good one.'

Most of the lawyers I know don't make house calls at that time of night. I called Jock and woke him instead. I could hear a female voice complaining in the background.

'Where are you?'

'Harrow Road Police Station.'

'What are you doing there?'

'I've been arrested.'

'Wow!' Only Jock could sound impressed at this piece of news.

'I need you to do me a favour. I want you to call Julianne and tell her I'm OK. Tell her I'm helping the police with an investigation. She'll know the one.'

'Why don't you tell her the truth?'

'Please, Jock, don't ask. I need time to work this through.'

Since then I've been pacing the cell. I stand. I sit. I walk. I sit on the toilet. My nerves have made me constipated, or maybe it's the medication. Ruiz thinks I've been holding things back or being economical with the truth. Hindsight is an exact science. Right now my mistakes keep dividing inside my head, fighting for space with all the questions.

People talk about the sins of omission. What does that mean? Who decides if something is a sin? I know that I'm being semantic, but judging by the way people moralise and jump to conclusions, anyone would think that the truth is real and solid; that it's something that can be picked up and passed around, weighed and measured, before being agreed upon.

But the truth isn't like that. If I were to tell you this story tomorrow, it would be different than today. I would have filtered the details through my defences and rationalised my actions. Truth *is* a matter of semantics, whether we like it or not.

I hadn't recognised Catherine from the drawing. And the body I saw in the morgue seemed more like a vandalised shopfront mannequin than a real human being. It had been five years. I told Ruiz as soon as I was sure. Yes, it could have been sooner, but he already knew her name.

Nobody likes admitting mistakes. And we all hate acknowledging the large gap between what we should do and what we actually do. So we alter either our actions or our beliefs. We make excuses, or redefine our conduct in a more flattering light. In my business it's called *cognitive dissonance*. It hasn't worked for me. My inner voice – call it my conscience or soul or guardian angel – keeps whispering, 'Liar, liar, pants on fire . . . '

Ruiz is right. I am in a shit-load of trouble.

I lie on the narrow cot, feeling the springs press into my back.

Summoning my sister's new boyfriend to a police station at six-thirty in the morning is an odd way to make somebody feel like part of the family. I don't know many criminal barristers. Usually I deal with Crown solicitors, who treat me like their new best friend or something nasty they stepped in, depending on what opinion I offer in court.

Simon arrives an hour later. There's no small talk about Patricia or appreciation for Sunday's lunch. Instead he motions for me to sit down and pulls up a chair. This is business.

The holding cells are on the floor below us. The charge room must be nearby. I can smell coffee and hear the tapping of computer keyboards. There are Venetian blinds at the windows of the interview room. The strips of sky are beginning to grow light.

Simon opens his briefcase and takes out a blue folder and a large legal notebook. I'm amazed at how he combines a Santa Claus physique with the demeanour of a lawyer.

'We need to make some decisions. They want to start the interviews as soon as possible. Is there anything you want to tell me?'

I feel myself blinking rapidly. What does he mean? Does he expect me to confess?

'I want you to get me out of here,' I say, a little too abruptly.

He begins by explaining that the Police and Criminal Evidence Act gives the police forty-eight hours in which to either charge a suspect or let them go, unless they've been granted leave by the courts.

'So I could be here for two days?'

'Yes.'

'But that's ridiculous!'

'Did you know this girl?'

'Yes.'

'Did you arrange to meet her on the night she died?'

218

'No.'

Simon is making notes. He leans over the notebook, scribbling bullet points and underlining some words.

'This is one of those no-brainers,' he says. 'All you have to do is provide an alibi for the thirteenth of November.'

'I can't do that.'

Simon gives me the weary look of a schoolteacher who hasn't received the answer he expects. Then he brushes a speck of fluff from his suit sleeve as if dismissing the problem. Standing abruptly, he knocks twice on the door to signal that he's finished.

'Is that all?'

'Yes.'

'Aren't you going to ask me if I killed her?'

He looks bemused. 'Save your plea for a jury and pray it never gets that far.'

The door closes after him but the room is still full of what he has left behind – disappointment, candour and the scent of aftershave. Five minutes later a WPC takes me along the corridor to the interrogation room. I have been in one before. Early in my career I sometimes acted as the 'responsible adult' when juveniles were being interrogated.

A table and four chairs take up most of the room. In the far corner is a large tape recorder, which is time-coded. There is nothing on the walls or the windowsill. The WPC stands immediately inside the door, trying not to look at me.

Ruiz arrives, along with a second detective who is younger and taller, with a long face and crooked teeth. Simon follows them into the interview room. He whispers in my ear, 'If I touch your elbow I want you to be quiet.'

I nod agreement.

Ruiz sits down opposite me, without bothering to remove his jacket. He rubs a hand across the whiskers on his chin.

'This is the second formal interview of Professor Joseph Paul O'Loughlin, a suspect in the murder of Catherine Mary McBride,' he says for the benefit of the tape. 'Present during the interview are Detective Inspector Vincent Ruiz, Detective Sergeant John Keebal and Dr O'Loughlin's legal representative, Simon Koch. The time is eight-fourteen a.m.'

A WPC checks the recorder is working. She nods to Ruiz. He places both his hands on the table and links his fingers together. His eyes settle on me and he says nothing. I have to admit it is a very eloquent pause.

'Where were you on the evening of November thirteenth this year?'

'I don't recall.'

'Were you at home with your wife?'

'No.'

'So you can recall that much?' he says sarcastically.

'Yes.'

'Did you work that day?'

'Yes.'

'What time did you leave the office?'

'I had a doctor's appointment at four o'clock.'

The questions go on like this, asking for specifics. Ruiz is trying to pin me down. He knows, as I do, that lying is a lot harder than telling the truth. The devil is in the detail. The more you weave into a story, the harder it is to maintain. It becomes like a straitjacket – binding you tighter, giving you less room to move.

Finally he asks about Catherine. Silence. I glance at

Simon who says nothing. He hasn't said a word since the interview began. Neither has the younger detective, sitting to the side and slightly behind Ruiz.

'Did you know Catherine McBride?'

'Yes.'

'Where did you first meet her?'

I tell the whole story – about the self-mutilation and the counselling sessions; how she seemed to get better and how she eventually left the Marsden. It feels strange talking about a clinical case. My voice sounds vaguely strident, as though I'm trying too hard to convince them.

When I finish I open the palms of my hands to signal the end. I can see myself reflected in Ruiz's eyes. He's waiting for more.

'Why didn't you tell the hospital authorities about Catherine?'

'I felt sorry for her. I thought it would be cruel to see a dedicated nurse lose her job. Who would that benefit?'

'That's the only reason?'

'Yes.'

'Were you having an affair with Catherine McBride?'

'No.'

'Did you ever have sexual relations with her?'

'No.'

'When was the last time you spoke to her?'

'Five years ago. I can't remember the exact date.'

'Why did Catherine call your office on the evening she died?'

'I don't know.'

'We have other telephone records which indicate that she called the number twice the previous fortnight.'

'I can't explain that.'

'Your name was in her diary.'

I shrug. It's another mystery. Ruiz slaps his open palm on the table and everyone jumps, including Simon.

'You met her on that night.'

'No.'

'You lured her away from the Grand Union Hotel.'

'No.'

'You tortured her.'

'No.'

'This is horse-shit!' he explodes. 'You have deliberately withheld information and have spent the last three weeks covering your arse, misdirecting the investigation, trying to steer police away from you.'

Simon touches my arm. He wants me to be quiet. I ignore him.

'I didn't touch her. I haven't seen her. You have NOTHING!'

'I want to speak with my client,' says Simon more insistently.

To hell with that! I'm done with being polite. 'What possible reason would I have for killing Catherine?' I shout. 'You have my name in a diary, a telephone call to my office and no motive. Do your job. Get some evidence before you come accusing me.'

The younger detective grins. I realise that something is wrong. Ruiz opens a thin green folder which lies on the table in front of him. From it he produces a photocopied piece of paper which he slides across in front of me.

'This is a letter dated the nineteenth of April 1997. It is addressed to the senior nursing administrator of the

Royal Marsden Hospital. In this letter, Catherine McBride makes an allegation that you sexually assaulted her in your office at the hospital. She says that you hypnotised her, fondled her breasts and interfered with her underwear—'

'She withdrew that complaint. I told you that.'

My chair falls backwards with a bang and I realise that I'm on my feet. The young detective is quicker than I am. He matches me for size and is bristling with intent.

Ruiz looks exultant.

Simon has hold of my arm. 'Professor O'Loughlin . . . Joe . . . I advise you to be quiet.'

'Can't you see what they're doing? They're twisting the facts—'

'They're asking legitimate questions.'

A sense of alarm spreads through me. Ruiz has a motive. Simon picks up my chair and holds it for me. I stare blankly at the far wall, numb with tiredness. My left hand is shaking. Both detectives stare at it silently. I sit and force my hand between my knees to stop the tremors.

'Where were you on the evening of November thirteenth?'

'In the West End.'

'Who were you with?'

'No one. I got drunk. I had just received some bad news about my health.'

That statement hangs in the air like a torn cobweb looking for something to cling to. Simon breaks first and explains that I have Parkinson's Disease. I want to stop him. It is *my* business. I'm not looking for pity.

Ruiz doesn't miss a beat. 'Is one of the symptoms memory loss?'

I'm so relieved that I laugh. I didn't want him treating me any differently. 'Exactly where did you go drinking?' Ruiz presses on.

'Different pubs and wine bars.'

'Where?'

'Leicester Square, Covent Garden . . . '

'Can you name any of these bars?'

I shake my head.

'Can anyone confirm your whereabouts?'

'No.'

'What time did you get home?'

'I didn't go home.'

'Where did you spend the night?'

'I can't recall.'

Ruiz turns to Simon. 'Mr Koch, can you please instruct your client—'

'My client has made it clear to me that he doesn't recall where he spent the night. He is aware that this does not help his situation.'

Ruiz's face is hard to read. He glances at his wristwatch, announces the time and then turns off the tape recorder. The interview is terminated. I glance from face to face, wondering what happens next. Is it over?

The young WPC comes back into the room.

'Are the cars ready?' asks Ruiz.

She nods and holds open the door. Ruiz strides out and the young detective snaps handcuffs on to my wrists. Simon starts to protest and is handed a copy of a search warrant. The address is typed in capital letters on both sides of the page. I'm going home.

* * *

My most vivid childhood memory of Christmas is of the St Mark's Anglican School nativity play in which I featured as one of the three wise men. The reason it is so memorable is that Russell Cochrane, who played the baby Jesus, was so nervous that he wet his pants and it leaked down the front of the Virgin Mary's blue robes. Jenny Bond, a very pretty Mary, was so angry that she dropped Russell on his head and swung a kick into his groin.

A collective groan went up from the audience, but it was drowned out by Russell's howls of pain. The entire production disintegrated and the curtain came down early.

The backstage farce proved even more compelling. Russell's father, a big man with a bullet-shaped head, was a police sergeant who sometimes came to the school to lecture us on road safety. He cornered Jenny Bond backstage and threatened to have her arrested for assault. Jenny's father laughed. It was a big mistake. Sergeant Cochrane handcuffed him on the spot and marched him along Stafford Street to the police station, where he spent the night.

Our nativity play made the national papers. 'Virgin Mary's Father Arrested', said the headline in the *Sun*. The *Star* wrote: 'Baby Jesus Kicked in the Baubles!'.

I think of it again because of Charlie. Is she going to see me in handcuffs, being flanked by policemen? What will she think of her father then?

The unmarked police car pulls up the ramp from the underground car park and emerges into daylight. Sitting next to me, Simon puts an overcoat over my head. Through the damp wool, I can make out the pyrotechnics of flashguns and TV lights. I don't know how many photographers and cameramen there are. I hear their voices and feel the police car accelerate away.

Traffic slows to a crawl in Marylebone Road. Pedestrians seem to hesitate and stare. I'm convinced they're looking at me – wondering who I am and what I'm doing in the back seat of a police car.

'Can I phone my wife?' I ask.

'No.'

'She doesn't know we're coming.'

'Exactly.'

'But she doesn't know I've been arrested.'

'You should have told her.'

I suddenly remember the office. I have patients coming today. Appointments need to be rescheduled. 'Can I call my secretary?'

Ruiz turns and glances over his shoulder. 'We are also executing a search warrant on your office.'

I want to argue but Simon touches my elbow. 'This is part of the process,' he whispers, trying to sound reassuring.

The convoy of three police cars pulls up in the middle of our road, blocking the street in either direction. Doors are flung open and detectives assemble quickly, some using the side path to reach the back garden.

Julianne answers the front door. She is wearing pink rubber gloves. A fleck of foam clings to her hair where she has brushed her fringe to one side. A detective gives her a copy of the warrant. She doesn't look at it. She is too busy focusing on me. She sees the handcuffs and the look on my face. Her eyes are wide with shock and incomprehension.

'Keep Charlie inside,' I shout.

I look at Ruiz. I plead with him. 'Not in front of my daughter. *Please.*'

I see nothing in his eyes, but he reaches into his jacket pocket and finds the keys to the handcuffs. Two detectives take my arms.

Julianne is asking questions – ignoring the officers who push past her into the house. 'What's happening, Joe? What are you . . . ?'

'They think I had something to do with Catherine's death.'

'How? Why? That's ridiculous. You were helping them with their investigation.'

Something falls and smashes upstairs. Julianne glances upwards and then back to me. 'What are they doing in our house?' She is on the verge of tears. 'What have you done, Joe?'

I see Charlie's face peering out of the sitting room. It quickly disappears as Julianne turns. 'You stay in that room, young lady,' she barks, sounding more frightened than angry.

The front door is wide open. Anybody walking by can look inside and see what is happening. I can hear cupboards and drawers being opened on the floor above; mattresses are being lifted and beds dragged aside. Julianne doesn't know what to do. Part of her wants to protect her house from being vandalised, but mostly she wants answers from me. I don't have any.

The detectives take me through to the kitchen, where I find Ruiz peering out of the French doors at the garden. Men with shovels and hoes are ripping up the lawn. D.J. is leaning against Charlie's swing with a cigarette hanging from his mouth. He looks at me through the smoke; inquisitive, insolent. A faint hint of a smile creases the corners of his mouth – as though he's watching a Porsche get a parking ticket.

Turning away reluctantly, he lets the cigarette fall into the gravel where it continues to glow. Then he bends and slices open the plastic packing surrounding a radiator.

'We interviewed your neighbours,' explains Ruiz. 'You were seen burying something in the garden.'

'A bug-eyed goldfish.'

Ruiz is totally baffled. 'I beg your pardon?'

Julianne laughs at the absurdity of it all. We are living in a Monty Python sketch.

'He buried Charlie's goldfish,' she says. 'It's under the plum tree next to Harold the Hamster.'

A couple of the detectives behind us can't stifle their giggles. Ruiz has a face like thunder. I know I shouldn't goad him, but it feels good to laugh.

2

The mattress has compressed to the hardness of concrete beneath my hip and shoulder. From the moment I lie down the blood throbs in my ears and my mind begins to race. I want to slip into peaceful emptiness. Instead I chase the dangerous thoughts, magnified in my imagination.

By now Ruiz will have interviewed Julianne. He'll have asked where I was on 13 November. She'll have told him that I spent the night with Jock. She won't know that's a lie. She'll repeat what I told her.

Ruiz will also have talked to Jock, who will tell them that I left his office at five o'clock that day. He asked me out for a drink, but I said no. I said I was going home. None of our stories are going to match.

Julianne has spent all evening in the charge room, hoping to see me. Ruiz told her she could have five minutes but I can't face her. I know that's appalling. I know she must be scared, confused, angry and worried sick. She just wants an explanation. She wants to hear me tell her it's going to be all right. I'm more frightened of confronting her than I am of Ruiz. How can I explain Elisa? How can I make things right?

Julianne asked me if I thought it unusual that a woman I hadn't seen in five years is murdered and then the police ask me to help identify her. Glibly, I told her that coincidences were just a couple of things happening simultaneously. Now the coincidences are starting to pile up. What are the chances of Bobby being referred to me as a patient? Or that Catherine would phone my office on the evening she died? When do coincidences stop being coincidences and become a pattern?

I'm not being paranoid. I'm not seeing shadows darting in the corner of my eye or imagining sinister conspiracies. But something is happening here that is bigger than the sum of its parts.

I fall asleep with this thought and sometime during the night I wake suddenly, breathing hard with my heart pounding. I cannot see who or what is chasing me, but I know it's there, watching, waiting, laughing at me.

Every sound seems exaggerated by the starkness of the cell. I lie awake and listen to the seesaw creaks of bedsprings, water dripping in cisterns, drunks talking in their sleep and guards' shoes echoing down corridors.

Today is the day. The police will either charge me or let me go. I should be more anxious and concerned. Mostly I feel remote and separate from what's happening. I pace out the cell, thinking how bizarre life can be. Look at all the twists and turns, the coincidences and bad luck, the mistakes and misunderstandings. I don't feel angry, or bitter. I have faith in the system. Pretty soon they're going to realise the evidence isn't strong enough against me. They'll have to let me go.

This sort of optimism strikes me as quite odd when I think about how naturally cynical I am concerning law and order. Innocent people get shafted every day. I've seen the evidence. It's incontrovertible. Yet I have no fears about this happening to me.

I blame my mother and her unwavering belief in authority figures such as policemen, judges and politicians. She grew up in a village in the Cotswolds, where the town constable rode a bicycle, knew every local by name and solved most crimes within half an hour. He epitomised fairness and honesty. Since then, despite the regular stories of police planting evidence, taking bribes and falsifying statements, my mother has never altered her beliefs. 'God made more good people than bad,' she says, as though a headcount will sort everything out. And when this seems highly unlikely, she adds, 'They will get their comeuppance in Heaven.'

A hatch opens in the lower half of the door and a wooden tray is propelled across the floor. I have a plastic bottle of orange juice, some grey-looking sludge that I assume to be scrambled eggs and two slices of bread that have been waved over a toaster. I put it to one side and wait for Simon to arrive.

He looks very jolly in his silk tie printed with holly and silver bells. It's the sort of tie Charlie will give me for Christmas. I wonder if Simon has ever been married or had children.

He can't stay long; he's due in court. I see strands of his horsehair wig sticking out of his briefcase. The police have requested a blood and hair sample, he says. I have no problem with that. They are also seeking permission to interview my patients, but a judge has refused them access to my files. Good for him.

The biggest piece of news concerns two of the phone calls Catherine made to my office. Meena, bless her cotton socks, has told detectives that she talked to Catherine twice in early November.

I had totally forgotten about the search for a new secretary. Meena had placed an advertisement in the Medical Appointments section of the *Guardian*. It asked for experienced medical secretaries, or applicants with nursing training. We had over eighty replies. I start explaining this to Simon, getting more and more excited. 'Meena was coming up with a shortlist of twelve.'

'Catherine made the shortlist.'

'Yes. Maybe. She must have done. That would explain the call. Meena will know.' Did Catherine know she was applying to be *my* secretary? Meena must have mentioned my name. Maybe Catherine wanted to surprise me. Or perhaps she thought I wouldn't give her an interview.

Simon scissors his fingers across his tie, as if pretending to cut it off. 'Why would a woman who accused you of sexual assault apply to become your secretary?' He sounds like a prosecutor.

'I didn't assault her.'

He doesn't comment. Instead he looks at his watch and closes his briefcase. 'I don't think you should answer any more police questions.'

'Why?'

'You're digging yourself into a deeper hole.'

Simon shrugs on his overcoat and leans down to brush a smudge of dirt from the mirror-like surface of his black shoes. 'They have eight more hours. Unless they come up with something new, you'll be home by this evening.'

Lying on the bunk with my hands behind my head, I stare at the ceiling. Someone has scrawled in the corner: 'A day without sunlight is like . . . night'. The ceiling must be twelve feet high. How on earth did anyone get up there?

It is strange being locked away from the world. I have no idea what's been happening in the past forty-eight hours. I wonder what I've missed. Hopefully my parents have gone back to Wales. Charlie will have started her Christmas break; the boiler will be fixed; Julianne will have wrapped the presents and put them under the tree . . . Jock will have dusted off his Santa suit and done his annual tour of the children's wards. And then there's Bobby – what has he been doing?

Midway through the afternoon, I am summoned to the interview room again. Ruiz and the same detective sergeant are waiting. Simon arrives out of breath from climbing the stairs. He's clutching a sandwich in a plastic prism and a bottle of orange juice.

'A late lunch,' he confesses apologetically.

The tape recorder is switched on.

'Professor O'Loughlin, help me out here.' Ruiz conspires to raise a polite smile. 'Is it true that killers often return to the scene of the crime?'

Where is he going with this? I glance at Simon who indicates I should answer.

'A "signature killer" will sometimes return, but more often than not it's an urban myth.'

'What's a "signature killer"?'

'Every killer has a behavioural imprint – it's like a criminal shadow that is left behind at a crime scene, a signature. It might be the way they tie a ligature or dispose of a body. Some feel compelled to return to the scene.'

'Why?'

'There are lots of possible reasons. Perhaps they want to fantasise and relive what they've done, or collect a souvenir. Some may feel guilty or just want to stay close.'

'Which is why kidnappers often help with the search?'

'Yes.'

'And arsonists help fight fires?'

I nod. The sergeant is pretending to be an Easter Island statue. Ruiz opens a folder and takes out several photographs.

'Where were you on Sunday November twenty-fourth?'

So this is it – this is what he's found.

'I was visiting my great auntie.'

A spark of excitement ignites in his eyes. 'What time was that?'

'In the morning.'

'Where does she live?'

'At Kensal Green Cemetery.'

The truth disappoints him. 'We have CCTV pictures of your car in the parking area.' He slides the photograph across the desk. I'm putting a box of leaves into Charlie's outstretched arms.

Ruiz pulls out another sheet of paper. 'Do you remember how we discovered the body?'

'You said a dog disturbed it.'

234

'The caller didn't leave a name or contact number. He phoned from a public phone box near the entrance to the cemetery. Did you see anyone in that vicinity?'

'No.'

'Did you use that phone box?'

Surely he's not suggesting that I made the call?

'You said the killer would know the area intimately.'

'Yes.'

'How would you describe your knowledge?'

'Detective Inspector, I think I see where you're going with this. Even if I did kill Catherine and then bury her by the canal, do you really think I'd bring my wife and daughter along to watch her being dug up?'

Ruiz slams the folder shut and snarls, 'I ask the fucking questions. You worry about answering them.'

Simon interrupts. 'Perhaps we should all cool down.'

Ruiz leans across the desk towards me, until I can see the capillaries beneath the skin of his nose. I swear he can breathe through those pores.

'Are you willing to talk to me without your lawyer present?'

'If you turn off the tape.'

Simon objects and wants to talk to me alone. Outside in the corridor we have a frank exchange of views. He tells me I'm being stupid. I agree. But if I can get Ruiz to listen, maybe I can convince him to look again at Bobby.

'I want it noted that I advised you against this.'

'Don't worry, Simon. Nobody's going to blame you.'

Ruiz is waiting for me. A cigarette is alight in the ashtray. He stares at it intently, watching it burn down. The grey

235

ash forms a misshapen tower that will tumble with the slightest breath.

'I thought you were quitting.'

'I am. I like to watch.'

The ash topples and Ruiz pushes the ashtray to one side. He nods.

The room seems so much larger with just the two of us. Ruiz pushes back his chair and puts his feet on the table. His black brogues have worn heels. Above one sock, on the white of his ankle, there is a streak of black shoe polish.

'We took your photograph to every pub and wine bar in Leicester Square and Charing Cross,' he says. 'Not one barman or barmaid remembers you.'

'I'm easy to forget.'

'We're going out again tonight. Maybe we'll trigger someone's memory. Somehow I don't think so. I don't think you were anywhere near the West End.'

I don't respond.

'We also showed your photograph to the regulars at the Grand Union Hotel. Nobody remembers seeing you there. They remembered Catherine. She was dressed real nice, according to some of the lads. One of them offered to buy her a drink but she said she was waiting for someone. Was it you?'

'No.'

'Who was it?'

'I still think it was Bobby Moran.'

Ruiz lets out a low rumble that ends with a hacking cough. 'You don't give up, do you?'

'Catherine didn't die on the night she disappeared. Her body wasn't found for eleven days. Whoever tortured her took a long time to break her spirit – days perhaps. Bobby could have done it.'

'Nothing points to him.'

'I think he knew her.'

Ruiz laughs ironically. 'That's the difference between what you do and what I do. You base your conclusions on bell curves and empirical models. A sob story about a lousy childhood and you're ready to put someone in therapy for ten years. I deal with facts and right now they're all pointing to you.'

'What about intuition? Gut instincts? I thought detectives used them all the time.'

'Not when I'm trying to get approval for a surveillance budget.'

We sit in silence, measuring the gulf between us. Eventually Ruiz speaks. 'I talked to your wife yesterday. She described you as being a little "distant" lately. You suggested the family go away on a trip . . . to America. It came up suddenly. She couldn't explain why.'

'It had nothing to do with Catherine. I wanted to see more of the world.'

'Before it's too late.' His voice softens, 'Tell me about your Parkinson's. Must be pretty gutting to get news like that – particularly when you've got a good-looking wife, a young daughter, a successful career. How many years are you going to lose? Ten? Twenty?'

'I don't know.'

'I reckon news like that would make a guy feel pretty pissed off with the world. You've worked with cancer patients. You tell me – do they get bitter and feel cheated?'

'Some of them do.'

'I bet some of them want to tear down the world. I mean, why should they get all the shitty luck, right? What are you going to do in a situation like that? Go quietly, or rail against the dying of the light? You could settle old scores and make amends. Nothing wrong with exacting a bit of rough justice if it's the only kind on offer.'

I want to laugh at his clumsy attempt at psychoanalysis. 'Is that what you'd do, Inspector?' It takes Ruiz a few moments to realise that I'm now scrutinising him. 'You think the vigilante spirit might take you?'

Doubt fills his eyes, but he won't let it stay there. He wants to move on; to change the subject, but first I want to set him straight about people with terminal illnesses or incurable diseases. Yes, some want to lash out in frustration at the sense of hopelessness and helplessness. But the bitterness and anger soon fade. Instead of feeling sorry for themselves, they face the fury of the ill wind and look ahead. And they resolve to enjoy every moment they have left; to suck the marrow out of life until it dribbles down their chin.

Sliding his feet to the floor, Ruiz puts both hands flat on the table and levers himself upwards. He doesn't look at me as he speaks. 'I want you charged with murder but the director of public prosecutions says I don't have enough evidence. He's right, but then so am I. I'm going to keep looking until we find some more. It's just a matter of time.' His eyes are gazing at something a great distance away.

'You don't like me, do you?' I ask.

'Not particularly.'

'Why?'

'Because you think I'm a dumb, foul-mouthed plod who

doesn't read books and thinks the theory of relativity has something to do with inbreeding.'

'That's not true.'

He shrugs and reaches for the door handle.

'How much of this is personal?' I ask.

His answer rumbles through the closing door. 'Don't flatter yourself.'

3

The same WPC who has shadowed me for the last forty-eight hours hands me my tennis racket and a parcel containing my watch, wallet, wedding ring and shoelaces. I have to count my money, including the loose change, and sign for it all.

The clock on the wall of the charge room says it's 9.45 p.m. What day is it? Wednesday. Seven days until Christmas. A small silver tree is perched on the front counter, decorated with a handful of baubles and a wonky star. Hanging on the wall behind it is a banner saying, 'Peace and Goodwill to All Men'.

The WPC offers to call me a cab. I wait in the reception area until the driver gives me a blast on the horn. I'm tired, dirty and smell of stale sweat. I should go home, yet when I slide on to the back seat of the cab I feel my courage leak away. I want to tell the driver to head in the opposite direction. I don't want to face Julianne. Semantics aren't going to wash with her. Only the unqualified truth.

I have never loved anyone as much as I love her – not until Charlie came along. There is no justification for cheating on her. I know what people will say. They'll call it classic mid-life paranoia. I hit my forties and, fearing my own mortality, had a one-night stand. Or they'll put it all down to self-pity. On the same day I learned of my progressive neurological disease I slept with another woman – getting my fill of sex and excitement before my body falls apart.

I have no excuses for what happened. It wasn't an accident or a moment of madness. It was a mistake. It was sex. It was tears, semen and someone other than Julianne.

Jock had just told me the bad news. I was sitting in his office, unable to move. A huge bloody butterfly must have flapped its wings in the Amazon because the vibrations knocked me down.

Jock offered to take me for a drink. I said no. I needed some air. For the next few hours I wandered around the West End, visiting bars and trying to feel like just another person having a few drinks to unwind.

First I thought I wanted to be alone. Then I realised that I really needed somebody to talk to. Somebody who wasn't part of my perfect life: somebody who didn't know Julianne, or Charlie, or any of my friends or family. So that's how I finished up on Elisa's doorstep. It wasn't an accident. I sought her out.

In the beginning we just talked. We talked for hours. (Julianne will probably say this makes my infidelity worse because it was more than just some insatiable male craving.)

What did we talk about? Childhood memories. Favourite holidays. Special songs. Maybe none of these things. The words weren't important. Elisa knew I was hurting, but didn't ask why. She knew I would either tell her or I wouldn't. It made no difference to her.

I have very little memory of what happened next. We kissed. Elisa rolled me on top of her. Her heels bumped against my back. She moved so slowly as she took me inside her. I moaned as I came and the pain leaked away.

I spent the night. The second time *I* took her. I pushed Elisa down and drove into her violently, making her hips jerk and her breasts quiver. When it was over, white tissues, wet with sperm, lay on the floor like fallen leaves.

The strange thing is that I expected to be consumed by guilt or doubt. Feeling normal didn't even enter my calculations. I was convinced Julianne would see straight through me. She wouldn't need to smell it on my clothes, or see lipstick on my collar. Instead she would know intuitively, just as she seems to know everything else about me.

I have never regarded myself as a risk-taker, or someone who gets a thrill from living close to the edge. Once or twice at university, before I met Julianne, I had one-night stands. It seemed natural then. Jock was right – the left-wing girls were easier to bed. This was different.

The cabbie is pleased to be rid of me. I stand on the footpath and stare at my house. The only light is a glow from the kitchen window, down the side path.

My key slips into the lock. As I step inside I see Julianne silhouetted against a rectangle of light at the far end of the hall. She is standing in the kitchen doorway.

'Why didn't you call me? I would have picked you up . . .'

'I didn't want Charlie to come to the police station.'

I can't see the look on her face. Her voice sounds OK. I put down my tennis things and walk towards her. Her cropped dark hair is tousled and her eyes are pouchy from lack of sleep. As I try to put my arms around her she slips away. She can hardly bear to look at me.

This is not just about a lie. I have brought police officers into her house: opening cupboards, looking under beds, searching through her personal things. Our neighbours have seen me in handcuffs. Our garden has been dug up. She has been interviewed by detectives and asked about our sex life. She has waited for hours in a police station, hoping to see me, only to be turned away – not by the authorities but by me. All of this and not one phone call or message to help her understand.

I glance at the kitchen table and see a scattered pile of newspapers. The pages are open at the same story. 'Psychologist Arrested in McBride Murder Probe', reads one headline. 'Celebrity Shrink Detained' says another. There are photographs of me sitting in the back seat of a police car with Simon's coat over my head. I look guilty. Put a coat over Mother Teresa's head and she would *look* guilty. Why do suspects do it? Surely it would be better to smile and wave.

I slump into a chair and look through the stories. One newspaper has used a telephoto shot of me perched on the roof of the Marsden, with Malcolm strapped in the harness in front of me. A second photo shows me covered in the coat. My hands are cuffed on my lap. The message is clear – I have gone from hero to zero.

Julianne fills the electric kettle and takes out two mugs.

She is wearing dark leggings and an oversized sweater that I bought for her at Camden Market. I told her it was for me, but I knew what would happen. She always borrows my sweaters. She says she likes the way they smell.

'Where's Charlie?'

'Asleep. It's nearly eleven.'

When the water boils, she fills each mug and jiggles the tea bags. I can smell peppermint. Julianne has a shelf full of different herbal teas. She sits opposite me. Her eyes rest on me without any emotion. She slightly rotates her wrists, turning her palms face up. With that one small movement she signifies that she is waiting for me to explain.

I want to say it was all a misunderstanding but I'm afraid it will sound trite. Instead I stick to the story – or what I know of it. How Ruiz thinks I had something to do with Catherine's murder because my name was in her diary when they fished it out of the canal; and how Catherine came to London for a job interview to be *my* secretary. I had no idea. Meena arranged the shortlist. Catherine must have seen the advertisement.

Julianne is a step ahead of me. 'That can't be the only reason they arrested you?'

'No. The telephone records show that she called my office on the evening she was killed.'

'Did you speak to her?'

'No. I had an appointment with Jock. That's when he told me about . . . you know what.'

'Who answered the call?'

'I don't know. Meena went home early.'

I lower my eyes from her gaze. 'They've dredged up the

sexual assault complaint. They think I was having an affair with her – that she threatened to destroy my career and our marriage.'

'But she withdrew the complaint.'

'I know, but you can see how it looks.'

Julianne pushes her cup to the centre of the table and slips off her chair. I feel myself relax a little because her eyes are no longer focused on me. Even without looking at her, I know exactly where she is – standing at the French windows, staring through her reflection at the man she thought she knew, sitting at the table.

'You told me you were with Jock. You said you were getting drunk. I knew you were lying. I've known all along.'

'I did get drunk, but not with Jock.'

'Who were you with?' The question is short, sharp and to the point. It sums up Julianne – spontaneous and direct, with every line of communication a trunk route.

'I spent the night with Elisa Velasco.'

'Did you sleep with her?'

'Yes.'

'You had sex with a prostitute?'

'She's not a prostitute any more.'

'Did you use a condom?'

'Listen to me, Julianne. She hasn't been a prostitute for years.'

'DID . . . YOU . . . USE . . . A . . . CONDOM?' Each word is clearly articulated. She is standing over my chair. Her eyes swim with tears.

'No.'

She delivers the slap with the force of her entire body. I reel sideways, clutching my cheek. I taste blood on the inside of my mouth and hear a high-pitched ringing inside my ears.

Julianne's hand is on my thigh. Her voice is soft. 'Did I hit you too hard? I'm not used to this.'

'I'm OK,' I reassure her.

She hits me again, this time even harder. I finish up on my knees, staring at the polished floorboards.

'You selfish, stupid, gutless, two-timing, lying bastard!' She is shaking her hand in pain.

I'm now an unmoving target. She beats me with her good fist, hammering on my back. She is screaming: 'A prostitute! Without a condom! And then you came home and you fucked me!'

'No! Please! You don't understand—'

'Get out of here! You are not wanted in this house! You will *not* see me. You will *not* see Charlie.'

I crouch on the floor, feeling wretched and pathetic. She turns and walks away, down the hallway to the front room. I pull myself up and follow her, desperate for some sign that this isn't the end.

I find her kneeling in front of the Christmas tree with a pair of garden shears in her hand. She has neatly lopped off the top third of the tree. It now looks like a large green lampshade.

'I'm so sorry.'

She doesn't answer.

'Please listen to me.'

'Why? What are you going to say to me? That you love me? That she meant nothing? That you *fucked* her and then you made *love* to me?'

That's the difficulty when arguing with Julianne. She

unleashes so many accusations at once that no single answer satisfies them collectively. And the moment you start trying to divide the questions up, she hits you again with a new series.

She is crying properly now. Her tears glisten in the lamplight like a string of beads draped down her cheeks.

'I made a mistake. When Jock told me about the Parkinson's it felt like a death sentence. Everything was going to change – all our plans. The future. I know I said the opposite. It's not true. Why give me this life and then give me this disease? Why give me the joy and beauty of you and Charlie and then snatch it away? It's like showing someone a glimpse of what life could be like and in the next breath telling them it can never happen.'

I kneel beside her, my knees almost touching hers.

'I didn't know how to tell you. I needed time to think. I couldn't talk to my parents or friends, who were going to feel sorry for me and give me chin-up speeches and brave smiles. That's why I went to see Elisa. She's a stranger, but also a friend. There's good in her.'

Julianne wipes her cheeks with the sleeve of her sweater and stares at the fireplace.

'I didn't plan to sleep with her. It just happened. I wish I could change that. We're not having an affair. It was one night.'

'What about Catherine McBride? Did you sleep with her?'

'No.'

'Well why did she apply to be your secretary? What would make her think you would ever give her a job after what she put us through?'

'I don't know.'

Julianne looks at her bruised hand and then at my cheek.

'What do you want, Joe? Do you want to be free? Is that it? Do you want to face this alone?'

'I don't want to drag you and Charlie down with me.'

My maudlin tone infuriates her. She bunches her fists in frustration.

'Why do you always have to be so fucking sure of yourself? Why can't you just admit you need help? I know you're sick. I know you're tired. Well, here's a news flash: we're all sick and we're all tired. I'm sick of being marginalised and tired of being pushed aside. Now I want you to leave.'

'But I love you.'

'Leave!'

'What about us? What about Charlie?'

She gives me a cold, unwavering stare. 'Maybe I still love you, Joe, but at the moment I can't stand you.'

4

When it is over – the packing, the walking out the door and the cab-ride to Jock's doorstep – I feel like I did on my first day at boarding school. Abandoned. A single memory comes back to me, with all the light and shade of reality: I am standing on the front steps of Charterhouse as my father hugs me and feels the sob in my chest. 'Not in front of your mother,' he whispers.

He turns to walk away and says to my mother, 'Not in front of the boy,' as she dabs at her eyes.

Jock insists I'll feel better after a shower, a shave and a decent meal. He orders takeaway from his local Indian, but I'm asleep on the sofa before it arrives. He eats alone.

In the motley half-light leaking through the blinds I can see tin foil trays stacked beside the sink, with orange and yellow gravy erupting over the sides. The TV remote is pressing into my spine and the weekly programme guide is wedged under my head. I don't know how I managed to sleep at all.

My mind keeps flashing back to Julianne and the look she gave me. It went far beyond disappointment. Sadness is not a big enough word. It was as though something had frozen inside her. Very rarely do we fight. Julianne can argue with passion and emotion. If I try to be too clever or become insensitive she accuses me of arrogance and I see the hurt in her eyes. This time I saw only emptiness. A vast, windswept landscape that a man could die trying to cross.

Jock is awake. I can hear him singing in the shower. I try to swing my legs to the floor but nothing happens. For a fleeting moment I fear I'm paralysed. Then I realise that I can feel the weight of the blankets. Concentrating my thoughts, my legs grudgingly respond.

The *bradykinesia* is becoming more obvious. Stress is a factor in Parkinson's Disease. I'm supposed to get plenty of sleep, exercise regularly and try not to worry about things. Yeah, right!

Jock lives in a mansion block overlooking Hampstead Heath. Downstairs there is a doorman who holds an umbrella over your head when it rains. He wears a uniform and calls people 'Guv' or 'Madam'. Jock and his second wife used to own the entire top floor, but since the divorce he can only afford a one-bedroom apartment. He also had to sell his Harley and give her the cottage in the Cotswolds. Whenever he sees an expensive sports car he claims it belongs to Natasha.

'When I look back, it's not the ex-wives that frighten me, it's the mothers-in-law,' he says. Since his divorce he has become, as Jeffrey Bernard would say, a sort of roving dinner guest on the outside looking in, and a fly on the wall of other people's marriages.

Jock and I go a lot further back than university. The same obstetrician, in the same hospital, delivered us both on the same day, only eight minutes apart. That was on 18 August 1960, at Queen Charlotte's Maternity Hospital in Hammersmith. Our mothers shared a delivery suite and the OB had to dash back and forth between the curtains.

I arrived first. Jock had such a big head that he got stuck and they had to pull him out with forceps. Occasionally he still jokes about coming second and trying to catch up. In reality, competition is never a joke with him. We were probably side-by-side in the nursery. We might have looked at each other, or kept each other awake.

It says something about the separateness of individual experience that we began our lives only minutes apart but didn't meet again until nineteen years later. Julianne says fate brought us together. Maybe she's right. Aside from being held upside down and smacked on the arse by the same doctor, we had very little in common. I can't explain why Jock and I became friends. What did I offer to the partnership? He was a big wheel on campus, always invited to the best parties and flirting with the prettiest girls. My dividend was obvious, but what did he get? Maybe that's what they mean when they say people just 'click'.

We long ago drifted apart politically, and sometimes morally, but we can't shake loose our history. He was best man at my wedding and I was best man at both of his. We have keys for each other's houses and copies of each other's wills. Shared experience is a powerful bond, but it's not just that.

Jock, for all his right-wing bluster, is actually a big softie, who has donated more money to charity than he settled on either of his ex-wives. Every year he organises a fundraiser for Great Ormond Street and he hasn't missed a London Marathon in fifteen years. Last year he pushed a hospital bed with a load of 'naughty' nurses in stockings and suspenders. He looked more like Benny Hill than Dr Kildare.

Jock emerges from the bathroom with a towel around his waist. He pads barefoot across the lounge to the kitchen. I hear the fridge door open and then close. He slices oranges and fires up an industrial-size juicer. The kitchen is full of gadgets. He has a machine to grind coffee, another to sift it and a third which looks like a cannon shell rather than a percolator. He can make waffles, muffins, pancakes or cook eggs in a dozen different ways.

I take my turn in the bathroom. The mirror is steamed up. I rub it with the corner of a towel, making a rough circle large enough to see my face. I look exhausted. Wednesday night's TV highlights are printed backwards on my right cheek. I scrub my face with a wet flannel.

There are more gadgets on the windowsill, including a battery-powered nasal hair trimmer that sounds like a demented bee stuck in a bottle. There are a dozen different brands of shampoo. It reminds me of home. I always tease Julianne about her 'lotions and potions' filling every available inch of our en suite. Somewhere in the midst of these cosmetics I have a disposable razor, a can of shaving foam and a deodorant stick. Unfortunately, retrieving them means risking a domino effect that will topple every bottle in the bathroom.

Jock hands me a glass of orange juice and we sit in silence staring at the percolator.

'I could call her for you,' he suggests.

I shake my head.

'I could tell her how you're moping around the place . . . no good to anyone . . . lost . . . desolate . . . '

'It wouldn't make any difference.'

He asks about the argument. He wants to know what upset her. Was it the arrest, the headlines or the fact that I lied to her?

'The lying.'

'I figured as much.'

He keeps pressing me for details. I don't really want to go there but the story comes out as my coffee grows cold. Perhaps Jock can help me make sense of it all.

When I reach the part about seeing Catherine's body in the morgue, I suddenly realise that he might have known her. He knew a lot more of the nurses at the Marsden than I did.

'Yeah, I was thinking that,' he says, 'but the photograph they put in the paper didn't ring any bells. The police wanted to know if you stayed with me on the night she died,' he adds.

'Sorry about that.'

'Where were you?'

I shrug.

'It's *true* then. You've been having a bit on the side.'

'It's not like that.'

'It never is, old son.'

Jock goes into his schoolboy routine, wanting to know all the 'sordid details'. I won't play along, which makes him grumpy.

'So why couldn't you tell the police where you were?'

'I'd rather not say.'

Frustration passes quickly across his face. He doesn't push any further. Instead he changes tack and admonishes me for not talking to him sooner. If I wanted him to provide me with an alibi, I should at least have told him.

'What if Julianne had asked me? I might have given the game away. And I could have told the police you were with me, instead of dropping you in the shit.'

'You told the truth.'

'I would have lied for you.'

'What if I *had* killed her?'

'I still would have lied for you. You'd do the same for me.'

I shake my head. 'I wouldn't lie for you if I thought you'd killed someone.'

His eyes meet mine and stay there. Then he laughs and shrugs. 'We'll never know.'

5

At the office I cross the lobby, aware that the security guards and receptionist are staring at me. I take the lift upstairs to find Meena at her desk and an empty waiting room.

'Where is everyone?'

'They cancelled.'

'Everyone?'

I lean over her desk and look down the appointments list for the day. All the names are crossed out with a red line. Except for Bobby Moran.

Meena is still talking. 'Mr Lilley's mother died. Hannah Barrymore has the flu. Zoe has to mind her sister's children . . . ' I know she's trying to make me feel better.

I point to Bobby's name and tell her to cross it out.

'He hasn't called.'

'Trust me.'

Despite Meena's best efforts to clean up, my office is still a mess. Evidence of the police search is everywhere, including the fine graphite powder they used to dust for fingerprints.

'They didn't take any of your files, but some of them were mixed up.'

I tell her not to worry. The notes cease to be important if I no longer have any patients. She stands at the door, trying to think of something positive to say. 'Did I get you into trouble?'

'What do you mean?'

'The girl who applied for the job . . . the one who was murdered . . . should I have handled it differently?'

'Absolutely not.'

'Did you know her?'

'Yes.'

'I'm sorry for your loss.'

This is the first time that anyone has acknowledged the fact that Catherine's death might have saddened me. Everybody else has acted as though I have no feelings one way or the other. Maybe they think I have some special understanding of grief or control over it. If that's the case, they're wrong. Getting to know patients is what I do. I learn about their deepest fears and secrets. A professional relationship becomes a personal one. It can be no other way.

I ask Meena about Catherine. How did she sound on the phone? Did she ask questions about me? The police took away her letters and job application but Meena has kept a copy of her CV.

She fetches it for me and I glance at the covering letter and the first page. The problem with curricula vitae is that they tell you virtually nothing of consequence about a person. Schools, exam results, tertiary education, work experience – none of it reveals an individual's personality or temperament. It is like trying to judge a person's height from their hair colour.

Before I can finish reading, the phone rings in the outer office. Hoping it might be Julianne, I pick up the call before Meena can patch it through. The voice on the line is like a force ten gale. Eddie Barrett lets loose with a string of colourful invective. He is particularly imaginative when it comes to describing uses for my Ph.D. in the event of a toilet paper shortage.

'Listen, you over-qualified head-shrinker, I'm reporting you to the British Psychological Society, the Qualifications Board and the UK Registrar of Expert Witnesses. Bobby Moran is also going to sue you for slander, breach of duty and anything else he can find. You're a disgrace! You should be struck off! More to the point, you're an arsehole!'

I have no time to respond. Each time I sense a break in Eddie's diatribe, he simply rolls on through. Maybe this is how he wins so many cases – he doesn't shut up for long enough to let anyone else get a word in.

The truth is I have no defence. I have broken more professional guidelines and personal codes than I can list, but I would do the same again. Bobby Moran is a sadist and a serial liar. Yet at the same time I feel a terrible sense of loss. By betraying a patient's trust I have opened a door and crossed a threshold into a place that is supposed to be out of bounds. Now I'm waiting for the door to hit me in the arse.

Eddie hangs up and I stare at the phone. I press the speed-dial. Julianne's voice is on the answering machine.

My guts contract. Life without her seems unthinkable. I have no idea what I want to say. I try to be cheerful because I figure Charlie might hear the message. I finish up sounding like Father Christmas. I call back and leave another message. The second one is even worse.

I give up and begin sorting out my files. The police emptied my filing cabinets, looking for anything hidden at the back of the drawers. I look up as Fenwick's head peers around the door. He is standing in the corridor, glancing nervously over his shoulder.

'A quick word, old boy.'

'Yes?'

'Terrible business, all this. Just want to say "Chin up" and all that. Don't let the rotters get you down.'

'That's very nice of you, Fenwick.'

He sways from foot to foot. 'Awful business. A real bugger. I'm sure you understand. What with the negative publicity and the like . . . ' He looks wretched.

'What's the matter, Fenwick?'

'Given the circumstances, old boy, Geraldine suggested it might be better if you weren't my best man. What would the other guests say? Awfully sorry. Hate kicking a man when he's down.'

'That's fine. Good luck.'

'Jolly good. Well . . . um . . . I'll leave you to it. I'll see you this afternoon at the meeting.'

'What meeting?'

'Oh dear, hasn't anyone told you? What a bugger!' His face turns bright pink.

'No.'

'Well, it's not really my place . . . ' He mumbles and

shakes his head. 'The partners are having a meeting at four. Some of us – not me, of course – are a little concerned about the impact of all this on the practice. The negative publicity and the like. Never good news having the police raid the place and reporters asking questions. You understand.'

'Of course.' I smile through gritted teeth. Fenwick is already backing out of the door. Meena flashes him a look that sends him into full retreat.

There are no benign possibilities. My esteemed colleagues are to discuss my partnership – banishment being the issue. My resignation will be sought. A choice of words will be agreed and a chat with the chief accountant will wrap the whole thing up without any fuss. Bollocks to that!

Fenwick is already halfway down the corridor. I call after him: 'Tell them I'll sue the practice if they try to force me out. I'm not resigning.'

Meena gives me a look of solidarity. It is mixed with another expression that could be mistaken for pity. I'm not used to people feeling sorry for me.

'I think you should go home. There's no point in staying,' I tell her.

'What about answering the phone?'

'I'm not expecting any calls.'

It takes twenty minutes for Meena to leave, fussing over her desk and glancing fretfully at me as though she is breaking some secretarial code of loyalty. Once alone, I close the blinds, push the unsorted folders to one side and lean back in my chair.

What mirror did I break? What ladder did I walk under? I am not a believer in God or fate or destiny. Maybe this is the 'law of averages'. Maybe Elisa was right. My life has been too easy. Having won nearly every important toss of the coin, my luck has now run out.

The ancient Greeks used to say that Lady Luck was a very beautiful girl with curly hair who walked among people in the street. Perhaps her name was Karma. She is a fickle mistress, a prudent woman, a tramp and a Manchester United supporter. She used to be mine.

It rains on the walk to Covent Garden. In the restaurant, I shake out my coat and hand it to a waitress. Drops of water leak down my forehead. Elisa arrives fifteen minutes later, warmly wrapped in a black overcoat with a fur collar. Underneath she's dressed in a dark blue camisole with spaghetti straps and a matching mini skirt. Her stockings are seamed and dark. She uses a linen napkin to dry herself and runs her fingers through her hair.

'I never remember to carry an umbrella any more.'

'Why is that?'

'I used to have one with a carved handle. It had a stiletto blade inside the shaft . . . in case of trouble. See how well you taught me.' She laughs and reapplies her lipstick. I want to touch the tip of her tongue with my fingers.

I cannot explain what it is like to sit in a restaurant with such a beautiful woman. Men covet Julianne, but with Elisa there is real hunger as their insides flutter and their hearts knock. There is something very pure, impulsive and innately sexual about her. It is as though she has refined, filtered and distilled her sexuality to a point where a man can believe that a single drop might be enough to satisfy him for a lifetime.

Elisa glances over her shoulder and instantly attracts a waiter's attention. She orders a salade niçoise and I choose the penne carbonara.

Normally I enjoy the confidence that comes with sitting opposite Elisa, but today I feel old and decrepit, like a gnarled olive tree with brittle bark. She talks quickly and eats slowly, picking at the seared tuna and slices of red onion.

Although I let her talk, I feel desperate and impatient. My salvation must start today. She is still watching me. Her eyes are like mirrors within mirrors. I can see myself. My hair is plastered to my forehead. I haven't slept for more than a few hours in what feels like weeks.

Elisa apologises for 'rabbiting on'. She reaches across the table and squeezes my hand. 'What did you want to talk to me about?'

I hesitate and then begin slowly – telling her about my arrest and the murder investigation. As I describe each new low point her eyes cloud with concern. 'Why didn't you just tell the police you were with me?' she asks. 'I don't mind.'

'It's not that easy.'

'Is it because of your wife?'

'No. She knows.'

Elisa shrugs her shoulders, neatly summing up her views on marriage. As a cultural institution she has nothing against it because it always provided some of her best customers. Married men were preferable to single men because they showered more often and smelled better.

'So what's stopping you telling the police?'

'I wanted to ask you first.'

She laughs at how old-fashioned that sounds. I feel myself blush.

'Before you say anything, I want you to think very carefully,' I tell her. 'I am in a very difficult position when I admit to spending the night with you. There are codes of conduct . . . ethics. You are a former patient.'

'But that was years ago.'

'It makes no difference. There are people who will try to use it against me. They already see me as a maverick because of my work with prostitutes and the TV documentary. And they're lining up to attack me over this . . . over you.'

Her eyes flash. 'They don't need to know. I'll go to the police and give a statement. I'll tell them you were with me. Nobody else has to find out.'

I try to muster all the kindness I have left, but my words still sting. 'Think for a moment what will happen if I get charged. You will have to give evidence. The prosecution will try everything they can to destroy my alibi. You are a former prostitute. You have convictions for malicious wounding. You have spent time in jail. You are also a former patient of mine. I met you when you were only fifteen. No matter how many times we tell them this was just one night, they'll think it was more . . . ' I run out of steam, stabbing my fork into my half-finished bowl of pasta.

Elisa's lighter flares. The flame catches in her eyes which are already blazing. I have never seen her so close to losing her poise. 'I'll leave it up to you,' she says softly. 'But I'm willing to give a statement. I'm not afraid.'

'Thank you.'

We sit in silence. After a while she reaches across the table and squeezes my hand again. 'You never told me why you were so upset that night.'

'It doesn't matter any more.'

'Is your wife *very* upset?'

'Yes.'

'She is lucky to have you. I hope she realises that.'

6

As I open the office door I'm aware of a presence in the room. The chrome-faced clock above the filing cabinet shows half past three. Bobby Moran is standing in front of my bookcase. He seems to have appeared out of thin air.

He turns suddenly. I don't know who is more startled.

'I knocked. There was no answer.' He drops his head. 'I have an appointment,' he says, reading my thoughts.

'Shouldn't that be with your lawyer? I heard you were suing me for slander, breach of confidentiality and whatever else he can dredge up.'

He looks embarrassed. 'Mr Barrett says I should do those things. He says I could get a lot of money.' He squeezes past me and stands at my desk. He's very close. I can smell fried dough and sugar. Damp hair is plastered to his forehead in a ragged fringe.

'Why are you here?'

'I wanted to see you.' There is something threatening in his voice.

'I can't help you, Bobby. You haven't been honest with me.'

'Are you always honest?'

'I try to be.'

'How? By telling the police I killed that girl?'

He picks up a smooth glass paperweight from my desk and weighs it in his right hand, then his left. He holds it up to the light. 'Is this your crystal ball?'

'Please, put it down.'

'Why? Scared I might bury it in your forehead?'

'Why don't you sit down?'

'After you.' He points to my chair. 'Why did you become a psychologist? Don't tell me, let me guess . . . A repressive father and an over-protective mother. Or is there a dark family secret? A relative who started howling at the moon or a favourite aunt who they had to lock away?'

I won't give him the satisfaction of knowing how close he is to the truth. 'I'm not here to talk about me.'

Bobby glances at the wall behind me. 'How can you hang that diploma? It's a joke! Until three days ago you thought I was someone completely different. Yet you were going to stand up in court and tell a judge whether I should be locked up or set free. What gives you the right to destroy someone's life? You don't know me.'

Listening to him I sense that for once I am talking to the real Bobby Moran. He lobs the paperweight on to the desk, where it rolls in slow-motion and drops into my lap.

'Did you kill Catherine McBride?'

'No.'

'Did you know her?'

His eyes lock on to mine. 'You're not very good at this, are you? I expected more.'

'This is not a game.'

'No. It's more important than that.'

We regard each other in silence.

'Do you know what a serial liar is, Bobby?' I ask eventually. 'It is someone who finds it easier to tell a lie rather than the truth, in any situation, regardless of whether it is important or not.'

'People like you are supposed to know when someone is lying.'

'That doesn't alter what you are.'

'All I did was change a few names and places – you got the rest of it wrong all by yourself.'

'What about Arky?'

'She left me six months ago.'

'You said you had a job.'

'I told you I was a writer.'

'You're very good at telling stories.'

'Now you're making fun of me. Do you know what's wrong with people like you? You can't resist putting your hands inside someone's psyche and changing the way they view the world. You play God with other people's lives . . . '

'Who are these "people like me"? Who have you seen before?'

'It doesn't matter,' Bobby says dismissively. 'You're all the same. Psychologists, psychiatrists, psychotherapists, tarot card readers, witch doctors—'

'You were in hospital. Is that where you met Catherine McBride?'

'You must think I'm an idiot.'

Bobby almost loses his composure but recovers himself quickly. He has almost no physiological response to lying. His pupil dilation, pore size, skin flush and breathing remain exactly the same. He's like a poker player who has no 'tells'.

'Everything I've done in my life and everyone I have come into contact with is significant – the good, the bad and the ugly,' he says with a note of triumph in his voice. 'We are the sum of our parts or the part of our sums. You say this isn't a game but you're wrong. It's good versus evil. White versus black. Some people are pawns and some are kings.'

'Which are you?' I ask.

He thinks about this. 'I was once a pawn but I reached the end of the board. I can be anything now.'

Bobby sighs and gets to his feet. The conversation has started to bore him. The session is only half an hour old but he's had enough. It should never have started. Eddie Barrett is going to have a field day.

I follow Bobby into the outer office. A part of me wants him to stay. I want to shake the tree and see what falls off the branches. I want the truth.

Bobby is waiting at the lift. The doors open.

'Good luck.'

He turns and looks at me curiously. 'I don't need luck.' The slight upturn of his mouth gives the illusion of a smile.

Back at my desk, I stare at the empty chair. An object on the floor catches my eye. It looks like a small carved figurine – a chess piece. Picking it up, I discover it's a wooden whale carved by hand. A key ring is attached with a tiny eyelet screw on the whale's back. It's the sort of thing you see hanging from a child's satchel or schoolbag.

Bobby must have dropped it. I can still catch him. I can call downstairs to the foyer and get the security guard to have him wait. I look at the clock. Ten minutes past four. The meeting has started upstairs. I don't want to be here.

Bobby's sheer size makes him stand out. He's a head taller than anybody else and pedestrians seem to divide and part to let him through. Rain is falling. I bury my hands in my overcoat. My fingers close around the smooth wooden whale.

Bobby is heading towards the underground station at Oxford Circus. If I stay close enough, hopefully I won't lose him in the labyrinthine walkways. I don't know why I'm doing this. I guess I want answers instead of riddles. I want to know where he lives and who he lives with.

Suddenly, he disappears from view. I suppress the urge to run forward. I keep moving at the same pace and pass an off-licence. I catch a glimpse of Bobby at the counter. Two doors further on I step inside a travel agency. A girl in a red skirt, white blouse and wishbone tie smiles at me.

'Can I help you?'

'I'm just looking.'

'To escape the winter?'

I'm holding a brochure for the Caribbean. 'Yes, that's right.'

Bobby passes the window. I hand her the brochure. 'You can take it with you,' she suggests.

'Maybe next year.'

On the pavement, Bobby is thirty yards ahead of me. He has a distinctive shape. He has no hips and it looks as though his backside has been stolen. He keeps his trousers pulled up high, with his belt tightly cinched.

Descending the stairs into the underground station, the crowd seems to swell. Bobby has a ticket ready. There is a queue at every ticket machine. Three underground lines cross at Oxford Circus – if I lose him now he can travel in any one of six different directions.

I push between people, ignoring their complaints. At the turnstile I place my hands on either side of it and lift my legs over the barrier. Now I'm guilty of fare evasion. The escalator descends slowly. A stale wind sweeps up from the tunnels, forced ahead of the moving engines.

On the northbound platform of the Bakerloo line, Bobby weaves through the waiting crowd until he reaches the far end. I follow him, needing to be close. At any moment I expect him to turn and catch sight of me. Four or five schoolboys, human Petri dishes of acne and dandruff, push along the platform, wrestling each other and laughing. Everyone else stares straight ahead in silence.

A blast of wind and noise. The train appears. Doors open. I let the crowd carry me forward into the carriage. Bobby is in my peripheral vision. The doors close auto matically and the train jerks forward and gathers speed. Everything smells of damp wool and stale sweat.

Bobby gets off the train at Warwick Avenue. It has grown dark. Black cabs swish past, the sound of their tyres louder than their engines. The station is only a hundred yards from the Grand Union Canal and perhaps two miles from where Catherine's body was found.

With fewer people around I have to drop further back. Now he's only a silhouette in front of me. I walk with my head down and collar turned up. As I pass a cement mixer on the footpath, I stumble sideways and put my shoe into a puddle. My balance is deserting me.

We follow Blomfield Road alongside the canal until Bobby crosses a footbridge at the end of Formosa Street. Spotlights pick out an Anglican church. The fine mist looks like falling glitter around the beams of light. Bobby sits on a park bench and looks at the church for a long time. I lean against the trunk of a tree, my feet growing numb with the cold.

What is he doing here? Maybe he lives nearby. Whoever killed Catherine knew the canal well: not just from a street map or a casual visit. He was comfortable here. It was his territory. He knew where to leave her body so that she wouldn't be found too quickly. He fitted in. Nobody recognised him as a stranger.

Bobby can't have met Catherine in the hotel. If Ruiz has done his job he will have shown photographs to the staff and patrons. Bobby isn't the sort of person you forget easily.

Catherine left the pub alone. Whoever she was supposed to meet had failed to show. She was staying with friends in Shepherd's Bush. It was too far to walk. What did she do? Look for a taxi. Or perhaps she started walking to Westbourne Park Station. From there it is only three stops to Shepherd's Bush. The walk would have taken her over the canal.

A London Transport depot is across the road. Buses are coming in and out all the time. Whoever she met must have been waiting for her on the bridge. I should have asked Ruiz which part of the canal they dredged to find Catherine's diary and mobile phone.

Catherine was five foot six and 134 pounds. Chloroform takes a few minutes to act, but someone of Bobby's size and strength would have had few problems subduing her. She would have fought back or cried out. She wasn't the sort to meekly surrender.

But if I'm right and he knew her, he might not have needed the chloroform – not until Catherine realised the danger and tried to escape.

What happened next? It isn't easy carrying a body. Perhaps he dragged her on to the towpath. No, he needed somewhere private. Somewhere he'd prepared in advance. A flat or a house? Neighbours can be nosy. There are dozens of derelict factories along the canal. Did he risk using the towpath? The homeless sometimes sleep under the bridges or couples use them for romantic rendezvous.

The shadow of a narrow boat moves past me. The rumble of the motor is so low that the sound barely reaches me. The only light on the vessel is near the wheel. It casts a red glow on the face of the helmsman. I wonder. Traces of machine oil and diesel were found on Catherine's buttocks and hair.

I peer around the tree. The park bench is empty. Damn! Where has he gone? There is a figure on the far side of the church, moving along the railings. I can't be sure it's him. My mind sets off at a run but my legs are left behind. I finish up doing a perfect limp fall. Nothing is broken. Only my pride hurts.

I stumble onwards and reach the corner of the church where the iron railings take a 90-degree turn. The figure is staying on the path but moving much more quickly. I doubt if I can keep up with him.

What is he doing? Has he seen me? Jogging slowly, I carry on, losing sight of him occasionally. Doubt gnaws at my resolve. What if he's stopped up ahead? Perhaps he's waiting for me. The six lanes of the Westway curve above me, supported by enormous concrete pillars. The glow of headlights is too high to help me.

Ahead I hear a splash and a muffled cry. Someone is in the canal. Arms are thrashing at the water. I start running. There is the faint outline of a figure beneath the bridge. The sides of the canal are higher there. The stone walls are black and slick.

I try to shrug off my overcoat. My right arm gets caught in the sleeve and I swing it around until it comes loose. 'This way! Over here!' I call.

He doesn't hear me. He can't swim.

I kick off my shoes and leap. The cold slaps me so hard I swallow a mouthful of water. I cough it out through my mouth and nose. Three strokes. I'm with him. I slide my arm around him from behind and pull him backwards, keeping his head above the surface. I talk to him gently, telling him to relax. We'll find a place to get out. Wet clothes weigh him down.

I swim us away from the bridge. 'You can touch the bottom here. Just hold on to the side.' I scramble up the stone wall and pull him up after me.

It isn't Bobby. Some poor tramp, smelling of beer and vomit, lies at my feet, coughing and spluttering. I check his head, neck and limbs for any sign of trauma. His face is smeared with snot and tears.

'What happened?'

'Some sick fuck threw me in the canal! One minute I'm

sleepin' and the next I'm flyin'.' He's resting on his knees, doubled over and swaying back and forth like an underwater plant. 'I tell yer, it ain't safe no more. It's like a fuckin' jungle . . . Did he take me blanket? If he took me blanket you can throw me back in.'

His blanket is still under the bridge, piled on a makeshift bed of flattened cardboard boxes.

'What about me teeth?'

'I don't know.'

He curses and scoops up his things, jealously clutching them to his chest. I suggest calling an ambulance and then the police but he wants none of it. My whole body has started to tremble and I feel like I'm inhaling slivers of ice.

Retrieving my overcoat and shoes, I give him a soggy twenty pound note and tell him to find somewhere to dry out. He'll probably buy a bottle and be warm on the inside. My feet squelch in my shoes as I climb the stairs on to the bridge. The Grand Union Hotel is on the corner.

Almost as an afterthought, I lean over the side of the bridge and call out, 'How often do you sleep here?'

His voice echoes from beneath the stone arch. 'Only when the Ritz is full.'

'Have you ever seen a narrow boat moored under the bridge?'

'Nah. They moor further along.'

'What about a few weeks ago?'

'I try not to remember things. I mind me own business.'

He has nothing to add. I have no authority to press him. Elisa lives close by. I contemplate knocking on her door but I've brought her enough trouble already.

273

After twenty minutes I manage to hail a cab. The driver doesn't want to take me because I'll ruin the seats. I offer him an extra twenty quid. It's only water. I'm sure he's had worse.

Jock isn't home. I am so tired I can barely get my shoes off before collapsing into the spare bed. In the early hours I hear his key in the lock. A woman laughs drunkenly and kicks off her shoes. She comments on all the gadgets.

'Just wait till you see what I keep in the bedroom,' says Jock, triggering more giggles.

I wonder if he has any earplugs.

It is still dark as I pack a sports bag and leave a note taped to the microwave. Outside, a street-sweeping machine is polishing the gutters. There isn't a burger wrapper in sight.

On the ride through the city I keep looking out the rear window. I change cabs twice and visit two cash-point machines before catching a bus along the Euston Road.

I feel as though I'm slowly coming out of an anaesthetic. Over the past few days I have been letting details slip. Even worse, I have stopped trusting my instincts.

I am not going to tell Ruiz about Elisa. She shouldn't have to face a grilling in the witness box. I want to spare her that ordeal, if possible. And when this is all over – if nobody knows about her – I might still have a career that can be resurrected.

Bobby Moran had something to do with Catherine McBride's death. I'm convinced of it. If the police won't put him under the microscope then it's up to me. People normally need a motive to kill, but not to stay free. I *will* not let them send me to prison. I *will* not be separated from my family.

At Euston Station I do a quick inventory. Apart from a change of clothes, I have Bobby Moran's notes, Catherine McBride's CV, my mobile phone and a thousand pounds in cash. I forgot to bring a photograph of Charlie and Julianne.

I pay for the train ticket in cash. With fifteen minutes to spare, I have time to buy a toothbrush, toothpaste, a recharger for my mobile phone and one of those travelling towels that looks like a car chamois.

'Do you sell umbrellas?' I ask hopefully. The shopkeeper looks at me as though I've asked for a shotgun.

Nursing a takeaway coffee, I board the train and find a double seat facing forwards. I keep my bag beside me, covered by my overcoat.

The empty platform slides past the window and the northern suburbs of London disappear the same way. The train leans on floating axles as it corners at high speed. We tear past tiny stations with empty platforms where trains no longer seem to stop. One or two vehicles are parked in the long-stay car parks that look so far beyond the pale that I half expect to see a hose running from an exhaust pipe and a body slumped over a steering wheel.

My head is full of questions. Catherine applied to be my secretary. She phoned Meena twice and then took a train down to London, arriving a day early.

Why did she phone the office that evening? Who answered the call? Did she have second thoughts about surprising me? Did she want to cancel? Perhaps she'd been stood up and just wanted to go out for a drink. Maybe she wanted to apologise about causing me so much trouble.

All of this is supposition. At the same time, it fits the framework of detail. It can be built upon. All the pieces can be made to fit a story except for one – Bobby.

His coat smelled of chloroform. Bobby had machine oil on his shirt cuffs. Catherine's post-mortem mentioned machine oil. 'It's all about the oil,' Bobby told me. Did he know she had twenty-one stab wounds? Did he lead me to the place where she disappeared?

Perhaps he's using me to construct an insanity defence. By playing 'mad' he might avoid a life sentence. Instead they'll send him to a prison hospital like Broadmoor. Then he can astound some prison psychiatrist with his responsiveness to treatment. He could be out within five years.

I'm sounding more and more like him – fashioning conspiracies out of coincidences. Whatever lies at the heart of this, I must not underestimate Bobby. He has played games with me. I don't know why.

My search has to start somewhere. Liverpool will do for now. I take out Bobby Moran's file and begin reading. Opening my new notebook, I make bullet points – the name of a primary school, the number of his father's bus, a club his parents used to visit . . .

These could be more of Bobby's lies. Something tells me they're not. I think he changed certain names and places, but not all of them. The events and emotions he described were true. I have to find the strands of truth and follow them back to the centre of the web.

7

The clock at Lime Street Station glows white with solid black hands pointing to eleven o'clock. I walk quickly across the concourse, past the coffee stand and closed public toilet. A gaggle of teenage girls, speaking at 110 decibels, communicate through a cloud of cigarette smoke.

It must be five degrees colder than in London, with a wind straight off the Irish Sea. I half expect to see icebergs on the horizon. St George's Hall is over the way. Banners snap in the wind, advertising the latest Beatles retrospective.

I walk past the large hotels on Lime Street and search the side streets for something smaller. Not far from the university I find the Albion. It has a worn carpet in the entrance hall and a family of Iraqis camped on the first-floor landing. Young children look at me shyly, hiding behind their mothers' skirts. The men are nowhere to be seen.

My room is on the second floor. It is just large enough for a double bed and a wardrobe held shut with a wire hanger. The hand basin has a rust stain in the shape of a teardrop beneath the tap. The curtains will only half close and the windowsill is dotted with cigarette burns.

There have been very few hotel rooms in my life. I am grateful for that. For some reason loneliness and regret seem to be part of their décor.

I press the memory button on my mobile and hear the singsong tones of the number being automatically dialled. Julianne's voice is on the answering machine. I know she's listening. I can picture her. I make a feeble attempt to apologise and ask her to pick up the phone. I tell her it's important.

I wait . . . and wait . . .

She picks up. My heart skips.

'What is so important?' Her tone is harsh.

'I want to talk to you.'

'I'm not ready to talk.'

'You're not giving me a chance to explain.'

'I gave you a chance two nights ago, Joe. I asked you why you slept with a whore and you told me that you found it easier to talk to her than to me . . . ' Her voice is breaking. 'I guess that makes me a pretty lousy wife.'

'You have everything planned. Your life runs like clock-work – the house, work, Charlie, school; you never miss a beat. I'm the only thing that doesn't work . . . not properly . . . not any more . . . '

'And that's my fault?'

'No, that's not what I mean.'

'Well, pardon me for trying so hard. I thought I was

278

making us a lovely home. I thought we were happy. It's fine for you, Joe, you have your career and your patients who think you walk on water. This is all I had – us. I gave up everything for this and I loved it. I loved you. Now you've gone and poisoned the well.'

'But don't you see – what I've got is going to destroy all that . . .'

'No, don't you dare blame a disease. You've managed to do this all by yourself.'

'It was only one night,' I say plaintively.

'No! It was someone else! You kissed her the way you kiss me. You fucked her! How could you?'

Even when sobbing and angry she manages to remain piercingly articulate. I am selfish, immature, deceitful and cruel. I try to pick out which of these adjectives doesn't apply to me. I fail. 'I made a mistake,' I say weakly. 'I'm sorry.'

'That's not enough, Joe. You broke my heart. Do you know how long I have to wait before I can get an AIDS test? Three months!'

'Elisa is clear.'

'And how do you know? Did you ask her before you decided not to use a condom? I'm going to hang up now.'

'Wait! Please! How's Charlie?'

'Fine.'

'What have you told her?'

'That you're a two-timing shit and a weak, pathetic, self-pitying, self-centred creep.'

'You didn't.'

'No, but I felt like it.'

'I'll be out of town for a few days. The police might ask

279

you questions about where I am. That's why it's best if I don't tell you.'

She doesn't reply.

'You can get me on my mobile. Call me, please. Give Charlie an extra hug from me. I'll go now. I love you.'

I hang up quickly, afraid to hear her silence.

Locking the door on my way out, I push the heavy key deep into my trouser pocket. Twice on my way down the stairs I feel for it. Instead I find Bobby's whale. I trace its shape with my fingers.

Outside, an icy wind pushes me along Hanover Street towards the Albert Docks. Liverpool reminds me of an old woman's handbag, full of bric-a-brac, odds and ends and half finished packets of boiled sweets. Edwardian pubs squat beside mountainous cathedrals and art deco office blocks that can't decide which continent they should be on. Some of the more modern buildings have dated so quickly they look like derelict bingo halls only fit for the bulldozer.

The Cotton Exchange in Old Hall Street is a grand reminder of when Liverpool was the centre of the international cotton trade, feeding the Lancashire spinning industry. When the exchange building opened in 1906 it had telephones, electric lifts, synchronised electric clocks and a direct cable to the New York futures market. Now it houses, among other things, thirty million records of births, deaths and marriages in Lancashire.

A strange mixture of people queue at the indexes – a class of school children on an excursion; American tourists on the trail of distant relations; matronly women in tweed skirts; probate researchers and fortune hunters.

I have a goal. It seems fairly realistic. I queue at the colour-coded volumes where I hope to find the registration of Bobby's birth. With this I can get a birth certificate, which in turn will give me the names of his mother, father, their place of residence and occupations.

The volumes are stored on metal racks, listed by month and year. The 1970s and 1980s are arranged in quarters for each year, with surnames in alphabetical order. If Bobby has told the truth about his age, I might only have four volumes to search.

The year should be 1980. I can find no entry for a Bobby Moran or Robert Moran. I start working through the years on either side, going as far back as 1974 and forward to 1984. Growing frustrated, I look at my notes. I wonder if Bobby could have changed the spelling of his name or altered it entirely by deed poll. If so, I'm in trouble.

At the front information desk I ask to borrow a phone book. I can't tell if I'm charming people with my smile or frightening them. The Parkinson's mask is unpredictable.

Bobby lied about where he went to school, but perhaps he didn't lie about the name. There are two St Mary's in Liverpool – only one of them is a junior school. I make a note of the number and find a quiet corner in the foyer to make the call. The secretary has a Scouse accent and sounds like a character in a Ken Loach film.

'We're closed for Christmas,' she says. 'I shouldn't even be here. I was just tidying up the office.'

I make up a story about a sick friend who wants to track down his old mates. I'm looking for yearbooks or class photographs from the mid-eighties. She thinks the library has a cupboard full of that sort of thing. I should call back in the New Year.

'It can't wait that long. My friend is very sick. It's Christmas.'

'I might be able to check,' she says sympathetically. 'What year are you looking for?'

'I'm not exactly sure.'

'How old is your friend.'

'Twenty-two.'

'What is his name?'

'I think his name might have been different back then. That's why I need to see the photographs. I'll be able to recognise him.'

She is suddenly less sure of me. Her suspicion increases when I suggest coming to the school. She wants to ask the headmistress. Better still, I should put my request in writing and send it by post.

'I don't have time. My friend—'

'I'm sorry.'

'Wait! Please! Can you just look up a name for me? It's Bobby Moran. He might have worn glasses. He would have started in about 1985.'

She hesitates. After a long pause she suggests that I call her back in twenty minutes.

I go in search of fresh air. Outside, at the entrance to an alley, a man stands beside a blackened barrow. Every so often he yells, 'Roooooost chestnoooooots', making it sound as plaintive as a gull's cry. He hands me a brown paper bag and I sit on the steps, peeling the sooty skin from the warm chestnuts.

One of my fondest memories of Liverpool is the food.

The fish and chips and Friday night curries. The jam roly-poly, bread and butter pudding, treacle sponge, bangers and mash . . . I also loved the odd assortment of people – Catholics, Protestants, Muslims, Irish, African and Chinese – good grafters, fiercely proud and not afraid to wear their hearts and wipe their noses on the same sleeve.

The school secretary is less circumspect this time. Her curiosity has been sparked. My search has become hers.

'I'm sorry but I couldn't find any Bobby Moran. Are you sure that you don't mean Bobby Morgan? He was here from 1985 to 1988. He left in year three.'

'Why did he leave?'

'I'm not sure.' Her voice is uncertain. 'I wasn't here then. A family tragedy?' There is someone she can ask, she says. Another teacher. She takes the name of my hotel and promises to leave a message.

Back at the colour-coded volumes, I go through the names again. Why would Bobby change his surname by a single letter? Was he breaking with the past or trying to hide from it?

In the third volume I find an entry for Robert John Morgan. Born 24th September 1980 at Liverpool University Hospital. Mother: Bridget Elsie Morgan (née Aherne). Father: Leonard Albert Edward Morgan (merchant seaman).

I still can't be absolutely sure that it's Bobby but the chances are good. I fill out a pink application form to order a copy of his full birth certificate. The clerical officer behind the glass screen has an aggressive chin and flared nostrils. He pushes the form back towards me. 'You haven't stated your reasons.'

'I'm tracing my family history.'

'What about your postal address?'

'I'll pick it up from here.'

Without ever looking up at me, he thumps the application with a fist-sized stamp. 'Come back in the New Year. We close from Monday for the holidays.'

'But I can't wait that long.'

He shrugs. 'We open until midday on Monday. You could try then.'

Ten minutes later I leave the exchange building with a receipt in my pocket. Three days. I can't wait that long. In the time it takes me to cross the pavement I make a new plan.

The offices of the *Liverpool Echo* look like a mirrored Rubik's cube. The foyer is full of pensioners on a day tour. Each has a souvenir bag and a stick-on nametag.

A young receptionist is sitting on a high stool behind a dark wooden counter. She is small and pale, with curry-coloured eyes. To her left is a metal barrier with a swipe-card entry that separates us from the lifts.

'My name is Professor Joseph O'Loughlin and I was hoping to use your library.'

'I'm sorry but we don't allow public access to the newspaper library.' A large bunch of flowers is sitting on the counter beside her.

'They're lovely,' I say.

'Not mine, I'm afraid. The fashion editor gets all the freebies.'

'I'm sure you get more than your share.'

She knows I'm flirting, but laughs anyway.

'What if I want to order a photograph?' I ask.

'You fill out one of these forms.'

'What if I don't know the date, or the name of the photographer?'

She sighs. 'You don't really want a photograph, do you?'

I shake my head. 'I'm looking for a death notice.'

'How recently?'

'About fourteen years.'

She makes me wait while she calls upstairs. Then she asks if I have anything official-looking, like a security pass or business card. She slides it into a plastic wallet and pins it to my shirt.

'The librarian knows you're coming. If anyone asks you what you're doing, say you're researching a story for the medical pages.'

I take the lift to the fourth floor and follow the corridors. Occasionally I glimpse a large open-plan newsroom through the swing doors. I keep my head down and try to walk with a sense of purpose. Every so often my leg locks up and swings forward as though in a splint.

The librarian is in her sixties, with dyed hair and half glasses that hang around her neck on a chain. She has a rubber thimble on her right thumb for turning pages. Her desk is surrounded by dozens of cacti.

She notices me looking. 'We have to keep it too dry in here for anything else to grow,' she explains. 'Any moisture will damage the newsprint.'

Long tables are strewn with newspapers. Someone is cutting out stories and placing them in neat piles. Another is reading each story and circling particular names or phrases. A third uses these references to sort the cuttings into files.

'We have bound volumes going back a hundred and fifty

years,' says the librarian. 'The cuttings don't last that long. Eventually they fall apart along the edges and crumble into dust.'

'I thought everything would be on computer by now,' I say.

'Only for the past ten years. It's too expensive to scan all the bound volumes. They're being put on to microfilm.'

She turns on a computer terminal and asks me what I need.

'I'm looking for a death notice published around 1988. Leonard Albert Edward Morgan . . . '

'Named after the old king.'

'I think he was a bus conductor. He might have lived or worked in a place called Heyworth Street.'

'In Everton,' she says, flicking at a keyboard with two fingers. 'Most of the local buses either start or finish at the Pier Head or Paradise Street.'

I make a note of this on a pad. I concentrate on making the letters large and evenly spaced. It reminds me of being back in pre-school – tracing huge letters on cheap paper with crayons that almost rested on your shoulder.

The librarian leads me through the maze of shelves that stretch from the wooden floor to the sprinklers on the ceiling. Eventually we reach a wooden desk, scarred by cutting blades. A microfiche machine sits at the centre. She flicks a switch and the motor begins to hum. Another switch turns on the bulb and a square of light appears on the screen.

She hands me six boxes of film covering January to June 1988. Threading the first film on to the spools, she presses fast forward, accelerating through the pages and knowing almost instinctively when to stop. She points to the public notices and I make a note of the page number, hoping it will be roughly the same each day.

I trace my finger down the alphabetical listing, looking for the letter 'M'. Having satisfied myself there are no Morgans, I accelerate forward to the next day . . . and the next. The focus control is finicky and has to be constantly adjusted. At other times I have to pan back and forth to keep the newspaper columns on screen.

Having finished the first batch I collect another six boxes of microfiche from the librarian. The newspapers around Christmas have more pages and take longer to search. As I finish November 1988 my anxiety grows. What if it's not here? I can feel knots in my shoulder blades from leaning forward. My eyes ache.

The film rolls on to a new day. I find the death notices. For several seconds I carry on down the page before realising what I've seen. I go back. There it is! I press my finger on the name as though frightened it might vanish.

<u>Lenny A. Morgan</u>, aged 55, died on Saturday December 10 from burns received in an explosion at the Carnegie Engineering Works. Mr Morgan, a popular bus conductor at the Green Lane Depot in Stanley, was a former merchant seaman and a prominent union delegate. He is survived by his sisters, Ruth and Louise, and sons Dafyyd, 19, and Robert, 8. A service will be conducted at 1 p.m. Tuesday at St James' Church in Stanley. The family requests that memorial tributes take the form of contributions to the Socialist Workers' Party.

I go back through papers for the week before. An accident like this must have been reported. I find the news story at the bottom of page five. The headline reads: 'Worker Dies in Depot Blast'.

A Liverpool bus conductor has died after an explosion at the Carnegie Engineering Works on Saturday afternoon. Lenny Morgan, 55, suffered 80 per cent burns to his body when welding equipment ignited gas fumes. The blast and fire severely damaged the workshop, destroying two buses.

Mr Morgan was taken to Rathbone Hospital where he died on Saturday evening without regaining consciousness. The Liverpool coroner has begun an investigation into what caused the explosion.

Friends and workmates paid tribute to Mr Morgan yesterday, describing him as extremely popular with the travelling public, who enjoyed his eccentricities. 'Lenny used to dress in a Santa hat and serenade the passengers with carols at Christmas,' said supervisor Bert McMullen.

At three o'clock I rewind the microfilm, pack it into boxes and thank the librarian for her help. She doesn't ask me if I found what I wanted. She's too busy trying to repair the spine of a bound volume that someone has dropped.

Despite looking through another two months of newspapers, I found no further references to the accident. There must have been an inquest. As I ride down in the lift I flick through my notes. What am I looking for? Some link to Catherine. I don't know where she grew up, but her grandfather certainly worked in Liverpool. My instincts tell me that she and Bobby met in care – either at a children's home or at a psych hospital.

Bobby didn't mention having a brother. Considering that Bridget was only twenty-one when she had Bobby, Dafydd was either adopted or, more likely, Lenny had an earlier marriage that produced a son.

Lenny had two sisters but I only have maiden names, which makes it harder to find them. Even if they didn't marry, how many Morgans are likely to be in the Liverpool phone book? I don't want to have to go there.

Pushing through the revolving door, I'm so lost in thought I go round twice before finding the outside. Taking the steps carefully, I fix my bearings and head towards Lime Street Station.

I hate to admit it, but I'm enjoying this: the search. I'm motivated. I have a mission. Last-minute shoppers fill the footpaths and queue for buses. I'm tempted to find the number 96 and see where it takes me. Lucky dips are for people who like surprises. Instead I hail a cab and ask for the Green Lane Bus Depot.

8

A mechanic holds a carburettor in one blackened hand and gives me directions with the other. The pub is called the Tramway Hotel and Bert McMullen is usually at the bar.

'How will I recognise him?'

The mechanic chuckles and turns back to the engine, leaning inside the bowels of a bus.

I find the Tramway easily enough. Someone has scrawled graffiti on the blackboard outside: 'A beer means never having to say, "I'm thirsty".' Pushing through the door, I enter a dimly lit room with stained floors and bare wooden furniture. Red bulbs above the bar give the place a pink tinge like a Wild West bordello. Black and white photographs of trams and antique buses decorate the walls, alongside posters for 'live' music.

I take my time and count eight people, including a handful of teenagers playing pool in the back alcove near the toilets. I stand in front of the beer taps, waiting to be served by a barman who can't be bothered to look up from the *Racing Post*.

Bert McMullen is at the far end of the bar. His crumpled tweed jacket is patched at the elbows and adorned by various badges and pins, all related to buses. In one hand he holds a cigarette and in the other an empty pint glass. He turns the glass in his fingers, as if reading some hidden inscription etched into the side.

Bert growls at me. 'Who you gawpin' at?' His thick moustache appears to sprout directly from his nose and droplets of foam and beer are clinging to the ends of the grey and black hairs.

'I'm sorry. I didn't mean to stare.' I offer to buy him another pint. He half turns and examines me. His eyes, like watery glass eggs, stop at my shoes. 'How much did them shoes cost?'

'I don't remember.'

'Gimme an estimate.'

I shrug. 'A hundred pounds.'

He shakes his head in disgust. 'I wouldn't pick 'em up with two shitty sticks. You couldn't walk more 'an twenty mile in them things before they fall apart.' He's still staring at my shoes. He waves the barman over. 'Hey, Phil, get a load of these shoes.'

Phil leans over the bar and peers at my feet. 'What d'you call them?'

'Loafers,' I answer self-consciously.

'Gerraway!' Both men look at each other in disbelief. 'Why would you want to wear a shoe called a loafer?' says Bert. 'You got more bum than brains.'

'They're Italian,' I say, as if that makes a difference.

'Italian! What's wrong with English shoes? You a wog?'

'No.'

'You're wearing wog shoes.' Bert presses his face close to mine. I can smell baked beans. 'I reckon anyone who wears shoes like that hasn't done a proper day's work in his life. You got to wear boots, kid, with a steel cap in the toe and some grip on the bottom. Them shoes of yours wouldn't last a week in a real job.'

'Unless, of course, he works behind a desk,' says the barman.

Bert looks at me warily. 'Are you one of the overcoat gang?'

'What's that?'

'Never get your coat off.'

'I work hard enough.'

'Do you vote Labour?'

'I don't think that's any of your business.'

'Are you a Hail Mary?'

'Agnostic.'

'Ag-fucking-what?'

'Agnostic.'

'Jesus wept! OK, this is your last chance. Do you support the mighty Liverpool?' He crosses himself.

'No.'

He sighs in disgust. 'Get off home, yer Mam's got custard waiting.'

I look between the two of them. That's the problem with Scousers. You can never tell whether they're joking or being serious until they put a glass in your face.

Bert winks at the barman. 'He can buy me a drink, but

he can't fiddle arse around. 'E's got five minutes before he can bugger off.'

Phil grins at me. His ears are laden with silver rings and dangling pendants.

The pub has tables arranged along the walls, leaving a dance floor in the centre. The teenagers are still playing pool. The only girl among them looks underage and is dressed in tight jeans and a singlet top, revealing her bare midriff. The boys are trying to impress her but her boyfriend is easy to spot. Bulked up by weight training, he looks like an abscess about to explode.

Bert is watching the bubbles rise to the head of his Guinness. Minutes pass. I feel myself getting smaller and smaller. Finally he raises the glass to his lips and his Adam's apple bobs up and down as he swallows.

'I wanted to ask you about Lenny Morgan. I asked at the depot. They said you were friends.'

He shows no emotion.

I keep going. 'I know he died in a fire. I know you worked with him. I just want to find out what happened.'

Bert lights a cigarette. 'I can't see how it's any of your business.'

'I'm a psychologist. Lenny's son is in a spot of bother. I'm trying to help him.' As I hear the words I feel a pinprick of guilt. Is that what I'm trying to do? Help him?

'What's his name?'

'Bobby.'

'I remember him. Lenny used to bring him down the depot during the holidays. He used to sit up back and ring the bell to signal the driver. So what's he done?'

'He beat up a woman. He's about to be sentenced.'

Bert smiles sardonically. 'That sort of shit happens. You ask my old lady. I've hit her once or twice but she punches harder than I do. It's all forgotten in the morning.'

'This woman was badly hurt. Bobby dragged her out of a cab and kicked her unconscious in a busy street.'

'Was he shagging her?'

'No. He didn't know her.'

'Whose side are you on?'

'I'm assessing him.'

'So you're trying to get him banged up?'

'I want to help him.'

Bert snorts. Headlights from the road outside slide over the walls. 'It's all gin and oranges to me, son, but I can't see what Lenny has to do with it. He's been dead fourteen years.'

'Losing a father can be very traumatic. Perhaps it might help explain a few things.'

Bert pauses to consider this. I know he's weighing up his prejudices against his instincts. He doesn't like my shoes. He doesn't like my clothes. He doesn't like strangers. He wants to snarl and push his face into mine, but he needs a good enough reason. Another pint of Guinness has the casting vote.

'You know what I do every morning?' Bert says.

I shake my head.

'I spend an hour lying in bed, with my back so fucked up I can't even roll over to reach my fags. I stare at the ceiling and think about what I'm going to do today. Same as every day: I'm going to get up, hobble to the bathroom, then to the kitchen, and after breakfast I'm going to hobble down here and sit on this stool. Do you know why?'

I shake my head.

''Cos I've discovered the secret of revenge. Outlive the bastards. I'll dance on their graves. You take Maggie Thatcher. She destroyed the working class in this country. She closed down the mines, the docks and the factories. But she's rusting away now – just like those ships out there. She had a stroke not so long ago. Don't matter whether you're a destroyer or a dinghy – the salt always gets you in the end. And when she goes I'm gonna *piss* on her grave.'

He drains his glass as though washing away the bad taste in his mouth. I nod to the barman. He starts pouring another.

'Did Bobby look like his father?'

'Nah. He was a big pudding of a lad. Wore glasses. He worshipped Lenny; trailed after him like a puppy dog; running errands and fetching him cups of tea. When Lenny brought him to work, he'd sit outside of here and drink lemonade while Lenny had a few pints. Afterwards they'd cycle home.'

Bert is warming up. 'Lenny used to be a merchant seaman. His forearms were covered in tattoos. He was a man of very few words, but if you got him talkin' he'd tell you stories about his tattoos and how he got each one of 'em. Everybody liked Lenny. People smiled when they spoke his name. He was too nice a bloke. Sometimes folks can take advantage of that . . . '

'What do you mean?'

'You take his wife. I can't remember her name. She was some Irish Catholic shopgirl, with big hips and a ripcord in her knickers. I heard tell that Lenny only screwed her the once. He was too much of a gentleman to say. She gets pregnant and tells Lenny the baby is his. Anyone else would have been suspicious, but straight away Lenny marries her. He buys a house – using up all the money he'd saved from going to sea. We all knew what his missus was like: a real Anytime Annie. Half the depot must have ridden her. We nicknamed her "number twenty-two" – our most popular route.'

Bert looks at me sadly, flicking ash from his sleeve. He explains how Lenny had started at the garage as a diesel mechanic and then taken a pay cut to go on the road. Passengers loved his funny hats and his impromptu songs. When Liverpool beat Real Madrid in the final of the European Cup in 1981, he dyed his hair red and decorated the bus in toilet paper.

Lenny knew about his wife's indiscretions, according to Bert. She flaunted her infidelity – dressing herself in mini skirts and high heels. Dancing every night at the Empire Ballroom and the Grafton.

Without warning, Bert windmills his arm as though wanting to punch something. His face twists in pain. 'He was too soft – soft in the heart, soft in the head. If it were raining soup Lenny would be stuck with a fork in his hand. Some women deserve a slap. She took everything . . . his heart, his house, his boy. Most men would have killed her. Most men weren't like Lenny. She sucked him dry. Drained his spirit. She spent a hundred quid a month more than he earned. He was working double shifts and doing the house-work as well. I used to hear him pleading with her over the phone – "Are you staying in tonight, pet?" She just laughed at him.'

'Why didn't he leave her?'

He shrugs. 'Guess he had a blind spot. Maybe she threatened to take the kid. Lenny wasn't a wimp. I once seen him throw four hooligans off his bus because they were upsetting the other passengers. He could handle himself, Lenny. He just couldn't handle *her*.'

Bert falls silent. For the first time I notice how the bar has filled up and the noise level has risen. The Friday night band is setting up in the corner. People are looking at me; trying to work out what I'm doing. There is no such thing as anonymity when you're the odd one out.

The red lights have started to sway and the wooden floor-boards echo. I've been trying to keep up with Bert, drink for drink.

I ask about the accident. Bert explains that Lenny sometimes used the engineering workshop of a weekend to build his inventions. The boss turned a blind eye. The weekend buses were running, but the workshop was empty.

'How much do you know about welding?' Bert asks.

'Not much.'

He pushes his beer aside and picks up two coasters. Then he explains how two pieces of metal are joined together by using concentrated heat. Normally the heat is generated in two ways. An arc welder uses a powerful arc of electricity, with low voltage and high current generating temperatures of 11,000°F. Then you have oxy-fuel welders, where gases such as acetylene or natural gas are mixed with pure oxygen and burned to create a flame that can carve through metal.

'You don't muck around with this sort of equipment,' he says. 'But Lenny was one of the best welders I ever saw in me life. Fellas used to say he could weld two pieces of paper together.

'We always took a lot of precautions in the workshop. All flammable liquids were stored in a separate room from the cutting or welding. We kept combustibles at least thirty-five feet away. We covered the drains and kept fire extinguishers nearby.

'I don't know what Lenny was building. Some people joked it was a rocket ship to send his ex-wife into outer space. The blast knocked an eight-ton bus on to its side. The acetylene tank blew a hole through the roof. They found it a hundred yards away.

'Lenny finished up near the roller doors. The only part of his body that hadn't been burned was his chest. They figured he must have been lying down when the fireball engulfed him because that part of his shirt was only slightly singed.

'A couple of the drivers dragged him clear. I still don't know how they managed it . . . what with the heat and all. I remember them saying afterwards how Lenny's boots were smoking and his skin had turned to crackling. He was still conscious but he couldn't speak. He had no lips. I'm glad I didn't see it. I'd still be having nightmares.' Bert puts his glass down and his chest heaves in a short sigh.

'So it was an accident?'

'That's what it looked like at first. Everyone figured a spark from the welder had ignited the acetylene tank. There might have been a hole in the hose, or some other fault. Maybe gas had accumulated in the tank he was welding.'

'What do you mean "at first"?'

'When they peeled off Lenny's shirt they found something written on his chest. They say every letter was inch-perfect –

298

but I don't believe that, not when he was writing upside down and left to right. He'd used a welding torch to burn the word "SORRY" into his skin. Like I said, he was a man of very few words.'

9

I don't remember leaving the Tramway. Eight pints and then I lost count. The cold air hits me and I find myself on my hands and knees, leaving the contents of my stomach over the broken rubble and cinders of a vacant block.

It seems to be a makeshift car park for the pub. The country and western band is still playing. They're doing a cover of a Willie Nelson song about mothers not letting their children grow up to be cowboys.

As I try to stand something pushes me from behind and I fall into an oily puddle. The four teenagers from the bar are standing over me.

'Ya got any money?' asks the girl.

'Piss off!'

A kick is aimed at my head but misses. Another connects with my abdomen. My bowels slacken and I want to vomit again. I suck in air and try to think.

'Jesus, Baz, you said nobody gets hurt!' says the girl.

'Shut the fuck up! Don't use names.'

'Fuck you!'

'Leave it out, you two,' argues the one called Ozzie, who is left-handed and drinks rum and cola.

'Don't you start, dickhead.' Baz stares him down.

Someone takes my wallet out of my jacket.

'Not the cards, just the cash,' says Baz. He's older – in his early twenties – and has a swastika tattooed on his neck. He lifts me easily and pushes his face close to mine. I smell beer, peanuts and cigarette smoke.

'Hey, listen, toss-bag! You're not welcome here.'

Shoved backwards, I land against a wire fence topped with razor wire. Baz is toe-to-toe with me. He's three inches shorter and solid like a barrel. A knife blade gleams in his hand.

'I want my wallet back. If you give it to me, I won't press charges,' I say.

He laughs at me and mimics my voice. *Do I really sound that frightened?*

'You followed me from the pub. I saw you in there playing pool. You lost the last game on the black.'

The girl pushes her glasses up her nose. Her fingernails are bitten to the quick.

'What's he mean, Baz?'

'Shut up! Don't fucking use my name.' He shapes to hit her, but she shoots him a fierce glance. The silence lingers. I don't feel drunk any more.

I focus on the girl. 'You should have trusted your instincts, Denny.'

She looks at me, wide-eyed. 'How do you know my name?'

'You're Denny and you're under age – thirteen, maybe fourteen. This is Baz, your boyfriend, and these two are Ozzie and Carl—'

'Shut the fuck up!'

Baz shoves me hard against the fence. He can sense he's losing the initiative.

'Is this what you want, Denny? What's your mum going to say when the police come looking for you? She thinks you're staying at a girlfriend's house, doesn't she? She doesn't like you hanging out with Baz. She thinks he's a loser, a no-hoper.'

'Make him stop, Baz.' Denny covers her mouth.

'Shut the fuck up!'

No one says anything. They're watching me. I take a step forward and whisper to Baz. 'Use your grey cells, Baz. I just want my wallet.'

Denny interrupts, on the verge of tears, 'Just give him his fucking wallet. I want to go home.'

Ozzie turns to Carl. 'C'mon.'

Baz doesn't know what to do. He could carve me up like a wisp of smoke, but now he's on his own. The others are already disappearing, loose-limbed and hooting with laughter.

He pushes me hard against the fence, pressing the knife to my neck and his face next to mine. His teeth close around my earlobe. White heat. Pain. Ripping his head to one side, he spits hard into a puddle and shoves me away.

'There's a little souvenir from Bobby!'

He wipes blood from his mouth. Then he swaggers away and kicks at the door of a parked car. I'm sitting in water, braced against the fence, my wallet at my feet. In the distance

I see navigation lights blinking from the top of industrial cranes on the far side of the Mersey.

Slowly, pulling myself upright, I try to stand. My right leg buckles and I fall to my knees. Blood leaks in a warm trail down my neck.

I stumble to the main road but there is no traffic. Glancing over my shoulder, I worry about them coming back. Half a mile down the road I find a mini-cab office with metal grilles over the door and windows. The inside is saturated with cigarette smoke and the smell of takeaway food.

'What happened to you?' asks a fat man behind the grille.

I catch a glimpse of my reflection in the window. The bottom part of my ear is missing and my shirt collar is soaked with blood.

'I got mugged.'

'Who by?'

'Kids.'

I open my wallet. The cash is still there . . . all of it.

The fat man rolls his eyes, no longer concerned about me. I'm just a drunk who got into a fight. He radios for a car and makes me wait outside on the footpath. I glance nervously up and down the street, looking for Baz.

A souvenir! Bobby has some charming friends. Why didn't they take the money? What was the point? Unless they were trying to warn me off. Liverpool is a big enough place to get lost and small enough to get noticed, particularly if you start asking questions.

Slumped on the back seat of an old Mazda 626, I close my eyes and let my heart slow. Sweat has cooled between my shoulder blades, making my neck feel stiff.

The mini-cab drops me at the University Hospital, where I wait for an hour to get six stitches in my ear. As the intern wipes the blood from my face with a towel, he asks if the police have been informed. I lie and say yes. I don't want Ruiz knowing where I am.

Afterwards, with a dose of paracetamol to dull the pain, I walk through the city until I reach Pier Head. The last ferry is arriving from Birkenhead. The engine makes the air throb. Lights leak towards me in a colourful slick of reds and yellows. I stare at the water and keep imagining I can see dark shapes. Bodies. I look again and they vanish. Why do I always look for bodies?

As a child I sometimes went boating on the Thames with my sisters. One day I found a sack containing five dead kittens. Patricia kept telling me to put the sack down. She was screaming at me. Rebecca wanted to see inside. She, like me, had never seen anything dead, except for bugs and lizards.

I emptied the sack and the kittens tumbled on to the grass. Their wet fur stood on end. I was attracted and repelled at the same time. They had soft fur and warm blood. They weren't so different from me.

Later, as a teenager, I imagined that I would be dead by thirty. It was in the midst of the Cold War, when the world teetered on the edge of an abyss, at the mercy of whichever madman in the White House or the Kremlin had one of those 'I-wonder-what-this-button-does?' moments.

Since then my internal doomsday clock has swung wildly back and forth, much like the official version. Marrying Julianne made me hugely optimistic and having Charlie added to this. I even looked forward to graceful old age when we'd trade our backpacks for suitcases on wheels, playing with grandchildren, boring them with nostalgic stories, taking up eccentric hobbies . . .

The future will be different now. Instead of a dazzling road to discovery, I see a twitching, stammering, dribbling spectacle in a wheelchair. 'Do we really have to go and see Dad today?' Charlie will ask. 'He won't know the difference if we don't show up.'

A gust of wind sets my teeth chattering and I push away from the railing. I walk from the wharf, no longer worried about getting lost. At the same time I feel vulnerable. Exposed.

At the Albion Hotel the receptionist is knitting, moving her lips as she counts the stitches. Canned laughter emanates from somewhere beneath her feet. She doesn't acknowledge me until she finishes a row. Then she hands me a note. It has the name and telephone number of a teacher who taught Bobby at St Mary's School. The morning will be soon enough.

The stairs feel steeper than before. I'm tired and drunk. I just want to sink down and sleep.

I wake up suddenly, breathing hard. My hand slides across the sheets looking for Julianne. She normally wakes when I cry out in my sleep. She puts her hand on my chest and whispers that everything is all right.

Taking deep breaths, I wait for my heartbeat to slow and then slip out of bed, tiptoeing across to the window. The street is empty except for a newspaper van making a delivery. I touch my ear gingerly and feel the roughness of the stitches.

There is blood on my pillow.

The door opens. There is no knock. No warning foot-steps. I'm positive that I locked it. A hand appears, red-nailed, long-fingered. Then a face coloured with lipstick and blusher. She is pale-skinned and thin, with short-cropped blonde hair.

'Shhhhhhhh!'

A person giggles behind her.

'For fuck's sake, will you be quiet?'

She's reaching for the light switch. I'm silhouetted against the window. 'This room is taken.'

Her eyes meet mine and she utters a single shocked expletive. Behind her, a large dishevelled man in an ill-fitting suit has his hand inside her top. 'You scared the crap out of me,' she says, pushing his hand away. He gropes drunkenly at her breasts again.

'How did you get into this room?'

She rolls her eyes apologetically. 'Made a mistake.'

'The door was locked.'

She shakes her head. Her male friend looks over her shoulder. 'What's he doing in *our* room?'

'It's *his* room, ya moron!' She hits him in the chest with a silver diamanté clutch bag and starts pushing him back-wards. As she closes the door, she turns and smiles. 'You want some company? I can piss this guy off.'

She's so thin I can see the bones in her chest above her breasts. 'No thanks.'

She shrugs and hikes up her tights beneath her mini skirt. Then the door closes and I hear them trying to creep along the hall and climb to the next floor.

For a moment I feel a flush of anger. Did I really forget to lock the door? I was drunk, maybe even partly concussed.

It is just after six. Julianne and Charlie will still be sleeping. I take out my mobile and turn it on, staring at the glowing face in the darkness. There are no messages. This is my penance . . . to think about my wife and daughter when I fall asleep and when I wake.

Sitting on the windowsill, I watch the sky grow lighter. Pigeons wheel and soar over the rooftops. They remind me of Varanasi in India, where the vultures circle high over funeral pyres, waiting for the charred remains to be dumped in the Ganges. Varanasi is a sorry slum of a city, with crumbling buildings, cross-eyed children and nothing of beauty except the brightly coloured saris and swaying hips of the women. It appalled and fascinated me. The same is true of Liverpool.

I wait until seven before calling Julianne. A male voice answers. At first I think I've dialled the wrong number but then I recognise Jock's voice.

'I was just thinking about you,' he says in a booming voice. Charlie is in the background saying, 'Is that Dad? Can I talk to him? Please let me.'

Jock covers the receiver but I can still hear him. He tells her to fetch Julianne. Charlie complains, but obeys.

Meanwhile, Jock is full of chummy bonhomie. I interrupt him. 'What are you doing there, Jock? Is everything OK?'

'Your plumbing still sucks.'

What does he know about my fucking plumbing? He matches my coldness with his own. I can picture his face changing. 'Someone tried to break in. Julianne got a bit spooked. She didn't want to be on her own in the house. I offered to stay.'

'Who? When?'

'It was probably just some addict. He came through the front door. The plumbers had left it open. D.J. found him in the study and chased him down the street. Lost him near the canal.'

'Was anything taken?'

'No.'

I hear footsteps on the stairs. Jock puts his hand over the phone.

'Can I talk to Julianne? I know she's there.'

'She says no.'

I feel a flush of anger. Jock tries to banter again. 'She wants to know why you called her mother at three in the morning.'

A vague memory surfaces: dialling the number; her mother's icy rebuke. She hung up on me.

'Just let me talk to Julianne.'

'No can do, old boy. She's not feeling very well.'

'What do you mean?'

'Just what I said. She's feeling a bit off-colour.'

'Is anything wrong?'

'No. She's in good order. I've given her a full physical.' He's trying to wind me up. It's working.

'Give her the *fucking* phone—'

'I don't think you're in any position to give me orders, Joe. You're only making things worse.'

I want to sink my fist into his 100-situps-a-day stomach. Then I hear a telltale click. Someone has picked up the phone in my office. Jock doesn't realise.

I try to sound conciliatory and tell him that I'll call later. He puts the phone down, but I wait, listening.

'Dad, is that you?' Charlie asks nervously.

'How are you, sweetheart?'

'Good. When are you coming home?'

'I don't know. I have to sort out a few things with Mummy.'

'Did you guys have a fight?'

'How did you know?'

'When Mum's angry at you I should never let her brush my hair.'

'I'm sorry.'

'That's OK. Was it your fault?'

'Yes.'

'Why don't you just say you're sorry? That's what you tell me to do when I have a fight with Taylor Jones.'

'I don't think that's going to be enough this time.'

I can hear her thinking about this. I can even picture her biting her bottom lip in concentration.

'Dad?'

'Yes.'

'Well . . . um . . . I want to ask you something. It's about . . . well . . . ' She keeps starting and stopping. I tell her to think of the whole question in her head and then ask me.

Finally it comes blurting out. 'There was this picture in the newspaper . . . someone with a coat over his head. Some of the kids were talking . . . at school. Lachlan O'Brien said it was you. I called him a liar. Then, last night, I took one of the newspapers from the bin. Mum had thrown them out. I sneaked them upstairs to my room—'

'Did you read the story?'

'Yes.'

My stomach lurches. How do I explain the concept of

wrongful arrest and mistaken identity to an eight-year-old? Charlie has been taught to trust the police. Justice and fairness are important – even in the playground.

'It was a mistake, Charlie. The police made a mistake.'

'Then why is Mum angry at you?'

'Because I made another mistake. A different one. It has nothing to do with the police or with you.'

She falls silent. I can almost hear her thinking.

'What's wrong with Mummy?' I ask.

'I don't know. I heard her tell Uncle Jock she was late.'

'Late for what?'

'She didn't say. She just said she was late.'

I ask her to repeat the statement word for word. She doesn't understand why. My mouth is dry. It isn't just the hangover. In the background I can hear Julianne calling Charlie's name.

'I have to go,' whispers Charlie. 'Come home soon.'

She hangs up quickly. I don't have a chance to say goodbye. My first instinct is to call straight back. I want to keep calling until Julianne talks to me. Does 'late' mean what I think it means? I feel sick to the stomach; hopeless in the head.

I could be home in three hours if I caught a train. I could stand on the doorstep until she agrees to talk to me. Maybe that's what she wants – for me to come running back to fight for her.

We've waited six years. Julianne never stopped believing. I was the one who gave up hope.

10

A bell tinkles above my head as I enter the shop. The aromas of scented oils, perfumed candles and herbal poultices curl into my nostrils. Narrow shelves made of dark wood stretch from the floor to the ceiling. These are crammed with incense, soap, oils and bell jars full of everything from pumice stones to seaweed.

A large woman emerges from behind a partition. She wears a brightly coloured kaftan that starts at her throat and billows outwards over huge breasts. Strings of beads sprout from her skull and clack as she walks.

'Come, come, don't be shy,' she says, waving me towards her. This is Louise Elwood. I recognise her voice from the phone. Some people look like their voices. She is one of them – deep, low and loud. Bangles clink on her arms as she shakes my hand. At the centre of her forehead is a pasted red dot.

'Oh my, oh my, oh my,' she says, holding her hand beneath my chin. 'You are just in time. Look at those eyes. Dull. Dry. You haven't been sleeping well, have you? Toxins in the blood. Too much red meat. Maybe a wheat allergy. What happened to your ear?'

'An overzealous hairdresser.'

She raises an eyebrow.

'We spoke on the phone,' I explain. 'I'm Professor O'Loughlin.'

'Typical! Look at the state of you! Doctors and academics make the worst patients. They never take their own advice.'

She pirouettes with remarkable agility and bustles deeper into the shop. At the same time she keeps talking. There are no obvious signs of a man in her life. Photographs of children on the noticeboard are probably nieces and nephews. She has a Burmese (cat hair), a drawer full of chocolates (tinsel on the floor) and a taste for romance writers (*The Silent Lady* by Catherine Cookson).

Behind the partition is a small back room with just enough space for a table, three chairs and a bench containing a small sink. An electric kettle and a radio are plugged into the lone socket. The centre of the table has a women's magazine open at the crossword.

'Herbal tea?'

'Do you have coffee?'

'No.'

'Tea will be fine.'

She rattles off a list of a dozen different blends. By the time she's finished I've forgotten the first few.

'Camomile.'

'Excellent choice. Good for relieving stress and tension.'
She pauses. 'You're not a believer, are you?'

'I have never been able to work out why herbal tea smells so wonderful but tastes so bland.'

She laughs. Her whole body shakes. 'The taste is subtle. It works in harmony with the body. Smell is the most immediate of all our senses. Touch might develop earlier and be the last to fade, but smell is hot-wired directly into our brains.'

She sets out two small china cups and fills a ceramic teapot with steaming water. The tea leaves are filtered twice through a silver sieve before she pushes a cup towards me.

'You don't read tea leaves then?'

'I think you're making fun of me, Professor.' She's not offended.

'Fifteen years ago you were a teacher at St Mary's.'

'For my sins.'

'Do you remember a boy called Bobby Morgan?'

'Of course I do.'

'What do you remember about him?'

'He was quite bright, although a little self-conscious about his size. Some of the other boys used to tease him because he wasn't very good at sports, but he had a lovely singing voice.'

'You taught the choir?'

'Yes. I once suggested singing lessons, but his mother wasn't the most approachable of women. I only saw her once at the school. She came to complain about Bobby stealing money from her purse to pay for an excursion to the Liverpool Museum.'

'What about his father?'

She looks at me quizzically. Clearly I'm expected to know something. Now she is trying to decide whether to continue.

'Bobby's father wasn't allowed at the school,' she says. 'He had a court order taken out against him when Bobby was in the second form. Didn't Bobby tell you any of this?'

'No.'

She shakes her head. Beads swing from side to side. 'I raised the alarm. Bobby had wet himself in class twice in a few weeks. Then he soiled his pants and spent most of the afternoon hiding in the boys' toilets. He was upset. When I asked him what was wrong he wouldn't say. I took him to the school nurse. She found him another pair of trousers. That's when she noticed the welts on his legs. It looked as though he'd been beaten.'

The school nurse followed the normal procedure and informed the deputy headmistress who, in turn, notified the Department of Social Services. I know the process off by heart. A duty social worker would have taken the referral. It was then discussed with an area manager. The dominoes started falling – medical examinations, interviews, allegations, denials, case conferences, 'at risk' findings, interim care orders, appeals – each tumbling into the next.

'Tell me about the court order,' I ask.

She recalls only scant details. Allegations of sexual abuse, which the father denied. A restraining order. Chaperoning Bobby between classes.

'The police investigated but I don't know the outcome. The deputy headmistress dealt with the social workers and police.'

'Is she still around?'

'No. She resigned eighteen months ago; family reasons.'

'What happened to Bobby?'

'He changed. He had a stillness about him that you don't see in most children. A lot of the teachers found it very unnerving.' She stares into her teacup, tilting it gently back and forth. 'When his father died he became even more isolated. It was as though he was on the outside, with his face pressed against the glass.'

'Do you think Bobby was abused?'

'St Mary's is in a very poor area, Professor O'Loughlin. In some households just waking up in the morning is a form of abuse.'

I know almost nothing about cars. I can fill them with petrol, put air in the tyres and water in the radiator, but I have no interest in makes, models or the dynamics of the modern combustion engine. Usually I take no notice of other vehicles on the road but today it's different. I keep seeing a white van. I noticed it first this morning when I left the Albion Hotel. It was parked opposite. The other cars were covered in frost but not the van. The windscreen and back window had ragged circles of clear glass.

The same white van – or another one just like it – is parked on a delivery ramp opposite Louise Elwood's shop. The back doors are open. I can see hessian sacks inside, lining the floor. There must be hundreds of white vans in Liverpool: perhaps a whole fleet of them belonging to a courier company.

After last night I'm seeing phantoms lurking in every doorway and now sitting in cars. I walk across the market square, stopping at a department store window. Studying the reflection, I can see the square behind me. Nobody is following.

I haven't eaten. Seeking out warmth, I find a café on the first floor of a shopping arcade, overlooking the atrium. From my table I can watch the escalators.

H.L. Mencken – journalist, beer-drinker and sage – said that for every complex problem there is a solution that is simple, neat and wrong. I share his mistrust for the obvious.

At university I drove my lecturers to distraction by constantly questioning straightforward assumptions. 'Why can't you just accept things as they are?' they asked. 'Why *can't* the easy answer be right?'

Nature isn't like that. If evolution had been about simple answers we would all have bigger brains and not watch *You've Been Framed*, or smaller brains and not invent weapons of mass destruction. Mothers would have four arms and babies would leave home after six weeks. We would all have titanium bones, UV-resistant skin, X-ray vision and the ability to have permanent erections and multiple orgasms.

Bobby Morgan – I'll call him by his real name now – had many of the hallmarks of sexual abuse. Even so, I don't want it to be true. I have grown to like Lenny Morgan. He did a lot of things right when he raised Bobby. People warmed to him. Bobby adored him.

Perhaps Lenny had two sides to his personality. There is nothing to stop an abuser being a safe, loving figure. It would certainly explain his suicide. It could also be the reason why Bobby needed two personalities to survive.

11

Social Services keep files on children who have been sexually abused. I once had full access to them but I'm no longer part of the system. The privacy laws are compelling.

I need help from someone I haven't seen in over a decade. Her name is Melinda Cossimo and I'm worried I might not recognise her. We arrange to meet in a coffee shop opposite the magistrates' court.

When I first arrived in Liverpool Mel was a duty social worker. Now she's an area manager (they call it a 'child protection specialist'). Not many people last this long in Social Services. They either burn out or blow up.

Mel was your original punk, with spiky hair and a wardrobe of distressed leather jackets and torn denim. She was always challenging everyone's opinions because she liked to see people stand up for their beliefs, whether she agreed with them or not.

317

Growing up in Cornwall, she had listened to her father, a local fisherman, pontificate on the distinction between 'men's work' and 'women's work'. Almost predictably, she became an ardent feminist and author of 'When Women Wear the Pants' – her doctoral thesis. Her father must be turning in his grave.

Mel's husband Boyd, a Lancashire lad, wore khaki trousers, turtleneck sweaters and smoked roll-ups. Tall and thin, he went grey at nineteen but kept his hair long and tied back in a ponytail. I only ever saw it loose once, in the showers after we had played badminton.

They were great hosts. We'd get together most weekends for dinner parties at Boyd's run-down terrace, with its 'wind chime' garden and cannabis plants growing in an old fishpond. We were all over-worked, under-appreciated and yet still idealistic. Julianne played the guitar and Mel had a voice like Joni Mitchell. We ate vegetarian feasts, drank too much wine, smoked a little dope and righted the wrongs of the world. The hangovers lasted until Monday and the flatulence until midweek.

Mel makes a face at me through the window. Her hair is straight and pinned back from her face. She's wearing dark trousers and a tailored beige jacket. A white ribbon is pinned to her lapel. I can't remember what charity it represents.

'Is this the management look?'

'No, it's middle age,' she laughs, grateful to sit down. 'These shoes are killing me.' She kicks them off and rubs her ankles.

'Shopping?'

'An appointment in the children's court. An emergency care order.'

'Good result?'

'It could have been worse.'

I get the coffees while she minds the table. I know she's checking me out – trying to establish how much has changed. Do we still have things in common? Why have I suddenly surfaced? The caring profession is a suspicious one.

'So what happened to your ear?'

'Got bitten by a dog.'

'You should never work with animals.'

'So I've heard.'

Mel watches as my left hand tries to stir my coffee. 'Are you still with Julianne?'

'Uh-huh. We have Charlie now. She's eight. I think Julianne might be pregnant again.'

'Aren't you sure?' she laughs.

I laugh with her, but feel a pang of guilt.

I ask about Boyd. I picture him as an ageing hippy, still wearing linen shirts and Punjabi pants. Mel turns her face away, but not before I see the pain drift across her eyes like a cloud.

'Boyd is dead.'

Sitting very still, she lets the silence grow accustomed to the news.

'When?'

'Over a year ago. One of those big four-wheel drives, with a bullbar, went through a stop sign and cleaned him up.'

I tell her that I'm sorry. She smiles sadly and licks milk froth from her spoon.

'They say the first year is the hardest. I tell you, it's like being fucked over by fifty cops with batons and riot shields.

I still can't get my head around the fact he's gone. I even blamed *him* for a while. I thought he'd abandoned me. It sounds silly, but out of spite I sold his record collection. It cost me twice as much to buy it back again.' She laughs at herself and stirs her coffee.

'You should have got in touch. We didn't know.'

'Boyd lost your address. He was hopeless. I know I could have found you.' She smiles apologetically. 'I just didn't want to see anyone for a while. It would just remind me of the good old days.'

'Where is he now?'

'At home in a little silver pot on my filing cabinet.' She makes it sound as though he's pottering around in the garden shed. 'I can't put him in the ground here. It's too cold. What if it snows? He hated the cold.' She looks at me mournfully. 'I know that's stupid.'

'Not to me.'

'I thought I might save up and take his ashes to Nepal. I could throw them off a mountain.'

'He was scared of heights.'

'Yeah. Maybe I should just tip them in the Mersey.'

'Can you do that?'

'Don't see how anyone could stop me.' She laughs sadly. 'So what brings you back to Liverpool? You couldn't get away from here fast enough.'

'I wish I could have taken you guys with me.'

'Down south! Not likely! You know what Boyd thought of London. He said it was full of people searching for something that they couldn't find elsewhere, not having bothered to look.'

I can hear Boyd saying exactly that.

'I need to get hold of a child protection file.'

'A red edge!'

'Yes.'

I haven't heard that term for years. It's the nickname given by social workers in Liverpool to child protection referrals because the initiating form has a dark crimson border.

'What child?'

'Bobby Morgan.'

Mel makes the connection instantly. I see it in her eyes. 'I dragged a magistrate out of bed at two in the morning to sign the interim care order. The father committed suicide. You must remember?'

'No.'

Her brow furrows. 'Maybe it was one of Erskine's.' Rupert Erskine was the senior psychologist in the department. I was the junior half of the team – a fact he pointed out at every opportunity. Mel had been the duty social worker on Bobby's case.

'The referral came from a schoolteacher,' she explains. 'The mother didn't want to say anything at first. When she saw the medical evidence she broke down and told us she suspected her husband.'

'Can you get me the file?'

I can see she wants to ask me why. At the same time, she realises it is probably safer to remain ignorant. Closed childcare files are stored at Hatton Gardens, the head office of the Liverpool Social Services Department. Files are held for eighty years and can only be viewed by an appropriate member of staff, an authorised agency or a court officer. All access becomes part of the record.

Mel stares at her reflection in her teaspoon. She has to

make a decision. Does she help me or say no? She glances at her watch. 'I'll make a few phone calls. Come to my office at one-thirty.'

She kisses me on the cheek as she leaves. Another coffee is ordered for the wait. Down times are the worst. They give me too much time to think. That's when random thoughts bounce through my head like a ping-pong ball in a jar. Julianne is pregnant. We'll need a child gate at the bottom of the stairs. Charlie wants to go camping this summer. What's the connection between Bobby and Catherine?

Another van – but it's not white. The driver tosses a bundle of papers on to the pavement in front of the café. The front-page headline reads: 'Reward Offered in McBride Murder Hunt'.

Mel has a clean desk with two piles of paperwork on either side in haphazard columns. Her computer is decorated with stickers, headlines and cartoons. One of them shows an armed robber pointing a gun and saying, 'Your money or your life!' The victim replies, 'I have no money and no life. I'm a social worker.'

We're on the third floor of the Social Services Department. Most of the offices are empty for the weekend. The view from Mel's window is of a half-built prefabricated warehouse. She has managed to get me three files, each held together by a loop of red tape. I have an hour before she gets back from shopping.

I know what to expect. The first rule of intelligent tinkering is to save all the parts. That's what the Social Services do. When they mess about with people's lives they make a careful note of every decision. There will be interviews, family assessments, psych reports and medical notes. There will be minutes of every case conference and strategy meeting, as well as copies of police statements and court rulings.

If Bobby spent time in a children's home or psych ward, this will have been recorded. There will be names, dates and places. With any luck I can cross-reference these with Catherine McBride's file and discover a link.

The first page of the file is a record of a telephone call from St Mary's School. I recognise Mel's handwriting. Bobby had 'displayed a number of recent behavioural changes'. Apart from wetting himself and soiling his pants, he had 'displayed inappropriate sexual behaviour'. He had removed his underpants and simulated sex with a seven-year-old girl.

Mel faxed through the information to the area manager. At the same time, she phoned the clerk in the area office and organised a check through the index files to see if Bobby, his parents or any siblings had ever come up on file. When this drew a blank, she started a new file. The injuries worried her most. She consulted with Lucas Dutton, the assistant director (children), who made the decision to launch an investigation.

The 'red edge' is easy to find because of the border. It records Bobby's name, date of birth, address and details of his parents, school, GP and known health problems. There are also details about the deputy headmistress of St Mary's, the original referrer.

Mel had organised a full medical examination. Dr Richard Legende found 'two or three marks about six inches long across both his buttocks'. He described the injuries as being consistent with 'two or three successive blows with a hard item such as a studded belt'.

Bobby had been distressed throughout the examination and had refused to answer any questions. Dr Legende noted what appeared to be old scar tissue around the anus. 'Whether the injury was caused accidentally or by deliberate penetration is not clear,' he wrote. In a later report he hardened his resolve and described the scarring as being 'consistent with abuse'.

Bridget Morgan was interviewed. Hostile at first, she accused Social Services of being busybodies. When told of Bobby's injuries and behaviour, she began to qualify her answers. Eventually she began making excuses for her husband.

'He's a good man, but he can't help himself. He gets angry and loses his rag.'

'Does he ever hit you?'

'Yeah.'

'What about Bobby?'

'He gets the worst of it.'

'When he beats Bobby, what does he use?'

'A dog collar . . . He'll kill me if he knows I'm here . . . You don't know what he's like . . .'

When asked about any inappropriate sexual behaviour, Bridget categorically denied her husband could have done such a thing. Her protests became more strident as the interview went on. She became tearful and asked to see Bobby.

All allegations of sexual abuse have to be reported to the police. After being told this, Bridget Morgan grew even more anxious. Clearly distressed, she admitted to having concerns about her husband's relationship with Bobby. She wouldn't or couldn't elaborate.

Bobby and his mother were taken to Marsh Lane police station to be formally interviewed. A strategy meeting was held at the station. Those present were Mel Cossimo, her immediate boss Lucas Dutton, Detective Sergeant Helena Bronte and Bridget Morgan. Having spent a few minutes alone with Bobby, Mrs Morgan accepted the need for an investigation.

Leafing through her police statement, I try to pick out the crux of her allegations. Two years earlier she claimed to have seen Bobby sitting on her husband's lap, not wearing any underwear. Her husband had had only a towel around his waist and he appeared to be pushing Bobby's hand between his legs.

During the previous year she had often found that Bobby had no underwear on when he undressed to have a bath. When asked why, he'd said, 'Daddy doesn't like me wearing underpants.'

The mother also claimed that her husband would only take a bath when Bobby was awake and would leave the bathroom door open. He would often invite Bobby to join him, but the boy made excuses.

Although not a strong statement, in the hands of a good prosecutor it could be damning enough. The next statement I expect to find is Bobby's. It isn't there. I turn several pages and find that no mention is made of a formal statement, which could explain why Lenny Morgan was never charged. Instead there is a videotape and a sheaf of handwritten notes.

A child's evidence is crucial. Unless he or she admits to

being molested, the chances of success are slim. The abuser would have to admit the crime, or the medical evidence would have to be incontrovertible.

Mel has a video and TV in her office. I slide the tape out of the cardboard sleeve. The label has Bobby's full name, as well as the date and place of the interview. As the first images flash on to the screen, the time is stamped in the bottom left hand corner.

A child protection evaluation is very different from a normal patient consultation because of the time constraints. It can often take weeks to establish the sort of trust that allows a child to slowly reveal his or her inner world. Evaluations have to be done quickly and the questions are therefore more direct.

The child-friendly interview room has toys on the floor and brightly coloured walls. Drawing paper and crayons have been left on the table. A small boy sits nervously on a plastic chair, looking at the blank piece of paper. He is wearing a school uniform with baggy shorts and scuffed shoes. He glances at the camera and I see his face clearly. He has changed a lot in fourteen years, but I still recognise him. He sits impassively, as if resigned to his fate.

There is something else. Something more. The details return like surrendered soldiers. I have seen this boy before. Rupert Erskine asked me to review a case. A young boy who wasn't responding to any of his questions. A new approach was needed. Perhaps a new face.

The video is still running. I hear *my* voice. 'Do you prefer to be called Robert, Rob or Bobby?'

'Bobby.'

'Do you know why you're here, Bobby?'

He doesn't answer.

'I have to ask you a few questions. Is that OK?'

'I want to go home.'

'Not just yet. Tell me, Bobby, you understand the difference between the truth and a lie, don't you?'

He nods.

'If I said that I had a carrot instead of a nose, what would that be?'

'A lie.'

'That's right.'

The tape continues. I ask non-specific questions about school and home. Bobby talks about his favourite TV shows and toys. He relaxes and begins doodling on a sheet of paper as he talks.

If he had three magic wishes what would they be? After two false starts and shuffling his choices, he came up with: 1) owning a chocolate factory; 2) going camping; and 3) building a machine that would make everybody happy. Who would he most like to be? Sonic the Hedgehog because 'he runs really fast and saves his friends'.

Watching the video, I can recognise some of the mannerisms and body language of the adult Bobby. He rarely smiled or laughed. He maintained eye contact only briefly.

I ask him about his father. At first Bobby is animated and open. He wants to go home and see him. 'We're making an invention. It's going to stop shopping bags from spilling in the boot of the car.'

Bobby draws a picture of himself and I get him to name the different body parts. He mumbles when he talks about his 'private parts'.

'Do you like it when you have a bath with your dad?'

'Yes.'

'What do you like about it?'

'He tickles me.'

'Where does he tickle you?'

'All over.'

'Does he ever touch you in a way that you don't like?' Bobby's brow furrows. 'No.'

'Does he ever touch your private parts?'

'No.'

'What about when he washes you?'

'I suppose.' He mumbles something else that I can't make out.

'What about your mum? Does she ever touch your private parts?'

He shakes his head and asks to go home. He screws up the piece of paper and refuses to answer any more questions. He isn't upset or scared. It is another example of the 'distancing' that is common in sexually abused children who try to make themselves smaller and less of a target.

The interview ends and the outcome was clearly inconclusive. Body language and mannerisms weren't enough to formulate an opinion.

Turning back to the files, I piece together the history of what happened next. Mel recommended that Bobby be placed on the Child Protection Register – a list of all children in the area who were considered to be at risk. She applied for an interim custody order – getting a magistrate out of bed at two a.m.

Police arrested Lenny Morgan. His house was searched, along with his bus depot locker and a neighbouring garage he rented as a workshop. He maintained his innocence throughout. He described himself as a loving father who had never done anything wrong or been in trouble with the police. He claimed to have no knowledge of Bobby's injuries, but admitted to 'giving him a whack' when he dismantled and broke a perfectly good alarm clock.

I knew none of this. My involvement ended after a single interview. It was Erskine's case.

A child protection case conference was held on Friday 15 August. The conference was chaired by Lucas Dutton and included the duty social worker, consultant psychologist Rupert Erskine, Bobby's GP, the deputy headmistress of his school and Detective Sergeant Helena Bronte.

The minutes of the meeting indicate Lucas Dutton ran proceedings. I remember him. At my first case conference he shot me down in flames when I offered an alternative suggestion to his own. Directors are rarely questioned – especially by junior psychologists whose diplomas are fresh enough to smudge.

The police didn't have enough evidence to charge Lenny Morgan, but the criminal investigation continued. Based on the physical evidence and Bridget Morgan's statement, the conference recommended that Bobby be removed from his family and placed in foster care unless his father agreed to voluntarily stay away. Daily contact would be arranged but father and son were never to be left alone.

Bobby spent five days in foster care before Lenny agreed to leave the family home and live separately until the allegations were fully investigated.

The second case file begins with a contents page. I scan the list and continue reading. For three months the Morgan family was shadowed by social workers and psychologists, who tried to discover exactly how it functioned. Bobby's behaviour was monitored and reviewed, particularly during the contact visits with his father. At the same time Erskine interviewed Bridget, Lenny and Bobby separately, taking detailed histories. He also spoke to the maternal grandmother, Pauline Aherne, and Bridget's younger sister.

Both seemed to confirm Bridget's suspicions about Lenny. In particular, Pauline Aherne claimed to have witnessed an example of inappropriate behaviour when father and son were wrestling at bedtime and she saw Lenny's hand inside Bobby's pyjamas.

When I compared her statement to Bridget's, I noticed how they used many of the same phrases and descriptions. This would have concerned me if it had been my case. Blood is thicker than water – never more so than in child custody cases.

Lenny Morgan's first wife had died in a car accident. A son from the first marriage, Dafyyd Morgan, had left home at eighteen without coming to the attention of Social Services.

Several attempts were made to find him. Child care workers traced his teachers and a swimming coach, who reported no cause for concern in his behaviour. Dafyyd had left school at fifteen and been apprenticed to a local building firm. He'd then dropped out and his last known address was a backpackers' hostel in South Australia.

The file contains Erskine's conclusions, but not his session notes. He described Bobby as 'anxious, fidgety, and temperamentally fragile', and displaying 'symptoms of post-traumatic stress disorder'.

'When questioned about any sexual abuse, Bobby became increasingly defensive and agitated,' Erskine wrote. 'He also seems defensive if anyone suggests his family is not ideal. It is as if he is working hard to hide something.'

Of Bridget Morgan he wrote: 'Her first concern is always for her son. She is particularly reluctant to allow any further interviews with Bobby because of the anxiety these create. Bobby has apparently been wetting the bed and has had problems sleeping.'

Her concern was understandable. At a rough count, I estimated Bobby was interviewed more than a dozen times by therapists, psychologists and social workers. Questions were repeated and rephrased.

During free play sessions he was observed undressing dolls and naming body parts. None of these sessions were recorded, but a therapist reported that Bobby placed one doll on top of the other and made grunting noises.

Erskine included two of Bobby's drawings in the file. I hold them at arm's length. They're rather good in an abstract sort of way – a cross between Picasso and the Flintstones. The figures are robot-like, with skewed faces. Adults are drawn excessively large and children very small.

Erskine concluded:

There are several significant pieces of evidence which, in my opinion, strongly support the possibility of sexual contact between Mr Morgan and his son.

First, there is the evidence of Bridget Morgan, as well as that of the maternal grandmother, Mrs Pauline Aherne. Neither woman appears to have any reason to be biased or embellish their accounts. Both witnessed occasions when Mr Morgan exposed himself to his son and removed his son's underwear.

Secondly, there is the evidence of Dr Richard Legende, who found 'two or three strap marks about six inches long across both of the child's buttocks'. More perturbing was the evidence of scar tissue around the anus.

Added to this we have the behavioural changes in Bobby. He has displayed an unhealthy interest in sex, as well as a working knowledge far beyond that of a normal eight-year-old.

Based on these facts, I believe there exists a strong likelihood that Bobby has been sexually abused, most probably by his father.

There must have been another case conference in mid-November. I can find no minutes. The police investigation was suspended but the file left open.

The third file is full of legal documents – some of them bound in ribbon. I recognise the paperwork. Satisfied that Bobby was at risk, Social Services had applied for a permanent care order. The lawyers were set loose.

'What are you mumbling about?' Mel is back from her shopping, balancing two cups of coffee on a ledger. 'Sorry I can't offer you anything stronger. Remember when we used to smuggle boxes of wine in here at Christmas?'

'I remember Boyd getting drunk and watering the plastic plants in the foyer.'

We both laugh.

'Bring back any memories?' She motions to the files.

'Sadly.' My left hand is trembling. I push it into my lap. 'What did you make of Lenny Morgan?'

She sits down and kicks off her shoes. 'I thought he was a pig. He was abusive and violent.'

'What did he do?'

'He confronted me outside the court. I went to use a phone in the foyer. He asked me why I was doing this – as if it was personal. When I tried to get past him, he pushed me against the wall and put his hand around my throat. He had this look in his eyes . . . ' She shudders.

'You didn't press charges?'

'No.'

'He was upset?'

'Yes.'

'What about the wife?'

'Bridget. She was all fur coat and no knickers. A real social climber.'

'But you liked her?'

'Yes.'

'What happened about the care order?'

'One magistrate agreed with the application and two claimed there was insufficient evidence to sustain the argument.'

'So you tried to get Bobby made a ward of court?'

'You bet. I wasn't letting the father anywhere near him. We went straight to the county court and got a hearing that afternoon. The papers should all be there.' She motions towards the files.

'Who gave evidence?'

'I did.'

'What about Erskine?'

'I used his report.'

Mel is getting annoyed at my questions. 'Any social worker would have done what I did. If you can't get the magistrates to see sense, you go to a judge. Nine times out of ten you'll get wardship.'

'Not any more.'

'No.' She sounds disappointed. 'They've changed the rules.'

From the moment Bobby became a ward, every major decision on his welfare was made by a court instead of his family. He couldn't change schools, get a passport, join the army or get married without the court's permission. It also guaranteed that his father would never be allowed back into his life.

Turning the pages of the file, I come across the judgement. It runs to about eight pages, but I scan them quickly, looking for the outcome.

The husband and wife are each genuinely concerned about the welfare of the child. I am satisfied that they have in the past, in their own way, attempted to discharge their obligations as parents to the best of their ability. Unfortunately in the husband's case, his ability to properly and appropriately discharge his obligations to the child has, in my view, been adversely affected by the allegations hanging over his head.

I have taken into consideration the countervailing evidence – namely the husband's denials. At the same time, I am aware that the child wishes to live with both his father and mother. Clearly, the weight given to those wishes must be balanced against other matters relevant to Bobby's welfare.

The child welfare guidelines and tests are clear. Bobby's interests are paramount. This court cannot grant custody or access to a parent if that custody or access would expose a child to an unacceptable risk of sexual abuse.

I hope that, in due course, when Bobby has acquired a level of self-protection, maturity and understanding, he will have an opportunity to spend time with his father. However, until that time arrives, which I see regrettably as being some time in the future, he should not have contact with his father.

The judgement bears a court seal and is signed by Mr Justice Alexander McBride, Catherine's grandfather.

Mel is watching me from the far side of the desk. 'Find what you were looking for?'

'Not really. Did you ever have much to do with Justice McBride?'

'He's a good egg.'

'I suppose you've heard about his granddaughter.'

'A terrible thing.'

She spins her chair slowly around and stretches out her legs until her shoes rest on the wall. Her eyes are fixed on me.

'Do you know if Catherine McBride had a file?' I ask casually.

'Funny you should ask that.'

'Why?'

'I've just had someone else ask to see it. That's two interesting requests in one day.'

'Who asked for the file?'

'A homicide squad detective. He wants to know if *your* name crops up in there.'

Her eyes are piercing. She is angry with me for holding something back. Social workers don't confide in people easily. They learn not to trust . . . not when dealing with abused children, beaten wives, drug addicts, alcoholics and parents fighting for custody. Nothing can be taken at face value. Never trust a journalist, or a defence lawyer, or a

335

parent who is running scared. Never turn your back in an interview or make a promise to a child. Never rely on foster carers, magistrates, politicians or senior public servants. Mel had trusted me. I had let her down.

'The detective says you're a subject of interest. He says that Catherine made a sexual assault complaint against you. He asked if any other complaints had ever been made.'

This is Mel's territory. She has nothing against men, just the things they do.

'The sexual assault is a fiction. I didn't touch Catherine.'

I can't hide the anger in my voice. Turning the other cheek is for people who want to look the other way. I'm sick of being accused of something I haven't done.

On the walk back to the Albion Hotel, I try to put the pieces together. My stitched ear is throbbing but it helps focus my thoughts. It's like being able to concentrate with the TV turned up full volume.

Bobby was about the same age as Charlie when he lost his father. A tragedy like that can take a terrible toll, but more than one person is needed to shape a child's mind. There are grandparents, uncles, aunts, brothers, sisters, teachers, friends and a huge cast of extras. If I could call on all of these people and interview them, maybe I could discover what happened to him.

What am I missing? A child is made a ward of court. His father commits suicide. A sad story, but not unique. Children aren't made wards of court any more. The law changed in the early nineties. The old system was too open to abuse. Precious little evidence was required and there were no checks and balances.

Bobby had shown all the signs of being sexually abused. Victims of child abuse find ways of protecting themselves. Some suffer from traumatic amnesia; others bury their pain in their unconscious minds or refuse to reflect on what has happened. At the same time, there are sometimes social workers who 'verify' rather than question allegations of abuse. They believe that accusers never lie and abusers always do.

The more Bobby denied anything had happened, the more people believed it had to be true. This one cast iron assumption underpinned the entire investigation.

What if we got it wrong?

Researchers at the University of Michigan once took a synopsis of an actual case involving a two-year-old girl and presented it to a panel of experts including eight clinical psychologists, twenty-three graduate students and fifty social workers and psychiatrists. The researchers knew from the outset that the child had *not* been sexually abused.

The mother alleged abuse based on her discovery of a bruise on her daughter's leg and a single pubic hair (that she thought looked like the father's) in the girl's nappy. Four medical examinations showed no evidence of abuse. Two lie detector tests and a joint police and Child Protection Service investigation cleared the father.

Despite this, three quarters of the experts recommended that the father's contact with the daughter be either highly supervised or stopped altogether. Several of them even concluded that the girl had been sodomised.

There is no such thing as presumed innocence in child abuse cases. The accused is guilty until proven otherwise. The stain is invisible, yet indelible.

I know all the defences to arguments like this. False accusations are rare. We get it wrong more times than we get it right.

Erskine is a good psychologist and a good man. He nursed his wife through MS until she died and he's raised a lot for a research grant in her name. Mel has passion and a social conscience that always puts me to shame. At the same time, she has never made any pretence of neutrality. She knows what she knows. Gut instinct counts.

I don't know where any of this leaves me. I'm tired and I'm hungry. I still don't have any evidence that Bobby *knew* Catherine McBride, let alone murdered her.

A dozen steps before I reach my hotel room I know something is wrong. The door is open. A wine-dark stain leaks across the carpet, heading for the stairs. A potted palm lies on its side across the doorway. The clay pot must have broken in half when it sheared off the door handle.

A cleaner's trolley is parked in the stairwell. It contains two buckets, mops, scrubbing brushes and a collection of wet rags. The cleaning lady is standing in the middle of my room. The bed is upside down, littered with the remains of a broken drawer. The sink – wrenched from the wall – lies beneath a broken pipe and a steady trickle of water.

My clothes are scattered across the sodden carpet, interspersed with torn pages of notes and ripped folders. My sports bag is crammed inside the bowl of the toilet, decorated with a turd.

'There is nothing like having your room properly cleaned, is there?' I say.

The cleaning lady looks at me in disbelief.

Spearmint toothpaste spells out a message on the mirror

338

that's full of local flavour: 'GO HOME OR GET BOXED'. Simple. Succinct. Precise.

The hotel manager wants to call the police. I have to open my wallet to change his mind. Picking through the debris, there isn't much worth salvaging. Gingerly, I lift a bundle of soggy papers smeared with ink. The only sheet legible is the last page of Catherine's CV. I had read the covering letter in the office but got no further. Glancing down the page, I see a list of three character referees. Only one of them matters: Dr Emlyn R. Owens. She gives Jock's Harley Street address and phone number.

12

Maintenance work, leaves on the line, signal failures, point faults . . . pick any one of them, they all add up to the same thing – the train will be late arriving in London. The conductor apologises frequently over the tannoy, keeping everyone awake.

I buy a cup of tea from the dining car, along with a 'gourmet' sandwich which is evidence of how culinary words can be devalued. It tastes of nothing except mayonnaise. Random thoughts keep nudging away at my tiredness. Missing pieces. New pieces. No pieces at all.

There are little lies, so tiny that it doesn't much matter whether you do or you don't believe them. Other lies seem small, but have huge ramifications. And sometimes it isn't a case of what you say but what you don't say. Jock's lies are always close to the truth.

Catherine was having an affair with someone at the

Marsden – a married man. She was in love with him. She reacted badly when he broke things off. On the night she died she arranged to meet someone. Was it Jock? Maybe *that's* why she called my office – because he didn't show up. Or maybe he *did* show. He's not married any more. An old flame rekindled.

It was Jock who introduced me to Bobby. He said it was a favour for Eddie Barrett.

Jesus! I can't get my head around this. I wish I could go to sleep and wake up in a different body – or a different life. Any scenario would be better than this one. My best friend – I want to be wrong about him. We've been together from the very beginning. I used to think that sharing a delivery suite made us like brothers; non-genetic twins, who breathed the same air and saw the same bright light as we entered the world.

I don't know what to think any more. He has lied to me. He's in my house and he's taking advantage of everything that has happened. I have seen the way he looks at Julianne – with an emotion far baser than envy.

Everything with Jock is a contest. A duel. And he hates it most if he thinks you're not trying because it cheapens his victories.

Catherine would have been an easy conquest. Jock could always pick the vulnerable ones, although they didn't excite him as much as girls who were self-assured and cool. His affairs caused two divorces. He couldn't help himself.

Why would Catherine have stayed in touch with someone who broke her heart? And why would she list Jock as a referee on her CV?

Someone must have told her that I needed a secretary. It's too big a coincidence to think she happened to answer an advertisement and discover that she was applying to work for me. Perhaps Jock had started seeing her again. He wouldn't have to keep it a secret this time. Not unless he was embarrassed about the trouble Catherine caused me.

What am I missing?

She left the Grand Union Hotel alone. Jock hadn't turned up, or perhaps he'd arranged to meet her later. No! This is stupid! Jock isn't capable of torturing someone – forcing her to drive a knife through her own flesh. He can be a bully but he's not a sadist.

I'm going round in circles. What do I know to be true? He knew Catherine. He knew about her self-harm. He lied about knowing her.

A touch of fear passes across my consciousness like a slight fever. Aunt Gracie would have said that someone had walked across my grave.

Euston Station on a cold clear evening. The taxi queue stretches along the footpath and up the steps. On the ride to Hampstead, watching the red digits climb on the meter, I formulate a plan.

The doorman at Jock's mansion block has gone home for the evening, but the caretaker recognises my face and buzzes me through to the foyer.

'What happened to your ear?'

'Insect bite. Infected.'

The internal staircase is stained deep mahogany and the stair-rods gleam brightly as they reflect light from the chandeliers. Jock's flat is in darkness. I open the door and notice the blinking red light of the alarm. It isn't armed. Jock has trouble remembering the code.

I leave the lights off and walk through the flat until I reach the kitchen. The black and white marble tiles are like a giant chessboard. The light above the stove illuminates the floor and lower cabinets. I don't know why I'm frightened of turning on the overhead lights. I guess this feels more like a break-in than a house call.

First I try the drawer beneath the phone, looking for some evidence that he knew Catherine – an address book or a letter or an old telephone bill. I move to the wardrobe in the main bedroom where Jock has his shirts and suits and ties arranged by colour. A dozen shirts, still wrapped in plastic, are set out on separate shelves.

At the back of the wardrobe I find a box full of hanging files, including one for bills and invoices. The most recent phone bill is in a clear plastic sleeve. The service summary provides a breakdown of STD and international calls as well as calls to mobiles.

Scanning the first list, I look for any numbers with '0151' as the prefix – the code for Liverpool. I don't have any of Catherine's numbers.

Yes I do! Her CV!

I pull the still-damp pages from my jacket and spread them carefully on the rug. The ink has run into the corners but I can still read the address. I compare the numbers with the phone bill, running down the calls made on 13 November. The numbers jump out at me – two calls to Catherine's mobile. The second was at 5:24 p.m. and lasted for just over three minutes – too long for it to be a wrong number and long enough to make a date.

343

Something doesn't make sense. Ruiz has Catherine's phone records. He must know about these calls.

Ruiz's card is in my wallet but it has almost turned to pulp after my swim in the canal. At first I get his answering machine, but before I can hang up a gruff voice curses the technology and tells me to wait. I can hear him trying to turn the machine off.

'Detective Inspector Ruiz.'

'Ah, the professor returns.' He's reading Jock's number on a display window. 'How was Liverpool?'

'How did you know?'

'A little birdie told me you needed medical treatment. Suspected assaults have to be reported. How's the ear?'

'Just a touch of frostbite.'

I can hear him eating. Shovelling down a microwave curry or takeaway.

'It's about time you and I had another little chat. I'll even send a car to pick you up.'

'I'll have to take a raincheck on that.'

'Maybe we don't understand each other. At ten o'clock this morning a warrant was issued for your arrest.'

I glance down the hallway towards the door and wonder how long it would take for Ruiz to have someone kick it off its hinges.

'Why?'

'Remember I said to you I'd find something else? Catherine McBride wrote letters to you. She kept copies. We found them on her computer disk.'

'That's impossible. I didn't get any letters.'

'Well then, you won't mind coming in to explain them.'

'There must be some mistake. This is crazy.' For a

moment I'm tempted to tell him everything – about Elisa and Jock and Catherine's CV. Instead I hold things back, bartering for information. 'You told me the last call Catherine made was to my office. But she must have made other calls that day. People must have called her. You have checked those, right? You didn't just drop everything when you saw my number on the list?'

Ruiz doesn't respond.

'There was someone else she knew from the Marsden. I think she was having an affair with him. And I think he contacted her that day – the thirteenth. Are you listening to any of this?'

I sound desperate. Ruiz isn't going to barter. He's sitting there with his crooked smile, thinking there's nothing new under the sun. Or maybe he's being sly. He's squeezing every drop out of me.

'You told me once that you collect bits of information until two or three pieces fit. Well, I'm trying to help you. I'm trying to find out the truth.'

After another age, Ruiz breaks his silence. 'You're wondering if I interviewed your friend Dr Owens about his relationship with Catherine McBride. The answer is yes. I talked to him. I asked where he was that night and, unlike you, he could give me an alibi. Shall I tell you who he was with? Or perhaps, if I let you stumble around for long enough, you'll trip over the truth. Ask your wife, Professor.'

'What's she got to do with this?'

'She's his alibi.'

13

The black cab drops me on Primrose Hill Avenue and I walk the last quarter-mile. My mind is spinning, but a cold, overwhelming current of energy has swept away my tiredness.

My vain attempts to protect people from something I don't understand have been ridiculed. Someone, somewhere, is laughing at me. What a fool! All this time I've been operating under the misapprehension that tomorrow will be different. 'Wake up and smell the roses,' Jock's always telling me. OK, now I get it – every day is going to get worse.

At the end of my street I pause, straighten my clothes and move quickly along the footpath, wary of uneven paving stones. The upper floors of my house are in darkness, except for the main bedroom and a bathroom light on the first landing.

Something makes me stop. On the far side of the road, in the deeper shadows of the plane trees, I see the faint glow of a wristwatch held up to a face. The light goes out. Nobody moves. Whoever it belongs to must be waiting.

Crouching behind a parked car, I move from vehicle to vehicle, peering over the bonnets. I can just make out a figure in the shadows. Someone else is sitting in a car. The glow of a cigarette end lights up his lips.

Ruiz has sent them. They're waiting for me.

I retrace my steps, keeping to the shadows, until I turn the corner of my street and double back around the block. In the next road over I recognise the Franklins' house directly behind ours.

I jump a side gate and cross their garden, staying away from the rectangles of light shining from the windows. Daisy Franklin is in the kitchen stirring something on the stove. Two cats appear and disappear from under her skirt. Perhaps there's a whole family under there.

I head for a gnarled cherry tree in the back corner of the garden and lever myself upwards, swinging one leg over the fence. The other leg locks up and doesn't follow. All my weight is moving forwards and I deny gravity for only a split second, flapping my arms in slow-motion before crashing head-first into the compost heap.

Cursing, I crawl on my hands and knees, crushing snails under my palms, until I emerge from the fuchsias. Light spills out from the French doors. Julianne is sitting at the kitchen table, her newly washed hair wrapped in a towel.

Her lips are moving. She's talking to someone. I crane my neck to see who it is – leaning on a large Italian olive jar, which begins to topple until I rescue it with a bear hug.

A hand reaches across the table and the fingers mesh with hers. It's Jock. I feel sick. She pulls her hand away and slaps him on the wrist like she would a naughty child. Then she crosses the kitchen and bends to put coffee cups in the dishwasher. Jock watches her every movement. I want to stick needles in his eyes.

I've never been the jealous type, but I suddenly get a bizarre flashback to a former patient who was obsessed with losing his wife. She had a great figure and he kept imagining that men were staring at her breasts. Gradually, in his eyes, her breasts grew bigger and her tops became smaller and tighter. Her every movement seemed provocative. All of this was nonsense, but not to him.

Jock is a breast man. Both his wives were surgically enhanced. Why be satisfied with nature's meagre bounty when you can be all that money can buy?

Julianne has gone upstairs to dry her hair. Jock fumbles in the pockets of his leather jacket. His shadow is framed in the French doors, just before he steps outside. Gravel crunches underfoot. A lighter flares. The cigar tip smoulders.

I kick his legs out from under him, sending him tumbling backwards, landing heavily in a shower of sparks.

'Joe!'

'Get out of my house!'

'Jesus! If there's a scorch mark on this jumper—'

'And stay away from Julianne!'

He edges away and tries to sit up.

'Stay down!'

'Why are you sneaking around out here?'

'Because the police are out front.' I make it sound so obvious.

He stares at his cigar and contemplates whether to light it again.

'You had an affair with Catherine McBride. Your name is on her fucking CV!'

'Steady on, Joe. I don't know what you're—'

'You told me that you didn't know her. You saw her that night.'

'No.'

'You arranged to meet her.'

'No comment.'

'What do you mean "no comment"?'

'Just that: no comment.'

'This is bullshit! You arranged to meet her.'

'I didn't show up.'

'You're lying.'

'All right, I'm lying,' he says sarcastically. 'Whatever you want to think, Joe.'

'Quit pissing about.'

'What do you want me to say? She was worth a poke. I arranged to meet her. I didn't show up. End of story. Don't preach to me. You screwed a hooker. You lost your chance to moralise.'

I swing a punch but this time he's ready. He sways to one side and then sinks his shoe into my groin. The pain comes as a shock and my knees buckle. My forehead is pressed against his chest as he stops me from falling.

'None of this matters, Joe,' he says in a soft voice.

Gasping for breath, I hiss, 'Of course it matters. They think I killed her.'

Jock helps me upright. I swat his hands away and step back.

'They think I had an affair with her. You could tell them the truth.'

Jock gives me a sly look. 'For all I know you were poking her as well.'

'That's bullshit and you know it!'

'You have to understand things from my point of view. I didn't want to get involved.'

'So you dump me even deeper in the shit.'

'You had an alibi – you just didn't use it.'

Alibis. That's what it comes down to. I should have been at home with my wife – my pregnant wife. She should have been *my* alibi!

It was a Wednesday night. Julianne had her Spanish class. She normally doesn't get home until after ten.

'Why didn't you keep your appointment with Catherine?'

There's a smile behind his eyes. 'I had a better offer.'

He's not going to tell me. He wants me to ask.

'You were with Julianne.'

'Yes.'

I feel something shift inside me. I'm scared now. 'Where did you see her?'

'Worry about your own alibi, Joe.'

'Answer the question.'

'We had dinner. She wanted to see me. She asked about your condition. She didn't trust you to tell her the truth.'

'And after dinner?'

'We came back here for coffee.'

'Julianne is pregnant.' I make it a statement, not a question.

I watch him contemplating another lie, but he decides

against it. We now have a mutual understanding. All his mediocre lies and half-truths have diminished him.

'Yes, she's pregnant.' Then he laughs quietly. 'Poor Joe, you don't know whether to be happy or sad. Don't you trust her? You should know her better than that.'

'I thought I knew *you*.'

A toilet flushes upstairs. Julianne is getting ready for bed.

'These letters that Catherine wrote – were they to you?'

He gives me a searching look but doesn't answer.

'Why would Catherine write to me?'

Again he doesn't respond. I have to understand this now.

His silence infuriates me. I want to take one of his tennis rackets and break his kneecaps. I have it! The answer. Jock and I have the same initials – J. O. That's how she must have addressed the letters. She wrote them to Jock.

'You have to tell the police.'

'Maybe I should tell them where you are.'

He isn't joking. Inwardly, I want to kill him. I'm sick of the contest.

'Is this about Julianne? Do you think I've been keeping the seat warm all these years? Forget it! She's not going to come running to you if something happens to me. Not if you betray me. You'll never be able to live with yourself.'

'I live with myself now, that's the problem.' His eyes are shining and his oboe voice is wavering. 'You're a very lucky man, Joe, to have a family like this. It never worked out for me.'

'You couldn't stay with any woman long enough.'

'I didn't find the right one.'

Frustration is etched on his face. Suddenly it becomes clear to me. I see Jock's life for what it is – a series of bitter, repetitive disappointments, in which his mistakes and failings have been recast over and over because he could never break the mould.

'Get out of my house, Jock, and stay away from Julianne.'

He collects his things – a briefcase and a jacket – and turns towards me as he holds up the front door key, leaving it on the kitchen counter. I see him glance upstairs as if contemplating whether to say goodbye to Julianne. He decides against it and leaves.

As the front door closes behind him I feel a hollow, nagging doubt. The police are waiting outside. He could so easily tell them.

Before I can rationalise the danger, Julianne appears downstairs. Her hair is almost dry and she's wearing pyjama bottoms and a rugby jumper. Completely still, I watch her from the garden. She gets a glass of water and turns towards the French doors to check they're locked. Her eyes meet mine and show no emotion. She reaches down and picks up a ski jacket which is hanging on the back of a chair. Slipping it around her shoulders, she steps outside.

'What happened to you?'

'I fell over the fence.'

'I'm talking about your ear.'

'A dodgy tattooist.'

She's in no mood for glib asides. 'Are you spying on me?'

'No. Why?'

She shrugs. 'Someone has been watching the house.'

'The police.'

'No. Someone else.'

'Jock said somebody tried to break in.'

'D.J. scared him off.' She makes him sound like a guard dog.

The light behind her, shining through her hair, creates a soft halo effect. She's wearing the 'ugliest slippers in the world', which I bought her from a farm-stay souvenir shop. I can't think of anything to say. I just stand there, not knowing whether to reach out for her. The moment has passed.

'Charlie wants a kitten for Christmas,' she says, hugging the jacket around her.

'I thought that was last year.'

'Yes, but now she's stumbled on the perfect formula. If you want a kitten, ask for a horse.'

I laugh and she smiles, never taking her eyes off me. The next question is framed with her usual directness.

'Did you have an affair with Catherine McBride?'

'No.'

'The police have her love letters.'

'She wrote them to Jock.'

Her eyes widen.

'They had an affair when they were both at the Marsden. Jock was the married man she was seeing.'

'When did you find out?'

'Tonight.'

Her eyes are still fixed on mine. She doesn't know whether to believe me or not.

'Why didn't Jock tell the police?'

'I'm still trying to work that out. I don't trust him. I don't want him here.'

'Why?'

'Because he lied to me and he's kept details from the

353

police and he arranged to meet Catherine on the night she died.'

'Surely you're not serious! This is Jock you're talking about. Your best friend—'

'With my wife as his alibi.' It sounds like an accusation.

Her eyes narrow to the points of knitting needles. 'An alibi for what, Joe? Do you think he killed someone or do you think he's screwing me?'

'That's not what I said.'

'No. That's right. You never say what you mean. You couch everything in parenthesis and inverted commas and open questions.' She's on a roll. 'If you're such a brilliant psychologist, you should start looking at your own defects. I'm tired of propping up your ego. Do you want me to tell you again? Here's the list. You are *nothing* at all like your father. Your penis *is* the right size. You spend more than enough time with Charlie. You don't have to be jealous of Jock. My mother really *does* like you. And I don't blame you for ruining my black cashmere jumper by leaving tissues in your pockets. Satisfied?'

Ten years of potential therapy condensed to six bullet points. My God, this woman is good. The neighbourhood dogs start barking and it sounds like a muffled chorus of 'Hear, hear!'.

She turns to go inside. I don't want her to leave so I start talking – telling her the whole story about finding Catherine's CV and searching Jock's apartment. I try to sound rational, but I'm afraid that I come across as though I'm clutching at straws.

Her beautiful face looks bruised.

'You met Jock that night. Where did you go?'

'He took me for supper in Bayswater. I knew you wouldn't tell me the truth about the diagnosis. I wanted to ask him.'

'When did you call him?'

'That afternoon.'

'What time did he leave here?'

She shakes her head sadly. 'I don't even recognise you any more. You're obsessed! I'm not the one who—'

I don't want to hear it. I blurt out: 'I know about the baby.'

She trembles slightly. It might be the cold. That's when I see the realisation in her eyes that we're losing each other. The pulse is getting weaker. She might want me but she doesn't need me. She is strong enough to cope on her own. She lived through the loss of her father; Charlie's meningitis scare when she was eighteen months old; a biopsy on her right breast. She is stronger than I am.

As I leave, breathing in the coldness of the air, I turn back to look at the rear of the house. Julianne has gone. The kitchen is in darkness. I can follow her progress as she moves upstairs, turning off the lights.

Jock has gone. Even if he tells Ruiz the truth, I doubt anyone will believe him. He will be seen as a friend trying to save my hide. I cross the Franklins' garden and slip down the side path. Then I walk towards the West End, watching my shadow appear and disappear beneath the streetlights.

A black cab slows as it passes. The driver glances at me. My hand pulls at the door handle.

Elisa doesn't see herself as a visionary and she dislikes being portrayed by journalists as some sort of evangelist who rescues girls from the streets. Nor does she see prostitutes as 'fallen women' or victims of a harsh society.

We all have undiscovered talents, but Elisa found a diamond in her hidden depths. Her reinvention came at her lowest point – six months after being released from prison. Out of the blue she left a message at the Marsden, simply giving her address and no other details. I don't know how she found me. She wore little make-up and her hair had been cut short. She looked like a junior executive in a dark skirt and jacket. She had an idea and wanted my opinion. As she talked I could sense the weather changing, not outside, but inside her head.

She wanted to set up a drop-in centre for young girls on the streets – giving advice about personal safety, health, accommodation and drug rehab programmes. She had some savings and had rented an old house near King's Cross station.

The drop-in centre proved to be just the start. Soon she had set up PAPT. I was always amazed at the people she could call upon for advice – judges, barristers, journalists, social workers and restaurateurs. I sometimes wondered how many were former clients. Then again, I helped her . . . and it had nothing to do with sex.

The 'inside out' house is in darkness. The Tudor beams glisten with frost and the small light above the doorbell flickers as I push the button. It must be after midnight and I can hear the buzzer echoing in the hall. Elisa isn't home.

I just need to put my head down for a few hours. Just to sleep. I know where Elisa hides her spare key. She won't mind. I can wash my clothes and I'll make her breakfast in the morning. That's when I'll tell her that I need her alibi after all.

Thumb and forefinger pinched together, I slide the key into the lock. Two turns. I swap keys. Another lock. The door opens. Mail spills out on the rug beneath the mail flap. She hasn't been home for a few days.

My footsteps echo on the polished floorboards. The lounge has the atmosphere of a boutique, with the embroidered pillows and Indian rugs. A light is flashing on her answering machine. The tape is full.

I see her legs first. She is sprawled on the Elizabethan love seat, with her ankles bound together with brown masking tape. Her torso is tilted back and her head is covered with a black plastic bin bag, secured with tape around her neck. Her hands are underneath her, tied behind her back. Her skirt is bunched up along her thighs and her stockings are laddered and torn.

In a heartbeat I am a doctor again, ripping plastic, feeling for a pulse, pressing my ear to her chest. Her lips are blue and her body is cold and stiff. Hair is stuck to her forehead. Her eyes are open, staring at me in wonder.

I feel a cold grinding in my chest as though a drilling machine is tunnelling through my insides. I see it all over again: the struggle and the dying; how she fought to get free. How much oxygen is in the bag? Ten minutes at most. Ten minutes to fight. Ten minutes to die. She sucked the plastic against her mouth as she twisted and kicked. There are CD cases on the floor and a trestle table is upside down. A framed photograph is lying face down, amid shattered glass. Her thin gold chain is broken at the clasp.

Poor Elisa. I can still feel the softness of her lips on my cheek when we said goodbye at the restaurant. She is wearing the same dark blue camisole and a matching mini skirt. It must have happened on Thursday, some time after she left me.

I walk from room to room, looking for evidence of a forced entry. The front door was locked from the outside. He must have taken a set of keys.

On the kitchen bench is a mug with a spoon full of coffee granules coagulated like dark toffee in the base. The kettle is lying on its side and one of the dining chairs has toppled over. A kitchen drawer is open. It contains neatly folded tea towels, a small toolbox, light fuses and a roll of black bin liners. The kitchen tidy is empty, with a fresh bag inside.

Elisa's coat is hanging on the edge of the door. Her car keys are on the table, next to her purse, two unopened letters and her mobile phone. The battery is dead. Where is her scarf? Retracing my steps, I find the scarf on the floor behind the chair. A single knot is pulled tight in the centre, forming a silken garrotte.

Elisa is far too careful to open the door to a stranger. Either she knew her killer or he was already inside. Where? How? The patio doors are made of reinforced glass and lead to a small brick courtyard. A sensor triggers the security lights.

The downstairs office is cluttered but tidy. Nothing obvious appears to have been taken, such as the DVD or Elisa's laptop.

Upstairs in the second bedroom, I check the windows again. Elisa's clothes are hanging undisturbed on racks. Her jewellery box, inlaid with mother of pearl, is in the bottom drawer of the vanity. Anyone looking would have found it soon enough.

In the bathroom the toilet seat is down. The bathmat is

hanging on a drying rail, over a large blue towel. A new tube of toothpaste sits in a souvenir mug from the House of Commons. I stand on the lever of the pedal bin and the lid swings open. Empty.

I'm about to move on when I notice a dusting of dark powder on the white tiles beneath the sink. I run my finger over the surface, collecting a fine grey residue which smells of roses and lavender.

Elisa had a painted ceramic bowl of pot pourri on the windowsill. Perhaps she accidentally broke it. She would have swept up the debris in a dustpan and emptied it into the pedal bin. Then she might have emptied the pedal bin downstairs, but there's nothing in the kitchen tidy.

Looking closely at the window, I see splinters of bare wood at the edges where paint chips have been lost. The window had been painted shut and forced open. Levering my fingers under the base, I manage to do the same, gritting my teeth as the swollen wood screeches inside the frame.

Peering outside, I see the sewage pipes running down the outside wall and the flat roof of the laundry ten feet below. Wisteria has grown over the brick wall on the right side of the courtyard, making it easy to climb. The pipes would give someone a foothold to reach the window.

Projecting the scene against my closed lids, I see someone standing on the pipes, jemmying the window. He hasn't come to steal or vandalise. He knocks over the pot pourri as he squeezes through the opening and then has to clean up. He doesn't want it to look like a break-in. Then he waits.

The cupboard beneath the stairs has a sliding bolt. It's

a storeroom for mops and brooms – big enough for someone to hide in, crouched down, staring through the gap where the hinges join the door.

Elisa arrives home. She picks up her mail from the floor and carries on to the kitchen. She drapes her coat over the door and tosses her things on the table. Then she fills the kettle and spoons coffee into a mug. One mug. He attacks her from behind – wrapping the scarf around her neck, making sure the knot compresses her windpipe. When she loses consciousness he drags her into the lounge, leaving faint tracks against the grain of the rug.

He tapes her hands and feet, carefully cutting the tape and collecting any scraps that fall on the floor. Then he puts the plastic bin liner over her head. At some point she regains consciousness and sees only darkness. By then she is dying.

A jolt of rage forces my eyes open. I see my reflection in the bathroom mirror – a despairing face full of confusion and fear. Dropping to my knees, I vomit into the toilet, bashing my chin against the seat. Then I stumble out the door and into the main bedroom. The curtains are closed and the bedclothes are crumpled and unkempt. My eyes are drawn to a wastepaper bin. Half a dozen crumpled white tissues lie inside it. Memories swim to the surface – Elisa's weight on my thighs; our bodies together; brushing her cervix each time I moved.

Suddenly I scrabble in the bin, collecting tissues. My eyes are drawn around the room. Did I touch that lamp? What about the toothbrush or the door, the windowsill, the banister . . . ?

This is madness. I can't sterilise a crime scene. There

will be traces of me all over this house. She brushed my hair. I slept in her bed. I used her bathroom. I drank wine from a wine glass, coffee from a coffee mug. I touched light switches; CD cases; dining chairs; we screwed on her sofa for God's sake!

The phone rings. My heart almost leaps out of my chest. I can't risk answering it. Nobody can know I'm here. I wait, listening to the ring and half expecting Elisa to suddenly stir and say, 'Can someone please get that? It could be important.'

The noise stops. I breathe again. What am I going to do? Call the police? No! I have to get out. At the same time, I can't leave her here. I have to tell someone.

My mobile starts to ring. I fumble through my jacket pockets and need both hands to hold it steady. I don't recognise the number.

'Is that Professor Joseph O'Loughlin?'

'Who wants to know?'

'This is the Metropolitan Police. Someone has called us about an intruder at an address in Ladbroke Grove. The informant gave this mobile as a contact number. Is that correct?'

My throat closes and I can hardly get the vowels out. I mumble something about being nowhere near that address. *No, no, that's not good enough!*

'I'm sorry. I can't hear you,' I mumble. 'You'll have to call back.' I turn off the phone and stare at the blank screen in horror. I can't hear myself thinking over the roar in my head. The volume has been steadily building until now it rattles inside my skull like a freight train entering a tunnel.

I have to get out. Run! Taking the stairs two at a time, I trip towards the bottom and fall. Run! Scooping up Elisa's car keys, I think only of fresh air, a place far away and the mercy of sleep.

14

An hour before daybreak the roads are varnished with rain and patches of fog appear and disappear between the drizzle. Stealing Elisa's car is the least of my worries. Working the clutch with a useless left leg is the more immediate problem.

Somewhere near Wrexham I pull into a muddy farm track and fall asleep. Images of Elisa sweep into my head like the headlights that periodically brush across hedgerows. I see her blue lips and her wide eyes; eyes that follow me still.

Questions and doubts go round in my head like there's a needle stuck in the groove. Poor Elisa.

'Worry about your own alibi,' was what Jock had said. What did he mean? Even if I could prove I didn't kill Catherine – which I now can't – they're going to blame me for this. They're coming for me now. In my mind I can picture policemen crossing the fields in a long straight line, holding Alsatians on leashes, riding horses, hunting me down. I stumble into ditches and claw my way up embankments. Brambles tear at my clothes. The dogs are getting closer.

There is a tap, tap, tapping sound on the window. I can see nothing but a bright light. My eyes are full of grit and my body stiff with cold. I fumble for the handle and roll down the window.

'Sorry to wake you, mister, but yer blockin' the track.' A grizzled head under a woollen hat peers at me through the window. A dog is barking at his heels and I hear the throb of a tractor engine, parked behind me.

'You don't want to go falling asleep for too long out here. It's bloody cold.'

'Thanks.'

Light grey cloud, stunted trees and empty fields lie ahead of me. The sun is up but struggling to warm the day. I reverse out of the track and watch the tractor pass through a gate and bounce over puddles towards a half-ruined barn.

As the engine idles, I turn the heater up to full blast and call Julianne on the mobile. She's awake and slightly out of breath from her exercises.

'Did you give Jock Elisa's address?'

'No.'

'Did you ever mention her name to him?'

'What's this all about, Joe? You sound scared.'

'Did you say anything?'

' . . . I don't know what you're talking about. Don't get paranoid on me . . . '

I'm shouting at her, trying to make her listen, but she gets angry.

'Don't hang up! Don't hang up!'

It's too late. Just before the connection is cut off, I yell down the phone, 'Elisa is dead!'

I hit redial. My fingers are stiff and I almost drop the phone. Julianne picks up instantly. 'What do you mean?'

'Someone killed her. The police are going to think I did it.'

'Why?'

'I found her body. My fingerprints and God knows what else are all over her flat—'

'You went to her flat!' There is disbelief in her voice. 'Why did you go there?'

'Listen to me, Julianne. Two people are dead. Someone is trying to frame me.'

'Why?'

'I don't know. That's what I'm trying to work out.'

Julianne takes a deep breath. 'You're frightening me, Joe. You're sounding crazy.'

'Didn't you hear what I said?'

'Go to the police. Tell them what happened.'

'I have no alibi. I'm their only suspect.'

'Well, talk to Simon. Please, Joe.'

Tearfully, she hangs up and this time leaves the phone off the hook. I can't get through.

God's personal physician-in-waiting opens the door in his dressing gown. He has a newspaper in one hand and an angry scowl designed to frighten off uninvited guests.

'I thought you were the blasted carol singers,' he grumbles. 'Can't stand them. None of them can hold a tune in a bucket.'

'I thought the Welsh were supposed to be great choristers.'

'Another blasted myth.' He looks over my shoulder. 'Where's your car?'

'I parked around the corner,' I lie. I had left Elisa's Beetle at the local railway station and walked the last half-mile.

He turns and I follow him along the hallway towards the kitchen. His battered carpet slippers make slapping noises against his chalk-white heels.

'Where's Mum?'

'She was up and out early. Some protest rally. She's turning into a bloody leftie – always protesting about something.'

'Good for her.'

He scoffs, clearly not in agreement.

'The garden looks good.'

'You should see out back. Cost a bloody fortune. Your mother will no doubt give you the grand tour. Those bloody lifestyle programmes on TV should be banned. Garden "make-overs" and backyard "blitzes" – I'd drop a bomb on all of them.'

He isn't the slightest bit surprised to see me, even though I've turned up unannounced. He probably thinks that Mum mentioned it to him when he wasn't listening. He fills the kettle and empties the old tealeaves from the pot.

The tablecloth is dotted with flotsam gathered on various holidays, like a St Mark's Cross tea caddie and a jam pot from Cornwall. The Silver Jubilee spoon had been a present from Buckingham Palace when they were invited to one of the Queen's garden parties.

'Would you like an egg? There isn't any bacon.'

'Eggs will be fine.'

'There might be some ham in the fridge if you want an omelette.'

He follows me around the kitchen, trying to second-guess what I need. His dressing gown is tied at the waist with a tasselled cord and his glasses are clipped to the pocket with a gold chain so that he doesn't lose them. He knows about my arrest. Why hasn't he said anything? This is his chance to say, 'I told you so.' He can blame it on my choice of career and tell me that none of this would have happened if I'd become a doctor.

He sits at the table, watching me eat, occasionally sipping his tea and folding and unfolding the *Times*. I ask him if he's playing any golf. Not for three years.

'Is that a new Mercedes out front?'

'No.'

The silence seems to stretch out, but I'm the only one who finds it uncomfortable. He sits and reads the headlines, occasionally glancing at me over the top of the paper.

The farmhouse has been in the family since before I was born. For most of that time, until my father semi-retired, it was our holiday house. He had other places in London and Cardiff. Elsewhere, teaching hospitals and universities would provide him with accommodation if he accepted visiting fellowships.

When he bought the farmhouse it had ninety acres, but he leased most of the land to the dairy farmer next door. The main house, built out of local stone, has low ceilings and strange angles, where the foundations have settled over more than a century.

I want to clean up before Mum gets home. I ask Dad if

I can borrow a shirt and maybe a pair of trousers. He shows me his wardrobe. On the end of the bed is a man's track-suit, neatly folded.

He notices me looking. 'Your mother and I go walking.'

'I didn't know.'

'It's only been the last few years. We get up early if the weather is OK. There are some nice walks in Snowdonia.'

'So I hear.'

'Keeps me fit.'

'Good for you.'

He clears his throat and goes looking for a fresh towel. 'I suppose you want a shower instead of a bath.' He makes it sound newfangled and disloyal. A true Welshman would use a tin tub in front of the coal fire.

I push my face into the jets of water, hearing it rush past my ears. I'm trying to wash away the grime of the past few days and drown out the voices in my head. This all began with a disease; a chemical imbalance; a baffling neurolog-ical disorder. It feels more like a cancer – a blush of wild cells that have infected every corner of my life, multiplying by the second and fastening on to new hosts.

I lie down in the guest bedroom and close my eyes. I just want a few minutes' rest. Wind beats against the windows. I can smell sodden earth and coal fires. I vaguely remember my father putting a blanket over me. Maybe it's a dream. My dirty clothes are hanging over his arm. He reaches down and strokes my forehead.

A while later I hear the ring of spoons in mugs and the sound of my mother's voice in the kitchen. The other sound – almost as familiar – is my father breaking ice for the ice bucket.

Opening the curtains, I see snow on the distant hills and the last of the frost retreating across the lawn. Maybe we'll have a white Christmas – just like the year Charlie was born.

I can't stay here any longer. Once the police find Elisa's body they will put the pieces together and come looking, instead of waiting for me to turn up somewhere. This is one of the first places they'll search.

Urine splatters into the bowl. My father's trousers are too big for me but I cinch in the belt, making the material gather above the pockets. They don't hear me padding along the hallway. I stand in the doorway watching them.

My mother, as always, is dressed to perfection, wearing a peach-coloured cashmere sweater and a grey skirt. She thickened around her middle after she turned fifty and has never managed to lose the weight.

She puts a cup of tea in front of my father and kisses him on the top of his head with a wet smacking sound. 'Look at this,' she says. 'My stockings have a ladder. That's the second pair this week.' He slips his hand around her waist and gives her a squeeze. I feel embarrassed. I don't remember ever seeing them share such an intimate moment.

My mother jumps in surprise and admonishes me for having 'crept up on her'. She begins fussing about what I'm wearing. She could easily take the trousers in, she says. She doesn't ask about my own clothes.

'Why didn't you tell us you were coming?' she asks. 'We've been worried sick, especially after all those ghastly *stories* in the newspapers.' She makes the tabloids sound as attractive as a soggy furball deposited on a carpet.

'Well, at least that's all over with now,' she says sternly, as if determined to draw a line under the whole episode. 'Of course, I'll have to avoid the bridge club for a while, but I daresay it will all be forgotten soon enough. Gwyneth Evans will be insufferably smug. She will think she's off the hook now. Her eldest boy, Owen, ran off with the nanny and left his poor wife with two boys to look after. Now the ladies will have something else to talk about.'

My father seems oblivious to the conversation. He is reading a book with his nose so close to the pages that it looks as though he's trying to inhale them.

'Come on, I want to show you the garden. It looks wonderful. But you must promise to come back in the spring when the blooms are out. We have our own green-house and there are new shingles on the stable roof. All that damp is gone. Remember the smell? There were rats nesting behind the walls. Awful!'

She fetches two pairs of Wellingtons. 'I can't remember your size.'

'These are fine.'

She makes me borrow Dad's Barbour and then leads the way down the back steps on to the path. The pond is frozen the colour of watery soup and the landscape is pearl grey. She points out the dry stone wall which had crumbled during my childhood but now stands squat and solid, pieced together like a three-dimensional jigsaw. A new greenhouse with glass panels and a framework of freshly milled pine backs on to the wall. Trays of seedlings cover trestle tables and spring baskets, lined with moss, hang from the ceiling. She flicks a switch and a fine spray fogs the air.

'Come and see the old stables. We've had all the junk cleared out. We could make it into a granny flat. I'll show you inside.'

We follow the path between the vegetable patch and the orchard. Mum is still talking, but I'm only half-listening. I can see her scalp beneath the parting of her grey hair.

'How was your protest meeting?' I ask.

'Good. We had over fifty people.'

'What was it all about?'

'We're trying to stop that blasted wind farm. They want to build it right on the ridge.' She points in the general direction. 'Have you ever heard a wind turbine? The noise is monstrous. Blades flashing around. The air screaming in pain.'

Standing on tiptoes, she reaches above the stable door to get the key from its hiding place.

The tightness in my chest returns. 'What did you say?'

'When?'

'Just then . . . "the air screaming in pain".'

'Oh, the windmills; they make such a horrible sound.'

She has the key in her hand. It is tied to a small piece of carved wood. Unconsciously, my hand flashes out and grips her wrist. I turn it over and the pressure makes her fingers open.

'Who gave you that?' My voice is trembling.

'Joe, you're hurting me.' She looks at the keyring. 'Bobby gave me that. He's the young man I've been telling you about. He fixed the stone wall and the shingles on the stable. He built the greenhouse and did the planting. Such a hard worker. He took me to see the windmills . . . '

For a brief moment I feel myself falling, but nothing

happens. It's like someone has tilted the landscape and I'm leaning into it, clutching the doorframe.

'When?'

'He stayed with us for three months over the summer—'

'What did he look like?'

'How can I put it politely? He's very tall, but perhaps a little overweight. Big-boned. Sweet as can be. He only wanted room and board.'

The truth isn't a blinding light or a cold bucket of water in the face. It leaks into my consciousness like a red wine stain on a pale carpet, or a dark shadow on a chest X-ray. Bobby knew things about me; things I dismissed as coincidences. Tigers and lions; Charlie's painting of the whale; Aunt Gracie . . . He knew things about Catherine and how she died. A mind-reader. A stalker. A medieval conjurer who disappears and reappears in a puff of smoke.

But how did he know about Elisa? He saw us having lunch together and then followed her home. No. I saw him that afternoon. He turned up for his appointment. That's when I lost him, by the canal – close to Elisa's house.

'*No comprenderas todavía lo que comprenderas en el futuro.*' You do not understand yet what you will understand in the end . . .

Moving suddenly, I stumble and land awkwardly on the path. Scrambling upwards, I set off in a limping run towards the house, ignoring my mother's questions about not seeing the stable.

Bursting through the door, I ricochet off the laundry wall, upsetting a washing basket and a box of detergent on a shelf. A pair of my mother's knickers catches on the toe of my boot. The nearest telephone is in the kitchen.

Julianne answers on the third ring. I don't give her time to speak.

'You said someone was watching the house.'

'Hang up, Joe, the police are trying to find you.'

'Did you see someone?'

'Hang up and call Simon.'

'Please Julianne!'

She recognises the desperation in my voice. It matches her own.

'Did you see anyone?'

'No.'

'What about the person D.J. chased out of the house – did he get a good look at him?'

'No.'

'He must have said something. Was he big, tall, over-weight?'

'D.J. didn't get that close.'

'Do you have someone in your Spanish class called Bobby or Robert or Bob? He's tall, with glasses.'

'There *is* a Bobby.'

'What's his last name?'

'I don't know. I gave him a lift home one night. He said he used to live in Liverpool—'

'Where's Charlie? Get her out of the house! Bobby wants to hurt you. He wants to punish me . . .'

I try to explain but she keeps asking me why Bobby would do such a thing? It's the one question I can't answer.

'Nobody is going to hurt us, Joe. The street is crawling with police. One of them followed me around the super-market today. I shamed him into carrying my shopping bags . . .'

Suddenly I realise that she's probably right. She and Charlie are safer at the house than anywhere else because the police are watching them . . . waiting for me.

Julianne is still talking. 'Call Simon, please. Don't do anything silly. '

'I won't.'

'Promise me.'

'I promise.'

Simon's home number is written on the back of his business card. When he answers I can hear Patricia in the background. He's sleeping with my sister. Why does that seem strange?

His voice drops to a whisper and I can hear him taking the phone somewhere more private. He doesn't want Patricia to hear the conversation.

'Did you have lunch with anyone on Thursday?'

'Elisa Velasco.'

'Did you go home with her?'

'No.'

He takes a deep breath. I know what's coming.

'Elisa was found dead at her flat. She was suffocated with a bin liner. They're coming for you, Joe. They have a warrant. They want you for murder.'

My voice is high-pitched and shaking. 'I know who killed her. He's a patient of mine – Bobby Morgan. He's been watching me . . . '

Simon isn't listening. 'I want you to go to the nearest police station. Give yourself up. Call me when you get there. Don't say anything unless I'm with you—'

'But what about Bobby Morgan?'

374

Simon's voice is more insistent. 'You *have* to do as I say. They have DNA evidence, Joe. Traces of your semen and strands of your hair; your fingerprints were in the bedroom and bathroom. On Thursday afternoon a cab driver picked you up less than a mile from the murder scene. He remembers you. You flagged him down outside the same pub where Catherine McBride went missing—'

'You wanted to know where I spent the night of the thirteenth. I'll tell you. It was with Elisa.'

'Well, your alibi is dead.'

The statement is so blunt and honest I stop trying to convince him. The facts have been laid out, one by one, revealing how hopeless my position is. Even my denials sound hollow.

My father is standing in the doorway, dressed in his tracksuit. Behind him, through the open curtains of the lounge, two police cars have pulled into the drive.

Book Three

In the real dark night of the soul it is always three o'clock in the morning, day after day.

F. Scott Fitzgerald
The Crack-up

1

Three miles is a long way when you're running in Wellington boots. It is even further when your socks have slipped down and gathered in a ball beneath your arches, making you run like a penguin.

Scrambling along muddy sheep tracks and jumping between rocks, I follow a partly frozen stream cutting through the fields. In spite of the boots I manage to keep up a good pace and only occasionally glance behind me. Right now, I'm doing everything automatically. If I stop for anything I'm finished.

My childhood holidays were spent exploring these fields. I used to know every copse and hillock; the best fishing spots and hiding places. I kissed Ethelwyn Jones in the hayloft of her uncle's barn on her thirteenth birthday. It was my first kiss with tongues and I got an instant hard-on. She leaned right into it and let out a scream, biting down hard on my bottom lip. She wore braces and had a mouth like Jaws in the James Bond films. I had a blood blister on my lip for a fortnight, but it was worth it.

When I reach the A55 I slip beneath the concrete pylons of a bridge and carry on along the stream. The banks grow steeper and twice I slide sideways into the water, breaking thin ice at the edges.

I reach a waterfall about ten feet high and drag myself upwards using tufts of grass and rocks as handholds. My knees are muddy and trousers wet. Ten minutes further on, I duck under a fence and find a track marked for ramblers.

My lungs have started to hurt but my mind is clear. As clear as the cold air. As long as Julianne and Charlie are safe, I don't care what happens to me. I feel like a rag that has been tossed around in a dog's mouth. Someone is playing with me, ripping me to shreds: my family, my life, my career . . . Why? This is all bullshit. It's like trying to read mirror writing – everything is back to front.

A hundred yards on – over a farm gate – I reach the road to Llanrhos. The narrow blacktop has hedgerows down either side, broken by farm gates and pot-holed tracks. Staying close to the ditch along one side, I head towards a church spire in the distance. Patches of mist have settled in the low ground like pools of spilled milk. Twice I leap off the road when I hear a vehicle coming. The second is a police van, with dogs barking from behind the mesh-covered windows.

The village seems deserted. The only places open are a café and an estate agent with a 'back in ten minutes' sign on the door. There are coloured lights in some of the windows and a Christmas tree in the square, opposite the war memorial. A man walking a dog nods hello to me. My teeth are clenched so hard that I can't reply.

I find a park bench and sit down. Steam is rising off my oilskin jacket. My knees are covered in mud and blood. The palms of my hands are scratched and my fingernails are bleeding. I want to close my eyes to think but I need to stay alert.

The houses around the square are like storybook cottages, with picket fences and wrought iron arbours. They have Welsh names written in flowery script beside each front door. At the top of the square, white streamers are threaded through the railings of the church and soggy confetti clings to the steps.

Welsh weddings are like Welsh funerals. They use the same cars, florists and church halls, with their ancient tea urns operated by the same ample-breasted women wearing spacious floral dresses and support hose.

The cold leaks into my limbs as the minutes tick by. A battered Land Rover turns into the square and crawls slowly around the park. I watch and wait. Nobody is following. Stiff-legged, I stand. My sweat-soaked shirt clings to the small of my back.

The passenger door groans with age and neglect. I slide into the seat. A large pillow of foam covers the rusting springs and torn vinyl. The engine is so badly tuned that it sets off a thousand rattles and clinks as my father struggles to find first gear.

'Damn machine! Hasn't been driven in months.'

'What about the police?'

'They're searching the fields. I heard them say they'd found a car at the station.'

'How did you get away?'

'I told them I had surgery. I took the Merc and swapped it for the Land Rover. Thank God it started.'

Each time we hit a puddle, water spouts like a fountain from a hole in the floor. The road twists and turns, dipping and rising through the valley. The sky is clearing to the west and the shadows of clouds sweep across the landscape on a freshening breeze.

'I'm in a lot of trouble, Dad.'

'I know.'

'I didn't kill anyone.'

'I know that too. What does Simon say?'

'I should give myself up.'

'That sounds like good advice.'

In the same breath he accepts that it won't happen and nothing he can say will change things. We're driving along the Vale of Conwy towards Snowdonia. Fields have given way to sparse woodland, with thicker forests in the distance.

The road loops through the trees and a large manor house is visible on a ridge overlooking the valley. The iron gates are closed and a 'For Sale' sign is propped against them.

'That used to be a hotel,' he says without taking his eyes off the road. 'I took your mother there on our honeymoon. It was very grand in those days. People came to tea dances of a Saturday afternoon and the hotel had its own band . . . '

Mum has told me the story before, but I've never heard it from my father.

' . . . we borrowed your uncle's Austin Healey and went touring for a week. That's when I found the farmhouse. It wasn't for sale back then, but we stopped to buy apples.

We were stopping quite often because your mother was sore. She had to sit on a pillow over the rough roads.'

He's giggling now and I realise what he means. This is more information than I really require about my mother's sexual initiation, but I laugh along with him. Then I tell him the story of my friend Scott, who knocked his new bride unconscious on a dance floor in Greece during their wedding reception.

'How did he do that?'

'He was trying to show her "the flip" and he dropped her. She woke up in hospital and didn't know what country she was in.'

Dad laughs and I laugh too. It feels good. It feels even better when we stop laughing and the silence isn't awkward. Dad glances at me out of the corner of his eye. He wants to tell me something but doesn't know how to start.

I remember when he gave me the 'coming of age' speech. He told me he had something important to tell me and took me for a walk in Kew Gardens. This was such an unusual event – spending time together – that I felt my chest swell with pride.

Dad made several attempts to start his speech. Each time he became tongue-tied he seemed to lengthen his stride. By the time he reached the bit about intercourse and taking precautions I was sprinting alongside him, trying to catch the words and stop my hat from falling off.

Now he nervously drums his fingers on the steering wheel as though trying to send me the message in Morse Code. Clearing his throat unnecessarily, he begins telling me a convoluted story about choices, responsibility and opportunities. I don't know where he's going with this.

Finally he starts telling me about when he studied medicine at university.

'. . . after that I did two years of behavioural science. I wanted to specialise in educational psychology . . . '

Hold on! Behavioural science? Psychology? He glances at me balefully and I realise that he's not joking.

'. . . my father discovered what I was doing. He was on the university board and was a friend of the Vice Chancellor. He made a special trip to see me and threatened to cut off my allowance.'

'What did you do?'

'I did what he wanted. I became a surgeon.'

Before I can ask another question he raises a hand. He doesn't want to be interrupted.

'My career was mapped out for me. I had my placements, tenures and appointments handed to me. Doors were opened. Promotions were approved . . . ' His voice drops to a whisper. 'I guess what I'm trying to say is that I'm proud of you. You stuck to your guns and did what you wanted. You succeeded on your own terms. I know I'm not an easy man to love, Joe. I don't give anything in return. But I *have* always loved you. And I will always be here for you.'

He pulls off the road into a lay-by and leaves the engine running as he gets out and retrieves a bag from the back seat.

'This is all I managed to bring,' he says, showing me the contents. There is a clean shirt, some fruit, a thermos, my shoes and an envelope stuffed with £50 notes.

'I also picked up your mobile.'

'The battery is dead.'

'Well, take mine. I never use the damn thing.'

He waits for me to slide behind the wheel and tosses the bag on the passenger seat.

'They'll never miss the Land Rover . . . not for a while. It's not even registered.'

I glance at the bottom corner of the windscreen. A beer bottle label is stuck to the glass. He grins. 'I only drive her around the fields. Decent run will do her good.'

'How will you get home?'

'Hitchhike.'

I doubt if he's thumbed a ride in his entire life. What do I know? He's been full of surprises today. He still looks like my father, but at the same time he's different.

'Good luck,' he says, shaking my hand through the window. Maybe if we'd both been standing it would have been a hug. I like to think so.

I wrestle the Land Rover into gear and pull on to the asphalt. I can see him in the rear mirror, standing at the edge of the road. I remember something he told me when Aunt Gracie died and I was hurting inside.

'Remember, Joseph, the blackest hour of your life only lasts for sixty minutes.'

The police will track me on foot along the stream. The roadblocks will take longer to organise. With any luck I will be outside any cordon they throw up. I don't know how much time this gives me. By tomorrow my face will be all over the newspapers and on TV.

My mind seems to be speeding up as my body slows down. I can't do what they expect. Instead I have to bluff and double bluff. This is one of those he-thinks-that-I-think-that-he-thinks scenarios, where each participant is trying to guess the other's next move. I have two minds to consider. One belongs to a deeply pissed-off policeman who thinks I've played him like a fool, and the other to a sadistic killer who knows how to reach my wife and daughter.

The engine of the Land Rover cuts out every few seconds. Fourth gear is almost impossible to find and, when I do, I have to hold it in place with one hand on the gearstick.

I reach over the back seat and feel for the mobile phone. I need Jock's help. I know I'm taking a risk. He's a lying bastard but I'm running out of people to trust.

He answers and fumbles the phone. I can hear him cursing. 'Why do people always call when I'm taking a piss?' I picture him trying to balance the phone under his chin and zip up his fly.

'Have you told the police about the letters?'

'Yeah. They didn't believe me.'

'Convince them. You must have something from Catherine that can help prove you were sleeping with her.'

'Yeah. Sure. I kept Polaroids so I could show my wife's divorce lawyers.'

God he can be a smug bastard. I don't have time for this. Yet I'm smiling to myself. I was wrong about Jock. He's not a killer.

'The patient you referred to me, Bobby.'

'What about him?'

'How did you meet him?'

'Like I told you – his solicitor wanted neurological tests.'

'Who suggested my name – was it you or Eddie Barrett?'

'Eddie suggested you.'

Rain has started spitting down. The wipers have only one speed – slow.

'There is a cancer hospital in Liverpool called the Clatterbridge. I want to know if they have any record of a patient by the name of Bridget Morgan. She may be using her maiden name, Bridget Aherne. She has breast cancer. Apparently it's well advanced. She might be an outpatient, or be in a hospice. I need to find her.'

I'm not asking as a favour. He either does this or our long association is irredeemably ended. Jock fumbles for an excuse but can't find one. Mostly he wants to run for cover. He has always been a coward unless he can physically intimidate someone. I won't give him the chance to wheedle out. I know that he's lied to the police. I also have too many details about the assets he kept hidden from his ex-wives.

His voice is sharp. 'They're going to catch up with you, Joc.'

'They catch up to all of us,' I say. 'Call me on this number as soon as you can.'

2

In the third form, during a holiday in Wales, I took some matches from the china bowl on the mantelpiece to make a campfire. It was near the end of a dry summer and the grass was brittle and brown. Did I mention the wind?

My smouldering bundle of twigs sparked a grass fire that destroyed two fences, a 200-year-old hedgerow and threatened a neighbouring barn full of winter-feed. I raised the alarm, screaming at the top of my lungs as I ran home with blackened cheeks and smoky hair.

I crawled into the far corner of the loft in the stables, wedging myself against the sloping roof. I knew my father was too big to reach me. I lay very still, breathing in the dust and listening to the sirens of the fire engines. I imagined all sorts of horrors. I pictured entire farms and villages ablaze. They were going to send me to jail. Carey Moynihan's brother had been sent to borstal because he set fire to a train carriage. He came out meaner than when he went in.

I spent five hours in the loft. Nobody shouted or threatened me. Dad said I should come out and take my punishment like a man. Why do young boys have to act like men? The look of disappointment on my mother's face was far more painful than the sting of my father's belt. What would the neighbours say?

Prison seems much closer now than it did then. I can picture Julianne holding up our baby across the table. 'Wave to Daddy,' she tells him (it's a boy, of course) as she tugs down her skirt self-consciously, aware of the dozens of inmates staring at her legs.

I picture a red brick building rising out of the asphalt. Iron doors with keys the size of a man's palm. I see metal landings, meal queues, exercise yards, swaggering guards, nightsticks, pisspots, lowered eyes, barred windows and a handful of snapshots taped to a cell wall.

What happens to someone like me in jail?

Simon is right. I can't run. And just like I learned in third form, I can't hide for ever. Bobby wants to destroy me. He doesn't want me dead. He could have killed me a dozen times over but he wants me alive so I can *see* what he's doing and *know* that it's him.

Will the police keep watching my home or will they call off the surveillance to focus on Wales? I don't want that. I need to know that Julianne and Charlie are safe.

The phone rings. Jock has an address for a Bridget Aherne at a hospice in Lancashire.

'I talked to the senior oncologist. They give her only weeks.'

I can hear him unwrapping the plastic from a cigar. It's early. Maybe he's celebrating. Both of us have settled for an uneasy truce. Like an old married couple, we recognise the half-truths and ignore the irritations.

'There's a photograph of you in today's papers,' he says. 'You look like a banker rather than a "Most Wanted".'

'I don't photograph well.'

'Julianne gets a mention. They describe her as being "overwrought and emotional when visited by reporters".'

'She told them to fuck off.'

'Yeah, that's what I figured too.'

I can hear him blowing smoke. 'I got to hand it to you, Joe. I always took you for a boring fart. Likeable enough, but virtuous. Look at you now! Two mistresses and a wanted man.'

'I didn't sleep with Catherine McBride.'

'Shame. She was good in the sack.' He laughs wryly.

'You should listen to yourself sometimes, Jock.'

To think I once envied him. Look at what he's become: a crude parody of a right-wing, middle-class chauvinist and bigot. I no longer trust him, but I need another favour.

'I want you to stay with Julianne and Charlie – just until I sort this out.'

'You told me not to go near her.'

'I know.'

'Sorry, I can't help you. Julianne isn't returning my calls. I figure you must have told her about Catherine and the letters. She's pissed off at both of us now.'

'At least call her; tell her to be careful. Tell her to let no one into the house.'

3

The Land Rover has a top speed of forty and a tendency to oversteer into the centre of the road. It looks more like a museum piece than a motor car and people honk when they overtake as if I'm driving for charity. This could be the most perfect getaway vehicle ever conceived because nobody expects a wanted man to escape so slowly.

I use the back roads to reach Lancashire. A mouldy road map from the glove compartment, circa 1965, keeps me on track. I pass through villages with names like Puddinglake and Woodplumpton. On the outskirts of Blackpool, at a near-deserted petrol station, I use the restroom to clean up. I sponge the mud from my trousers and hold them under the hand dryer, before changing my shirt and washing the cuts on my hands.

The Squires Gate Hospice is fixed to a rocky headland as though rusted there by the salt air. The turrets, arched windows and slate roof look Edwardian, but the out-buildings are newer and less intimidating.

Flanked by poplar trees, the driveway curves around the front of the hospital and emerges into a parking area. I follow the signs to the palliative care ward on the ocean-side. The corridors are empty and the stairways almost tidy. A black nurse with a shaved head sits behind a glass partition staring at a screen. He is playing a computer game.

'You have a patient called Bridget Aherne.'

He looks down at my knees, which are no longer the same colour as the rest of my trousers.

'Are you family?'

'No. I'm a psychologist. I need to speak to her about her son.'

His eyebrows arch. 'Didn't know she had a son. She doesn't get many visitors.'

I follow his smooth, rolling walk along the corridor, where he turns beneath the staircase and takes me through double doors leading outside. A loose gravel pathway dissects the lawn where two bored-looking nurses share a sandwich on a garden seat.

We enter a single-storey annexe nearer to the cliffs and emerge into a long shared ward with maybe a dozen beds, half of them empty. A skinny woman with a smooth skull is propped up on pillows. She is watching two young chil-dren who are scribbling on drawing paper at the end of her bed. Elsewhere, a one-legged woman in a yellow dress sits in a wheelchair in front of a television with a crocheted blanket on her lap.

At the far end of the ward, through two doors, are the

private rooms. He doesn't bother to knock. The room is dark. At first I don't notice anything except the machines. The monitors and dials create the illusion of medical mastery: as though everything is possible if you calibrate the machinery and press the right buttons.

A middle-aged woman, with sunken cheeks, is lying at the centre of the web of tubes and leads. She has a blonde wig, pendulous breasts and tar-coloured lesions on her neck. A pink chemise covers her body, with a tattered red cardigan hanging over her shoulders. A bag of solution drips along tubing that snakes in and out of her body. There are black lines around her wrists and ankles – not dark enough to be tattoos and too uniform to be bruises.

'Don't give her any cigarettes. She can't clear her lungs. Every time she coughs it shakes the tubes loose.'

'I don't smoke.'

'Good for you.' He takes a cigarette from behind his ear and transfers it to his mouth. 'You can find your own way back.'

The curtains are drawn. Music is coming from somewhere. It takes me a while to realise there is a radio playing softly on the bedside table, next to an empty vase and a copy of the Bible.

She's asleep. Sedated. Morphine, perhaps. A tube sticks out of her nose and another comes from somewhere near her stomach.

I lean my shoulder against the wall and rest my head.

'This place gives you the creeps,' she says, without opening her eyes.

'Yes.'

I sit down on a chair so she doesn't have to turn her

head to see me. Her eyes open slowly. Her face is whiter than the walls. We stare at each other in the semi-darkness.

'Have you ever been to Maui?'

'It's in Hawaii.'

'I know where it fucking is.' She coughs and the bed rattles. 'That's where I should be now. I should be in America. I should have been born American.'

'Why do you say that?'

'Because the Yanks know how to live. Everything is bigger and better. People laugh about it. They call them arrogant and ignorant, but the Yanks are just being honest. They eat little countries like this for breakfast and shit them out before lunch.'

'Have you ever been to America?'

She changes the subject. Her eyes are puffy and dribble has leaked from the corner of her mouth. 'Are you a doctor or a priest?'

'A psychologist.'

She laughs sarcastically. 'No point getting to know me. Not unless you like funerals.'

The cancer must have struck quickly. Her body hasn't had time to waste away. She is pale, with a neat chin, graceful neck and flaring nostrils. If it weren't for her surroundings and the harshness of her voice, she would still be an attractive woman.

'The problem with cancer is that it doesn't feel like cancer, you know. A head cold feels like a cold. And a broken leg feels like a broken leg. But with cancer, you don't know unless you have X-rays and scans. Except for the lump, of course. Who can forget the lump? Feel it!'

394

'That's OK.'

'Don't make a fuss. You're a big boy. Have a feel. You're probably wondering if they're real. Most men do.'

Her hand shoots out and closes around my wrist. Her grip is surprisingly strong. I fight the urge to pull away. She puts my hand under her chemise. My fingers fold into the softness of her breast. 'Just there. Can you feel it? It used to be the size of a pea – small and round. Now it's the size of an orange. Six months ago it spread to my bones. Now it's in my lungs.'

My hand is still on her breast. She brushes it over the nipple, which hardens under my palm. 'You can fuck me if you like.' She's serious. 'I'd like to feel something other than this . . . this decay.'

The look of pity on my face infuriates her. She thrusts my hand away and wraps her cardigan tightly around her chest. She won't look at me.

'I need to ask you a few questions.'

'Forget it! I don't need any of your buck-up-now speeches. I'm not in denial and I've stopped making bargains with God.'

'I'm here about Bobby.'

'What about him?'

I haven't planned what I'm going to ask her. I'm not even sure what I'm looking for.

'When was the last time you saw him?'

'Six, maybe seven years ago. He was always in trouble. Wouldn't listen to anyone. Not me, anyway. Give a kid the best years of your life and he'll always be ungrateful.' Her sentences are ragged and short. 'So what has he done now?'

'He's been convicted of a serious assault. He kicked a woman unconscious.'

'A girlfriend?'

'No, a stranger.'

Her features soften. 'You've talked to him. How is he?'

'He's angry.'

She sighs. 'I used to think they gave me the wrong baby at the hospital. It didn't feel like mine. He looked like his father, which was a shame. I couldn't see any of me in him, except his eyes. He had two left feet and a round loaf of a face. He could never keep anything clean. He had to put his hands into things, open them up, find out how they worked. He once ruined a perfectly good radio and leaked battery acid all over my best rug. Just like his father . . . '

She doesn't finish the statement, but starts again. 'I never felt what a mother is supposed to feel. I guess I'm not maternal, but that doesn't make me cold, does it? I didn't want to get pregnant and I didn't want to inherit a stepson. I was only twenty-one, for Christ's sake!'

She arches a pencil-thin eyebrow. 'You're itching to get inside my head, aren't you? Not many people are interested in what someone else is thinking or what they have to say. Sometimes people act like they're listening, when really they're waiting for their turn, or getting ready to jump in. What are you waiting to say, Mr Freud?'

'I'm trying to understand.'

'Lenny was like that; always asking questions; wanting to know where I was going and when I was coming home.' She mimics his pleading voice. ' "Who are you with, petal? Please, come home. I'll wait up for you." It was so pathetic! No wonder I got to thinking is this the best I can do. I wasn't going to lie next to his sweaty back for the rest of my life.'

'He committed suicide.'

'I didn't think he had it in him.'

'Do you know why?'

She doesn't seem to hear me. Instead she stares at the curtains. The window must look directly over the ocean.

'You don't like the view?'

She shrugs. 'There's a rumour going around that they don't bother burying us. They throw us off the cliff instead.'

'What about your husband?'

She doesn't look at me. 'He called himself an inventor. What a joke! Do you know that if he made any money – fat chance of that – he was going to give it away? "To enrich the world," he said. That's what he was like: always rambling on about empowering the workers and the proletariat revolution, making speeches and moralising. Communists don't believe in heaven or hell. Where do you think he is?'

'I'm not a religious person.'

'But do you think he might have gone somewhere?'

'I wouldn't know.'

Her armour of indifference shows a weakness. 'Maybe we're all in hell and we just don't realise it.' She pauses and half closes her eyes. 'I wanted a divorce. He said no. I told him to get himself a girlfriend. He wouldn't let me go. People say I'm cold, but I *feel* more than they do. I knew how to find pleasure. I knew how to use what I was given. Does that make me a slut? Some people spend their entire lives in denial, or making other people happy, or collecting points they think can be redeemed in the next life. Not me.'

'You accused your husband of sexually abusing Bobby.'

She shrugs. 'I just loaded the gun. I didn't fire it. People like you did that. Doctors, social workers, schoolteachers, lawyers, do-gooders . . .'

'Did we get it wrong?'

'The judge didn't think so.'

'What do you think?'

'I think that sometimes you can forget what the truth is if you hear a lie often enough.' She reaches up and pushes the buzzer above her head.

I can't leave yet. 'Why does your son hate you?'

'We all end up hating our parents.'

'You feel guilty.'

She clenches her fists and laughs hoarsely. A chrome stand holding a morphine drip swings back and forth. 'I'm forty-three years old and I'm dying. I'm paying the price for anything I've done. Can you say the same?'

The nurse arrives, looking pissed off at being summoned. One of the monitor leads has come loose. Bridget holds up her arm to have it reconnected. In the same motion she dismissively waves her hand. The conversation is over.

It has grown dark outside. I follow the path lights between the trees until I reach the car park. Taking the thermos from the bag, I swig from it greedily. The whisky tastes fiery and warm. I want to keep drinking until I can't feel the cold or notice my arm trembling.

4

Melinda Cossimo answers the door reluctantly. Visitors this late are rarely good news for a social worker, particularly on a Sunday. Weekends are when family tensions are inclined to simmer and anger boils over. Wives get beaten and children run away from home. Social workers look forward to Mondays.

I don't give her time to speak. 'The police are looking for me. I need your help.'

She blinks at me wide-eyed, but looks almost calm. Her hair is swept up and pinned high on her head with a large tortoise shell clip. Wispy strands have escaped to stroke her cheeks and neck. As the door closes, she motions me onwards, telling me to march straight up the stairs to the bathroom. She waits outside the door while I pass her my clothes.

I protest about not having the time, but she doesn't react

to the urgency in my voice. It won't take long to wash a few things, she says.

I stare at the naked stranger in the mirror. He has lost weight. That can happen when you don't eat. I know what Julianne would say: 'Why can't I lose weight that easily?' The stranger in the mirror smiles at me.

I come downstairs wearing a robe and hear Mel hang up the phone. By the time I reach the kitchen she has opened a bottle of wine and is filling two glasses.

'Who did you call?'

'Nobody important.'

She curls up in a large armchair, with the stem of her wine glass slotted between the first and second fingers of her outspread palm. Her other hand rests on the back of an open book, lying face down across the armrest. The reading lamp above her casts a shadow beneath her eyes and gives her mouth a harsh downward curve.

This has always been a house I associate with laughter and good times, but now it seems too quiet. One of Boyd's paintings hangs above the mantelpiece and another is on the opposite wall. There is a photograph of him and his motorbike at the Isle of Man TT track.

'So what have you done?'

'The police think I killed Catherine McBride, among others.'

'Among others?' One eyebrow arches like an oxbow.

'Well, just *one* "other". A former patient.'

'You're going to tell me that you've done nothing wrong.'

'Not unless being foolish is a crime.'

'Why are you running?'

'Because someone wants to frame me.'

'Bobby Morgan.'

'Yes.'

She raises her hand. 'I don't want to know any more. I'm in enough trouble for showing you the files.'

'We got it wrong.'

'What do you mean?'

'I just talked to Bridget Morgan. I don't think Bobby's father abused him.'

'She told you that!'

'She wanted out of the marriage. He wouldn't give her a divorce.'

'He left a suicide note.'

'One word.'

'An apology.'

'Yes, but for what?'

Mel's voice is cold. 'This is ancient history, Joe. Leave it alone. You know the unwritten rule – never go back, never re-open a case. I have enough lawyers looking over my shoulder without another bloody lawsuit . . .'

'What happened to Erskine's notes? They weren't in the files.'

She hesitates. 'He might have asked to have them excluded.'

'Why?'

'Perhaps Bobby asked to see his file. He's allowed to do that. A ward can see the write-ups by the duty social worker and some of the minutes of the meetings. Third-party submissions like doctors' notes and psych reports are different. We need to get permission from the specialist to release them.'

'Are you saying that Bobby saw his file?'

'Maybe.' In the same breath she dismisses the idea. 'It's an old file. Things get misplaced.'

'Could Bobby have removed the notes?'

She whispers angrily, 'You can't be serious, Joe! Worry about yourself.'

'Could he have seen the video?'

She shakes her head, refusing to say anything more. I can't let it go. Without her help, my frail improbable theory goes south. Talking quickly, as though afraid she might stop me, I tell her about the chloroform, the whales and the windmills: how Bobby has stalked me for months, infiltrating the lives of everyone around me.

At some point she puts my washed clothes in the dryer and refills my wine glass. I follow her to the kitchen and shout over the whine of the blender as it pulverises warm chickpeas. She puts a dollop of humus on slices of toast, seasoned with crushed black pepper.

'So that's why I need to find Rupert Erskine. I need his notes or his memories.'

'I can't help you any more. I've done enough.' She glances at the clock on the stove.

'Are you expecting someone?'

'No.'

'Who did you call earlier?'

'A friend.'

'Did you call the police?'

She hesitates. 'No. I left instructions with my secretary. If I didn't call her back in an hour she had to contact the police.'

I glance at the same clock, counting backwards. 'Christ, Mel!'

'I'm sorry. I have my career to think about.'

'Thanks for nothing.' My clothes aren't quite dry, but I wrestle on the trousers and shirt. She grabs at my sleeve. 'Give yourself up.'

I brush her hand aside. 'You don't understand.'

My left leg is swinging as I try to move quickly. My hand is on the front door.

'Erskine. You wanted to find him.' She blurts it out. 'He retired ten years ago. Last I heard he was living near Chester. Someone from the department contacted him a while back. We had a chat . . . caught up.'

She remembers the address – a village called Hatchmere. Vicarage Cottage. I scribble the details on a scrap of paper balanced on the hallway table. My left hand refuses to budge. My right hand will have to do.

All mornings should be so bright and clear. The sun angles through the cracked back window of the Land Rover, fracturing into a disco ball of beams. With two hands on the handle, I force a side window open and peer outside. Someone has painted the world white; turned colour into monochrome.

Cursing the stiffness of the door, I shove it open and swing my legs outside. The air smells of dirt and wood smoke. Scooping a handful of snow, I rub it into my face, trying to wake up. Then I undo my fly and pee on the base of a tree, painting it a darker brown. How far did I travel last night? I wanted to keep going but the headlights on the Land Rover kept cutting out and plunging me into darkness. Twice I nearly finished up in a ditch.

How did Bobby spend the night? I wonder if he's looking for me or watching Julianne and Charlie? He's not going to wait for me to figure this out. I need to hurry.

Hatchmere lake is fringed with reeds and the water reflects the blueness of the sky. I stop at a red and white painted house and ask for directions. An old lady, still in her dressing gown, answers the door and mistakes me for a tourist. She starts giving me the history of Hatchmere, which segues into her own life story about her son who works in London and her grandchildren whom she only sees once a year.

I keep thanking her and backing away. She stands at her front gate as I struggle to start the Land Rover. That's just what I need. She's probably an expert on cribbage, crosswords and remembering licence plates. 'I never forget a number,' she'll say as she rattles it off to police.

The engine kindly turns over and fires, belching smoke from the exhaust. I wave and smile. She looks concerned for me.

Vicarage Cottage has Christmas lights strung over the windows and doors. Parked on the front path are a handful of toy cars, circled like wagons around an old milk crate. Hanging diagonally across the path is a rust-stained bed sheet with two ends tied to a tree. A boy squats underneath with a plastic ice-cream bucket on his head. He points a wooden stick at my chest.

'Are you a Slytherin?' he says with a lisp.

'Pardon?'

'You can only come in here if you're from Gryffindor.' The freckles on his nose are the colour of toasted corn.

A young woman appears at the door. Her blonde hair

is sleep-tossed and she's fighting a cold. A baby is perched on her hip, sucking on a small piece of toast.

'You leave the man alone, Brendan,' she says, smiling at me tiredly.

Stepping around the toys, I reach the door. I can see an ironing board set up behind her.

'I'm sorry about that. He thinks he's Harry Potter. Can I help you?'

'Hopefully, yes. I'm looking for Rupert Erskine.'

A shadow crosses her face. 'He doesn't live here any more.'

'Do you know where I might find him?'

She swaps her baby on to her opposite hip and does up a loose button on her blouse. 'You'd be better asking someone else.'

'Would one of the neighbours know? It's very important that I see him.'

She bites her bottom lip and looks past me towards the church. 'Well, if you want to see him you'll find him over there.'

I turn to look.

'He's in the cemetery.' Realising how blunt the statement sounds, she adds, 'I'm sorry if you knew him.'

Without making a conscious decision I find myself sitting down on the steps. 'We used to work together,' I explain. 'It was a long time ago.'

She glances over her shoulder. 'Would you like to come in and sit down?'

'Thank you.'

The kitchen smells of sterilised bottles and porridge. There are crayons and pieces of paper spread over the table and chair. She apologises for the mess.

'What happened to Mr Erskine?'

'I only know what the neighbours told me. Everyone in the village was pretty shook up by what happened. You don't expect that sort of thing – not round these parts.'

'What sort of thing?'

'They say he came across someone trying to rob the place, but I don't see how that explains anything. What sort of burglar ties an old man to a chair and tapes his mouth? He lived for two weeks. Some folks say he had a heart attack, but I heard he died of dehydration. It was the hottest fortnight of the year . . . '

'When was this?'

'August just gone. I reckon some folks are feeling guilty because nobody noticed him missing. He was always pottering in the garden and taking walks by the lake. Someone from the church choir knocked on the door and a man came to read the gas meter. The front door was unlocked, but nobody thought to go inside.' The baby is squirming in her arms. 'Are you sure you won't have a cup of tea? You don't look too good.'

I can see her lips moving and hear the question, but I'm not really listening. The ground has dropped away beneath me like a plunging lift. She's still talking, ' . . . a really nice old man, people say. A widower. You probably know that already. Don't think he had any other family . . . '

I ask to use her phone and need both hands to hold the receiver. The numbers are barely legible. Louise Elwood answers. I have to stop myself from shouting.

'The deputy headmistress at St Mary's – you said that she resigned for family reasons.'

'Yes. Her name was Alison Gorski.'

'When was that?'

'About eighteen months ago. Her mother died in a house fire and her father was badly burned. She moved to London so she could nurse him. I think he's in a wheelchair.'

'How did the fire start?'

'They think it was a case of mistaken identity. Someone put a petrol bomb through the letterbox. The newspapers thought it might have been an anti-Jewish thing, but there was never anything more said.'

A rush of fear becomes liquid on my skin. My eyes fix on the young woman who is watching me anxiously from beside the stove. She is frightened of me. I have brought something sinister into her house.

I make another call. Mel picks up immediately. I don't give her time to speak. 'The car that hit Boyd: what happened to the driver?' My voice sounds strident and thin.

'The police have been here, Joe. A detective called Ruiz—'

'Just tell me about the driver.'

'It was a hit and run. They found the four-wheel drive a few blocks away.'

'And the driver?'

'They think it was probably a teenage joy-rider. There was a thumbprint on the steering wheel but it matched nothing on file.'

'Tell me exactly what happened.'

'Why? What's this got to do—'

'Please, Mel.'

She stumbles over the first part of the story, trying to remember whether it was seven-thirty or eight-thirty that evening when Boyd went out. It upsets her to think she

407

could have forgotten a detail like this. She worries that Boyd might be growing fainter in her memories.

It was bonfire night. The air was laced with gunpowder and sulphur. Neighbourhood kids, giddy with excitement, had gathered round bonfires built from scrap wood on allotments and waste ground. Boyd often went out of an evening for tobacco. He went to his local for a quick pint and picked up his favourite blend from an off-licence on the way. He wore a fluorescent vest and a canary yellow helmet. His grey ponytail hung down his back. He paused at an intersection on Great Homer Street.

Perhaps he turned at the last moment, when he heard the car. He might even have seen the driver's face in that fraction of a second before he disappeared beneath the bullbar. His body was dragged for a hundred yards beneath the chassis, caught in the twisted frame of the motorbike.

'What's going on?' asks Mel. I imagine her wide red mouth and timid grey eyes.

'Lucas Dutton: where is he now?'

Mel answers in a calm, quavering voice. 'He works for some government advisory body on teenage drug use.'

I remember Lucas. He dyed his hair; played golf off a low handicap; collected matchbooks and blends of Scotch. His wife was a drama teacher; they drove a Skoda and went on holidays to a caravan in Bognor; they had twin girls . . .

Mel is demanding an explanation but I talk over her. 'What happened to the twins?'

'You're scaring me, Joe.'

'What happened to them?'

'One of them died last Easter of a drug overdose.'

I am ahead of her now, reading a list of names: Justice

McBride, Melinda Cossimo, Rupert Erskine, Lucas Dutton, Alison Gorski – all were involved in the same child protection case. Erskine is dead. The others have all lost someone close to them. What has this got to do with me? I only interviewed Bobby the once. Surely that isn't enough to explain the windmills, the Spanish lessons, the Tigers and Lions . . . Why did he spend months living in Wales, landscaping my parents' garden and fixing the old stables?

Mel is threatening to hang up on me. I can't let her go. 'Who put together the legal submission for the care order?'

'I did, of course.'

'You said Erskine was on holiday. Who signed off on the psych report?'

She hesitates. Her breathing changes. She is about to lie. 'I don't remember.'

More insistent this time: 'Who signed the psych report?'

She speaks straight through me, directly into the past. 'You did.'

'How? When?'

'I put the form in front of you and you signed. You thought it was a foster parent authorisation. It was your last day in Liverpool. We were having farewell drinks at the Windy House.'

I moan inwardly, the phone still to my ear. 'My name was in Bobby's files?'

'Yes.'

'You took it out of the folders before you showed them to me?'

'It was a long time ago. I thought it didn't matter.'

I can't answer her. I let the phone fall from my hand. The young mother is clutching her baby tightly in her arms, jiggling him up and down to calm his cries. As I retreat down the steps, I hear her calling her older son inside. Nobody wants to be near me. I am like an infectious disease. An epidemic.

5

George Woodcock called the ticking of the clock a mechanical tyranny that turned us into servants of a machine that we created. We are held in fear of our own monster – just like Baron von Frankenstein.

I once had a patient, a widower living alone, who became convinced that the ticking of a clock above his kitchen table sounded like human words. The clock would give him short commands. 'Go to bed!' 'Wash the dishes!' 'Turn off the lights!' At first he ignored the sound, but the clock repeated the instructions over and over, always using the same words. Eventually he began to follow the orders and the clock took over his life. It told him what to have for dinner and what to watch on TV; when to do the laundry; which phone calls to return . . .

When he first sat in my consulting room, I asked him whether he wanted a tea or a coffee. He didn't reply at first. He nonchalantly wandered over to the wall clock and after a moment he turned and said that a glass of water would be fine.

Strangely, he didn't want to be cured. He could have removed all clocks from his house or gone digital, but there was something about the voices that he found reassuring and even comforting. His wife, by all accounts, had been a fusspot and a well-organised soul, who hurried him along, writing him lists, choosing his clothes and generally making decisions for him.

Instead of wanting me to stop the voices, he needed to be able to carry them with him. The house already had a clock in every room, but what happened when he went outside?

I suggested a wristwatch, but for some reason these didn't speak loudly enough or they babbled incoherently. After much thought, we went shopping at Gray's Antique Market and he spent more than an hour listening to old-fashioned pocket watches, until he found one that quite literally spoke to him.

The clock I hear ticking could be the knocking of the Land Rover's engine. Or it could be the doomsday clock – seven minutes to midnight. My perfect past is fading into history and I can't stop the clock.

Two police cars pass me on the road out of Hatchmere, heading in the opposite direction. Mel must have finally given them Erskine's address. They can't know about the Land Rover – not yet, at least. The little old lady with the photographic memory will tell them. With any luck she'll recount her life story first, giving me time to get away.

I keep glancing in the rear mirror, half expecting to see

flashing blue lights. This will be the opposite of a high-speed police chase. They could overtake me on bicycles unless I can find fourth gear. Maybe we'll have one of those O.J. Simpson moments, a slow-motion motorcade, filmed from the news helicopters.

I remember the final scene of *Butch Cassidy and the Sundance Kid*, when Redford and Newman keep wisecracking as they go out to face the Mexican army. Personally, I'm not quite as fearless about dying. And I can't see anything glorious about a hail of bullets and a closed coffin.

Lucas Dutton lives in a red brick house in a suburban street, where the corner shops have disappeared and been replaced by drug dealers and brothels. Every blank wall is covered in spray paint. Even the folk art and Protestant murals have been spoiled. There is no sense of colour or creativity. It is mindless, malicious vandalism.

Lucas is perched on a ladder in the driveway, unbolting a basketball hoop from the wall. His hair is even darker, but he's thickened around the waist and his forehead is etched with frown lines that disappear into bushy eyebrows.

'Do you need a hand?'

He looks down and takes a moment to put a name to my face.

'These things are rusted on,' he says, tapping the bolts. Descending the ladder, he wipes his hands on his shirt-front and shakes my hand. At the same time he glances at the front door, betraying his nerves. His wife must be inside. They will have seen the news reports or heard the radio.

I can hear music coming from an upstairs window:

something with lots of thumping bass and shuffling turn-tables. Lucas follows my eyes.

'I tell her to turn it down but she says that it has to be loud. Sign of age, I guess.'

I remember the twins. Sonia was a good swimmer – in the pool, in the sea, she had a beautiful stroke. I was invited to a barbecue one weekend when she must have been about nine. She announced that she was going to swim the Channel one day.

'It'll be much quicker to take the tunnel,' I'd told her.

Everyone had laughed. Sonia had rolled her eyes. She didn't like me after that.

Her twin sister Claire was the bookish one, with steel-framed glasses and a lazy eye. She spent most of the barbecue in her room, complaining that she couldn't hear the TV because everyone outside was 'gibbering like monkeys'.

Lucas is folding up the ladder and explaining that 'the girls don't use the hoop any more'.

'I was sorry to hear about Sonia,' I say.

He acts as though he doesn't hear me. Tools are packed away in a toolbox. I'm about to ask him what happened when he starts telling me that Sonia had just won two titles at the national swimming championships and had broken a distance record.

'Yet even after all that training, all those early morning laps, mile after mile, she knew she wasn't going to be good enough. There is a fine line between being good and being great . . .'

I let him talk because I sense he's making a point. The story unfolds. Sonia Dutton, not quite twenty-three, dressed

414

up for a rock concert. She went with Claire and a group of friends from university. Someone gave her a white pill imprinted with a shell logo. She had always been so careful about medication and health supplements. She danced all night until her heartbeat grew rapid and her blood pressure soared. She felt faint and anxious. She collapsed in a toilet cubicle.

Lucas is still crouched over the toolbox as though he's lost something. His shoulders are shaking. In a rasping voice, he describes how Sonia spent three weeks in a coma, never regaining consciousness. Lucas and his wife argued over whether to turn off her life-support. He was the pragmatist. He wanted to remember her gliding through the water, with her smooth stroke. His wife accused him of giving up hope; of thinking only of himself; of not praying hard enough for a miracle.

'She hasn't said more than a dozen words to me since – not all together in a sentence. Last night she told me that she saw your photograph on the news. I asked her questions that she answered. It was the first time in ages . . . '

'Who gave Sonia the tablet? Did they ever catch anyone?'

Lucas shakes his head. Claire gave them a description. She looked at mugshots and a police line-up.

'What did she say he looked like?'

'Tall, skinny, tanned . . . he had slicked-back hair.'

'How old?'

'Mid-thirties.'

He closes the toolbox and flips the metal catches, before glancing despondently at the house, not yet ready to go inside. Chores like the basketball hoop have become important because they keep him busy and out of the way.

'Do you remember Bobby Morgan?'

'Yes.'

'When was the last time you saw him?'

'Fourteen . . . fifteen years ago. He was only a kid.'

'Not since then?'

He shakes his head and then narrows his eyes as if something has just occurred to him. 'Sonia knew someone called Bobby Morgan. It could have been the same person. He worked at the swimming centre.'

'You never saw him?'

'No.' He sees the curtains moving in the lounge. 'I wouldn't stick around if I were you,' he says. 'She'll call the police if she sees you.'

The toolbox is weighing down his right hand. He swaps it over and glances up at the basketball hoop. 'Guess that'll have to stay there a bit longer.'

I thank him and he hurries inside. The door shuts and the silence amplifies my steps as I walk away. I used to think Dutton was conceited and dogmatic, unwilling to listen or alter his point of view when it came to case conferences. He was the sort of autocratic, nit-picking public servant who is brilliant at making the trains run on time but fails miserably when it comes to dealing with people. If only his staff could be as loyal as his Skoda – starting first time on cold mornings and reacting immediately to every turn of the steering wheel. Now he has been diminished, lessened, beaten down by circumstances.

The man who gave Sonia the tainted white tablet doesn't sound like Bobby but eyewitness accounts are notoriously unreliable. Stress and shock can alter perceptions. Memory is flawed. Bobby is a chameleon, changing colours, camouflaging himself, moving backwards and forwards, but always blending in.

There is a poem that Aunt Gracie used to recite to me – a politically incorrect piece of doggerel called Ten Little Indian Boys. It started off with ten little Indian boys going out to dine, but one chokes himself and then there were nine. All nine little Indian boys stay up late, but one oversleeps and then there are eight . . .

Indian boys are stung by bees, eaten by fish, hugged by bears and chopped in half until only one remains, left alone. I feel like that last little Indian boy.

I understand what Bobby is doing now. He is trying to take away what each of us holds most dear – the love of a child, the closeness of a partner, the sense of belonging. He wants us to suffer as he suffered, to lose what we most love, to experience *his* loss.

Mel and Boyd had been soulmates. Anyone who knew them could see that. Jerzy and Esther Gorski had survived the Nazi gas chambers and settled in north London, where they raised their only child, Alison, who became a schoolteacher and moved to Liverpool. Firemen discovered Jerzy's body at the bottom of the stairs. He was still alive, despite the burns. Esther suffocated in her sleep.

Catherine McBride, a favoured granddaughter in a well-connected family – wayward, spoiled and smothered, she had never lost the heart of her grandfather, who doted on her and forgave her indiscretions.

Rupert Erskine had no wife or children. Perhaps Bobby couldn't discover what he held most dear or perhaps he knew all along. Erskine was a cantankerous old sod, about as likeable as a carpet burn. We made excuses for him because it can't have been easy looking after his wife for all those years. Bobby didn't give him any latitude. He left him alive long enough – tied to a chair – to regret his limitations.

There might be other victims. I don't have time to find them all. Elisa is my failure. I didn't discover Bobby's secret soon enough. Bobby has grown more sophisticated with each death but I am to be the prize. He could have taken Julianne or Charlie from me, but instead he has chosen to take it all – my family, friends, career, reputation and finally my freedom. And he wants me to *know* that he's responsible.

The whole point of analysis is to understand, not to take the essence of something and reduce it to something else. Bobby once accused me of playing God. He said people like me couldn't resist putting our hands inside someone's psyche and changing the way they view the world.

Maybe he is right. Maybe I've made mistakes and fallen into the trap of not thinking hard enough about cause and effect. And I know it isn't good enough, in the wash-up, to make excuses and say, 'I meant well.' That's what they told Gracie when they took her baby away. I've used the same words. 'With the best possible intentions . . . ' and 'with all the goodwill in the world . . . '

In one of my first cases in Liverpool I had to decide if a mentally handicapped twenty-year-old, with no family support and a lifetime of institutionalised care, could keep her unborn child.

I can still picture Sharon with her summer dress stretched tightly over the swell of her pregnancy. She had taken great care, washing and brushing her hair. She knew how important the interview was for her future. Yet despite her efforts, she had forgotten little things. Her socks were the same colour but different lengths. The zipper at the side of her dress was broken. A smudge of lipstick stained her cheek.

'Do you know why you're here, Sharon?'

'Yes, sir.'

'We have to decide whether you can look after your baby. It's a very big responsibility.'

'I can. I can. I'll be a good mother. I'm going to love my baby.'

'Do you know where babies come from?'

'It's growing inside me. God put it there.' She spoke very reverentially and rubbed her tummy.

I couldn't fault her logic. 'Let's play a "what if" game, OK? I want you to imagine that you're bathing your baby and the telephone rings. The baby is all slippery and wet. What do you do?'

'I . . . I . . . I . . . put my baby on the floor, wrapped in a towel.'

'While you are on the telephone, someone knocks on the front door. Do you answer it?'

She momentarily looked unsure. 'It might be the fire brigade,' I added. 'Or maybe it's your social worker.'

'I'd answer the door,' she said, nodding her head forcefully.

'It turns out to be your neighbour. Some young boys have thrown a rock through her window. She has to go to work. She wants you to sit inside her flat and wait for the glaziers to come.'

'Those little shits – they're always throwing rocks,' Sharon said, bunching her fists.

'Your neighbour has satellite TV: movie channels; cartoons; daytime soap operas. What are you going to watch while you're waiting?'

419

'Cartoons.'

'Will you have a cup of tea?'

'Maybe.'

'Your neighbour has left you some money to pay the glazier. Fifty quid. The job is only going to cost forty-five, but she says you can keep the change.'

Her eyes lit up. 'I can keep the money?'

'Yes. What are you going to buy?'

'Chocolate.'

'Where are you going to buy it?'

'Down the shops.'

'When you go to the shops, what do you normally take?'

'My keys and my purse.'

'Anything else?'

She shook her head.

'Where is your baby, Sharon?'

A look of panic spread across her face and her bottom lip began to tremble. Just when I thought she was going to cry, she suddenly announced, 'Barney will look after her.'

'Who's Barney?'

'My dog.'

A couple of months later, I sat outside the delivery suite and listened to Sharon sobbing as her baby boy was swaddled in a blanket and taken away from her. It was my job to transfer the boy to a different hospital. I strapped him in a carrycot on the back seat of my car. Looking down at the sleeping bundle, I wondered what he'd think, years from then, about the decision I had made for him? Would he thank me for rescuing him or blame me for ruining his life?

A different child has come back. His message is clear. We have failed Bobby. We failed his father – an innocent man, arrested and questioned for hours about his sex life and the length of his penis. His house and workplace were searched for child pornography that didn't exist and his name put on a central index of sex offenders despite him never having been charged, let alone convicted.

This indelible stain was going to blot his life for ever. All his future relationships would be tainted. Wives and partners would have to be told. Fathering a child would become a risk. Coaching a kids' soccer team would be downright reckless. Surely this is enough to drive a man to suicide.

Socrates – the wisest of all Greeks – was wrongly convicted of corrupting the youth of Athens and sentenced to death. He could have escaped but he drank the poison. Socrates believed that our bodies are less important than our souls. Maybe he had Parkinson's.

I share the blame for Bobby. I was part of the system. Mine was the cowardice of acquiescence. Rather than disagree I said nothing. I went along with the majority view. I was young, just starting my career, but that is no excuse. I acted like a spectator instead of a referee.

Julianne called me a coward when she threw me out. I know what she means now. I have sat in the grandstand, not wanting to get drawn into my marriage or my disease. I kept my distance, scared of what might happen. I have let my own state of mind absorb me. I was so worried about rocking the boat, I failed to spot the iceberg.

6

Three hours ago I came up with a plan. It wasn't my first. I worked my way through about a dozen, looking at all the fundamentals, but each had a fatal flaw. I have enough of those already. My ingenuity has to be tempered by my physical limitations. This meant jettisoning anything that requires me to abseil down a building, overpower a guard, short-circuit a security system or crack open a safe.

I also shelved any plan that didn't have an exit strategy. That's why most campaigns fail. The players don't think far enough ahead. The end game is the boring bit, the mopping-up operation, without the glamour and excitement of the principal challenge. Therefore, people get frustrated and only plan so far. From then on they imagine winging it, confident in their ability to master their retreat as skilfully as their advance.

I know this because I have had people in my consulting

room who cheat, steal and embezzle for a living. They own nice houses, send their children to private schools and play off single figure handicaps. They vote Tory and view law and order as an important issue because the streets just aren't safe any more. These people rarely get caught and hardly ever go to prison. Why? Because they plan for every outcome.

I am sitting in the darkest corner of a car park in Liverpool. On the seat beside me is a waxed paper shopping bag with a pleated rope handle. My old clothes are inside it and I'm now wearing new charcoal grey trousers, a woollen jumper and an overcoat. My hair is neatly trimmed and my face is freshly shaved. Lying between my legs is a walking stick. Now that I'm walking like a cripple I might as well get some sympathy for it.

The phone rings. I don't recognise the number on the screen. For a split second I wonder whether Bobby could have found me. I should have known it would be Ruiz.

'You surprise me, Professor O'Loughlin.' His voice is all gravel and phlegm. 'I figured you for the sort who would turn up at the nearest police station with a team of lawyers and a PR man.'

'I'm sorry if I disappoint you.'

'I lost twenty quid. Not to worry – we're running a new book. We're taking bets on whether you get shot or not.'

'What are the odds?'

'I can get three to one on you dodging a bullet.'

I hear traffic noise in the background. He's on a motorway.

'I know where you are,' he says.

'You're guessing.'

'No. And I know what you're trying to do.'

'Tell me.'

'First you tell me why you killed Elisa.'

'I didn't kill her.' Ruiz draws deeply on a cigarette. He's smoking again. I feel a curious sense of achievement. 'Why would I kill Elisa? That's where I spent the night on the thirteenth of November. She was my alibi.'

'That's unfortunate for you.'

'She wanted to give a statement, but I knew you wouldn't believe her. You'd drag up her past and humiliate her. I didn't want to put her through it all again . . . '

He laughs the way Jock often does, as though I'm soft in the head.

'We found the shovel,' he says. 'It was buried under a shit-load of leaves.'

What's he talking about? Think! There was a shovel leaning on Gracie's grave.

'The boys and girls at the lab did us proud again. They matched the soil samples found on the shovel with those taken from Catherine's grave. And then they matched the fingerprints on the handle with yours.'

When does this end? I don't want to know any more. Instead I talk over Ruiz, trying to keep the desperation out of my voice. I tell him to go back to the beginning and look for the red edge.

'His name is Bobby Morgan – not Moran. Read the case notes. All the pieces are there. Put them together . . . '

He's not listening to me. It's too big for him to comprehend.

'Under different circumstances I might admire your enthusiasm, but I have enough evidence already,' he says.

'I have motive, opportunity and physical evidence. You couldn't have marked your territory any better if you'd pissed in every corner.'

'I can explain—'

'Good! Explain it to a jury! That's the beauty of our legal system – you get plenty of chances to state your case. If the jury don't believe you, you can appeal to the High Court and then the House of Lords and the European Court of Human Sodding Rights. You can spend the rest of your life appealing. It obviously helps pass the time when you're banged up for life.'

I press the 'end call' button and turn off the phone.

Leaving the car park, I descend the stairs and emerge on street level. I dump my old clothes and shoes in a rubbish bin, along with the holdall and the soggy scraps of paper from my hotel room. As I head along the street, I swing my cane in what I hope is a jaunty, cheerful way. The shoppers are out and every store is bedecked with tinsel and playing Christmas carols. It makes me feel homesick. Charlie loves that sort of stuff – the department store Santas, window displays and watching old Bing Crosby movies set in Vermont.

As I'm about to cross the road, I spot a poster on the side of a newspaper van. 'MANHUNT FOR CATHERINE'S KILLER'. My face is underneath, pinned beneath the plastic ties. Instantly I feel like I'm wearing a huge neon sign on my head with the arrow pointing downwards.

The Adelphi Hotel is ahead of me. I push through the revolving door and cross the foyer, fighting the urge to quicken my stride. I tell myself not to walk too quickly or hunch over. Head up. Eyes straight ahead.

It's a grand old railway hotel, dating back to a time when steam trains arrived from London and steam ships left for New York. Now it looks as tired as some of the waitresses, who should be at home putting curlers in their hair.

The business centre is on the first floor. The secretary is a skinny thing called Nancy, with permed red hair and a red cravat around her neck that matches her lipstick. She doesn't ask for a business card or check if I have a room number.

'If you have any questions, just ask,' she says, keen to help.

'I'll be fine. I need to check my e-mails.' I sit at a computer terminal and turn my back to her.

'Actually, Nancy, you could do something for me. Can you find out if there are any flights to Dublin this afternoon?'

A few minutes later she rattles off a list. I choose the late afternoon shuttle and I give her my credit card details.

'Can you also see about getting me to Edinburgh?' I ask.

She raises an eyebrow.

'You know what head offices are like,' I explain. 'They can never make a decision.'

She nods and smiles.

'And see if there's a sleeper available on the Isle of Man ferry.'

'The tickets are non-refundable.'

'That's OK.'

In the meantime, I search for the e-mail addresses of all the major newspapers and gather the names of news editors, chief reporters and police roundsmen. I start typing an e-mail using my right hand, pressing one key at a time. I tuck my left hand under my thigh to stop it trembling.

I start with proof of my identity – giving my name, address, National Insurance number and employment details. They can't think this is a hoax. They have to believe that I am Joseph O'Loughlin – the man who killed Catherine McBride and Elisa Velasco.

It is just after 4.00 p.m. Editors are deciding the running order for stories in the first edition. I need to change tomorrow's headlines. I need to knock Bobby off his stride – to keep him guessing.

Up until now he's always been two, three, four steps ahead of me. His acts of revenge have been brilliantly conceived and clinically executed. He didn't simply apportion blame. He turned it into an art form. But for all his genius, he is capable of making a mistake. Nobody is infallible. He kicked a woman unconscious because she reminded him of his mother.

To whom it may concern:

This is my confession and testament. I, Joseph William O'Loughlin, do solemnly, sincerely and truly affirm that I am the man responsible for the murders of Catherine McBride and Elisa Velasco. I apologise to those who grieve at their loss. And for those of you who thought better of me, I am genuinely sorry.

I intend to give myself up to the police within the next 24 hours. At that point I will not seek to hide behind lawyers or to excuse the suffering I have caused. I will not claim there were voices inside my head. I wasn't high on drugs or taking instructions from Satan. I could have stopped this. Innocent people have died. My every hour is long with guilt.

I list the names, starting with Catherine McBride. I put down everything I know about her murder. Boyd Cossimo is next. I describe Rupert Erskine's last days; Sonia Dutton's overdose; the fire that killed Esther Gorski and crippled her husband. Elisa comes last.

I do not plead any kind of mitigation. Some of you may wish to know more about my crimes. If so, you must walk in my shoes, or find someone who has done so. There is such a person. His name is Bobby Moran (aka Bobby Morgan) and he will appear at the Central Criminal Court in London tomorrow morning. He, more than anyone, understands what it means to be both victim and perpetrator.

Sincerely yours,
Joseph O'Loughlin.

I have thought of everything, except what this will mean to Charlie. Bobby was a victim of a decision made beyond his control. I'm doing the same thing to my daughter. My finger hovers over the send button. I have no choice. The e-mail disappears into the labyrinth of the electronic post office.

Nancy thinks I'm mad but has made my travel arrangements, booking flights to Dublin, Edinburgh, London, Paris and Frankfurt. In addition there are first-class seats on trains to Birmingham, Newcastle, Glasgow, London, Swansea and Leeds. She has also managed to hire me a white Vauxhall Cavalier, which is waiting downstairs.

Everything has been paid for with a debit card that doesn't require authorisation from a bank. The card is linked to a trust account set up by my father. Inheritance tax is another of his pet hates. I'm assuming Ruiz will have frozen all my accounts but he can't touch this one.

The lift doors open and I set out across the foyer, staring straight ahead. I bump into a potted palm and realise that I'm drifting sideways. Walking has become a constant assortment of adjustments and corrections, like landing a plane.

The hire car is parked outside. As I walk down the front steps of the hotel I keep expecting to feel a hand on my shoulder or to hear a shout of recognition or alarm. My fingers fumble with the keys. Black cabs are queued in front of me but one of them eases out of my way. I follow the stream of traffic, glancing in the mirrors and trying to remember the quickest way out of the city.

Stopped at a red light, I look beyond the stream of pedestrians at the multi-storey car park. Three police cars are blocking the entry ramp and another is on the pavement. Ruiz is leaning on an open door, talking on the radio. He has a face like thunder.

As the lights change to green, I imagine him looking up and me saluting him like a World War I flying ace in a crippled plane, living to fight another day.

One of my favourite songs is on the radio - - 'Jumpin' Jack Flash'. At university I played bass guitar for a band called the Screaming Dick Nixons. We weren't as good as the Rolling Stones but we were louder. I knew nothing about playing the bass guitar but it was the easiest instrument to fake. Mostly my ambition was to get laid but that only ever happened to our lead singer, Morris Whiteside, who had long hair and a crucifixion scene tattooed on his torso. He's now a senior accountant working for Deutsche Bank.

I head west towards Toxteth and park the Cavalier in a vacant plot, among the cinders and weeds. A handful of teenagers watch me from the shadows beside a boarded-up community hall. I'm driving the sort of fancy car they normally only see on bricks.

I phone home. Julianne answers. Her voice sounds close, crystal clear, but already starting to shake. 'Thank God! Where have you been? Reporters keep ringing the door-bell. They say you're dangerous. They say the police are going to shoot you.'

I try to steer the conversation away from firearms. 'I know who did this. Bobby is trying to punish me for some-thing that happened a long time ago. It isn't just me. He has a list of names—'

'What list?'

'Boyd is dead.'

'How?'

'He was murdered. So was Erskine.'

'My God!'

'Are the police still watching the house?'

'I don't know. There was someone in a white van yesterday. At first I thought D.J. had come to finish the central heating but he's not due until tomorrow.'

I can hear Charlie singing in the background. A rush of tenderness catches in my throat.

The police will be trying to trace this call. With mobile phones, they have to work backwards, identifying which towers are relaying the signals. There are probably half a dozen transmitters between Liverpool and London. As each one is ticked off, the search area narrows.

'I want you to stay on the line, Julianne. If I don't

come back, just leave the line open. It's important.' I slide the phone under the driver's seat. The car keys are still in the ignition. I close the car door and walk away, head down, retreating into the darkness, wondering if he's watching me still.

Twenty minutes later, on a railway platform that looks abandoned and burned out, I step gratefully on to a suburban train. The carriages are almost empty.

Ruiz will know about the ferry, train and airline bookings by now. He'll realise I'm trying to stretch his resources but he will have to check them anyway.

The express to London leaves from Lime Street Station. The police will search each carriage but I'm hoping they won't stay on the train. Edgehill is one stop further, which is where I board a train to Manchester just after 10.30 p.m. After midnight I catch another, this one bound for York. I have a three-hour wait until the Great North Eastern Express leaves for London, sitting in a poorly lit ticket hall, watching the cleaners compete to do the least work.

I pay for the tickets with cash and choose the busiest carriage. Staggering drunkenly along the aisles, I topple into people and mumble apologies.

Only children stare at drunks. Adults avoid eye contact, hoping that I keep moving and choose somewhere else to sit. When I fall asleep, leaning against a window, the entire carriage lets out a silent collective sigh.

7

The train journeys of my youth were to and from boarding school, when I'd gorge myself on bags of sweets and chewing gum, which weren't allowed at Charterhouse. Sometimes I think Semtex would have been more acceptable than bubblegum. One of the seniors, Peter Clavell, swallowed so much that it clogged his intestines and doctors had to remove the blockage through his rectum. Not surprisingly, gum wasn't so popular after that.

My father's back-to-school pep-talk normally boiled down to a seven-word warning: 'Don't let me hear from the head-master.' When Charlie started school I promised that I'd be a different sort of parent. I sat her down and gave her a talk best saved for secondary school, or perhaps even university. Julianne kept giggling, which set Charlie off.

'Don't be scared of maths,' I finished up saying.

'Why?'

'Because a lot of girls are scared of numbers. They talk themselves out of being good at things.'

'OK,' Charlie replied, having absolutely no idea what I was talking about.

I wonder if I'm going to get to see her start secondary school. For weeks I've been worried about this disease denying me things. Now it pales into insignificance when set alongside murder.

As the train pulls into King's Cross I walk slowly through the carriages, studying the platform for any sign of the police. I fall into step with an elderly woman pulling a large suitcase. As we reach the barrier I offer to help her and she nods gratefully. At the ticket booth I turn to her. 'Where's your ticket, Mum?'

She doesn't bat an eyelid as she hands it to me. I give both tickets to the guard and give him a weary smile.

'Don't you hate these early starts?' he says.

'I'll never get used to them,' I reply as he hands me the stubs.

Weaving my way through the crowded concourse, I pause at the entrance to WH Smith where the morning papers are stacked side by side. KILLER CONFESSES – 'I KILLED CATHERINE' screams the headline in the *Sun*.

The broadsheets are reporting rising interest rates and a threatened strike by postal workers. Catherine's story – my story – is beneath the fold. People reach past me and pick up copies. Nobody makes eye contact. This is London, a city where people walk bolt upright with fixed expressions as though ready to face anything and avoid everything. They have somewhere else to be. Don't interrupt. Just keep moving.

* * *

Finding a rhythm to my stride, I weave my way through Covent Garden, past the restaurants and expensive boutiques. Reaching the Strand, I turn left and follow Fleet Street until the gothic façade of the Old Bailey comes into view.

A courthouse has stood on this site for nearly five hundred years and even before that, in medieval times, they held public executions here every Monday morning.

I take up position over the road, tucked against a wall in an alley that runs down towards the Thames. There are brass plates on nearly every doorway. I glance occasionally at my watch, to give the impression of waiting for someone. Men and women in black suits and gowns glide past me, clutching box files and bundles of paper tied with ribbon.

At half past nine the first of the news crews arrives – a cameraman and sound recordist. Others join them. Some of the stills photographers carry stepladders and milk crates. The reporters stick together in the background – sipping take-away coffee, swapping gossip and misinformation.

Shortly before ten, I notice a cab pull up on my side of the road. Eddie Barrett gets out first, looking like Danny DeVito with hair. Bobby is behind him, at least two heads taller but still having somehow managed to find a suit that looks too big for him.

Both are less than fifteen feet away from me. I lower my head and blow into my hands. Bobby's overcoat pockets are bulging with paper and his eyes are watery blue. The warmth of the cab meets the coldness of the air and fogs up his glasses. He pauses to wipe them clean. His hands are steady. The reporters have spotted Eddie and are waiting for him with cameras poised and TV lights at the ready.

I see Bobby lower his head. He is too tall to hide his face. Reporters are firing questions at him. Eddie Barrett puts his hand on Bobby's arm. Bobby pulls away as though scalded. A TV camera is right in his face. Flashguns flare. He wasn't expecting this. He doesn't have a plan.

Barrett is trying to hustle him up the stone steps and through the arches. Photographers are jostling each other and one of them suddenly tumbles backwards. Bobby is standing over him, his fist raised. Bystanders grab at his shoulders and Eddie swings his briefcase like a scythe, clearing a path in front of them. The last thing I see as the doors close is Bobby's head above the throng.

I allow myself a fleeting smile, but nothing more. I can't afford to get my hopes up. Nearby, a gift shop window is crammed with marshmallow Santas and Christmas crackers in red and green. There are reindeer clocks with noses that glow in the dark. I use the reflection in the glass to watch the courthouse steps.

I can picture the scene inside. The press bench will be packed and the public gallery standing room only. Eddie loves working a crowd. He will ask for an adjournment due to my unprofessional conduct and claim his client has been denied natural justice because of my malicious allegations. A new psych report will have to be commissioned, which could take weeks. Blah, blah, blah . . .

There is always a chance the judge might say no and sentence Bobby immediately. More likely, he will grant the adjournment and Bobby will walk free – even more dangerous than before.

Rocking back and forth on my heels, I have to remind myself of the rules. Avoid standing with my feet too close together. Consciously lift feet to avoid shuffling and foot drag. Don't instinctively pivot. My favourite suggestion for breaking a 'frozen pose' is to step over an imaginary obstacle in front of me. I have visions of looking like Marcel Marceau.

I walk to the end of the block, turn and come back again, never taking my eye off the photographers still milling outside the court entrance. Suddenly, they surge forward, cameras raised. Eddie must have had a car waiting. Bobby comes out in a half crouch, pushing through the mêlée and falling on to the back seat. The car door closes as the flash-guns continue firing.

I should have seen this coming. I should have been prepared. Limping on to the road, I wave both arms and a walking stick at a black cab. It swerves out of my way and swings past, forcing a line of traffic to brake hard. A second cab has an orange beacon. The driver either stops or runs me over.

He doesn't bat an eyelid when I tell him to follow that car. Maybe cab drivers hear that all the time.

The silver sedan carrying Bobby is ahead of us, sand-wiched between two buses and a line of cars. My driver manages to nudge into gaps and dodge between lanes, never losing touch. At the same time I notice him sneaking glances at me in the rear mirror. He looks away quickly when our eyes meet. He is young, perhaps in his early twenties, with rust-coloured hair and freckles on the back of his neck. His hands uncurl and flutter on the steering wheel.

'You know who I am.'

He nods.

'I'm not dangerous.'

He looks into my eyes, trying to find some reassurance. My face can't give him any. My Parkinson's mask is like cold chiselled stone.

8

This stretch of the Grand Union Canal is graceless and untidy, with the asphalt towpath pitted and broken. A rusting iron fence leans at a precarious angle, separating the terraced back gardens from the water. A graffiti-daubed caravan, missing a door, sits on bricks instead of wheels. A half-buried child's tricycle sprouts from a vegetable patch.

Bobby hasn't looked over his shoulder since the car dropped him at Camley Street, behind St Pancras Station. I know the rhythm of his walk now. He passes the Lock Keeper's cottage and keeps going. The gas works cast a shadow over the abandoned factories that lie along the south bank. A redevelopment sign announces a new industrial estate.

Four narrow boats are moored against a stone wall on the curve. Three are brightly painted in reds and greens. The fourth has a tug-style bow, with a black hull and a maroon trim to the cabin.

Bobby steps lightly on board and appears to knock on the deck. He waits for several seconds and then unlocks the sliding hatch. He pushes it forward and unlatches the door below. He steps down into the cabin, out of sight. I wait on the edge of the towpath, hidden by a bramble that is trying to swallow a fence. A woman in a grey overcoat pulls at a dog lead, dragging the animal quickly past me.

Five minutes pass. Bobby emerges and glances in my direction. He slides the hatch closed and steps ashore. Reaching into his pocket, he counts loose change in his hand. Then he sets off along the path. I follow at a distance until he climbs a set of steps on to a bridge. He turns south towards a garage.

I return to the boat. I need to see inside. The lacquered door is closed, but not locked. The cabin is dark. Curtains are drawn across the window slits and portholes. Two steps lead me down into the galley. The stainless steel sink is clean. A lone cup sits draining on a tea towel.

Six steps further is the saloon. It looks more like a workshop than a living area, with a bench down one side. My eyes adjust to the light and I see a pegboard dotted with tools – chisels, wrenches, spanners, screwdrivers, metal cutters, planes and files. There are boxes of pipes, washers, drill bits and waterproof tape on shelves. The floor is partly covered with drums of paint, rust proofing, epoxy, wax, grease and machine oil. A portable generator squats under the bench. An old radio hangs on a cord from the ceiling. Everything has its proper place.

On the opposite wall there is another pegboard, but this one is clear. The only attachments are four leather cuffs –

two near the floor and a matching set near the roof. My eyes are drawn to the floor. I don't want to look. The bare wood and skirting boards are stained by something deeper than the darkness.

Reeling backwards, I strike the bulkhead and emerge into a cabin. Everything seems slightly askew. The mattress is too large for the bed. The lamp is too large for the table. The walls are covered in scraps of paper but it's too dark for me to see them properly. I turn on a lamp and my eyes take a moment to adjust.

Suddenly I'm sitting down. Newspaper cuttings, photographs, maps, diagrams and drawings cover the walls. I see images of Charlie on her way to school, playing soccer, singing in the school choir, shopping with her grandmother, on a merry-go-round, feeding the ducks. Others show Julianne at her yoga class, at the supermarket, painting the garden furniture, answering the door . . . Looking closer, I recognise receipts, ticket stubs, soccer newsletters, business cards, photocopies of bank statements and telephone bills, a street map, a library card, a reminder for school fees, a parking notice, registration papers for the car . . .

The small bedside table is stacked high with ring-bound notebooks. I take the top one and open it. Neat, concise handwriting fills each page. The left-hand margin logs the time and date. Alongside are details of my movements, including places, meetings, duration, modes of transport, relevance. It is a 'how to' manual of my life. How to be me!

There is a sound on the deck above my head. Something is being dragged and poured. I switch off the light and sit

440

in darkness, trying to breathe quietly. Someone swings through the hatch into the saloon. He moves through to the galley and opens cupboards. I lie on the floor, squeezed between the bulkhead and the end of the bed, feeling my pulse throbbing at the base of my jaw.

The engine starts up. The pistons rise and fall, then settle into a steady rhythm. I see Bobby's legs through the portholes and feel the boat pitch as he steps along the sides, casting off the lines.

I glance to the galley and saloon. If I move quickly I might be able to get ashore before he comes back to the wheelhouse. I try to stand and knock over a rectangular frame leaning against the wall. As it topples, I manage to catch it with one hand. The painting is frozen momentarily in the light leaking through the curtains: a beach scene, bathing sheds, ice-cream stalls and a Ferris wheel. On the horizon, Charlie's stout, grey whale.

I fall backwards with a groan, unable to make my legs obey me. They belong to someone else.

The narrow boat rocks again as the footsteps return. He has cast off the bowline. The engine is put into gear and we swing away from the mooring. Water slides along the hull. Pulling myself upwards, I ease the curtain open a few inches and lift my face to the porthole. I can only see the treetops.

There is a new sound – a whooshing noise, like a strong wind. All the oxygen seems to disappear from the air. Fuel runs along the floor and soaks into my trousers. Varnished wood crackles as it burns. Fumes sting my eyes and the back of my throat. On my knees, I crawl down the boat into the gathering smoke.

Pulling myself through the U-shaped galley, I reach the saloon. The engine is close by. I can hear it thudding on the far side of the bulkhead. My head hits the stairs and I climb upwards. The hatchway is locked from the outside. I slam my shoulder against it. Nothing moves. My hand feels heat through the door. I need another way out.

The air feels like molten glass in my lungs. I can't see a thing but I can feel my way. On the benches in the workroom my fingers close around a hammer and a sharp, flat chisel. I retreat along the boat, away from the seat of the blaze, ricocheting off walls and hammering on the portholes with the hammer. The glass is reinforced.

Against the bulkhead in the cabin there is a small storage door. I squeeze through it, flopping like a stranded fish until my legs follow me. Oily tarpaulins and ropes snake beneath me. I must be in the bow. I reach above my head and feel the indentation of a hatch. Running my fingers around the edge, I search for a latch, then try wedging the chisel into a corner and swinging the hammer, but the angle is all wrong.

The boat has started to list. Water has invaded the stern. I lie on my back and brace both my feet against the underside of the hatch. Then I kick upwards . . . once, twice, three times. I'm screaming and cursing. The wood splinters and gives way. A square of blinding light fills the hold. I glance back as the petrol in the cabin ignites and a ball of orange flame erupts towards me. At the same moment, I drag myself upwards into daylight, rolling over and over. Fresh air embraces me for a split second and then water wraps itself around me. I sink slowly, inexorably, screaming inside my head, until I settle in the silt. I don't think about drowning. I'll just stay down here for a while where it's cool and dark and green.

When my lungs start to hurt, I reach upwards, grasping for handfuls of air. My head breaks the surface and I roll on to my back, sucking greedily. The stern of the boat has slipped under. Drums in the workroom are exploding like grenades. The engine has stopped but the boat is turning slowly away from me.

I wade towards the bank with mud sucking at my shoes and pull myself upwards using handfuls of reeds. I ignore the outstretched hand. I just want to lie down and rest. My body twists. My legs bump over the edge of the canal. I am sitting on the deserted towpath. Giant cranes are silhouetted against grey clouds.

I recognise Bobby's shoes. He reaches under my arms and grabs me around the chest. I'm being lifted. His chin digs into the top of my head as he carries me. I can smell petrol on his clothes or maybe on mine. I don't cry out. Reality seems far away.

A scarf loops around my neck and is pulled tight, with a knot pressing into my windpipe. The other end is tied to something above me, forcing me up on to my toes. My legs jerk like a marionette because I can't get any purchase on the ground to stop myself choking. I squeeze my fingers inside the scarf and hold it away from my throat.

We are in the courtyard of an abandoned factory. Wooden pallets are stacked against a wall. Sheets of roofing iron have fallen in a storm. Water leaks down the walls, weaving a tapestry of black and green slime. Bobby shifts away from me. His face is damp with sweat.

'I know why you're doing this,' I say.

He doesn't answer. He strips off his suit jacket and rolls up the sleeves of his shirt as if there is business to be taken care of. Then he sits on a packing crate and takes out a white handkerchief to clean his glasses. His stillness is remarkable.

'You won't get away with killing me.'

'What makes you think I want to kill you?' He hooks his glasses over his ears and looks at me. 'You're a wanted man. They'll probably give me a reward.' His voice betrays him. He isn't sure. In the distance I can hear a siren. The fire brigade is coming.

Bobby will have read the morning papers. He *knows* why I confessed. The police will have to re-open every case and examine the details. They will cross-reference the times, dates and places, putting my name into the equation. And what will they discover? That I couldn't have killed all of them. Then they'll begin to wonder why I confessed. And maybe – just maybe – they'll put Bobby's name into the same equation. How many alibis can he have tucked away? How well did he cover his tracks?

I have to keep him off-balance. 'I visited your mother yesterday. She asked about you.'

Bobby stiffens slightly and the pattern of his breathing quickens.

'I don't think I've met Bridget before, but she must have been very beautiful once. Alcohol and cigarettes aren't very kind to the skin. I don't think I met your father either, but I think I would have liked him.'

'You know nothing about him.' He spits the words.

'Not true. I think I have something in common with

444

Lenny . . . and with you. I need to take things apart – to understand how they work. That's why I came looking for you. I thought you might help me figure something out.'

He doesn't answer.

'I've got most of the story now – I know about Erskine and Lucas Dutton, Justice McBride and Mel Cossimo. But what I can't fathom is why you punished everyone except the person you hate the most.'

Bobby is on his feet, blowing himself up like one of those fish with the poisonous spikes. He shoves his face close to mine. I can see a vein, a faint blue pulsing knot above his left eyelid.

'You can't even say her name, can you? She says you look like your father but that's not entirely true. Every time you look in the mirror you must see your mother's eyes . . .'

A knife is gripped between his fingers. He holds the point of the blade against my bottom lip. If I open my mouth it will draw blood. I can't stop now.

'Let me tell you what I've worked out so far, Bobby. I see a small boy, suckled on his father's dreams but polluted by his mother's violence . . . ' The blade is so sharp I don't feel a thing. Blood is leaking down my chin and dripping on to my fingers, still pressed against my neck. ' . . . he blames himself. Most victims of abuse do. He thought of himself as a coward – always running, tripping, mumbling excuses; never good enough, always late, born to disappoint. He thinks he should have been able to save his father, but he didn't understand what was happening until it was too late.'

'Shut the fuck up! You were one of them. *You* killed him! You mind-fucker!'

'I didn't know him.'

'Yeah, that's right. You condemned a man you didn't know. How arbitrary is that? At least I choose. You haven't got a clue. You haven't got a heart.'

Bobby's face is still inches from mine. I see hurt in his eyes and hatred in the curl of his lips.

'So he blames himself, this boy, who is already growing too quickly and becoming awkward and uncoordinated. Tender and shy, angry and bitter – he can't untangle these feelings. He hasn't the capacity to forgive. He hates the world, but no more than he hates himself. He cuts his arms to rid himself of the poison. He clings to memories of his father and of how things used to be. Not perfect, but OK. Together.

'So what does he do? He withdraws from his surroundings and becomes isolated, making himself smaller, hoping to be forgotten, living inside his head. Tell me about your fantasy world, Bobby. It must have been nice to have somewhere to go.'

'You'll only try to spoil it.' His face is flushed. He doesn't want to talk to me, but at the same time he's proud of his achievements. This is something *he* has made. A part of him does want to draw me into his world – to share his exhilaration.

The blade is still pressing into my lip. He pulls it away and waves it in front of my eyes. He tries to make it look practised but fails. He isn't comfortable with a knife.

My fingers are growing numb holding the scarf away from my windpipe. And the lactic acid is building in my calves as I balance on my toes. I can't hold myself up much longer.

'How does it feel to be omnipotent, Bobby? To be judge, jury and executioner, punishing all those who deserve to be punished? You must have spent years rehearsing all of this. Amazing. But who were you doing it for, exactly?'

Bobby reaches down and picks up a plank. He mumbles at me to shut up.

'Oh, that's right, your father. A man you can hardly remember. I bet you don't know his favourite song or what movies he liked or who his heroes were. What did he carry in his pockets? Was he left- or right-handed? Which side did he part his hair?'

'I told you to SHUT YOUR MOUTH!'

The plank swings in a wide arc, striking me across the chest. Air blasts out of my lungs and my body spins, tightening the scarf like a tourniquet. I kick my legs to try to spin back. My mouth is flapping like the gills of a stranded fish.

Bobby tosses the plank aside and looks at me as if to say, 'I told you so.'

My ribs feel broken, but my lungs are working again. 'Just one more question, Bobby. Why are you such a coward? I mean, it's pretty obvious who deserved all this hatred. Look at what she did. She belittled and tormented your dad. She slept with other men and made him a figure of pity, even to his friends. And then, to top it all off, she accused him of abusing his own son . . . '

Bobby has turned away from me but even the silence is speaking to him.

'She ripped up the letters he wrote to you. I bet she even found the photographs you kept and destroyed them. She wanted Lenny out of her life and out of yours. She hated hearing his name . . . '

Bobby is growing smaller, as if collapsing from the inside. His anger has turned to grief.

'Let me guess what happened. She was going to be the first. You went looking for her and found her easily enough. Bridget had never been the shy, retiring type. Her stilettos made big footprints.

'You watched her and waited. You had it all planned . . . every last detail. Now was the moment. The woman who had destroyed your life was just a few feet away, close enough for you to put those fingers around her throat. She was right there, *right there*, but you hesitated. You couldn't do it. You were twice her size. She had no weapon. You could have crushed her so easily.'

I pause, letting the memory live in his mind. 'Nothing happened. You couldn't do it. Do you know why? You were scared. When you saw her again you became that little boy, with his trembling bottom lip and his stutter. She terrified you then, and she terrifies you now.'

Bobby's face is twisted in self-loathing. At the same time, he wants to wipe me from his world.

'Someone had to be punished. So you found your child protection files and the list of names. And you set about punishing all those responsible, by taking away what each of them loved most. But you never lost the fear of your mother. Once a coward, always a coward. What did you think when you discovered she was dying? Has her cancer done the job for you, or has it robbed you?'

'Robbed me.'

'She's dying a terrible death. I've seen her.'

448

He explodes. 'It's not enough. She is a MONSTER!' He kicks at a metal drum, sending it spinning across the courtyard. 'She destroyed my life. She *made* me into this.'

Spittle hangs from his lips. He looks at me for validation. He wants me to say, 'You poor bastard. It *is* all her fault. It's no wonder you feel like this.' I can't give him that. If I sanction his hatred there is no way back.

'I'm not going to give you any bullshit excuses, Bobby. Terrible things happened to you. I wish it could have been different. But look at the world around you – there are children starving in Africa; jets are being flown into buildings; bombs are being dropped on civilians; people are dying of disease; prisoners are being tortured; women are being raped . . . Some of these things we can change, but others we can't. Sometimes we just have to accept what happened and get on with our lives.'

He laughs bitterly. 'How can you say that?'

'Because it's true. You know it is.'

'I'll tell you what's true.' He is staring at me unblinkingly. His voice is a low rumble. 'There is a lay-by on the coast road through Great Crosby – about eight miles north of Liverpool. It's on the dual carriageway, set back from the road. If you drive in there after ten o'clock at night, you will sometimes see another car parked up. You put on your indicator – either left or right, depending on what you want – and you wait for the car in front to respond with the same indicator. Then you follow it.'

His voice is ragged. 'I was six when she first took me to the lay-by. I just watched the first time. It was in a barn somewhere. She was laid out on a table like a smorgasbord. Naked. There were dozens of hands on her. Anyone could do what they wanted. She had enough for all of them. Pain. Pleasure. It was all the same to her. And every time she opened her eyes she looked directly at me. 'Don't be selfish, Bobby,' she said. 'Learn to share.'

He rocks slightly, back and forth, staring straight ahead, picturing the scene in his mind. 'Private clubs and swingers bars were too middle class for my mother. She preferred her orgies to be anonymous and unsophisticated. I lost count of how many people shared her body. Women and men. That's how I learned to share. At first they took from me, but later I took from them. Pain and pleasure – my mother's legacy.'

His eyes are brimming with tears. I don't know what to say. My tongue has grown thick and prickly. My peripheral vision has started to fail because I can't get enough oxygen to my brain.

I want to say something. I want to tell him that he isn't alone. That a lot of people fret through the same dreams, yell into the same emptiness and walk past the same open windows and wonder whether to jump. I know he's lost. He's damaged. But he still has choices. Not every abused child turns out like this.

'Let me down, Bobby. I can't breathe properly.'

I can see the back of his square neck and his badly trimmed hair. He turns in slow motion, never looking at my face. The blade sweeps above my head and I collapse forwards, still clutching the remnants of the scarf. The muscles in my legs go into spasm. I taste concrete dust, mingled with blood. There are more loose planks leaning against one wall and industrial sinks against another. Where is the canal from here? I have to get out.

Lifting myself on to my knees, I start crawling. Bobby has disappeared. Metal shavings dig into my hands. Broken concrete and rusting drums are like an obstacle course. As I reach the entrance I can see a fire engine beside the canal and the flashing lights of a police car. I try to shout but no sound emerges.

Something is wrong. I've stopped moving. I turn to see Bobby standing on my coat.

'Your fucking arrogance blows me away,' he says, grasping my collar and lifting me to my feet. 'You think I'd fall for your cereal box psychology. I've seen more therapists, counsellors and psychiatrists than you've had crappy birthday presents. I've been to Freudians, Jungians, Adlerians, Rogerians – you name it – and I wouldn't give any of them the steam off my piss on a cold day.' He puts his face close to mine once more. 'You *don't* know me. You think you're inside my head. Shit! You're not even close!' He places the blade under my ear. We're breathing the same air.

A flick of his wrist and my throat will open like a dropped melon. That's what he's going to do. I can feel the metal against my neck. He is going to end this now.

At that moment I picture Julianne looking at me across her pillow, with her hair mussed up from sleep. And I see Charlie in her pyjamas, smelling of shampoo and tooth-paste. I wonder if it's possible to count the freckles on her nose. Wouldn't it be a terrible thing to die without trying?

Bobby's breath is warm on my neck – the blade is cold. His tongue comes out, wetting his lips. There is a moment of hesitation – I don't know why.

'I guess we both underestimated each other,' I say, inching my hand inside my coat pocket. 'I knew you wouldn't let me go. Your kind of vengeance isn't negotiable. You've invested too much in it. It's the reason you get up in the morning. That's why I had to get off that wall.'

He wavers, trying to work out what he hasn't prepared for. My fingers close around the handle of the chisel.

'I have a disease, Bobby. Sometimes I have difficulty walking. My right hand is OK, but see how my left arm trembles.' I hold up the limb that no longer feels as if it belongs to me. It draws his gaze like a birthmark on someone's face or a disfiguring burn.

With my right hand I drive the chisel through my coat into Bobby's abdomen. It strikes his pelvic bone and twists, puncturing the transverse colon. Three years at medical school are never wasted.

Still holding my collar, he falls to his knees. I swing around and hit him as hard as I can with my fist, aiming for his jaw. He puts his arm up, but I still manage to connect with the side of his head, throwing him backwards. Everything has slowed down. Bobby tries to stand but I move forward a pace and catch him under the chin with a clumsy but effective kick that snaps his head back.

For a moment I stare at him, crumpled on the ground. Then, crablike, I scuttle across the courtyard. Once I get my legs moving they still do the job. It might not be pretty but I've never been Roger Bannister.

A police dog handler is searching for a scent along the canal bank. He sees me coming and takes a step back. I keep going. It takes two of them to hold me. Even then I want to keep running.

Ruiz has me by the shoulders. 'Where is he?' he yells. 'Where's Bobby?'

9

Aunt Gracie made the best milky tea. She would always put an extra scoop of tealeaves in the pot and another slurp of milk in my cup. I don't know where Ruiz managed to find such a brew, but it helps to wash the taste of blood and petrol from my mouth.

Sitting in the front seat of a squad car, I hold the cup with both hands in a vain attempt to stop them trembling.

'You should really get that seen to,' Ruiz says. My bottom lip is still bleeding. I touch it gingerly with my tongue.

Ruiz takes the cellophane off a packet of cigarettes and offers me one.

I shake my head. 'I thought you'd given up.'

'I blame you. We chased that stolen bloody hire car for near on fifty miles. Found two fourteen-year-olds and a kid of eleven inside it. We also staked out the railway stations, airports, bus terminals . . . I had every officer in the north-west looking for you.'

'Wait till you get my invoice.'

He regards his cigarette with a mixture of affection and distaste. 'Your confession was a nice touch. Very creative. I had the press hyenas sniffing everything except my arse – asking questions, talking to relatives, stirring up the silt. You gave me no choice.'

'You found the red edge?'

'Yeah.'

'What about the other names on the list?'

'We're still looking into them.'

He leans against the open door, studying me thoughtfully. The glint of sunlight off the canal picks up the Tower of Pisa pin on his tie. His distant blue eyes have fixed on the ambulance parked a hundred feet away, framed against the factory wall.

The pain in my chest and throat is making me feel light-headed. I wince as I pull a rough grey blanket around my shoulders. Ruiz tells me how he spent all night checking the details from the child protection file. He ran the names through the computer and pulled up the unsolved deaths.

Bobby had worked in Hatchmere as a council gardener up until a few weeks before Rupert Erskine died. He and Catherine McBride attended the same group therapy sessions for self-mutilators at an outpatients clinic in West Kirkby in the mid-nineties.

'What about Sonia Dutton?' I ask.

'Nothing. He doesn't match the description of the pusher who sold her the drug.'

'He worked at her swimming club.'

'I'll check it out.'

'How did he get Catherine to come to London?'

'She came for the job interview. You wrote her a letter.'

'No I didn't.'

'Bobby wrote it for you. He stole stationery from your office.'

'How? When?'

Ruiz can see I'm struggling. 'You mentioned the word Nevaspring sewn into Bobby's shirt. It's a French company that delivers water coolers to offices. We're checking the CCTV footage from the medical centre.'

'He made deliveries—'

'Walked right past security with a bottle over his shoulder.'

'That explains how he managed to get into the building when he arrived late for several of his appointments.'

Across the waste ground, visible above the broken fence, Bobby is lying on a stretcher. A paramedic holds a transfusion bottle above his head.

'Is he going to be OK?' I ask.

'You haven't saved the taxpayer the cost of a trial, if that's what you're asking.'

'No.'

'You're not feeling sorry for him, are you?'

I shake my head. Maybe one day – a long while from now – I'll look back at Bobby and see a damaged child who grew into a defective adult. Right now, after what he did to Elisa and the others, I'm happy to have half killed the bastard.

Ruiz watches as two detectives climb into the back of the ambulance and sit either side of Bobby. 'You told me that Catherine's killer was going to be older . . . more practised.'

456

'I thought he would be.'

'And you said it was sexual.'

'I said her pain aroused him, but the motive wasn't clear. Revenge was one of the possibilities. You know, it's strange, but even when I was sure it was Bobby, I still couldn't picture him being there, making her cut herself. It was too sophisticated a form of sadism. But then again, he infiltrated all those lives – my life. He was like a piece of scenery that nobody notices because we concentrate on the foreground.'

'You saw him before anyone else did.'

'I tripped over him in the dark.'

The ambulance pulls away. Water birds lift out of the reeds. They twist and turn across the pale sky. Skeletal trees stretch upwards as if trying to pluck the birds from the air.

Ruiz gives me a ride to the hospital. He wants to be there when Bobby gets out of surgery. We follow the ambulance along St Pancras Way and turn into the accident and emergency bay. My legs have seized up almost completely now the adrenalin has drained out of them. I struggle to get out of the car. Ruiz commandeers a wheelchair and pushes me into a familiar white-tiled public hospital waiting room.

As usual, the Detective Inspector gets off on the wrong foot by calling the triage nurse 'sweetheart' and telling her to get her 'priorities sorted'. She takes her annoyance out on me, shoving her fingers between my ribs with unnecessary zeal. I feel like I'm going to pass out.

The young doctor who stitches up my lip has bleached hair, an old-fashioned feather-cut and a necklace of crushed shells. She has been on holiday somewhere warm and the skin on her nose is pink and peeling.

Ruiz has gone upstairs to keep tabs on Bobby. Not even an armed guard outside the surgery and a general anaesthetic is insurance enough for him to relax. Maybe he's trying to make amends for not believing me sooner. I doubt it.

Lying on a gurney, I try to keep my head still as I feel the needle slide into my lip and the thread tug at the skin. Scissors snip the ends and the doctor takes a step back, appraising her handiwork.

'And my mother told me I'd never be able to sew.'

'How does it look?'

'You should have waited for the plastic surgeon but I've done OK. You'll have a slight scar, just there.' She points to the hollow beneath her bottom lip. 'Guess it'll match your ear.' She tosses her latex gloves into a bin. 'You still need an X-ray. I'm sending you upstairs. Do you need someone to push you or can you walk?'

'I'll walk.'

She points to the lift and tells me to follow the green line to Radiology on the fourth floor. Half an hour later, Ruiz finds me in the waiting room. I'm hanging around for the radiologist to confirm what I already know from viewing the X-rays: two fractured ribs but no internal bleeding.

'When can you make a statement?'

'When they strap me up.'

'It can wait till tomorrow. Come on, I'll give you a lift home.'

A twinge of regret elevates me above the pain. Where is home? I haven't had time to contemplate where I'll spend tonight, and the night after that. Sensing my quandary, Ruiz murmurs, 'Why don't you go and listen to her? You're supposed to be good at that sort of thing.' In the same breath he adds, 'There's no frigging room at my place!'

Downstairs, he continues bossing people around until my chest is strapped and my stomach is rattling with painkillers and anti-inflammatories. I float along the corridor, following Ruiz to his car.

'There is one thing that puzzles me,' I say as we drive north towards Camden. 'Bobby could have killed me. He had the blade at my throat, yet he hesitated. It was as though he couldn't cross that line.'

'You said he couldn't kill his mother'

'That's different. He was scared of her. He had no trouble with the others.'

'Well, he doesn't have to worry about Bridget any more. She died at eight o'clock this morning.'

'So that's it. He has no one left.'

'Not quite. We found his half-brother. I left a message for him, telling him Bobby was in hospital.'

Uneasiness washes over me, inching upwards like an incoming tide. 'Where did you find him?'

'He's a plumber in north London. Dafyyd John Morgan.'

Ruiz is shouting into the two-way radio. He wants cars sent to the house. I'm shouting too – trying to reach Julianne on a mobile, but the line is engaged. We're five minutes away but the traffic is murder. A truck has run a red light at a five-way intersection, blocking Camden Road.

Ruiz is weaving on to the pavement, forcing pedestrians to scatter. He leans out of the window. 'Dumbassfuck! Dickhead! Go, go! Just fucking move!'

This is taking way too long. He has been inside my house – inside my walls. I can see him standing in my basement, laughing at me. And I remember his eyes when he watched the police digging up the garden, the lazy insolence and his half-smile.

Now it makes sense. The white van that followed me in Liverpool; it was a plumber's van. Magnetic mats were taken off the doors, making it look nondescript. The fingerprint on the stolen four-wheel drive didn't belong to Bobby. And the drug dealer who gave Sonia Dutton the adulterated Ecstasy matched the description of D.J., Dafyyd – one and the same.

At the narrow boat, Bobby knocked on the deck before opening the hatch. It wasn't his boat. The workroom was full of tools and plumbing equipment. They were D.J.'s diaries and notes. Bobby torched the boat to destroy the evidence.

I can't sit here waiting. The house is less than a quarter of a mile away. Ruiz tells me to wait but I'm already out of the door, running along the street, dodging between pedestrians, joggers, mothers with toddlers, nannies with prams. Traffic is backed up in both directions as far as I can see. I hit 'redial' on the mobile. The line is still engaged.

There had to be two of them. How could one person have done it all? Bobby was too easy to recognise. He stood out in a crowd. D.J. had the intensity and the power to control people. He didn't look away.

When it came to the moment of truth, Bobby couldn't kill me. He couldn't make that leap because he'd never done it before. Bobby could do the planning but D.J. was the foot soldier. He was older, more practised, more ruthless.

I vomit into a rubbish bin and keep running, passing the local off-licence, the betting shop, a pizzeria, discount store, pawnbroker, bakery and the Rag and Firkin pub. Nothing is coming quickly enough. My legs are slowing down.

I round the final corner and see the house ahead of me. There are no police cars. A white van is parked out front with the sliding side door open. Hessian sacks cover the floor . . .

I fall through the front gate and up the steps. The phone is off the hook.

I scream Charlie's name but it comes out as a low moan. She is sitting in the living room, dressed in jeans and a sweatshirt. A yellow Post-It note is stuck to her forehead. Like a new puppy, she throws herself at me, crushing her head to my chest. I almost black out with the pain.

'We were playing a game of "Who Am I?",' she explains. 'D.J. had to guess he was Homer Simpson. What did he choose for me?'

She lifts her face to mine. The note is curling at the edges but I recognise the small, neat print.

YOU'RE DEAD.

I find enough air to speak. 'Where's Mum?'

The urgency in my voice frightens her. She takes a step back and sees the bloodstains on my shirt and the sheen of sweat. My bottom lip is swollen and the stitches are crusted with blood.

'She's downstairs in the basement. D.J. told me to wait here.'

'Where is he?'

'He's coming back in a minute, but he said that ages ago.'

I push her towards the front door. 'Run, Charlie!'

'Why?'

'RUN! NOW! Keep running!'

The basement door is shut and wet paper towels have been pushed into the doorjamb. There is no key in the lock. I turn the handle and gently pull it open.

Dust is swirling in the air – the sign of leaking gas. I can't yell and hold my breath at the same time. Halfway down the steps, I stop to let my eyes adjust to the light. Julianne is slumped on the floor beside the new boiler. She's lying on her side, with her right arm under her head and her left reaching out as though pointing to something. A dark fringe has fallen over one eye.

Crouching next to her, I slip my hands under her arms and drag her backwards. The pain in my chest is unbelievable. White dots dance in front of my eyes like angry insects. I still haven't taken a breath but the time is close. I take the stairs one at a time, dragging Julianne upwards and sitting down heavily after each exertion. One step, two steps, three steps . . .

I hear Charlie coughing behind me. She takes hold of my collar, trying to help me, pulling when I pull.

Four steps, five steps . . .

We reach the kitchen and Julianne's head bounces off the floor as I set her down. I'll apologise later. Hauling her over my shoulder, I roar in pain, and totter down the hallway. Charlie is ahead of me.

What is the trigger? A timer or a thermostat; the central heating; a refrigerator; the security lights?

'Run, Charlie. Run!'

When did it grow dark outside? Police cars fill the street

with flashing lights. I don't stop this time. I scream one word, over and over. I cross the road, dodge the cars and get to the far end of the street before my knees buckle and Julianne falls on to the muddy grass. I kneel beside her.

Her eyes are open. The blast begins as a tiny spark in the midst of her deep brown corneas. The sound arrives a split second later, along with the shock wave. Charlie is thrown backwards. I try to shield them both. There is no orange ball like you see in the movies, only a cloud of smoke and dust. Debris rains down and I feel the warm breath of fire drying the sweat on my neck.

The blackened van lies upside down in the middle of the street. Chunks of roofing and ribbons of gutters are draped over trees. Rubble and splintered wood covers the road.

Charlie sits up and looks at the desolation. The note is still stuck to her forehead, blackened at the edges but still legible. I pull her against my chest, holding her close. At the same time, my fingers close around the yellow square of paper and crush it within my fist.

Epilogue

The nightmares of my recent past still see me running –
escaping the same monsters and rabid dogs and Neanderthal
second-row forwards – but now they seem more real. Jock
says it is a side effect of the Levodopa, my new medication.

The dosage has halved in the past two months. He says
I must be under less stress. What a comedian! He phones
me every day and asks if I fancy a game of tennis. I tell
him no and he tells me a joke. 'What's the difference between
a nine months pregnant woman and a *Playboy* centrefold?'

'I don't know.'

'Nothing, if her husband knows what's good for him.'

This is one of the cleaner ones and I risk telling Julianne.
She laughs, but not as loudly as I do.

We're living in Jock's flat while we decide whether to
rebuild or buy a new place. This is Jock's way of trying to

make amends, but he hasn't been forgiven. In the meantime, he's moved in with a new girlfriend, Kelly, who hopes to be the next Mrs Jock Owens. She will need a harpoon gun or a cast-iron pre-nup to get him anywhere near an altar.

Julianne has thrown away all his gadgets and the out-of-date frozen meals in the freezer. Then she went out and bought fresh sheets for the beds and new towels.

Her morning sickness is over, thankfully, and her body is getting bigger each day (everything except her bladder). She is convinced we're having a boy, because only a man could cause her so much grief. She always looks at me when she says this. Then she laughs, but not as loudly as I do.

I know she's watching me closely. We watch each other. Maybe it's the disease she's looking for, or perhaps she doesn't trust me entirely. We had an argument yesterday – our first since nursing things back together. We're going to Wales for a week and she complained that I always leave my packing until the last possible minute.

'I never forget anything.'

'That's not the point.'

'What is the point?'

'You should do it earlier. It's less stressful.'

'For who?'

'For you.'

'But I'm not the one who is getting stressed.'

After tiptoeing around her for five months, grateful for her forgiveness, I decided to draw a line in the sand. I asked her: 'Why do women fall in love with men and then try to change them?'

'Because men need help,' she replied, as if this was common knowledge.

'But if I become the man you want, I won't be the man I am.'

She rolled her eyes and said nothing, but since then she's been less prickly. This morning she came and sat on my lap, putting her arms around my neck and kissing me with the sort of passion that marriage is supposed to kill. Charlie said 'Yuck!' and hid her eyes.

'What's wrong?'

'You guys are French kissing.'

'What do you know about French kissing?'

'It's when you slobber over each other.'

I rubbed my hand across Julianne's stomach and whispered, 'I want our children never to grow up.'

Our architect has arranged to meet me at the hole in the ground. The only thing left standing is the staircase, which goes nowhere. The force of the blast sent the concrete floor of the kitchen through the roof and blew the boiler into a yard two streets over. The shockwave shattered almost every window in the block and three houses have had to be demolished.

Charlie says she saw someone at a first floor window just before the blast. Anyone on that floor would have been vaporised, say the experts, which might explain why they didn't find so much as a fingernail or a fibre or a stray tooth. Then again, I keep asking myself, why would D.J. stick around once the gas had been turned on and the timer set to fire the boiler? He had plenty of time to get out, unless he planned this as a 'final' act in every sense of the word?

Charlie doesn't understand that he could have done these things. She asked me the other day if I thought he was in heaven. I felt like saying, 'I just hope he's dead.'

His bank accounts haven't been touched in two months and nobody has seen him. There is no record of him leaving the country, applying for a job, renting a room, buying a car or cashing a cheque.

Ruiz has pieced together the early facts. D.J. was born in Blackpool. His mother, a sewing machinist, married Lenny in the late sixties. She died in a car accident when D.J. was seven. His grandparents (her parents) raised him until Lenny remarried. Then he fell under Bridget's spell.

I suspect that he experienced everything Bobby did, although no two children react the same way to sexual abuse or to sadism. Lenny was the most important figure in both their lives and his death lay at the heart of everything.

D.J. finished his apprenticeship in Liverpool, becoming a master plumber. He joined a local firm where people remember him more with apprehension than fondness. At a bar one night he drove a broken bottle into a woman's face because she didn't laugh at the punchline of his joke.

He disappeared in the late eighties and reappeared in Thailand, running a bar and a brothel. Two teenage junkies who tried to smuggle of kilo of heroin out of Bangkok told police they had met their supplier in D.J.'s bar, but he skipped the country before anyone could link him to the bust.

He turned up in Australia, working his way down the east coast on building sites. In Melbourne he befriended an Anglican minister and became the manager of a homeless shelter. For a while he seemed to have mended his ways.

No more sucker punches, broken noses or snapping ribs with his boots.

Appearances can be deceptive. The police in Victoria are now investigating the disappearance of six people from the hostel over a four-year period. Many of their welfare cheques were still being cashed up until eighteen months ago when D.J. appeared in the UK again.

I don't know how he found Bobby, but it can't have been too hard. Given the difference in their ages when D.J. left home, they must have been virtually strangers. Yet they discovered a shared desire.

Bobby's fantasies of revenge were just that – fantasies – but D.J. had the experience and the lack of empathy to make them come true. One was the architect, the other the builder. Bobby had the creative vision, D.J. had the tools. The end result was a psychopath with a plan.

Catherine was probably tortured and killed on the narrow boat. Bobby had watched me for so long, he knew exactly where to bury the body. He also knew that ten days later I'd be at the cemetery. One of them must have phoned the police from the call box near the gates. And leaving the shovel resting on Gracie's grave was a touch of the macabre with an explosive outcome.

Other small pieces have fallen into place as the weeks have passed. Bobby learned about our plumbing problems from my mother. She is notorious for boring people with stories of her children and grandchildren. She even showed him the photo albums and the building plans we submitted to the council for the renovations.

D.J. dropped leaflets through every letterbox in the street. Each small job provided another reference and helped convince Julianne to hire him. Once inside it was easy, although he almost came unstuck when Julianne caught him in my study one afternoon. That's when he made up the story of disturbing an intruder and chasing him out. He'd gone into the study to check to see if anything had been taken.

Bobby goes on trial at the end of next month. He hasn't entered a plea, but they expect it to be 'not guilty'. The case, though strong, is circumstantial. None of the physical evidence puts a murder weapon in his hand – not for Cathcrine or Elisa or Boyd or Erskine or Sonia Dutton or Esther Gorski.

Ruiz says it will be over after that, but he's wrong. This case will never be closed. People tried to shut this away years ago and look what happened. Ignore our mistakes and we are doomed to repeat them. Don't stop thinking of the white bear.

The events leading up to Christmas have almost become a surreal blur. Rarely do we talk about it, but I know from experience that it will come out one day. Sometimes, late at night, I hear a car door slam or heavy steps on the footpath and my mind won't be still. I have feelings of sadness, depression, frustration and anxiety. I am easily startled. I imagine people are watching me from doorways and parked cars. I can't see a white van without trying to make out the driver's face.

These are all common reactions to shock and trauma. Maybe it's good that I know these things, but I would prefer to stop analysing myself.

I still have my disease, of course. I am part of a study

being conducted at one of the research hospitals. Fenwick put me on to it. Once a month I drive to the hospital, clip a card to my shirt pocket and flip through the pages of *Country Life* while waiting my turn.

The head technician always offers me a cheery, 'How are you today?'

'Well, since you ask, I have Parkinson's Disease.'

He smiles wearily, gives me an injection and runs a few tests on my coordination, using video cameras to measure the degree and frequency of my tremors.

I know it will get worse. But what the hell! I'm lucky. A lot of people have Parkinson's. Not all of them have a beautiful wife, a loving daughter and a new baby to look forward to.

THE NIGHT
FERRY

This one is for Alpheus 'Two Dogs' Williams,
a mentor and a mate.

Acknowledgements

This is a story that could not have been told without Esther Brandt and Jacqueline de Jong who were invaluable in helping my research. Through them I met Sytze van der Zee, Leo Rietveld and the remarkable Joep de Groot, my guide through Amsterdam's famous Red Light District.

Elsewhere I am indebted to Ursula Mackenzie and Mark Lucas for their friendship, advice and belief that I have something inside me that is worth writing. For their hospitality I am grateful to Richard, Emma, Mark and Sara. And I'd be lost without my three daughters: Alex, Charlotte and Bella who make me laugh and forget work.

Yet again, however, it is Vivien who deserves most of the credit. My researcher, plotter, reader, reviewer, lover and wife, she is *my* love story.

Book One

'When the first baby laughed for the first time, the laugh broke into a thousand pieces and they all went skipping about, and that was the beginning of fairies.'

Sir James Barrie (*Peter Pan*)

1

It was Graham Greene who said that a story has no beginning or end. The author simply chooses a moment, an arbitrary point, and looks either forward or back. That moment is now – an October morning – when the clang of a metallic letter flap heralds the first post.

There is an envelope on the mat inside my front door. Inside is a small stiff rectangle of paper that says nothing and everything.

Dear Ali,
I'm in trouble. I must see you. Please come to the reunion.
Love, Cate

Sixteen words. Long enough to be a suicide note. Short enough to end an affair. I don't know why Cate has written to me now. She hates me. She told me so the last time we spoke, eight years ago. The past. Given long enough I could tell you the month, the day and the hour but these details are unimportant.

All you need to know is the year – 1998. It should have been the summer we finished university; the summer we went backpacking across Europe; the summer I lost my virginity to Brian Rusconi instead of to Cate's father. Instead it was the summer she went away and the summer I left home – a summer not big enough for everything that happened.

Now she wants to see me again. Sometimes you know when a story begins . . .

2

When the day comes that I am asked to recalibrate the calendar, I am going to lop a week off January and February and add them to October, which deserves to be forty days long, maybe more.

I love this time of year. The tourists have long gone and the kids are back at school. The TV schedules aren't full of reruns and I can sleep under a duvet again. Mostly I love the sparkle in the air, without the pollen from the plane trees so that I can open my lungs and run freely.

I run every morning – three circuits of Victoria Park in Bethnal Green, each one of them more than a mile. Right now I'm just passing Durward Street in Whitechapel. Jack the Ripper territory. I once took a Ripper walking tour, a pub crawl with ghost stories. The victim I remember best was his last one, Mary Kelly, who died on the same date as my birthday, November the ninth.

People forget how small an area Jack roamed. Spitalfields, Shoreditch and Whitechapel cover less than a square mile, yet in 1888 more than a million people were crammed into the slums, without decent water and sewerage. It is still overcrowded and poor but that's only compared with places like Hampstead or Chiswick or Holland Park. Poverty is a relative state in a rich country where the wealthiest are the first to cry poor.

It is seven years since I last ran competitively, on a September night in Birmingham, under lights. I wanted to get to the Sydney Olympics but only two of us were going to make it. Four-hundredths of a second separated first from fifth; half a metre, a heartbeat – a broken heart.

I don't run to win any more. I run because I can and because I'm fast. Fast enough to blur at the edges. That's why I'm here now, flirting with the ground while perspiration leaks between my breasts, plastering my T-shirt to my stomach.

When I run, my thoughts become clearer or at least more concentrated. I think about work and imagine that today someone will call and offer me my old job back.

A year ago I helped solve a kidnapping and find a missing girl. One of the kidnappers dropped me onto a wall, crushing my spine. After six operations and nine months of physio-therapy I am fit again, with more steel in my spine than England's back four. Unfortunately, nobody seems to know what to do with me at the Metropolitan Police. They think I am a wonky wheel on the machine.

As I pass the playground, I notice a man sitting on a bench, reading a newspaper. There is no child on the climbing frame behind him and other benches are in sunshine. Why has he chosen the shade?

6

In his mid-thirties, dressed in a shirt and tie, he doesn't raise his eyes as I pass. He's studying a crossword. What sort of man does a crossword in a park at this hour of the morning? A man who can't sleep. A man who waits.

Up until a year ago I used to watch people for a living. I guarded diplomats and visiting heads of state, ferrying their wives on shopping trips to Harrods and dropping their children at school. It is probably the most boring job in the Metropolitan Police but I was good at it. During five years with the Diplomatic Protection Group I didn't fire a shot in anger or miss one of the wives' hair appointments. I was like one of those soldiers who sit in the missile silos, praying the phone never rings.

On my second circuit of the park the man is still there. His suede jacket is lying across his lap. He has freckles and smooth brown hair, cut symmetrically and parted to the left. A leather briefcase is tucked close to his side.

A gust of wind tears the newspaper from his fingers. Three steps and I reach it first. It wraps around my thigh.

For a moment he wants to retreat, as if he's too close to the edge. His freckles make him look younger. His eyes don't meet mine. Instead he bunches his shoulders shyly and says 'Thank you'. The front page is still wrapped around my thigh. For a moment I'm tempted to have some fun. I could make a joke about feeling like tomorrow's fish and chips.

The breeze feels cool on my neck. 'Sorry, I'm rather sweaty.'

He touches his nose nervously, nods and touches his nose again.

'Do you run every day?' he asks suddenly.

'I try to.'

'How far?'

'Four miles.'

It's an American accent. He doesn't know what else to say.

'I have to keep going. I don't want to cool down.'

'OK. Sure. Have a nice day.' It doesn't sound so trite coming from an American.

On my third circuit of the park the bench is empty. I look for him along the street but there are no silhouettes. Normal service has been resumed.

Further along the street, just visible on the corner, a van is parked at the kerb. As I draw nearer, I notice a white plastic tent over missing paving stones. A metal cage is propped open around the hole. They've started work early.

I do this sort of thing – take note of people and vehicles. I look for things that are out of the ordinary: people in the wrong place, or the wrong clothes; cars parked illegally; the same face in different locations. I can't change what I am.

Unlacing my trainers, I pull a key from beneath the insole and unlock my front door. My neighbour, Mr Mordecai, waves from his window. I once asked him his first name and he said it should be Yo'man.

'Why's that?'

'Because that's what my boys call me: "Yo man, can I have some money?" "Yo man, can I borrow the car?"'

His laugh sounded like nuts falling on a roof.

In the kitchen I pour myself a large glass of water and drink it greedily. Then I stretch my quads, balancing one leg on the back of a chair.

The mouse living under my fridge chooses that moment

to appear. It is a very ambivalent mouse, scarcely bothering to lift its head to acknowledge me. And it doesn't seem to mind that my youngest brother Hari keeps setting mouse-traps. Perhaps it knows that I disarm them, taking off the cheese when Hari isn't around.

The mouse finally looks up at me, as though about to complain about the lack of crumbs. Then it sniffs the air and scampers away.

Hari appears in the doorway, bare-chested and barefoot. Opening the fridge, he takes out a carton of orange juice and unscrews the plastic lid. He looks at me, considers his options, and gets a glass from the cupboard. Sometimes I think he is prettier than I am. He has longer lashes and thicker hair.

'Are you going to the reunion tonight?' I ask.

'Nope.'

'Why not?'

'Don't tell me *you*'re going! You said you wouldn't be caught dead.'

'I changed my mind.'

There is a voice from upstairs. '*Hey, have you seen my knickers?*'

Hari looks at me sheepishly.

'*I know I had a pair. They're not on the floor.*'

Hari whispers, 'I thought you'd gone out.'

'I went for a run. Who is she?'

'An old friend.'

'So you must know her name?'

'Cheryl.'

'Cheryl Taylor!' (She's a bottle blonde who works behind the bar at the White Horse.) 'She's older than I am.'

9

'No, she's not.'

'What on earth do you see in her?'

'What difference does that make?'

'I'm interested.'

'Well, she has assets.'

'Assets?'

'The best.'

'You think so?'

'Absolutely.'

'What about Phoebe Griggs?'

'Too small.'

'Emma Shipley?'

'Saggy.'

'Mine?'

'Very funny.'

Cheryl is coming down the stairs. I can hear her rummaging in the sitting room. 'Found them,' she shouts.

She arrives in the kitchen still adjusting the elastic beneath her skirt.

'Oh, hello,' she squeaks.

'Cheryl, this is my sister, Alisha.'

'Nice to see you again,' she says, not meaning it.

The silence seems to stretch out. I might never talk again. Finally, I excuse myself and go upstairs for a shower. With any luck Cheryl will be gone by the time I come down.

Hari has been living with me for the past two months because it's closer to university. He is supposed to be safe-guarding my virtue and helping pay the mortgage but he's four weeks behind in his rent and is using my spare room as a knocking shop.

My legs are tingling. I love the feeling of lactic acid

leaking away. I look in the mirror and pull back my hair. Yellow flecks spark in my irises like goldfish in a pond. There are no wrinkles. Black don't crack.

My 'assets' aren't so bad. When I was running competitively I was always pleased they were on the small side and could be tightly bound in a sports bra. Now I wouldn't mind being a size bigger so I could have a cleavage.

Hari yells up the stairs. 'Hey, Sis, I'm taking twenty from your purse.'

'Why?'

'Because when I take it from strangers they get angry.'

Very droll. 'You still owe me rent.'

'Tomorrow.'

'You said that yesterday.' *And the day before.*

The front door closes. The house is quiet.

Downstairs, I pick up Cate's note again, holding it lightly between my fingertips. Then I prop it on the table against the salt and pepper shakers, staring at it for a while.

Cate Elliot. Her name still makes me smile. One of the strange things about friendship is that time together isn't cancelled out by time apart. One doesn't erase the other or balance it on some invisible scale. You can spend a few hours with someone and they will change your life, or you can spend a lifetime with a person and remain unchanged.

We were born at the same hospital and raised in Bethnal Green in London's East End, although we managed to more or less avoid each other for the first thirteen years. Fate brought us together, if you believe in such things.

We became inseparable. Almost telepathic. We were partners in crime, stealing beer from her father's fridge, window shopping on the King's Road, eating chips with vinegar on our way home from school, sneaking out to see bands at the Hammersmith Odeon and movie stars on the red carpet at Leicester Square.

In our gap year we went to France. I crashed a moped, got cautioned for having a fake ID and tried hash for the first time. Cate lost the key to our hostel during a midnight swim and we had to climb a trellis at two a.m.

There is no break-up worse than that of best friends. Broken love affairs are painful. Broken marriages are messy. Broken homes are sometimes an improvement. Our break-up was the worst.

Now, after eight years, she wants to see me. The thrill of compliance spreads across my skin. Then comes a nagging, unshakeable dread. She's in trouble.

My car keys are in the sitting room. As I pick them up I notice marks on the glass-topped coffee table. Looking closer, I can make out two neat buttock prints and what I imagine to be elbow smudges. I could kill my brother!

3

Someone has spilled a Bloody Mary mix on my shoes. I wouldn't mind so much, but they're not mine. I borrowed them, just like I borrowed this top, which is too big for me. At least my underwear is my own. 'Never borrow money or underwear,' my mother always says, in an addendum to her clean-underwear speech which involves graphic descriptions of road accidents and ambulance officers cutting off my tights. No wonder I have nightmares.

Cate isn't here yet. I've been trying to watch the door and avoid talking to anyone.

There should be a law against school reunions. They should come with warning stickers on the invitations. There is never a right time for them. You're either too young or too old or too fat.

This isn't even a proper school reunion. Somebody burned down the science classrooms at Oaklands. A vandal with a can of petrol rather than a rogue Bunsen burner. Now they're opening a brand new block, with a junior Minister of something-or-other doing the honours.

The new building is functional and sturdy, with none of the charm of the Victorian original. The cathedral ceilings and arched windows have been replaced by fibrous cement panels, strip lighting and aluminium frames.

The school hall has been decorated with streamers, and balloons hang from the rafters. A school banner is draped across the front of the stage.

There is a queue for the mirror in the girls' toilets. Lindsay Saunders leans past me over the sink and rubs lipstick from her teeth. Satisfied, she turns and appraises me.

'Will you stop acting like a Punjabi princess and loosen up. Have fun.'

'Is *that* what this is?'

I'm wearing Lindsay's top, the bronze one with shoe-string straps, which I don't have the bust to carry off. A strap falls off my shoulder. I tug it up again.

'I know you're acting like you don't care. You're just nervous about Cate. Where is she?'

'I don't know.'

Lindsay reapplies her lipstick and adjusts her dress. She's been looking forward to the reunion for weeks because of Rocco Manspiezer. She fancied him for six years at school but didn't have the courage to tell him.

'What makes you so sure you'll get him this time?'

'Well, I didn't spend two hundred quid on this dress and squeeze into these bloody shoes to be ignored by him again.'

Unlike Lindsay, I have no desire to hang around with people I have spent twelve years avoiding. I don't want to hear how much money they make or how big their house is or see photographs of their children who have names that sound like brands of shampoo.

That's the thing about school reunions – people only come to measure their life against others and to see the failures. They want to know which of the beauty queens has put on seventy pounds and seen her husband run off with his secretary; and which teacher got caught taking photographs in the changing rooms.

'Come on, aren't you curious?' Lindsay asks.

'Of course I'm curious. I *hate* the fact I'm curious. I just wish I was invisible.'

'Don't be such a spoilsport.' She rubs her finger across my eyebrows. 'Did you see Annabelle Trunzo? My God, that dress! And what about her hair?'

'Rocco doesn't even have any hair.'

'Ah, but he's still looking fit.'

'Is he married?'

'Hush your mouth.'

'Well, I think you should at least find out before you shag him.'

She gives me a wicked grin. 'I'll ask afterwards.'

Lindsay acts like a real man-eater, but I know she's not really so predatory. I tell myself that all the time, but I still wouldn't let her date my brothers.

Back in the hall, the lights have been turned down and the music turned up. Spandau Ballet has been replaced by 1980s anthems. The women are wearing a mixture of cocktail dresses and saris. Others are pretending not to care, in leather jackets and designer jeans.

There were always tribes at Oaklands. The whites were

15

a minority. Most of the students were Banglas (Bangladeshis) with a few Pakis and Indians thrown into the mix.

I was a 'curry', a 'yindoo', an 'elephant trainer'. Brown Indian in case you're wondering. As defining details go, nothing else came close at Oaklands – not my black hair, braces or skinny legs; not having glandular fever at seven, or being able to run like the wind. Everything else paled into insignificance alongside my skin colour and Sikh heritage.

It's not true that all Sikhs are called Singh. And we don't all carry curved blades strapped to our chests (although in the East End having this sort of rep isn't such a bad thing).

Even now the Banglas are sticking together. People are sitting next to the same people they sat alongside at school. Despite everything that has happened in the intervening years, the core facets of our personalities are untouched. All our flaws and strengths are the same.

On the far side of the hall I see Cate arriving. She is pale and striking, with a short expensive haircut and cheap sexy shoes. Dressed in a long light khaki skirt and a silk blouse, she looks elegant and, yes, pregnant. Her hands are smoothing her neat, compact bump. It's more than a bump. A beach ball. She hasn't long to go.

I don't want her to see me staring. I turn away.

'Alisha?'

'Sure. Who else?' I turn suddenly and put on a goofy smile.

Cate leans forward and kisses my cheek. I don't close my eyes. Neither does she. We stare at each other. Surprised. She smells of childhood.

There are fine lines at the corners of her eyes. I wasn't

there to see them drawn. The small scar on her left temple, just beneath her hairline – I remember that one.

We're the same age, twenty-nine, and the same shape, except for the bump. I have darker skin and hidden depths (like all brunettes) but I can categorically state that I will never look as good as Cate. She has learned – no, that makes it sound too practised – she was born with the ability to make men admire her. I don't know the secret. A movement of the eye, a cock of the head, a tone of voice or a touch of the arm, creates a moment, an illusion that all men gay or straight, old or young buy in to.

People are watching her now. I doubt if she even realises.

'How are you?'

'I'm fine,' I answer too quickly and start again. 'I'm all right.'

'Just all right?'

I try to laugh. 'But look at you – you're pregnant.'

'Yes.'

'When are you due?'

'In four weeks.'

'Congratulations.'

'Thank you.'

The questions and answers are too abrupt and matter-of-fact. Conversation has never been this hard – not with Cate. She looks nervously over my shoulder, as if worried we might be overheard.

'Didn't you marry—?'

'Felix Beaumont. He's over there.'

I follow her eyes to a tall, heavy-set figure in casual trousers and a loose white shirt. Felix didn't go to Oaklands and his real name is Buczkowski and not 'Beaumont'. His

17

father was a Polish shopkeeper who ran an electronics shop on Tottenham Court Road.

Now he's deep in conversation with Annabelle Trunzo whose dress is a scrap of material held up by her chest. If she exhales it's going to be bunched around her ankles.

'You know what I used to hate most about nights like this?' says Cate. 'Having someone who looks immaculate telling me how she spent all day ferrying children to ballet or football or cricket. And then she asks the obvious question: "Do you have any kids?" And I say, "Nope, no children." And she jokes, "Hey, why don't you have one of mine?" God, that pisses me off.'

'Well, it won't happen any more.'

'No.'

She takes a glass of wine from a passing tray. Again she glances around, looking distracted.

'Why did we fall out? It must have been my fault.'

'I'm sure you remember,' I say.

'It doesn't matter any more. By the way, I want you to be a godparent.'

'I'm not even a Christian.'

'Oh, that doesn't matter.'

Cate is avoiding whatever she really wants to talk about.

'Tell me what's wrong.'

She hesitates. 'I've gone too far this time, Ali. I've risked everything.'

Taking her arm, I steer her towards a quiet corner. People are starting to dance. The music is too loud. Cate puts her mouth close to my ear. 'You have to help me. Promise me you'll help me . . .'

'Of course.'

She holds back a sob, seeming to bite down upon it. 'They want to take my baby. They can't. You have to stop them . . .'

A hand touches her shoulder and she jumps, startled.

'Hello, gorgeous pregnant lady, who have we here?'

Cate backs away a step. 'No one. It's just an old friend.' Something shifts inside her. She wants to escape.

Felix Beaumont has perfect teeth. My mother has a thing about dental work. It is the first thing she notices about people.

'I remember you,' he says. 'You were behind me.'

'At school?'

'No, at the bar.'

He laughs and adopts an expression of amused curiosity.

Cate has backed further away. My eyes find hers. The faintest shake of her head tells me to let her go. I feel a rush of tenderness towards her. She motions with her empty glass. 'I'm just going to get a refill.'

'Go easy on that stuff, sweetheart. You're not alone.' Felix brushes her bump.

'Last one.'

He watches her leave with a mixture of sadness and longing. Finally he turns back to me.

'So is it Miss or Mrs?'

'Pardon?'

'Are you married?'

I hear myself say, 'Ms', which makes me sound like a lesbian. I change it to 'Miss' and then blurt, 'I'm single,' which appears desperate.

'That explains it.'

'What?'

'Those with children have photographs. Those without have nicer clothes and fewer lines.'

Is that supposed to be a compliment?

The skin around his eyes crinkles into a smile. He moves like a bear, rocking from foot to foot.

I hold out my hand. 'My name is Alisha Barba.'

He looks astonished. 'Well, well, well, you *really* do exist. Cate has talked about you a lot, but I thought you might be one of those imaginary childhood friends.'

'She talked about me?'

'Absolutely. So what do you do, Alisha?'

'I sit at home all day in my slippers, watching daytime soaps and old movies on Channel 4.'

He doesn't understand.

'I'm on medical leave from the Metropolitan Police.'

'What happened?'

'I broke my back. Someone dropped me across a wall.'

He flinches. My gaze drifts past him.

'She's coming back,' he says, reading my mind. 'She never leaves me talking to a pretty woman for too long.'

'You must be thrilled – about the baby.'

The smooth hollow beneath his Adam's apple rolls like a wave as he swallows. 'It's our miracle baby. We've been trying for so long.'

Someone has started a conga line on the dance floor, which snakes between the tables. Gopal Dhir grabs at my waist, pivoting my hips from side to side. Someone else pulls Felix into another part of the line and we're moving apart.

Gopal yells into my ear. 'Well, well, Alisha Barba. Are you still running?'

'Only for fun.'

'I always fancied you but you were far too quick for me.' He yells to someone over his shoulder. 'Hey, Rao! Look who it is – Alisha Barba. Didn't I always say she was cute?'

Rao has no hope of hearing him over the music, but nods vigorously and kicks out his heels.

I drag myself away.

'Why are you leaving?'

'I refuse to do the conga without a person from Trinidad being present.'

Disappointed, he lets me go and rocks his head from side to side. Someone else tries to grab me but I spring away.

The crowd around the bar has thinned out. I can't see Cate. People are sitting on the steps outside and spilling into the quadrangle. Across the playground I can see the famous oak tree, almost silver in the lights. Someone has put chicken wire around the trunk to stop children climbing. One of the Banglas fell off and broke his arm during my last year – a kid called Paakhi, which is Bengali for bird. What's in a name?

The new science block squats on the far side of the quadrangle. Deserted. Crossing the playground, I push open a door and enter a long corridor with classrooms to the left. Taking a few steps, I look inside. Chrome taps and curved spouts pick up faint light from the windows.

As my eyes adjust to the darkness, I see someone moving. A woman with her dress pushed up over her waist is arched over a bench with a man between her legs.

Backing away towards the door, I sense that someone else is watching. The smallest shift of my gaze finds him.

He whispers. 'Like to watch, do you, yindoo?'

I catch my breath. A half-breath. Paul Donavon pushes

21

his face close to mine. The years have thinned his hair and fleshed out his cheeks but he has the same eyes. It's amazing how I can hate him with the same intensity after all this time.

Even in the half-light I notice the tattooed cross on his neck. He sniffs at my hair. 'Where's Cate?'

'You leave her alone,' I say too loudly.

There are curses from the darkness. Lindsay and partner pull apart. Rocco is dancing on one leg, trying to hoist his trousers. At the far end of the corridor a door opens and light washes from outside as Donavon disappears.

'Jesus, Ali, you frightened the crap out of me,' says Lindsay, tugging down her dress.

'Sorry.'

'Who else was here?'

'Nobody. I'm really sorry. Just carry on.'

'I think the moment's gone.'

Rocco is already heading down the corridor.

'Give my best to your wife,' she calls after him.

I have to find Cate now. She should be told that Donavon is here. And I want her to explain what she meant. Who wants to take her baby?

I check the hall and the quadrangle. There is no sign of her. She might have left already. How strange it is to be conscious of losing her when I've only just met her again.

I walk to the school gates. Cars are parked on either side of the road. The pavement is dotted with people. I catch a glimpse of Cate and Felix on the far side. She is talking to someone. Donavon. She has her hand on his arm.

Cate looks up and waves. I'm closing the distance between

22

us, but she signals me to wait. Donavon turns away. Felix and Cate step between parked cars.

From somewhere behind them I hear Donavon cry out. Then comes a tortured high-pitched screech of rubber against tarmac. The wheels of a car are locked and screaming. Heads turn as if released from a catch.

Felix vanishes beneath the wheels, which rise and fall over his head with scarcely a bump. At the same moment Cate bends over the bonnet and springs back again. She turns her head in mid-air and for a moment she seems to be looking at me before the windscreen snaps her skull in a different direction. She tumbles through the air in slow motion like a trapeze artist ready to be caught. But nobody waits with chalky hands.

The driver brakes and slews. Cate rolls forward, landing on her back with her arm outstretched and one leg twisted beneath her.

Like an explosion in reverse, people are sucked towards the detonation. They scramble from cars and burst from doorways. Donavon reacts quicker than most and reaches Cate first. I drop to my knees beside him.

In a moment of suspended stillness, the three of us are drawn together again. She is lying on the road. Blood seeps from her nose in a deep soft satin blackness. Spittle bubbles and froths between her slightly parted lips. She has the prettiest mouth.

I cradle her head in the crook of my arm. What happened to her shoe? She only has one of them. Suddenly, I'm fixated on a missing shoe, asking people around me. It's important that I find it. Black, with a half-heel. Her skirt has ridden up. She's wearing maternity knickers to cover her bump.

A young chap steps forward politely. 'I've called 999.'

23

His girlfriend looks like she might be sick.

Donavon pulls down Cate's skirt. 'Don't move her head. She has to be braced.' He turns to the onlookers. 'We need blankets and a doctor.'

'Is she dead?' someone asks.

'Do you know her?' asks another.

'She's pregnant!' exclaims a third person.

Cate's eyes are open. I can see myself reflected in them. A burly man with a grey ponytail leans over us. He has an Irish accent.

'They just stepped out. I didn't see them. I swear.'

Cate's whole body goes rigid and her eyes widen. Even with blood in her mouth she tries to cry out and her head swings from side to side.

Donavon leaps to his feet and grabs the driver's shirt. 'You could have stopped, you bastard!'

'I didn't see them.'

'LIAR!' His voice is hoarse with hate. 'You ran them down.'

The driver glances nervously around the crowd. 'I don't know what he's talking about. It was an accident, I swear. He's talking crazy—'

'You saw them.'

'Not until it was too late . . .'

He pushes Donavon away. Buttons rip and the driver's shirt flaps open. The tattoo on his chest is of Christ on the cross.

People have piled out of the reunion to see what the commotion is about. Some of them are yelling and trying to clear the street. I can hear the sirens.

A paramedic pushes through the crowd. My fingers are

slick and warm. I feel like I'm holding Cate's head together. Two more crews arrive. The paramedics team up. I know the drill: no fire, no fuel leaks and no fallen power lines – they secure their own safety first.

I look for Felix. A dark shape is pinned beneath the rear axle of the car. Unmoving.

A paramedic crawls beneath the wheel arch. 'This one's gone,' he yells.

Another slides his hands beneath mine, taking hold of Cate's head. Two of them work on her.

'Airways are blocked. Using the Guedels.'

He puts a plastic curved tube in her mouth and suctions out blood.

'One seventy systolic over ninety. Right pupil dilated.'

'She's hypertensive.'

'Put a collar on.'

Someone talks into a two-way. 'We got serious head trauma and internal bleeding.'

'She's pregnant,' I hear myself saying. I don't know if they hear me.

'BP is climbing. Low pulse.'

'She's bleeding into her skull.'

'Let's get her inside.'

'She needs volume now.'

The spine board is placed beside her and Cate is logrolled onto her side and lifted onto a stretcher.

'She's pregnant,' I say again.

The paramedic turns to me.

'Do you know her?'

'Yes.'

'We got room for one. You can ride up front.' He is

pumping a rubber bag, forcing air into her lungs. 'We need her name, DOB, address – is she allergic to any drugs?'

'I don't know.'

'When is she due?'

'In four weeks.'

The stretcher is in the ambulance. The paramedics climb inside. A medical technician hustles me into the passenger seat. The door shuts. We're moving. Through the window I see the crowd staring at us. Where did they all come from? Donavon is sitting in the gutter, looking dazed. I want him to look at me. I want to say thank you.

The paramedics continue working on Cate. One of them talks into a two-way using words like 'bradycardic' and 'intracranial pressure'. A heart monitor beeps out a broken message.

'Is she going to be all right?'

Nobody answers.

'What about the baby?'

A paramedic starts to unbutton her blouse. 'I'm running two units.'

'No, wait. I've lost her pulse.'

The monitor flatlines.

'She's asystolic!'

'Starting compressions.'

He rips open the final buttons, exposing her bra and torso.

Both paramedics stop suddenly and raise their eyes to each other – a single look, no words, but it conveys everything. Strapped to Cate's midriff is a large piece of upholstery foam, trimmed to fit over her stomach. The prosthetic is pulled away. She is 'pregnant' no more.

Pushing down hard on her chest, a paramedic counts the compressions by yelling the numbers. The heart monitor is competing with the siren.

'No response.'

'We might have to crack her open.'

'One amp of adrenalin.' He bites off the cap and stabs the contents into her neck.

The next few minutes pass in a blur of flashing lights and fractured conversations. I know they're losing her. I guess I've known it all along. The dilated pupils, the bleeding inside her head – the classic signs of brain injury. Cate is broken in too many places to fix.

A thin green line on the monitor rises and falls and flattens again. They're counting each inflation with the chest compressions. One squeeze to every five compressions.

'Thommo.'

'What?'

'I'm stopping the chest compressions.'

'Why?'

'Because they're making her brains come out of her head.'

Cate's skull is broken behind her right ear.

'Keep going.'

'But—'

'Just keep going.'

Half a minute passes. Hard as they try, Cate's heart won't respond.

'What are you going to do?'

'Crack her chest.'

A wave of nausea washes into my mouth. I don't remember the rest of the journey or arriving at the

27

hospital. There are no crashing doors or white coats rushing down corridors. Instead, everything appears to slow down.

The building swallows Cate whole – less than whole, damaged.

Hospitals, I hate them. The smell, the pall of uncertainty, the whiteness. White walls, white sheets, white clothes. The only thing not white is the blood and the Afro-Caribbean nurses.

I'm still standing near the ambulance. The paramedics return and begin cleaning up.

'Are you gonna be OK?' one of them asks. The pillow of upholstery foam hangs from his fist. The dangling straps look like the legs of a strange sea creature.

He hands me a damp paper towel. 'You might want to use this.'

I have blood on my hands; blood all over my jeans.

'You missed a bit.' He motions to my cheek. I wipe the wrong one.

'Here, do you mind?'

He takes the towel and holds my chin in the palm of his hand, wiping my cheek. 'There.'

'Thank you.'

He wants to say something. 'Is she a close friend?'

'We went to school together.'

He nods. 'Why would she – I mean – why did she fake a pregnancy?'

I glance past him, unable to answer. It doesn't serve any purpose and makes even less sense. Cate needed to see me. She said they wanted to take her baby. What baby?

'Is she – will she be OK?'

It's his turn not to answer. The sadness in his eyes is rationed carefully because others will need it later.

A hose spits. Pink water swirls down the drain. The paramedic hands me the prosthetic and I feel something break inside me. Once I thought I had lost Cate for ever. Maybe this time I have.

4

Hospital waiting rooms are useless, helpless places, full of whispers and prayers. Nobody wants to look at me. Maybe it's the blood on my clothes. I have tried to clean Lindsay's top in the bathroom, scrubbing it under the tap with hand soap. I only managed to spread the stain around.

Doctors and nurses wander in and out, never able to relax. One patient on a trolley looks like a fly caught in a web of tubes and wires. The skin around his mouth is puckered and dry.

I have never really thought about death. Even when I was lying in hospital with pins holding my spine together, it didn't occur to me. I have faced off suspects, pursued cars, charged through doorways and walked into abandoned buildings but have never thought that I might die. Maybe that's one of the advantages of having little self-value.

A nurse has taken down details of Cate's family. I don't

know about Felix. His mother might still be alive. Nobody can tell me anything except that Cate is in surgery. The nurses are relentlessly positive. The doctors are more circumspect. They have the truth to contend with – the reality of what they can and cannot fix.

In the midst of an ordinary evening, on a quiet street, a couple are hit by a car. One is dead. The other has horrific injuries. What happened to Cate's other shoe? What happened to her baby?

A policeman arrives to interview me. He is my age, wearing a uniform with everything polished and pressed. I feel self-conscious about my appearance.

He has a list of questions – what, where, when and why. I try to remember everything that happened. The car came out of nowhere. Donavon yelled.

'So you think it was an accident?'

'I don't know.'

In my head I can hear Donavon accusing the driver of running them down. The policeman gives me a card. 'If you remember anything more, give me a call.'

Through the swing doors I see Cate's family arriving. Her father, her mother in a wheelchair, her older brother Jarrod.

Barnaby Elliot's voice is raised. 'What do you mean, there's no baby? My daughter is pregnant.'

'What are they saying, Barnaby?' his wife asks, tugging at his sleeve.

'They're saying she wasn't pregnant.'

'Then it mustn't be our Cate. They have the wrong person.'

The doctor interrupts. 'If you'll just wait here, I'll send someone to talk to you.'

Mrs Elliot is growing hysterical. 'Does that mean she lost the baby?'

'She was never pregnant. She didn't *have* a baby.'

Jarrod tries to intervene. 'I'm sorry but there must be some mistake. Cate was due in four weeks.'

'I want to see my daughter,' demands Barnaby. 'I want to see her right this minute.'

Jarrod is three years older than Cate. It is strange how little I can recall of him. He kept pigeons and wore braces until he was twenty. I think he went to university in Scotland and later got a job in the City.

In contrast, nothing about Cate is remote or diffuse or gone small. I still remember when I first saw her. She was sitting on a bench outside the school gates at Oaklands wearing white socks, a short grey pleated skirt and Doc Martens. Heavy mascara bruised her eyes, which seemed impossibly large. And her teased hair had all the colours of the rainbow.

Although new to the school, within days Cate knew more kids and had more friends than I did. She was never still – always wrapping her arms around people, tapping her foot or bouncing a crossed leg upon her knee.

Her father was a property developer, she said: a two-word profession, which like a double-barrelled surname gave a man gravitas. 'Train driver' is also two words but my father's job didn't sound so impressive or have the same social cachet.

Barnaby Elliot wore dark suits, crisp white shirts and ties that were from one club or another. He stood twice for the Tories in Bethnal Green and each time managed to turn a safe Labour seat into an even safer one.

I suspect the only reason he sent Cate to Oaklands was to make him more electable. He liked to portray himself as a battler from 'Struggle Street', with dirt under his finger-nails and machine oil in his veins.

In reality, I think the Elliots would have preferred their only daughter to attend a private school, Anglican and all-girls rather than Oaklands. Mrs Elliot, in particular, regarded it as a foreign country that she had no desire to visit.

Cate and I didn't talk to each other for almost a year. She was the coolest, most desirable girl in the whole school, yet she had a casual, almost unwanted beauty. Girls would hang around her, chatting and laughing, seeking her approval, yet she didn't seem to notice.

She talked like someone in a teen movie, smart-mouthed and sassy. I know teenagers are supposed to talk that way but I never met anyone who did, except for Cate. And she was the only person I knew who could distil her emotions into drops of pure love, anger, fear or happiness.

I came from the Isle of Dogs, further east, and went to Oaklands because my parents wanted me educated 'out of the area'. Sikhs were a minority, but so were the whites, who were the most feared. Some regarded themselves as the true East Enders, as if there was some royal cockney bloodline to be protected. The worst of them was Paul Donavon, a thug and a bully who fancied himself as a ladies' man and as a footballer. His best mate, Liam Bradley, was almost as bad. A head taller, with a forehead that blazed with pimples, Bradley looked as if he scrubbed his face with a cheese grater instead of soap.

New kids had to be initiated. Boys copped it the worst, of course, but girls weren't immune, particularly the pretty ones. Donavon and Bradley were seventeen and they were always going to find Cate. Even at fourteen she had 'potential', as the older boys would say, with full lips and a J-Lo bottom that looked good in anything tight. It was the sort of bottom that men's eyes follow instinctively. Men and boys and grandfathers.

Donavon cornered her one day during fifth period. He was standing outside the headmaster's office, awaiting punishment for some new misdemeanour. Cate was on a different errand – delivering a bundle of permission notes to the school secretary.

Donavon saw her arrive in the admin corridor. She had to walk right past him. He followed her onto the stairs.

'You don't want to get lost,' he said, in a mocking tone, blocking her path. She stepped to one side. He mirrored her movements.

'You got a sweet sweet arse. A peach. And beautiful skin. Let me see you walk up them stairs. Go on. I'll just stand here and you go right on ahead. Maybe you could hitch your skirt up a little. Show me that sweet sweet peach.'

Cate tried to turn back but Donavon danced around her. He was always light on his feet. On the football field he played up front, ghosting past defenders, pulling them inside and out.

Big heavy fire doors with horizontal bars sealed off the stairwell. Sound echoed off the cold hard concrete but stayed inside. Cate couldn't keep focused on his face without turning.

'There's a word for girls like you,' he said. 'Girls that wear skirts like that. Girls that shake their arses like peaches on the trees.'

Donavon put his arm around her shoulders and pressed his mouth against her ear. He pinned her arms above her head by the wrists, holding them in his fist. His other hand ran up her leg, under her skirt, pulling her knickers aside. Two fingers found their way inside her, scraping dry skin.

Cate didn't come back to class. Mrs Pulanski sent me to look for her. I found her in the girls' toilets. Mascara stained her cheeks with black tears and it seemed like her eyes were melting. She wouldn't tell me what had happened at first. She took my hand and pressed it into her lap. Her dress was so short that my fingers brushed her thigh.

'Are you hurt?'

Her shoulders shook.

'Who hurt you?'

Her knees were squeezed together. Locked tight. I looked at her face. Slowly I parted her knees. A smear of blood stained the whiteness of her cotton knickers.

Something stretched inside me. It kept stretching until it was so thin it vibrated with my heart. My mother says I should never use the word 'hate'. You should never hate anyone. I know she's right but she lives in a sanitised Sikh-land.

The bell sounded for lunch time. Screams and laughter filled the playground, bouncing off the bare brick walls and pitted asphalt. Donavon was on the southern edge in the 'quad', in the shadow of the big oak tree that had been carved with so many initials it should rightly have been dead.

'Well, what have we here,' he said, as I marched towards him. 'A little yindoo.'

'Look at her face,' said Bradley. 'Looks like she's gonna explode.'

'Turkey thermometer just popped out her bum – she's done.'

It drew a laugh and Donavon enjoyed his moment. To his credit he must have recognised some danger because he didn't take his eyes off me. By then I had stopped a yard in front of him. My head reached halfway up his chest. I didn't think of his size. I didn't think of my size. I thought of Cate.

'That's the one who runs,' said Bradley.

'Well, run away, little yindoo, you're smelling up the air.'

I still couldn't get any words out. Disquiet grew in Donavon's eyes. 'Listen, you sick Sikh, get lost.'

I rediscovered my voice. 'What did you do?'

'I did nothing.'

A crowd had started to gather. Donavon could see them coming. He wasn't so sure any more.

It didn't feel like me who was standing in the playground, confronting Donavon. Instead I was looking down from the branches of the tree, watching him from above like a bird. A dark bird.

'Fuck off, you crazy bitch.'

Donavon was fast but I was the runner. Later people said I flew. I crossed the final yard in the beat of a butterfly's wing. My fingers found his eye sockets. He roared and tried to throw me off. I clung on in a death grip, attacking the soft tissue.

Snarling my hair in his fists, he wrenched my head backwards, trying to pull me away, but I wasn't letting go. He pummelled my head with his fists, screaming, 'Get her off! Get her off!'

Bradley had been watching, too shocked to react. He

was never sure what to do unless Donavon told him. First he tried to put me in a headlock, forcing my face into the dampness of his armpit, which smelled of wet socks and cheap deodorant.

My legs were wrapped around Donavon's waist. My fingers gouged his eyes. Bradley tried another tack. He grabbed one of my hands and uncurled my fingers, pulling my arm backwards. My grip broke. I raked my fingernails across Donavon's face. Although he couldn't see anything from his streaming eyes he lashed out, kicking me in the head. My mouth filled with blood.

Bradley had hold of my left arm, but my right was still free. In a family of boys you learn how to fight. When you're the only girl you learn how to fight dirty.

Spinning to my feet, I swung my hand at Donavon's face. My index finger and middle finger speared up his nose, hooking him like a fish. My fist closed. No matter what happened next Donavon would follow me. Bradley could break my arm, drag me backwards, kick me through the goalposts and Donavon would come with me like a bull with a ring through his nose.

A moan was all I heard escape from his mouth. His arms and legs were jerking.

'Don't touch her. Don't touch her,' he sniffled. 'Just let her go.'

Bradley loosened his grip on my left arm.

Donavon's eyes were swollen and closing. His nasal passages were turned inside out by my fingers. I held him with his head tilted back and his lower jaw flapping open as he sucked air.

Miss Flower, the music teacher, was on playground duty

that day. In truth she was having a cigarette in the staffroom when someone came hurtling up the stairs to get her.

Donavon blubbered on about being sorry. I didn't say a word. It felt like none of this had happened to me. I still seemed to be watching from the branches of the tree.

Miss Flower was a fit, youthful, jolly-hockey-sticks type with a fondness for French cigarettes and the sports mistress. She took in the scene with very little fuss and realised that nobody could force me to let Donavon go. So she adopted a conciliatory approach full of comforting words and calming appeals. Donavon had gone quiet. The less he moved, the less it hurt.

I didn't know Miss Flower well but I think she got me, you know. A skinny Indian girl with braces and glasses doesn't take on the school bully without a good reason. She sat with me in the infirmary as I spat blood into a bowl. Two front teeth had been ripped out of the wire braces and were trapped in the twisted metal.

I had a towel around my neck and another across my lap. I don't know where they took Donavon. Miss Flower held an ice pack to my mouth.

'You want to tell me why?'

I shook my head.

'Well, I don't doubt he deserved it – but you will have to give a reason.'

I didn't answer.

She sighed. 'OK, well, it can wait. First you need a clean uniform. There might be one in lost property. Let's clean up before your parents arrive.'

'I want to go back to class,' I lisped.

'First you need to get those teeth fixed, dear.'

Finding an emergency dentist on the NHS normally meant promising your first-born to the Church but I had family connections. My Uncle Sandhu has a dental practice in Ealing. (He's not really my uncle, but every older Asian who knew my family was referred to as uncle or aunt.) Uncle Sandhu had fitted my braces 'at cost'. Bada was so pleased that he would make me smile for visitors, showing off my teeth.

Mama rang my sister-in-law Nazeem and the two of them caught a minicab to the school. Nazeem had the twins and was pregnant again. I was whisked off to Uncle Sandhu who dismantled my braces and took photographs of my teeth. I looked six years old again and had a lisp.

The next morning was fresh and bright and possessed of an innocence so pristine that it made a lie of the previous day. Cate didn't come to school. She stayed away for two weeks until we broke up for the summer holidays. Miss Flower said she had pleurisy.

Sucking on my glued teeth, I went back to my classes. People treated me differently. Something had happened that day. The scales had fallen from my eyes; the earth had rotated the required number of times and I said goodbye to childhood.

Donavon was expelled from Oaklands. He joined the army, the Parachute Regiment, just in time for Bosnia. Other wars would turn up soon enough. Bradley left during the holidays and became an apprentice boilermaker. I still see him occasionally, pushing his kids on the swings on Bethnal Green.

Nobody ever mentioned what happened to Cate. Only I knew. I don't think she even told her parents – certainly not her father. Digital penetration isn't classified as rape because the law differentiates between a penis and a finger, or fist, or bottle. I don't think it should, but that's an argument for fancy defence lawyers.

People were nicer to me after my fight with Donavon. They acknowledged my existence. I was no longer just 'the runner'; I had a name. One of my teeth took root again. The other turned yellow and Uncle Sandhu had to replace it with a false one.

During the holidays I had a phone call from Cate. I don't know how she found my number.

'I thought maybe you might like to catch a movie.'

'You mean, you and me?'

'We could see *Pretty Woman*. Unless you've already seen it. I've been three times but I could go again.' She kept talking. I had never heard her sound nervous.

My mother wouldn't let me see *Pretty Woman*. She said it was about a whore.

'Julia Roberts is a hooker with a heart,' I explained, which only got me into trouble. Apparently, it was OK for my mother to use the term 'whore' but I wasn't allowed to say 'hooker'. In the end we went to see *Ghost* with Patrick Swayze and Demi Moore.

Cate didn't say anything about Donavon. She was still beautiful, still clear-skinned, still wearing a short skirt. Sitting in the darkness, our shoulders touched and her fingers found mine. She squeezed my hand. I squeezed hers.

And that was the start of it. Like Siamese twins, we were. Salt and pepper, Miss Flower called us but I preferred 'milk and cookies', which was Mr Nelson's description. He was American and taught biology and protested when people said that it was the easiest of the science electives.

Through school and then university Cate and I were best friends. I loved her. Not in a sexual way, although I don't think I understood the difference at fourteen.

Cate claimed she could predict the future. She would map out our paths, which included careers, boyfriends, weddings, husbands and children. She could even make herself miserable by imagining that our friendship would be over one day.

'I have never had a friend like you and I never shall again. Never ever.'

I was embarrassed.

The other thing she said was this: 'I am going to have lots of babies because they will love me and never leave me.'

I don't know why she talked like this. She treated love and friendship like a small creature trapped in a blizzard, fighting for survival. Maybe she knew something then that I didn't.

5

Another morning. The sun is shining somewhere. I can see blue sky bunched between buildings and a construction crane etched in charcoal against the light. I cannot say how many days have passed since the accident – four or fourteen. Colours are the same – the air, the trees, the buildings – nothing has changed.

I have been to the hospital every day, avoiding the waiting room and Cate's family. Instead I sit in the cafeteria or wander the corridors, trying to draw comfort from the technology and the smiles of the staff.

Cate is in a coma. Machines are helping her to breathe. According to the hospital bulletin she suffered a perforated lung, a broken back and multiple fractures to both her legs. The back of her skull was pulverised but two operations have stopped the bleeding.

Her neurosurgeon tells me the coma is a good thing. Her body has shut down and is trying to repair itself.

'What about brain damage?'

He toys with his stethoscope and won't look me in the eye. 'The human brain is the most perfectly designed piece of equipment in the known universe,' he explains. 'Unfortunately, it is not designed to withstand a ton of metal at high speed.'

'Which means?'

'We classify severe head injury as a coma score of eight or less. Mrs Beaumont has a score of four. It is a *very* severe head injury.'

At eleven o'clock the ICU posts another bulletin. Cate's condition hasn't changed. I bump into Jarrod in the cafeteria and we drink coffee and talk about everyday incidental things: jobs and families, the price of eggs, the frailty of modern paper bags. The conversation is punctuated by long pauses as though silence has become part of the language.

'The doctors say she was never pregnant,' he says. 'She didn't *lose* the baby. There was no miscarriage or termination. Mum and Dad are beside themselves. They don't know what to think.'

'She must have had a reason.'

'Yeah, well, I can't think of one.' A trickle of air from the ceiling vents ruffles his hair.

'Do you think Felix knew?'

'I guess. How do you keep a secret like that from your husband?' He glances at his watch. 'Have you been to see her?'

'No.'

'Come on.'

Jarrod leads me upstairs to the intensive-care unit, along painfully white corridors that all look the same. Only two visitors per patient are allowed in the ICU. Masks must be worn and hands must be scrubbed with disinfectant.

Jarrod isn't coming with me. 'There's someone already with her,' he says, adding as an afterthought, 'she won't bite.'

My stomach drops. It's too late to back out.

The curtains are open and daylight casts a square on the floor. Mrs Elliot in her wheelchair is trapped in the light like a hologram, her skin as pale and fine as white china.

Cate lies beside her, hostage to a tangle of tubing, plasma bags and stainless steel. Needles have been driven into her veins and her head is swathed in bandages. Monitors and machines blink and buzz, reducing her existence to a digital computer game.

I want her to wake now. I want her eyes to open and for her to pluck away the breathing tube like a strand of hair caught in the corner of her mouth.

Wordlessly, Mrs Elliot points to a chair beside the bed. 'The last time I watched my daughter sleeping she was eight years old. She had come down with pneumonia. I think she caught it at one of those public swimming pools. Every time she coughed it sounded like someone drowning on dry land.'

I reach across the marble sheets and take Cate's fingers in mine. I can feel her mother's eyes upon me. A cold scrutiny. She does not want me here.

I remember Mrs Elliot when she could still walk – a tall, thin woman who always offered Cate her cheek to kiss so as not to smudge her lipstick. She used to be an actress who did mainly TV commercials and was always impeccably made-up, as though perpetually ready for her close-up. Of course, that was before she suffered a stroke that paralysed her down her right side. Now one eyelid droops and no amount of make-up can hide the nerve damage around her mouth.

In a whisper, she asks, 'Why would she lie about the baby?'

'I don't know. She was coming to see me. She said she had done something foolish and that someone wanted to take her baby.'

'What baby? She was never pregnant. Never! Now they say her pelvis is so badly shattered that even if she survives she'll never be able to carry a baby.'

Something shudders inside me. A déjà vu from another hospital and a different time, when *my* bones were being mended. A price is paid with every surgery.

Mrs Elliot clutches a cushion to her chest. 'Why would she do this? Why would she lie to us?'

There is no warmth in her voice, only accusation. She feels betrayed. Embarrassed. What will she tell the neighbours? I feel like lashing out and defending Cate, who deserves more than this. Instead I close my eyes and listen to the wind washing over the rooftops and the electronic beeping of the machines.

How did she do it – maintain such a lie for weeks and months? It must have haunted her. A part of me is strangely envious. I don't think I've ever wanted something *that* much; not even Olympic medals. When I missed out on the team for the Sydney Games I cried on the edge of the track but they were tears of frustration rather than disappointment. The girl who took my place *wanted* it more.

I know that I shouldn't compare Olympic selection with

motherhood. Perhaps my opinions are clouded by the medical reality of a patched pelvis and a reinforced spine that can never withstand the trials of pregnancy and labour. Wanting children is a dangerous ambition for me.

Squeezing Cate's hand, I hope she knows I'm here. For years I wanted her to call, to be friends again, to need me. And just when it finally happened, she's been snatched away like a half-finished question. I have to find out what she wanted. I have to understand why.

Euston Traffic Garage is in Drummond Crescent, tucked between Euston Station and the British Library. The spire of St Aloysius's church rises above it like a rocket on a launch pad.

The Collision Investigation Unit is an odd place, a mixture of high-tech gadgetry and old-fashioned garage, with hoists, grease traps and machine tools. This is where they do the vehicular equivalents of autopsies and the process is much the same. Bodies are opened, dismantled, weighed and measured.

The duty officer, a roly-poly sergeant in overalls, peers up from the twisted front end of a car. 'Can I help you?'

I introduce myself, showing him my badge. 'There was a traffic accident on Friday night on Old Bethnal Green Road. A couple were knocked down.'

'Yeah, I looked at that one.' He wipes his hands on a rag and tucks it back into his pocket.

'One of them is a friend of mine.'

'She still alive?'

'Yes.'

'Lucky.'

'How far are you with the investigation?'

'Finished. Just got to write it up.'

'What do you think happened?'

'Thought it was pretty obvious. Your friend and her husband tried to tackle a minicab.' He doesn't mean to sound callous. It's just his way. 'Maybe the driver could've put the brakes on a bit sooner. Sometimes you can be unlucky. Choose the wrong moment to check your mirrors and that fraction of a second comes off your reaction time. Might've made a difference. Might not. We'll never know.'

'So you're not going to charge him?'

'What with?'

'Dangerous driving, negligence – there must be something.'

'He was licensed, insured, registered and roadworthy – I got nothing on this guy.'

'He was travelling too fast.'

'He says they stepped out in front of him. He couldn't stop.'

'Did you examine the car?'

'At the scene.'

'Where is it now?'

He sighs. 'Let me explain the facts of life to you, Detective Constable. You see that yard out there?' He motions to an open roller door leading to a walled yard. 'There are sixty-eight vehicles – every one of them involved in a serious accident. We have thirteen reports due for the coroner, two dozen submissions for criminal trials and I spend half my time in the witness box and the other half up to me elbows in motor oil and blood. There are no *good* traffic accidents but from my point of view the one on Friday night was

47

better than most because it was simple – sad, but simple. They stepped out from between parked cars. The driver couldn't stop in time. End of story.'

The genial curiosity on his face has vanished. 'We checked the brakes. We checked his licence. We checked his driving record. We checked his blood alcohol. We took a statement at the scene and let the poor guy go home. Sometimes an accident is just an accident. If you have evidence to the contrary, hand it over. Otherwise, I'd appreciate if you let me get on with my job.'

There is a moment when we eyeball each other. He's not so much angry as disappointed.

'I'm sorry. I didn't mean to question your expertise.'

'Yes, you did.' His expression softens. 'But that's OK. I'm sorry about your friend.'

'Would you mind if I took a look at the driver's statement?'

He doesn't see a problem with that. He leads me to an office and motions to a chair. A computer hums on the desk and box files line the shelves like cardboard bricks. The sergeant hands me a file and a video. For a moment he hovers near the door, unwilling to leave me alone.

The driver's name was Earl Blake and his occupation is listed as stevedore. He was moonlighting as a minicab driver to make extra money, he said.

The video is time-coded down to the second and begins with wide-angle shots of the street, taken in the shaky camera style of a holiday video. Party-goers are milling outside the gates of Oaklands, some still holding drinks or draped with streamers.

Earl Blake is in the distance, talking to a policeman. He

notices the camera and seems to turn away. It might mean nothing.

There are statements from a dozen witnesses. Most heard the screech of brakes and saw the impact. Further along the road, two cabbies were parked near the corner of Mansford Street. The minicab came past them slowly, as though searching for an address.

I look for any mention of Donavon. His name and address were taken down by investigators but there isn't a statement.

'Yeah, I remember him,' says the sergeant. 'He had a tattoo.' He points to his neck, tracing a cross below his Adam's apple. 'He said he didn't see a thing.'

'He *saw* it happen.'

The sergeant raises an eyebrow. 'That ain't what he told me.'

I make a note of Donavon's address on a scrap of paper.

'You're not trying to run a private investigation here, are you, Detective Constable?'

'No, sir.'

'If you have any important information regarding this accident, you are obliged to make it known to me.'

'Yes, sir. I have no information. Mr Donavon tried to save my friend's life. I just want to thank him. Good manners, you see. My mother bred them into me.'

6

Earl Blake's address is a small terrace off Pentonville Road at the neglected end of King's Cross. There is nobody home. My legs have gone to sleep I've been sitting here for so long, staring out the windscreen, tapping a rhythm on the wheel.

A drug pusher leans against a low wall outside a pub on the corner, his face half-hidden under the brim of a baseball cap. Two teenage girls walk by and he says something, smiling. They toss back their hair and sashay a little faster.

A red hatchback pulls into a parking space ahead of me. A woman in her fifties emerges, dressed in a nurse's uniform. She collects a bag of groceries from the boot and walks to the terrace, cursing as she drops her keys.

'Are you Mrs Blake?' I ask.

'Who wants to know?' Her blue-grey hair is lacquered into place.

'I'm looking for your husband.'

'You trying to be funny?'

She has opened the door and stepped inside. I stand in the doorway.

'Your husband was involved in a car accident last Friday night.'

'Not bloody likely.'

She is disappearing down the hallway.

'I'm talking about *Earl* Blake.'

'That's his name.'

'I need to speak to him.'

Shouting over her shoulder, 'Well, missy, you're six years too late. That's when I buried him.'

'He's *dead*?'

'I sure hope so.' She laughs wryly.

The house smells of damp dog and toilet freshener.

'I'm a police officer,' I call after her. 'I'm sorry if there's been a mistake. Do you have a *son* called Earl?'

'Nope.'

Dumping her shopping on a table in the kitchen, she turns. 'Listen, love, either come in or stay out. This place costs a fortune to bloody heat.'

I follow her into the house and shut the door. She has taken a seat at the table and kicked off her shoes, rubbing her feet through her support hose.

I look around. There are medications lined up on the windowsill and food coupons stuck under fridge magnets. A picture of a baby in a hollowed-out pumpkin is on the calendar.

'Put the kettle on, will you, love?'

The tap spits and belches.

'I'm sorry about your husband.'

51

'Nowt for you to be sorry about. He dropped dead right there – face first into his egg and chips. He was whingeing about how I overcooked the eggs and then *whump*!' Her hand slaps the table top. 'I told him not to wear his underwear to breakfast but he never did listen. All the neighbours watched him wheeled out of here in his old Y-fronts.'

She tosses her shoes in the corner beside the back door. 'I know all men leave eventually but not when you've just made 'em egg 'n' chips. Earl was always bloody inconsiderate.'

Mrs Blake pushes herself upwards and warms the teapot. 'You're not the first, you know.'

'What do you mean?'

'Some bloke came here yesterday. He didn't believe me either when I said Earl was dead. He said Earl owed him money. As if! Can't see him gambling from beyond.'

'What did this man look like?'

'Had this tattoo on his neck. A cross.'

Donavon is searching for Blake.

'I hate tattoos,' she continues. 'Earl had 'em on his forearms. He was in the merchant navy before I met him. Travelled all over the place and came back with these *souvenirs*. I call 'em skin complaints.'

'Did he have one just here?' I point to my chest. 'A crucifixion scene.'

'Earl weren't religious. He said religion was for people who believed in hell.'

'Do you have a photograph of him?'

'Yeah, a few. He was handsome once.'

She leads me to the sitting room, which is full of 1970s furniture and faded rugs. Rummaging in a cupboard next to the gas fire, she pulls out a photo album.

'Course, it's easier keeping the place clean now. He was a real slob. Dropped clothes like they was crumbs.'

She hands me a snapshot. Earl is wearing a jacket with a fur collar and fluorescent strips. He looks nothing like the driver of the minicab, although both are roughly the same age.

'Mrs Blake, do you ever get mail for your late husband?'

'Yeah, sure, junk stuff. Banks are always sending him applications for credit cards. What's he going do with a credit card, eh?'

'Did you cancel his driver's licence?'

'Didn't bother. I sold his old van. Bought meself the hatchback. Reckon the dealer ripped me off, the Paki bastard. No way that thing had done only four thousand miles.'

She realises her mistake. 'No offence, love.'

'I'm not Pakistani.'

'Right. I don't know much about the difference.'

She finds me another photograph.

'Do you ever take in lodgers or have visitors staying?'

'Nah.'

'Ever had a break-in?'

'Yeah, a few years back.' She looks at me suspiciously.

I try to explain that someone has stolen her husband's identity, which is not as difficult as it sounds. A bank statement and a gas bill is all it takes to get a credit report, which will yield a National Insurance number and a list of previous addresses. The rest falls into place – birth certificates, credit cards, a passport.

'Earl never did anything wrong,' says Mrs Blake. 'Never did much right, either.' She overbalances a little as she stands and her forearms wobble beneath the short sleeves of her uniform.

I don't stay for a cup of tea, which disappoints her. Letting myself out, I stand for a moment on the front steps, raising my face to the misty rain. Three kids are practising their literacy skills on a wall across the road.

Further down the street is a triangular garden with benches and a playground surrounded by a semicircle of plane trees and a copper beech. Something catches my eye beneath the lower branches.

When soldiers are trained to hide in the jungle, they are told that four main things will give them away: movement, shape, shine and silhouette. Movement is the most important. That's what I notice. A seated figure stands from a bench and begins walking away. I recognise his gait.

It is strange how I react. For years, whenever I have conjured up Donavon's face, panic has swelled in the space between my heart and lungs. I'm not frightened of him now. I want answers. Why is he so interested in Cate Beaumont?

He knows I've clocked him. His hands are out of his pockets, swinging freely as he runs. If I let him reach the far side of the park I'll lose him in the side streets.

Rounding the corner, I accelerate along the path which is flanked by a railing fence and tall shrubs. An old Royal Mail sorting office is on the opposite corner, with tall windows edged in painted stone. Turning left, I follow the perimeter fence. The exit is ahead. Nobody emerges. He should be here by now.

I pause at the gate, listening for hard heels on the

pavement. Nothing. A motorcycle rumbles to life on the far side of the park. He doubled back. Clever.

Run, rabbit, run. I know where you live.

My hallway smells of bleach and the stale backdraught of a vacuum cleaner. My mother has been cleaning. That's one of the signs that my life isn't all that it should be. No matter how many times I complain that I don't need a cleaner, she insists on catching a bus from the Isle of Dogs just to 'straighten a few things up'.

'I am defrosting the freezer,' she announces from the kitchen.

'It doesn't need defrosting. It's automatic.'

She makes a 'pfffhh' sound. Her blue and green sari is tucked up into her support stockings, making her backside appear enormous. It is an optical illusion just like her eyes behind her glasses, which are as wet and brown as fresh cow dung.

She is waiting for a kiss on the cheek. I have to bend. She is scarcely five feet tall and shaped like a pear, with sticky-out ears that help her hear like a bat and X-ray vision that only mothers possess. She also has an oddly selective sense of smell, which can pick up the scent of perfume from fifty feet yet allows her to sniff the crotches of my four brothers' underpants to establish if they need washing. I feel like retching at the thought of it.

'Why is there a padlock on my Hari's door?'

'Privacy, perhaps.'

'I found it open.'

That's strange. Hari is always very careful about locking the door.

Mama holds my face in her hands. 'Have you eaten today?'

'Yes.'

'You're lying. I can tell. I have brought some dahl and rice.'

She uses perfect school-book English, the kind they used to teach in the dark ages when she went to school.

I notice a suitcase in the corner. For a moment I fear that she might be planning to stay but one suitcase would never be enough.

'Your father was cleaning out the attic,' she explains.

'Why?'

'Because he has nothing else to do.' She sounds exasperated.

My father has retired after thirty-five years driving main-line trains and is still making the adjustment. Last week he went through my pantry checking use-by dates and putting them in order.

Mama opens the suitcase. Lying neatly across the top is my old Oaklands school uniform. I feel a stab of recognition and remember Cate. I should phone the hospital for an update on her condition.

'I didn't want to throw things away without asking you,' she explains. There are scarves, scrapbooks, photo albums, diaries and running trophies. 'I had no idea you had a crush on Mr Elliot.'

'You read my *diary*!'

'It fell open.'

Matricide is a possibility.

She changes the subject. 'Now, you're coming early on Sunday to help us cook. Make sure Hari wears something nice. His ivory shirt.'

My father is having his sixty-fifth birthday and the party has been planned for months. It will include at least one eligible Sikh bachelor, no doubt. My parents want me to marry a good Sikh boy – bearded, of course; not one of those clean-shaven Indians who thinks he's a Bollywood film star. This ignores the fact that all my brothers cut their hair, apart from Prabakar, the eldest, who is the family's moral guardian.

I know that all parents are considered eccentric by their children, but mine are particularly embarrassing. My father, for example, is a stickler for conserving energy. He studies the electricity bill every quarter and compares it to previous quarters and previous years.

Mama crosses entire weeks off the calendar in advance so that she 'doesn't forget'.

'But how will you know what day it is?' I once asked her.

'Everyone knows what day it is,' she replied.

You cannot argue with logic like that.

'By the way, your phone is fixed,' she announces. 'A nice man came this afternoon.'

'I didn't report a problem.'

'Well, he came to fix it.'

A chill travels across my skin as if someone has left a door open. I fire off questions: what did he look like? What was he wearing? Did he have identification? Mama looks concerned and then frightened.

'He had a clipboard and a box of tools.'

'But no ID?'

'I didn't ask.'

'He should have shown it to you. Did you leave him alone?'

'I was cleaning.'

My eyes dart from one object to the next, taking an inventory. Moving upstairs, I search my wardrobes and drawers. None of my jewellery is missing. My bank statements, passport and spare set of keys are still in the drawer. Carefully, I count the pages of my chequebook.

'Perhaps Hari reported the fault,' she says.

I call him on his mobile. The pub is so noisy he can barely hear me.

'Did you report a problem with the phone?'

'What?'

'Did you call British Telecom?'

'No. Was I supposed to?'

The conversation is going round in circles. 'It doesn't matter,' I say, hanging up.

My mother rocks her head from side to side and makes concerned noises. 'Should we call the police?'

The question had already occurred to me. What would I report? There was no break-in. Nothing has been taken as far as I can tell. It is either the perfect crime or no crime at all.

'Don't worry about it, Mama.'

'But the man—'

'He was just fixing the telephone.'

I don't want her worrying. She spends enough time here already.

Mama looks at her watch. If she doesn't leave now she won't be home for dinner. I offer to drive her and she smiles. It is the widest, most radiant smile ever created. No wonder people do as she says – they want to see her smile.

On the bedside table is a book that I started reading last

night. The bookmark is in the wrong place – twenty pages forward. Perhaps I moved it inadvertently. Paranoia is not reality on a finer scale: it is a foolish reaction to unanswered questions.

7

On her very last day of being sixteen Cate found her mother lying unconscious in the kitchen. She had suffered something called a haemorrhagic stroke, which Cate explained as being like a 'brain explosion'.

Ruth Elliot had two subsequent strokes in hospital, which paralysed her down her right side. Cate blamed herself. She should have been at home. Instead we'd sneaked out to watch the Beastie Boys at the Brixton Academy. Cate let a guy kiss her that night. He must have been at least twenty-five. Ancient.

'Maybe I'm being punished for lying,' she said.

'But your Mum is the one *really* being punished,' I pointed out.

Cate started going to church after that – for a while at least. I went with her one Sunday, kneeling down and closing my eyes.

'What are you doing?' she whispered.

'Praying for your Mum.'

'But you're not an Anglican. Won't your god think you're changing teams?'

'I don't think it matters which god fixes her up.'

Mrs Elliot came home in a wheelchair, unable to talk properly. In the beginning she could only say one word: 'when', uttered more as a statement than a question.

No matter what you said to her she answered the same way.

'How are you today, Mrs Elliot?'

'When, when, when.'

'Have you had your tea?'

'When, when, when.'

'I'm just going to study with Cate.'

'When, when.'

I know it sounds horrible but we used to play tricks on her.

'We have a biology test, Mrs E.'

'When, when.'

'On Friday.'

'When, when, when.'

'In the morning.'

'When, when.'

'About half-nine.'

'When, when.'

'Nine thirty-four, to be precise. Greenwich Mean Time.'

They had a nurse to look after her. A big Jamaican called Yvonne, with pillow breasts and fleshy arms and mottled pink hands. She used to wear electric colours and men's shoes and she blamed her bad complexion on the English weather. Yvonne was strong enough to scoop Mrs Elliot up in her arms and lift her into the shower and back into her wheelchair. And she talked to her all the time, having long conversations that sounded completely plausible unless you listened closely.

Yvonne's greatest gift, however, was to fill the house with laughter and songs, lifting the gloom. She had children of her own – Caspar and Bethany – who had steel-wool hair and neon smiles. I don't know about her husband – he was never mentioned – but I know Yvonne went to church every Sunday and had Tuesdays off and baked the best lime cheesecake in creation.

On weekends I sometimes slept over at Cate's place. We rented a video and stayed up late. Her Dad didn't come home until after nine. Tanned and tireless, he had a deep voice and an endless supply of corny jokes. I thought him unbelievably handsome.

The tragedy of his wife's condition gained a lot of sympathy for Barnaby. Women, in particular, seemed to admire his devotion to his crippled wife and how he went out of his way to make her feel special.

Ruth Elliot, however, didn't seem to share this admiration. She recovered her speech after months of therapy and attacked Barnaby at every opportunity, belittling him in front of Yvonne and his children and his children's friends.

'Did you hear that?' she'd say as the front door opened. 'He's *home*. He *always* comes home. Who does he smell like tonight?'

'Now, now, Ruth, please,' Barnaby would say, but she wouldn't stop.

'He smells of soap and shampoo. He always smells of

soap and shampoo. Why does a man shower *before* he comes home?'

'You know the reason. I've been playing tennis at the club.'

'He washes before he comes home. Washes the smell away.'

'Ruth, darling,' Barnaby tried to say. 'Let's talk about this upstairs.'

She would fight at his hands and then surrender as he lifted her easily from her chair and carried her up the sixteen stairs. We would hear her screaming and finally crying. He would put her to bed, settle her like a child, and then rejoin us in the kitchen for hot chocolate.

When I first met Cate, Barnaby was already forty but looked good for his age. And he could get away with things because he was so supremely confident. I saw him do it countless times at restaurants, on school open days and in the middle of the street. He could say the most outrageous things, using double entendres and giving playful squeezes and women would simply giggle and go weak at the knees.

He called me his 'Indian Princess' and his 'Bollywood Beauty' and, one time, when he took us horse riding, I actually felt dizzy when he put his hands around my waist and lifted me down from the saddle.

I would never have confessed it to anyone, but Cate guessed the truth. It wasn't hard. I was always inviting myself back to her place and making excuses to talk to her father. She didn't even know about the times I rode my bicycle past his office, hoping he might see me and wave. Twice I ran into open car doors.

Cate, of course, found my infatuation hilarious beyond

measure, thus ensuring I have never admitted to loving any man.

See the sort of stuff I remember! It's all coming back, the good, the bad and the ugly. My mind aches.

I've been dreading this moment – seeing Barnaby again. Ever since the accident he has slept at Cate's house, according to Jarrod. He hasn't been to work or answered calls.

The front door has stained-glass panels and a tarnished knocker in the shape of a naked torso. I grab her hips and knock. Nobody answers. I try again.

A lock turns. The door opens a crack. Unshaven and unwashed, Barnaby doesn't want to see me. Self-pity needs his full attention.

'Please, let me in.'

He hesitates but the door opens. I move inside, stepping around him as though he's surrounded by a force field. The place smells musty and closed up. Windows need opening. Plants need watering.

I follow him to the kitchen and dining area – open-plan, looking out into the garden. Cate's touches are everywhere from the French provincial dining table to the art deco posters on the walls. There are photographs on the mantel. One of them, a wedding picture, shows Cate in a 1920s flapper dress trimmed with mother-of-pearl.

Folding himself onto a sofa, Barnaby crosses his legs. A trouser cuff slides up to reveal a bald shin. People used to say that he was ageless and joke about him having a portrait in his attic. It's not true. His features are too feminine to age well. Instead of growing character lines he has wrinkled and one day, ten years from now, he'll wake up an old man.

I never imagined speaking to him again. It doesn't seem so hard, although grief makes everything more intimate.

'They always say that a father is the last person to know anything,' he says. 'Cate used to laugh at me. "Dear old Dad," she said. "Always in the dark."'

Confusion clouds his eyes. Doubt.

'Did Felix know?'

'They weren't sleeping together.'

'He told you that?'

'Cate wouldn't let him touch her. She said it might harm the baby. They slept in different beds – in different rooms.'

'Surely a husband would—'

'Marriage and sex aren't mutually inclusive,' he says, perhaps too knowingly. I feel myself growing uncomfortable. 'Cate even told Felix he could see a prostitute if he wanted. Said she wouldn't mind. What sort of wife says that? He should have seen something was wrong.'

'Why couldn't she conceive?'

'Her womb destroyed his sperm. I don't know the medical name for it. They tried for seven years. IVF, drugs, injections, herbal remedies; they exorcised the house of evil spirits and sprinkled Chinese lemon-grass oil on the garden. Cate was a walking bloody textbook on infertility. That's why it came as such a surprise. Cate was over the moon – I've never seen her happier. I remember looking at Felix and he was trying hard to be excited – I guess he was – but it's like he had a question inside him that wouldn't go away.'

'He had doubts?'

'For years his wife rejects his sperm and then suddenly she's pregnant. Any man would have doubts.'

'But if that's the case—'

'He *wanted* to believe, don't you see? She convinced everyone.'

Standing, he motions me to follow him. His slippers flap gently against his heels as he climbs the stairs. The nursery door is open. The room is freshly painted and papered. The furniture new. A cot, a changing table, a comfortable chair with a Winnie the Pooh pillow.

Opening a drawer, he takes out a folder. There are receipts for the furniture and instructions for assembling the cot. He upends an envelope, shaking it gently. Two sheets of photographs, monochrome images, drop into his hand. Ultrasound pictures.

Each photograph is only a few inches square. The background is black, the images white. For a moment it's like looking at one of those magic-eye pictures where a 3-D image emerges from within. In this case I see tiny arms and legs. A face, eyes, a nose . . .

'They were taken at twenty-three weeks.'

'How?'

'Felix was supposed to be there but Cate messed up the days. She came home with the photographs.'

The rest of the file contains testimony of an unborn baby's existence. There are application forms to the hospital, appointment slips, medical reports, correspondence and receipts for the nursery furniture. An NHS pamphlet gives details of how to register the birth. Another lists the benefits of folic acid in early pregnancy.

There are other documents in the drawer, including a

bundle of private letters tucked in a corner, bank statements, a passport and health-insurance certificates. A separate file contains details of Cate's IVF treatments. There appear to have been five of them. Sohan Banerjee, a fertility specialist in Wimbledon, is mentioned several times.

'Where was she planning to have the baby?'

'Chelsea and Westminster Hospital.'

I look at a brochure for prenatal classes. 'What I can't understand is how it was supposed to end. What was Cate going to do in four weeks?'

Barnaby shrugs. 'She was going to be exposed as a liar.'

'No, think about it. That prosthetic was almost a work of art. She must have altered it two or three times over the months. She also had to forge medical letters and appointment slips. Where did she get the ultrasound pictures? She went to all that effort. Surely she had a plan.'

'Like what?'

'Maybe she organised a surrogacy or a private adoption.'

'Why keep it a secret?'

'Perhaps she couldn't let anyone know. Commercial surrogacy is illegal. Women can't accept money to have a baby. I know it sounds far-fetched but isn't it worth considering?'

He scoffs and smites at the air between us. 'So a month from now my daughter was going to nip off somewhere, dump the padding and come back with a baby, custom-made, ready-to-order, from the baby factory. Maybe Ikea do them nowadays.'

'I'm just looking for reasons.'

'I *know* the reason. She was obsessed. Desperate.'

'Enough to explain these?' I point to the ultrasound pictures.

Reaching down, he opens the second drawer and retrieves a different file. This one contains court transcripts, charge sheets and a judgement.

'Eighteen months ago Cate was caught stealing baby clothes from Mothercare. She said it was a misunderstanding, but we knew it was a cry for help. The magistrates were very kind. They gave her a suspended sentence.

'She had counselling for about six months, which seemed to help. She was her old self again. There were obvious places she had to avoid like parks and playgrounds, schools. But she couldn't stop torturing herself. She peered into prams and struck up conversations with mothers. She got angry when she saw women who already had big families and who were pregnant again. It was unfair, she said. They were being greedy.

'She and Felix looked into adopting a baby. They went for the interviews and were screened by social workers. Unfortunately, the shoplifting conviction came back to haunt Cate. The adoption committee deemed her mentally unstable. It was the final straw. She lost it completely. Felix found her sitting on the floor of the nursery, clutching a teddy bear, saying, "Look! It's a beautiful baby boy." She was taken to hospital and spent a fortnight in a psych ward. They put her on antidepressants.'

'I had no idea.'

He shrugs. 'So you see, Alisha, you shouldn't make the mistake of putting rational thoughts in my daughter's head. Cate didn't have a plan. Desperation is the mother of bad ideas.'

Everything he says makes perfect sense but I can't forget the image of Cate at the reunion, begging me to help her. She said they wanted to take her baby. Who did she mean?

There is nothing as disarming as a heartfelt plea. Barnaby's natural caution wavers.

'What do you want?'

'I need to see telephone records, credit-card receipts, cheque stubs and diaries. Have any large sums of money been withdrawn from Cate or Felix's bank accounts? Did they travel anywhere or meet anyone new? Was she secretive about money or appointments? I also need to see her computer. Perhaps her e-mails can tell me something.'

Unable to push his tongue around the word no, he hedges. 'What if you find something that embarrasses this family?'

His wretchedness infuriates me. Whatever Cate might have done, she needs him now.

The doorbell rings. He turns toward the sound, surprised. I follow him down the stairs and wait in the hallway as he opens the front door.

Yvonne gives a deep-throated sob and throws her arms around his shoulders, crushing his head to her chest.

'I'm sorry. I'm so sorry,' she wails. Her eyes open. 'Alisha?'

'Hello, Yvonne.'

Manhandling Barnaby out of the way, she smothers me in her cleavage. I remember the feeling. It's like being wrapped in a fluffy towel, fresh from the dryer. Gripping my forearms, she holds me away. 'Look at you! You're all grown up.'

'Yes.'

'You cut your lovely hair.'

'Ages ago.'

Yvonne hasn't changed. If anything she is a little fatter

and her pitted face has fleshed out. Overworked veins stand out on her calves and she's still wearing men's shoes.

Even after Ruth Elliot recovered her speech, Yvonne stayed with the family, cooking meals, washing clothes and ironing Barnaby's shirts. She was like an old-fashioned retainer, growing old with them.

Now she wants me to stay, but I make excuses to leave. As I reach the car, I can still feel Barnaby's stubble on my cheeks where he kissed me goodbye. Glancing back at the house I remember a different tragedy, another goodbye. Voices from the past jostle and merge. The sadness is suffocating.

8

Donavon gave the police an address in Hackney, not far from London Fields. Set back from the road, the crumbling terrace house has a small square front yard of packed dirt and broken concrete. A sun-faded red Escort van is parked in the space, alongside a motorcycle.

A young woman answers the door. She's about twenty-five with a short skirt, a swelling pregnancy and acne scars on her cheeks. Cotton wool is wedged between her toes and she stands with her heels planted and toes raised.

'I'm looking for Donavon.'

'Nobody here by that name.'

'That's too bad. I owe him some money.'

'I can give it to him.'

'You said he didn't live here.'

'I meant he wasn't here right now,' she says curtly. 'He might be around later.'

'I'd prefer to give it to him personally.'

She considers this for a moment, still balancing on her heels. 'You from the council?'

'No.'

'A welfare officer?'

'No.'

She disappears and is replaced by Donavon.

'Well, well, if it isn't yindoo.'

'Give it a rest, Donavon.'

He runs his tongue along a nick in his front tooth while his eyes roam up and down over me. My skin is crawling.

'Didn't your mother ever tell you it's not polite to stare?'

'My mother told me to beware of strangers who tell lies about owing me money.'

'Can I come in?'

'That depends.'

'On what?'

'I'm fucking certain I ordered a Thai girl but I guess you'll do.'

He hasn't changed. The pregnant girl is standing behind him. 'This is my sister Carla,' he says.

She nods, sullenly.

'It's nice to meet you, Carla. I went to school with your brother. Did you go to Oaklands?'

Donavon answers for her. 'I sort of shat in that particular nest.'

'Why did you run yesterday?'

He shrugs. 'You got the wrong guy.'

'I know it was you.'

He holds up his hands in mock surrender. 'Are you gonna

arrest me, officer? I hope you brought your handcuffs. That's always fun.'

I follow him along the hallway, past a coat rack and assorted shoes. Carla continues painting her nails at the kitchen table. She is flexible and short-sighted, pulling her foot almost up to her nose as she dabs on the varnish with a thin brush, unconcerned about exposing her knickers.

A dog beneath the table thumps its tail several times but doesn't bother rising.

'You want a drink?'

'No. Thank you.'

'I do. Hey, Carla, nip up the road and get us a few cans.'

Her top lip curls as she snatches the twenty-quid note from his fist.

'And this time I want the change back.'

Donavon gives a chair a gentle shake. 'You want to sit down?'

I wait for him to be seated first. I don't feel comfortable with him standing over me. 'Is this your place?' I ask.

'My parents'. My Dad's dead. Mum lives in Spain.'

'You joined the army.'

'Yeah, the Paras.' His fingers vibrate against the table top.

'Why did you leave?'

He motions to his leg. 'A medical discharge. I broke my leg in twelve places. We were on a training jump above Andover. One of the newbies wrapped his chute around mine and we came down under the one canopy. Too fast. They wouldn't let me jump after that. They said I'd get a pension but the government changed the rules. I got to work.'

I glance around the kitchen, which looks like a craft workshop with boxes of leather strips, crystals, feathers and painted clay beads. On the table I notice a reel of wire and pliers.

'What are you making?'

'I sell stuff at the markets. Trinkets and shit. Don't make much, you know . . .'

The statement trails off. He talks a little more about the Paras, clearly missing army life, until Carla returns with a six-pack of draught and a packet of chocolate biscuits. She retreats to the stairs with the biscuits, eating them while listening to us. I can see her painted toes through a gap in the stair rails.

Donavon opens a can and drinks noisily. He wipes his mouth.

'How is she?'

'She might be brain-damaged.'

His face tightens. 'What about the baby?'

'She wasn't pregnant.'

'*What?*'

'She was faking it.'

'What do you mean – faking it? Why would she . . . ? Makes no fucking sense.'

The phantom pregnancy seems harder for him to accept than Cate's medical condition.

'Why are you interested in Earl Blake?'

'Same reason as you.'

'Yeah, sure. What difference does it make to you?'

'You wouldn't understand.'

'Try me.'

'Fuck you!'

74

'You wish!'

'The bastard could have stopped,' he says suddenly, his anger bordering on violence.

'Did you see the car speed up? Did it veer towards them?'

A shake of the head.

'Then why are you so sure?'

'He was lying.'

'Is that it?'

He raises one shoulder as if trying to scratch his ear. 'Just forget it, OK?'

'No, I want to know. You said the driver was lying. Why?'

He goes quiet. 'I just know. He lied. He ran them down.'

'How can you be sure?'

He turns away, muttering, 'Sometimes I just am.'

My mother always told me that people with green eyes are related to fairies, like the Irish, and that if I ever met someone with one green eye and one brown one it meant that person had been taken over by a fairy, but not in a scary way. Donavon is seriously scary. The bones of his shoulders shift beneath his shirt.

'I found out some stuff about Blake,' he says, growing calmer. 'He signed on with the minicab firm a week ago and only ever worked days. At the end of every shift he handed over eighty quid for the lease of the car but the mileage didn't match the fares. He can't have done more than a few miles. He told another driver that he had regular customers who liked to have him on call. One of them was a film producer but there's no way some hotshot film producer is going around London in a beat-up Vauxhall Cavalier.'

He straightens up, into the story now. 'So I ask myself,

"Why does a guy need a car all day if it's not going anywhere?" Maybe he's watching someone – or waiting for them.'

'That's a big leap.'

'Yeah, well, I saw the look Cate gave him. She recognised him.'

He noticed it too.

Kicking back his chair, he stands and opens a kitchen drawer.

'I found this. Cate must have dropped it.'

He hands me a crumpled envelope. My name is on the front of it. The swirls and dips of the handwriting belong to Cate. Lifting the flap, I pull out a photograph. A teenage girl gazes absently at the camera. She has fine limbs and ragged dark hair, trimmed by the wind. Her wide lips curl down at the edges, making her look melancholy rather than gloomy. She is wearing jeans, sandals and a cotton shirt. Her hands are by her sides, palms open, with a white band on her wrist.

I turn the photograph over. There is a name written on the back. Samira.

'Who is she?' asks Donavon.

'I don't know.'

'What about the number?'

In the bottom right-hand corner there are ten digits. A phone number, perhaps.

I study the image again as a dozen different questions chase each other. Cate faked her pregnancy. Does this girl have anything to do with it? She looks too young to be a mother.

I take out my mobile and punch in the number. A

recorded voice announces it is unavailable. The area code doesn't belong in the UK. It could be international.

The fight seems to have gone out of Donavon. Maybe alcohol mellows him.

'What are you gonna do?' he asks.

'I don't know yet.'

On my feet, I turn to leave. He calls after me, 'I want to help.'

'Why?'

He's still not going to tell me.

Carla intercepts me before I reach the front door.

'He's losing it,' she whispers. 'He used to have it together but something happened in Afghanistan or wherever the hell they sent him. He's not the same. He doesn't sleep. He gets obsessed about stuff. I hear him at night, walking about.'

'You think he needs help?'

'He needs something.'

9

Chief Superintendent Lachlan North has an office on the eleventh floor of New Scotland Yard overlooking Victoria Street and Westminster Abbey. He is standing by the window beside a telescope, peering into the eyepiece at the traffic below.

'If that moron thinks he can turn there . . .'

He picks up a two-way radio and communicates a call sign to traffic operations.

A tired voice answers. *'Yes, sir.'*

'Some idiot just did a U-turn in Victoria Street. Did you see it?'

— *'Yes, sir, we're onto him.'*

The Chief Super is still peering through the telescope. 'I can get his number plate.'

— *'It's under control, sir.'*

'Good work. Over and out.'

Reluctantly, he turns away from the window and sits down. 'There are some dangerous bloody morons loose on our roads, Detective Constable Barba.'

'Yes, sir.'

'In my experience, the morons are more dangerous than the criminals.'

'There are more of them, sir.'

'Yes. Absolutely.'

He dips his head into a drawer and retrieves a dark green folder. Shuffling through the contents, he clears his throat and smiles, attempting to appear warmer and fuzzier. A nagging doubt hooks me in the chest.

'The results of your medical have been reviewed, DC Barba, along with your psychological evaluation. I must say that you have made a remarkable recovery from your injuries. Your request to return to active duty with the Diplomatic Protection Group has also been noted. Courageous is the word that comes to mind.' He tugs at his cuffs. Here it comes. 'But under the circumstances, having reviewed the matter thoroughly, it has been decided to transfer you out of the DPG. You might be a little gun-shy, you see, which is hardly a good thing when protecting diplomats and foreign heads of state. Could be embarrassing.'

'I'm not gun-shy, sir. Nobody fired a gun at me.'

He raises his hand to stop me. 'Be that as it may, we have a responsibility to look after our foreign guests and, while I have every confidence in you, there is no way of testing your fitness when push comes to shove and Abdul the terrorist takes a pot-shot at the Israeli ambassador.' He taps the folder several times with his finger to stress the point.

'The most important part of my job is shuffling people and priorities. It is a thankless task but I don't ask for medals or commendations. I am simply a humble servant of the public.' His chest swells. 'We don't want to lose you, DC Barba. We need more women like you in the Met, which is why I am pleased to offer you a position as a recruitment officer. We need to encourage more young women into the Met, particularly from minority communities. You can be a role model.'

A mist seems to cloud my vision. He stands now, moving back to the window where he bends to peer through his telescope again.

'Unbelievable! Moron!' he screams, shaking his head.

He turns back to me, settling a haunch on a corner of his desk. A painting behind his head depicts the Bow Street Runners, London's renowned early police force.

'Great things are expected of you, DC Barba.'

'With all due respect, sir, I am not gun-shy. I am fitter than ever. I can run a mile in four and a half minutes. I'm a better shot than anyone at the DPG. My high-speed defensive driving skills are excellent. I am the same officer as before—'

'Yes, yes, you're very capable, I'm sure, but the decision has been made. It's out of my hands. You'll report to the Police Recruitment Centre at Hendon on Monday morning.'

He opens his office door and waits for me to leave. 'You're still a very important member of the team, Alisha. We're glad to have you back.'

Words have dried up. I know I should argue with him or slam my fist on his desk and demand a review. Instead, I meekly walk out the door. It closes behind me.

Outside, I wander along Victoria Street. I wonder if the chief superintendent is watching me. I'm tempted to look up at his window and flip him the bird. Isn't that what the Americans call it?

Of course, I don't. I'm too polite, you see. That's my problem. I don't intimidate. I don't bully. I don't talk in sporting clichés or slap backs or have a wobbly bit between my legs. Unfortunately, it's not as though I have outstanding feminine wiles to fall back upon such as a killer cleavage or a backside like J-Lo's. The only qualities I bring to the table are my gender and ethnic credibility. The Metropolitan Police want nothing else from me.

I am twenty-nine years old and I still think I'm capable of something remarkable in my life. I am different, unique, beyond compare. I don't have Cate's luminous beauty or infinite sadness, or her musical laugh or the ability to make all men feel like warriors. I have wisdom, determination and steel.

At sixteen I wanted to win Olympic gold. Now I want to make a difference. Maybe falling in love will be my remarkable deed. I will explore the heart of another human being. Surely that is challenge enough. Cate always thought so.

When I need to think I run. When I need to forget I run. It can clear my thoughts completely or focus them like a magnifying glass that dwarfs the world outside the lens. When I run the way I know I can, it all happens in the air, the pure air, floating above the ground, levitating the way great runners imagine themselves in their dreams.

The doctors said I might never walk again. I confounded predictions. I like that idea. I don't like doing things that are predictable. I don't want to do what people expect.

I began with baby steps. Crawl before you can walk, Simon my physiotherapist said. Walk before you can run. He and I conducted an ongoing skirmish. He cajoled me and I cursed him. He twisted my body and I threatened to break his arm. He said I was a cry-baby and I called him a bully.

'Rise up on your toes.'

'I'm trying.'

'Hold on to my arm. Close your eyes. Can you feel the stretch in your calf?'

'I can feel it in my eyeballs.'

After months in traction and more time in a wheelchair, I had trouble telling where my legs stopped and the ground began. I bumped into walls and stumbled on pavements. Every set of stairs was another Everest. My living room was an obstacle course.

I gave myself little challenges, forcing myself out on the street every morning. Five minutes became ten minutes, became twenty minutes. After every operation it was the same. I pushed myself through winter and spring and a long hot summer when the air was clogged with exhaust fumes and heat rose from every brick and slab.

I have explored every corner of the East End, which is like a huge, deafening factory with a million moving parts. I have lived in other places in London and never even made eye contact with neighbours. Now I have Mr Mordecai next door, who mows my postage-stamp-sized lawn; and Mrs Goldie across the road picks up my dry-cleaning.

There is a jangling, squabbling urgency to life in the East End. Everyone is on the make – haggling, complaining, gesticulating and slapping their foreheads. These are the 'people of the abyss' according to Jack London. That was a century ago. Much has changed. The rest remains the same.

For nearly an hour I keep running, following the Thames past Westminster, Vauxhall and the old Battersea Power Station. I recognise where I am – the back streets of Fulham. My old boss lives near here, in Rainville Road: Detective Inspector Vincent Ruiz, retired. We talk on the phone every day or so. He asks me the same two questions: are you OK and do you need anything? My answers are always: yes, I'm OK and no, I don't need anything.

Even from a distance I recognise him. He is sitting in a folding chair by the river, with a fishing rod in one hand and a book on his lap.

'What are you doing, sir?'

'I'm fishing.'

'You can't really expect to catch anything.'

'No.'

'So why bother?'

He sighs and puts on his 'Ah-grasshopper-you-have-much-to-learn' voice.

'Fishing isn't always about catching fish, Alisha. It isn't even about the expectation of catching fish. It is about endurance, patience and most importantly . . .' He raises a can of draught. 'It is about drinking beer.'

Sir has put on weight since he retired – too many pastries

over coffee and *The Times* crossword – and his hair has grown longer. It's strange to think that he's no longer a detective – just an ordinary citizen.

Reeling in his line, he folds up his chair.

'You look like you've just run a marathon.'

'Not quite that far.'

I help him carry his gear across the road and into a large terrace house, with lead-light windows above empty flower boxes. He fills the kettle and moves a bundle of typed pages from the kitchen table.

'So what have you been doing with yourself, sir?'

'I wish you wouldn't call me sir.'

'What should I call you?'

'Vincent.'

'How about DI?'

'I'm not a detective inspector any more.'

'It could be like a nickname.'

He shrugs. 'You're getting cold. I'll get you a sweater.'

I hear him rummaging upstairs and he comes down with a cardigan that smells of lavender and mothballs. 'My mother's,' he says apologetically.

I have met Mrs Ruiz just the once. She was like something out of a European fairy tale – an old woman with missing teeth, wearing a shawl, rings and chunky jewellery.

'How is she?'

'Mad as a meat-axe. She keeps accusing the staff at the hostel of giving her enemas. Now *there*'s one of life's lousy jobs. You got to feel sorry for that poor bastard.'

Ruiz laughs out loud, which is a nice sound. He's normally one of the most taciturn of men, with a permanent scowl and a generally low opinion of the human race, but that has never put me off. Beneath his gruff exterior I know there *isn't* a heart of gold. It's more precious than that.

I spy an old-fashioned typewriter in the corner.

'Are you writing, DI?'

'No.' He answers too abruptly.

'You're writing a book.'

'Don't be daft.'

I try not to smile but I know my lips are turning up. He's going to get cross now. He hates people laughing at him. He takes the manuscript and tries to stuff it into an old briefcase. Then he sits back at the table, nursing his cup of tea.

I let a decent interval go by. 'So what's it about?'

'What?'

'Your book.'

'It's not a book. It's just some notes.'

'Like a journal.'

'No. Like *notes*.' That settles the issue.

I haven't eaten since breakfast. Ruiz offers to make me something. *Pasta Putanesca*. It is perfect – far too subtle for me to describe and far better than anything I could have cooked. He puts shavings of Parmesan on slices of sourdough and toasts them under the griller.

'This is very good, DI.'

'You sound surprised.'

'I *am* surprised.'

'Not all men are useless in the kitchen.'

'And not all women are domestic goddesses.' I talk to my local Indian more often than I do to my mother. It's called the Tandoori Diet.

85

Ruiz was there the day my spine was crushed. We have never really spoken about what happened. It's like an undeclared pact. I know he feels responsible but it wasn't his fault. He didn't force me to be there and he can't make the Met give me my old job back.

The dishes are washed and packed away.

'I am going to tell you a story,' I tell him. 'It's the sort of story you like because it has a puzzle at the centre. I don't want you to interrupt and I won't tell you if it's real or invented. Just sit quietly. I need to put all the details in order to see how it sounds. When I'm finished I will ask you a question and you can tell me if I'm totally mistaken. Then I will let you ask me one question.'

'Just one?'

'Yes. I don't want you to tear apart my logic or pick holes in my story. Not now. Tomorrow, maybe. Is it a deal?'

He nods.

Carefully, I set out the details, telling him about Cate, Donavon and Earl Blake. Like a tangle in a fishing line, if I pull too tightly the story knots together and it becomes harder to separate fact from supposition.

'What if Cate arranged a surrogacy and something went wrong? There could be a baby out there somewhere. Cate's baby.'

'Commercial surrogacy is illegal,' he says.

'It still happens. Women volunteer. They get their expenses paid, which is allowed, but they cannot profit from the birth.'

'Usually they're related in some way – a sister or a cousin.'

I show him the photograph of Samira. He searches her face for a long time as though she might tell him something. Turning it over he notices the numbers.

'The first four digits could be a mobile-phone prefix – but not in the UK,' he says. 'You need the exact country code or you won't be able to call it.'

It's my turn to be surprised again.

'I'm not a complete technophobe,' he protests.

'You're typing your *notes* on an ink ribbon.'

He glances at the old typewriter. 'Yeah, well, it has sentimental value.'

The clouds have parted just long enough to give us a sunset. The last golden rays settle on the river. In a few minutes they'll be gone, leaving behind a raw, damp cold.

'You promised me a question,' he says.

'One.'

'Do you want a lift home?'

'Is that it?'

'I thought maybe we could swing by Oaklands and you could show me where it happened.'

The DI drives an old Mercedes with white leather seats and soft suspension. It must guzzle petrol and makes him look like a lawn bowler, but Ruiz has never been one to worry about the environment or what people think of him.

I feel strange sitting in the passenger seat instead of behind the wheel. For years it was the other way around. I don't know why he chose me to be his driver, but I heard the gossip about the DI liking pretty faces. He's really not like that.

When I first moved out of uniform into the Serious Crime Group, the DI showed me respect and gave me a chance to prove myself. He didn't treat me any differently because of my colour or my age or my being a woman.

I told him I wanted to become a detective. He said I had to be better, faster and cleverer than any man who wanted the same position. Yes, it was unfair. He wasn't defending the system – he was teaching me the facts of life.

Ruiz was already a legend when I did my training. The instructors at Hendon used to tell stories about him. In 1963, as a probationary constable, he arrested one of the Great Train Robbers, Roger Cordrey, and recovered £141,000 of the stolen money. Later, as a detective, he helped capture the Kilburn Rapist, who had terrorised North London for eight months.

I know he's not the sort to reminisce or talk about the good old days but I sense that he misses a time when it was easier to tell the villains from the constabulary and the general public respected those who tried to keep them safe.

He parks the car in Mansford Street and we walk towards the school. The Victorian buildings are tall and dark against the ambient light. Fairy lights still drip from the windows of the hall. In my imagination I can see the dark stain on the tarmac where Cate fell. Someone has pinned a posy to the nearest lamp-post.

'It's a straight line of sight,' he says. 'They can't have looked.'

'Cate turned her head.'

'Well, she can't have seen the minicab. Either that or he pulled out suddenly.'

'Two cab drivers say they saw the minicab further along the street, barely moving. They thought he was looking for an address.'

I think back, mentally replaying events. 'There's something else. I think Cate recognised the driver.'

'She knew him?'

'He might have picked her up earlier as a fare.'

'Or followed her.'

'She was frightened of him. I could see it in her eyes.'

I mention the driver's tattoo. The Crucifixion. It covered his entire chest.

'A tattoo like that might be traceable,' says the DI. 'We need a friend on the inside.'

I know where he's going with this.

'How is "New Boy" Dave?' he asks. 'You two still bumping uglies?'

'That would be none of your business.'

Sikh girls blush on the inside.

Dave King is a detective with the Serious Crime Group (Western Division), Ruiz's old squad. He's in his early thirties with a tangle of gingery hair that he cuts short so that it doesn't escape. He earned the nickname 'New Boy' when he was the newest member of the SCG but that was five years ago. He's now a detective sergeant.

Dave lives in a flat in West Acton, just off the Uxbridge Road, where gas towers dominate the skyline and trains on the Paddington line rattle him awake every morning.

It is a typical bachelor pad in progress, with a king-size

bed, a wide-screen TV, a sofa, and precious little else. The walls are half-stripped and the carpet has been ripped up but not replaced.

'Like what you've done to the place,' observes Ruiz sardonically.

'Yeah, well, I been sort of busy,' says Dave. He looks at me as if to say, 'What's going on?'

Pecking him on the cheek, I slip my hand under his T-shirt and run my fingers down his spine. He's been playing rugby and his hair smells of mown grass.

Dave and I have been sleeping together, on and off, for nearly two years. Ruiz would smirk over the 'on and off' part. It's the longest relationship of my life – even discounting the time I spent convalescing in hospital.

Dave thinks he wants to marry me but he hasn't met my family. You don't marry a Sikh girl. You marry her mother, her grandmother, her aunties, her brothers . . . I know all families have baggage but mine belongs in one of those battered suitcases, held together with string, that you see circling endlessly on a luggage carousel.

Dave tries to outdo me by telling stories about his family, particularly his mother who collects road kill and keeps it in her freezer. She is on a mission to save badgers, which includes lobbying local councils to build tunnels beneath busy roads.

'I don't have anything to drink,' he says apologetically.

'Shame on you,' says Ruiz, who is pulling faces at the photographs on the fridge. 'Who's this?'

'My mother,' says Dave.

'You take after your father, then.'

Dave clears the table and pulls up chairs. I go through

90

the story again. Ruiz then adds his thoughts, giving the presentation added gravitas. Meanwhile, Dave folds and unfolds a blank piece of paper. He wants to find a reason not to help us.

'Maybe you should wait for the official investigation,' he suggests.

'You know things get missed.'

'I don't want to tread on any toes.'

'You're too good a dancer for that, New Boy,' says Ruiz, cajoling him.

I can be shameless. I can bat my big brown eyelashes with the best of them. Forgive me, sisters. Taking the piece of paper from Dave's hand, I let my fingers linger on his. He chases them, not wanting to lose touch.

'He had an Irish accent but the most interesting thing is the tattoo.' I describe it to him.

Dave has a laptop in the bedroom on a makeshift desk made from a missing bathroom door and saw-horses. Shielding the screen from me, he types in a username and a password.

The Police National Computer is a vast database that contains the names, nicknames, aliases, scars, tattoos, accents, shoe size, height, age, hair colour, eye colour, offence history, associates and modus operandi of all known offenders and 'persons of interest' in the UK. Even partial details can sometimes be enough to link cases or throw up names of possible suspects.

In the good old days almost every police officer could access the PNC via the Internet. Unfortunately, one or two officers decided to make money selling the inform-ation. Now every request – even a licence check – has to be justified.

Dave types in details of the driver's age range, accent and tattoo. It takes less than fifteen seconds for eight possible matches. He highlights the first name and the screen refreshes. Two photographs appear – a front view and a profile of the same face. The date of birth, antecedents and last known address are printed across the bottom. He is too young; too smooth-skinned.

'That's not him.'

Candidate number two is older, with horn-rimmed glasses and bushy eyebrows. He looks like a librarian caught in a paedophile sweep. Why do all mugshots look so unflattering? It isn't just the harsh lighting or plain white background with its black vertical ruler measuring the height. Everybody looks gaunt, depressed – worst of all, guilty.

A new photograph appears. A man in his late forties with a shaved head. Something about his eyes makes me pause. He looks arrogant: as if he knows that he is cleverer than the vast majority of his fellow human beings and this inclines him to be cruel.

I reach towards the computer screen and cup my hand over the top of the image, trying to imagine him with a long grey ponytail.

'That's him.'

'Are you sure?'

'Absolutely.'

His name is Brendan Dominic Pearl – born in 1958 in Rathcoole, a Loyalist district of north Belfast.

'IRA,' whispers Dave.

'How do you know?'

'It's the classic background.' He scrolls down the screen

to the biography. Pearl's father was a boilermaker on the Belfast docks. His elder brother Tony died in an explosion in 1972 when a bomb accidentally detonated in a warehouse being used as a bomb-making factory by the IRA.

A year later, aged fifteen, Brendan Pearl was convicted of assault and firearms offences. He was sentenced to eighteen months of juvenile detention. In 1977 he launched a mortar attack on a Belfast police station that wounded four people. He was sentenced to twelve years.

At the Maze Prison in 1981 he joined a hunger strike with two dozen Republican prisoners. They were protesting about being treated as common criminals instead of prisoners of war. The most celebrated of them, Bobby Sands, died after sixty-six days. Pearl slipped into a coma in the hospital wing but survived.

Two years later, in July 1983, he and fellow inmate Frank Farmer climbed out of their compound onto the prison roof and gained access to the Loyalist compound. They murdered a paramilitary leader, Patrick McNeill, and maimed two others. Pearl's sentence was increased to life.

Ruiz joins us. I point to the computer screen. 'That's him – the driver.'

His shoulders suddenly shift and his eyes search mine.

'Are you sure?'

'Yes. Why? What's wrong?'

'I know him.'

It's my turn to be surprised.

Ruiz studies the picture again as if the knowledge has to be summoned up or traded for information he doesn't need.

'There are gangs in every prison. Pearl was one of the IRA's enforcers. His favourite weapon was a metal pole with a curved hook, something like a marlinspike or a fishing gaff. That's why they called him the Shankhill Fisherman. You don't find many fish in the Maze but he found another use for the weapon. He used to thread it through the bars while prisoners were sleeping and open their throats with a flick of the wrist, taking out their vocal cords in the process so they couldn't scream for help.'

Cotton wool fills my oesophagus. Ruiz pauses, his head bent, motionless.

'When the Good Friday peace agreement was signed more than four hundred prisoners were released from both sides – Republicans and Loyalists. The British Government drew up a list of exemptions – people they wanted kept inside. Pearl was among them. Oddly enough, the IRA agreed. They didn't want Pearl any more than we did.'

'So why isn't he still in prison?' asks Dave.

Ruiz smiles wryly. 'That's a very good question, New Boy. For forty years the British Government told people it wasn't fighting a war in Northern Ireland – it was a "police operation". Then they signed the Good Friday Agreement and declared, "The war is over."

'Pearl got himself a good lawyer and that's exactly what he argued. He said he was a prisoner of war. There should be *no* exemptions. Bombers, snipers and murderers had been set free. Why was *he* being treated differently? A judge agreed. He and Frank Farmer were released on the same day.'

A palm glides over his chin, rasping like sandpaper. 'Some soldiers can't survive the peace. They need chaos. Pearl is like that.'

'How do you know so much about him?' I ask.

There is sadness in his eyes. 'I helped draw up the list.'

10

'New Boy' Dave shifts beside me, draping his arm over my breasts. I lift it away and tuck it under his pillow. He sleeps so soundly that I can rearrange his body like a stop-motion animation puppet.

A digital clock glows on the bedside table. I lift my head. It's after ten on Sunday morning. Where are the trains? They didn't wake me. I have less than an hour and a half to shower, dress and get ready for my father's birthday.

Rolling out of bed, I look for my clothes. Dave's clothes. My running gear is still damp from yesterday.

He reaches for me, running his thumbs beneath the underside of my breast, tracing a pattern that only men can find.

'You trying to sneak away?'

'I'm late. I have to go.'

'I wanted to make you breakfast.'

'You can drive me home. Then you have to find Brendan Pearl.'

'But it's Sunday. You never said . . .'

'That's the thing about women. We don't *say* exactly what we want but we reserve the right to be mighty pissed off when we don't get it. Scary, isn't it?'

Dave makes coffee while I use the shower. I keep pondering how Brendan Pearl and Cate Beaumont could possibly know each other. They come from different worlds, yet Cate recognised him. It doesn't *feel* like an accident. It never did.

On the drive to the East End, Dave chats about work and his new boss. He says something about being unhappy but I'm not really listening.

'You could come over later,' he says, trying not to sound needy. 'We could get a pizza and watch a movie.'

'That would be great. I'll let you know.'

Poor Dave. I know he wants something more. One of these days he's going to take my advice and find another girlfriend. Then I'll have lost something I never tried to hold.

Things I like about him: he's sweet. He changes the sheets. He tolerates me. I feel safe with him. He makes me feel beautiful; and he lets me win at darts.

Things I don't like about him: his laugh is too loud. He eats junk food. He listens to Mariah Carey CDs. And he has hair growing on his shoulders. (*Gorillas* have hair on their shoulders.) Christ, I can be pedantic!

His rugby mates have nicknames like Bronco and Sluggo and they talk in this strange jargon that nobody else can understand unless they follow rugby and appreciate the finer points of mauling, rucking and lifting. Dave took me to watch a game one day. Afterwards we all went to the pub – wives and girlfriends. It was OK. They were all really nice and I felt comfortable. Dave didn't leave my side and kept sneaking glances at me and smiling.

I was only drinking mineral water but I shouted a round. As I waited at the bar I could see the corner tables reflected in the mirror.

'So what are we doing after?' asked Bronco. 'I fancy a curry.'

Sluggo grinned. 'Dave's already had one.'

They laughed and a couple of the guys winked at each other. 'I bet she's a tikka masala.'

'No, definitely a vindaloo.'

I didn't mind. It was funny. I didn't even care that Dave laughed too. But I knew then, if not before, that my initial instincts were right. We could share a bath, a bed, a weekend, but we could never share a life.

We pull up in Hanbury Street and straight away I realise that something is missing.

'I'll kill him!'

'What's wrong?'

'My car. My brother has taken it.'

I'm already calling Hari's mobile. Wind snatches at his words. He's driving with the window open.

'Hello?'

'Bring back my car.'

'Sis?'

'Where are you?'

'Brighton.'

'You're joking! It's Dad's birthday.'

'Is that *today*?' He starts fumbling for excuses. 'Tell him I'm on a field trip for university.'

'I'm not going to lie for you.'

'Oh, come on.'

'No.'

'All right, I'll be there.'

I look at my watch. I'm already late. 'I hate you, Hari.'

He laughs. 'Well, it's a good thing I love you.'

Upstairs I throw open wardrobes and scatter my shoes. I have to wear a sari to keep my father happy. Saris and salvation are mixed up in his mind – as though one is going to bring me the other, or at least get me a husband.

'New Boy' Dave is downstairs.

'Can you call me a cab, please?'

'I'll take you.'

'No, really.'

'It won't take more than a few minutes – then I'll go to work.'

Back in my room, I wrap the sari fabric around my body, right to left, tucking the first wrap into my petticoat, making sure the bottom edge is brushing my ankles. Then I create seven pleats down the centre, making sure they fall with the grain of the fabric. Holding the pleats in place, I take the remaining length of sari behind my back, across my body and drape it over my left shoulder.

This one is made of Varanasi silk, elaborately brocaded in red and green, with delicate figures of animals sewn with metallic silver thread along the border.

Pinning up my hair with a golden comb, I put on

make-up and jewellery. Indian women are expected to wear lots of jewellery. It is a sign of wealth and social standing.

Sitting on the stairs, I buckle my sandals. Dave is staring at me.

'Is something wrong?'

'No.'

'Well, what are you gawping at?'

'You look beautiful.'

'Yeah, right.' *I look like a Ratner's display window.*

I bat his hands away as he reaches out for me. 'No touching the merchandise! And for God's sake don't have an accident. I don't want to die in these clothes.'

My parents live in the same house where I grew up. My mother doesn't like change. In her perfect world, children would never leave home or discover how to cook or clean for themselves. Since this is impossible, she has preserved our childhoods in bric-a-brac and become the full-time curator at the Barba family museum.

As soon as I turn into the cul-de-sac I feel a familiar heat in my cheeks. 'Just drop me off here.'

'Where's the house?'

'Don't worry. This will be fine.'

We pull up outside a small parade of shops. Fifty yards away my niece and nephew play in the front garden. They go tearing inside to announce my arrival.

'Quick, quick. Turn round!'

'I can't turn round.'

It's too late! My mother appears, waddling down the road. My worst nightmare is coming true.

She kisses me three times, squeezing me so hard that my breasts hurt.

'Where is Hari?'

'I reminded him. I even ironed his shirt.'

'That boy will be the death of me.' She points to her temple. 'See my grey hairs.'

Her gaze falls on 'New Boy' Dave. She waits for an introduction.

'This is a friend from work. He has to go.'

Mama makes a 'pfffhh' sound. 'Does he have a name?'

'Yes, of course. Detective Sergeant Dave King. This is my mother.'

'It's nice to meet you, Mrs Barba. Ali has told me so much about you.'

My mother laughs. 'Will you stay for lunch, Detective Sergeant?'

'No, he has to go.'

'Nonsense. It's Sunday.'

'Police have to work weekends.'

'Detectives are allowed to have lunch breaks. Isn't that right?'

Then my mother smiles and I know I've lost. Nobody can ever say no to that smile.

Small feet patter down the hallway ahead of us. Harveen and Daj are fighting over who's going to break the news that Auntie Ali has brought someone with her. Harveen comes back and takes my hand, dragging me into the kitchen. There are frown lines on her forehead at the age of seven. Daj is two years older and, like every male member of my family, is improbably handsome (and spoilt).

'Have you brought anything for us?' he asks.

'Only a kiss.'

'What about a present?'

'Only for Bada.'

Benches are covered with food and the air is heavy with steam and spices. My two aunts and my sisters-in-law are talking over one another amid the clatter and bang of energetic cooking. There are hugs and kisses. Glasses graze my cheekbones and fingers tug at my sari or straighten my hair, without my relatives ever taking their eyes from 'New Boy' Dave.

My aunties, Meena and Kala, couldn't be less alike as sisters. Meena is quite masculine-looking and striking, with a strong jaw and thick eyebrows. Kala, by contrast, is unexceptional in almost every way, which might explain why she wears such decorative spectacles, to give her face more character.

Meena is still fussing with my hair. 'Such a pretty thing to be unmarried; such lovely bones.'

A baby is thrust into my arms – the newest addition to the family. Ravi is six weeks old, with coffee-bean-coloured eyes and rolls of fat on his arms that you could lose a sixpence inside.

Cows might be sacred to Hindus, but babies are sacred to Sikhs, boys more so than girls. Ravi latches on to my finger and squeezes it until his eyes fold shut.

'She's so good with children,' says Mama, beaming. Dave should be squirming but he's actually enjoying this. Sadist!

The men are outside in the garden. I can see my father's blue turban above them all. His beard is swept back from his cheeks and crawls down his neck like a silver trickle of water.

I count heads. There are extras. My heart sinks. They've invited someone for me to meet.

My mother ushers Dave outside. He glances over his shoulder at me, hesitating before obeying her instructions. Down the side steps, along the mildewed path, past the door to the laundry, he reaches the rear garden. Every face turns towards him and the conversation stops.

It's like the parting of the Red Sea, as people step back and 'New Boy' Dave faces my father. It's eyeball to eyeball but Dave doesn't flinch, which is to his credit.

I can't hear what they're saying. My father glances up towards the kitchen window. He sees me. Then he smiles and thrusts out his hand. Dave takes it and suddenly conversation begins again.

My mother is at the sink, peeling and slicing mangoes. She slides the knife blade easily beneath the pale yellow flesh. 'We didn't know you were going to bring a friend.'

'I didn't bring him.'

'Well, your father has invited someone. You must meet his guest. It's only polite. He is a doctor.'

'A very fine one,' echoes Auntie Kala. 'Very successful.'

I scan the gathering and pick him out. He is standing with his back to me, dressed in a Punjabi suit that has been laundered and starched to attention.

'He's fat.'

'A sign of success,' says Kala.

'It takes a big hammer to hammer a big nail,' adds Meena, cackling like a schoolgirl. Kala disapproves.

'Oh, don't give me that look, sister. A wife has to learn how to keep her husband happy in the boudoir.' The two of them continue arguing while I go back to the window.

The stranger in the garden turns and glances up at me. He holds up his glass, as if offering me a toast. Then he shakes it from side to side, indicating its emptiness.

'Quickly, girl, take him another drink,' says Meena, handing me a jug.

Taking a deep breath, I walk down the side steps into the garden. My brothers whistle. They know how much I hate wearing a sari. All the men turn towards me. I keep my eyes focused on my sandals.

My father is still talking to Dave and my Uncle Rashid, a notorious butt squeezer. My mother claims it is an obsessive-compulsive disorder but I think he's just a lech. They are talking about cricket. The men in my family are obsessed with the game even when the summer is over.

Most Indian men are small and elegant with delicate hands but my brothers are strapping, rugged types, except for Hari, who would make a beautiful woman.

Bada kisses my cheek. I bow to him slightly. He ushers his guest closer and makes the formal introductions.

'Alisha, this is Dr Sohan Banerjee.'

I nod, still not raising my eyes.

The name is familiar. Where have I heard it before?

Poor Dave doesn't understand what's going on. He's not a Sikh, which is probably a good thing. If I'd brought a Sikh home my parents would have killed a goat.

Dr Banerjee stands very straight and bows his head. My father is still talking. 'Sohan contacted me personally and asked if he could meet you, Alisha. Family to family – that is how it should be done.'

I'm not meant to comment.

'He has more than one medical degree,' he adds.

He has more than one chin.

I don't know how much worse this day could get. People are watching me. Dave is on the far side of the garden talking to my eldest brother, Prabakar, the most religious member of the family, who won't approve.

The doctor is talking to me. I have to concentrate on his words. 'I believe you are a police officer.'

'Yes.'

'And you live separately from your parents. Very few single Indian girls have property. So why aren't you married?'

The bluntness of the question surprises me. He doesn't wait for an answer. 'Are you a virgin?'

'Excuse me?'

'I'm assuming your mother explained the facts of life to you.'

'It's none of your business.'

'No comment means yes.'

'No, it doesn't.'

'In my experience it does. Do you drink?'

'No.'

'See? You don't have to be so defensive. My parents think I should marry a girl from India because village girls are hard workers and good mothers. This may be so but I don't want a peasant girl who can't eat with a knife and fork.'

Anger rises in my throat and I have to swallow hard to keep it down. I give him my politest smile. 'So tell me, Dr Banerjee –'

'Call me Sohan.'

'Sohan, do you ever masturbate?'

His mouth opens and closes like a ventriloquist's dummy. 'I hardly think . . .'

'No comment means yes.'

The flash of anger in his eyes is like a blood-red veil. He grinds his teeth into a smile. 'Touché.'

'What kind of doctor are you?'

'An obstetrician.'

Suddenly I remember where I've read his name. It was in the file that Barnaby Elliot showed me. Sohan Banerjee is a fertility specialist. He performed Cate's IVF procedures.

There are one hundred thousand Sikhs in London and, what – maybe four hundred obstetricians? What are the chances of Cate's doctor showing up here?

'We have a mutual acquaintance,' I announce. 'Cate Beaumont. Did you hear about the accident?'

He shifts his gaze to the mottled green roof of my father's shed. 'Her mother telephoned me. A terrible thing.'

'Did she tell you that Cate faked her pregnancy?'

'Yes.'

'What else did she say?'

'It would be highly unethical to reveal the details of our conversation.' He pauses and adds, 'Even to a police officer.'

My eyes search his or perhaps it's the other way round. 'Are you deliberately trying to withhold information from a police investigation?'

He smiles warily. 'Forgive me. I thought this was a birthday party.'

'When did you last see Cate?'

'A year ago.'

'Why couldn't she conceive?'

'No reason at all,' he says blithely. 'She had a laparoscopy, blood tests, ultrasounds and a hysteroscopy. There were no abnormalities, adhesions or fibroids. She *should* have been able to conceive. Unfortunately, she and her husband were incompatible. Felix had a low sperm count, but married to someone else he may well have fathered a child without too much difficulty. However, in this case his sperm were treated like cancerous cells and were destroyed by his wife's immune system. Pregnancy was theoretically possible but realistically unlikely.'

'Did you ever suggest surrogacy as an option?'

'Yes, but there aren't many women willing to have a child for another couple. There was also another issue . . .'

'What issue?'

'Have you heard of achondrogenesis?'

'No.'

'It is a very rare genetic disorder, a form of lethal dwarfism.'

'What does that have to do with Cate?'

'Her only known pregnancy resulted in a miscarriage at six months. An autopsy revealed severe deformities of the foetus. By some twisted chance of fate, a reverse lottery, she and Felix each carried a recessive gene. Even if by some miracle she could conceive, there was a twenty-five per cent chance that it would happen again.'

'But they kept trying.'

He raises his hand to stop me. 'Excuse me, Alisha, but am I to understand from your questions that you are investigating this matter in some official capacity?'

'I'm just looking for answers.'

'I see.' He ponders this. 'If I were you, I would be very careful. People can sometimes misconstrue good intentions.'

I'm unsure if this is advice or a warning but he holds my gaze until I feel uncomfortable. There is an arrogance about Banerjee that is typical of his generation of educated Sikhs, who are more pukka than any Englishman you will ever meet.

Finally, he relaxes. 'I will tell you this much, Alisha. Mrs Beaumont underwent five IVF implants over a period of two years. This is very complex science. It is not something you do at home with a glass jar and a syringe. It is the last resort, when all else fails.'

'What happened in Cate's case?'

'She miscarried each time. Less than a third of IVF procedures result in a birth. My success rate is at the high end of the scale, but I am a doctor, not a miracle worker.'

For once the statement doesn't sound conceited. He seems genuinely disappointed.

Aunt Meena calls everyone inside for lunch. The tables have been set up with my father at the head. I am seated among the women. The men sit opposite. 'New Boy' Dave and Dr Banerjee are side by side.

Hari arrives in time for pudding and is treated like a prodigal son by my aunts, who run their fingers through his long hair. Leaning down, he whispers into my ear. 'Two at once, Sis. And I had you down as an old maid.'

My family are noisy when we eat. Plates are passed around. People talk over each other. Laughter is like a spice. There is no ceremony but there are rituals (which are not the same thing). Speeches are made, the cooks must be thanked, nobody talks over my father and all disagreements are saved for afterwards.

I don't let Dave stay that long. He has work to do. Sohan Banerjee also prepares to leave. I still don't understand why he's here. It can't be just a coincidence.

'Would you accede to seeing me again, Alisha?' he asks.

'No, I'm sorry.'

'It would make your parents very happy.'

'They will survive.'

He rocks his head from side to side and up and down. 'Very well. I don't know what to say.'

'"Goodbye" is traditional.'

He flinches. 'Yes. Goodbye. I wish your friend Mrs Beaumont a speedy recovery.'

Closing the front door, I feel a mixture of anxiety and relief. My life has enough riddles without this one.

Hari meets me in the hallway. His dark eyes catch the light and he puts his arms around me. My mobile is open in his hand.

'Your friend Cate died at one o'clock this afternoon.'

11

There are cars parked in the driveway and in the street outside the Elliots' house. Family. A wake. I should leave them alone. Even as I debate what to do I find myself standing at the front door ringing the bell.

It opens. Barnaby is there. He has showered, shaved and tidied himself up but his eyes are watery and unfocused.

'Who is it, dear?' asks a voice from inside.

He stiffens and steps back. Wheels squeak on the parquetry floor and Cate's mother, Ruth Elliot, rolls into view. She is dressed in black, making her face appear even more spectral.

'You must come in,' she says, her lips peeled back into a pained smile.

'I'm so sorry about Cate. If there's anything I can do . . .'

She doesn't answer. Wheels roll her away. I follow them inside to the sitting room, which is full of sad-eyed friends and family. A few of them I recognise. Judy and Richard Sutton, a brother and sister. Richard was Barnaby's campaign manager in two elections and Judy works for Chase Manhattan. Cate's Aunt Paula is talking to Jarrod and in the corner I spy Reverend Lunn, an Anglican minister.

Yvonne is crumpled on a chair, talking and sobbing at the same time. Her clothes, normally so bright and vibrant, now mirror her mood: black. Her two children are with her, both grown up, more English than Jamaican. The girl is beautiful. The boy could name a thousand places he'd prefer to be.

Yvonne cries a little harder when she sees me, groaning as she raises her arms to embrace me.

Before I can speak, Barnaby grips my forearm, pulling me away.

'How did you know about the money?' he hisses. I can smell the alcohol on his breath.

'What are you talking about?'

The words catch in his throat. 'Somebody withdrew eighty thousand pounds from Cate's account.'

'Where did she get that sort of money?'

He lowers his voice even further. 'From her late grandmother. I checked her bank account. Half the money was withdrawn last December and the other half in February.'

'A bank cheque?'

'Cash. The bank won't tell me any more.'

'And you have no idea why?'

He shakes his head and stumbles forward a pace. I steer him towards the kitchen where 'get well soon' cards lie open on the table, amid torn envelopes. They seem pointless now: forlorn gestures swamped by a greater grief.

Filling a glass from the tap, I hand it to him. 'The other day you mentioned a doctor, a fertility specialist.'

'What about him?'

'Did you ever meet him?'

'No.'

'Do you know if he ever suggested alternatives to IVF, like adoption or surrogacy?'

'Not that I heard. He didn't overstate Cate's chances, I know that much. And he wouldn't implant more than two embryos each time. He had another policy – three strikes and you're out. Cate begged him to let her try again so he gave her five chances.'

'Five?'

'They harvested eighteen eggs but only twelve were viable. Two embryos were implanted each time.'

'But that only accounts for ten – what about the remaining two eggs?'

He shrugs. 'Dr Banerjee wouldn't go again. He saw how fragile Cate had become, emotionally. She was falling apart.'

'She could have gone to another clinic.'

'Felix wouldn't let her. The hormones, the tests, the tears – he wouldn't put her through it again.'

None of this explains the money. Eighty thousand pounds isn't something you just give away. Cate was trying to buy a baby but something went wrong. That is why she contacted me.

I go over the story again, laying out the evidence. Some of the details and half-truths have taken on the solidity of facts. I can see what Barnaby's thinking. He's worried about his political ambitions. This sort of scandal would kill his chances stone dead.

'That's why I need to see Cate's computer,' I say.

'She doesn't have one.'

'Have you looked?'

'Yes.'

The glass clinks against his teeth. He's lying to me.

'The files you showed me – and Cate's letters – can I borrow them?'

'No.'

My frustration is turning to anger. 'Why are you doing this? How can I make you understand?'

His hand touches my knee. 'You could be nicer to me.'

Ruth Elliot materialises in the kitchen, her wheels silent this time. She looks at me as though she's spat out a frog.

'People are beginning to leave, Barnaby. You should come and say goodbye.'

He follows her to the front door. I grab my coat and slip past them.

'Thank you for coming, dear,' she says mechanically, reaching up from her wheelchair. Her lips are as dry as paper on my forehead.

Barnaby puts his arms around me and his lips brush my left ear lobe. He leans into me. I move my weight so that our thighs lose contact.

'Why do women always do this to *me*?'

Driving away, I can still feel the warmth of his breath. Why do men always think it is about *them*?

I'm sure I could find an excuse or make an argument for what I'm about to do, but whatever way you dress it up, it's still breaking the law. A half-brick. An overcoat. The pane of glass shatters and falls inwards. So far it's vandalism

113

or criminal damage. I reach inside and unlock the door. Now it's illegal entry. If I find the laptop it's going be theft. Is this what they mean by the slippery slope of crime?

It's after midnight. I'm wearing black jeans, leather gloves and a royal-blue turtleneck sweater that Auntie Meena knitted me. I have brought with me a large roll of black plastic, some duct tape, a torch and a USB drive for downloading computer files.

I close my eyes. The layout of the ground floor rises up in front of me. I remember it from three days ago. Glass crunches under my sneakers. A red light blinks on the answering machine.

It shouldn't have come to this. Barnaby lied to me. It's not that I suspect him of anything serious. Good people protect those they love. But sometimes they don't recognise how good intentions and blind loyalty can twist their reasoning.

He's frightened of what I might find. *I*'m frightened. He's worried that he didn't really know his daughter. *I*'m worried too.

I climb the stairs. In the nursery I take the roll of black plastic and cover the window, sealing the edges with duct tape. Now it's safe to turn on the torch.

Precautions like this might be unnecessary but I can't afford to have the neighbours investigating or someone calling the police. My career (what career?) already hangs on a thread. I open the dresser drawer. The files have gone, along with the bundle of letters.

Moving from room to room I repeat the process, searching wardrobes and drawers beneath beds.

Next to the main bedroom there is a study with a desk

and filing cabinet. The lone window is partially open. I glance outside to a moonlit garden, blanketed by shadows and fallen leaves.

Unfurling another sheet of plastic, I seal the window before turning on my torch. Beneath the desk, just above the skirting board, I notice a phone outlet. The top drawer contains software and instructions for an ADSL connection. I was right about the computer. Right about Barnaby.

Opening the remaining drawers, I find the usual office supplies – marker pens, a stapler, paper clips, a ball of rubber bands, Post-It notes, a cigarette lighter . . .

Next I search the filing cabinet, leafing through the hanging files. There are no labels or dates. I have to search each one. Plastic sheaths contain the domestic bills. Each telephone account has a list of outgoing calls to mobiles and long-distance numbers. I can possibly trace them but it will take days.

Among the invoices there is one from an Internet company. People sometimes leave copies of their e-mails on their server but I need Cate's password and username.

Having finished in the study I move on to the main bedroom, which is paper-free except for the bookshelves. Barnaby said Felix was sleeping in the guest room. His side of the wardrobe is empty. Cate slept on the right side of the queen-size bed. Her bedside drawer has night cream, moisturiser, emery boards and a picture frame lying face down. I turn it over.

Two teenage girls are laughing at the camera; arms draped over each other's shoulders; sea water dripping from their hair. I can almost taste the salt on their skin and hear the waves shushing the shingles.

Every August the Elliot family used to rent a cottage in Cornwall and spend their time sailing and swimming. Cate invited me one year. I was fifteen and it was my first proper beach holiday.

We swam, rode bikes, collected shells and watched the boys surfing at Widemouth Bay. A couple of them offered to teach Cate and me how to surf but Barnaby said that surfers were deadbeats and potheads. Instead he taught us how to sail in a solo dinghy on Padstow Harbour and the Camel Estuary. He could only take one of us out at a time.

I was embarrassed by my lime-green gingham seersucker one-piece, which my mother had chosen. Cate let me borrow one of her bikinis. As we sat side by side, Barnaby's leg would sometimes touch mine. And to balance the boat we had to lean out over the water and he put his arm around my waist. I liked the way he smelled of salt and suntan lotion.

Of an evening we played games like charades and Trivial Pursuit. I tried to sit next to him because he would nudge me in the ribs when he told one of his jokes or lean against me until we toppled over.

'You were flirting with him,' said Cate after we'd gone to bed. We were sharing the loft. Mr and Mrs Elliot had the largest bedroom on the floor below and Jarrod had a room to himself at the back of the house.

'No, I wasn't.'

'You *were*.'

'Don't be ridiculous.'

'It's disgusting. He's old enough to be—'

'—Your father?'

She laughed. She was right, of course. I did flirt with

him and he flirted back because he knew no other way to behave with women or girls.

Cate and I were lying on top of the bedclothes, unable to sleep because it was so hot. The loft had no insulation and seemed to trap the heat from the day.

'Do you know your problem?' she said. 'You've never actually kissed a boy.'

'Yes, I have.'

'I'm not talking about your brothers. I mean a proper French kiss – with tongues.'

I grew embarrassed.

'You should practise.'

'Pardon?'

'Here, do this.' She pressed her thumb and forefinger together. 'Pretend this is a boy's lips and kiss them.'

She held my hand and kissed it, snaking her tongue between my thumb and forefinger until they were wet with saliva.

'Now you try it.' She held out her hand. It tasted of toothpaste and soap. 'No, too much tongue. Yeuch!'

'*You* used a lot of tongue.'

'Not *that* much.' She wiped her hand on the sheets and looked at me with impatient affection. 'Now, you have to remember positioning.'

'What do you mean?'

'You have to tilt your head to the right or left so you don't bang noses. We're not Eskimos.'

She tossed her ponytail over her shoulder and pulled me close. Cupping my face, she pressed her lips against mine. I could feel her heart beating and the blood pulsing beneath her skin. Her tongue brushed along my lips and danced over my teeth. We were breathing the same air. My eyes stayed closed. It was the most amazing feeling.

'Wow, you're a fast learner,' she said.

'You're a good teacher.'

My heart was racing.

'Maybe we shouldn't do that again.'

'It did feel a bit weird.'

'Yeah. Weird.'

I rubbed my palms down the front of my nightdress.

'Yeah, well, now you know how to do it,' said Cate, picking up a magazine.

She had kissed a lot of boys, even at fifteen, but she didn't brag about it. Many more followed – pearls and pebbles strung around her neck – and as each one came and went there was scarcely a shrug of resignation or sadness.

I brush my fingers over the photograph and contemplate whether to take it with me. Who would know? At the same moment an answer occurs to me. Retracing my steps to the study, I open the desk drawer and spy the cigarette lighter. When we were kids and I stayed the night with Cate, she would sneak cigarettes upstairs and lean out the window so that her parents didn't smell the smoke.

Tearing the plastic sheet from the sash window, I slide the lower pane upwards and brace my hands on the sill as I lean outside, sixteen feet above the garden.

In the darkness I follow the line of a rainwater pipe that is fixed to the bricks with metal brackets. I need more light. Risking the torch, I direct the beam onto the pipe. I can just make out the knotted end of a thin cord, looped over the nearest bracket, beyond reach.

What did she use?

I look around the study. At the back of the desk, hard against the wall, is a wire coat hanger stretched to create a diamond shape with a hook on one end. Back at the window, I lean out and snag the loop of cord on the hook, pulling it towards me. The cord runs across the wall and over a small nail before dropping vertically. As I pull it tighter a paint can emerges from the foliage of the garden. It rises towards me until I can lean out and grab it.

Pulling it inside, I use a coin to lever open the lid. Inside is a half-full packet of cigarettes and a larger package wrapped in plastic and held together with rubber bands. Retrieving it, I close the lid of the paint can and let the nylon cord slip through my fingers as I lower it back into the shrubs.

Returning to the main bedroom, I slip off the rubber bands from the package and unfold what turns out to be a plastic bag with documents pressed into the bottom corner. I spread the contents on the duvet: two airline boarding passes, a tourist map of Amsterdam and a brochure.

The boarding passes are for a British Midlands flight from Heathrow to Schiphol Airport in the Netherlands on the ninth of February, returning on the eleventh.

The tourist map has a picture of the Rijksmuseum on the front cover and is worn along the folds. It seems to cover the heart of Amsterdam where the canals and streets follow a concentric horseshoe pattern. The back of the map has bus, tram and train routes, flanked by a list of hotels. One of them is circled: the Red Tulip Hotel.

I pick up the brochure. It appears to promote a charity – the 'New Life Adoption Centre' – which has a phone number and a post-office box address in Haywards Heath, West Sussex. There are pictures of babies and happy couples, along with a quote: *'Isn't it nice to know when you're not ready to be a mother, somebody else is?'*

Unfolding the brochure I find more photographs and testimonials.

'HOPING TO ADOPT? If you are looking for a safe, successful adoption we can help! Since 1995 we have helped hundreds of couples adopt babies. Our select group of caring professionals can make your dream of a family come true.'

On the opposite page is a headline: *'ARE YOU PREGNANT AND CONSIDERING WHAT TO DO?'*

And underneath: *'We can help you! We offer assistance and encouragement during and after your pregnancy and can provide birth-parent scholarships. Open adoption means YOU make the choices.'*

Alongside the text is a photograph of a child's hand clinging to the finger of an adult.

Someone called Julie writes: *'Thank you for turning my unexpected pregnancy into a gift from God to all involved.'*

On the opposite page are further testimonials, this time from couples.

'Choosing adoption brought us a beautiful daughter and made our lives complete.'

A loose page slips from the centre of the brochure.

'This child could be yours,' it reads. *'Born this month: a boy, white, with an unknown father. The mother, 18, is a prostitute and former drug user but is now clean. This baby could be yours for a facilitation fee and medical expenses.'*

Returning the documents to the plastic bag, I snap the rubber bands into place.

The phone number on the back of Samira's photograph

needed a foreign prefix. Cate visited the Netherlands in February. She announced she was twelve weeks pregnant in May.

I pick up the telephone next to the bed and call international enquiries. It feels wrong to call from the scene of the crime, as though I'm confessing. An operator gives me the country code for the Netherlands. Adding '31' this time, I call the number.

It connects. The ring tone is long and dull.

Someone picks up. Silence.

'Hello?'

Nothing.

'Hello, can you hear me?'

Someone is breathing.

'I'm trying to reach Samira. Is she there?'

A guttural voice, bubbling with phlegm, answers me. 'Who is calling?'

The accent might be Dutch. It sounds more East European.

'A friend.'

'Your name?'

'Actually, I'm a friend of a friend.'

'Your name and your friend's name?'

Distrust sweeps over me like a cold shadow. I don't like this voice. I can feel it searching for me, reaching inside my chest, feeling blindly for my soft centre, my soul.

'Is Samira there?'

'There is nobody here.'

I try to sound calm. 'I am calling on behalf of Cate Beaumont. I have the rest of the money.'

I am extrapolating on the known facts, which is just a

fancy way of saying that I'm winging it. *How much further can I go?*

The phone goes dead.

Not far enough.

Putting the receiver back on its cradle, I smooth the bed and pick up my things. As I turn towards the door I hear a tinkling sound. I know what it is. I made just such a sound when I smashed a pane of glass in the French doors.

Someone is in the house. What are the chances of two intruders on the same night? Slim. None. Tucking the package into the waistband of my jeans, I peer over the banister. There are muffled voices in the hall. At least two. A torch beam passes the bottom of the stairs. I pull back.

What to do? I shouldn't be here. Neither should they. Ahead of me are the stairs to the loft. Climbing them quickly, I reach a door that opens on stiff hinges.

From downstairs: 'Did you hear something?'

'What?'

'I thought I heard something.'

'Nah.'

'I'll check upstairs.'

One of them sounds Irish. It could be Brendan Pearl.

'Hey!'

'What?'

'You notice that?'

'What?'

'The windows are covered in plastic. Why would they do that?'

'Fucked if I know. Just get on with it.'

The loft seems to be full of odd angles and narrow corners. My eyes are getting used to the dark. I can make out a single bed, a cabinet, a fan on a stand and cardboard boxes of clutter and bric-a-brac.

Squeezing into a space formed by the cabinet and the sloping roof, I pull boxes in front of me. I need a weapon. The iron bed has heavy brass balls on the bedposts. I unscrew one of them quietly and peel off a sock, slipping the ball inside. It slips down to the toe and I weigh it in my hands. It could break bones.

Returning to my hiding place, I listen for footsteps on the stairs and watch the door. I have to call the police. If I flip open my phone the screen will light up like a neon sign saying, 'Here I am! Come and get me!'

Shielding it in both hands, I dial 999. An operator answers.

'Officer in trouble. Intruders on premises.'

I whisper the address and my badge number. I can't stay on the line. The phone closes and the screen goes dark. Only my breathing now and the footsteps . . .

The door opens. A torch beam flashes and swings across the room. I can't see the figure behind it. He can't see me. He stumbles over a box and sends Christmas baubles spilling across the floor. The light finds one of them close to my feet.

He puts the torch on the bed, facing towards him. It reflects off his forehead. Brendan Pearl. All my weight is on the balls of my feet, ready to fight. What's he doing?

There is something in his fist. A boxlike can. He presses it and a stream of liquid arcs from the nozzle, shining silver in the torch beam. He presses again, soaking the boxes and

123

drawing patterns on the walls. Fluid splashes across my fore-head, leaking into my eyes.

Red-hot wires stab into my brain and the smell catches in the back of my throat. Benzine? Lighter fluid? Fire!

The pain is unimaginable, but I mustn't move. He's going to set fire to the house. I have to get out. I can't see. Vibrations on the stairs. He's gone. Crawling from my hiding place, I reach the door and press my ear against it.

My eyes are useless. I need water to flush them out. There's a bathroom on the first floor as well as an en-suite in the main bedroom. I can find them but only if Pearl has gone. I can't afford to wait.

Something breaks with a crack and topples over down-stairs. My vision is blurred but I see a light. Not light. Fire!

The ground floor is ablaze and the smoke is rising. Clinging to the handrail, I make it down to the landing. Feeling my way along the wall, I reach the en-suite and splash water into my eyes. I can see only blurred outlines, shadows instead of sharp detail.

The smoke is getting thicker. On my hands and knees, I feel my way across the bedroom, smelling the lighter fluid on the carpet. When the fire reaches this floor it will accel-erate. The study window is still open. I crawl across the landing, bumping my head against a wall. My fingers find the skirting board. I can feel the heat.

Finding the window, I lean outside and take deep breaths between spluttering coughs. There is a whooshing sound behind me. Flames sweep past the open door. Hungry. Feeding on the accelerant.

Climbing onto the window ledge I look down. I can just make out the garden, sixteen feet below. A jump like that will break both my legs. I turn my head towards the down pipe bolted to the wall. My eyes are useless. How far was it? Four feet. Maybe a little more.

I can feel the heat of the fire on the backs of my legs. A window blows out beneath me. I hear glass scattering through the shrubbery.

I have to back myself to do this. I have to trust my memory and my instincts. Toppling sideways, I reach out, falling.

My left hand brushes past the pipe. My right hand hooks around it. Momentum will either pull me loose or rip my shoulder out. Two hands have it now. My hip crashes against the bricks and I hang on.

Hand below hand, I shimmy towards the ground. Sirens are coming. My feet touch soft earth and I wheel around, stumbling a dozen paces before tripping over a flower bed and sprawling on my face.

Every window at the rear of the house is lit up. Through my watery eyes it sounds and looks like a university party. The ultimate house-warming.

12

Two detectives have turned up. One of them, Eric Softell, I remember from training college. His surname sounds like a brand of toilet paper, which was why they nicknamed him 'Arsewipe' at training college. Not me, of course. Sikh girls don't risk calling people names.

'I heard you were off the force,' he says.

'No.'

'Still running?'

'Yes.'

'Not fast enough from what I hear.' He grins at his partner, Billy Marsh, a detective constable.

Stories about the camaraderie of police officers are often sadly overstated. I don't find many of my colleagues particularly lovable or supportive, but at least most of them are honest and some of them are keepers like DI Ruiz.

A paramedic has flushed out my eyes with distilled water.

I'm sitting on the back ramp of the ambulance, head tilted, while he tapes cotton wool over my left eye.

'You should see an eye specialist,' he says. 'It can sometimes take a week before the full damage is clear.'

'Permanent damage?'

'See the specialist.'

Behind him fire hoses snake across the gleaming road and firemen in reflective vests are mopping up. Structurally, there is still a house on the block, but the insides are gutted and smoking. The loft collapsed under the weight of water.

I called Hari to come and get me. Now he's watching the firemen with a mixture of awe and envy. What boy doesn't want to play with a hose?

Sensing the animosity between Softell and me, he tries to step in and play the protective brother, which doesn't really suit him.

'Listen, punka wallah, why don't you run along and fetch us a cup of tea?' says Softell.

Hari doesn't understand the insult but he recognises the tone.

I should be angry but I'm used to remarks like this from people like Softell. During probationer training a group of us were given riot shields and sent to the parade ground. Another band of recruits were told to attack us verbally and physically. There were no rules, but we weren't able to retaliate. Softell spat in my face and called me a 'Paki whore'. I practically thanked him.

My left thigh is slightly corked; my knuckles are scraped and raw. There are questions. Answers. The name Brendan Pearl means nothing to them.

'Explain to me again what you were doing in the house.'

'I was driving by. I saw a burglary in process. I called it in.'

'From inside the house?'

'Yes, sir.'

'So you followed them inside?'

'Yes.'

Softell shakes his head. 'You just happened to be driving past a friend's house and you saw the same man who was driving the car that ran her down. What do you think, Billy?'

'Sounds like bullshit to me.' Marsh is the one taking notes.

'How did you get lighter fluid in your eyes?'

'He was spraying it around.'

'Yeah, yeah, while you were *hiding* in the corner.'

Arsehole!

Casually, he props his foot on the tray of the ambulance. 'If you were just gonna hide in there – why bother going in at all?'

'I thought there was only one of them.'

I'm digging myself into a hole.

'Why didn't you phone for back-up *before* you went in?'

Deeper and deeper.

'I don't know, sir.'

Drops of water have beaded on the polished toe of his shoe.

'You see how it looks, don't you?' Softell says.

'How does it look?'

'A house burns down. A witness comes forward who is covered in lighter fluid. Rule number one when dealing with arson – nine times out of ten, the person who yells "Fire!" is the person who starts the fire.'

'You can't be serious. Why would I do that?'

His shoulders lift and drop. 'Who knows? Maybe you just like burning shit.'

The whole street has been woken. Neighbours are standing on the pavement in dressing gowns and overcoats. Children are jumping on a hose and dancing away from a leak that sprays silver under the street light.

A black cab pulls up outside the ring of fire engines. Ruiz emerges. He steps through the ring of rubbernecks, ignoring the constable who is trying to keep them back.

After pausing to appraise the house, he continues along the road until he reaches me. The white eyepatch makes me look like a reverse pirate.

'Do you ever have a *normal* day?' he asks.

'Once. It was a Wednesday.'

He looks me up and down. I'm putting most of my weight on one leg because of my thigh. Surprisingly, he leans forward and kisses my cheek, an absolute first.

'I thought you retired,' says Billy Marsh.

'That's right, son.'

'Well, what are you doing here?'

'I asked him to come,' I explain.

Ruiz is sizing up the detectives. 'Mind if I listen in?'

It sounds like a question only it isn't. The DI manages to do that sometimes – turn questions into statements.

'Just don't get in the bloody way,' mumbles Softell.

Marsh is on the phone calling for a SOCO team to sweep the house and garden for clues. The fire brigade will launch its own investigation. I hobble away from the ambulance, which has another call. Ruiz takes my arm.

Hari is still here. 'You can go home now,' I tell him.

'What about you?'

129

'I could be a while.'

'You want me to stay?'

'That's OK.'

He glances at Softell and whispers, 'Do you know that prick?'

'He's OK.'

'No wonder people dislike coppers.'

'Hey!'

He grins. 'Not you, sis.'

There are more questions to answer. Softell becomes less interested in what I was doing in the house and more interested in Brendan Pearl.

'So you think this arson attack is linked to the deaths of the Beaumonts?'

'Yes.'

'Why would Pearl burn down their house?'

'Perhaps he wanted to destroy evidence – letters, e-mails, phone records – anything that might point to him.'

I explain about Cate's fake pregnancy and the money missing from her account. 'I think she arranged to buy a baby, but something went wrong.'

Marsh speaks. 'People adopt foreign kids all the time – Chinese orphans, Romanians, Koreans – why would you *buy* a child?'

'She tried to adopt and couldn't.'

'How do you buy one?'

I don't have the answers. Softell glances at Billy Marsh. There is a beat of silence and something invisible passes between them.

'Why didn't you report any of this earlier?'

'I couldn't be sure.'

'So you went looking for evidence. You broke into the house.'

'No.'

'Then you tried to cover your tracks with a can of lighter fluid and a cock and bull story.'

'Not true.'

Ruiz is nearby, clenching and unclenching his fists. For the first time I notice how old he looks in a shapeless overcoat, worn smooth at the elbows.

'Hey, Detective Sergeant, I know what you're thinking,' he says. 'You want some kitchen-sink, bog-standard example of foul play that you can solve by nine o'clock and still make your ballet lesson. This is one of your colleagues, one of your own. Your job is to believe her.'

Softell puffs up, too stupid to keep his mouth shut. 'And who do you think you are?'

'Godzilla.'

'Who?'

Ruiz rolls his eyes. 'I'm the monster that's going to stomp all over your fucking career if you don't pay this lady some respect.'

Softell looks like he's been bitch-slapped. He takes out his mobile and punches in a number. I overhear him talking to his superintendent. I don't know what he's told. Ruiz still has a lot of friends in the Met, people who respect what he's done.

When the call finishes Softell is a chastened man. A taskforce investigation has been authorised and a warrant issued for the arrest of Brendan Pearl.

'I want you at the station by midday to make a statement,' he says.

'I can go?'

'Yeah.'

Ruiz won't let me drive. He takes me home in my car. Squeezed behind the wheel of my hatchback, he looks like a geriatric Noddy.

'Was it Pearl?'

'Yes.'

'Did you see him?'

'Yes.'

Taking one hand off the wheel, he scratches his chin. His ring finger is severed below the first knuckle, courtesy of a high-velocity bullet. He likes to tell people his third wife attacked him with a meat cleaver.

I tell Ruiz about the boarding passes and the brochure for the New Life Adoption Centre. We both know stories about stolen and trafficked babies. Most stray into the realm of urban myth – baby farms in Guatemala and runaways snatched from the streets of São Paulo for organ harvesting.

'Let's just say you're right and Cate Beaumont organised some sort of private adoption or to buy a baby. Why go through the pretence of pregnancy?'

'Perhaps she wanted to convince Felix that the baby was his.'

'That's a pretty ambitious goal. What if the kid looks nothing like him?'

'A lot of husbands are happy to *believe* they've fathered a child. History is littered with mistakes.'

Ruiz raises an eyebrow. 'You mean lies.'

I rise to the bait. 'Yes, women can be devious. Sometimes we have to be. We're the ones who get left changing nappies when some bloke decides he's not ready to commit or to get rid of his Harley or his porn collection.'

Silence.

'Did that sound like a rant?' I ask.

'A little.'

'Sorry.'

Ruiz begins thinking out loud – trawling through his memory. That's the thing about the DI – nothing is ever forgotten. Other people grimace and curse, trying to summon up the simplest details, but Ruiz does it effortlessly, recalling facts, figures, quotes and names.

'Three years ago the Italian police smashed a ring of Ukrainian human traffickers who were trying to sell an unborn baby. They ran a kind of auction, looking for the highest bidder. Someone offered to pay quarter of a million pounds.'

'Cate travelled to Amsterdam in February. She could have arranged a deal.'

'Alone?'

'I don't know.'

'How did they communicate with her?'

I think back to the fire. 'We might never know.'

Ruiz drops me home and arranges to meet me in the morning.

'You should see an eye specialist.'

'First I have to make a statement.'

Upstairs, I pull the phone jack from the wall and turn off my mobile. I have talked to enough people today. I want a shower and a warm bed. I want to cry into a pillow and fall asleep. A girl should be allowed.

13

Wembley Police Station is a brand new building decked in blue and white on the Harrow Road. The new national stadium is almost a mile away with soaring light towers visible above the rooftops.

Softell keeps me waiting before taking my statement. His attitude has changed since last night. He has looked up Pearl on the computer and the interest sparks in his eyes like a gas ring igniting. Softell is the sort of detective who goes through an entire career with his head under his armpit, not understanding people's motives or making any head-line arrests. Now he can sense an opportunity.

The deaths of Cate and Felix Beaumont are a side issue. A distraction. I can see what he's going to do: he'll dismiss Cate as a desperate woman with a history of psychiatric problems and a criminal record. Pearl is the man he wants.

'You have no evidence a baby ever existed,' he says.

'What about the missing money?'

'Someone probably ripped her off.'

'And then killed her.'

'Not according to the vehicle accident report.'

Softcell hands me a typed statement. I have to sign each page and initial any changes. I look at my words. I have lied about why I was at the house and what happened before the fire. Does my signature make it worse?

Taking back the statement, he straightens the pages and punches the stapler. 'Very fucking professional,' he sneers. 'You know it never stops – the lying. Once you start it just keeps getting worse.'

'Yeah, well, you'd know,' I say, wishing I could think of a put-down that wasn't so lame. Mostly, I wish I could tear up the statement and start again.

Ruiz is waiting for me in the foyer.

'How's the eye?'

'The specialist said I should wear an eyepatch for a week.'

'So where is it?'

'In my pocket.'

We step on a black rubber square and the doors open automatically.

'Your boyfriend has called six times in the last hour. Ever thought of getting a dog instead?'

'What did you tell him?'

'Nothing. That's why he's here.'

I look up and see Dave leaning on Ruiz's car. He wraps me in a bear hug with his face in my hair. Ruiz turns away as though embarrassed.

'Are you smelling me, Dave?'

'Yup.'

'That's a bit creepy.'

'Not to me. I'm just glad you're in one piece.'

'Only bruises.'

'I could kiss them better.'

'Perhaps later.'

Dressed in a dark blue suit, white shirt and maroon tie, Dave has tidied up since his promotion, but I notice a brown sauce stain on the tie that he hasn't managed to sponge away. My mother would recognise a detail like that. Scary.

My stomach is empty. I haven't eaten since yesterday.

We find a café near Wembley Central with a smudged blackboard menu and enough grease in the air to flatten Dave's hair. It's an old-fashioned 'caff' with Formica tables, paper napkins, and a nervy waitress with a nose stud.

I order tea and toast. Ruiz and Dave choose the all-day breakfast – otherwise known as the '999' because it's a heart attack on a plate. Nobody says anything until the food is consumed and tea has been poured. The DI takes milk and sugar.

'There is a guy I used to play rugby with,' he says. 'He never talked about his job, but I know he works for MI5. I called him this morning. He told me an interesting thing about Brendan Pearl.'

'What's that?'

Ruiz takes out a tattered notebook held together with a rubber band. Loose pages tumble through his fingers. A lot of detectives don't believe in keeping notes. They want their memories to be 'flexible' should they ever get in the witness box. Ruiz has a memory like the proverbial steel trap, yet he still backs it up on paper.

'According to my friend, Pearl was last known to be working as a security consultant for a construction company in Afghanistan. Three foreign contractors were killed in mid-September 2004 in a convoy travelling on the highway leading from the main airport to central Kabul when a suicide bomber drove into them. Pearl was among the wounded. He spent three weeks in a German hospital and then signed himself out. Nobody has heard from him since then.'

'So what's he doing here?' asks Dave.

'And how did Cate meet him?' I add.

Ruiz gathers up the pages and slips the rubber band around them. 'Maybe we should check out this New Life Adoption Centre.'

Dave disagrees. 'It's not *our* investigation.'

'Not *officially*,' concedes the DI.

'Not even unofficially.'

'It's an *independent* investigation.'

'Unauthorised.'

'*Unconstrained.*'

Interrupting them, I suggest, 'You could come with us, Dave.'

He hesitates.

Ruiz spies an opening. 'That's what I like about you, Dave. You're a freethinker. Some people think the modern British detective has become timid and punctilious, but not you. You're a credit to the Met. You're not frightened to have an opinion or act on a hunch.'

It's like watching a fisherman casting a fly. It curls through the air, settles on the water and drifts downstream, drifting, drifting . . .

'I suppose it wouldn't hurt to check it out,' says Dave.

There are no signs pointing out the New Life Adoption Centre, either in the nearest village or at the gates, which are flanked by sandstone pillars. A loose gravel driveway curves through fields and crosses a single-lane stone bridge. Friesians dot the pasture and scarcely stir as we pass.

Eventually, we pull up in front of a large Adam-style house, in the noise shadow of Gatwick Airport. I take Dave's arm.

'OK, we've been married for six years. It was a big Sikh wedding. I looked beautiful, of course. We've been trying for a baby for five years but your sperm count is too low.'

'Does it have to be *my* sperm count?'

'Oh, don't be so soft! Give me your ring.'

He slides a white-gold band from his pinkie and I place it on my wedding finger.

Ruiz has stayed behind in the village pub, chatting with the locals. So far we've established that the adoption centre is a privately run charity operating out of a stately home, Followdale House. The founder, Julian Shawcroft, is a former executive director of the Infertility and Planned Parenthood Clinic in Manchester.

A young woman, barely out of her teens, answers the doorbell. She's wearing woolly socks and a powder-blue dressing gown that struggles to hide her pregnancy.

'I can't really help you,' she confides immediately. 'I'm just minding the front desk while Stella has a tinkle.'

'Stella?'

'She's in charge. Well, not really in charge. Mr Shawcroft is *really* in charge but he's often away. He's here today, which is unusual. He's the chairman or the managing director. I can never work out the difference. I mean, what does an MD do and what does a chairman do? I'm talking too much, aren't I? I do that sometimes. My name is Meredith. Do you think Hugh is a nice boy's name? Hugh Jackman is very cute. I can't think of any other Hughs.'

'Hugh Grant,' I suggest.

'Cool.'

'Hugh Heffner,' says Dave.

'Who's he?' she asks.

'It doesn't matter,' I tell her, glancing at Dave.

Her hair is just long enough to pull into a ponytail and her nail polish is chipped where she has picked it off.

The lobby of the house has two faded Chesterfields on either side of a fireplace. The staircase, with its ornate banister, is sealed off by a blue tasselled rope hung from brass posts.

Meredith leads us to an office in a side room. Several desks have computers on them and a photocopier spits out pages as a light slides back and forth beneath the glass.

There are posters on the wall. One of them shows a couple swinging an infant between their outstretched hands, except the child is cut out like a missing piece of a jigsaw puzzle. Underneath the caption reads: *'Is There a Child-Sized Hole in Your Life?'*

Through French doors I can see a rose garden and what might once have been a croquet lawn.

'When are you due?' I ask.

'Two weeks.'

'Why are you here?'

She giggles. 'This is an adoption centre, silly.'

'Yes, but people come to adopt a baby, not to have one.'

'I haven't decided yet,' she says in a matter-of-fact way.

A woman appears – Stella – apologising for the delay. She looks very businesslike in a dark polo-neck, black trousers and imitation-snakeskin shoes with pointed toes and kitten heels.

Her eyes survey me up and down, as though taking an inventory. 'Nope, the womb is vacant,' I feel like saying. She glances at her diary.

'We don't have an appointment,' I explain. 'It was rather a spur-of-the-moment decision to come.'

'Adoption should never be spur-of-the-moment.'

'Oh, I don't mean *that* decision. We've been talking about it for months. We were in the neighbourhood.'

Dave chips in, 'I have an aunt who lives close.'

'I see.'

'We want to adopt a baby,' I add. 'It's all we think about.'

Stella takes down our names. I call myself Mrs King, which doesn't sound as weird as it probably should.

'We've been married six years and trying to have a baby for five.'

'So you're looking to adopt because you can't have your own baby?'

It's a loaded question. 'I come from a big family. I wanted the same. But even though we want our own children, we always talked about adopting.'

'Are you prepared to take an older child?'

'We'd like a baby.'

'Yes, well, that may be so, but there are very few newborn

babies put up for adoption in this country. The waiting list is very long.'

'How long?'

'Upwards of five years.'

Dave blows air through his cheeks. He's better at this than I expected. 'Surely it can be fast-tracked in some way,' he says. 'I mean, even the slowest of wheels can be *oiled*.'

Stella seems to resent the suggestion. 'Mr King, we are a non-profit charity governed by the same rules and regulations as local-authority adoption services. The interests of the child come *first* and *last*. *Oil* doesn't enter into it.'

'Of course not. I didn't mean to suggest—'

'My husband works in management,' I explain contritely. 'He believes that almost any problem can be solved by throwing more people or money at it.'

Stella nods sympathetically and for the first time seems to consider my skin colour. 'We do facilitate inter-country adoptions, but there are no children made available from the subcontinent. Most people are choosing to adopt from Eastern Europe.'

'We're not fussy,' adds Dave. I kick him under the desk. 'We're not fazed, I mean. It's not a race thing.'

Stella is eyeing him cautiously. 'There are many *bad* reasons to adopt. Some people try to save their marriage, or replace a child who has died, or they want a fashion accessory because all their friends have one.'

'That's not us,' I say.

'Good. Well, even with inter-country adoptions the assessment and approval process is exactly the same as for adopting a child in this country. This includes full medicals, home visits, criminal-record checks and interviews with social workers and psychologists.'

She stands and opens a filing cabinet. The form is thirty pages long.

'I was wondering if Mr Shawcroft was here today.'

'Do you know him?'

'Only by reputation. That's how I heard about the centre – through a friend.'

'And what's your friend's name?'

'Cate Beaumont.'

I get no sense of whether she's heard the name before.

'Mr Shawcroft is normally very busy fund-raising but fortunately he's here today. He might be able to spare you a few minutes.'

She excuses herself and I can hear her walking upstairs.

'What do you think?' whispers Dave.

'Watch the door.' Skirting the desk, I open the drawer of the filing cabinet.

'That's an illegal search.'

'Just *watch* the *door*.'

My fingers are moving over the files. Each adoptive family appears to have one but there is no 'Beaumont' or 'Elliot'. Some folders are marked by coloured stickers. There are names typed on the labels. At first glance I think they might be children, but the ages are all wrong. These are young women.

One name jumps out at me. Carla Donavon. Donavon's younger sister. His *pregnant* sister. A coincidence? Hardly.

'Those files are confidential.' The disembodied voice startles me.

I look to Dave. He shakes his head. There is an intercom

on the desk. I scan the ceiling and spy a small security camera in the corner. I should have seen it earlier.

'If you want to know something, Mrs King, you should ask,' says the voice. 'I assume that's your real name or perhaps you have lied about that as well.'

'Do you always eavesdrop on people?' I ask.

'Do you always illegally search someone's office and look at highly confidential files? Who exactly are you?'

Dave answers, 'Police officers. I'm Detective Sergeant Dave King. This is Detective Constable Alisha Barba. We are making inquiries about a woman we believe may have been one of your clients.'

The faint buzzing of the intercom goes silent. A side door opens. A man enters, in his mid-fifties, with a sturdy frame and a broad face that creases momentarily as he smiles disarmingly. His hair, once blond, now grey, has tight curls like wood shavings from a lathe.

'I'm sure there must be a law against police officers misrepresenting who they are and conducting unauthorised searches.'

'The drawer was open. I was simply closing it.'

This triggers a smile. He has every right to be angry and suspicious. Instead he finds it amusing. He makes a point of locking the filing cabinet before addressing us again.

'Now that we know exactly who we are, perhaps I could give you a guided tour and you could tell me what you're doing here.'

He leads us into the lobby and through the French doors onto the terrace. The young woman we saw earlier is sitting on a swing in the garden. Her dressing gown billows as she rocks back and forth, getting higher and higher.

'Be careful, Meredith,' he calls. And then to us. 'She's a clumsy young thing.'

'Why is she here?'

'Meredith hasn't decided what she wants to do. Giving up a baby is a difficult and courageous decision. We help young women like her to decide.'

'You try to convince her.'

'On the contrary. We offer love and support. We teach parenting skills so she'll be ready. And if she decides to give up her baby we have scholarships that can help her find a flat and get a job. We operate open adoptions.'

'Open?'

'The birth mothers and adoptive parents get to know one another and often stay in touch afterwards.'

Shawcroft chooses an unraked gravel path around the southern end of the house. Large bay windows reveal a lounge. Several young women are playing cards in front of a fire.

'We offer prenatal classes, massage therapy and have quite a good gymnasium,' he explains.

'Why?'

'Why not?'

'I don't understand why it's necessary.'

Shawcroft has an eye for an opening. It gives him the opportunity to explain his philosophy and he does so passionately, haranguing the historical attitudes that saw young unmarried mothers demonised or treated like outcasts.

'Single motherhood has become more acceptable but it is still a challenging choice,' he explains. 'That's why I established this centre. There are far too many orphans and unwanted children in our society and overseas, with too few options available to improve their lives.

'Have you any idea how slow, bureaucratic and unfair our adoption system is? We leave it in the hands of people who are underfunded, understaffed and inexperienced – people who play God with the lives of children.'

Dave has dropped back.

'I began out of a small office in Mayfair. There was just me. I charged fifty pounds for a two-hour consultancy session. Two years later I had a full-time staff of eight and had completed more than a hundred adoptions. Now we're here.' He gestures towards Followdale House.

'How can you afford this place?'

'People have been very generous – new parents and grandparents. Some leave us money as bequests or make donations. We have a staff of fourteen, including social workers, counsellors, career advisers, health visitors and a psychologist.'

In one corner of the garden I notice a golf bag propped beneath an umbrella and a bucket of balls waiting to be hit. There are calluses on his fingers.

'My one indulgence,' he explains, gazing over the fence into the pasture. 'The cows are rather ball-shy. I have developed an incurable slice since my operation.'

'Operation?'

'My hip. Old age catching up on me.'

He picks up a club and swings it gently at a rose bush. A flower dissolves in a flurry of petals. Examining his fingers, he opens and closes his fist.

'It's always harder to hold a club in the winter. Some people wear gloves. I like being able to *feel* the grip.'

He pauses and turns to face me. 'Now, detective constable, let's dispense with the pretence. Why are you here?'

'Do you know someone called Cate Beaumont?'

'No.' The answer is abrupt.

'You don't need to check your client files?'

'I remember all of them.'

'Even those who don't succeed?'

'*Especially* those who don't succeed.'

Dave has joined us. He picks a metal-headed driver and eyes a Friesian in the distance before thinking better of it.

'My friend faked her pregnancy and emptied her bank account. I think she arranged to buy a baby.'

'Which is illegal.'

'She had one of your brochures.'

'Which is *not* illegal.' Shawcroft doesn't take offence or become defensive. 'Where is your friend now?'

'She's dead. Murdered.'

He repeats the word with renewed respect. His hands are unfailingly steady.

'The brochure contained an advertisement for a baby boy whose mother was a prostitute and a former drug addict. It mentioned a facilitation fee and medical expenses.'

Shawcroft lets his palm glide over his cheek, giving himself time. For a moment something struggles inside him. I want a denial. There isn't one.

'The facilitation fee is to cover paperwork such as visas and birth certificates.'

'Selling children is illegal.'

'The baby was not for sale. Every applicant is properly vetted. We require referees and assessment reports. There are group workshops and familiarisation. Finally, there is an adoption panel that must approve the adopter before a child can be matched to them.'

'If these adoptions are above board, why are they advertised using post-office box numbers?'

He gazes straight ahead as if plotting the distance of his next shot.

'Do you know how many children die in the world every year, Alisha? Five million. War, poverty, disease, famine, neglect, landmines and predators. I have seen children so malnourished they don't have the energy to swat flies away and starving women holding babies to their withered breasts desperate to feed them. I have seen them throw their babies over the fences of rich people's houses or, worse still, into the River Ganges because they can't afford to look after them. I have seen Aids orphans, crack babies and children sold into slavery for as little as fifteen pounds. And what do we do in this country? We make it *harder* for people to adopt. We tell them they're too old, or the wrong colour, or the wrong religion.'

Shawcroft makes no attempt to hide the bitterness in his voice. 'It takes courage for a country to admit it can't take care of its smallest and weakest. Many countries who are not so brave would prefer to see abandoned children starve than to leave for a better life.

'The system is unfair. So, yes, I sometimes cut corners. In some countries contracts can be signed with birth mothers. Hollywood movie stars do it. Government ministers do it. Children can be rescued. Infertile couples can have families.'

'By *buying* babies.'

'By *saving* them.'

For all his avuncular charm and geniality, there is steel in this man's nature and something vaguely dangerous. A

147

mixture of sentimentality and spiritual zeal that fortifies the hearts of tyrants.

'You think that what I'm doing is immoral. Let me tell you what's more immoral. Doing *nothing*. Sitting back in your comfortable chair in your comfortable home thinking that just because you sponsor a child in Zambia you're doing enough.'

'It shouldn't mean breaking the law.'

'Every family that adopts here is vetted and approved by a panel of experts.'

'You're profiting from their desperation.'

'All payments go back into the charity.'

He begins listing the number of foreign adoptions the centre has overseen and the diplomatic hurdles he has had to overcome. His arguments are marshalled so skilfully that I have no line of reasoning to counter them. My objections sound mean-spirited and hostile. I should apologise.

Shawcroft continues talking, railing against the system, but then makes his only mistake: emotional blackmail.

'Your friend's death is very unfortunate, DC Barba, but I would strongly counsel you against making any rash or unfounded claims about what we do here. Police knocking on doors, asking questions, upsetting families. Is that what you want?'

Stella appears on the terrace and calls to him: miming a phone call with her hand.

'I have to go,' he says, smiling tiredly. 'The baby you referred to was born in Washington four weeks ago. A boy. A young couple from Oxford are adopting him.'

I watch him return along the path, gravel rasping beneath

his soft-soled shoes. Meredith is still in the garden. He motions for her to come inside. It is getting cold.

'New Boy' Dave falls into step beside me and we follow the path in the opposite direction towards the car park, passing a statue of a young girl holding an urn and another of a Cupid with a missing penis.

'So what do you think?' he asks.

'What sort of adoption centre has surveillance cameras?'

14

'Finding Donavon' sounds like the title of an Irish art-house movie directed by Neil Jordan. 'Deconstructing Donavon' is another good title and that's exactly what I plan to do when I find him.

Maybe it's a coincidence, maybe it's not but I don't like the way that his name keeps popping up whenever I trace Cate's movements. Donavon claims to know when someone is lying. That's because he's an expert on the subject – a born deceiver.

On the drive back to London we go over the details of our meeting with Shawcroft. Ruiz doesn't see a problem with adoption having a financial element if couples are vetted properly. Too much control allows black markets to flourish. Perhaps he's right, but a zealot like Shawcroft can turn compassion into a dangerous crusade.

'New Boy' Dave has work to do. We drop him at the

Harrow Road police station and I make him promise to run a check on Shawcroft. He kisses my cheek and whispers, 'Leave this alone.'

I can't. I won't. He adds something else. 'I *did* like being married to you.'

Time-wise it was even shorter than Britney Spears's first wedding, but I don't tell him that.

Nobody answers the door at Donavon's house. The curtains are drawn and his motorbike isn't parked outside. A neighbour suggests we try the markets in Whitechapel Road. Donavon has a weekend stall there.

Parking behind the Royal London Hospital, we follow the insurrection of noise, colour and movement. Dozens of stalls spill out from the pavement. Everything is for sale – Belgian chocolates from Poland, Greek feta from Yorkshire, Gucci handbags from China and Rolex watches draped inside trench coats.

Traders yell over one another.

– 'Fresh carnations. Two-fifty a bunch!'

– 'Live mussels!'

– 'Garden tomatoes as red as your cheeks!'

I can't see Donavon but I recognise his stall. Draped from the metal framework there are dozens of intricate necklaces or perhaps they're wind chimes. They twirl in the light breeze, fragmenting the remains of the sunlight. Beneath them, haphazardly displayed, are novelty radios, digital clocks and curling tongs from Korea.

Carla looks cold and bored. She's wearing red woollen tights and a short denim skirt stretched over her growing bump.

I close the gap between us and slide my hand under her

sweater, across her abdomen until I feel the warmth of her skin.

'Hey!'

I pull my hand away as if scalded. 'I just wanted to be sure.'

'Sure about what?'

'It doesn't matter.'

Carla looks at me suspiciously and then at Ruiz. A faint, fast vibration is coming off her, as though something terrible and soundless is spinning inside.

'Have you seen him?' she asks anxiously.

'Who?'

'Paul. He hasn't been home in two days.'

'When did you last see him?'

'On Saturday. He had a phone call and went out.'

'Did he say where?'

'No. He never leaves it this long. He always calls me.'

Female intuition is often a myth. Some women just *think* they're more intuitive. I know I'm letting the sisters down by saying that, but gender isn't a factor. It's blood. Families can tell when something is wrong. Carla's eyes dart across the crowd as though assembling a human jigsaw puzzle.

'When are you due?' I ask.

'Christmas.'

'What can you tell me about the New Life Adoption Centre?'

Her mouth seems to frame something she's too embarrassed to admit. I wait for her.

'I don't know what sort of mother I'm gonna make. Paul says I'll be fine. He says I learned from one of the *worst* so

I won't make the same mistakes our Mum did.' Her hands are trembling. 'I didn't want an abortion. It's not because of any religious thing. It's just how I feel, you know. That's why I thought about adoption.'

'You went to see Julian Shawcroft.'

'He offered to help me. He said there were scholarships, you know. I always wanted to be a make-up artist or a beautician. He said he could arrange it.'

'If you gave up the baby?'

'Yeah, well, you can't do both, eh? Not look after a baby and work full-time – not without help.'

'So what did you decide?' asked the DI.

Her shoulders grow rounder. 'I keep changing me mind. Paul wants me to keep it. He says he'll look after us all.' She gnaws at a reddened fingernail.

A crew-cutted teenager stops and picks up a transistor radio shaped like a Pepsi can.

'Don't waste your money – this stuff is shite,' says Carla. The youth looks hard-done-by rather than grateful.

'How did you hear about the New Life Adoption Centre?'

'A friend told Paul about it.'

'Who?'

Carla shrugs.

Her mauve-tinted eyelids tremble. She doesn't have the wherewithal to lie to me. She can't see a reason. Glancing above her head, I notice the feathers and beads.

I have seen one of these ornaments before – at Cate's house, in the nursery. It was hanging above the new cot.

'What are they?' I ask.

Carla unhooks one from the metal frame above her and hangs it from her finger, watching me through a wooden circle criss-crossed with coloured threads and hung with feathers and beads.

'This is a dream catcher,' she explains. 'American Indians believe the night air is filled with dreams, some good and some bad. They hang a dream catcher over a child's bed so it can catch dreams as they flow by. The good dreams know how to slip through the holes and slide down the soft feathers where they land gently on the child's head. But the bad dreams get tangled in the web and perish when the sun comes up.'

Blowing gently, she makes the feathers bob and swirl.

Donavon didn't go to the reunion to 'make his peace' with Cate. He had seen her before. He gave her a dream catcher or she bought one from him.

'How well did your brother know Cate Beaumont?'

Carla shrugs. 'They were friends, I guess.'

'That's not possible.'

She bridles. 'I'm not lying. When Paul was in the Paras she wrote to him. I seen the letters.'

'Letters?'

'He brought them home from Afghanistan. He kept her letters.'

I hear myself quizzing her, wanting to know the where, when and why, but she can't answer for her brother. Trying to pin her down to specific dates and times makes her even more confused.

Ruiz intervenes and I feel a twinge of guilt at having browbeaten a pregnant woman who's worried about her brother.

The afternoon sun is sliding below rooftops, leaving behind shadows. Stallholders are shutting up, loading wares into boxes, bags and metal trunks. Buckets of ice are tipped into the gutter. Plastic awnings are rolled and tied.

After helping Carla load up the red Escort van we follow her home. The house is still empty. There are no messages waiting for her on the answerphone. I should be angry with Donavon, yet I feel a nagging emptiness. This doesn't make any sense. Why would Cate write letters to someone who sexually assaulted her? She was talking to him the night of the reunion. What were they saying?

Ruiz drops me home. After turning off the engine we stare at the streetscape as if expecting it to change suddenly after more than a century of looking almost the same.

'You want to come in?'

'I should go.'

'I could cook.'

He looks at me.

'Or we could get takeaway.'

'Got any alcohol?'

'There's an off-licence on the corner.'

I can hear him whistling his way up the street as I open the front door and check my answering machine. All the messages are for Hari. His girlfriends. I should double his rent to pay the phone bill.

The doorbell rings. It should be Ruiz – only it's not. A younger man has come to the door, dressed in a pepper-grey suit, clean-shaven with broad shoulders and Nordic features. His rectangular glasses seem too small for his face. Behind him are two more men, who are standing beside cars that are double-parked and blocking the street. They look official, but not like police officers.

'DC Barba, we need you to accompany us.' He makes a clicking sound with his tongue that might be a signal or a sign of nerves.

'Why? Who are you?'

He produces a badge. SOCA. The Serious Organised Crime Agency. The organisation is less than a year old and the media have labelled it Britain's answer to the FBI, with its own Act of Parliament, budget and extraordinary powers. What do they want with me?

'I'm a police officer,' I stammer.

'I know who you are.'

'Am I under arrest?'

'Important people wish to speak to you.'

I look for Ruiz. He's hurrying down the pavement with a half-bottle of Scotch tucked in his coat pocket. One of the men beside the cars tries to step in front of him. The DI feints left and drops his shoulder, propelling him over a low brick wall into a muddy puddle. This could get ugly.

'It's all right, sir.'

'Who are they?'

'SOCA.'

The look on his face says it all. Fear and loathing.

'You might want to pack a few things for the journey,' says the senior officer. He and Ruiz are sizing each other up like roosters in a hen house.

I pack a sports bag with a pair of jeans, knickers and a lightweight sweater. My gun is wrapped in a cloth on top of a kitchen cabinet. I contemplate whether I should take it with me, but dismiss the idea as being too hostile. I have no idea what these people want but I can't risk antagonising them.

Ruiz follows me to the car. A hand is placed on the back of my head as I slide onto the rear seat. The brake is released suddenly and I'm thrown back against the new-smelling leather.

'I hope we haven't spoiled your plans for the evening, DC Barba,' says the grey-suited man.

'You know my name – can I have yours?'

'Robert Forbes.'

'You work for SOCA?'

'I work for the government.'

'Which *part* of the government?'

'The part people don't often talk about.' He makes the clicking sound again.

The car has reached the end of Hanbury Street. Beneath a street light a solitary spectator, clad in black leather, leans against a motorcycle. A helmet dangles from his right hand. A fag end burns in his fist. It's Donavon.

Traffic meanders at an agonisingly slow pace, shuffling and pausing. I can only see the back of the driver's head. He has a soldier's haircut and wrap-around sunglasses like Bono, who also looks ridiculous wearing sunglasses at night.

I'm trying to remember what I've read about SOCA. It's an amalgam of the old National Crime Squad and National Criminal Intelligence Service, along with elements of Customs & Excise and the Immigration Service. Five thousand officers were specially chosen with the aim of targeting criminal gangs, drug smugglers and people traffickers. The boss of the new agency is a former head of M15.

'Where are you taking me?'

'To a crime scene,' says Forbes.

'What crime? There must be some mistake.'

'You are Alisha Kaur Barba. You are twenty-nine years of age. You work for the London Metropolitan Police, most recently for the Diplomatic Protection Group. You have four brothers. Your father is a retired train driver. Your mother takes in sewing. You went to Falcon Street Primary School and to Oaklands Secondary. You graduated from London University with a degree in sociology and topped your class at Hendon Police Training College. You are an expert markswoman and former champion athlete. A year ago you were injured trying to apprehend a suspect who almost snapped your spine. You accepted a bravery medal but refused a disability pension. You seem to have recovered quite well.'

'I set off metal detectors at airports.'

I don't know if his knowledge is supposed to impress or intimidate me. Nothing else is said. Forbes is not going to answer my questions until he's ready. Silence is part of the softening-up process. Ruiz taught me that.

We take the A12 through Brentwood and out of London. I don't like the countryside at night. Even in moonlight it looks bruised and sullen like a week-old fall down the stairs.

Forbes takes several phone calls, answering yes or no but offering nothing more apart from the clicking sound in his throat. He is married. The gold band on his wedding finger is thick and heavy. Someone at home irons his shirts and polishes his shoes. He is right-handed. He's not carrying a gun. He knows so much about me that I want to even the scales.

We continue through Chelmsford in Essex before

bypassing Colchester and turning east towards Harwich along the A120. Convoys of prime-movers and semi-trailers begin to build up ahead of us. I can smell the salt in the air.

A large sign above the road welcomes us to Harwich International Port. Following the New Port Entrance Road through two roundabouts we come to the freight entrance. Dozens of trucks are queuing at the gates. A Customs officer with a light wand and a fluorescent vest waves us through.

In the distance I see the Port of Felixstowe. Massive gantry cranes tower above the ships, lifting and lowering containers. It looks like a scene from *War of the Worlds* where alien machines have landed and are creating hatchlings for the next generation. Row after row of containers are stacked on top of one another, stretching for hundreds of yards in every direction.

Now Forbes decides to speak to me again.

'Have you ever been here before, DC Barba?'

'No.'

'Harwich is a freight and passenger port. It handles cruise ships, ferries, bulk carriers and roll-on roll-off vessels. Thousands of vehicles pass through here every day from Denmark, Sweden, Belgium, Germany and the Hook of Holland.'

'Why am I here?'

He motions ahead of us. The car slows. In the middle of the Customs area a Scene of Crime tent has been erected. Police cars are circled like wagons around it.

Arc lights inside the tent throw shadows against the fabric walls, revealing the outline of a truck and people moving inside, silhouetted like puppets in a kabuki theatre.

Forbes is out of the car, walking across the tarmac. The ticking of the cooling engine sounds like a clock. At that moment a side flap of the tent is pushed open. A SOCO emerges, wearing overalls and white rubber gloves that peel off his hands like a second skin.

I recognise him. George Noonan, a forensic pathologist. They call him 'the Albino' because of his pale skin and snow-white hair. Dressed in white overalls, white gloves and a white hat, he looks like a fancy-dress spermatozoon.

He spends a few minutes talking to Forbes. I'm too far away to hear what they say.

Forbes turns towards me, summoning me forward. His face is set hard like the wedge of an axe.

The tent flap opens. Plastic sheets cover the ground, weighed down with silver boxes of forensic equipment and cameras. A truck is parked at the centre, with its twin rear doors open. Inside there are wooden pallets holding boxes of oranges. Some of these have been shifted to one side to form a narrow aisle just wide enough for a person to squeeze through to the far end of the lorry.

A camera flash illuminates a cavity within the pallets. At first I think there might be mannequins inside it, broken models or clay figurines. Then the truth reaches me. Bodies – I count five of them – are piled beneath a closed air vent. There are three men, a woman and a child. Their mouths are open. Breathless. Lifeless.

They appear to be Eastern European, dressed in cheap mismatched clothes. An arm reaches up as if suspended by a wire. The lone woman has her hair pulled back. A tortoise-shell hair-clip has come loose and dangles on her cheek from a strand of hair. The child in her arms is wearing a Mickey Mouse sweatshirt and clutching a doll.

The flashgun pops again. I see the faces frozen in place, trapped in that moment when their oxygen ran out and their dreams turned to dust on dry tongues. It is a scene to haunt me. A scene that changes everything. And although I can't picture the world they came from, which seems impossibly strange and remote, their deaths are somehow unbearably close.

'They died in the past twelve hours,' says Noonan.

Automatically, I transfer this into personal time. What was I doing? Travelling to West Sussex. Talking to Julian Shawcroft at the adoption centre.

Noonan is holding several bloody fingernails collected in a plastic bag. I feel my stomach lurch.

'If you're going to puke, detective constable, you can get the hell away from *my* crime scene,' he says.

'Yes, sir.'

Forbes looks at Noonan. 'Tell her how they died.'

'They suffocated,' the pathologist replies wearily.

'Explain it to us.'

The request is for my benefit. Forbes wants me to hear this and to smell the sweet stench of oranges and faeces. Noonan obliges.

'It begins with a rising panic as one fights for each breath, sucking it in, wanting more. The next stage is quiescence. Resignation. And then unconsciousness. The convulsions and incontinence are involuntary, the death throes. Nobody knows what comes first – oxygen deprivation or carbon dioxide poisoning.'

Taking hold of my elbow, Forbes leads me out of the

truck. A makeshift morgue has been set up to take the bodies. One of them is already on a gurney, lying face up, covered in a white sheet. Forbes runs his fingers over the cloth.

'Someone inside the truck had a mobile,' he explains. 'When they began to suffocate they tried to call someone and reached an emergency number. The operator thought it was a hoax because the caller couldn't give a location.'

I look towards the massive roll-on, roll-off ferry with its open stern doors.

'Why am I here?'

He flicks his wrist and the sheet curls back. A teenage boy with fleshy limbs and dark hair lies on the slab. His head is almost perfectly round and pink except for the blueness around his lips and the overlapping folds of flesh beneath his chin.

Forbes hasn't moved. He's watching me from behind his rectangular glasses.

I drag my eyes away. With a birdlike quickness he grips my arm. 'This is all he was wearing – a pair of trousers and a shirt. No labels. Normally, clothes like this tell us nothing. They're cheap and mass-produced.' His fingers are digging into me. 'These clothes are different. There was something sewn into the lining. A name and address. Do you know whose name? Whose address?'

I shake my head.

'Yours.'

I try not to react but that in itself is a reaction.

'Can you explain that?' he asks.

'No.'

'Not even a vague notion.'

My mind is racing through the possibilities. My mother

used to put labels on my clothes because she didn't want me losing things. My name, not my address.

'You see how it looks,' he says, clicking his tongue again. 'You have been implicated in a people-trafficking investigation and potentially a murder investigation. We think his name is Hasan Khan. Does that mean anything to you?'

'No.'

'The lorry is Dutch-registered. The driver is listed on the passenger manifest as Arjan Molenaar.'

Again I shake my head.

Numbness rather than shock seeps through me. It feels like someone has walked up and hit me in the back of the head with a metal tray and the noise is still ringing in my ears.

'Why weren't they found sooner?'

'Do you know how many lorries pass through Harwich every day? More than ten thousand. If Customs searched every one of them there'd be ships queued back to Rotterdam.'

Noonan joins us, leaning over the body and talking as though the teenager were a patient and not a corpse.

'All right, young fellow, *please* try to be candid. If you open up to the process in good faith we'll find out more about you. Now let's take a look.'

He peers closer, almost putting his lips on the boy's cheek. 'There is evidence of petechial haemorrhages, pinpoint, less than one millimetre on the eyelids, lips, ears, face and neck, consistent with lack of oxygen to the tissue . . .'

He holds up an arm, examining the skin.

'The scarring indicates an old thermal injury to the left forearm and hand. Something very intense, perhaps a blast.'

163

I notice dozens of smaller scars on the boy's chest. Noonan takes an interest, using a ruler to measure them.

'Very unusual.'

'What are they?'

'Knife wounds.'

'He was stabbed?'

'Someone sliced him up.' He flicks an imaginary knife through the air. 'None of the wounds are particularly deep. The blade threatened no organs or major blood vessels. Excellent control.'

The pathologist sounds impressed – like one surgeon admiring the work of another.

He sees something else. Lifting the boy's right arm, he turns it outward, displaying the wrist. A small tattooed butterfly hovers halfway between the palm and elbow. Noonan takes a measurement and speaks into a digital recorder.

Forbes has shown me enough.

'I wish to go home now,' I say.

'I still have questions.'

'Do I need a lawyer?'

The question disappoints him. 'I can provide you with someone if you wish.'

I know I should be more concerned but the desire for knowledge overrides my natural caution. It's not about being invincible or believing that my innocence will protect me. I've seen too many miscarriages of justice to be so optimistic.

The terminal has a café for freight drivers. Forbes takes a table and orders coffee and a bottle of water.

For the next hour he dissects my personal life, my friends and associates. Over and over I make the same point. I

164

have no idea how my name and address were sewn into the clothes of Hasan Khan.

'Is it my colour?' I ask him eventually.

His countenance falls. 'Why do people *always* do that – play the race card? Whenever someone from a minority background is questioned I can guarantee it's coming. This has nothing to do with your colour or your religion or where you were born. *Your* name and address were sewn into a dead kid's clothes. An illegal. That's what makes you a person of interest.'

I wish I could take the question back.

He takes out a half-packet of cigarettes and counts them, rationing himself. 'Have you any idea how big it is – people trafficking?' He puts the cigarettes away, clicking his tongue as though admonishing himself.

'More than four hundred thousand people were trafficked into Western Europe last year. The Italian Mafia, the Russians, the Albanians, the Japanese Yakuza, the Chinese Snakeheads – they're all involved. And beneath the big syndicates are thousands of smaller freelance gangs that operate with nothing more than a couple of mobile phones, a speedboat and a Transit van. They corrupt border guards, politicians, police and Customs officers. They are bottom-feeding scum, who prey on human misery. I hate them. I really do.'

His eyes are locked on mine. His tongue is making that sound again. I suddenly realise what he reminds me of – the road runner. Wile E. Coyote was always trying to catch that arrogant beeping bird, coming up with ridiculous booby traps and snares. Just *once* I wanted the coyote to win. I wanted the hundred-pound barbell or the bundle of dynamite or the slingshot to work, so he could ring that scrawny bird's neck.

As if on cue there is a 'beep beep' from Forbes's pager. He makes a phone call on the far side of the cafeteria. Something significant must have been said because his demeanour changes.

'I'm sorry for keeping you so long, DC Barba.'

'So I can leave?'

'Yes, of course, but it's very late. Accommodation has been arranged in town. The pub looks quite nice. I can have you driven back to London in the morning.'

He tugs nervously at the cuffs of his jacket, as though worried the sleeves might be shrinking. I wonder who called. Sikh girls don't have friends in high places.

The pub is quaint and rustic, although I've never been exactly sure what 'rustic' means. The restaurant annexe has low ceilings with fishing nets strung from the beams and a harpoon bolted above the bar.

Forbes invites me to dinner. 'I'm a detective inspector but you don't have to consider it an order,' he says, trying to be charming.

I can smell the kitchen. My stomach rumbles. Perhaps I can find out more about Hasan Khan.

Shrugging off his grey jacket, Forbes stretches his legs beneath the table and makes a fuss over ordering and tasting the wine.

'This is very good,' he comments, holding his glass up to the light. 'Are you sure you won't have some?' Without waiting for me to answer he pours himself another glass.

I have been calling him Mr Forbes or sir. He says I should

call him Robert. I don't give him permission but he calls me Alisha anyway. He asks if I'm married.

'You know that already.'

'Yes, of course.'

He has Nordic eyes and his bottom teeth are crooked but he has a pleasant smile and an easy laugh. The clicking sound seems to go away when he relaxes. Perhaps it's a nervous thing, like a stutter.

'So what about your family?' he asks. 'When did they come to Britain?'

I tell him about my grandfather who was born in a small village in Gujarat and joined the British Army at fourteen where he became a kitchen hand and then a chef. After the war a major in the Royal Artillery brought him back to England to cook for his family. My grandfather travelled on a steamer that took three weeks to get from Bombay to England. He came alone. That was in 1947.

He earned three pounds a week, but still managed to save enough for my grandmother to join him. They were the first Indians in Hertfordshire but they later moved to London.

My only memory of my grandparents is a story they told me about their first winter in England. They had never seen snow and said it looked like a scene from a Russian fairy tale.

I don't always understand irony, but my grandfather spent his entire life trying to become white only to be crushed by an overturned coal truck on Richmond Hill that painted him as black as soot.

Forbes has finished a second bottle of wine and grown melancholy.

'I have to use the bathroom,' he says.

I watch him weave between tables, leading with his left shoulder and then his right. On his way back he orders a brandy. He talks about growing up in Milton Keynes, a planned town that didn't exist before the 1960s. Now he lives in London. He doesn't mention a wife but I know there's one at home.

I want to talk to him about the illegals before he gets too drunk. 'Have you managed to trace the truck?' I ask.

'Shipping containers have codes. They can be tracked anywhere in the world.'

'Where did it come from?'

'The truck left a factory on the outskirts of Amsterdam early yesterday. The locks are supposed to be tamper-proof.'

'How did you know Hasan Khan's name?'

'He had papers. We found a cloth bag tied around his waist. According to the Dutch police, he arrived in Holland nineteen months ago from Afghanistan. He and a group of asylum seekers were living above a Chinese restaurant in Amsterdam.'

'What else was in the bag?'

Forbes lowers his eyes. 'Drawings and photographs. I could show them to you . . .' He pauses. 'We could go to my room.'

'Alternatively, you could bring the bag downstairs,' I suggest.

He runs his socked foot up my calf and gives me his bad-little-boy smile.

I want to say something disagreeable but can't find the words. I'm never good at put-downs. Instead I smile politely and tell him to quit while he's ahead.

He frowns. He doesn't understand.

For the love of God, you're not even attractive. Call your wife and wish her goodnight.

Forbes stumbles as he climbs the stairs. 'I guess we hit the old vino pretty hard, eh?'

'One of us did.'

He fumbles in his pocket for his key and makes several unsuccessful attempts to find the keyhole. I take it from him. He collapses on the bed and rolls over, spreadeagled like a sacrifice to the demon god of drink.

I take off his shoes and hang his jacket over the chair. The calico bag is on the bedside table. As I leave I slide the security bar across the door frame so that the door doesn't close completely.

Back in my room I call Ruiz and 'New Boy' Dave. Dave wants to come and get me. I tell him to stay put. I'll call him in the morning.

Fifteen minutes later I go back to Forbes's room. The door is still ajar and he's snoring. I cross the floor, listening for a change in his breathing. My fingers close around the calico bag. He doesn't stir.

Suddenly there's another sound. A sing-song ring tone.

I drop to the floor and crouch between the radiator and the curtain.

If Forbes turns on the lamp he'll see me or he'll notice that the bag is missing.

Rolling half out of bed, he reaches for his jacket, fumbling with his mobile.

'Yeah. I'm sorry, babe, I should have called. I got in late and I didn't want to wake you or the kids – No, I'm fine, not drunk. Just a few glasses – No, I didn't see the news tonight – that's really great

– Yeah – OK – I'll call you in the morning – Go to sleep now –
Love you too.'

He tosses the phone aside and stares at the ceiling. For a moment I think he's falling back to sleep until he groans and rolls out of bed. The bathroom light blinks on. Behind him, my hiding place is neatly framed by the radiance. He drops his boxers and urinates.

Sliding out of the light, I cross the floor and ease the door shut behind me. Dizzy and trembling, I have broken one of Ruiz's fundamental rules: when under stress always remember to breathe.

Back in my room, I tip the contents of the calico bag onto the bed. There is a pocket knife with one blade broken and the other intact, a small mirror, a medicine bottle full of sand, a charcoal drawing of two children and a battered circular biscuit tin.

Every object is significant. Why else would he carry them? These are the worldly possessions of a sixteen-year-old boy. They can't possibly breathe life into his lungs or tell me his fears and desires. They aren't enough. He deserves more.

The biscuit tin contains a tarnished military medal and a black and white photograph folded in half. It appears to show a group of workers standing in front of a factory with a corrugated iron roof and wooden shutters on the windows. Packing crates are stacked against the wall, along with drums and pallets.

There are two lines of workers. Those in the front row are sitting on stools. At the centre is a patriarch or the factory owner in a high-backed chair. Ramrod straight, he has a stern countenance and a far-off stare. One hand is on his knee. The other is missing and the sleeve of his coat is tied off at the elbow.

Beside him is another man, physically similar, perhaps his brother. He is wearing a small fez and has a neatly trimmed beard. He also is missing a hand and his left eye appears to be an empty socket. I glance along the two rows of workers, many of whom are maimed or crippled or incomplete. There are people on crutches, others with skin like melted plastic. A boy in the front row is kneeling on a skateboard. No, not kneeling. What I first imagine are his knees, poking out from beneath short trousers, are the stumps of his thighs.

None of the workers is smiling. They are olive-skinned men with blurred features and no amount of magnifying will make the image any clearer or the men appear any less stiff and glowering.

I put the photograph back in the tin and examine the rest of the curios and ornaments. The charcoal drawing is creased at the corners. The two children, a boy and a girl, are about six and eight. Her arm is around his shoulders. She has a high forehead and a straight parting in her hair. He looks bored or restless, with a spark of light in his eyes from an open window. He wants to be outside.

The paper is soft in my fingers. A fixative has been sprayed on the charcoal to stop it smudging. In the bottom left-hand corner there is a signature. No, it's a name. Two names. The drawing is of Hasan as a young boy and his sister, Samira.

Lying back, I stare at the ceiling and listen to the deep night. It is so quiet I can hear myself breathing. What a beautiful sound.

This is a story of parts. A chronicle of fictions. Cate faked her pregnancy. Brendan Pearl ran her and Felix down. Her doctor lied. Donavon lied. An adoption agency lied. People are being trafficked. Babies are being bought and sold.

I once read that people caught in avalanches can't always tell which way is up or down and don't know which direction to dig. Experienced skiers and climbers have a trick. They dribble. Gravity shows them the way.

I need a trick like that. I am submerged in something dark and dangerous and I don't know if I'm escaping or burying myself deeper. I'm an accidental casualty. Collateral damage.

My dreams are real. As real as dreams can be. I hear babies crying and mothers singing to them. I am being chased by people. It is the same dream as always but I never know who they are. And I wake at the same moment, as I'm falling.

I call Ruiz again. He picks up on the second ring. The man never sleeps.

'Can you come and fetch me?'

He doesn't ask why. He puts down the phone and I imagine him getting dressed and getting in his car and driving through the countryside.

He is thirty years older than me. He has been married three times and has a private life with more ordnance than a live-firing range but I know and trust him more than anyone else.

I know what I'm going to do. Up until now I have been trying to imagine Cate's situation – the places she went to, what she tried to hide – but there is no point in calling the same phone numbers or mentally piecing together her movements. I have to follow her footsteps, to catch up.

I am going to Amsterdam to find Samira. I look at the clock. Not tomorrow. Today.

Two hours later I open the door to Ruiz. Sometimes I wonder if he knows my thoughts or if he's the one who puts them in my mind in the first place and then reads them like he's counting cards in a poker game.

'We should go to Amsterdam,' he says.

'Yes.'

Book Two

'*The bitterest tears shed over graves are for words left unsaid and deeds left undone.*'

Harriet Beecher Stowe

1

In our second year at university in London Cate missed a period and thought she was pregnant. We were synchronised – same time, same place, same moods. I can't remember which of her bad boyfriends had breached her defences, but I remember her reaction clearly enough. Panic.

We did a home pregnancy test and then another. I went with her to the family planning clinic, a horrible green building in Greenwich not far from the Observatory. Where time began, life ended.

The nurse asked Cate some questions and told her to go home and wait another seven days. Apparently, the most common reason for a false negative is testing too early.

Her period arrived.

'I might have been pregnant and miscarried,' she said afterwards. 'Perhaps if I had wanted it more.'

Later, apropos of nothing, she asked, 'What do they do with them?'

'With what?'

'With the aborted babies.'

'They don't call them babies. And I guess they get rid of them.'

'Get rid of them?'

'I don't know, OK?'

I wonder if a scare such as this, a near miss, came back to haunt her during the years of trying to fall pregnant. Did she tell Felix? Did she wonder if God was punishing her for not loving the first one enough?

I *remember* the name of the bad boyfriend. We called him Handsome Barry. He was a Canadian ski instructor with a year-round suntan and incredibly white teeth. What is it about male ski instructors? They take on this Godlike aura in the mountains as if the rarefied air makes them look more handsome or (more likely) women less discerning.

We were working during the Christmas break at a ski lodge in the French Alps in the shadow of Mont Blanc (which didn't ever throw a shadow since the clouds never lifted).

'Have you ever seen a Sikh ski?' I asked Cate.

'You can be the first,' she insisted.

We shared a room in Cell Block H, the nickname for the staff quarters. I worked as a chambermaid, five days a week, from six in the morning until mid-afternoon. I rarely saw Cate who worked nights at a bar. She practised her Russian accent by pretending to be Natalia Radzinsky, the daughter of a countess.

'Where on earth did you sleep with Barry?' I asked.

'I borrowed your house key. We used one of the guest suites.'

'You did *what*?'

'Oh, don't worry. I put down a towel.'

She seemed more interested in my love life. 'When are you going to lose your virginity?'

'When I'm ready.'

'Who are you waiting for?'

I told her 'Mr Right', when really I meant 'Mr Considerate' or 'Mr Worthy' or any 'mister' who *wanted* me enough.

Maybe I was my mother's daughter after all. She was already trying to find me a husband, my cousin Anwar, who was reading philosophy at Bristol University. Tall and thin, with large brown eyes and little wire spectacles, Anwar had great taste in clothes and liked Judy Garland records. He ran off with a boy from the university bookshop, although my mother still won't accept that he's gay.

Ruiz has scarcely said a word since our flight left Heathrow. His silences can be so eloquent.

I told him that he didn't have to come. 'You're retired.'

'True, but I'm not dead,' he replied. The faintest of smiles wrinkled the corners of his eyes.

It's amazing how little I know about him after six years. He has children – twins – but doesn't talk about them. His mother is in a retirement home. His stepfather is dead. I don't know about his real father as he's never come up in conversation.

I have never met anyone as self-sufficient as Ruiz. He

doesn't appear to hunger for human contact or *need* anyone. You take those survivor shows on TV where people are separated into competing tribes and try to win 'immunity'. Ruiz would be a tribe of one – all on his own. And the grumpy old bugger would come out on top every time.

Amsterdam. It makes me think of soft drugs, sanctioned prostitution and wooden shoes. This will be my first visit. Ruiz is also a 'Dutch virgin' (his term, not mine). He has already given me his thumbnail appraisal of the Dutch. 'Excellent lager, a few half-decent footballers and the cheese with the red wax.'

'The Dutch are very polite,' I offered.

'They're probably the nicest people in the world,' he agreed. 'They're so amenable they legalised prostitution and marijuana rather than say no to anyone.'

For all his gypsy blood Ruiz has never been a wanderer. His only foreign holiday was to Italy. He is a creature of habit – warm beer, stodgy food and rugby – and his xenophobia is always worse the further he gets from home.

We managed to get bulkhead seats which means I can take off my shoes and prop my feet against the wall, showing off my pink and white striped socks. The seat between us is empty. I've claimed it with my book, my bottle of water and my headphones. Possession is nine-tenths of the law.

Outside the window the Dutch landscape is like an old snooker table, patched with different squares of felt. There are cute farmhouses, cute windmills and occasional villages. This whole below-sea-level thing is quite strange. Even the bridges would be underwater if the dykes ever failed. But the Dutch are so good at reclaiming land that they'll probably fill in the North Sea one day and the M11 will stretch all the way to Moscow.

On the journey from the airport our taxi driver seems to get lost and drives us in circles, crossing the same canals and the same bridges. The only clue we have to Cate's movements is the tourist map of central Amsterdam and a circle drawn around the Red Tulip Hotel.

The desk clerk greets us with a wide smile. She is in her mid-twenties, big-boned and a pound or two away from being overweight. Behind her is a noticeboard with brochures advertising canal-boat cruises, bicycle tours and day trips to a tulip farm.

I slide a photograph of Cate across the check-in counter. 'Have you seen her?'

She looks hard. Cate is worth a long look. The woman doesn't recognise her.

'You could ask some of the other staff,' she says.

A porter is loading our cases onto a trolley. In his fifties, he's wearing a red waistcoat stretched tight over a white shirt and a paunch: putting the buttons under pressure.

I show him the photograph. His eyes narrow as he concentrates. I wonder what he remembers about guests – their faces, their cases, the tips they leave?

'Room twelve,' he announces, nodding vigorously. His English is poor.

Ruiz turns back to the desk clerk. 'You must have a record. She might have stayed here during the second week of February.'

She glances over her shoulder, worried about the manager, and then taps at the keyboard. The screen refreshes and I glance down the list. Cate isn't there. Wait! There's another name I recognise: 'Natalia Radzinsky.'

The porter claps his hands together. 'Yes, the countess. She had one blue bag.' He measures the dimensions in the air. 'And a smaller one. Very heavy. Made of metal.'

'Was she with anyone?'

He shakes his head.

'You have a very good memory.'

He beams.

I look at the computer screen again. I feel as though Cate has left me a clue that nobody else could recognise. It's a silly notion, of course, to imagine the dead leaving messages for the living. The arrogance of archaeologists.

The Red Tulip Hotel has sixteen rooms, half of them overlooking the canal. Mine is on the first floor and Ruiz's room is above me. Sunlight bounces off the curved windows of a canal boat as it passes, taking tourists around the city. Bells jangle and bike riders weave between pedestrians.

Ruiz knocks on my door and we make a plan. He will talk to the Immigration and Naturalisation Service (IND), which deals with asylum seekers in the Netherlands. I will visit Hasan Khan's last known address.

I take a taxi to Gerard Doustraat in a quarter known as de Pijp, or 'The Pipe' as my driver explains. He calls it the 'real Amsterdam'. Ten years ago it had a seedy reputation but is now full of restaurants, cafés and bakeries.

The Flaming Wok is a Chinese restaurant with bamboo blinds and fake bonsai trees. The place is empty. Two waiters are hovering near the kitchen door. Asian. Neat, wearing black trousers and white shirts.

From the front door I can see right through to the kitchen where pots and steamers hang from the ceiling. An older man, dressed in white, is preparing food. A knife stutters in his hand.

The waiters speak menu English. They keep directing me to a table. I ask to see the owner.

Mr Weng leaves his kitchen, wiping his hands on a towel. He bows to me.

'I want to know about the people who were living upstairs.'

'They gone now.'

'Yes.'

'You want to rent frat? One bedroom. Very crean.'

'No.'

He shrugs ambivalently and points to a table, motioning me to sit, before he orders tea. The waiters, his sons, compete to carry out the instructions.

'About the tenants,' I say.

'They come, they go,' he replies. 'Sometimes full. Sometimes empty.' His hands flutter as he talks and he clasps them occasionally, as if fearful they might fly away.

'Your last tenants – where were they from?'

'Everywhere. Estonia, Russia, Uzbekistan . . .'

'What about this boy?' I show him the charcoal drawing of Hasan. 'He's older now. Sixteen.'

He nods energetically. 'This one OK. He wash the dishes for food. Others take food from bins.'

The green tea has arrived. Mr Weng pours. Tea leaves circle in the small white cups.

'Who paid the rent?'

'Pay money up front. Six months.'

'But you must have had a lease.'

Mr Weng doesn't understand.

'A contract?'

'No contract.'

'What about the electricity, the telephone?'

He nods and smiles. He's too polite to tell me that he doesn't have an answer.

I point to the girl in the drawing and take out the photograph of Samira. 'What about this girl?'

'Many girls in and out.' He makes a circle with his left forefinger and thumb and thrusts another finger through the hole. 'Prostitutes,' he says apologetically, as though sorry for the state of the world.

I ask to see the flat. One of his sons will show me. He takes me through a fire door that opens into an alley and leads me up a rear staircase to where he unlocks a door.

I have been in depressing flats before but few have disheartened me as quickly as this one. It has one bedroom, a lounge, a kitchen and a bathroom. The only furniture is a low chest of drawers with a mirror on top and a sofa with cigarette burns.

'The mattresses were thrown away,' Mr Weng's son explains.

'How many lived here?'

'Ten.'

I get the impression he knew the occupants better than his father.

'Do you remember this girl?' I show him the photograph.

'Maybe.'

'Did she stay here?'

'She visited.'

'Do you know where she lives?'

'No.'

The tenants left nothing behind except a few cans of food, some old pillows and a couple of used international phone cards. There are no clues here.

Afterwards I catch a taxi and meet Ruiz at a bar in Nieuwmarkt, a paved open square not far from the Oude Kerk. Most of the outside tables are empty. It is getting too late in the year for backpackers and American tourists.

'I didn't think you were going to buy one of those, sir,' I say, pointing to his guidebook.

'Yeah, well, I hate asking directions,' he grumbles. 'I'm sure someone is going to say, "You want to go *where*?" That's when I'll discover I'm in the wrong bloody country.'

A couple at the next table are locals. They could be having an argument or agreeing completely. I can't tell.

'The Dutch can squeeze more vowels into a sentence than anyone else in the world,' says Ruiz, too loudly. 'And that Dutch "j" is a deliberate bloody provocation.'

He goes back to his guidebook. We're sitting on the western flank of the red-light district, in an area known as de Walletjes ('the Little Walls').

'That building with all the turrets is the Waag,' he explains. 'It used to be a gatehouse to the old city.'

A young waitress has come to take our order. Ruiz wants another beer, 'with less froth and more Heineken.' She smiles at me sympathetically.

Opening his marbled notebook, Ruiz relates how Hasan and Samira Khan were smuggled across the German border into the Netherlands in the luggage compartment of a tourist coach in April 2005. They were taken to an Application Centre at Ter Apel and were interviewed by the Immigration and Naturalisation Service. Hasan claimed to be fifteen and Samira seventeen. They told the authorities they were born in Kabul and had spent three years living in a refugee camp in Pakistan. After their mother died of dysentery, their father Hamid Khan took the children back to Kabul where he was shot dead in 1999. Hasan and Samira were sent to an orphanage.

'That's the story they told in every interview, together and independently. Never wavered.'

'How did they get here?'

'Traffickers, but they both refused to name names.' Ruiz consults his notebook again. 'After they were screened they were housed at a centre for under-age asylum seekers operated by the Valentine Foundation. Three months later they were moved to the campus at Deelen where a hundred and eighty children are housed. In December last year both their visas were revoked.'

'Why?'

'I don't know. They were given twenty-eight days to leave the Netherlands. An appeal was lodged but they disappeared.'

'Disappeared?'

'Not many of these people hang around to get deported.'

'What do you mean, "these people"?'

Ruiz looks at me awkwardly. 'Slip of the tongue.' He pauses to sip his beer. 'I have the name of a lawyer who represented them. Lena Caspar. She has an office here in Amsterdam.'

White froth clings to his top lip. 'There's something else.

The boy made an earlier North Sea crossing. He was picked up and sent back to the Netherlands within twenty-four hours.'

'Guess he tried again.'

'Second time unlucky.'

2

The lawyer's office is on Prinsengracht in a four-storey building that deviates from the vertical by a degree or two, leaning out over the brick-paved street. A high-arched doorway leads to a narrow courtyard where an old woman is swabbing flagstones with a mop and bucket. She points to the stairs.

On the first floor we enter a waiting room full of North Africans, many with children. A young man looks up from a desk, pushing his Harry Potter glasses higher up his nose. We don't have an appointment. He flicks through the pages of a daily schedule.

At that moment a door opens behind him and a Nigerian woman appears, dressed in a voluminous floral dress. A young girl clings to her hand and a baby is asleep on her shoulder.

For a moment I don't see anyone else. Then a small

woman emerges, as if appearing from the folds of the Nigerian's dress.

'I'll send you a copy of the papers once I've lodged the appeal,' she says. 'You must let me know if you change your address.'

Dressed in a long-sleeved cotton blouse, black cardigan and grey trousers, she looks very lawyerly and businesslike despite her diminutive stature. Smiling absently at me as though we might have met, she glances at Ruiz and shudders.

'Mrs Caspar, excuse this interruption. Could we have a word?'

She laughs. 'How very English that sounds. Just the one word? I'm almost tempted to say yes just to hear which one you might choose.' The skin around her eyes wrinkles like peach stones. 'I'm very busy today. You'll have to wait until—'

She stops in mid-sentence. I am holding up a photograph of Samira. 'Her brother is dead. We have to find her.'

Mrs Caspar holds her office door open until we follow her inside. The room is almost square, with highly polished wood floors. The house has belonged to her family for generations, she explains. The law practice was her grandfather's and then her father's.

Despite volunteering this information, Mrs Caspar has a lawyer's natural caution.

'You don't look like a police officer,' she says to me. 'I thought you might require my services.' She turns her attention to Ruiz. '*You*, however, look *exactly* like a policeman.'

'Not any more.'

'Tell me about Hasan,' she says, turning back to me. 'What happened to him?'

'When did you last see him?'

'Eleven months ago.'

I describe the discovery of his body in the truck and how my name and address were sewn into his clothes. Turning her face to the window, Mrs Caspar might be close to tears, but I doubt if such a woman would let strangers see her emotions.

'Why would he have your name?'

'I don't know. I was hoping you could tell me.'

She shakes her head.

'I am trying to find Samira.'

'Why?'

How do I answer this? I plunge straight in. 'I think a friend of mine who couldn't have children tried to buy a baby in Amsterdam. I think she met Samira.'

'Samira doesn't have a baby.'

'No, but she has a womb.'

Mrs Caspar looks at me incredulously. 'A Muslim girl doesn't rent her womb. You must be mistaken.'

The statement has the bluntness and certainty of fact or dogma. She crosses the office, opens a filing cabinet and takes out a folder. Sitting at her desk, she scans the contents.

'My government does not welcome asylum seekers. They have made it more and more difficult for them. We even have a Minister for Immigration who claims that only twenty per cent of applicants are "real refugees" – the rest are liars and frauds.

'Unfortunately, legitimate asylum seekers are being demonised. They are treated like economic refugees,

190

roaming between countries looking for someone to take them in.'

The bitterness in her voice vibrates her tiny frame.

'Samira and Hasan had no papers when they arrived. The IND claimed they destroyed them on purpose. They didn't believe Samira was a minor. She looked closer to twelve than twenty, but they sent her for tests.'

'Tests?'

'An age-evaluation test. They X-rayed her collarbone, which is supposed to establish if someone is older or younger than twenty. Hasan had his wrist X-rayed. A report was prepared by Harry van der Pas, a physical anthropologist at Tilburg University.

'It backfired on them. Samira appeared to be even younger. Poor diet and malnutrition had stunted her growth. They gave them both temporary visas. They could stay, but only until further checks were done.'

Mrs Caspar turns a page in the folder.

'Nowadays the policy is to return under-age asylum seekers to their own country. Hasan and Samira *had* no family. Afghanistan can scarcely feed its own people. Kabul is a city of widows and orphans.'

She slides a page of notes towards me – a family history. 'They were orphans. Both spoke English. Their mother was educated at Delhi University. She worked as a translator for a publishing company until the Taliban took over.'

I look at the notes. Samira was born in 1987 during the Soviet occupation of Afghanistan. She was two years old when the Soviets left and ten when the Taliban arrived.

'And their father?'

'A factory owner.'

191

I remember Hasan's photograph.

'They made fireworks,' explains Mrs Caspar. 'The Taliban closed the factory down. Fireworks were forbidden. The family fled to Pakistan and lived in a refugee camp. Their mother died of dysentery. Hamid Khan struggled to raise his children. When he grew tired of living like a beggar in a foreign country he took his family back to Kabul. He was dead within six months.'

'What happened?'

'Samira and Hasan witnessed his execution. A teenager with a Kalashnikov made him kneel on the floor of their apartment and shot him in the back of the head. They threw his body from a window into the street and wouldn't let his children collect it for eight days, by which time the dogs had picked it over.'

Her voice is thick with sadness. 'There is an Afghan proverb. I heard Samira say it: "*To an ant colony dew is a flood.*"'

It doesn't need any further explanation.

'When did you last see her?'

'Mid-January. She surprised me on my birthday. She made me fireworks. I don't know how she managed to buy the chemicals and powder. I had never seen anything so beautiful.'

'What about their application for asylum?'

The lawyer produces another letter. 'Eighteen is a very important age for an asylum seeker in this country. Once you reach this age you are treated as an adult. Samira's temporary residency was revoked. She was deemed to be old enough to look after Hasan, so his visa was also cancelled. Both were denied asylum and told they had to leave.

'I lodged an appeal, of course, but I couldn't prevent them being forced onto the street. They had to leave the campus at Deelen. Like a lot of young people denied asylum they chose to run rather than wait to be deported.'

'Where?'

She opens her arms, palms upward.

'How can we find Samira?'

'You can't.'

'I have to try. Did she have any friends at the campus?'

'She mentioned a Serbian girl. I don't know her name.'

'Is she still there?'

'No. She was either deported or she ran away.'

Mrs Caspar looks at Ruiz and back to me. The future is mapped out in the lines on her face. It is a difficult journey.

'I have a friend – a retired policeman like you, Mr Ruiz. He has spent half his life working in the red-light district. He knows everyone: the prostitutes, pimps, dealers and drug addicts. Walls have mice and mice have ears. He can hear what the mice are saying.'

She takes down the name of our hotel and promises to leave a message.

'If you find Samira, be careful with her. When she finds out about her brother she will hurt in places where it matters most.'

'You think we'll find her?'

She kisses my cheeks. 'There is always a way from heart to heart.'

Back at the Red Tulip I call DI Forbes. Straight away he demands to know where I am. A quiet inner voice tells me to lie. It's a voice I've been hearing a lot lately.

'Have you interviewed the truck driver?' I ask.

'Are you in Amsterdam?' he counters.

'What did he tell you?'

'You can't just *leave* the fucking country. You're a suspect.'

'I wasn't made aware of any restrictions.'

'Don't give me that crap! If you're running a parallel investigation I'll have you up on disciplinary charges. You can forget about your career. You can forget about coming home.'

I can hear the annoying click in his voice. It must drive his wife mad – like living with a human metronome.

Eventually, he calms down when I tell him about Hasan. We swap information. 'The truck driver has been charged with manslaughter, but there is a complication. UK immigration officers received a tip-off about a suspect vehicle before the roll-on roll-off ferry docked in Harwich. They had the licence number and were told to look for a group of illegal immigrants.'

'Who provided the tip-off?'

'The Port Authority in Rotterdam received an anonymous phone call two hours after the ferry sailed. We think it came from the traffickers.'

'Why?'

'They were setting up a decoy.'

'I don't understand.'

'They were sacrificing a small number of illegals who would tie up resources. Customs and Immigration would be so busy that they wouldn't notice a much larger shipment.'

'On the same boat?'

'Two articulated lorries haven't been accounted for. The

companies listed on the freight manifest are non-existent. They could have smuggled a hundred people in the back of those trucks.'

'Could the air vents have been closed deliberately – to create a more effective decoy?'

'We may never know.'

'I don't want a health club, I want a gym,' I tell the desk clerk who doesn't appreciate the difference. I shadow-box and she backs away. Now she understands.

I know a little about gyms. In our last year at Oaklands I convinced Cate to take karate classes with me. They were held in a grungy old gym in Penwick Street, mostly used by boxers and old guys in sleeveless vests whose veins would pop out of their heads when they were on the bench press.

The karate instructor was Chinese with a cockney accent and everyone called him 'Peking' which got shortened to 'PK' which he didn't seem to mind.

There was a boxing ring and a weight-training room with mirrors and a separate annexe with mats on the floor for karate. PK spent the first few lessons explaining the principles behind karate, which didn't particularly interest Cate. 'The mental discipline, physical training and study help build respect towards our fellow man,' he said.

'I just want to be able to kick them in the balls,' said Cate.

'The two Japanese characters that make up the word "karate" have the literal meaning of "empty hands",' explained PK. 'It is a system of self-defence that has evolved over hundreds of years. Every move is based on a knowledge of

the muscles and joints and the relationship between movement and balance.'

Cate raised her hand. 'When do I learn to hit people?'

'You will be taught the techniques of counter-attack.'

He then described how the word 'karate' came from
Mandarin and Cantonese phrases like 'Chan Fa' and 'Ken
Fat', which sent Cate into a fit of giggles. The literal meaning
is 'The Law of the Fist'. Attacks to the groin of an oppo-
nent are frowned upon by most martial arts. Karate also
doesn't approve of targeting the hip joints, knee joints,
insteps, shins, upper limbs and face.

'What's the bloody point?' muttered Cate.

'I think he means in competition.'

'Forget competition. I want to hurt their balls.'

She persevered with learning the theory but every week
she pestered him with the same question: 'When do we
learn the groin kick?'

PK finally relented. He gave Cate a private lesson after
the gym had closed. The blinds were drawn and he turned
off all the lights except for the one over the ring.

She came out looking flushed and smiling, with a mark
on her neck that looked suspiciously like a love bite. She
didn't go back to self-defence classes again.

I kept going, working my way through the belts. PK
wanted me to go for black but I was already at the police
training college.

Ruiz is on his second beer when I get to the restaurant.
He's watching the pizza chef spin a disc of dough in the
air and draping it over his knuckles before launching it
again.

The waiters are young. Two of them are watching me, commenting to each other. They're trying to fathom my relationship with Ruiz. What is a young Asian woman doing with a man twice her age? I'm either a mail-order bride or his mistress, they think.

The café is nearly empty. Nobody eats this early in Amsterdam. An old man with a dog sits near the front door. He slips his hand beneath the table with morsels of food.

'She could be anywhere,' says Ruiz.

'She wouldn't have left Amsterdam.'

'What makes you so sure?'

'Hasan was only sixteen. She wouldn't leave him.'

'He made *two* North Sea crossings without her.'

I have no answer.

So far we have been trying to make inquiries without drawing attention to ourselves. Why not change our tactics? We could print up posters or place an advertisement.

Ruiz doesn't agree. 'Cate Beaumont tried to take this public and look what happened. This isn't some seat-of-the-pants operation where someone panicked and killed the Beaumonts. We're dealing with an organised gang – guys like Brendan Pearl.'

'They won't expect it.'

'They'll know we're looking.'

'We'll flush them out.'

Ruiz continues to argue, but he understands my point. Chance or fate will not decide what takes place next. We can *make* things happen.

Single hotel rooms in strange cities are lonely places where the human spirit touches rock-bottom. I lie on the bed but cannot sleep. My head refuses to abandon the image of a child in a Mickey Mouse T-shirt, lying next to his mother, beneath a closed air vent.

I want to rewind the clock, back to the night of the reunion and further. I want to sit down with Cate and take turns at talking and crying and saying we're sorry. I want to make up for the last eight years. Most of all, I want to be forgiven.

3

A mobile vibrates gently beneath my pillow.

I hear Ruiz's voice. 'Rise and shine.'

'What time is it?'

'Just gone seven. There's someone downstairs. Lena Caspar sent him.'

Pulling on my jeans, I splash water on my face and brush my hair back in a band.

Nicolaas Hokke is in his mid-sixties, with short springy grey hair and a beard. His six-foot frame helps hide the beginnings of a paunch beneath a scuffed leather jacket.

'I understand you need a guide,' he says, taking my hand in both of his. He smells of tobacco and talcum powder.

'I'm looking for a girl.'

'A girl?'

'An asylum seeker.'

'Hmm. Let's talk over breakfast.'

He knows a place. We can walk. The intersections are a flurry of trams, cars and bicycles. Hokke negotiates them with the confidence of a deity crossing a lake.

Already I am falling for Amsterdam. It is prettier and cleaner than London with its cobbled squares, canals and wedding-cake façades. I feel safer here: the anonymous foreigner.

'Often people want tours of the red-light district,' Hokke explains. 'Writers, sociologists, foreign politicians. I take them twice – once during daylight and again at night. It is like looking at different sides of the same coin, light and dark.'

Hokke has an ambling gait and walks with his hands clasped behind his back. Occasionally he stops to point out a landmark or explain a sign. 'Straat' means 'street' and 'steeg' means 'lane'.

'This was your beat?' asks Ruiz.

'Of course.'

'When did you retire?'

'Two years ago. And you?'

'A year.'

They nod to each other as if they share an understanding.

Turning a corner, I get my first glimpse of Amsterdam's famous 'windows'. Initially they appear to be simple glass doors with wooden frames and brass numbers. The curtains are drawn across some of them. Others are open for business.

Only when I draw closer do I see what this means. A skinny dark woman in a sequinned bra and G-string is sitting on a stool with her legs crossed and boots zipped up to her knees. Under the black lights the bruises on her thighs appear as pale blotches.

The blatancy of her pose and her purpose diminishes a small part of me. She watches me aggressively. She doesn't want me with these men. I will stop them coming to her door.

Negotiating more of the narrow lanes, we pass windows that are so close on either side that it is like being at a tennis match and following the ball back and forth across the net. In contrast, Ruiz looks straight ahead.

A large Dominican woman calls out to Hokke and waves. Dressed in a red tasselled push-up bra that underpins a massive bust, she is perched on a stool with her legs crossed and her stomach bulging over her crotch.

Hokke stops and talks to her in Dutch.

'She has four children,' he explains. 'One of them is at university. Twenty years a prostitute but she's still a woman.'

'What do you mean, a woman?'

'Some of them turn into whores.'

He waves to several more prostitutes, who blow him kisses or tease him by slapping their wrists. Further down the street an older woman comes out of a shop and throws her arms around him like he's her long-lost son. She presses a bag of cherries into his hand.

'This is Gusta,' he explains, introducing us. 'She still works the windows.'

'Part-time,' she reminds him.

'But you must be—'

'Sixty-five,' she says proudly. 'I have five grandchildren.'

Hokke laughs at our surprise. 'You're wondering how many customers would sleep with a grandmother.'

Gusta puts her hands on her hips and rolls them seductively. Hokke looks for a polite way to answer our question.

'Some of the younger, prettier girls have men queuing up outside their windows. They are not concerned if a man comes back to them. There will be plenty more waiting. But a woman like Gusta cannot rely on a sweet smile and a firm body. So she has to offer quality of service and a certain expertise that comes with experience.'

Gusta nods in agreement.

Hokke doesn't seem to resent or disapprove of the prostitutes. The drug addicts and dealers are a different story. A North African man is leaning on the railing of a bridge. He recognises Hokke and dances towards him. Hokke doesn't stop moving. The African has betel-stained teeth and dilated pupils. Hokke's face is empty, neutral. The African jabbers in Dutch, grinning wildly. Hokke carries on walking.

'An old friend?' I ask.

'I've known him for thirty years. He's been a heroin addict for this much time.'

'It's remarkable he's still alive.'

'Addicts do not die from the drugs, they die from the lifestyle,' he says adamantly. 'If drugs were less expensive he wouldn't have to steal to afford them.'

On the far side of the bridge we meet another junkie, younger and even less appealing. He points the glowing end of a cigarette at me and talks to Hokke in a wheedling voice. An argument ensues. I don't know what they're saying.

'I asked him if he was clean,' Hokke explains.

'What did he say?'

'He said: "I am always clean."'

'You argued.'

'He wanted to know if you were for sale.'

'Is he a pimp?'

'When it suits him.'

We reach the café and take a table outside under the bare branches of a large tree that is threaded with fairy lights. Hokke drinks his coffee black and orders a slice of sourdough toast with jam. Afterwards he fills a pipe, so small that it seems almost designed for an apprentice smoker.

'My one vice,' he explains.

Ruiz laughs. 'So in all those years you were never tempted.'

'Tempted?'

'To sleep with some of the women in the windows. There must have been opportunities.'

'Yes, opportunities. I have been married for forty years, Vincent – I hope I can call you Vincent? I have slept with only my wife. She is enough for me. These women are in business. They should not be expected to give away their bodies for free. What sort of businesswoman would do that?'

His face almost disappears behind a cloud of pipe smoke.

'This girl you want to find, you think she might be a prostitute?'

'She was trafficked out of Afghanistan.'

'Afghani prostitutes are rare. The Muslim girls are normally Turkish or Tunisian. If she is illegal she won't be working the windows unless she has false papers.'

'Are they difficult to get?'

'The Nigerians and Somalis swap papers because they all look alike but the windows are normally the easiest to police. The streets and private clubs are more difficult. It is like an iceberg – we see only the tip. Beneath the waves there are hundreds of prostitutes, some under-age, working

203

from parking lots, toilets and private houses. Customers find them through word of mouth and mobile telephones.'

I tell him about Samira disappearing from the care centre.

'Who brought her to the Netherlands?' he asks.

'Traffickers.'

'How did she pay them?'

'What do you mean?'

'They will want something in return for smuggling her.'

'She and her brother are orphans.'

He empties his pipe, tapping it against the edge of an ashtray.

'Perhaps they haven't yet paid.' Refilling it again he explains how gangs operate within the asylum centres. They pick up girls and turn them into prostitutes, while the boys are used as drug runners or beggars.

'Sometimes they don't even bother kidnapping children from the centres. They collect them for the weekend and bring them back. This is safer for the pimps because the girls don't disappear completely and trigger an investigation. Meanwhile, they are fed, housed and learn a bit of Dutch – paid for by the Dutch government.'

'You think that's what happened to Samira?'

'I don't know. If she is young she will be moved between cities or sold to traffickers in other countries. It is like a carousel. Young and new girls are prized as fresh meat. They generate more money. By moving them from place to place it is harder for the police or their families to find them.'

Hokke gets to his feet and stretches. He beckons us to follow him. We turn left and right down the cobbled lanes, moving deeper into the red-light district. More windows are open. Women tap on the glass to get Hokke's attention. A Moroccan shakes her breasts at him. Another slaps her rump and sways to a song that only she can hear.

'Do you know them all?' I ask.

He laughs. 'Once perhaps, yes. I heard all their stories. Now there is a kind of wall between the police and the prostitutes. In the old days most of them were Dutch. Then the Dominicans and Colombians moved in. Then the Surinamese. Now we have Nigerians and girls from Eastern Europe.'

Each of the streets is different, he explains. The Oudekerksteeg is the African quarter. The South Americans are on Boomsteeg, the Asians on Oudekennissteeg and Barndesteeg, while Bloedstraat has the transsexuals. The Eastern European girls are on Molensteeg and along the Achterburgwal.

'It is getting harder to make money. A prostitute needs at least two clients before her rent for the window is paid. Another four clients are needed for the pimp's share. Six men have used her and she still hasn't earned anything for herself.

'In the old days prostitutes would save up to buy a window and then become the landlady, renting to other girls. Now companies own the windows and sometimes use them to launder money by claiming the girls earn more than they do.'

Hokke doesn't want to sound melancholy but can't help himself. He yearns for the old days.

'The place is cleaner now. Less dangerous. The problems have gone out further,' he says, 'but they never disappear.'

We are walking alongside a canal, past strip clubs and

cinemas. From a distance the sex shops look like souvenir sellers. Only up close do the bright novelty items become dildos and fake vaginas. I am fascinated and disturbed in equal parts; torn between looking away and peering into the window to work out what the various things are for.

Hokke has turned into a lane and knocks on a door. It is opened by a large man with a bulging stomach and side-burns. Behind him is a small room barely big enough for him to turn around in. The walls are lined with porn videos and film reels.

'This is Nico, the hardest-working projectionist in Amsterdam.'

Nico grins at us, wiping his hands on his shirt-front.

'This place has been here longer than I have,' explains Hokke. 'Look! It still shows Super-8 films.'

'Some of the actresses are grandmothers now,' says Nico.

'Like Gusta,' adds Hokke. 'She was very beautiful once.'

Nico nods in agreement.

Hokke asks him if he knows of any Afghani girls working the windows or clubs.

'Afghani? No. I remember an Iraqi. You remember her, Hokke? Basinah. You had a beating heart for her.'

'Not me,' laughs the former policeman. 'She had problems with her landlord and wanted me to help.'

'Did you arrest him?'

'No.'

'Did you shoot him?'

'No.'

'You weren't a very successful policeman, were you, Hokke? Always whistling. The drug dealers heard you coming from two streets away.'

Hokke shakes his head. 'When I wanted to catch them I didn't whistle.'

I show Nico the photograph of Samira. He doesn't recognise her.

'Most of the traffickers deal with their own. Girls from China are smuggled by the Chinese; Russians smuggle Russians.' He opens his hands. 'The Afghanis stay at home and grow poppies.'

Nico says something to Hokke in Dutch.

'This girl. Why do you want to find her?'

'I think she knows about a baby.'

'A baby?'

'I have a friend.' I correct myself. 'I *had* a friend who faked her pregnancy. I think she arranged to get a baby from someone in Amsterdam. My friend was murdered. She left behind this photograph.'

Hokke is filling his pipe again. 'You think this baby was being smuggled?'

'Yes.'

He stops in mid-movement, the match burning in his fingers. I have surprised him – a man who thought he had seen and heard it all after thirty years in this place.

Ruiz is waiting outside, watching the carnival of need and greed. There are more people now. Most have come to see but not touch the famous Red-Light District. One group of Japanese tourists is shepherded by a woman holding a bright yellow umbrella above her head.

'Samira had a brother,' I explain to Hokke and Nico. 'He went missing from the care centre at the same time. Where would he go?'

'Boys can also become prostitutes,' says Hokke, in a

matter-of-fact way. 'They also carry drugs or pick pockets or become beggars. Look at Central Station. You'll see dozens of them.'

I show them the charcoal drawing of Hasan. 'He had a tattoo on the inside of his wrist.'

'What sort of tattoo?'

'A butterfly.'

Hokke and the projectionist exchange glances.

'It is a property tattoo,' says Nico, scratching his armpit. 'Somebody owns him.'

Hokke stares into the blackened bowl of his pipe. Clearly, it is not good news.

I wait for him to explain. Choosing his words carefully, he reveals that certain criminal gangs control areas of the city and often claim ownership over asylum seekers and illegals.

'She should stay away from de Souza,' says Nico.

Hokke holds a finger to his lips. Something passes between them.

'Who is de Souza?' I ask.

'Nobody. Forget his name.'

Nico nods. 'It is for the best.'

There are more windows open. More customers. The men don't raise their eyes as they pass each other.

Prostitution has always confused me. When I was growing up, movies like *Pretty Woman* and *American Gigolo* glamorised and sanitised the subject. My first glimpse of real prostitutes was with Cate. We were in Leeds for an athletics meeting. Near the railway station, where most of the cheap hotels could be found, we saw women on street corners. Some of them appeared washed-out and unclean – nothing like Julia Roberts. Others looked so carnivorous that they were more like angler fish than objects of desire.

Maybe I have a naive view of sex as being beautiful or magical or other-worldly. It *can* be. I have never liked dirty jokes or overtly sexual acts. Cate called me a prude. I can live with that.

'What are you thinking, sir?'

'I'm wondering why they do it,' Ruiz replies.

'The women?'

'The men. I don't mind someone warming my toilet seat for me but there's some places I don't want to come second, or third . . .'

'You think prostitution should be illegal?'

'I'm just making an observation.'

I tell him about an essay I read at university by Camille Paglia who claimed that prostitutes weren't the victims of men but their conquerors.

'That must have set the feminists a-fighting.'

'Rape alarms at ten paces.'

We walk in silence for a while and then sit down. A swathe of sunshine cuts across the square. Someone has put up a soapbox beneath a tree and is preaching or reciting something in Dutch. It could be *Hamlet*. It could be the telephone directory.

Back at the hotel we start making calls – working through a list of charities, refugee advocates and support groups. Hokke has promised us more names by tomorrow. We spend all afternoon on the phones but nobody has any knowledge of Samira. Perhaps we are going to have to do this the old-fashioned way – knocking on doors.

On Damrak I find a print shop. A technician enlarges the photograph of Samira and uses a colour copier to produce a bundle of images. The smell of paper and ink fills my head.

Ruiz will take the photograph to Central Station and show it around. I'll try the women in the windows, who are more likely to talk to me. Ruiz is completely happy with the arrangement.

Before I leave I call Barnaby Elliot to ask about the funerals. The moment he hears my voice he starts accusing me of having burned down Cate and Felix's house.

'The police say you were there. They say you reported the fire.'

'I reported a break-in. I didn't start a fire.'

'What were you doing there? You wanted her computer and her letters. You were going to steal them.'

I don't respond, which infuriates him even more.

'Detectives have been here asking questions. I told them you were making wild allegations about Cate. Because of you they won't release the bodies. We can't arrange the funerals – the church, the readings, the death notices. We can't say goodbye to our daughter.'

'I'm sorry about that, Barnaby, but it's not my fault. Cate and Felix were murdered.'

'SHUT UP! JUST SHUT UP!'

'Listen to me—'

'No! I don't want to hear any more of your stories. I want you to leave my family alone. Stay away from us.'

As soon as he hangs up my mobile chirrups like a fledgling.

'Hello? Alisha? Hello.'

'I can hear you, Mama.'

'Is everything OK?'

'Yes, fine.'

'Did Hari call you?'

'No.'

'A Chief Superintendent North has been trying to reach you. He said you didn't turn up for work.'

Hendon! My new job as a recruitment officer. I totally forgot.

'He wants you to call him.'

'OK.'

'Are you sure everything is all right?'

'Yes, Mama.'

She starts telling me about my nieces and nephews – which ones are teething, smiling, walking or talking. Then I hear about the dance recitals, soccer games and school concerts. Grandchildren are at the centre of her life. I should feel usurped but the emotion is closer to emptiness.

'Come round for lunch on Sunday. Everyone will be here. Except for Hari. He has a study date.'

That's a new name for it.

'Bring that nice sergeant.' She means 'New Boy' Dave.

'I didn't *bring* him last time.'

'He was very nice.'

'He's not a Sikh, Mama.'

'Oh, don't worry about your father. He's all bark and no bite. I thought your friend was very polite.'

'Polite.'

'Yes. You can't expect to marry a prince. But with a little patience and hard work, you can *make* one. Look how well I did with your father.'

I can't help but love her. She kisses the receiver. Not many people still do that. I kiss her back.

As if on cue I get a call from 'New Boy' Dave. Maybe they're working in cahoots.

'Hello, sweet girl.'

'Hello, sweet boy.' I can hear him breathing as distinctly as if he were standing next to me.

'I miss you.'

'A *part* of you misses me.'

'No. All of me.'

The odd thing is that I miss him too. It's a new feeling.

'Have you found her?'

'No.'

'I want you to come home. We need to talk.'

'So let's talk.'

He has something he wants to say. I can almost hear him rehearsing it in his mind. 'I'm quitting the force.'

'Good God!'

'There's a little sailing school on the South Coast. It's up for sale.'

'A sailing school.'

'It's a good business. It makes money in the summer and in the winter I'll work on the fishing boats or get a security job.'

'Where will you get the money?'

'I'm going to buy it with Simon.'

'I thought he was working in San Diego?'

'He is, but he and Jacquie are coming home.'

Simon is Dave's brother. He is a sailmaker or a boat designer; I can never remember which one.

'But I thought you *liked* being a detective.'

'It's not a good job if I ever have a family.'

Fair point. 'You'll be closer to your Mum and Dad.' (They live in Poole.)

'Yeah.'

'Sailing can be fun.' I don't know what else to say.

'Here's the thing, Ali. I want you to come with me. We can be business partners.'

'Partners?'

'You know I'm in love with you. I want to get married. I want us to be together.' He's talking quickly now. 'You don't have to say anything yet. Just think about it. I'll take you down there. I've found a cottage in Milford-on-Sea. It's beautiful. Don't say no. Just say maybe. Let me show you.'

I feel something shift inside me and I want to take his large hand in my two small hands and kiss his eyelids. Despite what he says, I know he wants an answer. I can't give him one. Not today, nor tomorrow. The future is an hour-by-hour panorama.

4

Once more I walk past the Oude Kerk and Trompettersteeg. Hokke was right – the red-light district is different at night. I can almost smell the testosterone and used condoms.

As I pass each window, I press a photograph against the glass. Some of the prostitutes shout at me or shake their fingers angrily. Others offer seductive smiles. I don't want to meet their eyes, but I must make sure they look at Samira.

I walk through Goldbergersteeg and Bethlemsteeg, making a mental note of those windows where the curtains are closed so I can return later. Only one woman tries to encourage me indoors. She puts two fingers to her lips and pokes her tongue between them. She says something in Dutch. I shake my head.

In English this time. 'You want a woman.' She shakes her claret-covered breasts.

'I don't sleep with women.'

'But you've thought about it.'

'No.'

'I can be a man. I have the tools.' She is laughing at me now.

I move on, around the corner, along the canal through Boomsteeg to Molensteeg. There are three windows side by side, almost below ground. The curtain is open on the centre one. A young woman raises her eyes. Black lights make her blonde hair and white panties glow like neon. A tiny triangle barely covers her crotch and two higher on her chest are pulled together to create a cleavage. The only other shadows darken the depression on either side of her pubic bone where the bikini is stretched tightly across her hips.

A balloon hangs from the window. Streamers. Birthday decorations? I hold the photograph against the glass. A flash of recognition. Something in her eyes.

'You know her?'

She shakes her head. She's lying.

'Help me.'

There are traces of beauty in her cheekbones and the curve of her jaw. Her hair is parted. The thin scalp line is dark instead of white. She lowers her eyes. She's curious.

The door opens. I step inside. The room is scarcely wide enough for a double bed, a chair and a small sink attached to the wall. Everything is pink – the pillows, sheets and the fresh towel lying on top. One entire wall is a mirror, reflecting the same scene so it looks like we're sharing the room with another 'window'.

'My name is Eve – just like the first woman,' she says, laughing sarcastically. 'Welcome to my Garden of Eden.'

Leaning down, she picks up a packet of cigarettes beneath

her stool. Her breasts sway. She hasn't bothered closing the curtain. Instead, she stays by the window. I look at the bed and the chair, wondering where to sit.

Eve points to the bed. 'Twenty euros, five minutes.'

Her accent is a mixture of Dutch and American. It's another testament to the power of Hollywood which has taught generations of people in distant corners of the world to speak English.

I hand over the money. She palms it like a magician making a playing card disappear.

I hold up the photograph again. 'Her name is Samira.'

'She's one of the pregnant ones.'

I feel myself straighten. Invisible armour. Knowledge.

Eve shrugs. 'Then again, I could be wrong.'

The thumbprint on her forearm is a bruise. Another on her neck is even darker.

'Where did you see her? When?'

'Sometimes I get asked to help with the new ones. To show them.'

'To show them what?'

She laughs and lights a cigarette. 'What do *you* think? Sometimes they watch me from the chair or from the bed, depending on what the customer has paid for. Some of them like being watched. Makes it quicker.'

I'm about to ask why she needs a chair when I notice the strip of carpet on the floor to protect her knees.

'But you said she was pregnant. Why would you need to show her this?'

She rolls her eyes. 'I'm giving you the *five*-minute version. That's what you paid for.'

I nod.

'I saw her the first time in January. I remember because it was so cold that day.' She motions to the sink. 'Cold water only. Like ice. They brought her to watch. Her eyes were bigger than this.' The prostitute makes fists with her hands. 'I thought she was going to throw up. I told her to use the sink. I knew she was never going to make it as one of us. It's only sex. A physical act. Men come and go. They cannot touch me here or here,' she says, pointing to her heart and her head. 'This girl acted as though she was saving herself. Another fucking virgin!' She flicks the ash from her cigarette.

'What happened?'

'Time's up.' She holds out her hand for more money.

'That wasn't five minutes.'

She points to the wall behind me. 'You see that clock? I lie on my back and watch it for a living. Nobody judges five minutes like I do.'

I hand her another twenty euros. 'You said she was pregnant.'

'That was the next time I saw her.' Eve mimes the bump. 'She was at a doctor's clinic in Amersfoort. She was in the waiting room with a Serbian girl. Both of them were pregnant. I figured it was a welfare scam or they were trying to stay in the country by having a baby.'

'Did you talk to her?'

'No. I remember being surprised because I thought she was going to be the world's last virgin.' The cigarette is burning near her knuckles.

'I need the name and address of the clinic.'

'Dr Beyer. You'll find him in the book.'

She crushes the cigarette beneath a slingback shoe. A

knock on the glass catches her attention. A man outside points first to me and then to Eve.

'What's your name?' she whispers conspiratorially.

'Alisha.'

She reaches for the door. 'He wants both of us, Alisha.'

'Don't open it!'

'Don't be so shy. He looks clean. I have condoms.'

'I'm not a—'

'Not a whore. Not a virgin, either. You can make some money. Buy some decent clothes.'

There is a small commotion outside. More men are peering through the window. I'm on my feet. I want to leave. She is still trying to convince me. 'What have you got to lose?'

I want to say my self-respect.

She opens the door. I have to squeeze past her. Her fingernail runs down my cheek and the tip of her tongue moistens her bottom lip. Men crowd the passageway, where the cobbles are slick and hard. I have to shoulder my way past them, smelling their bodies, brushing against them. My foot strikes a step and I stumble. A hand reaches out to help me but I slap it away irrationally, wanting to scream abuse at him. I was right about Samira. Right about the baby. That's why Cate faked her pregnancy and carried Samira's photograph.

A small patch of grey sky appears above the crush. Suddenly I'm out, in a wider street, drawing deep breaths. The dark water of the canal is slashed with red and lilac. I lean over a railing and vomit, adding to the colour.

My mobile vibrates. Ruiz is on the move.

'I might have found someone,' he says, puffing slightly.

'I was showing Samira's photograph around Central Station. Most people didn't want to know but this one kid acted real strange when he saw the picture.'

'You think he knew her?'

'Maybe. He wouldn't tell the truth if God Almighty asked him for it.'

'Where is he now?'

'He took off. I'm fifty yards behind him.'

The DI rattles off a description of a teenage boy in a khaki camouflage jacket, jeans and sneakers.

'Damn!'

'What's up?'

'My mobile is running low. Should have charged it last night. Nobody ever bloody calls me.'

'I do.'

'Yeah, well, that just goes to show you should get a life. I'll try to give you a cross street. There's a canal up ahead.'

'Which one?'

'They all look the same.'

I hear music in the background and a girl shouting from the windows.

'Hold on. Barndesteeg,' Ruiz says.

Standing in the ochre glow of a street light, I open a tourist map and run my finger down the names until I find the street grid reference. They're not far away.

Movies and TV shows make it look easy to follow someone and not be seen, but the reality is very different. If this were a proper police tail, we'd have two cars, a motor-cyclist and two, maybe three officers on foot. Every time the target turned, someone new would be behind him. We don't have that luxury.

Crossing over Sint Jansbrug, I walk quickly along the canal. Ruiz is a block further east, heading towards me along Stoofsteeg. The teenager is going to walk straight past me.

The pavement is crowded. I have to step left and right, brushing shoulders with passers-by. The air is thick with hashish and fried-food smells.

I don't see him until the last moment. He's almost past me. Gaunt-cheeked, hair teased with fingers and gel, he skips from the pavement to the gutter and back again, dodging people. He's carrying a canvas bag over his shoulder. A bottle of soft drink protrudes from the top. He looks over his shoulder. He knows he's being followed but he's not scared.

Ruiz has dropped back. I take over. We reach the canal and cross the bridge, almost retracing my steps. The boy walks nearer the water than the buildings. If he wants to lose a tail, why take the open side of the street?

Then it dawns on me – he's leading Ruiz away. Someone at the station must have known Samira. He didn't want Ruiz finding them.

The teenager stops moving and waits. I walk past him. The DI doesn't appear. The kid thinks he's safe but doubles back to make sure.

When he moves again he doesn't look back. I follow him through the narrow lanes until he reaches Warmoesstraat and then Dam Square. He waits near a sculpture until a slender girl appears, dressed in jeans and a pink corduroy jacket. Her hair is short and straight, the colour of unmilked tea.

The boy argues and gesticulates, miming with his hands. I call Ruiz on the mobile. 'Where are you?'

'Behind you.'

'Was there a girl at the station in jeans and a pink jacket? Dark-haired. Late teens. Pretty for now.'

'Samira?'

'No. Another girl. I think he was trying to lead you away. He didn't want you finding her.'

They're still arguing. The girl shakes her head. The boy tugs at her coat sleeve. She pulls away. He shouts something. She doesn't turn.

'They're splitting up,' I whisper into my mobile. 'I'll follow the girl.'

She has a curious body, a long torso and short legs, with slightly splayed feet when she walks. She takes a blue scarf from her pocket and wraps it over her head, tying it beneath her chin. It is a hijab – a head covering. She could be Muslim.

I stay close behind her, aware of the crowds and the traffic. Trams joust on tracks that divide the wider roads. Cars and bicycles weave around them. She is so small. I keep losing sight of her.

One moment she's in front of me and the next—. Where has she gone? I sprint forward, looking vainly in doorways and shop windows. I search the side streets, hoping for a glimpse of her pink jacket or the blue of her hijab.

Standing on a traffic island, I turn full circle and step forward. A bell sounds urgently. My head turns. An unseen hand wrenches me backward as a tram washes past in a blur of noise and rushing air.

The girl in the pink jacket is staring at me, her heart beating faster than mine. The smudges beneath her eyes are signs of the premature or the beaten-down. She knew I was following her. She saved me.

'What's your name?'

Her lips don't move. She turns to leave. I have to sprint several yards to get in front of her.

'Wait! Don't leave. Can we talk?'

She doesn't answer. Perhaps she doesn't understand.

'Do you speak English?' I point to myself. 'My name is Alisha.'

She steps around me.

'Wait, please.'

She steps around me again. I have to dodge people as I try to walk backwards and talk to her at the same time. I hold my hands together as if praying. 'I'm looking for Samira.'

She doesn't stop. I can't *make* her talk to me.

Suddenly she enters a building, pushing through a heavy door. I don't see her use a key or press a buzzer. Inside, smells of soup and electric warmth. A second door reveals a large stark room full of tables and scraping chairs. People are sitting and eating. A nun in a black tunic fills bowls of soup from a trolley. A biker type with a long beard hands out plates and spoons. Someone else distributes bread rolls.

An old man at the nearest table leans low over his food, dipping chunks of bread into the steaming mixture. He crooks his right arm around the bowl as though protecting it. Beside him a tall figure in a woollen cap is trying to sleep with his head on the table. There must be thirty people in the dining room, most with ragtag clothes, body tics and empty stomachs.

'Wou je iets om te eten?'

I turn to the voice.

In English this time: 'Would you like something to eat?'

The question belongs to an elderly nun with a narrow face and playful eyes. Her black tunic is trimmed with green and her white hair sweeps back from her brow until it disappears beneath a wimple.

'No, thank you.'

'There is plenty. It is good soup. I made it myself.'

A work apron, the width of her shoulders, reaches down to her ankles. She is collecting plates from the tables, stacking them along her arm. Meanwhile, the girl has lined up metal tins in front of the soup pot.

'What is this place?'

'We are Augustinians. I am Sister Vogel.'

She must be in her eighties. The other nuns are of similar vintage although not quite so shrunken. She is tiny, scarcely five feet tall, with a voice like gravel spinning in a drum.

'Are you sure you won't eat?'

'No. Thank you.' I don't take my eyes off the girl.

The nun steps in front of me. 'What do you want with her?'

'Just to talk.'

'That's not possible.'

'Why?'

'She will not hear you.'

'No, you don't understand. If I can just speak—'

'She *cannot* hear you.' Her voice softens. 'She is one of God's special children.'

I finally understand. It's not about language or desire. The girl is deaf.

The soup tins have been filled. The girl screws a lid on each tin and places them in a shoulder bag. She raises the strap over her head, adjusting it across her chest. She unfolds

223

a paper napkin and wraps up two pieces of bread. A third piece she takes with her, nibbling at the edges.

'Do you know her name?' I ask.

'No. She comes three times a week and collects food.'

'Where does she live?'

Sister Vogel isn't going to volunteer the information. There is only one voice she obeys – a higher authority.

'She's done nothing wrong,' I reassure her.

'Why do you wish to speak with her?'

'I'm looking for someone. It's very important.'

Sister Vogel puts down the soup dishes and wipes her hands on her apron. Rather than walking across the room she appears to float a fraction above the wooden floorboards in her long tunic. I feel leaden-footed alongside her.

She steps in front of the girl and taps the palm of her hand before making shapes with her fingers.

'You can sign!' I say.

'I know some of the letters. What do you wish to ask?'

'Her name.'

They sign to each other.

'Zala.'

'Where is she from?'

'Afghanistan.'

I take the photograph from my pocket. Sister Vogel takes it from me. The reaction is immediate. Zala shakes her head adamantly. Fearfully. She won't look at the image again.

Sister Vogel tries to calm her down. Her voice is soft. Her hands softer. Zala continues to shake her head, without ever lifting her gaze from the floor.

'Ask her if she knows Samira.'

Sister Vogel tries to sign but Zala is backing away.

'I need to know where Samira is.'

The nun shakes her head, scolding me. 'We don't frighten people away from here.'

Zala is already at the door. She can't run with the soup weighing her down. As I move to follow her, Sister Vogel grabs my arm. 'Please leave her alone.'

I look at her imploringly. 'I can't.'

Zala is on the street. She looks back over her shoulder. Her cheeks are shining under the street lamps. She's crying. Hair has escaped from beneath her hijab. She cannot spare a hand to brush it away from her face.

The DI isn't answering his mobile. His battery must be dead. Dropping back, I stay behind Zala as she leads me away from the convent. The streets and canals are no longer familiar. They are lined with ageing, psoriatic houses, subdivided into bedsits, flats and maisonettes. Doorbell buttons form neat lines.

We pass a small row of shops that are shuttered and locked. At the next corner Zala crosses the road and enters a gate. It belongs to a large run-down apartment block at the heart of a T-junction. The shrubs outside are like puffs of green against the darkness of the bricks. There are bars on the downstairs windows and shutters on the upper floors. Lights burn behind them.

I walk past the gate and check that there are no other entrances. I wish Ruiz were here. What would he do? Knock on the door? Introduce himself? No, he'd wait and watch. He'd see who was coming and going. Study the rhythm of the place.

I look at my watch. It has just gone eight. Where is he? With luck, he'll get my text message with the address.

The wind has picked up. Leaves dance with scraps of paper at my feet. Hidden in a doorway, I'm protected by the shadows.

I don't have the patience for stake-outs. Ruiz is good at them. He can block everything out and stay focused, without ever daydreaming or getting distracted. When I stare at the same scene for too long it becomes burned into my subconscious, playing over and over on a loop until I don't register the changes. That's why police surveillance teams are rotated every few hours. Fresh eyes.

A car pulls up. Double-parks. A man enters the building. Five minutes later he emerges with three women. Neatly groomed. Dressed to kill. Ruiz would say it smells like sex.

Two different men step outside to smoke. They sit on the steps with their legs splayed, comfortable. A young boy creeps up behind one of them and covers his eyes playfully. Father and son wrestle happily until the youngster is sent back inside. They look like immigrants. It's the sort of place Samira would go, seeking safety in numbers.

I can't stay here all night. And I can't afford to leave and risk losing my link to her. It's almost nine. Where the hell is Ruiz?

The men on the steps look up as I approach.

'Samira Khan?'

One of them tosses his head, indicating upstairs. I step around them. The door is open. The foyer smells of cooking spices and a thousand extinguished cigarettes.

Three children are playing at the base of the stairs. One of them grabs hold of my leg and tries to hide behind me before dashing off again. I climb to the first landing. Empty gas bottles have collected against the walls beside bags of rubbish. A baby cries. Children argue. Canned laughter escapes through thin walls.

Two teenage girls are sitting outside a flat, heads together, swapping secrets.

'I'm looking for Samira.'

One of them points upstairs.

I climb higher, moving from landing to landing, aware of the crumbling plaster and buckling linoleum. Laundry hangs over banisters and somewhere a toilet has overflowed.

I reach the top landing. A bathroom door is open at the far end of the corridor. Zala appears in the space. A bucket of water tilts her shoulders. In the dimness of the corridor I notice another open door. She wants to reach it before I do. The bucket falls. Water spills at her feet.

Against all my training I rush into a strange room. A dark-haired girl sits on a high-backed sofa. She is young. Familiar. Even dressed in a baggy jumper and peasant skirt she is obviously pregnant. Her shoulders pull forward as if embarrassed by her breasts.

Zala pushes past me, putting her body between us. Samira is standing now, resting a hand on the deaf girl's shoulder. Her eyes travel over me, as though putting me in context.

'I don't want to hurt you.'

In textbook English: 'You must leave here. It is not safe.'

'My name is Alisha Barba.'

Her eyes bloom. She knows my name.

'Please leave. Go now.'

'Tell me how you know me.'

Samira doesn't answer. Her right hand moves to her distended belly. She caresses it gently and sways slightly

227

from side to side as if rocking her passenger to sleep. The motion seems to take the fight out of her.

She signs for Zala to lock the door and pushes her towards the kitchen where speckled linoleum is worn smooth on the floor and a shelf holds jars of spices and a sack of rice. The soup canisters are washed and drying beside the sink.

I glance around the rest of the apartment. The room is large and square. Cracks edge across the high ceiling and leaking water has blistered the plaster. Mattresses are propped against the wall, with blankets neatly folded along the top. A wardrobe has a metal hanger holding the doors shut.

There is a suitcase, a wooden trunk, and on the top a photograph in a frame. It shows a family in a formal pose. The mother is seated, holding a baby. The father is standing behind them, a hand on his wife's shoulder. At her feet is a small girl – Samira – holding the hem of her mother's dress.

I turn back to her. 'I've been looking for you.'

'Please go.'

I glance at the swell of her pregnancy. 'When are you due?'

'Soon.'

'What are you going to do with the baby?'

She holds up two fingers. For a moment I think she's signing something to Zala but this has nothing to do with deafness. The message is for me. Two babies! Twins.

'A boy and a girl,' she says, clasping her hands together, beseeching me. 'Please go. You cannot be here.'

Hair prickles on the nape of my neck. Why is she so terrified?

228

'Tell me about the babies, Samira. Are you going to keep them?'

She shakes her head.

'Who is the father?'

'Allah the Redeemer.'

'I don't understand.'

'I am a virgin.'

'You're pregnant, Samira. You understand how that happens.'

She confronts my scepticism defiantly. 'I have never lain down with a man. I *am* a virgin.'

What fantasies are these? It's ridiculous. Yet her certainty has the conviction of a convert.

'Who put the babies inside you, Samira?'

'Allah.'

'Did you see him?'

'No.'

'How did he do it?'

'The doctors helped him. They put the eggs inside me.'

She's talking about IVF. The embryos were implanted. That's why she's having twins.

'Whose eggs were put inside you?'

Samira raises her eyes at the question. I know the answer already. Cate had twelve viable embryos. According to Dr Banerjee and Barnaby there were five IVF procedures using two eggs per treatment. That left two eggs unaccounted for. Cate must have carried them to Amsterdam. She arranged a surrogacy.

That's why she'd had to fake her pregnancy. She was going to give Felix his *own* child – a perfect genetic match that nobody could prove wasn't theirs.

'Please leave,' says Samira. Tears are close.

'Why are you so frightened?'

'You don't understand.'

'Just tell me why you're doing this.'

She pushes back her hair with her thumb and forefinger. Her eyes hold mine until the precise moment that it becomes uncomfortable. She is strong-willed. Defiant.

'Did someone pay you money? How much? Did Cate pay you?'

She doesn't answer. Instead she turns her face away, gazing at the window, a dark square against a dark wall.

'Is that how you know my name? Cate gave it to you. She said that if anything happened, if anything went wrong, you had to contact me. Is that right?'

She nods.

'I need to know why you're doing this. What did they offer you?'

'Freedom.'

'From what?'

She looks at me as though I'll never understand. 'Slavery.'

I kneel down and take her hand, which is surprisingly cool. There is a speck of sleep in the corner of her eye. 'I need you to tell me exactly what happened. What were you told? What were you promised?'

There is a noise from the corridor. Zala reappears. Terror paints her face and her head swings from side to side, looking for somewhere to hide.

Samira motions for her to stay in the kitchen. She then turns to face the door. Waiting. A brittle scratching. A key in the lock. My nerve ends are twitching.

The door opens. A thin man with pink-rimmed eyes and

bad teeth seems to spasm at the sight of me. His right hand reaches into a zipped nylon jacket.

'Wie bent u?' he barks.

I think he's asking who I am.

'I'm a nurse,' I say.

He looks at Samira. She nods.

'Dr Beyer asked me to drop by and check on Samira on my way home. I live not far from here.'

The thin man makes a sucking sound with his tongue and his eyes dart about the room as though accusing the walls of being part of the deceit. He doesn't believe me, but he's not sure.

Samira turns towards me. 'I have been having cramps. They keep me awake at night.'

'You are *not* a nurse,' he says accusingly. 'You don't speak Dutch!'

'I'm afraid you're mistaken. English is the official language of the European Union.' I use my best Mary Poppins voice. Officious. Matter-of-fact. I don't know how far I can push him.

'Where do you live?'

'Like I said, it's just around the corner.'

'The address?'

I remember a cross street. 'If you don't mind, I have an examination to conduct.'

He screws his mouth into a sneer: something about his defiance hints at hidden depths of brutality. Whatever his relationship to Samira or Zala, he terrifies them. Samira mentioned slavery. Hasan had a property tattoo on his wrist. I don't have all the answers but I have to get them away from here.

The thin man barks a question in Dutch.

Samira nods her head, lowering her eyes.

'Lieg niet tegen me, kutwijf. Ik vermoord je.'

His right hand is still in his jacket. Lithe and sinewy like a marathon runner, he weighs perhaps a hundred and eighty pounds. With the element of surprise I could possibly take him.

'Please leave the room,' I tell him.

'No. I stay here.'

Zala is watching from the kitchen. I motion her towards me and then unfold a blanket, making her hold it like a curtain to give Samira some privacy.

Samira lies back on the couch and lifts her jumper, bunching it beneath her breasts. My hands are damp. Her thighs are smooth and a taut triangle of white cotton lies at the top of them. The skin of her swollen belly is like tracing paper, stretched so tightly I can see the faint blue veins beneath the surface.

The babies move. Her entire torso seems to ripple. An elbow or a knee creates a peak and then slips away. I can feel the outline of tiny bodies beneath her skin, hard little skulls and joints.

She lifts her knees and raises her hips, indicating that I should remove her underwear. She has more of an idea of what to do than I have. Her minder is still at the door. Samira fixes him with a defiant glare as if to say. 'You want to see this?'

He can't hold her gaze. Instead he turns away and walks into the kitchen, lighting a cigarette.

'You lie so easily,' Samira whispers.

'So do you.'

'Who is he?'

'Yanus. He looks after us.'

I look around the room. 'He's not doing such a good job.'

'He brings food.'

Yanus is back at the doorway.

'Well, the babies are in good position,' I say loudly. 'They're moving down. The cramps could be Braxton Hicks, which are like phantom contractions. Your blood pressure is a little higher than it has been.'

I don't know where this information is coming from; some of it must be via verbal osmosis, having heard my mother's graphic descriptions of my nieces and nephews arriving in the world. I know far more than I want to about mucus plugs, fundal measurements and crowning. In addition to this, I am a world authority on pain relief – epidurals, pethidine, Entonox, TENS machines and every homeopathic, mind-controlling family remedy in existence.

Yanus turns away again. I hear him punch buttons on his mobile phone. He's calling someone. Taking advice. Time is running out.

'You met a friend of mine. Cate Beaumont. Do you remember her?'

Samira nods.

'Do your babies belong to her?'

The same nod.

'Cate died last Sunday. She was run down and killed. Her husband is also dead.'

Samira doubles over as though her unborn have understood the news and are grieving already. Her eyes flood with a mixture of disbelief and knowing.

233

'I can help you,' I plead.

'Nobody can help me.'

Yanus is standing in the doorway. He reaches into his jacket again. I can see his shadow lengthening on the floor. I turn to face him. He has a can of beans in his fist. He swings it; a short arc from the hip. I sense it coming but have no time to react. The blow sends me spinning across the room. One side of my head is on fire.

Samira screams. Not so much a scream as a strangled cry.

Yanus is coming for me again. I can taste blood. One side of my face is already beginning to swell. He hits me, using the can like a hammer. A knife flashes in his right hand.

His eyes are fixed on mine with ecstatic intensity. This is his calling – inflicting pain. The blade twirls in front of me, doing figures of eight. *I* was supposed to take *him* by surprise. The opposite happened. I underestimated him.

Another blow connects. Metal on bone. The room begins to blur.

Some things, real things, seem to happen half in the mind and half in the world: trapped in between. The mind sees them first – like now: a boot swings towards me. I glimpse Zala hanging back. She wants to look away but can't drag her gaze from me. The boot connects and I see a blaze of colour.

Fishing roughly in my pockets, Yanus takes out my mobile, my passport, a bundle of euros . . .

'Who are you?'

'I'm a nurse.'

'Leugenaar!'

He holds the knife against my neck. The point pricks my skin. A ruby teardrop is caught on the tip of the blade.

Zala moves towards him. I yell at her to stop. She can't hear me. Yanus swats her away with the can of beans. Zala drops and holds her face. He curses. I hope he broke his fingers.

My left eye is closing and blood drips from my ear, warming my neck. He forces me upright, pulling my arms back and looping plastic cuffs around my wrists. The ratchets pull them tighter, pinching my skin.

He opens my passport. Reads the name.

'Politieagent! How did you find this place?' He spits towards Zala. '*She* led you here.'

'If you leave us alone I won't say anything. You can walk out of here.'

Yanus finds this amusing. The point of his knife traces across my eyebrow.

'My partner knows I'm here. He's coming. He'll bring others. If you leave now you can get away.'

'What are you doing here?'

'Looking for Samira.'

He speaks to Samira in Dutch. She begins gathering her things. A few clothes, the photograph of her family . . .

'Wait for me outside,' he tells her.

'Zala.'

'Outside.'

'Zala,' she says again, more determined.

He waves the knife in her face. She doesn't flinch. She is like a statue. Immovable. She's not leaving without her friend.

The door suddenly blasts inwards as if blown from its

hinges. Ruiz fills the frame. Sometimes I forget how big he can make himself.

Yanus barely flinches. He turns, knife first. Here is a fresh challenge. The night holds such promise for him. Ruiz takes in the scene and settles on Yanus, matching his intensity.

But I can see the future. Yanus is going to take Ruiz apart. Kill him slowly. The knife is like an extension of him, a conductor's baton directing an invisible orchestra. Listening to voices.

The DI has something in his hand. A half-brick. It's not enough. Yanus braces his legs apart and raises a hand, curling a finger to motion him onwards.

Ruiz swings his fist, creating disturbance in the air. Yanus feints to the left. The half-brick comes down and misses. Yanus grins. 'You're too slow, old man.'

The blade is alive. I scarcely see it move. A dark stain blossoms on Ruiz's shirtsleeve, but he continues stepping forward, forcing Yanus to retreat.

'Can you walk, Alisha?'

'Yes, sir.'

'Get up and get out.'

'Not without you, sir.'

'Please, for once in your life—'

'I'll kill you both,' says Yanus.

My hands are bound behind me. I can't do anything. The acid sting of nausea rises in my throat. Samira goes ahead of me, stepping into the corridor. Zala follows, still holding her cheek. Yanus yells to her in Dutch, threateningly. He lunges at Ruiz who dodges the blade. I turn outside the door and run towards the stairs, waiting for the sound of a body falling.

On every landing I shoulder the locked doors, banging my head against them and yelling for help. I want someone to untie my hands, to call the police, to give me a weapon. Nobody answers. Nobody wants to know.

We reach the ground floor and the street, turning right and heading for the canal. Samira and Zala are ahead of me. What a strange trio we make, hustling through the darkness. We reach the corner. I turn to Samira. 'I have to help him.' She understands. 'I want you to go straight to the police.'

She shakes her head. 'They'll send me back.'

I haven't time to argue. 'Then go to the nuns. Quickly. Zala knows the way.'

I can feel the adrenalin still pumping through my body. Running now, aware of the void in my stomach, I sprint towards the house. There are people milling around outside. They're surrounding a figure slumped on the steps. Ruiz. Someone has given him a cigarette. He sucks it greedily, drawing in his cheeks and then exhaling slowly.

Relief flows through me like liquid beneath my skin. I don't know whether to weep or laugh or do both. Blood soaks his shirt. A fist is pressed against his chest.

'I think maybe you should take me to a hospital,' he says, struggling to breathe.

Like a crazy woman, I begin yelling at people to call an ambulance. A teenager summons the courage to tell me there's one coming.

'I had to get close,' Ruiz explains in a hoarse whisper. His brow and upper lip are dotted with beads of sweat. 'I had to let him stab me. If he could reach me I could *reach* him.'

'Don't talk. Just be still.'

'I hope I killed the bastard.'

More people emerge from the flats. They want to come and see the bleeding man. Someone cuts away my cuffs and the plastic curls like orange peel at my feet.

Ruiz gazes at the night sky above the rooftops.

'My ex-wives have been wishing this on me for a long while,' he says.

'That's not true. Miranda is still in love with you.'

'How do you know?'

'I can see it. She flirts with you all the time.'

'She can't help herself. She flirts with everyone. She does it to be nice.'

His breathing is laboured. Blood gurgles in his lungs.

'Wanna hear a joke?' he says.

'Don't talk. Sit quietly.'

'It's an old one. I like the old ones. It's about a bear. I like bears. Bears can be funny.'

He's not going to stop.

'There's this family of polar bears living in the Arctic in the middle of winter. The baby polar bear goes to his mother one day and says, "Mum? Am I really a *polar* bear?"

'"Of course you are, son," she says.

'And the cub replies, "Are you sure I'm not a panda bear or a black bear?"

'"No, you're definitely not. Now run outside and play in the snow."

'But he's still confused so the baby polar bear goes looking for his father and finds him fishing at the ice hole. "Hey, Dad, am I a polar bear?"

'"Well, of course, son," he replies gruffly.

"'Are you sure I don't have any grizzly in me or maybe koala?'"

"'No, son, I can tell you now that you're a hundred per cent pure bred polar bear, just like me and your mother. Why in the world do you ask?'"

"'Because I'm freezing my butt off out here!'"

The DI laughs and groans at the same time. I put my arms around his chest, trying to keep him warm. A mantra, unspoken, grows louder in my head: 'Please don't die. Please don't die. Please don't die.'

This is my fault. He shouldn't be here. There's so much blood.

5

Regret is such an odd emotion because it invariably comes a moment too late, when only imagination can rewrite what has happened. My regrets are like pressed flowers in the pages of a diary. Brittle reminders of summers past; like the last summer before graduation, the one that wasn't big enough to hold its own history.

It was supposed to be the last hurrah before I entered the 'real world'. The London Metropolitan Police had sent me an acceptance letter. I was part of the next intake for the training college at Hendon. The class of 1998.

When I went to primary school I never imagined getting to secondary school. And at Oaklands I never imagined the freedom of university. Yet there I was, about to graduate, to grow up, to become a full-fledged, paid-up adult with a tax-file number and a HECS debt. 'Thank God we'll never be forty,' Cate joked.

I was working two jobs – answering phones at my brothers' garage and working weekends on a market stall. The Elliots invited me to Cornwall again. Cate's mother had suffered her stroke by then and was confined to a wheelchair.

Barnaby Elliot still had political ambitions but no safe seat had become available. He wasn't made of the right stuff – not old-school enough to please the die-hard Conservatives and not female, famous or ethnic enough to satisfy modernisers in the party.

I still thought he was handsome. And he continued to flirt with me, finding reasons to lean against me or punch my arm or call me his 'Bollywood Beauty' or his 'Indian Princess'.

On Sunday mornings the Elliots went to church in the village, about ten minutes' walk away. I stayed in bed until after they'd gone.

I don't know why Barnaby came back; what excuse he made to the others. I was in the shower. Music videos were turned up loud on the TV. The kettle had boiled. The clock ticked as if nothing had happened.

I didn't hear him on the stairs. He just appeared. I held the towel against me but didn't cry out. He ran his fingers slowly over my shoulder and along my arms. Perfect fingernails. I looked down. I could see his grey trousers and the tips of his polished shoes protruding from under his turn-ups.

He kissed my throat. I had to throw my head back to make room for him. I looked up at the ceiling and he moved his lips lower to the space between my breasts. I held his head and pushed against him.

241

My hair was long back then, plaited in a French braid that reached down to the small of my back. He held it in his fists, wrapping it around his knuckles like a rope. Whispering in my ear, sweet nothings that meant more, he pushed down on my shoulders, wanting me to kneel. Meanwhile, the TV blared and the clock ticked and the water in the kettle cooled.

I didn't hear the door open downstairs or footsteps on the stairs. I don't know why Cate came back. Some details don't matter. She must have heard our voices and the other noises. She must have known but she kept coming closer until she reached the door, drawn by the sounds.

In real estate, location is everything. Barnaby was standing naked behind me. I was on all fours with my knees apart. Cate didn't say a word. Having seen enough she still stayed there, watching more. She didn't see me fighting or struggling. I *didn't* fight or struggle.

This is the way I remember it. The way it happened. All that was left was for Cate to tell me to leave and that she never wanted to see me again. And time enough for her to lie sobbing on her bed. A single bed away, I packed my bag, breathing in her grief and trying to swallow something that I couldn't spit out.

Barnaby drove me to the station in silence. The seagulls were crying, accusing me of betrayal. The rain had arrived, drowning summer.

It was a long journey back to London. I found Mama at her sewing machine, making a dress for my cousin's wedding. For the first time in years I wanted to crawl onto her lap. Instead I sat next to her and put my head on her shoulder. Then I cried.

Later that night I stood in front of the bathroom mirror with Mama's big dressmaking scissors, and cut my hair for the first time. The blades carved through my tresses and sent them rocking to the tiles. I trimmed it as short as the scissors allowed, nicking my skin so that blood stained the blades and tufts of hair stood out from my skull like sprouts of wheatgerm.

I can't explain why. Somehow the act was palliative. Mama was horrified. (She would have been less shocked if I'd sliced open my wrists.)

I left messages for Cate and wrote her notes. I couldn't visit her house without risking meeting her father or, worse, her mother. What if Ruth Elliot knew? I caught the same buses and trains as Cate. I orchestrated chance meetings and sometimes I simply stalked her, but it made no difference. Being sorry wasn't enough. She didn't want to see me or talk to me.

Eventually I stopped trying. I locked myself away for hours, coming out only to run and to eat. I ran a personal best a month later. I no longer wanted to catch up with the future – I was running away from the past. I threw myself into my police training, studying furiously. Filling notebooks. Blitzing exams.

My hair grew back. Mama calmed down. I used to daydream in the years that followed that Cate and I would find each other and somehow redeem the lost years. But a single image haunted me – Cate standing silently in the doorway, watching her father fuck her best friend to the rhythm of a ticking clock and a cooling kettle.

In all the years since, not a day has passed when I haven't wanted to change what happened. Cate did not forgive me.

She hated me with a hatred more fatal than indifference because it was the opposite of love.

After enough time had passed, I didn't think about her every hour or every day. I sent her cards on her birthday and at Christmas. I heard about her engagement and saw the wedding photographs in a photographer's window in Bethnal Green Road. She looked happy. Barnaby looked proud. Her bridesmaids (I knew all their names) wore the dresses she'd always said she wanted. I didn't know Felix. I didn't know where they'd met or how he'd proposed. What did she see in him? Was it love? I could never ask her.

They say time is a great healer and a lousy beautician but it didn't heal *my* wounds. It covered them over with layers of regret and awkwardness like pancake make-up. Wounds like mine don't heal. The scars simply grow thicker and more permanent.

The curtains sway back and forth, breathing in and then out like lungs drawing restless air. Light spills from around the edges. Another day.

I must have dozed off. I rarely sleep soundly any more. Not like I did as a child when the world was still a mystery. Now I snatch awake at the slightest noise or movement. The scars on my back are throbbing, telling me to stand and stretch.

Ruiz is lying on a bed in the dimness. Wires, fluids and machines have captured him. A mask delivers oxygen. Three hours ago surgeons inserted a tube in his chest and rein-flated his right lung. They stitched his arm, commenting on his many scars.

My ear is taped with sticking plaster. An ice pack has

melted on my cheek and the swelling has gone down. The bruising will be ugly but I can let down my hair and hide the worst of it.

The doctors and nurses have been very kind. They wanted me to leave the DI's room last night. I argued. I begged. Then I seem to remember lying down on the linoleum floor, challenging them to carry me out. They let me stay.

I feel numb. Shell-shocked. This is my fault. I close my eyes to the darkness and listen to him breathing. Someone has delivered a tray with a glass of orange juice under a frilled paper lid on it. There are biscuits, too. I'm not hungry.

So this is all about a baby. Two babies. Cate Beaumont tried unsuccessfully to get pregnant through IVF. She then met someone who convinced her that for eighty thousand pounds another woman would have a baby for her. Not just any baby. Her own genetic offspring.

She travelled to Amsterdam where two of her fertilised embryos were implanted into the womb of an Afghani teenager who owed money to people smugglers. Both embryos began growing.

Meanwhile, in London, Cate announced that she was pregnant. Friends and family celebrated the news. She began an elaborate deception that she had to maintain for nine months. What went wrong? Cate's ultrasound pictures – the fake ones – showed only one baby. She didn't expect twins.

Someone must have arranged the IVF procedure. Doctors were needed. Fertility specialists. Midwives. Minders.

A nurse appears at the door, an angel in off-white. She walks around the bed and whispers in my ear. A detective has come to interview me.

'He won't wake yet,' she whispers, glancing at Ruiz. 'I'll keep watch.'

A local *politieagent* has been sitting outside the room all night. He looks very smart in dark blue trousers, light blue shirt, tie and jacket. Now he's talking to a more senior colleague. I wait for them to finish.

The senior detective introduces himself as Spijker, making it sound like a punishment. He doesn't give me a first name. Maybe he only has the one. Tall and thin, with a narrow face and thinning hair, he looks at me with watery eyes as though he's already having an allergic reaction to what I might say.

A small mole on his top lip dances up and down as he speaks. 'Your friend will be all right, I think.'

'Yes, sir.'

'I shall need to talk to him when he wakes up.'

I nod.

We walk to the patients' lounge, which is far smarter than anything I've seen in a British hospital. There are eggs and cold meats and slices of cheese on a platter, along with a basket of bread rolls. The detective waits for me to be seated and then takes out a fountain pen, resting it on a large white pad. His smallest actions have a purpose.

Spijker explains that he works for the Youth and Vice Squad. Under normal circumstances, this might sound like an odd combination but not when I look at Samira's age and what she's been through.

As I tell him the story, explaining events, it strikes me how implausible it all sounds. An English woman transports fertilised embryos to Amsterdam inside a small cooler box. The eggs are placed in the womb of an unwilling surrogate. A virgin.

246

Spijker leans forward, with his hands braced on either side of his chair. For a moment I think he might suffer from piles and want to relieve some of the pressure.

'What makes you think this girl was forced to become pregnant?'

'She told me.'

'And you believe her?'

'Yes, sir.'

'Perhaps she agreed.'

'No. She owed money to traffickers. Either she became a prostitute or she agreed to have a baby.'

'Trafficking is a very serious crime indeed. Commercial surrogacy is also illegal.'

I tell him about the prostitute on Molensteeg who mentioned seeing a second pregnant girl. A Serb. Samira had a Serbian friend on the campus, according to Lena Caspar.

There could be others. Babies born at a price, ushered into the world with threats and blackmail. I have no idea how big this is; how many people it touches.

Spijker's face gives nothing away. He speaks slowly, as if practising his English. 'And this has been the purpose of your visit to Amsterdam?'

The question has a barbed tip. I have been waiting for this – the issue of jurisdiction. What is a British police officer doing investigating possible crimes in the Netherlands? There are protocols to be followed. Rules to be obeyed.

'I was making private inquiries. It is not an official investigation.'

Spijker seems satisfied. His point has been made. I have no authority in the Netherlands.

'Where is this woman – the pregnant one?'

'Safe.'

He waits, expecting an address. I explain about Samira's asylum appeal and the deportation order. She's frightened of being sent back to Afghanistan.

'If this girl is telling the truth and becomes a witness there are laws to protect her.'

'She could stay?'

'Until the trial.'

I want to trust him – I want Samira to trust him – yet there is something in his demeanour that hints at scepticism. The notepad and fountain pen have not been touched. They are merely props.

'You tell a very interesting story, detective constable. A very interesting story, indeed.' The mole on his top lip is quivering. 'However, I have heard a different version. The man we found unconscious at the scene says he returned home and found you in his apartment. You claimed to be a nurse and that you were trying to examine his fiancée.'

'His fiancée!'

'Yes, indeed his fiancée. He says that he asked you for some proof of your identity. You refused. Did you conduct a physical examination of Miss Khan?'

'She *knew* I wasn't a nurse. I was trying to help her.'

'Mr Yanus further claims that he was attacked by your colleague as he endeavoured to protect his fiancée.'

'Yanus had a knife. Look at what he did!'

'In self-defence.'

'He's lying.'

Spijker nods, but not in agreement. 'You see my dilemma, DC Barba. I have two different versions of the same event.

Mr Yanus wants you both charged with assault and abducting his fiancée. He has a good lawyer. A very good lawyer indeed.'

'This is ridiculous! Surely you can't believe him.'

The detective raises a hand to silence me. 'We Dutch are famous for our open minds but do not mistake this openness for ignorance or naivety. I need evidence. Where is the pregnant girl?'

'I will take you there, but I must talk to her first.'

'To get your stories straight, perhaps?'

'No!' I sound too strident. 'Her brother died three days ago. She doesn't know.'

We drive in silence to my hotel. I am given time to shower and change. Spijker waits in the lobby.

Peeling off my clothes, I slip on a hotel robe and sit cross-legged on the bed, leafing through the messages that were waiting at reception. 'New Boy' Dave has phoned four times, my mother twice and Chief Superintendent North has left a terse six-word 'please explain'. I screw it into a ball and flush it away. Maybe this is what he meant by shuffling people and priorities.

I should call Ruiz's family. Who, exactly? I don't have numbers for his children or any of his ex-wives – not even the most recent, Miranda.

I pick up the phone and punch the numbers. Dave is at the station. I hear other voices in the background.

'Hello, sweet girl, where have you been?'

'My mobile was stolen.'

'How?'

'There was an accident.'

His mood alters. 'An accident!'

'Not really an accident.' *I'm not doing this very well.*

'Hang on.' I hear him apologising to someone. He takes me somewhere private.

'What's wrong? Are you all right?'

'The DI is in hospital. Someone stabbed him.'

'Shit!'

'I need a favour. Find a number for his ex-wife.'

'Which one?'

'Miranda. Tell her that he's in the Academisch Medisch Centrum. It's a hospital in Amsterdam.'

'Is he going to be all right?'

'I think so. He's out of surgery.'

Dave wants the details. I try to fudge them, making it sound like a wrong-place-at-the-wrong-time scenario. Bad luck. He isn't convinced. I know what's coming now. He's going to get clingy and pathetic and ask me to come home and I'll be reminded of all the reasons I don't want to be married to someone.

Only he doesn't. He is matter-of-fact and direct, taking down the number of the hospital, along with Spijker's name. He's going to find out what the Dutch police are doing.

'I found Samira. She's pregnant.'

I can hear Dave's mind juddering through the consequences. He is careful and methodical, like a carpenter who measures twice and cuts once.

'Cate paid for a baby. A surrogate.'

'Jesus, Ali.'

'It gets worse. She donated the embryos. There are twins.'

'Who owns the babies?'

'I don't know.'

250

Dave wants the whole story but I don't have time. I'm about to hang up when he remembers something.

'I know it's probably not the time,' he says. 'But I had a phone call from your mother.'

'When?'

'Yesterday. She invited me to lunch on Sunday.'

She threatened to do it and she went and did it!

He's waiting for a response.

'I don't know if I'll be home by then,' I say.

'But you *knew* about the invite?'

'Yes, of course,' I lie. 'I told her to invite you.'

He relaxes. 'For a moment I thought she might have gone behind your back. How embarrassing would that be – my girlfriend's mother arranging dates for me? Story of my life – mothers liking me and their daughters running a mile.'

Now he's blathering.

'It's all right, Dave.'

'Brilliant.'

He doesn't want to hang up. I do it for him. The shower is running. I step beneath the spray and flinch as the hot water hits my cheek and the cut on my ear. Washed and dried, I open my bag and take out my Dolce & Gabbana pants and a dark blouse. I see less of me in the mirror than I remember. When I ran competitively my best weight was a hundred and twenty-three pounds. I got heavier when I joined the Met. Night shifts and canteen food will do that to you.

I have always been rather un-girlie. I don't have manicures or pedicures and I only paint my nails on special occasions (so I can chip it off when I get bored).

The day I cut my hair was almost a rite of passage. When it grew back I had got a sensible layered shag cut. My mother cried. She's never been one to ration tears.

Ever since my teens I have lived in fear of saris and skirts. I didn't wear a bra until I was fourteen and my periods started after everyone else's. I imagined them banked up behind a dam wall and when the gates opened it was going to be like a scene from a Tarantino film, without Harvey Keitel to clean up afterwards.

In those days I didn't imagine ever feeling like a woman, but slowly it happened. Now I'm almost thirty and self-conscious enough to wear make-up – a little lip-gloss and mascara. I pluck my eyebrows and wax my legs. I still don't own a skirt and every item in my wardrobe, apart from my jeans and my saris, is a variant on the colour black. That's OK. Small steps.

I make one more phone call. It diverts between numbers and Lena Caspar answers. A public address system echoes in the background. She is on a railway platform. There is a court hearing in Rotterdam, she explains. An asylum seeker has been charged with stealing groceries.

'I found Samira.'

'How is she?'

'She needs your help.'

The details can wait. I give her Spijker's name and phone number. Samira will need protection and guarantees about her status if they want her to give evidence.

'She doesn't know about Hasan.'

'You have to tell her.'

'I know.'

The lawyer begins thinking out loud. She will find

someone to take over the court case in Rotterdam. It might take a few hours.

'I have a question.'

My words are drowned out by a platform announcement. She waits. 'I'm sorry. What did you say?'

'I have a hypothetical question for you.'

'Yes?'

'If a married couple provided a fertilised embryo to a surrogate mother who later gave birth, who would the baby belong to?'

'The birth mother.'

'Even if genetically it had the DNA of the couple?'

'It doesn't matter. The law in the Netherlands is the same as the law in the UK. The birth mother is the legal mother. Nobody else has a claim.'

'What about the father?'

'He can apply for access, but the court will favour the mother. Why do you want to know?'

'Spijker will explain.'

I hang up and take another look in the mirror. My hair is still wet. If I wear it out it will hide the swelling on my cheek. I'll have to stop my natural inclination to push it behind my ears.

Downstairs I find the detective and desk clerk in conversation. A notebook is open. They stop talking when they see me. Spijker is checking my details. I would do the same.

It is a short drive to the Augustinian convent. We turn along Warmoesstraat and pull into a multi-storey car park. The African parking attendant comes running over. Spijker shows him a badge and tears up the parking stub.

Against his better judgement he has agreed to let me see

Samira first. I have twenty minutes. Descending the concrete steps, I push open a heavy fire door. Across the street is the convent. A familiar figure emerges from the large front door. Dressed in her pink jacket and a long ankle-length skirt, Zala puts her head down and hustles along the pavement. Her blue hijab hides the bruising on her face. She shouldn't be outside. I fight the urge to follow her.

A large ruddy-faced nun answers the door. Like the others she is creased and crumbling, trying to outlive the building. I am led down a corridor to Sister Vogel's office, which contains a curious mixture of the old and the new. A glass-fronted cabinet, full of books, is stained the same dark colour as the mahogany desk. In the corner there is a fax machine and a photocopier. A heart-shaped box of candies sits on the mantel, alongside photographs that could be of her nieces and nephews. I wonder if Sister Vogel ever regrets her calling. God can be a barren husband.

She appears beside me. 'You didn't tell me you were a police officer.'

'Would it have made a difference?'

She doesn't answer. 'You sent more people for me to feed.'

'They don't eat very much.'

She folds her arms. 'Is this girl in trouble?'

'Yes.'

'Has she been abandoned?'

'Abused.'

Sorrow fills every crease and wrinkle of her face. She notices the bruising on my cheek and reaches towards it sympathetically. 'Who did this to you?'

'It doesn't matter. I must talk to Samira.'

She takes me to a room on the second floor which is stained with the same dark panels. Samira is at the window when the door opens. She's wearing a long dress, buttoned down the middle with a Peter Pan collar. The light from the window paints an outline of her body inside it. Watching me carefully, she takes a seat on the sofa. Her pregnancy rests on her thighs.

Sister Vogel doesn't stay. As the door closes, I glance around the room. On the wall there is a painting of the Virgin Mary and the baby Jesus. Both are pictured beside a stream, where fruit hangs from trees and fat naked cherubs dance above the water.

Samira notices me looking at it. 'Are you a Christian?'

'A Sikh.'

She nods, satisfied.

'Do you dislike Christians?'

'No. My father told me that Christians believe less than we believe. I don't know if that is true. I am not a very good Muslim. I sometimes forget to pray.'

'How often are you supposed to pray?'

'Five times a day, but my father always said that three was enough.'

'Do you miss him, your father?'

'With every breath.'

Her copper-coloured eyes are flecked with gold and uncertainty. I can't imagine what they've seen in her short life. When I picture Afghanistan I see women draped in black like covered statues, mountains capped with snow, old caravan trails, unexploded mines, scorching deserts, terracotta houses, ancient monuments and one-eyed madmen.

I introduce myself properly this time and tell Samira

how I found her. She looks away self-consciously when I mention the prostitute on Molensteeg. At the same time she holds her hand to her chest, pressing down. I see pain etched in the furrows on her forehead.

'Are you OK?'

'Heartburn. Zala has gone to get medicine.' She glances at the door, already missing her friend.

'Where did you meet her?'

'At the orphanage.'

'You didn't leave Afghanistan together?'

'No. We had to leave her behind.'

'How did she get here?'

'In the back of a truck and then by train.'

'By herself?'

Samira's face softens. 'Zala can always find a way to make herself understood.'

'Has she always been deaf?'

'No.'

'What happened?'

'Her father fought with the mujahedin against the Taliban. When the Talibs took over they punished their enemies. Zala and her mother were imprisoned and tortured with acid and melted plastic. Her mother took eight days to die. By then Zala could not hear her screaming.'

The statement sucks the oxygen from the room and I feel myself struggling for breath. Samira looks towards the door again, waiting for Zala. Her fingers are splayed on her belly as if reading the bumps and kicks. What must it feel like – to have something growing inside you? A life, an organism that takes what it needs without asking or sharing, stealing sleep, changing hormones, bending bones and squeezing organs. I have heard my friends and sisters-in-law complain of weak nails, moulting hair, sore breasts and stretch marks. It is a sacrifice men could not make.

Samira is watching me. She has something she wants to ask.

'You said Mrs Beaumont is dead.'

'Yes.'

'What will happen now to her babies?'

'It is your decision.'

'Why?'

'They belong to you.'

'No!'

'They're your babies.'

Her head pivots from side to side. She is adamant.

Standing suddenly, she rocks slightly and reaches out her hand, bracing it on the back of the sofa. Crossing the room, she stares out the window, hoping to see Zala.

I'm still contemplating her denial. Does she love her unborn twins? Does she imagine a future for them? Or is she simply carrying them, counting down the days until the birth, when her job is done?

'When did you meet Mrs Beaumont?'

'She came to Amsterdam. She bought me clothes. Yanus was there. I had to pretend that I didn't speak English but Mrs Beaumont talked to me anyway. She gave me a piece of paper with your name. She said if I was ever in trouble I had to find you.'

'When was this?'

'In February I saw her the first time. She came to see me again in September.'

'Did she know you were having twins?'

Samira shrugs.

'Did she know why?'

'What do you mean?'

'Did she know about the debt? Did she know you were *forced* to get pregnant?'

Her voice softens. 'She thanked me. She said I was doing a good thing.'

'It is a crime to force someone to have a baby. She did a very *foolish* thing.'

Samira shrugs, unwilling to be so harsh. 'Sometimes friends do foolish things,' she says. 'My father told me that true friends are like gold coins. Ships are wrecked by storms and lie for hundreds of years on the ocean floor. Worms destroy the wood. Iron corrodes. Silver turns black but gold doesn't change in sea water. It loses none of its brilliance or colour. It comes up the same as it went down. Friendship is the same. It survives shipwrecks and time.'

The swelling in my chest suddenly hurts. How can someone so young be so wise?

'You must tell the police what happened.'

'They will send me back.'

'These people have done very bad things. You owe them nothing.'

'Yanus will find me. He will never let me go.'

'The police can protect you.'

'I do not trust them.'

'Trust me.'

She shakes her head. She has no reason to believe me. Promises don't fill stomachs or bring back dead brothers. She still doesn't know about Hasan. I can't bring myself to tell her.

'Why did you leave Kabul?'

'Brother.'

'Your brother?'

'No. An Englishman. We called him "Brother".'

'Who is he?'

'A saint.'

Using her forefinger she traces the outline of a cross on her neck. I think of Donavon's tattoo. Is it possible?

'This Englishman – was he a soldier?'

'He said he was on a mission from God.'

She describes how he visited the orphanage, bringing food and blankets. There were sixty children aged between two and sixteen who slept in dormitories, huddling together in winter, surviving on scraps and charity.

When the Taliban were in control they took boys from the orphanage to fill their guns with bullets and the girls were taken as wives. The orphans cheered when the Northern Alliance and the Americans liberated Kabul, but the new order proved to be little different. Soldiers came to the orphanage looking for girls. The first time Samira hid under blankets. The second time she crawled into the latrine. Another girl threw herself off the roof rather than be taken.

I'm amazed at how ambivalent she sounds. Fateful decisions, issues of life and death, are related with the matter-of-factness of a shopping list. I can't tell if she's inured to shock or overcome by it.

'Brother' paid off the soldiers with medicine and money. He told Samira that she should leave Afghanistan because it wasn't safe. He said he would find her a job in London.

'What about Hasan?'

'Brother said he had to stay behind. I said I would not go without him.'

They were introduced to a trafficker called Mahmoud, who arranged their passage. Zala had to stay behind because no country would accept a deaf girl, Mahmoud told them.

Hasan and Samira were taken overland to Pakistan by bus and smuggled south through Quetta and west into Iran until they reached Tabriz near the Turkish border. In the first week of spring they walked across the Ararat mountain range and almost succumbed to the freezing nights and the wolves.

On the Turkish side of the mountains, sheep farmers smuggled them between villages and arranged their passage to Istanbul in the back of a truck. For two months brother and sister worked in a sweatshop in the garment districts of Zeytinburnu, sewing sheepskin waistcoats.

The trafficking syndicate demanded more money to get them to England. The price had risen to ten thousand American dollars. Samira wrote a letter to 'Brother' but didn't know where to send it. Finally they were moved. A fishing boat took them across the Aegean Sea to Italy where they caught a train to Rome with four other illegals. They were met at the station and taken to a house.

Two days later they met Yanus. He took them to a bus depot and put them inside the luggage compartment of a tourist coach that travelled through Germany to the Netherlands. 'Don't move, don't talk – otherwise you will be found,' he told them. When the coach arrived at the Dutch border they were to claim asylum. He would find them.

'We are supposed to be going to England,' Samira said.

'England is for another day,' he replied.

The rest of the story matches what I've already learned from Lena Caspar.

Sister Vogel knocks softly on the door. She is carrying a tray of tea and biscuits. The delicate cups have chipped handles. I pour the tea through a broken strainer. Samira takes a biscuit and wraps it in a paper napkin, saving it for Zala.

'Have you ever heard the name "Paul Donavon"?'

She shakes her head.

'Who told you about the IVF clinic?'

'Yanus. He said we had to pay him for our passage from Kabul. He threatened to rape me. Hasan tried to stop him but Yanus cut him over and over. A hundred cuts.' She points to her chest. Noonan found evidence of these wounds on Hasan's torso.

'What did Yanus want you to do?'

'To become a whore. He showed me what I would have to do – sleep with many men. Then he gave me a choice. He said a baby would pay off my debt. I could remain a virgin.'

She says it almost defiantly. This is a truth that sustains Samira. I wonder if that's why they chose a Muslim girl. She would have done almost anything to protect her virginity.

I still don't know how Cate became involved. Was it her idea or Donavon's?

Spijker is waiting outside. I can't delay this. Opening my satchel I take out the charcoal drawing, smoothing the corners.

Samira lets out a short cry. Excitement lights her eyes from within. 'Hasan! You've seen him!'

She waits. I shake my head. 'Hasan is dead.'

Her head jerks up as though tied to a cord. The light in her eyes is replaced by anger. Disbelief. I tell her quickly, hoping it might spare her, but there is no painless way to do this. His journey. His crossing. His fight to stay alive.

She puts her hands over her ears.

'I'm sorry, Samira. He didn't make it.'

'You're lying! Hasan is in London.'

'I'm telling the truth.'

She rocks from side to side, her eyes closed and her mouth opening and closing soundlessly. The word she wants to say is no.

'Surely you must be wondering why you haven't heard from him,' I say. 'He should have called by now or written to you. You sewed my name into his clothes. That's how I found you.' I close the gap between us. 'I have no reason to lie to you.'

She stiffens and pulls away, fixing me with a gaze of frightening intensity.

Spijker's voice echoes from downstairs. He has grown tired of waiting.

'You must tell the police everything you have told me.'

She doesn't answer. I don't know if she understands.

Turning towards the window, she utters Zala's name.

'Sister Vogel will look after her.'

She shakes her head stubbornly, her eyes full of imbecile hope.

'I will find her. I'll look after her.'

For a moment something struggles inside her. Then her mind empties and she surrenders. Fighting fate is too difficult. She must save herself to fight whatever fate throws up.

There is a pharmacy in the heart of de Walletjes, explains Sister Vogel. The pharmacist is a friend of hers. This is where she sent Zala. She was carrying a note.

Turning each corner I expect to see a flash of pink or her blue hijab coming towards me. I pass a greengrocer and catch the scent of oranges, which makes me think of Hasan. What will happen to Samira now? Who will look after her?

I turn into Oudekerksteeg. There is still no sign of Zala. A touch on my arm makes me turn. For a second I don't recognise Hokke, who is wearing a woollen cap. With his light beard it makes him look like a North Sea fisherman.

'Hello, my friend.' He looks at me closely. 'What have you done to yourself?' His finger traces the bruising on my cheek.

'I had a fight.'

'Did you win?'

'No.'

I look over his shoulder, scanning the square for Zala. My sense of urgency makes him turn his own head.

'Are you still looking for your Afghani girl?'

'No, a different one this time.'

It makes me sound careless – as though I lose people all the time. Hokke has been sitting in a café. Zala must have passed by him but he doesn't remember her.

'Perhaps I can help you look.'

I follow him, scanning the pedestrians, until we reach the pharmacy. The small shop has narrow aisles and neatly stacked shelves. A man in a striped shirt and white coat is serving customers at a counter. When he recognises Hokke he opens his arms and they embrace. Old friends.

'A deaf girl – I'd remember her,' he announces, breaking into English.

'She had a note from Sister Vogel.'

The pharmacist yells to his assistant. A head pops out from behind a stand of postcards. More Dutch. A shrug. Nobody has seen her.

Hokke follows me back onto the street. I walk a few paces and stop, leaning against a wall. A faint vibration is coming off me: a menacing internal thought spinning out of control. Zala has not run away. She would not leave Samira willingly. Ever.

Police headquarters is on one of the outer canals, west of the city. Fashioned by the imagination of an architect, it looks scrubbed clean and casts a long shadow across the canal. The glass doors open automatically. CCTV cameras scan the foyer.

A message is sent upstairs to Spijker. His reply comes back: I'm to wait in the reception area. None of my urgency has any effect on the receptionist, who has a face like that of the farmer's daughter in *American Gothic*. This is not my jurisdiction. I have no authority to make demands or throw my weight around.

Hokke offers to keep me company. At no point has he asked how I found Samira or what happened to Ruiz. He is content to accept whatever information is offered rather than seeking it out.

So much has happened in the past week yet I feel as though I haven't moved. It's like the clock on the wall above the reception desk, with its white face and thick black hands that refuse to move any faster.

Samira is somewhere above me. I don't imagine there are many basements in Amsterdam – a city that seems to float on fixed pontoons held together by bridges.

Perhaps it is slowly sinking into the ooze like a Venice of the north.

I can't sit still. I should be at the hospital with Ruiz. I should be starting my new job in London – or resigning from it.

Across the foyer the double doors of a lift slide open. There are voices, deep, sonorous, laughing. One of them belongs to Yanus. His left eye is swollen and partially closed. Head injuries are becoming a fashion statement. He isn't handcuffed, nor is he being escorted by police.

The man beside him must be his lawyer. Large and care-worn, with a broad forehead and broader arse, his rumpled suit has triple vents and permanent creases.

Yanus looks up at me and smiles with his thin lips.

'I am very sorry for this misunderstanding,' he says. 'No hard feelings.'

He offers me his hand. I stare at it blankly. Spijker appears at his left shoulder, standing fractionally behind him.

Yanus is still talking. 'I hope Mr Ruiz is being looked after. I am very sorry I stabbed him.'

My eyes search for an explanation from Spijker.

'Mr Yanus is being released,' he explains. 'We may need to question him again later.'

The fat lawyer is tapping his foot on the floor impatiently. It has the effect of making his face wobble. 'Samira Khan has confirmed that Mr Yanus is her fiancé. She is pregnant by him.' His tone is extravagantly pompous, with just a hint of condescension. 'She has also given a statement corroborating his account of what happened last night.'

'No!'

'Fortunately for you, Mr Yanus has agreed not to make a formal complaint against you or your colleague for assault, malicious wounding and abducting his fiancée. In return, the police have decided not to lay charges against him.'

'Our investigations are continuing,' counters Spijker.

'Mr Yanus has cooperated fully,' retorts the fat lawyer, dismissively.

Lena Caspar is so small that I almost don't see her behind him. I can sense my gaze flicking from face to face like a child waiting for a grown-up to explain. Yanus has withdrawn his hand. Almost instinctively he slides it inside his jacket, where his knife would normally be.

I imagine that I must look dazed and dumbstruck, but the opposite is true. I can see myself reflected in the dozens of glass panels around the walls and the news hasn't altered my demeanour at all. Internally, the story is different. Of all the possible outcomes, this one couldn't be anticipated.

'Let me talk to Samira.'

'That's not possible.'

Lena Caspar puts her hand on my arm. 'She doesn't want to talk to anyone.'

'Where is she?'

'In the care of the Immigration and Naturalisation Service.'

'Is she going to be deported?'

The fat lawyer answers for her. 'My client is applying for a visa that will allow his fiancée to remain in the Netherlands.'

'She's *not* his fiancée!' I snap.

The lawyer inflates even further (it barely seems possible): 'You are very fortunate, Miss Barba, that my client is so willing to forgive. You would otherwise be facing very serious charges. Mr Yanus now demands that you leave him alone, along with his fiancée. Any attempt by you to approach either of them will be taken very seriously.'

Yanus looks almost embarrassed by his own generosity. His entire persona has softened. The cold, naked, unflinching hatred of last night has gone. It's like a watching a smooth ocean after a storm front has passed. He extends his hand again. There is something in it this time – my mobile phone and passport. He hands them to me and turns away. He and the fat lawyer are leaving.

I look at Spijker. 'You know he's lying.'

'It makes no difference,' he replies.

Mrs Caspar wants me to sit down.

'There must be something,' I say, pleading with her.

'You have to understand. Without Samira's testimony there is no case to answer, no evidence of forced pregnancies or a black market in embryos and unborn babies. The proof might lie in DNA or paternity tests, but these can't be done without Samira's permission and invasive surgery that could endanger the twins.'

'Zala will confirm my story.'

'Where is she?'

The entrance doors slide open. The fat lawyer goes first. Yanus pulls a light blue handkerchief from his pocket and wipes his forehead. I recognise the fabric. He rolls it over and over in his fingers. It's not a handkerchief. It's a head-scarf. Zala's hijab!

Spijker sees me moving and holds me back. I fight against his arms, yelling accusations out the door. Yanus turns and smiles, showing a few teeth at the sides of his mouth. A shark's smile.

267

'See! In his hand – the scarf!' I cry. 'That's why she lied.'

Mrs Caspar steps in front of me. 'It's too late, Alisha.'

Spijker releases my arms slowly and I shake his fingers loose. He's embarrassed at having touched me. There's something else in his demeanour. Understanding. He *believes* me! He had no choice but to release Yanus.

Frustration, disappointment and anger fill me until I feel like screaming. They have Zala. Samira is sure to follow. For all the bruises and bloodshed, I haven't even slowed them down. I'm like Wile E. Coyote, flattened beneath a rock, listening to the Road Runner's infernal, triumphant, infuriating 'beep, beep!'

6

Ruiz's skin is a pallid grey and his eyes are bloodshot from the morphine. The years have mugged him in his sleep and he looks every one of his sixty years.

'I knew you were gonna be OK,' I say. 'Your hide is thicker than a rhino's.'

'Are you saying my arse looks big in these pyjamas?'

'Not in *those* pyjamas.'

The curtains are open and the remains of the day are collecting on the far horizon.

It might be the morphine or his ridiculous male pride, but the DI keeps bragging about the number of stitches he needed in his chest and arm. Next we'll be comparing scars. I don't need a comparison – mine are bigger than his.

Why is it always a competition with men? Their egos are so fragile or their hormones so strong that they have to prove themselves. What tossers!

I give him a big wet kiss on his cheek. He's lost for words.

'I brought you something, sir.'

He gives me a quick look, unsure whether to trust me. I pull a bottle of Scotch from a paper bag. It's a private joke. When I was lying in hospital with a busted spine Ruiz brought me a bottle. It's still the only time I've ever had alcohol. A one-off drink, sucked through a crazy straw, that made my eyes water and my throat burn. What do people see in alcohol?

I crack the seal and pour him a drink, adding a little water.

'You're not having one?'

'Not this time. You can have mine.'

'That's very generous of you.'

A nurse walks in. The DI hides the glass. I hide the bottle. She hands him a little plastic cup with two pills in it. The fact that we've stopped talking and look guilty encourages her to pause at the door. She says something in Dutch. It might be 'Bottoms up', but I doubt it.

'I think I'm going to stay here,' says Ruiz. 'The food is much better than the NHS muck and the nurses have a certain charm. They remind me of my house mistresses at boarding school.'

'That sounds disturbingly like a sexual fantasy.'

He half grins. 'Not completely.'

He takes another sip. 'Have you ever thought about what you'd like to happen when you die? The arrangements.'

'I've made a will.'

'Yeah, but did you stipulate anything for the funeral? Cremation or burial or having your ashes sprinkled off the end of Margate Pier?'

'Not specifically.' This is getting rather morbid.

'I want my ashes put into a rocket.'

'Sure, I'll put in a call to NASA.'

'In a *firework* rocket. I want to be blasted into a thousand falling stars. They can do that now – put ashes in fireworks. I read about it somewhere.'

'Go out with a bang.'

'A blaze of glory.'

He smiles and holds out his glass for more. 'Not yet, of course.'

'Of course.'

The truth is, I *have* thought about it. Dying. During the autumn and winter of my discontent – the months of surgery and physiotherapy, when I couldn't wash, feed or care for myself – a small, secret, childlike part of me feared that I would never walk again. And an unspoken, guilt-ridden, adult part of me decided I would rather die if that happened.

Everyone thinks I'm so strong. They expect me to face autumns and winters like that and bitch-slap them down; make them come to heel. I'm not so strong. I only pretend.

'I had a phone call from Miranda today,' the DI announces. 'I still don't know how she got the number or knew I was in hospital. As far as I can tell I was unconscious for most of yesterday.' His eyes narrow. 'Try not to look so sheepish, my little lambkin.'

'I told you she still cares about you.'

'But can't *live* with me.'

'That's because you're grumpy.'

'And you're an expert in these things, I suppose.'

'Well, "New Boy" Dave has asked me to marry him.' The statement blurts from me, unplanned, spontaneous.

Ruiz ponders it. 'I didn't think he had the courage.'

'You think he's afraid of me?'

'Any man with any sense should be a little bit afraid of you.'

'Why?'

'I mean that in the nicest possible way.' His eyes are dancing.

'You said I was too sharp for him.'

'And you said that any man who could *fit* into your pants couldn't *get* into your pants.'

'He loves me.'

'That's a good start. How about you?'

I can't answer. I don't know.

It's strange, talking about love. I used to hate the word. Hate is too strong. I was sick of reading about it in books, hearing it in songs, watching it in films. It seemed such a huge burden to place on another person – to love them; to give them something so unbelievably fragile and expect them not to break it or lose it or leave it behind on the No. 96 bus.

I thought I had a choice. Fall in love. Don't fall in love. He loves me. He loves me not. See, I'm not so smart!

My mind drifts back to Samira. I don't know what to do. I'm out of ideas. Up until now I've been convinced that I would find Cate's babies and then – what then? What did I imagine would happen? Cate broke the law. She rented a womb. Perhaps she didn't realise that Samira would be forced to cooperate. I can give her the benefit of *that* doubt.

Cate always walked close to the edge. Closer to death, closer to life. She had a crazy streak. Not all the time, just occasionally. It's like when the wind changes suddenly before a storm and kids go wild, running around in circles like swirling scraps of paper caught in the updraught. Cate would get that same gleam in her eye and drift onto the wrong side of crazy.

She is more memory than reality. She belongs to a time of teenage crushes, first kisses, crowded lecture halls and smoky pubs. Even if she had lived, we might have had nothing in common except the past.

I should let it go. When Ruiz is well enough I'll take him home. I'll swallow my pride and take whatever job I'm offered or I'll marry Dave and we'll live in Milford-on-Sea. I shouldn't have come to Amsterdam. Why did I ever imagine I could make a difference? I can't bring Cate back. Yet for all this, I still can't shake one fundamental question: what will happen to the babies?

Yanus and his cronies will sell them to the highest bidder. Either that or they'll be born in the Netherlands and put up for adoption. Worse still, they'll be sent back to Kabul along with Samira, who will be ostracised and treated as an outcast. In some parts of Afghanistan they still stone women for having children out of wedlock.

Cate lied and deceived. She broke the law. I still don't know why Brendan Pearl killed her, although I suspect it was to stop her talking. She came to me. I guess that makes me partially responsible.

Am I guilty of anything else? Is there something else I should have done? Perhaps I should tell Felix's family that their son would have become a father in a few weeks. Barnaby and Mrs Elliot are pseudo-grandparents to surrogate twins.

I didn't imagine ever feeling sorry for Barnaby – not

after what happened. I thought I saw his true nature on the day he dropped me at the railway station in Cornwall. He couldn't even look at me or say the word goodbye.

I still don't know if he told his wife. I doubt it. Barnaby is the type to deny, deny and deny, until faced with incontrovertible proof. Then he will shrug, apologise and play the tragic hero, brought down by loving too much rather than too little.

When I first saw him at the hospital, when Cate was in a coma, it struck me how he was still campaigning, still trying to win votes. He caught glimpses of his reflection in the glass doors, making sure he was doing it right, the grieving. Maybe that's unfair – kicking a man when he's down.

Ruiz is asleep. I take the glass from his hand and rinse it in the sink. Then I tuck the bottle into my bag.

I'm still no closer to knowing what to do. It's like running a race where I cannot tell how many laps there are to go or who's winning or who's been lapped. How do I know when to kick on the final bend and start sprinting for home?

A taxi drops me at the hotel. The driver is listening to a football game being broadcast on the radio. The commentator has a tenor voice that surges with the ebb and flow of the action. I have no idea who is playing but I like the thunderous sound of the crowd. It makes me feel less melancholy.

There is a white envelope poking out of my pigeon-hole at the reception desk. I open it immediately.

Three words: 'Hello, sweet girl.'

The desk clerk shifts her gaze. I turn. 'New Boy' Dave is standing behind mc.

His arms wrap around me and I bury my face in his shirt. I stay there. Holding him tightly. I don't want him to see my tears.

7

One second I'm sleeping and the next I'm awake. I look at the clock. Four a.m. Dave is lying next to me on his side with his cheek pressed flat against the sheet and his lips vibrating gently.

Last night we didn't talk. Exhaustion and a hot shower and the touch of his hands put me to sleep. I'll make it up to him when he wakes. I'm sure it doesn't do much for the male ego, having a woman fall asleep on them.

Propped on one elbow, I study him. His hair is soft and rumpled like a tabby cat, with tiny flecks of blond amid the ginger. He has a big head. Does that mean he would father big babies, with big heads? Unconsciously I squeeze my thighs together.

Dave scratches his ear. He has nice ears. The one I can see bears the faintest hint that at one time it might have been pierced. His hand is stretched towards me on the sheet.

The nails are wide and flat, trimmed straight across. I touch his fingers with mine, awkward at being so happy.

Yesterday was perhaps the worst day of my life and I held him last night like a shipwrecked sailor clinging to the debris. He made me feel safe. He wrapped his arms around me and the pain leaked away.

Maybe that's why I feel this way; lying so still – not wanting this moment to end.

I have no experience of love. Ever since adolescence I have avoided it, renounced it, longed for it. (Such a dichotomy is one of the symptoms.) I have been an agony aunt for all my girlfriends, listening to their sob stories about arranged marriages, unfaithful husbands, men who won't call or commit, missed periods, sexual neuroses, wedding plans, post-natal depression and failed diets. I know all about other people's love affairs but I am a complete novice when it comes to my own. That's why I'm scared. I'm sure to mess it up.

Dave touches my bruised cheek. I flinch. 'Who did that?' he asks.

'His name is Yanus.'

I can almost see him storing this information away for future reference. He and Ruiz are similar in that way. There is nothing half-cocked or hot-headed about them. They can wait for their shot at revenge.

'You were lucky he didn't break your cheekbone.'

'He could have done a lot worse.'

I step closer and kiss him on the lips, quickly, impulsively. Then I turn and go to shower. Spinning back to say something, I catch him punching the air in victory.

He blushes.

'It wasn't *that* good a kiss.'

'It was to me.'

Later, he sits on the bed and watches me dress, which makes me feel self-conscious. I keep my back to him. He reaches across and cups my breasts before my bra embraces them.

'I volunteer for this job,' he says.

'That's very noble, but you're not holding my breasts all day.'

I gently push his hands away and continue dressing.

'You really like me, don't you?' he says. His big goofy grin is reflected in the wardrobe mirror.

'Don't push it,' I warn him.

'But you do. You *really* like me.'

'That *could* change.'

His laugh isn't entirely convincing.

We breakfast at a café on Paleisstraat near Dam Square. Blue and white trams clatter and fizz past the window beneath humming wires. A weak sun is barely breaking through the clouds and a wind tugs at the clothes of pedestrians and cyclists.

The café has a zinc-topped counter running the length of one side. Arranged above it is a blackboard menu and barrels of wine or port. The place smells of coffee and grilled cheese. My appetite is coming back. We order sliced meats, bread and cheese, coffee with frothed milk.

I take Dave through everything that's happened. Occasionally he interrupts with a question but mostly he eats and listens. This whole affair is laced with half-truths

278

and concocted fictions. The uncertainties and ambiguities seem to outweigh the facts and they nag at me, making me fretful and uncomfortable.

I borrow his notebook and write down names.

Brendan Pearl
Yanus
Paul Donavon
Julian Shawcroft

On the opposite side of the page I write another list: the victims.

Cate and Felix Beaumont.
Hasan Khan
Samira Khan

There are likely to be others. Where do I list those who fall in-between, people like Barnaby Elliot? I still think he lied to me about Cate's computer. And Dr Banerjee, her fertility specialist. It was more than a coincidence that he turned up at my father's birthday party.

I'm not sure what I hope to achieve by writing things down. Perhaps it will give me a fresh slant on events or throw up a new link. I have been searching for a central figure behind events but maybe that's too simplistic a notion. People could all be linked like spokes of a wheel that only touch in the centre.

There is another issue. Where was the baby handover going to occur? Perhaps Cate planned to take a holiday or a weekend break to the Netherlands. She would go into 'labour'; tell everyone she had given birth and then bring the baby home to live happily ever after.

Even a newborn baby needs travel documents. A passport. Which means a birth certificate, statutory declarations and signed photographs. I should call the British Consulate in The Hague and ask how British nationals register a foreign birth.

In a case like this it would be much easier if the baby were born in the same country as the prospective parents. It could be a home birth or in a private house, without involving a hospital or even a midwife.

Once the genetic parents took possession of the baby nobody could ever prove it didn't belong to them. Blood samples, DNA and paternity tests would all confirm their ownership.

Samira said Hasan was going to the UK ahead of her. She expected to follow him. What if that's where they planned to take her? It would also explain why Cate gave Samira my name in case something went wrong.

'Last night you said you were giving up and going home,' says Dave.

'I know. I just thought . . .'

'You said yourself that these babies belong to Samira. They always have.'

'Someone killed my friend.'

'You can't bring her back.'

'They torched her house.'

'It's not your case.'

I feel a surge of anger. Does he really expect me to leave this to Softell and his imbecile mates? And Spijker doesn't fill me with confidence after letting Yanus go.

'Last night you were crying your eyes out. You said it was over.'

'That was last night.' I can't hide the anger in my voice.

'What's changed?'

'My mind. It's a woman's prerogative.'

I want to say, *Don't be a fucking jerk, Dave, and stop quoting me back to myself.*

What is it about men? Just when you think they're rational members of the human race they go all Neanderthal and protective. Next he'll be asking me how many partners I've had and if the sex was any good.

We're drawing stares from other patrons. 'I don't think we should talk about it here,' he whispers.

'We're not going to talk about it at all.' I get up to leave.

'Where are you going?'

I want to tell him it's none of his damn business. Instead I say that I have an appointment with Samira's lawyer, which isn't entirely true.

'I'll come with you.'

'No. You go and see Ruiz. He'll appreciate that.' My voice softens. 'We'll meet up later.'

Dave looks miserable but doesn't argue. Give him his due – he's a quick learner.

Lena Caspar's waiting room is being vacuumed and tidied. Magazines sit neatly stacked on a table and the toys have been collected in a polished wooden crate. Her desk is similarly neat and empty except for a box of tissues and a jug of water on a tray. Even the waste-paper basket is clean.

The lawyer is dressed in a knee-length skirt and a matching jacket. Like many women of a certain age, her make-up is applied perfectly.

'I cannot tell you where Samira is,' she announces.

'I know. But you can tell me what happened yesterday.'

She points to a chair. 'What do you want to know?'

'Everything.'

The lawyer places her palms flat on the desk. 'I knew something was wrong when I saw the interpreter. Samira's English is perfect, yet she pretended not to understand what I said to her. Everything had to be translated back and forth. Samira volunteered no information without being prompted.'

'Did Yanus spend any time alone with her?'

'Of course not.'

'Did she see him?'

'Yanus took part in a line-up. She picked him out through a two-way mirror.'

'He couldn't see Samira?'

'No.'

'Did Yanus have anything in his hands?'

She sighs, irritated at my pedantry.

I press her. 'Did he have something in his hands?'

She is about to say no but remembers something. 'He had a blue handkerchief. He was pushing it into his fist like a magician preparing a conjuring trick.'

How did he find Zala? Nobody knew she was at the convent except the nuns. Sister Vogel wouldn't have given her up. De Walletjes is a small place. What did the lawyer once say to me? 'The walls have mice and the mice have ears.'

Mrs Caspar listens patiently while I explain what I think happened. Zala is not her concern. She has four hundred asylum seekers on her books.

'What will happen to Samira now?' I ask.

'She will be sent back to Afghanistan, which is I think a better option than marrying Yanus.'

'He is not going to marry her.'

'No.'

'He is going to find her and take her babies.'

She shrugs. How can she blithely accept such an outcome? Leaning on the windowsill, she looks down at the courtyard where pigeons peck at the base of a lone tree.

'Some people are born to suffer,' she says pensively. 'It never stops for them, not for a second. Look at the Palestinians. The same is true of Afghanis and Sudanese, Ethiopians and Bangladeshis. War, famine, droughts, flood, the suffering never stops. They are made for it – sustained by it.

'We in the West like to think it can be different; that we can change these countries and these people because it makes us feel better when we tuck our own children into their warm beds with full stomachs and then pour ourselves a glass of wine and watch someone else's tragedy unfold on CNN.' She stares down at her hands as if she despises them. 'Unless we truly understand what it's like to walk in their shoes, we should not judge people like Samira. She is only trying to save what she has left.'

Something else trembles in her voice. Resignation. Acceptance. Why is she so ready to give up? In that split second I realise there is something that she's not telling me. Either she can't bring herself to do it or Spijker has warned her off. With her innate sense of honesty and justice, she will not lie to me directly.

'What happened to Samira?'

'She went missing last night from the migrant centre at Schiphol Airport.'

8

There is a scientific theory called the 'uncertainty principle' that states it is impossible to truly observe something without altering it. I have done more than observe. By finding Samira I have changed the course of events.

During the taxi journey to police headquarters my fists are clenched and my fingernails dig into the soft flesh. I want to scream. I warned Spijker this would happen. I said Samira would run or Yanus would find her.

I don't expect him to see me. He will hide behind his workload or make excuses that I've wasted enough of his time already. Again I wait in the foyer. This time the summons comes. Perhaps he has a conscience after all.

The corridors are lined in light grey carpet and dotted with palms. It feels more like a merchant bank than a police station.

Spijker is jacketless. His sleeves are rolled up. The hair

on his forearms is the colour of his freckles. The door closes. His jacket swings from a hanger behind it.

'How long are you intending to remain in Amsterdam?' he asks.

'Why, sir?'

'You have already stayed longer than is usual. Most visitors are here for a day or two.'

'Are you advising me to leave?'

'I have no authority to do that.' He spins on his chair, gazing out the window. His office looks east across the theatre district to the neo-Gothic spires of the Rijksmuseum. Lined on the windowsill are tiny cacti in painted clay pots. This is his garden – fleshy, bulbous and spiky.

I had a speech prepared during my taxi ride, when I vented my spleen and caused the taxi driver a few anxious moments, peering into the rear-view mirror. Now all my best lines seem pointless and wasted. I wait for the detective to speak.

'I know what you think, DC Barba. You think I have dropped the ball on this. That is a rugby term, yes? A British game, not a Dutch one. In the Netherlands we do not *pick up* the ball. Only a goalkeeper can do this.'

'You should have protected her.'

'She *chose* to escape.'

'She's eight months pregnant and eighteen years old. You couldn't hold her for twenty-four hours?'

'Did you want me to handcuff her?'

'You could have stopped her.'

'I am trying to keep this investigation low-key. I don't want it reaching the media. Black-market babies make dramatic headlines.'

'So it was a political decision?'

'There is no politics in the Dutch police.'

'No?'

'No one has talked politics to me.'

Despite his turned-down mouth and sad eyes, Spijker comes across as an optimist, a man who has faith in the human condition.

'I have twenty years' service. I know how to make a case. I am like the little pig that builds his house out of bricks. You are like the little pig who builds her house from straw. Do you remember what happens to such a house?' He puffs out his cheeks and blows. A flake of cigarette ash swirls from his desk into my lap.

Sporting metaphors and fairy-tale metaphors – what next? Spijker opens the top drawer of his desk, withdrawing a file.

'There is a fertility clinic in Amersfoort. It has a very good reputation and has helped thousands of couples to begin a family. Occasionally, when IVF has been unsuccessful, the clinic has agreed to implant embryos into the uterus of a surrogate mother. This is called gestational surrogacy. In 2002 there were only four such procedures and fifteen hundred normal IVF implantations. In 2003 and 2004 there were two in total.' He glances at the file. 'In the past year there have been twenty-two.'

'Twenty-two! That's an increase of more than tenfold.'

'Gestational surrogacy is legal in the Netherlands. Commercial surrogacy is not. Nor is blackmail or bonded slavery.

'Directors of the clinic and staff insist they are unaware of any wrongdoing. They also insist that the surrogate

286

mothers were properly screened. They were examined physically, financially and psychologically.

'On 26 January this year Samira Khan underwent this examination. She was asked questions about her menstrual cycle and was given pills and injections – oestrogen and progesterone – to prepare her uterus for the implantation.

'On 10 February she returned to the clinic. The embryo transfer took less than fifteen minutes. A soft tube was inserted through her vagina to a predetermined position. A small inner catheter was then loaded with two embryos and these were injected into the uterus. Samira Khan was told to lie still for thirty minutes and then discharged. She was taken to the car park in a wheelchair and driven away by Yanus. Her pregnancy was confirmed two weeks later. Twins.'

Spijker finally looks up at me. 'But you know this already.'

There are other papers in his file.

'Do you have the names of the intended parents?'

'Legal contracts are required between couples and the surrogate mothers. The clinic does not draw up these contracts, but requires a written statement from a lawyer confirming they exist.'

'Have you seen the contracts?'

'Yes.'

For a moment I think he's going to wait for me to ask, but he is not a cruel man.

'Each copy of the contract was signed by Samira Khan and countersigned by Cate Beaumont. Is this what you wish to know?'

'Yes.'

He returns the folder to the drawer and rises from his

seat, surveying the view from his window with a mixture of pride and protectiveness.

'Of the twenty-two procedures I mentioned, eighteen resulted in pregnancies. One of the failures involved a woman named Zala Haseeb. Doctors discovered that she was unable to fall pregnant because of earlier damage to her reproductive organs caused by blunt-force trauma.'

'She was tortured by the Taliban.'

He doesn't turn from the window but I know he hears me.

'Twelve of the surrogate mothers are past term but we have no confirmation of the births. Normally the clinic monitors every stage of the pregnancy and keeps a record of each outcome for statistical purposes. In this case, however, it lost track of the women.'

'Lost track of them!'

'We are in the process of finding them. The clinic has provided us with their names but the addresses appear to be fictitious.'

'I don't think you'll find any trace of the births in the Netherlands,' I say. 'I think the mothers were smuggled across borders or overseas to where the intended parents live. This meant the babies could be handed over immediately after they were born and registered without any questions.'

Spijker sees the logic of this. 'We are tracking the intended parents through financial transactions. There are receipts and statutory declarations.'

'Who drew up the contracts?'

'A legal firm here in Amsterdam.'

'Are they being investigated?'

Spijker pauses for a brief moment. 'You met the senior partner yesterday. He represents Mr Yanus.'

His gaze builds into a stare. For the first time I realise what a burden he carries. I have been chasing the truth about a single woman. He now has a case that touches dozens, perhaps hundreds of people's lives.

Spijker turns away from the window. After a long silence he speaks. 'Do you have children?'

'No, sir.'

'I have four of them.'

'Four!'

'Too many, not enough – I can't decide.' A smile flirts with his lips. 'I understand what it means to people: how they can want a child so badly that they will do almost anything.' He leans slightly forward, inclining his head to one side. 'Do you know the legend of Pandora's Box, DC Barba?'

'I've heard the term.'

'The box didn't belong to Pandora: it was built by the Greek god Zeus and it was crammed full of all the diseases, sufferings, vices and crimes that could possibly afflict humanity. I cannot imagine such a malignant brew. The god Zeus also created Pandora – a beautiful woman, inquisitive by nature. He knew that she wouldn't be able to resist peeking inside the mysterious box. She heard pitiful whispers coming from inside. So she raised the lid just a little. And all the ills of the world flew out, fastening upon the carefree and innocent, turning their cries of joy into wails of despair.'

Spijker's fingers open, showing me his palms. Empty. This is what he fears. An investigation like this risks tearing apart entire families. How many of these babies are in loving homes? Consider how lucky they are when so many children are abused and unwanted. The argument triggers a feeling of déjà vu. Julian Shawcroft had made a similar case when I visited him at the adoption centre.

I understand the concerns – but my best friend was murdered. Nothing anyone says to me will justify her death and their ominous warnings sound hollow when I picture Cate lying broken on the road.

The briefing is over. Spijker stands rather formally and escorts me downstairs.

'I spoke to a Chief Superintendent North of Scotland Yard yesterday evening. He informed me that you are absent without leave from the London Metropolitan Police. You are facing disciplinary proceedings for neglect of duty.'

There is nothing I can say.

'I also spoke to a Detective Inspector Forbes who is investigating the deaths of illegals on a ferry at Harwich. You are helping him with this investigation. There was also, I think, a Detective Sergeant Softell, who wishes to speak to you about a suspicious fire.'

Spijker could have used the term 'suspect' but is far too polite.

'These men have asked me to put you on the first available flight back to London, but, as I explained to them, I have no authority for this.' He pinches the bridge of his nose between his thumb and forefinger. 'I also assume that you do not wish to leave Amsterdam without your friend Mr Ruiz. I spoke to him this morning. He is recovering well.'

'Yes, sir.'

'He has great affection for you.'

'We have known each other a long time.'

'He believes that you will make a very fine investigator. He used a term I am not familiar with. He said you were "sharper than a pointy stick".'

That sounds like the DI.

'I understand why you are here and why you will stay a little longer, but now it is time for you to leave this investigation to me.'

'What about Samira?'

'I will find her.'

9

I don't normally notice people when I run. I shut out the world, floating over the ground like a vague impression. Today is different. I can hear people talking, arguing and laughing. There are muffled footsteps and car doors closing, the hum of traffic and machines.

'New Boy' Dave is at the hospital with Ruiz. That's where I'm heading, although the strangeness of the city makes it difficult to get my bearings. There are twin church steeples ahead of me. I turn again, running past flat-fronted shops that have barred windows or metal shutters. Some of the alleys and lanes are only wide enough for bicycles or pedestrians.

By the time I find the hospital it is almost dark. The corridors are quiet and rain streaks the windows. 'New Boy' Dave puts his jacket around my shoulders to stop me getting cold. Ruiz is asleep.

'How is he?'

'Bored shitless. Today he tried to organise a mass escape from the hospital to the nearest pub. He convinced two guys to join him – both amputees. He said they were legless already so it shouldn't matter.'

'How far did they get?'

'As far as the hospital gift shop. One of the nurses uncovered the escape plot and called security.'

'What did the DI say?'

'He said the Resistance would spring him tomorrow.'

Dave has been talking to the doctors. Ruiz should be able to leave hospital in a few days but he won't be able to fly for a month.

'We can take the ferry,' I suggest.

Dave is toying with my fingers, running his thumb across the palm. 'I was sort of hoping you might fly home with me tomorrow. I have an Old Bailey trial on Monday.'

'I can't leave the DI. We started this together.'

He understands. 'What are you going to do about the job?'

'I haven't decided.'

'You're supposed to have started.'

'I know.'

There's something else he wants to ask. His forehead creases, wrestling with the question.

'Have you thought about the other thing?' he asks. He's referring to the sailing school and the cottage by the sea. Marriage. The future. I'm still amazed that he plucked up the courage to ask me. The sense of expectation and dread must be killing him. Sometimes life is like the movies, with the audience barracking, 'Just ask her. Just ask her.'

'I thought you always wanted to be a detective,' I say.

'I wanted to be a fireman when I was six. I got over it.'

'I fell in love with Mr Sayer my piano teacher and wanted to be a concert pianist.'

'I didn't know you played.'

'It's still open to debate.'

He's waiting for my answer.

'So what happened, Dave? What made you decide to quit?'

He shrugs.

'Something must have triggered it.'

'You remember Jack Lonsdale?'

'I heard he got wounded.'

Dave stills his hands by putting them in his pockets. 'We were following up a tip-off about a bail jumper on the White City Estate. A drug dealer. It's a God-awful place at the best of times but this was Saturday night in mid-July. Hot. We found the place OK and knocked on the door. It was supposed to be a simple pick-up. I was putting handcuffs on the dealer when his fifteen-year-old kid came out of the kitchen and stuck a knife in Jack's chest. Right there.' He points to the spot. 'The kid was hanging off the blade, trying to scramble his guts, but I managed to pry him loose. His eyes were like saucers. He was higher than a 747. I tried to get Jack out to the car but there were two hundred people outside the flat, most of them West Indian, screaming abuse and throwing shit. I thought we were gonna die.'

'Why didn't you tell me?'

'You had your own shit to deal with.'

'How's Jack now?'

'They had to take out part of his bowel and he's taken

early retirement. The dealer finished up in Brixton. His kid went to a foster home. His mother was dead, I think.'

Dave lowers his eyes, unwilling to look at me. 'I know it makes me sound like a coward but I keep thinking how it could have been me spilling blood on that filthy floor – or worse, it could have been you.'

'It doesn't make you a coward. It makes you human.'

'Yeah, well, that's when I got to thinking about doing something else.'

'Maybe you just need a sea change.'

'Maybe.'

'Maybe you don't really want to marry me.'

'Yes, I do.'

'Would you still want to marry me if we didn't have children?'

'What do you mean?'

'I'm asking.'

'But you *want* children, right?'

'What if I couldn't have children?'

Dave straightens up. He doesn't understand.

I try to explain. 'Sometimes children just don't arrive. Look at Cate. She couldn't get pregnant and it twisted her up inside until she did something foolish. Don't you think if two people love each other that should be enough?'

'Yeah, I guess.'

He still doesn't get my point. There is nowhere else for me to go except the truth. Words tumble out and I'm surprised at how organised they sound. Almost perfect sentences.

'A woman's pelvis is meant to expand and tilt forward as a baby grows inside her. Mine can't do this. I have metal plates and rods holding my spine together. My pelvis cannot bend or twist. Pregnancy would put enormous strain on the discs and joints of my lower back. I risk being paralysed and nursing a baby from a wheelchair.'

He looks stunned. Desolate. It doesn't matter what he says now because I have glimpsed his soul. He wants to raise a child. And, for the first time in my life, I realise that I want one too. I *want* to be a mother.

In the hours that follow all possibilities are considered. On the taxi ride to the hotel, over dinner, afterwards in bed, Dave talks of second opinions, alternatives and operations. We use up so much air in the room that I can scarcely breathe. He hasn't answered my original question. The most important one. He hasn't said if it matters.

While on the subject of true confessions, I tell him about sleeping with Barnaby Elliot and falling out with Cate. There are moments when I see him flinch but he needs to hear this. I am not the person he imagines.

My mother says the truth is unimportant when it comes to love. An arranged marriage is all about the fictions that one family tells another. Perhaps she's right. Perhaps falling in love is about inventing a story and accepting the truth of it.

10

I wake in the early hours, with Dave's heart beating against my back and his arm around me. A part of me wants to stay like this, not moving, scarcely breathing. Another part wants to run down the hotel corridor, the stairs, along the street, out of the city, away!

Slipping out of bed and into the bathroom, I dress in jeans and a blouse and fill the pockets of my jacket with cash and my mobile. I bend to lace my boots, accepting the dull ache in my spine for what it is, a part of me now.

Daylight is leaking over the rooftops and the streets are beginning to stir. A machine with spinning brushes seems to be polishing the cobblestones with overnight rain. Most of the windows are closed in de Walletjes, with curtains drawn. Only the desperate and the lonely are on the streets at this hour.

I wonder if this is what it feels like to be a refugee – to be a stranger in a place, despairing and hopeful all at once. Waiting for what will come next. I have never lived like this.

Hokke is waiting for me at the café. He knows about Samira. 'A bird told me,' he says, raising his eyes. As if signalled, a pigeon flutters onto a branch above us.

The air inside the café is noisy with whistling steam and banging pots. Counter staff and waitresses acknowledge Hokke with waves, shouts and handshakes. He leaves me for a moment, threading his way between tables. The kitchen door is open. Bending low over sinks, scrubbing pans, are three young men who greet Hokke with respect. He ruffles their hair and shares a joke.

I glance around the café, which is almost empty except for a table of hippies who seem to be communicating in a code of clicks and clacks from their beaded hair. On her own, a young teenage girl nurses a hot drink. Waiflike and hollow-eyed, she is just the sort pimps prey upon with warm meals and promises.

Hokke has returned. He too notices the girl. Summoning a waitress, he quietly orders breakfast for the girl: thick toast, jam, cheese and ham. She accepts it warily, expecting there to be strings attached, and eats greedily.

His attention turns to me.

'I have to find Samira,' I tell him.

'Again.'

'Refugees have networks. You said so. You mentioned a name: de Souza. Could he help me?'

Hokke puts a finger to his lips. He leans closer, speaking out of the corner of his mouth like a prisoner under the eye of a warder. 'Please be very careful when you speak such a name.'

'Who is he?'

Hokke doesn't answer immediately. He pours coffee from a pot, tapping metal against glass. 'Despite what you have read, the Netherlands is defined more by what it forbids than by what it permits. We do not have slums. Graffiti is cleaned away quickly. Broken windows are repaired. Abandoned vehicles are towed. We expect our trains and trams to run on time. We queue. It doesn't change the people, of course, just the aesthetics.'

He gestures with a slight nod towards the kitchen. 'There are half a million illegal workers in the Netherlands – Iranians, Sudanese, Afghans, Bosnians, Kosovars, Iraqis. They work in restaurants, hotels, laundries and factories. Newspapers wouldn't be delivered without them, hotel sheets wouldn't be laundered, houses wouldn't be cleaned. People complain, but we cannot do without them.'

A pipe appears in his hand. He packs it slowly, pressing tobacco into the bowl with his thumb. A match flares and flickers as he sucks in a breath.

'Imagine a person who could control a workforce such as this. He would be more powerful than any trade union leader or politician.'

'Is there such a person?'

His voice drops to a whisper. 'His name is Eduardo de Souza. Nobody has more real power in this city than he does. He has an army of couriers, cleaners, drivers and spies. He can get you anything – a pistol, a fake passport, a kilo of the finest Afghani heroin. Drugs and prostitution are only a small part of it. He knows which politicians are

–299

sleeping with which girls and which illegals are looking after their children or cleaning their houses or tending their gardens. That is *real* power. Destiny-making.'

Hokke sits back, his soft blue eyes blinking through the smoke.

'You admire him.'

'He is a very interesting man.'

His answer strikes me as peculiar. It carries a hint that there are things he hasn't told me.

'How long have you known him?'

'Many years.'

'Is he a friend?'

'Friendship is something I find harder to understand as I get older.'

'Will he help me find Samira?'

'He could be behind it all.'

'Why do you say that?'

'Yanus once worked for him.'

He places his hands on the table and wearily pushes himself to his feet.

'I will get a message to him.'

His pipe slips into his jacket pocket. He won't let me pay for breakfast. The bill has been covered, he says, nodding towards the owner.

Outside it is raining again. The puddles are shiny and black as oil. Hokke offers me an umbrella. 'I will call you in a few hours. Give my regards to DI Ruiz. Tell him that old policemen never die. They just miss a beat.'

Barnaby answers his mobile quickly as if he's been expecting a call. It must also be raining in London. I hear car tyres swishing on a wet road and raindrops on his umbrella. I ask about the funerals. There is a long pause. I swap the phone between hands.

'Saturday at the West London Crematorium. They won't release the bodies until Wednesday.'

There is another silence. The knowledge of Samira and the twins expands in my chest. Lawyers and medical ethicists can debate all they want about who 'owns' the twins, but it doesn't change the fact that Cate provided the embryos. Barnaby should know.

'There's something I have to tell you.'

He grunts a response.

'I know why Cate faked her pregnancy. She arranged a surrogate. Her embryos were implanted in someone else's womb.'

Something shifts deep in his chest. A groan. 'I told you to leave my daughter's affairs alone.'

I don't expect this reaction. Surely he must be curious. Doesn't he want to know the outcome? Then it dawns on me that none of this is new. He knows already.

He lied about finding Cate's computer, which means he must have read her e-mails. If he knows, why hasn't he gone to the police?

'What are you doing, Barnaby?'

'I'm getting my grandchildren.'

He has no idea what he's dealing with. 'Listen to me, Barnaby. This isn't what you think. Cate broke the law.'

'What's done is done.'

'These men are killers. You can't negotiate with them. Look what happened to Cate.'

301

He isn't listening. Instead he charges ahead, trying to attach logic and fairness to what should happen next.

'Stop, Barnaby. This is crazy.'

'It's what Cate would have wanted.'

'No. You'll get yourself killed. Just tell me where you are. Let's sit down and talk.'

'Stay out of this. Don't interfere.'

The line goes dead. He won't answer again.

Before I can dial Spijker there is another call. DI Forbes's voice is hoarse with a cold and the clicking sound in his throat is muffled by phlegm. I can imagine one of his children bringing the infection home from school and spreading it through the house like a domestic plague.

'Having a nice holiday?'

'It's not a holiday.'

'You know the difference between you and me? I don't run away when things get tough. I'm a professional. I stick with the job. I got a wife and kids; responsibilities . . .' *And wandering hands.*

He sneezes and blows his nose. 'I'm still waiting for your fucking statement.'

'I'm coming home.'

'When?'

'By Friday.'

'Well, you can expect a warm welcome. A Chief Superintendent North has been on the phone. Says you didn't show up for work. He's not happy.'

'It's not important,' I say, trying to change the subject. I ask him about the two trucks that couldn't be accounted for on the ferry that carried Hasan and the other illegals.

One was stolen from a German freight yard three months ago, he says. It was resprayed and registered in Holland. According to the manifest it was carrying plumbing supplies from a warehouse in Amsterdam, but the pick-up address doesn't exist. The second truck was leased from an owner-driver five weeks ago. He thought it was doing a run from Spain to the Netherlands. The leasing documents and bank accounts are in false names.

This case is populated with people who seem to be ghosts, floating across borders with false papers. People like Brendan Pearl.

'I need a favour.'

He finds this amusing. 'I shouldn't even be talking to you.'

'We're on the same side.'

'Cellar-dwellers.'

'Running into form.'

'What do you want?'

'I need you to check the Customs and Immigration files for the past two years. Among the stowaways and illegals, were any of them pregnant?'

'Off the top of my head I can think of two in the past three months. They were hidden in the back of a container.'

'What happened to them?'

'I don't know.'

'Can you find out?'

'Yeah, sure. Along with a thousand other fucking things on my plate.'

I feel the heat in my cheeks.

'There's something else. Hasan Khan has a sister, Samira. She's pregnant. I think traffickers are going to try to move her into the UK.'

303

'When?'

'I don't know. You might want to give Customs a heads-up.'

'I'm not a free agent here.'

'It's only a phone call. If you don't want to do it, just say so.'

'How are they going to move her?'

'They'll probably stick to what they know.'

'We can't search every truck and container.'

I can hear him scratching a note on a pad. He asks me about Spijker and I give him the nuts and bolts of the surrogacy scam.

'I've never known anyone who attracts trouble like you do,' he says.

'You sound like my mother.'

'Do you take any notice of *her*?'

'Not much.'

The call ends and I close my eyes for a moment. When I open them again, I see a class of schoolchildren with their teacher. The girls are dressed like Madeline in navy-blue raincoats with yellow hats, and they are all holding hands as they wait for the traffic lights to change. Inexplicably, I feel a lump forming in my throat. I'll never have one of those.

A police car is parked outside the hotel. A uniformed officer waits in reception, standing almost to attention.

'New Boy' Dave hovers like a jealous suitor. 'Where have you been?'

'I had to see someone.'

He grips my hand tightly.

The officer introduces himself and holds out a police radio. I place it against my ear. Spijker's voice comes from far away. I can hear water. Seagulls. 'We've found someone.'

'Who is it?'

'I'm hoping you can tell me.'

Something soft and wet flips over in my stomach.

The officer takes back the radio to receive further instructions.

'I'll come with you,' says Dave.

'What about your flight?'

'There's still time.'

We sit in silence on the journey. Frustration is etched into his forehead. He wants to say something planned, thought-out, about last night, but it's not the right time.

I feel oddly ambivalent. Maybe that means I'm not ready to marry and I'm not really in love. The whole idea was one of those 'what-if' moments that doesn't survive the hangover or the harsh light of day.

The Dutch officer has a vocabulary of four English words and is unwilling or unable to explain where we're going. Meanwhile he navigates the narrow streets and bridges, taking us through an industrial area with docks and warehouses. We seem to pass the same grey squares of water several times before pulling up beside a weathered wooden pier. Police cars nose together as though drinking from the same trough.

Spijker is a head taller than the other detectives. He is wearing a dark suit and polished shoes and still seems miscast in life – as though he's playing dress-up in his father's clothes.

There is a wooden ramp that slopes into the water from the dock. Halfway down it is a Zodiac made of heavy rubberised canvas with a wooden bottom. Another is already waiting on the water with four men on board.

Spijker hands me a pair of rubber boots and a waterproof jacket to wear over my sweater. He finds similar clothes for Dave and then pulls on his own rubber boots.

The Zodiac launches in a fluid movement. Spijker holds out his hand and helps me step on board. The throttle engages and we pull away. The sky is like a solid grey sheet with no depth at all. A quarter-mile off I see the flat of a paddle, lifting and dipping as a canoeist follows the shore. Further out is a ferry, snub-nosed and puffing smudges of black smoke.

I try to orientate myself. Some six miles to the west is the North Sea. We seem to be following a western dock. The air smells sweet – of chocolate. Perhaps there is a factory nearby. Dave is beside me. I feel him when I rock sideways, brushing his left arm with my breast.

Spijker is comfortable steering a boat. Perhaps it rubs off, living below sea level, protected by dykes and flood barriers.

'How much do you know about the sea, DC Barba?'

What is there to know? It's cold, it's wet, it's salty . . .

'My father was a merchant seaman,' he explains without waiting for me to answer. 'He divorced my mother when I was seven but I used to spend holidays with him. He didn't go to sea any more and he wasn't the same man on shore. He seemed smaller.'

Dave hasn't said much since I introduced them to one another. But now he mentions the sailing school he wants to buy. Soon they're discussing skiffs and sail area. I can actually picture Dave in an Aran sweater, ducking beneath a boom. He seems suited to the outdoors, big spaces full of wind and sky and water.

Five hundred yards ahead of us is a container ship. The port of Amsterdam spent millions thinking they could match Rotterdam as a hub for international trade, explains Spijker. 'It is never going to be so.'

Passing the ship we come to a wooden pier rising twenty feet above the waterline, supported by pylons and beams. A floating platform is moored on the nearside.

Spijker disengages the throttle and the engine idles. He steadies the Zodiac and throws a rope around a rusting cleat on the platform, drawing us closer. At the same moment a spotlight is switched on and swings into the darker shadows beneath the pier, searching amid the weathered grey wood. A flash of white appears. A figure suspended above the water, gazing down at me. A noose is looped around her neck. Another rope around her waist disappears into the water: obviously weighted down.

The body swings slightly as if moved by an unseen hand and her outstretched toes seem to pirouette on the surface of the water.

'Is it the deaf girl?' asks Spijker.

Zala's eyes are open. Two crimson orbs. Blood vessels have burst in the whites and her pupils seem to have disappeared. She's dressed in the same skirt and pink jacket that I last saw her wearing. Salt in the air has stiffened the fabric.

The Zodiac is rising and sinking on the slight swell. Spijker steadies it and I step onto the platform. A metal ladder, bolted to a pylon, leads up to the pier. Seagulls watch from the navigation buoys and a nearby barge. The other Zodiac has arrived, carrying ropes and a stretcher cage.

Spijker climbs the ladder and I follow him. Dave is behind me. The planks of the pier are old and deeply furrowed, with gaps in between that are wide enough for me to see the top of Zala's head and her shoulders.

The rope around her neck is tied to a metal bollard normally used for mooring ships.

A police officer in climbing gear abseils over the side. He swings in a harness beside her body and we watch in silence as Zala is lashed into a stretcher cage. The rope around her waist is tied to a breeze-block. I can see the cement dust on her hands and the front of her jacket.

They made her jump. The certainty is like a vision. She held the breeze-block in her arms and they pushed her the final step. She dropped fifteen feet before the rope stopped her. The cement brick tore from her fingers and kept falling until the second rope, tied around her waist, pulled taut. My stomach shares the drop.

'A fisherman found her just before nine-thirty,' says Spijker. 'He reported it to the coastguard.' He swivels to a junior officer, seeking confirmation.

'What made you think . . . ?' I can't finish the question.

'She fitted the description.'

'How did she get out here?'

Spijker motions along the pier. 'It's fenced off. Warning signs. Of course, that only encourages people.'

'You're not thinking suicide?'

'Your deaf girl didn't carry that lump of concrete out here by herself.'

In the distance there are whitecaps where the water is less sheltered from the wind. A fishing boat is coming in, its windows flashing in a rare shaft of sunlight.

Despite his veteran's cynicism, Spijker needs to show compassion and offer condolences. Somehow I have become his only link to this girl.

'She came from Kabul. She was an orphan,' I explain.

'Another one.'

'What do you mean?'

'The list of surrogates from the IVF clinic. At least ten of them were orphans. It's making them difficult to find.'

Orphans. Illegal immigrants. What a perfect combination of the unwanted and the desperate.

'Samira mentioned a visitor to the orphanage. A westerner who said he could organise a job for her. He had a cross on his neck. I might know who it is.' I give him Donavon's name and he promises to check the files.

The dock gates have been unlocked at the far end of the pier. A forensic team arrives in a van. A second car is summoned to take us back to our hotel.

As I walk along the pier I feel that Amsterdam has changed and become darker and more dangerous. I long for the familiar. Home.

Dave falls into step beside me.

'Are you all right?'

'Fine.'

'It's not your fault.'

'What do you know about it?' I snap. Straight away, I feel angry with myself. He's done nothing wrong. After a few minutes I try to assuage my guilt. 'Thanks for being here. I'm sorry about last night. Forget everything I said.'

'I think we should talk about it some more.'

'There's nothing to talk about.'

'I love you.'

'But it's different now, isn't it?'

Dave puts his hand on my forearm to stop me. 'I don't care. I want to be with you.'

'You say that now, but think about in five years or ten years. I couldn't do that to you.'

An abandoned crane is rusting on the shoreline. It looks like wreckage from an ancient war. Zala's body is still spinning in my mind, pirouetting on her toes in the waves.

I have been a fool. My good intentions have set off a chain of events that have led to this. And I don't know where it ends or who else will be hurt. I am certain of only one thing. I want to spend every waking moment hunting down the people who took Cate from me and who did this to Zala. This is not about an eye for an eye. It's bigger than that. I want to make their misery more poignant and horrific than anything they have inflicted upon others. Never in my life have I felt so capable of killing someone.

Dave's hair is combed. His bag is packed. A taxi is booked for the airport. The clock hasn't moved. Not even a second. I swear it. I hate the last hour before someone leaves. Everything has been said and done. Minutes drag out. Statements are repeated. Tickets are checked.

'It's time to leave this alone,' he says, rinsing his toothbrush. 'It's over.'

'How did we get to "over"?'

'Maybe you think,' he says, choosing his words with care, 'that this is about you and me. It's not. I'd tell you the same thing if I didn't love you.'

'But that's why you *should* understand.'

He picks up his bag and puts it down again.

'You could come with me.'

'I'm not leaving Ruiz.'

He puts on his jacket.

'You could stay,' I suggest.

'I have to give evidence in court.'

'I need you.'

'You don't *need* anyone.'

It's not meant to wound but I flinch as though struck.

He opens the door slowly. All the while I'm hoping that he'll turn back, take me in his arms, force me to look in his eyes, tell me he doesn't care about anything except me, that he understands.

The door closes behind him. My chest is suddenly empty. He's taken my heart.

11

For twenty minutes I stare at the door, wishing it would open, hoping that Dave will come back.

When I was lying in hospital with my damaged spine, fearing I would never walk again, I started to say cruel things to people. I criticised nurses and complained about the food. I called one male orderly Fat Albert after the Bill Cosby character.

'New Boy' Dave came to visit me every day. I remember screaming at him and calling him a moron. He didn't deserve it. I felt sorry for myself because everybody else felt sorry for me. And being cruel to people took my mind off myself for a while.

Dave didn't come to see me after that. I wanted to call him. I wanted to say that I was sorry for being mad and could he please come back. I didn't. Instead I wrote him a letter. What a gutless wonder! I don't deserve him.

My mobile rattles on the table.

'You didn't come to lunch today.'

'I'm still overseas, Mama.'

'Your Auntie Meena made kulfi. It's your favourite.'

It was my favourite at age six.

'All the boys came. Even Hari.'

Typical. He doesn't show up unless he can show me up.

'Your friend Detective King phoned to say that he couldn't make it.'

'I know, Mama.'

'But another very eligible gentleman was here. He was disappointed not to see you.'

'Whose arm did you twist this time?'

'Dr Banerjee seems to be very fond of you.'

It cannot be a coincidence. 'What did he want?'

'He brought you flowers – such a thoughtful man. And his table manners are impeccable.'

If we get married I'll have clean tablecloths.

'Where did you tell him I was?'

'I said you were in Amsterdam. You're being very secretive about this. You know I don't like secrets.'

She carries on describing the good doctor and a funny story that he told her about his baby nephew. I don't hear the punchline. I'm too busy trying to connect him to Samira.

Banerjee collected twelve viable embryos from Cate. Instead of six cycles of IVF, there were only five, which meant that two embryos remained, frozen and stored in liquid nitrogen. He gave them to Cate, which means he knew about her surrogacy plan. That's why he arranged an invitation to my father's birthday party. He tried to warn me off.

'I have to go, Mama.'

'When will you be home?'

'Soon.'

I hang up and call 'New Boy' Dave, who is just boarding his flight.

'Does this mean you miss me?'

'It's a given. I need a favour.'

He sighs. 'Just the one?'

'When you get back to London, run a ruler over Dr Sohan Banerjee.'

'He was at your father's party.'

'That's him.'

'What do you want to know?'

'Does he have any links with fertility clinics outside the UK? Also, check if he has any links with adoption agencies or children's charities.'

'I'll see what I can do.'

A stewardess is telling him to turn off his phone.

'Safe journey.'

'You too.'

Forbes's cold is getting worse and he's developed a seal-like cough punctuated by the clicking in his throat. He sounds like a beat box.

'You should have stayed home,' I suggest.

'My house is full of sick people.'

'So you decided to infect the rest of the population.'

'That's me. Patient Zero.'

'Did you find them – the pregnant asylum seekers?'

'I should have locked you up when I had the chance.' He blows his nose. 'They arrived in early July, hidden in a shipping container. A Russian, aged eighteen, and an Albanian, twenty-one. Both looked ready to pop any time. They were fingerprinted, issued with identification papers and taken to a reception centre in Oxfordshire. Three days later they were taken to bed-and-breakfast accommodation in Liverpool. They had two weeks to fill out a Statement of Evidence form and meet with a lawyer but neither of them showed up. They haven't been seen since.'

'What about the babies?'

'There's no record of the births at any NHS hospital but that doesn't prove anything. A lot of people have them at home these days – even in the bath. Thank Christ our tub wasn't big enough.'

I have a sudden mental image of his wife, whale-like in the family bath tub.

'It still doesn't make much sense,' he says. 'One of the main attractions of the UK for asylum seekers is free health care. These women could have had their babies in an NHS hospital. The government also provides a one-off grant of three hundred pounds for a newborn baby, as well as extra cash for milk and nappies. This is on top of the normal food vouchers and income support. These women claimed to have no family or friends in the UK who could support them, yet they didn't take advantage of the welfare benefits on offer. Makes you wonder how they survived.'

'Or *if* they did.'

He doesn't want to go there.

Ruiz is waiting for me downstairs at the Academisch Medisch Centrum. He looks like a kid being picked up from summer camp, but without the peeling nose or nettle stings.

'The staff wished me a long and healthy life,' he says. 'They also told me never to get sick in the Netherlands again.'

'Touching.'

'I thought so. I'm a medical bloody miracle.' He holds up the stump of his missing finger and begins counting. 'I've been shot, almost drowned and now stabbed. What's left?'

'They could blow you up, sir.'

'Been tried. Brendan Pearl and his IRA chummies fired a mortar into a Belfast police station. Missed me by that much.' He does his Maxwell Smart impersonation.

He pauses at the revolving door. 'Have you been crying, grasshopper?'

'No, sir.'

'I thought you might have been pining.'

'Not pining, sir.'

'Women are allowed to be warm and fuzzy.'

'You make me sound like a stuffed animal.'

'With very sharp teeth.'

He's in a good mood. Maybe it's the morphine. It doesn't last long. I tell him about Zala and can see the tension rise to his shoulders and move to his neck. His eyes close and he takes a ragged breath as though the pain has suddenly returned.

'They're going to smuggle Samira into Britain,' I say.

'You can't be certain of that.'

'It happened to the others. The babies are delivered in the same country as the parents live.'

'The Beaumonts are dead.'

'They'll find other buyers.'

'Who are *they*?'

'Yanus. Pearl. Others.'

'What does Spijker say?'

'He says I should go home.'

'A wise man.'

'Hokke says there is someone who might help us find Samira.'

'Who is he?'

'Eduardo de Souza. Yanus used to work for him.'

'This gets better and better.'

My mobile is ringing. Hokke is somewhere noisy. The red-light district. He spends more time there now than when he was walking the beat.

'I will pick you up at seven from the hotel.'

'Where are we going?'

'Answers at seven.'

12

An enormous dish-water moon has risen in the east and seems to move across the sky, following our taxi. Even in darkness I recognise some of the roads. Schiphol Airport is not far from here.

This is a different area of Amsterdam. The chocolate box façades and historic bridges have been replaced by the functional and harsh cement-grey apartment blocks and shops protected by metal shutters. Only one store is open. A dozen black youths are standing outside.

De Souza doesn't have a fixed address, Hokke explains. He moves from place to place, never staying more than a night in any one bed. He lives with the people he employs. They protect him.

'Be very careful what you say to him. And don't interrupt when he speaks. Keep your eyes down and your hands by your sides.'

We have pulled up outside an apartment block. Hokke opens the door for me.

'Aren't you coming with me?'

'You must go alone. We will wait here.'

'No,' declares Ruiz. 'I am going with her.'

Hokke responds with equal passion. 'She goes alone or there will be nobody waiting to meet her.'

Ruiz continues to protest but I push him back into the car where he grimaces as he folds his arms across his bandaged chest.

'Remember what I told you,' says the Dutchman, pointing towards a building that is identical to the one next to it and the one next to that. A teenage boy leans against a wall. A second one watches us from an upstairs window. Lookouts. 'You must go now. Phone me if there's a problem.'

I walk away from the taxi. The boy leaning against the wall has gone. The second teenager is still at the window. I walk through a concrete archway and into a quadrangle. Lights shine on water. Chinese lanterns are strung from the branches of a leafless tree growing amid the weeds.

Pushing through a fire door, I climb the stairs, counting off the floors. Turning left at the landing, I find the second door. A bell sounds when I push a small white button.

Another teenager appears at the door. His gleaming black eyes examine me but turn away when I meet his gaze. Shoes and sandals are lined up in the narrow hallway. The teenager points to my boots. I take them off.

The floor creaks idly as I follow him to a living area. A group of five men in their forties and fifties are seated on cushions arranged at the edges of a woven rug.

Eduardo de Souza is immediately recognisable because

of his place at the centre. Dressed in white pantaloons and a dark shirt, he looks Turkish or possibly Kurdish, with a high forehead and carved cheekbones. Unfurling his legs, he rises and touches my hand briefly.

'Welcome, Miss Barba. I am Eduardo de Souza.'

His neatly trimmed beard is black and grey – the grey like slivers of ice hanging on dark fur. Nobody speaks or moves, yet there is a perceptible energy in the air, a sharpening of focus. I keep my gaze lowered as eyes roam over me.

Through the doorway to the kitchen I spy a young Nigerian woman in a flowing dress of bright colours. Three children, two boys and a girl, jostle at the doorway, regarding me with fascination.

De Souza speaks again. 'These are friends of mine. This is Sunday. He is our host this evening.'

Sunday smiles. He is Nigerian and his teeth are a brilliant white. Each of the men introduces himself in turn. The first is Iranian with a Swiss German accent. His name is Farhad and his eyes are set so deep in his skull that I can scarcely see them. Beside him is Oscar, who looks Moroccan and speaks with a French accent.

Finally, there is Dayel, a smooth-shaven Indian with an oil burn on his neck.

'One of your countrymen, although not a Sikh,' says de Souza. Dayel smiles at the introduction.

How does he know I'm a Sikh?

There is a spare brocade cushion beside him. I am expected to sit. Sunday's wife enters the room carrying a tray of mismatched glasses and begins pouring sweet tea. Her hair is braided into a curtain of long beaded plaits.

She smiles shyly at me. Her teeth are perfect and her wide nose flares gently as she breathes.

Dishes arrive. A meal. Holding his hands together, de Souza studies me above his steepled fingers, weighing up whether or not to help me. His English is perfect, overlaid with an educated British accent that is especially noticeable on the long vowels.

'This area of Amsterdam is called Bijlmermeer,' he says, glancing at the window. 'In October 1992 a cargo jet took off from Schiphol and lost two engines. It buried itself into an apartment block like this one, full of immigrant families who were sitting down to an evening meal. Fifty apartments were destroyed by the initial impact. Another hundred burned afterwards as jet fuel ran through the streets like a river of fire. People threw themselves off balconies and rooftops to escape the flames.

'At first they said the death toll was two hundred and fifty. Later they dropped the estimate to seventy-five and officially only forty-three people died. The truth is, nobody knows the true number. Illegal immigrants have no papers and they hide from the police. They are ghosts.'

De Souza hasn't touched the food but seems particularly satisfied to see the others eating.

'Forgive me, Miss Barba, I talk too much. My friends here are too polite to tell me to be quiet. It is customary for a guest to bring something to the feast or provide some form of entertainment. Do you sing or dance?'

'No.'

'Perhaps you are a storyteller.'

'I don't really understand.'

'You will tell us a story. The best of them seem to me

to be about life and death, love and hate, loyalty and betrayal.' He waves his hand as if stirring the air. His amber eyes are fixed on mine.

'I am not a very good storyteller.'

'Let us be the judge of that.'

I tell him the story of two teenage girls who met at school and became best friends. Soulmates. Later, at university, one of them slept with the other's father. He seduced her. She allowed herself to be seduced. The friendship was over.

I don't mention names – but why would I tell them such a personal story?

Seamlessly I begin talking about a second pair of teenage girls, who met in a city of widows and orphans. People traffickers smuggled them out of Afghanistan as far as Amsterdam. They were told that they owed a debt for their escape. Either they became prostitutes or carried a baby for a childless couple. Virgins were implanted with embryos in a ritualised form of medical rape. They were the perfect incubators. Factories. Couriers.

Even as I tell this story, a sense of alarm dries my throat. Why have I told de Souza such personal stories? For all I know he is involved. He could be the ringleader. I don't have time to consider the implications. I don't know if I care. I have come too far to back out.

There is a moment of silence when I finish. De Souza leans forward and takes a chocolate from a platter, rolling it over his tongue before chewing it slowly.

'It is a good story. Friendship is a difficult thing to define. Oscar here is my oldest friend. How would you define friendship, Oscar?'

Oscar grunts slightly, as though the answer is obvious.

'Friendship is about choice and chemistry. It cannot be defined.'

'But surely there is something more to it than that.'

'It is a willingness to overlook faults and to accept them. I would let a friend hurt me without striking back,' he says, smiling. 'But only once.'

De Souza laughs. 'Bravo, Oscar, I can always rely on you to distil an argument down to its purest form. What do you think, Dayel?'

The Indian rocks his head from side to side, proud that he has been asked to speak next.

'Friendship is different for each person and it changes throughout our lives. At age six it is about holding hands with your best friend. At sixteen it is about the adventure ahead. At sixty it is about reminiscing.' He holds up a finger. 'You cannot define it with any one word, although honesty is perhaps the closest word—'

'No, not honesty,' Farhad interrupts. 'On the contrary, we often have to protect our friends from what we truly think. It is like an unspoken agreement. We ignore each other's faults and keep our confidences. Friendship isn't about being honest. The truth is too sharp a weapon to wield around someone we trust and respect. Friendship is about self-awareness. We see ourselves through the eyes of our friends. They are like a mirror that allows us to judge how we are travelling.'

De Souza clears his throat now. I wonder if he is aware of the awe that he inspires in others. I suspect he is too intelligent and too human to do otherwise.

'Friendship cannot be defined,' he says sternly. 'The moment we begin to give reasons for being friends with someone we begin to undermine the magic of the relationship. Nobody wants to know that they are loved for their money or their generosity or their beauty or their wit. Choose one motive and it allows a person to say, "Is that the *only* reason?"'

The others laugh. De Souza joins in with them. This is a performance.

He continues: 'Trying to explain why we form particular friendships is like trying to tell someone why we like a certain kind of music or a particular food. We just do.'

He focuses on me now. 'Your friend's name is Cate Beaumont.'

How does he know that?

'Were you ever jealous of her?'

'I don't know what you mean?'

'Friends can be jealous of each other. Oscar here is envious of my position and my wealth.'

'Not at all, my friend,' Oscar beseeches.

De Souza smiles knowingly. 'Did you envy Cate Beaumont's beauty or her success?'

'Sometimes.'

'You wished she had less and you had more.'

'Yes.'

'That is natural. Friendships can be ambiguous and contradictory.'

'She is dead now,' I add, although I sense he knows this already.

'She paid money for a baby. A criminal act,' he states piously.

'Yes.'

'Are you trying to protect her?'

'I'm trying to rescue the surrogate mother and the babies.'

'Perhaps you want a baby for yourself?'

My denial is too strident. I make it worse. 'I have never . . . I don't . . .'

He reaches into a small pouch tied to the belt of his tunic. 'Do you think I am a criminal, Miss Barba?'

'I don't know enough—'

'Give me your opinion.'

I pause. The faces in the circle watch with a mixture of amusement and fascination.

'It's not up to me to say,' I stammer.

Silence. Perspiration leaks into the hollow of my back, weaving between the bumps of my vertebrae.

De Souza is waiting. He leans close, his face only inches from mine. His bottom teeth are brittle and jagged, yellowing like faded newsprint. It is not such a perfect face after all.

'You can offer me nothing,' he says dismissively.

I can feel the situation slipping away from me. He is not going to help me.

The anger fermenting inside me, fuelled by hostile thoughts and by images of Zala, suddenly finds an escape valve. Words tumble out. 'I think you're a criminal and a misogynist but you're not an evil man. You don't exploit children or sell babies to the highest bidder.' I point to Sunday's wife who has come to collect our plates. 'You would not ask this woman, the wife of a friend, to give up one of her children or force her to have another woman's baby. You support asylum seekers and illegal immigrants; you give them jobs and find them homes. They respect and admire you. We can stop this trade. I can stop it. Help me.'

Sunday's wife is embarrassed at having been singled out.

She continues collecting the plates, eager to get away. The tension in the room is amplified by the stillness. Every man's eyes are upon me. Oscar makes a choking noise. He would slit my throat in a heartbeat.

De Souza stands abruptly. The meeting is finished. Oscar takes a step towards me. De Souza signals for him to stop. Alone, he walks me to the front door and takes my hand. Pressed between his fingers is a small scrap of paper.

The door closes. I do not look at the message. It's too dark to read it. The taxi is waiting. I slide into the back seat and lean against Ruiz as I close the car door. Hokke tells the driver to go.

The note is rolled into a tube, wedged between my thumb and forefinger. My hands are shaking as I unroll it and hold it up to the internal light.

Five words. Handwritten. 'She leaves tonight from Rotterdam.'

13

Our taxi driver takes an entry ramp onto a motorway.

'How far is it?'

'Seventy-five kilometres.'

'What about the port?'

'Longer.'

I look at my watch. It's eight p.m.

'The port of Rotterdam is forty kilometres long,' says Hokke. 'There are tens of thousands of containers, hundreds of ships. How are you going to find her?'

'We need a ship's name,' says Ruiz.

'Or a sailing time,' echoes Hokke.

I stare at the slip of paper. It's not enough. We can't phone ahead and alert Customs or the police. What would we tell them?

'Most likely they want to smuggle her into the UK,' I say. 'They've used Harwich before.'

'They might choose an alternative port this time.'

'Or stick to what they know.'

Hokke shakes his head. It is a wild, impossible chase. Rotterdam is the biggest container port in Europe. He has an idea. A friend, a former police officer, works for a private security firm that patrols some of the terminals.

Hokke calls him. They chat to each other gruffly, in stern sentences full of Dutch consonants. Meanwhile, I follow the brightly lit motorway signs, counting down the kilometres and the minutes. In the moonlight I can make out wind turbines like ghostly giants marching across the fields.

Trucks and semis are nose to tail in the outside lane. I wonder if Samira could be inside one of them. What must it be like? Deafening. Black. Lonely.

Hokke finishes the call and outlines the possibilities. Security is tight around the terminals and docks, with CCTV cameras on the fences and regular dog patrols. Once inside there are Customs checks, heat-seeking scanners and more dogs. More than six and a half million shipping containers pass through the port every year. These have to be specially sealed. Empty containers awaiting transfer are a different story but even if someone breached the security and reached the containers they wouldn't know which ship a container was meant to be loaded onto unless they had inside information.

'Which means they're more likely to target a truck *before* it reaches the port,' says Ruiz. 'One they know is travelling to the UK.'

Hokke nods. 'We're probably looking at roll-on roll-off ferries. There are two major ferry operators doing North Sea crossings out of Rotterdam. Stena Line has a terminal on the Hook of Holland. P&O operates from a dock fifteen kilometres further east, closer to the city.'

We're still twenty miles away and it's nearly eight-thirty.

Hokke makes another call, getting a timetable of departures, calling out the details. A P&O ferry sails for Hull at nine o'clock. The Stena Line night ferry to Harwich leaves at eleven. Both arrive in the UK in the early hours of tomorrow morning.

'Are you carrying a passport, grasshopper?'

'Yes, sir.'

'You want to take the first ferry or the second?'

'I'll take the second.'

He nods in agreement. 'Anyone know the weather forecast?'

Hokke is on the mobile to P&O, seeing if they will hold the passenger gates open. They're supposed to close fifteen minutes before departure, which means we won't make it.

We're basing our assumptions on a ratio of about two per cent detail and ninety-eight per cent desire. Even if Samira is on board one of the ferries, she won't be mingling with other passengers. They'll keep her hidden. How are we going to find her?

My mind aches when I think about her. I made promises. I said I would find Zala and keep her safe. What am I going to say to her?

De Souza asked if I wanted the babies for myself. It was a ridiculous suggestion. Why would he say that? I'm doing this for Cate and for Samira. For the twins.

The docks are lit up for miles. Cranes and gantries act as massive lighting towers, painting the hulls of ships and rows of stacked containers. The water is dark and solid in between and the waves are hardly waves at all; they're wrinkles on a sluggish river.

The taxi pulls up outside the P&O terminal. Ruiz is out the door before we stop moving. A week of maddening pain and morphine won't slow him down.

'Good luck,' he yells without turning back. 'I'm going to find her first.'

'Yeah, right. You'll spend your entire time throwing up.'

His hand rises. One finger extends.

The Stena Line terminal is at the western edge of the port where the Hook of Holland reaches out into the North Sea. The taxi drops me and I say goodbye to Hokke.

'I can never repay you.'

'But you will,' he laughs, pointing to the meter.

I give him all my remaining euros for he still has to get home.

He kisses me three times – left cheek, right cheek and left cheek again.

'Be careful.'

'I will.'

I have an hour until the *Stena Britannica* leaves. The ship dominates the skyline, towering over the surrounding structures. It is the length of two football fields and the height of a fifteen-storey building, with twin stacks that slope backwards and give the impression – although not the conviction – of speed.

Seagulls circle and swoop for insects in the beams of the spotlights. They appear so graceful in flight yet they squabble like fishwives on the ground. And they always sound so desperately sad, wailing in misery like creatures already condemned to hell.

Many trucks and trailers are already on board. I can see them lined up on the open decks, a few feet apart, buttressed hard against the stern railings. More trucks are queuing, on the loading ramp. Meanwhile, cars and vans are being marshalled in a different parking area waiting their turn.

A young woman in the ticket office wears a light blue skirt and matching jacket, like a maritime stewardess. 'You will need to write down the details of your vehicle,' she says.

'I don't have a vehicle.'

'I'm sorry but there is no pedestrian footbridge on this service. We cannot board foot passengers.'

'But I have to catch this ferry.'

'That is not possible.' She glances over my shoulder. 'Perhaps . . . ?'

An elderly couple have just pulled up in an early-model Range Rover, towing an old-fashioned caravan that looks like a Cinderella pumpkin carriage. The man is bald, with a small goatee that could be a shaving oversight. His wife is twice his size, wearing acres of denim across her hips. They look and sound Welsh.

'What is it, pet?' she asks as I interrupt their cup of thermos tea.

'They won't let me onto the ferry as a foot passenger. I really need to get back to England. I was wondering if I could ride with you.'

Husband and wife look at each other.

'Are you a terrorist?' he asks.

'No.'

'Are you carrying drugs?'

'No.'

'Do you vote Tory?'

'No.'

'Are you a Catholic?'

'No.'

He winks at his wife. 'Clear on all counts.'

'Welcome aboard,' she announces, thrusting out her hand. 'I'm Bridget Jones. Not the fat one from the movies – the fatter one from Cardiff. This is Bryce, my husband.'

The Range Rover is packed to the gunwales with suit-cases, shopping bags and duty-free: Dutch cheeses, French sausage, two cases of Stella Artois, a bottle of Bailey's Irish Cream and assorted souvenirs.

They are very cute. A twee couple, with matching lumbar cushions and travelling mugs. Mr Jones is wearing driving gloves with cut-off fingers and she has road maps, colour-coded, in a pocket on the dashboard.

'We've been to Poland,' she announces.

'Really?'

'Nobody we know has ever been to Poland. Not even our friends Hettie and Jack from the caravanning club, who think they've been everywhere.'

'And to Estonia,' her husband adds. 'We've done 3,264 miles since we left home on August twenty-eighth.' He strokes the steering wheel. 'She's managed eighteen mile to the gallon, which is pretty bloody good for an old girl, espe-cially after that bad batch of diesel in Gdansk.'

'Gdansk was very dodgy,' agrees his wife.

'It must be cold to be caravanning.'

'Oh, we don't mind,' she giggles. 'A spouse is better than a hot water bottle.'

332

Mr Jones nods. 'I get pretty good mileage out of this old girl.'

I don't know if he's referring to his wife or still talking about the car.

Ahead of us the traffic is moving. Vehicles pull onto the ramp and disappear inside, manoeuvred into marked lanes barely wide enough for their axles. Engines are turned off. The caravan is strapped down. Men in fluorescent vests direct us to the airlock doors, which lead to stairs and lifts.

'Don't dawdle, pet,' says Mrs Jones. 'The buffet is included in the price. You want to beat the queue.'

Mr Jones nods. 'They do a fine apple crumble and custard.'

A key-card is included with my ticket. It corresponds to a cabin on one of the accommodation decks. Deck Eight has signs asking passengers to be quiet because truck drivers are sleeping. Some of them must have boarded hours ago. How am I going to find Samira?

I don't bother visiting my cabin. I have no luggage to stow. Instead I study the ship's floor plan, which is bolted to the wall near an emergency exit. There are four vehicle decks, which are restricted to authorised personnel during the voyage. Deck 10 is for crew only. It must be the bridge.

The corridors between the cabins are just wide enough for two people to pass. I search them, looking for the familiar or the unfamiliar. This used to be my job when I worked for the Diplomatic Protection Group – looking for small changes, trying to sense the presence of someone in a crowd or notice their absence in the instant of looking. It could be a person who doesn't belong or who tries too hard to belong or who draws the eye for some other reason.

333

The ship's engines have started. I can feel the faint vibrations through my feet and they seem to transfer to my nerve endings.

The buffet is being served in the Globetrotter Restaurant. Most of the passengers seem to be truck drivers, dressed in jeans and T-shirts. Food is piled high on their plates – congealed curries, cottage pie, vegetarian lasagne. Big engines need refuelling.

The Dutch drivers are playing cards, while the British drivers smoke and read tabloids. The ferry has slipped its moorings and pulled out into the river. As the shore lights slide past the window, it feels as though the land is moving and not the ferry. England is five hours away.

Hokke was right. This haystack is too big. I could search the ferry for weeks and not find Samira. She could be locked in a truck or in one of the cabins. She might not even be on board. Perhaps de Souza had no intention of letting me find her and was simply getting me out of the Netherlands.

The cavernous vehicle decks are below me. Some are open to the elements while others are enclosed. I have to search them. How? Do I hammer on the side of each truck, calling her name? Will she answer?

If there's any chance at all that she's on board I have to find her. Running along the gangways and up the stairs, I stop people and show them Samira's photograph. I'm doubling back on myself, lost in a maze. Have I been down this corridor before? Is that the same passenger I asked earlier? Most of them are in their cabins now, lying down to sleep.

I turn another corner and suddenly I feel it. A shiver in

the air. It's an uncanny sensation, as if I'm prescient. Along a long corridor, a figure with his back to me pauses to unlock a cabin door. I see a quarter-profile and suddenly flatten myself against a wall. My phantoms are following me.

14

The ferry shifts and I brace myself. We must have reached open water. I am sure it's *him*. Brendan Pearl. He is here because *she* is here.

My first reaction is to retreat. I pull back and take a few deep breaths on the stairwell while contemplating what to do. Taking out my mobile, I check the signal. Nothing. The ferry has moved out of range. I should talk to the captain. He can radio ahead and get a message to Forbes.

A member of the crew is climbing the stairs. Although dressed in dark trousers and a white shirt with epaulettes, he looks too young to be at sea. He has a name tag on his chest. Raoul Jakobson.

'Do you have keys to all the cabins?' I ask.

'Is there a problem?'

'There is a man on board who is wanted by the British police. He is staying in cabin 8021.' I point along the passage.

His gaze follows my outstretched hand. 'I am a British police officer. A detective constable. Is there a passenger list?' I show him my badge.

'Yes, of course.'

He opens a door marked 'Authorised Personnel Only' and retrieves a clipboard, running his finger down the page until he finds the cabin number.

'That cabin is occupied by a Patrick Norris. He is a British driver.'

Pearl has a new identity.

'Is it possible to find out what vehicle he drove on board?'

Raoul consults the list again: 'V743 LFB. On Deck Five.'

'I need to check this vehicle.'

'Passengers are not authorised to be on that deck.'

'I'm looking for an illegal passenger. She could be locked inside the truck.'

'Perhaps you should talk to the captain.'

'Yes, of course, but there isn't time right now. *You* go to the captain. I need him to send a message to this man,' I scribble a phone number on the clipboard. 'His name is Detective Inspector Robert Forbes. Mention my name. Tell him that Brendan Pearl is on this ferry.'

'Is that it?'

'He'll understand.'

Raoul looks at the phone number and glances down the passage towards Pearl's cabin.

'Is he dangerous, this man?'

'Yes, but nobody is to panic. Let him sleep.' I look at my watch. 'We'll be in Harwich in four hours.' Moving towards the stairwell, I nod goodbye. 'Tell the captain. I have to go.'

Taking the stairs two at a time, I swing through the

landings and reach Deck Five. Hitting the red button, I hear the air hiss out as the seal is broken. The metal door slides open. The noise of the ship's engines is amplified in the cavernous space and transfers through the floor in pulsing vibrations.

Stepping over the lip of the door, I begin walking down the first line of vehicles. The trucks are parked seven abreast and nose-to-tail, so close together there is just enough room to squeeze between them. I wish I had a torch. The strip lighting can barely cut through the gloom and I have difficulty reading the vehicle numbers.

I walk the length of the deck and back again, following the lanes. When the ferry pitches and rolls in the swell I brace my hand against a wheel arch or trailer. My imagination puts me inside them. I can picture Hasan and the others, trapped, suffocating. I want to hammer on the metal sides and fling open the doors, filling them with air.

I'm in the second lane on the starboard side when I find it. The rig has a maroon Mercedes cab and a white box trailer. Stepping onto the running-board, I grip the side mirror and pull myself up to peer into the cab. Takeaway coffee cups and food wrappers litter the floor.

Stepping down, I slowly circle the trailer. Pressing my ear against the steel skin I listen for a sneeze or a cough or a whisper, any sound at all. Nothing. The rear doors are sealed with a metal rod-and-cam lock. The barrel is closed and padlocked.

Someone holding a torch is walking towards me. The beam swings from side to side, blinding me momentarily. I edge away from the trailer. Darkness feathers around me.

'You're not supposed to be down here,' says a voice.

At that same moment a hand snakes around my face, cupping my mouth. Smothering all sound away.

I can't breathe. My feet are off the ground. My assailant's fingers are digging into my cheek, tearing at my gums. His other forearm wraps around my neck, searching for my windpipe. I brace my hands against it and kick backwards, trying to find his instep or his knee. The blow barely touches him.

He lifts me higher. My toes scrabble at the floor, unable to get leverage. I can hear blood pulsing in my ears. I need to breathe.

Karate training taught me about pressure points. There is one in the soft flesh between the thumb and forefinger, above the webbing. I find the spot. My attacker grunts in pain, releasing his grip on my mouth and nose. I still can't breathe. My windpipe is being crushed. I keep driving my thumb into his flesh.

A knee snaps into my kidneys. The pain is like a blast of heat. I don't let go of his right hand but at the same time I can't see his left fist cocking. The punch is like a punctuation mark. Darkness sweeps away the pain and the memories. I am free of the ferry and the incessant noise of the engines. Free of Cate and Samira. Free of the unborn twins. Free at last.

Slowly the world becomes wider. Lighter. I am suspended for a moment a few inches above my body, staring down at a strange scene. My hands are bound with electrical tape behind my back. Another piece of tape covers my mouth, wrapped around my head like a mask, pulling at my split and swollen lip.

339

There is a weak light from a torch, lying on the floor near my feet. My head is on Samira's lap. She leans forward and whispers something in my ear. She wants me to lie still. Light catches her pupils. Her fingers are like ice.

My head is pressed to her womb. I feel her babies moving. I can hear the sough and gurgle of the fluid, the melody of their heartbeats. Blood slides back and forth beneath her skin, squeezing into smaller and smaller channels, circulating oxygen.

I wonder if twins are aware of each other's existence. Do they hear each other's heartbeat? Do they hold each other or communicate by touch?

Bit by bit the confusion and darkness work their way into some semblance of order. If I stay relaxed I can breathe through the tape.

Samira's body suddenly spasms and jackknifes from the waist, squeezing my head against her thighs. Regaining control, she leans back and breathes deeply. I try to lift my head. She wants me to lie still.

I can't talk through the gag. She hooks her fingers beneath the plastic tape and lifts it away from my lips just enough for me to speak.

'Where are we?'

'In a truck.'

Our whispers are magnified by the trailer's emptiness.

'Are you all right?'

She shakes her head. Tears form at the edge of her eyes. Her body convulses again. She's in labour.

'Who brought me here?'

'Yanus.'

340

He and Pearl must be working together.

'You have to untie me.'

Her eyes sweep to the closed rear doors and she shakes her head.

'Please.'

'They will kill you.'

They will kill me anyway.

'Help me to sit up.'

She lifts my head and shoulders until I'm leaning with my back against a wall. My inner gyroscope is totally messed up. I may have ruptured an eardrum.

The trailer appears to be full of pallets and crates. Through a square narrow opening I see a crawl space with a mattress and three plastic bottles. Someone has built a false wall to create a secret compartment in the trailer. Customs officers wouldn't notice the difference unless they measured the outside and inside of the truck.

'When did the contractions start?'

She looks at me helplessly. She has no way of judging time.

'How far are they apart?'

'A minute.'

How long was I unconscious? Raoul will have gone to the ferry's captain by now. They will telephone Forbes and come looking for me. Forbes will tell them to be careful.

'Undo my hands.'

Samira shakes her head.

Letting go of the tape she tugs a blanket around my shoulders. She is more worried about me than she is about herself.

'You should not have come.'

I can't reply. Another contraction contorts her face. Her entire body seems to lock up.

The rear doors swing open. I feel the draught and hear the intake of Samira's breath.

'I told you not to touch her,' says Yanus, springing into the trailer. He seizes her, smearing his hands over her face as if covering her with filth. Then he peels back her lips, forcing her jaw open, and spits into her mouth. She gags and tries to turn away.

Then he confronts me, ripping off the gag. It feels as though half my face is torn off with it.

'Who knows you're here?'

My voice is slurred: 'The captain. The crew . . . they're radioing ahead.'

'Liar!'

Another figure is standing in the open end of the trailer. Brendan Pearl. He can't have been there for more than a few seconds yet I have the sensation that he's been watching me for a long time.

The light behind him washes out his features, but I can see how he's changed his appearance since I saw him last. His hair is shorter and he's wearing glasses. The walking stick is a nice touch. He's holding it upside down. Why? It's not a walking stick. It has a curved hook like a fishing gaff or a marlinspike. I remember what Ruiz called him – the Shankhill Fisherman.

Yanus kicks me in the stomach. I roll once and he places a shoe on my neck, forcing it down, concentrating his weight on the point where my spine joins my skull. Surely it must snap.

Samira cries out, her body racked by another contraction.

342

Pearl says something and Yanus lifts his foot. I can breathe. He circles the empty trailer and returns, putting his heel on my neck again.

I force my arm out, pointing towards Samira. She is staring at her hands in horror. Liquid stains her skirt and pools beneath her knees.

Pearl pushes Yanus aside.

'Her waters have broken,' I gasp desperately, choking the words out.

'She pissed herself,' sneers Yanus.

'No. She's having the babies.'

'Make them stop,' says Pearl.

'I can't. She needs a doctor.'

Another contraction arrives, stronger than before. Her scream echoes from the metal walls. Pearl loops the barbed hook around her neck. 'She makes another sound like that and I'll take out her throat.'

Samira shakes her head, covering her mouth with her hands.

Pearl pulls me into a sitting position and cuts the electrical tape away from my wrists. He pauses for a moment, chewing at his cheek like a cud.

'She don't look so healthy, does she?' he says, in an Irish lilt.

'She needs a doctor.'

'Can't have no doctors.'

'But she's having twins!'

'I don't care if she's having *puppies*. You'll have to deliver them.'

'I don't know how to deliver a baby!'

'Then you better learn quick.'

'Don't be stupid—'

The stave of the marlinspike strikes my jaw. When the pain passes I count teeth with my tongue. 'Why should I help you?'

'Because I'll kill you if you don't.'

'You're going to kill me anyway.'

'Know that, do you?'

Samira's hand shoots out and grips my wrist. Her knuckles are white and the pain is etched on her face. She wants help. She wants the pain to go away. I glance at Pearl and nod.

'That's grand as grand can be.' He stands and stretches, twirling the spike in his fist.

'We can't do it here,' I say. 'We need to get her to a cabin. I need light. Clean sheets. Water.'

'No.'

'Look at this place!'

'She stays here.'

'Then she dies! And her babies die! And whoever is paying you will get nothing.'

I think Pearl is going to hit me again. Instead he weighs the marlinspike in both hands before swinging it down until the metal hook touches the floor and leaning upon it like a walking stick. He and Yanus converse in whispers. Decisions have to be made. Their plan is unravelling.

'You have to try to hold on,' I tell Samira. 'It's going to be OK.'

She nods, far calmer than I am.

Why hasn't anyone come looking for me? Surely they will have called Forbes by now. He'll tell them what to do.

Pearl comes back.

'OK, we move her.' He raises his shirt to show me a pistol tucked into his belt. 'No fuckin' tricks. You escape and Yanus here will cut the babies out of her. He's a frustrated fuckin' surgeon.'

The Irishman collects Samira's things – a small cotton bag and a spare blanket. Then he helps her to stand. She cups her hands beneath her pregnancy as though taking the weight. I wrap the blanket around her shoulders. Her damp grey skirt sticks to her thighs.

Yanus has gone ahead to check the stairs. I can picture crew members waiting for him. He'll be overpowered. Pearl will have no choice but to surrender.

He lifts Samira down from the trailer. I follow, stumbling slightly as I land. Pearl pushes me out of the way and closes the rear doors, sliding the barrel lock into place. Something is different about the truck. The colour. It's not the same.

My stomach turns over. There are two trucks. Yanus and Pearl must have each driven a vehicle on board. Glancing towards the nearest stairwell, I see the glowing exit sign. We're on a different deck. They don't know where to look for me.

Samira goes first. Her chin is drawn down to her clavicle and she seems to be whispering a prayer. A contraction stops her suddenly and her knees buckle. Pearl puts his arm around her waist. Although in his late forties, he has the upper-body strength of someone who has bulked up in prison weight rooms. You don't work a regular job and have a physique like his.

We move quickly up the stairs and along empty passageways. Yanus has found a cabin on Deck Nine, where there are fewer passengers. He takes Samira from Pearl and I glance at them, fleetingly, sidelong. Surely they can't expect to get away with this.

The two-berth cabin is oppressively neat. It has a narrow single bunk about a foot from the floor and another directly above it, hinged and folded flat against the wall. There is a square porthole with rounded corners. The window is dark. Land has ceased to exist and I can only imagine the emptiness of the North Sea outside. I look at my watch. It's twelve-thirty. Harwich is another three and a half hours away. If Samira can stay calm – and the contractions are steady – we may reach Harwich in time. In time for what?

Her eyes are wide and her forehead is beaded with perspiration. At the same time she is shivering. I sit on the bed, with my back to the bulkhead, pulling her against me with my arms wrapped around her, trying to keep her warm. Her belly balloons between her knees and her entire body jolts with each contraction.

I am running on instinct. Trying my best not to panic or show fear. The first-aid course I did when I joined the Met was comprehensive but it didn't include childbirth. I remember something my Mama said to my sisters-in-law: 'Doctors don't deliver babies, women do.'

Yanus and Pearl take turns guarding the door. There isn't enough room in the cabin for both of them. One will watch the passageway.

Yanus leans against the narrow cabin counter, watching with listless curiosity. Taking an orange from his pocket, he peels it expertly and separates it into segments that he lines up along the bench. Each piece is finally crushed between his teeth and he sucks the juices down his throat before spitting out the pith and seeds onto the floor.

I have never believed that people could be wholly evil. Psychopaths are made, not born. Yanus could be the exception. I try to picture him as a youngster and cling to the hope that there might be some warmth inside him. He must have loved someone, something – a pet, a parent, a friend. But I can see no trace of it.

One or twice Samira can't stifle her cries. He tosses a roll of masking tape into my lap. 'Shut her up!'

'No! She has to tell me when the contractions are coming.'

'Then keep her quiet.'

Where does he keep his knife? Strapped to his chest on his left side, next to his heart. He seems to read my mind and taps his jacket.

'I can cut them out of her, you know. I've done it before with animals. I start cutting just here.' He puts his finger just above his belt buckle and draws it upwards over his navel and beyond. 'Then I peel back her skin.'

Samira shudders.

'Just shut up, will you?'

He gives me his shark's smile.

Night presses against the porthole. There might be five hundred passengers on board the ferry, but right now it feels as though the cabin light is burning in a cold hostile wasteland.

Samira tilts her head back until she can look into my eyes. 'Zala?' she asks.

I wish I could lie to her but she reads the truth on my face. I can almost see her slipping backwards into blackness, disappearing. It is the look of someone who knows that fate has abandoned them to a sadness so deep that nothing can touch it.

'I should never have let her go,' she whispers.

'It's not your fault.'

Her chest rises and falls in a silent sob. She has turned her eyes away. It is a gesture that says everything. I vowed to find Zala and keep her safe. I broke my promise.

The contractions seem to have eased. Her breathing steadies and she sleeps.

Pearl has replaced Yanus.

'How is she?'

'Exhausted.'

He braces his back against the door, sliding down until he settles on his haunches, draping his arms over his knees. In such a small space he appears larger, overgrown, with big hands. Yanus has feminine hands, shapely and delicate, fast with a blade. Pearl's are like blunt instruments.

'You'll never get away with this, you know that.'

He smiles. 'There are many things I know and many more things I don't know.'

'Listen to me. You're only making this worse. If she dies or the babies die they'll charge you with murder.'

'They won't die.'

'She needs a doctor.'

'Enough talk.'

'The police know I'm here. I saw you earlier. I told the captain to radio ahead. There will be a hundred police officers waiting at Harwich. You can't get away. Let me take Samira. There could be a doctor on board or a nurse. They'll have medical supplies.'

Pearl doesn't seem to care. Is that what happens when you spend most of your life in prison or committing acts that should put you there?

My scalp tingles. 'Why did you kill my friend Cate and her husband?'

'Who?'

'The Beaumonts.'

His eyes, not quite level with each other, give the impression of lopsidedness until he talks and his features suddenly line up. 'She was greedy.'

'How?'

'She could only pay for one baby but wanted both of them.'

'You asked her to *choose*?'

'Not me.'

'Someone else did?'

He doesn't have to answer.

'That's obscene,' I say.

He shrugs. 'Pitter or Patter – seems simple enough. Life is about choices.'

That's what Cate meant – at the reunion – when she said they were trying to take her baby. They wanted her to pay double. Her bank account was empty. She had to choose: the boy or the girl. How can a mother make a decision like that and live for the rest of her life gazing into the eyes of one child and seeing a reflection of another that she never knew?

Pearl is still talking. 'She threatened to go to the police. We warned her. She ignored it. That's the problem with folks nowadays. Nobody takes responsibility for their actions. Make a mistake and you pay for it. That's life.'

'Have you paid for *your* mistakes?'

'All my life.' His eyes are closed. He wants to go back to ignoring me.

349

A knock. Pearl slides the pistol from his belt and points it towards me while holding a finger to his lips. He opens the door a fraction. I can't see a face. Someone is asking about a missing passenger. They're looking for me.

Pearl yawns. 'Is that why you woke me?'

A second voice: 'Sorry, sir.'

'What does she look like?'

I can't hear the description.

'Well, I ain't seen her. Maybe she went for a swim.'

'I hope not, sir.'

'Yeah, well, I got to sleep.'

'Sorry, sir, you won't be disturbed again.'

The door closes. Pearl waits for a moment, pressing his ear to the door. Satisfied, he tucks the pistol back in his belt.

There's another knock on the door. Yanus.

'Where the fuck were you?' demands Pearl.

'Watching,' replies Yanus.

'You were supposed to fucking warn me.'

'Would have made no difference. They're knocking on every door. They won't come back now.'

Samira sits bolt upright, screaming. The contraction is brutal and I scissor my legs around her, holding her still. An unseen force possesses her, racking her body in spasms. I find myself drawn to her pain. Caught up in it. Breathing when she breathes.

Another contraction comes almost immediately. Her back arches and her knees rise up.

'I have to push now.'

'No!'

'I have to.'

This is it. I can't stop her. Sliding out from behind her,

I lay her down and take off her underwear. Pearl is unsure of what to do.

'Take deep breaths, that's a good girl,' he says. 'Good deep breaths. You thirsty? I'll get you a drink of water.'

He fills a glass in the small bathroom and returns.

'Shouldn't you be checking the cervix?' he asks.

'And I suppose you know all about it.'

'I seen movies.'

'Take over any time you want.'

His tone softens. 'What can I do?'

'Run some hot water in the sink. I need to wash my hands.'

Samira unclenches her teeth as the pain eases. Short panting breaths become longer. She focuses on Pearl and begins issuing instructions. She needs things – scissors and string, clips and towels. For a moment I think she's delirious but I soon realise that she knows more about childbirth than any of us.

Pearl opens the door and passes on the instructions to Yanus. They argue. Pearl threatens him.

Samira has another instruction. Men cannot be present at the birth. I expect Pearl to say no but I see him wavering.

I tell him, 'Look at this place. We can't go anywhere. There's one door and a porthole fifty feet above the water.'

He accepts this and glances at his watch. It's after two. 'An hour from now she has to be back in the truck.' His hand is on the door handle. He turns and addresses me.

'My Ma is a good Catholic. Pro-life, you understand? She'd say there were already five people in this room, babies included. When I come back I expect to see the same number. Keep them alive.'

He closes the door and Samira relaxes a little. She asks me to fetch a flannel from the bathroom. She folds it several times and wedges it between her teeth when she feels a contraction coming.

'How do you know so much?'

'I have seen babies born,' she explains. 'Women would sometimes come to the orphanage to give birth. They left the babies with us because they could not take them home.'

Her contractions are coming forty seconds apart. Her eyes bulge and she bites down hard on the flannel. The pain passes.

'I need you to see if I'm ready,' she whispers.

'How?'

'Put two fingers inside me to measure.'

'How do I tell?'

'Look at your fingers,' she says. 'See how long they are. Measure with them.'

Opening her legs, I do as she asks. I have never touched a woman so intimately or been so terrified.

'I think you're ready.'

She nods, clenching the flannel between her teeth through the first part of the contraction and then breathing in short bursts, trying to ease the pain. Tears squeeze from her eyes and mingle with her sweat. I smell her exertions.

'I have to get to the floor,' she says.

'Are you going to pray?'

'No. I'm going to have a baby.'

She squats with her legs apart, bracing her arms between the bunk and the bench table. Gravity is going to help her.

'You must feel for the baby's head,' she says.

My hand is inside her, turning and dipping. I feel a baby's head. It's crowning. Should there be blood?

'They will kill you after the babies are born,' whispers Samira. 'You must get out of here.'

'Later.'

'You must go now.'

'Don't worry about me.'

There's a knock on the door. I undo the latch and Pearl hands me scissors, a ball of string and a rusty clip. Yanus hisses from behind him. 'Keep the bitch quiet.'

'Fuck you! She's having a baby.'

Yanus makes a lunge for me. Pearl pushes him back and closes the door.

Samira is pushing now, three times with each contraction. She has long slender lemur-like feet, roughly callused along the outer edges. Her chin is tucked to her throat and oily coils of her hair fall over her eyes.

'If I pass out, you must make sure you get the babies out. Don't leave them inside me.' Teeth pull at her bottom lip. 'Do whatever you have to.'

'Shhh.'

'Promise me.'

'I promise.'

'Am I bleeding a lot?'

'You're bleeding. I don't know if it's too much. I can see the baby's head.'

'It hurts.'

'I know.'

Existence narrows to just breathing, pain and pushing. I brush hair from her eyes and crouch between her legs. Her face contorts. She screams into the flannel. The baby's head is out. I hold it in my cupped hand, feeling the dips and hollows of the skull. The shoulders are trapped. Gently I put my finger beneath its chin and the tiny body rotates within her. On the next contraction the right shoulder appears, then the left, and the baby slides into my hands.

A boy.

'Rub your finger down his nose,' gasps Samira.

It takes only a fingertip to perform the task. There is a soft, shocked sob, a rattle and a breath.

Samira issues more instructions. I am to use the string and tie off the umbilical cord in two places, cutting between the knots. My hands are shaking.

She is crying. Spent. I help her back onto the bunk and she leans against the bulkhead wall. Wrapping the boy in a towel, I hold him close, smelling his warm breath, letting his nose brush against my cheek. Which one are you, I wonder, Pitter or Patter?

I look at my watch and make a mental note of the time: 2.55 a.m. What is the date? 29 October. Where will they say he was born? In the Netherlands or Britain? And who will be his true mother? What a mixed-up way to start a life.

The contractions have started again. Samira kneads her stomach, trying to feel the unborn twin.

'What's wrong?'

'She is facing the wrong way. You must turn her.'

'I don't know how.'

Each new contraction brings a groan of resignation. Samira is almost too exhausted to cry out; too tired to push. I have to hold her up this time. She squats. Her thighs part still further.

Reaching inside her, I try to push the baby back, turning her body, fighting gravity and the contractions. My hands are slick. I'm frightened of hurting her.

354

'It's coming.'

'Push now.'

The head arrives with a gush of blood. I glimpse something – white, with blue streaks – wrapped around its neck.

'Stop! Don't push!'

My hand slides along the baby's face until my fingers reach beneath her chin and untangle the umbilical cord.

'Samira, you *really* need to push the next time. It's very important.'

The contraction begins. She pushes once, twice . . . nothing.

'Push.'

'I can't.'

'Yes, you can. One last time, I promise.'

She throws back her head and muffles a scream. Her body stiffens and bucks. A baby girl emerges, blue, slick, wrinkled, cupped in both my hands. I rub her nose. Nothing. I hold her on her side, sweeping my index finger round her mouth and throat, trying to clear the dripping goo.

I drape her over my hand, with her arms and legs dangling, and slap her back, hard. Why won't she breathe?

Putting her on a towel I begin chest compressions with the tips of my index and middle fingers. At the same time I lower my head, purse my lips and puff into the baby's mouth and nose.

I know about resuscitation. I have done the training and I have witnessed paramedics do it dozens of times. Now I am breathing into a body that has never taken a breath. Come on, little one. Come on.

Samira is half on the bunk and half on the floor. Her

eyes are closed. The first twin is swaddled and lying between her arm and her side.

I continue the compressions and breathing. It is like a mantra, a physical prayer. Almost without my noticing, the narrowest of chests rises and eyelids flutter. Blue has become pink. She's alive. Beautiful.

15

A girl and a boy – Pitter and Patter, each with ten fingers and ten toes; squashed-up noses, tiny ears. Rocking back on my heels, I feel like laughing with relief, until I catch my reflection in the mirror. I am smeared with blood and tears yet have a look of complete wonderment on my face.

Samira groans softly.

'You're bleeding.'

'It will stop when I feed them.'

How does she know so much? She is massaging her belly, which ripples and sways in its emptiness. I swaddle the baby girl and tuck her next to Samira.

'Go now!'

'I can't leave you.'

'Please!'

An extraordinary calmness washes through me. I have

only two options – to fight or to fall. I take the scissors, weighing them in my hand. Maybe there is a way.

I open the door. Pearl is in the passage.

'Quickly! I need a drinking straw. The girl. Her lungs are full of fluid.'

'What if I can't?'

'A ballpoint pen, a tube – anything like that. Hurry!'

I close the door. He will leave Yanus to watch the passage.

Taking the babies from Samira, I lay them side by side on the floor of the bathroom, tucked between the sink and the toilet. Cupping my hands beneath the running water, I wash away the blood and clean my face.

I have been trained to use a firearm. I can shoot a perfect score with a pistol from thirty yards on an indoor range. What good is that now? My hand-to-hand skills are defensive but I know the vital organs. I glance again at the scissors.

It is a plan I can only try once. Lying on the bathroom floor, I face the bedroom, holding the scissors like an ice pick with a reverse grip. My thumb hooks through the handle. If I look towards my toes I can see the babies.

Taking a deep breath I open my lungs, screaming for help. How long will it take?

Yanus shoulders the door open, shattering the lock. He charges inside, holding the knife ahead of him. In mid-stride he looks down. Beneath his raised foot is the afterbirth – purple, slick and glistening. I don't know what he imagines it to be, but the possibilities are too much for him to comprehend. He rears back and I drive the scissors into the soft flesh behind his right knee, aiming for the artery and the tendons that work his leg. The knee buckles and he swings his arm down in an arc, trying to stab me, but I'm too low and the blade sweeps past my ear.

I grab his arm and lock it straight, spearing the scissors into the inside of his elbow, severing another artery. The knife slips from his fingers.

He tries to spin and grab me but I am already out of reach. Leaping to my feet, I jump onto his back and send him down. I could kill him if I wanted. I could drive the blade into his kidneys.

Instead, I reach into his pocket and find the masking tape. His right leg is flapping like the wooden limb of a marionette. Pulling his good arm behind his back, I tape it in a reverse sling around his neck. Another piece covers his mouth.

Yanus is groaning. I grab his face. 'Listen to me. I have severed the popliteal artery in your leg and the brachial artery in your arm. You know this already because you're a knife man. You also know that you will bleed to death unless you maintain pressure on these wounds. You will have to squat on your haunches and keep this arm bent. I will send someone to help you. If you do as I suggest, you might still be alive when they get here.'

Samira has been watching all this with a curious detachment. Crawling off the bed, she takes several painful steps towards Yanus before leaning down and spitting in his face.

'We have to go.'

'You go. Take the babies.'

'Not without you.'

I take the smaller twin, the girl, whose eyes are open, watching me. Samira takes the sleeping boy. Cautiously, I peer into the passageway. Pearl will be coming back soon.

Samira has a towel pressed between her thighs. We head towards the stairs, moving as quickly as she can stumble. The passage is so narrow that I bounce off the wall as I try to keep hold of Samira's arm. People are asleep. I don't know which cabins are occupied.

There is a service lift. I can't open the door. Samira's legs buckle. I stop her falling. This is Deck Nine. The bridge is on Deck Ten. She isn't strong enough to climb the stairs. I have to get her away from the cabin and hide her.

There is a linen room with shelves on either side, stacked with folded sheets and towels. I could leave her here and go for help. No, she shouldn't be left alone.

I hear movement. Someone is awake. After hammering on the cabin door, it opens hurriedly. A middle-aged man, wearing pyjamas and grey socks, looks irritated. A fuzz of red hair spills from the vee of his shirt and makes it seem like his stuffing is coming out.

I push Samira ahead of me. 'Help her! I have to find a doctor!'

The man says something in German. Then he spies the bloody towel between her thighs. I hand him the baby girl.

'Who are you?'

'Police. There's no time to explain. Help her.'

Samira curls up on the bunk, her arms around the other twin.

'Don't open the door. Don't let anyone know she's here.'

Before he can protest, I step back into the passage and run towards the stairs. The passenger lounge is deserted apart from two rough-looking men at the bar, hunched over pints. A woman files her nails at a cash register.

I yell for the captain. It isn't the desperation in my voice that affects them most. It's the blood on my clothes. I have come from a nightmare place, another dimension.

People are running. Members of the crew appear, yelling orders and ushering me further upstairs. Sentences stream out of me, between snorting sobs. They're not listening to me. They have to get Samira and the twins.

The captain is a large man with shaggy eyebrows and a semicircle of hair clinging to the scalp above his ears and neck. His uniform is white and blue, matching his eyes.

He stands in the middle of the bridge, his head thrust forward, listening without any hint of scepticism. The state of my clothes is proof enough. The chief engineer is a medic. He wants to examine me. We don't have time. The captain is on the radio, using emergency frequencies, talking to HM Coastguard, Customs and mainland police. A cutter has been sent from Felixstowe to intercept us and a Royal Navy helicopter is being scrambled from Prestwick in Scotland.

Pearl is somewhere on board. Yanus is bleeding to death. This is taking too long.

'You have to get Samira,' I hear myself say. My voice sounds shrill and frightened. 'She needs medical help.'

The captain won't be rushed. He is following the protocols and procedures set down for piracy or violent incidents at sea. He wants to know how many there are? Are they armed? Will they take hostages?

The information is relayed to the Coast Guard and police. We are twenty minutes from port. Huge glass windows frame the approaching coastline, which is still blanketed in darkness. The bridge is high up, overlooking the bow. Nothing approximates a steering wheel. Instead there are computer screens, buttons and keyboards.

I confront the captain, demanding that he listen to me.

'I understand that you're a British police officer,' he says abruptly. 'But this is a Dutch vessel and you have no authority here. My responsibility is to my passengers and crew. I will not endanger their safety.'

'A woman has just given birth. She's bleeding. She needs medical help.'

'We are twenty minutes from docking.'

'So you'll do nothing?'

'I am waiting for my instructions.'

'What about the passengers downstairs? They're waking up.'

'I don't believe they should be panicked. We have contingency plans to evacuate passengers to the Globetrotter Lounge, where most of them are due to have breakfast.'

The chief engineer is a neat little man with a college-boy haircut.

'Will you come with me?' I ask.

He hesitates. I pick up the first-aid box from the bench and turn to leave. The engineer looks at the captain, seeking permission. I don't know what passes between them but he's ready to follow me.

'Are there any weapons on board?'

'No.'

God, they make it hard! This time we use a service lift to reach Deck Nine. The doors open. The passage is empty. The deck below has the freight drivers who are due to disembark first.

At every corner I expect to see Pearl. He is a natural at this. Even my presence on the ferry didn't fluster him. He simply adjusted his sights and made a new plan. Yanus is

362

the more unpredictable but Pearl is the more dangerous because he can adapt. I can picture him, fazed for a moment by the loss of Samira and the twins but still calculating his chances of escape.

Even before I reach the cabin I can see that something is wrong. A handful of passengers crowd the passage, craning to look over one another's head. Among them is the Welsh couple. Mrs Jones looks naked without her lipstick and is squeezed into a grey tracksuit that struggles to encompass her buttocks.

'You can't escape them,' she says to the others. 'Thugs and criminals. And what do the police do? Nothing. Too busy giving out speeding tickets. Even if they do get charged, some judge or magistrate will let them off on account of their drug addiction or deprived childhood. What about the bloody victims, eh? Nobody cares about them.'

The cabin door is open, the lock broken. Sitting on his bunk, the German truck driver holds his head back to stop his nose bleeding. There is no sign of Samira or the twins.

'Where are they?' I grab his shoulder. 'Where?'

The worst thing is not the anger. It is the murderous desire behind the anger.

My mobile phone is ringing. We must be in range of a signal. I don't recognise the number.

'Hello.'

'And hello to you,' says Pearl. 'Have you ever seen that TV commercial about the Energizer bunny that keeps going and going and going? You're like that fucking bunny. You just don't quit.'

His voice has an echo. He's on the vehicle deck. 'Where is she?'

'I found her, bunny.'

'Yes.'

'Do you know how? The blood. You left a trail of it.' A baby is crying in the background. 'I also found Yanus. You cut him pretty good, but I patched him up.'

'He'll bleed to death.'

'Don't you worry about that, bunny. I don't leave *my* friends behind.'

I'm already on the move, running along the passage to the first cabin. The chief engineer struggles to keep up with me. Yanus has gone. The floor is polished red with blood and dozens of footprints stain the passageway.

People are amazing. They will walk past a scene like this and ignore it because it's beyond their ordinary, mundane, workaday comprehension.

Pearl is still on the line. 'You'll never get off the ferry,' I yell. 'Give them back. Please.'

'I need to talk to the captain.'

'He won't negotiate.'

'I don't wanna fuckin' negotiate! We have a mutual interest.'

'What's that?'

'We both want me off this ferry.'

My head is clearer now. Others are making decisions for me. It is three hours before dawn and the Essex coast is somewhere ahead of us in the darkness. I can't hear the engines from the bridge and without any points of reference the ferry doesn't appear to be moving. Two coastguard launches have joined the *Stena Britannica*, escorting us into port. The captain is communicating directly with his superiors in Rotterdam.

I am being kept away, at arm's length, as though I'm a liability or worse, a hysterical woman. What could I have done differently? Hindsight is a cruel teacher. I should never have left Samira or the twins. I should have stayed with them. Perhaps I could have fought Pearl off.

My mind goes further back. I should never have gone to Amsterdam looking for her. I have made things worse rather than better. That's the story of my life – good intentions. And being a hundredth of a second too slow – close enough to touch victory in a contest where first and last were separated by the width of a chest.

How can they negotiate with Pearl? He can't be trusted. The chief engineer hands me something hot to drink.

'Not long to go now,' he says, motioning to the windows. The lights of Harwich appear and disappear as we ride the swell. Massive cranes with four legs and oblong torsos seem to stand guard at the gates of the town. I stay at the window, watching it approach.

The captain and navigator stare at screens, using external cameras to manoeuvre the ferry, edging it against the dock. We are so high up that the stevedores look like Lilliputians trying to tie down a giant.

DI Forbes is first on board, pausing just long enough to look at my clothes with a mixture of awe and disgust. He takes the phone from the captain.

'Don't trust him,' I yell across the bridge. It is all I have a chance to say before the DI introduces himself to Pearl. I can only hear one side of their conversation but Forbes repeats each demand as it is made. The clicks in his throat are like punctuation marks.

Pearl wants the main ferry doors opened and vehicles moved to clear a path for his truck. Nobody is to approach. If he sees a police officer on the deck, or if he hears a fire alarm, or if anything is different or untoward he will kill Samira and the twins.

'*You have to give me more time,*' says Forbes. '*I'll need at least an hour . . . That's not long enough. I can't do it in fifteen minutes . . . Let me talk to Samira . . . Yes, that's why I want to talk to her . . . No, I don't want that. Nobody has to get hurt.*'

In the background one of the babies is crying – perhaps both of them. Do twins sound the same? Do they harmonise when they cry?

There are CCTV cameras on the vehicle decks. One of them is trained on the truck. Yanus can be seen clearly behind the wheel. Samira is in the passenger seat.

The rest of the passengers are being evacuated down gangways to the main terminal building. The port area has been closed and sealed off by armed response teams in black body armour. There are sharpshooters on surrounding rooftops.

The anguish of the past hours has swelled up inside me, making it hard to breathe. I can feel myself sinking into the background.

Forbes has agreed to take a limited number of vehicles off the ferry, clearing a path for the truck. I follow the detective down the footbridge to the dock as he supervises the evacuation. Men in yellow reflective vests wave the first of the rigs down the ramp.

Forbes has put Pearl onto a speakerphone. The Irishman sounds calm. Confident. Perhaps it's bravado. He is talking over the sound of engines, telling Forbes to hurry. Slowly a clear lane emerges on the vehicle deck. The Mercedes truck is at the far end, with its headlights blazing and engine running.

I still can't understand how he hopes to get away. There are unmarked police cars waiting outside and helicopters in the air. He can't outrun them.

Yanus is bleeding to death. Even with a bandaged leg and forearm his blood pressure will be dropping. How long before he loses consciousness?

'You definitely saw a gun?' asks Forbes, addressing me directly for the first time.

'Yes.'

'Could he have other firearms?'

'Yes.'

'What is the truck carrying?'

'This one is empty. There's another on Deck Five. I didn't see inside.' I give him the vehicle number.

'So it could be a trafficking run. There might be illegals on board.'

'It's possible.'

The last of the rigs has been moved. Yanus has a clear path to the ramp. Pearl is still issuing instructions. The twins are silent.

In a beat of tense silence I realise something is wrong. Pearl is too calm, too confident. His plan doesn't make sense. As the notion occurs to me, I'm moving, pushing past Forbes and sprinting up the ramp. A hundred metres is not my favourite distance but I can cover it in less time than it takes most people to tie their shoes.

Forbes is yelling at me to stop. He's too late. Reacting to the new development he orders his men to move. Heavy boots thunder up the ramp after me, sweeping between the outer rows of trucks.

Yanus is still behind the wheel, staring out through the windscreen, unperturbed by my approach. His eyes seem to follow me as I swing on the door handle and wrench it open. His hands are taped to the steering wheel. Blood has drained onto the floor at his feet. I press my hand to his neck. He's dead.

Samira's hands are also taped. I lean across Yanus and touch her shoulder. Her eyes open.

'Where are they?'

She shakes her head.

I swing down and run to the rear of the truck. A sledge-hammer pulverises the lock and the doors swing open. Guns sweep from side to side. The trailer is empty.

Forbes reaches us, puffing and wheezing, still clogged up with his cold. I snatch the phone from him. The line is dead.

Amid the commotion of the next few minutes I see things at half speed and struggle to find enough saliva to moisten my mouth. Forbes is bellowing orders and kicking angrily at the truck tyres. Someone will have to pop him with a tranquilliser gun if he doesn't calm down.

Teams of police have secured the ferry. Nobody is being allowed on or off. Passengers are being screened and interviewed in the terminal. Floodlights on the dock make it appear like a massive stage or film set, ready for the cameras to roll.

Yanus watches and waits, as though expecting his cue. My heart trips at the reality of having killed him. Yes, he deserved it – but *I did this*. I took his life. His blood still stains my clothes, along with Samira's.

Paramedics are lifting her onto a stretcher. The towel is still wedged between her thighs. A medic gently shunts me to one side when I approach. She can't talk to me now. I want to say I'm sorry – that it was my fault. I should never have left her. I should have stayed with them. Perhaps I could have stopped Pearl.

Some time later Forbes comes looking for me.

'Let's walk,' he says.

Instinctively, I take his arm. I'm frightened my legs might fail.

'What time is it?' I ask.

'Five-thirty.'

'My watch says five-fifteen.'

'It's slow.'

'How do you know yours isn't fast?

'Because the ferry company has those big fucking clocks on the wall that say *your* watch is wrong in four different time zones.'

We walk down the ramp, along the dock, away from the ferry. Refinery tanks and shipping containers create silhouettes against the brightening sky. Wind and smoke and scudding clouds are streaming over us.

'You don't think he's on the ferry, do you?' asks Forbes.

'No.'

There is another long pause. 'We found a lifebuoy missing from the starboard railing. He could have gone over the side.'

'Someone would have seen him.'

'We were distracted.'

'Even so.'

I can still smell the twins and feel the smoothness of their

369

skin. We're both thinking the same thing. What happened to them?

'You should never have put yourself on that ferry,' he says.

'I couldn't be sure she was on board.'

Taking a packet of cigarettes from his pockets, he counts the contents.

'You shouldn't smoke when you've got a cold.'

'I shouldn't smoke at all. My wife thinks men and women can have precisely the same ailment with the same symptoms but it's always the man who is sicker.'

'That's because men are hypochondriacs.'

'I've got a different theory. I think it's because no matter how sick a woman is there's always a small part of her brain thinking about shoes.'

'I bet you didn't tell her that.'

'I'm sick, not stupid.'

His demeanour is different now. Instead of sarcasm and cynicism I sense anxiety and a hardening resolve.

'Who's behind this?'

'Samira mentioned an Englishman who called himself "Brother". She said he had a cross on his neck. There's someone you should look at. His name is Paul Donavon. He went to school with Cate Beaumont – and with me. He was there on the night she was run down.'

'You think he's behind this?'

'Samira met "Brother" at an orphanage in Kabul. Donavon was in Afghanistan with the British Army. The traffickers targeted orphans because it meant fewer complications. There were no families to search for them or ask questions. Some were trafficked for sex. Others were given the option of becoming surrogates.'

'The pregnant illegals you asked about. Both claimed to be orphans.'

Forbes still hasn't lit his cigarette. It rests between his lips, wagging up and down as he talks. He glances over his shoulder at the ferry.

'About the other night.'

'What night?'

'When we had dinner.'

'Yeah?'

'Did I conduct myself in a proper fashion? I mean, did I behave?'

'You were a perfect gentleman.'

'That's good,' he mumbles. 'I mean, I thought so.' After a pause. 'You took something that didn't belong to you.'

'I prefer to think that we shared information.'

He nods. 'You might want to reconsider your career choice, DC Barba. I don't know if you're what I'd call a team player.'

He can't stay. There is a debriefing to attend, which is going to be rough. His superiors are going to want to know how he let Pearl get away. And once the media get hold of this story it's going to run and run.

Forbes looks at my clothes. 'If he's not on the ferry, how did he get off?'

'He could still be on board.'

'You don't believe that.'

'No. What about the crew?'

'You think he took a uniform?'

'It's possible.'

He turns abruptly and strides back towards the waiting police cars. The CCTV footage will most likely provide the answer. There are cameras on every corner of the dock and every deck of the ship. One of them will have recorded Pearl.

'Eat bananas,' I yell after him.

'Pardon?'

'My mother's remedy for a cold.'

'You said you never listened to her.'

'I said *almost* never.'

There have been too many hospitals lately. Too many long waits on uncomfortable chairs, eating machine snacks and drinking powdered coffee and synthetic whitener. This one smells of boiled food and faeces and has grim checked tiles in the corridors, worn smooth by the trolleys.

Ruiz called me from Hull after his ferry docked. He wanted to come and get me but I told him to go home and rest. He's done enough.

'Are they looking after you?'

'I'm fine.'

'Samira?'

'She's going to be OK.'

I hope I'm right. She's been asleep for ten hours and didn't even wake when they lifted her from the ambulance and wheeled her to a private room. I have been waiting here, dozing in my plastic chair, with my head on the bed near her shoulder.

It is mid-afternoon when she finally wakes. I feel the mattress shift and open my eyes to see her looking at me.

'I need the bathroom,' she whispers.

I take her by the elbow and help her to the en-suite.

'Where am I?'

'In a hospital.'

'What country?'

'England.'

There is a nod of acceptance but no hint of a journey completed or any sense of achievement.

Samira washes her face, ears, hands and feet, talking softly to herself. I take her arm again, leading her back to bed.

Motioning to the window, she wants to look outside. The North Sea is just visible over the rooftops and between buildings. It is the colour of brushed steel.

'As a child I used to wonder what the sea looked like,' she says. 'I had only ever seen pictures in books and on TV.' She gazes at the horizon.

'What do you think now?'

'I think it looks higher than the land. Why doesn't the water rush in and sweep us away?'

'Sometimes it does.'

I notice a towel in her hand. She wants to use it as a prayer mat but doesn't know in which direction she should face towards Mecca. She turns slowly round and round, like a cat trying to settle.

There are tears in her eyes and her lips tremble, struggling to form the words.

'They will be hungry soon. Who will feed them?'

Book Three

'Love and pain are not the same. Love is put to the test – pain is not. You do not say of pain, as you do of love, "That was not true pain or it would not have disappeared so quickly."'

William Boyd (*The Blue Afternoon*)

1

In the nights since the twins were born I have drowned countless times, twitching and kicking at the bedclothes. I see tiny bodies floating in fields of kelp or washed up on beaches. My lungs give out before I can reach them, leaving me choking and numb with an obscure anguish. I wonder if there's such a thing as a *swollen* heart?

Samira is also awake. She walks through the house at three a.m., moving as though her feet have an agreement with the ground that she will always tread lightly in return for never encountering another path that is too steep.

It has been five days since the twins went missing. Pearl has soaked through the cracks of the world and vanished. We know how he got off the ferry. A CCTV camera on Deck Three picked up a man in a hard hat and reflective jacket who couldn't be identified as one of the crew. The footage didn't show his face clearly but he was seen carrying a pets' travelling cage. The square grey plastic box was supposed to contain two Siamese cats but they were found wandering in a stairwell.

Another camera in the Customs area picked up the clearest images of the unidentified man. In the foreground trucks are being scanned with heat-seeking equipment designed to find illegals. But in the background, at the edge of the frame, a pumpkin-shaped caravan attached to an early-model Range Rover can be seen. Mr and Mrs Jones of Cardiff are seen repacking their duty-frees and souvenirs after being searched. As the car and caravan pull away, a square grey pet cage is visible on the tarmac next to where they were parked.

The Welsh couple were pulled over a little after midday on Sunday on the M4 just east of Reading. The caravan was empty but Pearl's fingerprints were lifted from the table and the aluminium door. The couple had stopped for petrol at a motorway service centre on the M25. A cashier remembered Pearl buying bottles and baby formula. Shortly afterwards, at 10.42 a.m., a car was reported stolen from an adjacent parking area. It still hasn't been found.

Forbes is running the investigation, liaising with Spijker in Amsterdam, combining resources, pitting their wills against the problem. They are cross-checking names from the IVF clinic with the UK immigration records.

There has been a news blackout about the missing twins. DI Forbes took the decision. Stolen children make dramatic headlines and he wants to avoid creating panic. A year ago a newborn was snatched from a hospital in Harrogate and there were 1,200 alleged sightings in the first two days. Mothers were accosted in the street and treated like kidnappers. Homes were raided needlessly. Innocent families suffered.

The only public statement has been about Pearl, who has a warrant out for his arrest. Another one. I have taken to carrying my gun again. As long as he's out there, I'm going to keep it with me. I am not going to lose Samira again.

She has been staying with me since leaving hospital on Wednesday. Hari has moved out of the spare room and is sleeping downstairs on a sofa bed. He seems quite taken by our lodger. He has started wearing a shirt around the house because he senses that she disapproves.

I am to face a Police Disciplinary Tribunal. Neglect of duty, deliberate falsehood and abuse of authority are just three of the charges. Failing to show up at Hendon is the least of my worries. Barnaby Elliot has accused me of harassment and arson. The investigation is being supervised by the Police Complaints Authority. I am guilty until proven innocent.

A toilet flushes along the hallway. A light switch clicks off. A few minutes later comes the hum of a machine and the rhythmic suction of a breast pump. Samira's milk has come in and she has to express every six hours. The sound of the pump is strangely soporific. I close my eyes again.

She hasn't said anything about the twins. I keep wondering when she is going to crack, fragmented by the loss. Even when she identified Hasan's body at Westminster Mortuary she held it all inside.

'It's OK to cry,' I told her.

'That is why Allah gave us tears,' she answered.

'You think God played a part in this?'

'He would not give me this suffering if he did not think I could endure it.'

How can she be so wise, yet so accepting? Can she really believe this is part of some grand master plan or that Allah would test her so cruelly?

Such faith seems positively medieval, yet she has an appetite for learning. Things that I take for granted she finds fascinating, like central heating, dual flush toilets and my washer/dryer. In Kabul she had to carry water upstairs to their flat and the power failed almost daily. London has lights along every street, burning through the night. Samira asked me if perhaps we British are scared of the dark. She didn't understand why I laughed.

I took her shopping for clothes at Canary Wharf yesterday. 'There is not so much glass in all of Afghanistan,' she said, pointing to the office towers that shone in the morning sun. I could see her studying the office workers queuing for coffee and 'skinny' muffins: the women dressed in narrow skirts, tight tops and jackets, flicking their short hair, chatting on mobile phones.

The clothing boutiques intimidated her. The shop assistants were dressed like mourners and the shops felt like funeral parlours. I told Samira there was a better place to find clothes. We left and went to Commercial Road where garments were crammed on racks and spilling from bins. She chose two skirts, a long-sleeved blouse and a cardigan. It came to less than sixty pounds.

She studied the twenty-pound notes.

'Is this your queen?'

'Yes.'

'She looks like she has been dipped in plaster.'

I laughed. 'I guess she does.'

The Christmas decorations were up. Even the bagel bakery and halal butcher had fairy lights and fake snow. Samira stopped and peered into a lobster tank in the window of a restaurant.

'I am never going to swim in the sea.'

'Why?'

'I don't want to meet one of them.'

I think she had visions of lobsters crawling over one another in the same density as in the tank.

'This must be like science fiction to you.'

'Science? Fiction?'

'It means like a fantasy. Unreal.'

'Yes, unreal.'

Seeing London through Samira's eyes has given me a different perspective on the city. Even the most mundane scene takes on a new life. When I took her underground to catch the Tube, she clutched my hand as an approaching train roared through the tunnel – sounding like a 'monster in a cave', she said.

The casual wealth on display is embarrassing. There are more vets in the East End than there were doctors in Kabul. And the animals are better fed than the orphans.

The breast pump has stopped. Samira has turned on Hari's TV and is flicking between channels. Slipping out of bed, I tiptoe along the hall and knock on her door. She's wearing my old dressing gown, the one with an owl sewn onto the pocket.

'Can't you sleep?'

'No.'

'I'll make us a sleeping potion.'

Her eyes widen.

She follows me down the stairs, along the hall into the kitchen. I close the door and take a bottle of milk from the fridge, pouring it into mugs. Two minutes in the microwave and they're steaming. Breaking up pieces of dark chocolate, I drop them in the liquid, watching them melt. Samira uses a spoon to catch the melting shards, licking it clean.

'Tell me about your family.'

'Most of them are dead.'

She licks the spoon. I break off more pieces of chocolate and add them to her mug.

'Did you have a big family?'

'Not so big. In Afghanistan people exaggerate what their family has done. Mine is no different. One of my ancestors travelled to China with Marco Polo, they say, but I don't believe it. I think he was a smuggler who brought the black powder from India to Afghanistan. The king heard of the magic and asked to see a demonstration. According to my father, a thousand rockets streamed back and forth across the sky. Bamboo castles dripped with fire. Fireworks became our family business. The formulas were passed down from father to son – and to me.'

I remember the photograph among Hasan's possessions that showed a factory with workers lined up outside, most of them missing limbs or eyes or incomplete in other ways. Hasan had burn scars on his arms.

'It must have been dangerous work.'

Samira holds up her hands, showing her fingers. 'I am one of the lucky ones.' She sounds almost disappointed. 'My father lost both his thumbs when a shell exploded. Uncle Yousuf lost his right arm and his wife lost her left arm. They helped each other to cook and sew and drive a car. My aunt changed gears and my uncle steered. My father's other brother, Fahad, lost his fingers during a display. He was a very good gambler but he began to lose when he couldn't shuffle the cards.

'I didn't meet my grandfather. He was killed in a factory explosion before I was born. Twelve others died in the same fire, including two of his brothers. My father said it was a sacrifice that only our family could make. One hand is enough to sin, he said. One hand is enough to save.'

She glances at the dark square of the window. 'It was our calling – to paint the sky. My father believed that one day our family would make a rocket that would light the way to Heaven. In the meantime, we would make rockets that drew the gaze of Allah in the hope that he would bless our family and bring us happiness and good health.' She pauses and considers the irony of such a statement. Perfectly still, she is canted forward over the table, firm yet fragile. Her stare seems to originate at the back of her eyes.

'What happened to the factory?'

'The Talibs closed it down. Fireworks were sinful, they said. People celebrated when they arrived. They were going to stop the warlords and end the corruption. Things changed but not in a good way. Girls could not go to school. Windows were painted over so women could not be seen. There was no music or TV or videos, no card games or kites. I was ten years old and they made me wear a burka. I could not buy things from male shopkeepers. I could not talk to men. I could not laugh in public. Women had to be ordinary. Invisible. Ignorant. My mother educated us in secret. Books were hidden each night and homework had to be destroyed.

'Men with beards and black turbans patrolled the streets, listening for music and videos. They beat people with whips soaked in water and with chains. Some were taken away and didn't come back.

'My father took us to Pakistan. We lived in a camp. My mother died there and my father blamed himself. One day he announced that we were going home. He said he would rather starve in Kabul than live like a beggar.'

She falls silent, shifting in her chair. The motor of the refrigerator rattles to life and I feel the same shudder pass through me.

'The Americans dropped leaflets from the sky saying they were coming to liberate us but there was nothing left to free us from. Still we cheered because the Talibs were gone, running like frightened dogs. But the Northern Alliance was not so different. We had learned not to expect too much. In Afghanistan we sleep with the thorns and not the flowers.'

The effort of remembering has made her sleepy. I wash the mugs and follow her upstairs. She pauses at my door, wanting to ask me something.

'I am not used to the quiet.'

'You think London is quiet?'

She hesitates. 'Would it be all right if I slept in your room?'

'Is there something wrong? Is it the bed?'

'No.'

'Are you frightened?'

'No.'

'What is it, then?'

'At the orphanage we slept on the floor in the same room. I am not used to being alone.'

My heart twists. 'You should have said something earlier. Of course you can sleep with me.'

She collects a blanket and spreads it on the floor beside my wardrobe.

'My bed is big enough. We can share.'

'No, this is better.'

She curls up on the floor and breathes so quietly that I want to make sure she's still there.

'Good night,' I whisper. 'May you sleep amid the flowers, not the thorns.'

DI Forbes arrives in the morning, early as usual. Dressed in a charcoal suit and yellow tie, he is ready to front a news conference. The media blackout is being lifted. He needs help to find the twins.

I show him to the kitchen. 'Your cold sounds better.'

'I can't stomach another bloody banana.'

Hari is with Samira in the sitting room. He is showing her his old Xbox and trying to explain what it does.

'You can shoot people.'

'Why?'

'For fun.'

'Why would you shoot people for *fun*?'

I can almost hear Hari's heart sinking. Poor boy. The two of them have something in common. Hari is studying chemical engineering and Samira knows more about chemical reactions than any of his lecturers, he says.

'She's an odd little thing,' says Forbes, whispering.

'How do you mean?'

'She doesn't say much.'

'Most people talk too much and have nothing to say.'

'What is she going to do?' he asks.

'I don't know.'

What would I do in her shoes? I have never been without friends or family or stranded in a foreign country (unless you count Wolverhampton, which is pretty bloody foreign).

Hari walks into the kitchen, looking pleased with himself.

'Samira is going to teach me to make fireworks,' he announces, taking a biscuit from Forbes's plate.

'So you can blow yourself up,' I say.

'I'm very careful.'

'Oh yes. Like the time you filled that copper pipe with black powder and blew a hole in the wooden siding.'

'I was fifteen.'

'Old enough to know better.'

'Sunday is Guy Fawkes' Night. We're going to make a whistling chaser.'

'Which is?'

'A rocket that whistles and has white and red stars with a salute at the end.'

'A salute?'

'A big bang.'

Hari has already compiled a list of ingredients: potassium nitrate, sulphur, barium chlorate and copper powder. I have no idea what this stuff does but I can almost see the fireworks exploding in his eyes.

Forbes looks at the list. 'Is this stuff legal?'

'We're only making three-inch shells.'

It doesn't answer the question but the detective lets it pass.

Although Samira doesn't mention the twins, I know she must think about them, just as I do. Rarely does a minute pass when my mind doesn't drift back to them. I can feel their skin against my lips and see their narrow ribcages moving with each breath. The baby girl had trouble breathing. Perhaps her lungs weren't fully developed. We have to find her.

Forbes has opened the car door and waits for Samira to sit in the rear seat. She is wearing her new clothes – a long woollen skirt and white blouse. She looks so composed. Still. There is a landscape inside her that I will never reach.

'You won't have to answer questions,' the DI explains. 'I'll help you prepare a statement.'

He drives hunched over the wheel, frowning at the road as if he hates city traffic. At the same time he talks about the investigations. With the help of Spijker he has managed to trace five asylum seekers impregnated at the fertility clinic in Amsterdam who subsequently turned up in the UK.

'All admit to giving birth and claim the babies were taken from them. They were each given five hundred pounds and told their debt had been repaid.'

'Where did they give birth?'

'A private address. They couldn't give an exact location. They were taken there in the back of a Transit van with blacked-out windows. Two of them talked of planes coming in to land.'

'It's under a flight path?'

'That's what I figure.'

'Births have to be registered. Surely we can find the babies that way.'

'It's not as easy as you think. Normally, the hospital or health authority informs the registrar of a birth but not when it happens in a private home or outside of the NHS. Then it's up to the parents. And how's this? Mum and Dad don't even have to turn up at the registry office. They can send along someone else – a witness to the birth or even just the owner of the house.'

'Is that it? What about doctors' certificates or medical records?'

'Don't need them. You need more paperwork to register a car than a baby.'

We're passing the Royal Chelsea Hospital on the Embankment before turning left over Albert Bridge and circling Battersea Park.

'What about Dr Banerjee?'

'He admits to providing Cate Beaumont with her surplus embryos but claims to have no knowledge of the surrogacy plan. She told him she was transferring to a different fertility clinic with a higher success rate.'

'And you believe him?'

Forbes shrugs. 'The embryos belonged to her. She had every right to take them.'

This still doesn't explain why Banerjee lied to me. Or why he turned up at my father's birthday party.

'What about Paul Donavon?'

'He did two tours of Afghanistan and six months in Iraq. Won the Queen's Gallantry Medal. The guy is a bona fide fucking hero.'

Samira hasn't said a word. Sometimes I feel as if she has turned off or tuned out, or is listening to different voices.

'We are contacting the orphanage in Kabul as well as one in Albania and another in Russia,' says Forbes. 'Hopefully they can give us more than just a nickname.'

The conference room is a stark, windowless place, with vinyl chairs and globe lights full of scorched moths. This used to be the old National Criminal Intelligence Service building, now refitted and rebranded to suit the new crime-fighting agency with new initials. Despite the headlines and high-tech equipment, SOCA still strikes me as being rather more Loch Ness than Eliot Ness – chasing shadowy monsters who live in dark places.

Radio reporters have taken up the front row, taping their station logos to the microphones. Press reporters slouch in the middle rows and their TV counterparts, with whiter teeth and better clothes, are at the rear.

When I did my detective training at Bramshill they sent us in groups to see an autopsy. I watched a pathologist working on the body of a hiker who had been dead for a fortnight.

Holding up a jar, he said, 'This little fellow is a sarcophagid fly, but I like to refer to him as a crime reporter. Notice the red boozer eyes and his grey-checked abdomen, which is perfect for hiding food stains. More importantly, he's always first to find a corpse . . .'

Forbes looks at his watch. It's eleven o'clock. He straightens his tie and tugs at the sleeves of his suit.

'You ready?'

Samira nods.

Flashguns explode and render me blind as I follow Samira to the conference table. Photographers are fighting for position, holding cameras above their heads in a strange jiggling dance.

Forbes holds a chair for Samira, then reaches across the table to a jug of water and pours her a glass. His slightly pock-marked face is bleached by the brightness of the TV lights.

Clearing his throat, he begins. 'We are investigating the abduction of two newborn babies, a twin boy and girl, born in the early hours of Sunday morning on board a ferry between the Hook of Holland and Harwich. The *Stena Britannica* docked at 3.36 a.m. (GMT) and the babies were last seen thirty minutes earlier.'

Flashguns fire in his eyes.

Forbes makes no mention of baby-broking or illegal surrogacy. Instead he concentrates on the details of the voyage and abduction. An image of Brendan Pearl is projected onto the screen behind him, along with a detailed description.

'DC Barba was returning from a short stay in Amsterdam when she stumbled upon a people-trafficking operation. She helped deliver the twins but was unable to prevent the babies being taken.

'I want to stress that this is not a domestic dispute and Brendan Pearl is not related to the missing infants. Pearl is on parole after being released as a result of the Good Friday Agreement. He is considered dangerous. We are advising people not to approach him under any circumstances and to call the police if they know his whereabouts. Miss Khan will now make a brief statement.'

He slides the microphone towards Samira. She looks at it suspiciously and unfolds a piece of paper. The flashguns create a wall of light and she stumbles over the first words. Someone shouts for her to speak up. She begins again:

'I wish to thank everyone who has looked after me these past few days, especially Miss Barba for helping me on the ferry when I was having the babies. I am also grateful to the police for all they have done. I ask the man who took the twins to give them back. They are very small and need medical care. Please take them to a hospital or leave them somewhere safe.'

Samira looks up from the page. She's departing from the script. 'I forgive you for this but I do not forgive you for Zala. For this I hope you will suffer eternal agony for every second of every day for the rest of your life.'

Forbes cups his hand over the microphone, trying to stop her. Samira stands to leave. Questions are yelled from the floor.

'*Who is Zulu?*'

'*Did you know Brendan Pearl?*'

'*Why did he take your babies?*'

The story has more holes than a Florida ballot card. The reporters sense a bigger story. Decorum breaks down.

'*Has there been a ransom demand?*'

'*How did Pearl get off the ferry with the twins?*'

'*Do you believe they're still alive?*'

Samira flinches. She's almost at the door.

'*What about names?*'

She turns to the questioner, blinking into the flashguns. 'A maiden can leave things nameless; a mother must name her children.'

The answer silences the room. People look at one another, wondering what she means. Mothers. Maidens. What does that have to do with anything?

Forbes's shoulders are knotted with rage.

'That was a fucking disaster,' he mutters as I chase him down the corridor.

'It wasn't so bad.'

'God knows what they're going to write tomorrow.'

'They're going to write about the twins. That's what we want. We're going to find them.'

He suddenly stops and turns. 'That's only the beginning.'

'What do you mean?'

'I want you to meet someone.'

'When?'

'Now.'

'The funerals are today.'

'It won't take long.' He glances ahead of us. Samira is waiting near the lift. 'I'll make sure she gets home.'

Twenty minutes later we pull up outside a Victorian mansion block in Battersea, overlooking the park. Twisting branches of wisteria, naked and grey, frame the downstairs windows. The main door is open. An empty pram is poised, ready for an excursion. I can hear the mother coming down the stairs. She is attractive, in her early forties. A baby – too old to be one of the twins – rests on her hip.

'Excuse me, Mrs Piper.'

'Yes?'

'I'm Detective Inspector Forbes. This is DC Barba.'

The woman's smile fades. Almost imperceptibly she tightens her hold on the child. A boy.

'How old is he?' I ask.

'Eight months.'

'Aren't you beautiful?' I lean forward. The mother leans away.

'What's his name?'

'Jack.'

'He looks like you.'

392

'He's more like his father.'

Forbes interrupts. 'We were hoping to have a brief word.'

'I'm just going out. I have to meet someone.'

'It won't take long.'

Her gaze flicks from his face to mine. 'I think I should call my husband.' Pointedly she adds, 'He works for the Home Office.'

'Where did you have your baby?' Forbes asks.

She stutters nervously. 'It was a home birth. I'm going upstairs to ring my husband.'

'Why?' asks Forbes. 'We haven't even told you why we're here, yet you're anxious about something. Why do you need your husband's permission to talk to us?'

There is a flaw in the moment, a ripple of disquiet.

Forbes continues: 'Have you ever been to Amsterdam, Mrs Piper? Did you visit a fertility clinic there?'

Backing away towards the stairs, she shakes her head, less in denial than in the vain hope that he'll stop asking her questions. She is on the stairs. Forbes moves towards her. He's holding a business card. She won't take it from him. Instead he leaves it in the pram.

'Please ask your husband to phone me.'

I can hear myself apologising for bothering her. At the same time I want to know if she paid for a baby. Who did she pay? Who arranged it? Forbes has hold of my arm, leading me down the steps. I imagine Mrs Piper upstairs on the phone, the tears and the turmoil.

'Their names came up among the files that Spijker sent me,' Forbes explains. 'They used a surrogate. A girl from Bosnia.'

'Then it's *not* their baby.'

'How do we prove that? You saw the kid. Paternity tests, DNA tests, blood samples – every one of them will show that young Jack belongs to the Pipers. And there isn't a judge in this country who would give us permission to take samples in the first place.'

'We can prove they visited an IVF clinic in the Netherlands. We can prove their embryos were implanted in a surrogate. We can prove that it resulted in a pregnancy and a successful birth. Surely that's enough?'

'It doesn't prove that money changed hands. We need one of these couples to give evidence.'

He hands me a list of names and addresses:

Robert & Helena Piper
Alan & Jessica Case
Trevor & Toni Jury
Anaan & Lola Singh
Nicholas & Karin Pederson

'I have interviewed the other four couples. In each case they have called a lawyer and stuck to their story. None of them are going to cooperate – not if it means losing their child.'

'They broke the law!'

'Maybe you're right, but how many juries are going to convict? If that was your friend back there, holding her baby, would *you* take it away from her?'

2

The funerals are at two o'clock. I am dressed in a black blouse, black jacket, black trousers and black shoes. The only splash of colour is my lipstick.

Samira uses the bathroom after me. It's hard to believe that she's just given birth. There are stretch marks across her belly but elsewhere her skin is flawless. Occasionally I notice a tic or twitch of pain when she moves, but nothing else betrays her discomfort.

She is laying out her clothes on the bed, taking care not to crease her blouse.

'You don't have to come,' I tell her, but she has already decided. She met Cate only twice. They spoke through Yanus in stilted sentences rather than having a proper conversation. Yet they shared a bond like no other. Unborn twins.

We sit side by side in the cab. She is tense, restless – as

if at any moment she might unfurl a set of hidden wings and take flight. In the distance a chimney belches a column of white smoke like a steam train going nowhere.

'The police are going to find the twins,' I announce, as if we're deep in conversation.

She doesn't answer.

I try again. 'You do *want* to find them?'

'My debt is paid,' she whispers, chewing at her lower lip.

'You *owe* these people nothing.'

Again, she doesn't answer. How can I make her understand? Then, without warning, she replies, placing her words in careful sentences.

'I have tried not to love them. I thought it would be easier to give them up if I did not love them. I have even tried to *blame* them for what happened to Hasan and Zala. This is unfair, yes? What else can I do? My breasts leak for them. I hear them crying in my dreams. I want the sound to stop.'

Twin hearses are parked outside the chapel at the West London Crematorium. A carpet of artificial grass leads to a ramp where a small black sign with movable white letters spells out Felix and Cate's names.

Samira walks with surprising grace along the gravel path – not an easy thing to do. She pauses to look at the marble and stone crypts. Gardeners lean on their shovels and watch her. She seems almost alien. Other-worldly.

Barnaby Elliot is welcoming people and accepting condolences. Ruth Elliot is next to him in her wheelchair, dressed in mourning clothes that make her skin seem bloodless and brittle.

She sees me first. Her mouth twists around my name.

Barnaby turns and walks towards me. He kisses me on each cheek and I smell the sharp alcohol scent of his aftershave.

'Who did you see in Amsterdam?' he asks.

'A detective. Why did you lie about Cate's computer?'

He doesn't answer. Instead he raises his gaze to the trees, some of which are clinging to the yellow and gold remnants of autumn.

'I feel you should know that I have instructed a lawyer to gain custody of the twins. I want both of them.'

I look at him incredulously.

'What about Samira?'

'They're *our* grandchildren. They belong with us.'

'Not according to the law.'

'The law is an ass.'

I glance across at Samira, who is hanging back, perhaps sensing trouble. Barnaby shows no such discretion. 'Does she even *want* them?' he says, too loudly.

I have to unclench my jaw to speak. 'You stay away from her.'

'Listen to me—'

'No! *You* listen! She has been through enough. She has lost *everything*.'

Glaring at me with a sudden crazed energy, he lashes out at a hedge with his fist. His coat sleeve snags and he jerks it violently, tearing the fabric, which billows and flaps. Just as quickly he regains his composure. It's like watching a deep-breathing exercise for anger management. Reaching into his pocket, he takes out a business card.

'The trustee of Felix and Cate's will is having a meeting in chambers at Gray's Inn on Monday afternoon at three. He wants you there.'

'Why?'

'He didn't say. This is the address.'

I take the card and watch Barnaby return to his wife. Reaching for his hand, she cocks her head into his palm, holding it against her cheek. I have never seen them share a moment – not like this. Maybe it takes one tragedy to mend another.

The chapel is softly lit with red lights flickering behind glass. Flowers cover the coffins and spill out down the centre aisle almost to Ruth Elliot's wheelchair. Barnaby is beside her, alongside Jarrod. All three of them are holding hands, as if steeling one another.

I recognise other family and friends. The only person missing is Yvonne. Perhaps she didn't think she could cope with a day like this. It must be like losing a daughter.

On the other side of the church are Felix's family, who look far more Polish than Felix ever did. The women are short and square, with veils on their heads and rosary beads in their fingers.

The funeral director is holding his top hat across his bent other arm. His son, dressed identically, mimics his pose, although I notice a wad of chewing gum behind his ear.

A hymn strikes up – 'Come Let Us Join Our Friends Above', which is not really Cate's cup of tea. Then again, it must be hard to find something appropriate for a person who once pledged her undying love to a photograph of Kurt Cobain.

Reading from the Bible, Reverend Lunn intones something about the Resurrection and how we're all going to rise together on the same day and live as God's children. At the same time, he rubs a finger along the edge of Cate's coffin as if admiring the workmanship.

398

'Love and pain are not the same,' he says. 'But sometimes it feels like they should be. Love is put to the test every day. Pain is not. Yet the two of them are inseparable because true love cannot bear separation.'

His voice sounds far away. I have been in a state of suspended mourning for Cate for the past eight years. Trivial, sentimental, everyday sounds and smells bring back memories – lost causes, jazz shoes, cola Slushies, Simply Red songs, a teenager singing into a hairbrush, purple eye shadow . . . These things make me want to smile or swell painfully in my chest. There it is again   love and pain.

I don't see the coffins disappear. During the final hymn I slip outside, needing fresh air. On the far side of the parking lot, in the shadows of an arch, I see a familiar silhouette, waiting, tranquil. He's wearing an overcoat and red muffler. Donavon.

Samira is walking through the rose garden at the side of the chapel. She is going to see him when she clears the corner.

Instinctively, I close the gap. Any witness would say that my body language borders on violence. I grab Donavon's arm, twisting it behind his back, before shoving him against a wall, pressing his face to the bricks.

'Where are they? What have you done with them?'

'I don't know what you're talking about.'

I want him to struggle. I want to hurt him. Samira is behind me, hanging back.

'Do you know this man?'

'No.'

'The Englishman you met at the orphanage. You said he had a cross on his neck.' I pull aside Donavon's muffler, revealing his tattoo.

She shakes her head. 'A gold cross. Here.' She traces the outline on her collar.

Donavon laughs. 'Wonderful detective work, yindoo.'

I want to hit him.

'You were in Afghanistan.'

'Serving Queen and country.'

'Spare me the patriotic who-dares-wins crap. You lied to me. You saw Cate before the reunion.'

'Yes.'

'Why?'

'You wouldn't understand.'

'Try me.'

I let him go and he turns, blinking slowly, his pale eyes a little more bloodshot than I remember. Mourners are leaving the chapel. He glances at the crowd with a mixture of embarrassment and concern. 'Not here. Let's talk somewhere else.'

I let him lead the way. Leaving the cemetery, we walk east along the Harrow Road, which is choked with traffic and a conga line of buses. Sneaking sidelong glances at Donavon, I watch how he regards Samira. He doesn't seem to recognise her. Instead he keeps his eyes lowered in a penitent's demeanour, framing answers to the questions that he knows are coming. More lies.

We choose a café with stools at the window and tables inside. Donavon glances at the menu, buying time. Samira slips off her chair and kneels at the magazine rack, turning the pages quickly, as though expecting someone to stop her.

'The magazines are free to read,' I explain. 'You're allowed to look at them.'

Donavon twists the skin on his wrist, leaving a white weal. Blood rushes back to the slackened skin.

'I met Cate again three years ago,' he announces. 'It was just before my first tour of Afghanistan. It took me a while to find her. I didn't know her married name.'

'Why?'

'I wanted to see her.'

I wait for something more. He changes the subject. 'Have you ever been skydiving?'

'No.'

'What a rush. There's no feeling like it – standing in the doorway of a plane at ten thousand feet, heart pounding, charged up. Take that last big step and the slipstream sucks you away. Falling – only it doesn't feel like falling at all. It's flying. Air presses hollows in your cheeks and screams past your ears. I've jumped high-altitude, low-opening with oxygen – from twenty-five thousand feet. I swear I could open my arms and embrace the entire planet.'

His eyes are shining. I don't know why he's telling me this but I let him continue.

'The best thing that ever happened to me was getting booted out of school and joining the Paras. Up until then I was drifting. Angry. I didn't have any ambition. It changed my life.

'I got a little girl now. She's three. Her mother doesn't live with me any more – they're in Scotland – but I send 'em money every month and presents on her birthday and at Christmas. I guess what I'm trying to say is that I'm a different person.'

'Why are you telling me this?'

'Because I want you to understand. You think I'm a thug and a bully but I changed. What I did to Cate was unforgivable but *she* forgave me. That's why I went looking for her. I wanted to find out how things turned out for her. I didn't want to think I screwed up her life because of what I did to her.'

I don't want to believe him, I want to keep hating him because that's the world according to me. *My* recorded history.

'Why would Cate agree to see you?'

'She was curious, I guess.'

'Where did you meet?'

'We had a coffee in Soho.'

'And?'

'We talked. I said I was sorry. She said it was OK. I wrote her a few letters from Afghanistan. Whenever I was home on leave we used to get together for lunch or a coffee.'

'Why didn't you tell me this before?'

'Like I said, you wouldn't understand.'

It's not a good enough reason. How could Cate forgive *Donavon* before she forgave me?

'What do you know about the New Life Adoption Centre?'

'Cate took me there. She knew that Carla couldn't decide what to do about the baby.'

'How did Cate know about the adoption centre?'

He shrugs. 'Her fertility specialist is on the adoption panel.'

'Dr Banerjee. Are you sure?'

'Yeah.'

Julian Shawcroft and Dr Banerjee *know* each other. More lies.

'Did Cate tell you why she went to Amsterdam?'

'She said she was going to have another round of IVF.'

I glance towards Samira. 'She paid for a surrogate.'

'I don't understand.'

'There are twins.'

Donavon looks dumbfounded. Speechless.

'Where?'

'They're missing.'

I can see the knowledge register in his mind and match up with other details. News of the twins is already on the radio and in the early editions of the *Evening Standard*. I have shaken him more than I thought possible.

'What Cate did was illegal,' I explain. 'She was going to blow the whistle. That's why she wanted to talk to me.'

Donavon has regained a semblance of composure. 'Is that why they killed her?'

'Yes. Cate didn't accidentally find Samira. Someone put them together. I'm looking for a man called "Brother" – an Englishman who came to Samira's orphanage in Kabul.'

'Julian Shawcroft has been to Afghanistan.'

'How do you know?'

'It came up in conversation. He was asking where I served.'

I flip open my mobile and punch the speed dial. 'New Boy' Dave answers on the second ring. I haven't talked to him since Amsterdam. He hasn't called. I haven't called. Inertia. Fear.

'Hello, sweet boy.'

He sounds hesitant. I don't have time to ask why.

'When you did the background check on Julian Shawcroft, what did you find?'

'He used to be executive director of a Planned-Parenthood Clinic in Manchester.'

'Before that.'

'He studied theology at Oxford and then joined some sort of religious order.'

'A religious order?'

'He became a Catholic brother.'

There's the link! Cate, Banerjee, Shawcroft and Samira – I can tie them together.

Dave is no longer on the phone. I can't remember saying goodbye.

Donavon has been talking to me, asking questions. I haven't been listening.

'Did they look like Cate?' he asks.

'Who?'

'The twins.'

I don't know how to answer. I'm not good at describing newborn babies. They all look like Winston Churchill. Why should Donavon care?

3

A silver-coloured Lexus pulls into the driveway of a detached house in Wimbledon, south London. It has a personalised number plate: BABYDOC. Sohan Banerjee collects his things from the back seat and triggers the central locking. Lights flash. If only everything in life could be achieved with the press of a button.

'The penalty for people trafficking is fourteen years,' I say.

The doctor wheels around, clutching his briefcase to his stomach like a shield. 'I don't know what you're talking about.'

'I don't know the penalty for commercial surrogacy, but when you add medical rape and kidnapping I'm sure you'll be in prison long enough to make new friends.'

'I've done nothing wrong.'

'And I almost forgot murder. An automatic life sentence.'

'You're trespassing,' he blusters.

'Call the police.'

He looks towards his house and then at the houses nearby, perhaps conscious of what his neighbours might think.

'You *knew* Cate Beaumont was going to Amsterdam. You gave her a liquid-nitrogen canister that contained her remaining embryos. You told her about the Dutch clinic.'

'No. No.' His chins are wobbling.

'Were you going to deliver the twins?'

'I don't know what you're talking about,' he says again.

'How well do you know Julian Shawcroft?'

'We have a professional relationship.'

'You were at Oxford together. He was studying theology. You were studying medicine. See how much I know, Dr Banerjee? Not bad for some uppity Sikh girl who can't get a husband.'

His briefcase is still resting on the shelf of his stomach. My skin prickles with something more physical than loathing.

'You're on his adoption panel.'

'An independent body.'

'You told Cate about the New Life Adoption Centre. You introduced her to Shawcroft. What did you imagine you were doing? This wasn't some humanitarian crusade to help the childless. You got into bed with sex traffickers and murderers. Young women have been raped and exploited. People have died.'

'You've got it all wrong. I had nothing to do with any of that. What motive would I have?'

Motive? I still don't understand why Banerjee would get mixed up in something like this. It can't be the money. Maybe he was trapped or tricked into doing a 'favour'. It takes only one mistake and the hooks are planted.

He looks towards the house again. There is no wife waiting for him inside. No children at the door.

'It's personal, isn't it?'

He doesn't answer.

Forbes showed me a list of names. They were couples who provided embryos to the IVF clinic in Amsterdam. A surname suddenly stands out – Anaan and Lola Singh from Birmingham.

'Do you have family in the UK, Dr Banerjee? A sister, perhaps? Any nieces or nephews?'

He wants to deny it but the truth is imprinted on his features like fingerprints in putty. Mama mentioned that he had a nephew. The good doctor was so proud that he told stories about him over Sunday lunch. I take a stab at the rest of the story. His sister couldn't get pregnant. And not even her very clever brother – a fertility specialist – could help her.

Julian Shawcroft suggested there might be another way. He organised a surrogate mother in the Netherlands and Banerjee delivered the baby. He thought it was a one-off – a family matter – but Shawcroft wanted him to deliver other babies. He couldn't say no.

'What do you want from me?'

'Give me Julian Shawcroft.'

'I can't do that.'

'Are you worried about your career; your reputation?'

Banerjee smiles wryly – a defeated gesture. 'I have lived in this country for two-thirds of my life, Alisha. I hold masters' and doctoral degrees from Oxford and Harvard. I have published papers, lectured and been a Visiting Fellow at the University of Toronto.' He glances again at his house, the drawn curtains and empty rooms beyond. 'My reputation is *all* I have.'

'You broke the law.'

'Is it so very wrong? I thought we were helping the childless and offering a new life to asylum seekers.'

'You exploited them.'

'We saved them from orphanages.'

'And forced some of them into brothels.'

His dense eyebrows are knitted together.

'Give me Shawcroft. Make a statement.'

'I must protect my sister and her child.'

'By protecting *him*?'

'We protect each other.'

'I could have you arrested.'

'I will deny everything.'

'At least tell me where the twins are.'

'I don't meet the families. Julian arranges that side of things.' His voice changes. 'I beg you, leave this alone. Only bad things can come of it.'

'For whom?'

'For everyone. My nephew is a beautiful boy. He's nearly one.'

'When he grows up are you going to tell him about the medical rape that led to his conception?'

'I'm sorry.'

Everyone is sorry. It must be the times.

4

Forbes shuffles a stack of photographs and lays them out on a desk in three rows as if he's playing solitaire. Julian Shawcroft's picture is on the right edge. He looks like a charity boss straight from central casting: warm, smiling, avuncular . . .

'If you recognise someone I want you to point to the photograph,' the detective says.

Samira hesitates.

'Don't worry about getting anyone in trouble – just tell me if there is someone here who you've met before.'

Her eyes travel over the photographs and suddenly stop. She points to Shawcroft.

'This one.'

'Who is he?'

'Brother.'

'Do you know his real name?'

She shakes her head.

'How do you know him?'

'He came to the orphanage.'

'In Kabul?'

She nods.

'What was he doing there?'

'He brought blankets and food.'

'Did you talk to him?'

'He couldn't speak Afghani. I translated for him.'

'What did you translate?'

'He had meetings with Mr Jamal, the director. He said he could arrange jobs for some of the orphans. He wanted only girls. I told him I could not leave without Hasan. He said it would cost more money but I could repay him.'

'How much?'

Five thousand American dollars for each of us.'

'How were you supposed to repay this money?'

'He said God would find a way for me to pay.'

'Did he say anything about having a baby?'

'No.'

Forbes takes a sheet of paper from a folder. 'This is a list of names. I want you to tell me if you recognise any of them.'

Samira's finger dips down the page and stops. 'This girl – Allegra – she was at the orphanage.'

'Where did she go?'

'She left before me. Brother had a job for her.'

The detective smiles tightly. 'He certainly did.'

Forbes's office is on the second floor, opposite a large open-plan incident room. There is a photograph of his wife on a filing cabinet. She looks like a no-nonsense country girl, who has never quite managed to shed the baby pounds.

He asks Samira to wait outside. There's a soft-drinks machine near the lift. He gives her change. We watch her walk away. She looks so young – a woman in progress.

'We have enough for a warrant,' I say. 'She identified Shawcroft.'

Forbes doesn't answer. What is he waiting for? He stacks the photographs, lining up the edges.

'We still can't link Shawcroft to the surrogacy plot. It's her word against his.'

'But the other orphans—'

'Talk about a saintly man who offered to help them. We can't *prove* Shawcroft arranged for them to be trafficked. And we can't *prove* he blackmailed them into getting pregnant. We need one of the buyers to give evidence, which means incriminating themselves.'

'Could we indemnify them from prosecution?'

'Yes, but we can't indemnify them against a civil lawsuit. Once they admit to paying for a surrogate baby, the birth mother could reclaim her child.'

I can hear it in his voice – resignation. The task is proving too hard. He won't give up but neither will he go the extra yard, make the extra call, knock on one more door. He thinks that I'm clutching at straws; that I haven't thought this through. But I have never been more certain.

'Samira should meet him.'

'What?'

'She could wear a wire.'

Forbes sucks air through his teeth. 'You gotta be kidding! Shawcroft would see right through it. He *knows* we have her.'

'Yes, but investigations are about building pressure. Right

now he thinks we can't touch him. He's comfortable. We have to shake him up – take him out of his comfort zone.'

There are strict rules governing the bugging of phones and properties. The Surveillance Commissioner has to grant permission. But a wire is different – as long as she stays in a public place.

'What would she say?'

'He promised her a job.'

'Is that it?'

'She doesn't *have* to say anything. Let see what *he* says.'

Forbes crunches a throat lozenge between his teeth. His breath smells of lemons.

'Is she up for it?'

'I think so.'

5

Any sport can be made to sound ridiculous if you break it down to its basics – stick, ball, hole – but I have never really understood the appeal of golf. I guess the courses are pretty in an artificial sort of way, like Japanese gardens planned down to the last pebble and shrub.

Julian Shawcroft plays every Sunday morning in the same foursome, with a town planner, a car dealer and a local businessman. They tee off just after ten.

Their club is on the border of Sussex and Surrey, somewhere in the Green Belt and the White Stockbroker Belt. Brown is a colour rarely seen out here – unless you take a big divot.

Samira has a battery the size of a matchbox taped to the small of her back and a thin red fibre threaded under her right armpit and attached to a button-sized microphone taped between her breasts.

Adjusting her blouse, I lift my gaze to hers and smile reassuringly. 'You don't have to go through with this.'

She nods.

'Do you know what you're going to say?'

Another nod.

'If you get frightened, walk away. If you feel threatened, walk away. Any sign of trouble – you understand?'

'Yes.'

Groups of golfers are milling around outside the locker room and on the practice green, waiting for the starter to call their names. Shawcroft has the loudest laugh but not the loudest trousers, which belong to one of his playing partners. He takes a practice swing beside the first tee and looks up to see Samira standing at the top of a set of stone steps with the sun behind her. He shields his eyes.

Without hesitation, she moves towards him, stopping six feet away.

'Can I help you?' asks one of the other golfers.

'I've come to see Brother.'

Shawcroft hesitates, looking past her. He is searching for us.

'Nobody called Brother here, lass,' says the car dealer.

Samira points. They turn to Shawcroft, who stutters a denial. 'I don't know who she is.'

Forbes adjusts the volume on the digital recording equipment. We're watching from eighty yards away, parked beneath the branches of a plane tree, opposite the pro shop.

Samira is a foot shorter than any of the men. Her long skirt flares out in the breeze.

'Maybe she can caddy for you, Julian?' one of them jokes.

'You remember me, Brother,' says Samira. 'You told me to come. You said you had a job for me.'

Shawcroft looks at his playing partners apologetically. Suspicion is turning to anger. 'Just ignore her. Let's play.'

Turning his back, he takes another hurried practice swing and then sprays his opening drive wildly to the right where it disappears into trees. He tosses his club to the ground in disgust.

The others tee off. Shawcroft is already at the wheel of a golf cart. It jerks forward and accelerates away.

'I told you he wouldn't fall for this,' says Forbes.

'Wait. Look.'

Samira floats down the fairway after them, the hem of her skirt growing dark with dew. The carts have separated. Shawcroft is looking for his wayward drive in the rough. He glances up and sees her coming. I hear him yelling to his partner. 'Lost ball. I'll hit another.'

'You haven't even looked for this one.'

'It doesn't matter.'

He drops another ball and hacks it out, looking more like a wood-chopper than a golfer. The cart takes off again. Samira doesn't break stride.

I feel a lump in my throat. This girl never ceases to amaze me. She follows them all the way to the green, skirting the bunkers and crossing a small wooden bridge over a brook. Constantly looking over his shoulder, Shawcroft thrashes at the ball and hurries forward.

'She's going to walk out of range,' says Forbes. 'We have to stop her.'

'Wait. Just a little longer.'

The foursome are more than three hundred yards away

but I can see them clearly enough through binoculars. Samira is standing on the edge of the green, watching and waiting.

Shawcroft finally snaps. 'Get off this golf course or I'll have you arrested.'

Waving his club, he storms towards her. She doesn't flinch.

'Steady on, old boy,' someone suggests.

'Who is she, Julian?' asks another.

'Nobody.'

'She's a pretty thing. She could be your ball-washer.'

'Shut up! Just shut up!'

Samira hasn't moved. 'I paid my debt, Brother.'

'I don't know what you're talking about.'

'You said God would find a way for me to pay. I paid it twice. Twins. I paid for Hasan and for me, but he's dead. Zala didn't make it, either.'

Shawcroft grabs her roughly by the arm and hisses, 'I don't know who sent you here. I don't know what you want, but I can't help you.'

'What about the job?'

He is walking her away from the group. One of his partners yells, 'Where are you off to, Julian?'

'I'm going to have her thrown off the course.'

'What about the round?'

'I'll catch up.'

The car dealer mutters, 'Not again.'

Another foursome is already halfway down the fairway. Shawcroft marches past them, still holding Samira by the arm. She has to run to keep from falling.

'You're hurting me.'

'Shut up, you stupid slut. I don't know what you're playing at but it won't work. Who sent you here?'

'I paid my debt.'

'Fuck the debt! There is no job! This is harassment. You come near me again and I'll have you arrested.'

Samira doesn't give up. God, she's good.

'Why did Hasan die?'

'It's called life. Stuff happens.'

I don't believe it. He's quoting Donald Rumsfeld. Why doesn't 'stuff' happen to people like Shawcroft?

'It took me a long while to find you, Brother. We waited in Amsterdam for you to come or to send word. In the end we couldn't wait any longer. They were going to send us back to Kabul. Hasan came alone. I wanted to go with him but he said I should wait.' Her voice is breaking. 'He was going to find you. He said you had forgotten your promise. I told him you were honourable and kind. You brought us food and blankets at the orphanage. You wore the cross . . .'

Shawcroft twists her wrist, trying to make her stop.

'I had the babies. I paid my debt.'

'Will you shut up!'

'Someone killed Zala . . .'

'I don't know what you're talking about.'

They're nearing the clubhouse. Forbes is out of the car, moving towards them. I hang back. Shawcroft flings Samira into a flower bed. She bangs her knee and cries out.

'That qualifies as assault.'

Shawcroft looks up and sees the detective. Then he looks past him and spots me.

'You have no right! My lawyer will hear about this.'

Forbes hands him an arrest warrant. 'Fine. For your sake I hope he's not playing golf today.'

6

Shawcroft regards himself as an intellectual and a textbook lawyer, although he seems to have mixed up the Crimes Act and the Geneva Convention as he yells accusations of inhuman treatment from his holding cell.

Intellectuals show off too much and wise people are just plain boring. (My mother is forever telling me to save money, go to bed early and not to lend things.) I prefer clever people who hide their talents and don't take themselves too seriously.

A dozen officers are going through the files and computer records of the New Life Adoption Centre. Others are at Shawcroft's house in Hayward's Heath. I don't expect them to find a paper trail leading to the twins. He's too careful for that.

There is, however, a chance that prospective buyers initially came to the centre looking to adopt legally. At our first meeting I asked Shawcroft about the brochure that I

418

found at Cate's house, which advertised a baby boy born to a prostitute. Shawcroft was adamant that all adopting parents were properly screened. This should mean interviews, psych reports and criminal-background checks. If he was telling me the truth then whoever has the twins could once have been on a waiting list at the adoption centre.

It is four hours since we arrested him. Forbes arranged to bring him through the front door, past the public waiting area. He wanted to cause him maximum discomfort and embarrassment. Although experienced, I sense that Forbes is not quite in the same league as Ruiz, who knows exactly when to be hard-nosed and when to let someone sweat for another hour in a holding cell, alone with their demons.

Shawcroft is waiting for his lawyer, Eddie Barrett. I could have guessed he would summon 'the Bulldog', an old-fashioned ambulance chaser with a reputation for courting the media and getting right up police noses. He and Ruiz are old adversaries, sharing a mutual loathing and grudging respect.

Wolf whistles and howls of laughter erupt in the corridor. Barrett has arrived, dressed in jeans, cowboy boots, a plaid shirt and a ten-gallon hat.

'Look, it's Willie Nelson!' someone calls.

'Is that a six-shooter in your pocket, Eddie, or are you just dawg gone pleased to see me?'

Someone breaks into a hoedown. Eddie tucks his thumbs into his belt and gives them a few boot-scootin' moves. He doesn't seem to mind them taking the mickey out of him. Normally it's the other way round and he makes police look foolish during interviews or in court.

Barrett is a strange-looking man with an upside-down

body (short legs and a long torso) and he walks just like George W. Bush with his arms held away from his body, his back unnaturally straight and his chin in the air. Maybe it's a cowboy thing.

One of the uniforms escorts him to an interview room. Shawcroft is brought upstairs. Forbes slips a plastic plug into his ear – a receiver that will allow us to talk to him during the interrogation. He takes a bundle of files and a list of questions. This is about *looking* prepared as much as *being* prepared.

I don't know if the DI is nervous but I can feel the tension. This is about the twins. Unless Shawcroft cracks or cooperates we may never find them.

The charity boss is still wearing his golfing clothes. Barrett sits next to him, placing his cowboy hat on the table. The formalities are dispensed with – names, the location and time of interview. Forbes then places five photographs on the table. Shawcroft doesn't bother looking at them.

'These five asylum seekers allege that you convinced them to leave their homelands and illegally enter the UK.'

'No.'

'You deny knowing them?'

'I may have met them. I don't recall.'

'Perhaps if you looked at their faces—'

Barrett interrupts. 'My client has answered your question.'

'Where might you have met them?'

'My charities raised more than half a million pounds last year. I visited orphanages in Afghanistan, Iraq, Albania and Kosova.'

'How do you know these women are orphans? I didn't mention that.'

Shawcroft stiffens. I can almost see him silently admonish himself for slipping up.

'So you *do* know these women?'

'Perhaps.'

'And you know Samira Khan?'

'Yes.'

'Where did you meet her?'

'At an orphanage in Kabul.'

'Did you talk about her coming to the UK?'

'No.'

'Did you offer her a job here?'

'No.' He smiles his blameless smile.

'You introduced her to a man who smuggled her to the Netherlands and then to Britain.'

'No.'

'The cost was five thousand US dollars but it rose to ten thousand by the time she and her brother reached Turkey. You told her that God would find a way for her to repay this money.'

'I meet many orphans on my travels, detective, and I don't think there has ever been one of them who hasn't wanted to leave. It is what they dream about. They tell each other bedtime stories of escaping to the West where even beggars drive cars and dogs are put on diets because there is so much food.'

Forbes places a photograph of Brendan Pearl on the table. 'Do you know this man?'

'I can't recall.'

'He is a convicted killer.'

'I'll pray for him.'

'What about his victims – will you pray for them?' Forbes is holding a photograph of Cate. 'Do you know this woman?'

'She might have visited the adoption centre. I can't be sure.'

'She wanted to adopt?'

Shawcroft shrugs.

'You will have to answer verbally for the tape,' says Forbes.

'I *can't* recall.'

'Take a closer look.'

'There's nothing wrong with my eyesight, Detective Inspector.'

'What about your memory?'

Barrett interrupts. 'Listen, Dr Phil, it's Sunday. I got better things to do than listen to you stroke your pole. How about you tell us what my client is supposed to have done?'

Forbes shows admirable restraint. He places another photograph on the table, this one of Yanus. The questions continue. The answers are the same: 'I cannot recall. I do not remember.'

Julian Shawcroft is not a pathological liar (why tell a lie when the truth can serve you better?) but he is a natural deceiver and it comes as easily to him as breathing. Whenever Forbes has him under pressure, he carefully unfurls a patchwork of lies, tissue-thin yet carefully wrought, repairing any flaw in the fabric before it becomes a major tear. He doesn't lose his temper or show any anxiety. Instead he projects a disquieting calmness and a firm, fixed gaze.

Among the files at the adoption centre are the names of at least twelve couples that also appear on paperwork from the IVF clinic in Amsterdam. I relay the information to Forbes via a transmitter. He touches his ear in acknowledgement.

'Have you ever been to Amsterdam, Mr Shawcroft?' he asks.

I speak it here, it comes out there – like magic.

'Several times.'

'Have you visited a fertility clinic in Amersfoort?'

'I don't recall.'

'Surely you would remember this clinic.' Forbes relates the name and address. 'I doubt if you visit *so* many.'

'I am a busy man.'

'Which is why I'm sure you keep diaries and appointment calendars.'

'Yes.'

'Why haven't we found any?'

'I don't keep my schedule more than a few weeks before throwing it out. I deplore clutter.'

'Can you explain how couples who were screened by your adoption centre also appear in the files of an IVF clinic in Amsterdam?'

'Perhaps they were getting IVF treatment. People who want to adopt often try IVF first.'

Barrett is gazing at the ceiling. He's in danger of getting bored.

'These couples didn't have IVF treatment,' says Forbes. 'They provided embryos that were implanted in the wombs of asylum seekers who were forced to carry pregnancies to term before the babies were taken from them.'

Forbes points to the five photographs on the table. 'These women, Mr Shawcroft: the same women you met at different orphanages; the same women you encouraged to leave. They have identified you. They have provided statements to the police. And each one of them remembers you telling them the same thing: "God will find a way for you to repay your debt."'

Barrett takes hold of Shawcroft's arm. 'My client wishes to exercise his right to silence.'

Forbes gives the textbook reply. 'I hope your client is aware that negative inferences can be drawn by the courts if he fails to mention facts that he later relies upon in his defence.'

'My client is aware of this.'

'Your client should also be aware that he has to remain here and listen to my questions, whether he answers them or not.'

Barrett's small dark eyes are glittering. 'You do what you have to, Detective Inspector. All we've heard so far is a bunch of fanciful stories masquerading as facts. So what if my client talked to these women? You have no evidence that he organised their illegal entry into this country. And no evidence that he was involved in this Goebbels-like fairy tale about forced pregnancies and stolen babies.'

Barrett is perfectly motionless, poised. 'It seems to me, Detective Inspector, that your entire case rests on the testimony of five illegal immigrants who would say anything to stay in this country. You want to make a case based on that – bring it on.'

The lawyer gets to his feet, smooths his boot-cut jeans and adjusts his buffalo-skull belt buckle. He glances at Shawcroft. 'My advice to you is remain silent.' He opens the door and swaggers down the corridor, hat in hand. There's that walk again.

7

'Penny for the guy.'

A group of boys with spiky haircuts are loitering on the corner. The smallest one has been dressed up as a tramp in oversized clothes. He looks like he's fallen victim to a shrinking ray.

One of the other boys nudges him. 'Show 'em yer teef, Lachie.'

Lachie opens his mouth sullenly. Two of them are blacked out.

'Penny for the guy,' they chorus again.

'You're not going to throw him on a bonfire, I hope.'

'No, ma'am.'

'Good.' I give them a pound.

Samira has been watching. 'What are they doing?'

'Collecting money for fireworks.'

'By begging?'

'Not exactly.'

Hari has explained to her about Guy Fawkes Night. That's why the two of them have spent the past two days in my garden shed, dressed like mad scientists in cotton clothes, stripped of anything that might create static electricity or cause a spark.

'So this Guy Fawkes, he was a terrorist?'

'Yes, I suppose he was. He tried to blow up the Houses of Parliament with barrels of gunpowder.'

'To kill the king?'

'Yes.'

'Why?'

'He and his co-conspirators weren't happy with the way the king was treating Catholics.'

'So it was about religion.'

'I guess.'

She looks at the boys. 'And they celebrate this?'

'When the plot failed, people set off fireworks in celebration and burned effigies of Guy Fawkes. They still do.' *Never let anyone tell you that Protestants don't hold a grudge.*

Samira silently contemplates this as we make our way towards Bethnal Green. It's almost six o'clock and the air is already heavy with the smell of smoke and sulphur. Bonfires are dotted across the grass with families clustered around them, wrapped up against the cold.

My entire family has come to see the fireworks. Hari is in his element, having emerged from the back shed carrying an old ammunition box that contains the fruits of his labour and Samira's expertise. I don't know how he managed to source what she needed: the various chemicals, special salts and metallic powders. The most important ingredient, black powder, came from a hobby shop in Notting Hill – or, more specifically, from model rocket motors that were carefully disassembled to obtain the solid fuel propellant.

Torches dance across the grass and small fireworks are being lit: Stick Rockets, Roman Candles, Flying Snakes, Crackle Dragons and Bags of Gold. Children are drawing in the air with sparklers and every dog in London is barking, keeping every baby awake. I wonder if the twins are among them. Perhaps they are too young to be frightened by the noise.

I hook my arm through Bada's and we watch Samira and Hari plant a heavy plastic tube in the earth. Samira has pulled her skirt between her legs and wrapped it tightly around her thighs. Her headscarf is tucked beneath the collar of her coat.

'Who would give him such knowledge?' says Bada. 'He'll blow himself up.'

'He'll be fine.'

Hari has always been a favourite among equals. As the youngest, he has had my parents to himself for the past six years. I sometimes think he's their last link to middle age.

Shielding a pale tapered candle in the palm of her hand, Samira crouches close to the ground. One or two seconds elapse. A rocket whizzes into the air and disappears. One, two, three seconds pass and it suddenly explodes high above us, dripping stars that melt into the darkness. Compared with the fireworks that have come before, it is higher, brighter and louder. People stop their own displays to watch.

Hari sings out the names – Dragon's Breath, Golden Phoenix, Glitter Palm, Exploding Apples – while Samira moves without fuss between the launch tubes. Meanwhile,

427

ground shells shoot columns of sparks around her and the explosions are mirrored in her eyes.

The finale is Hari's Whistling Chaser. Samira lets him light the fuse. It screams upwards until little more than a speck of light detonates into a huge circle of white like a dandelion. Just when it seems about to fade, a red ball of light explodes within the first. The final salute is a loud bang that rattles the neighbouring windows, setting off car alarms. The crowd applauds. Hari takes a bow. Samira is already cleaning up the scorched cardboard tubes and shredded paper, which she packs into the old ammunition box.

Hari is buzzing. 'We should celebrate,' he says to Samira. 'I'll take you out.'

'Out?'

'Yes.'

'Where is "out"?'

'I don't know. We could have a drink or see a band.'

'I do not drink.'

'You could have a juice or a soft drink.'

'I cannot go out with you. It's not good for a girl to be alone with a boy.'

'We wouldn't be alone. The pub is always packed.'

'She means without a chaperone,' I tell him.

'Oh. Right.'

I sometimes wonder why Hari is considered the brightest among my brothers. He looks crestfallen.

'It's a religious thing, Hari.'

'But I'm not religious.'

I give him a clip round the ear.

I still haven't told Samira about what happened at

Shawcroft's interview – or, more importantly, what *didn't* happen. The charity boss gave us nothing. Forbes had to let him go.

How do I explain the rules of evidence and the notion of burden of proof to someone who has never been afforded the luxury of justice or fairness?

On the walk home we drop behind the others and I hook my arm through Samira's.

'But he *did* these things,' she says, turning to face me. 'None of this would have happened without him. Hasan and Zala would still be here. So many people are dead.' She lowers her gaze. 'Perhaps they are the lucky ones.'

'You mustn't think such a thing.'

'Why not?'

'Because the twins are going to need a mother.'

She cuts me off with a slash of her hand. 'I will *never* be their mother!'

Her face has changed. Twisted. I am looking at another face beneath the first, a dangerous one. It lasts only a fraction of a second – long enough to unsettle me. She blinks and it's gone. I have her back again.

We are almost home. A car has slowed about fifty yards behind us, edging forward without closing the gap. Fear crawls down my throat. I reach behind my back and untuck my shirt. The Glock is holstered at the base of my spine.

Hari has already turned into Hanbury Street. Mama and Bada have gone home. Opposite the next street light is a footpath between houses. Samira has noticed the car.

'Don't look back,' I tell her.

As we pass under the street light I push her towards the

footpath, yelling at her to run. She obeys without question. I spin to face the car. The driver is in shadow. I aim the pistol at his head and he raises his hands, palms open like a mime artist pressing against a glass wall.

A rear window lowers. The interior light blinks on. I swing my gun into the opening. Julian Shawcroft has one hand on the door and the other holding what could be a prayer book.

'I want to show you something,' he says.

'Am I going to disappear?'

He looks disappointed. 'Trust in God to protect you.'

'Will you take me to the twins?'

'I will help you understand.'

A gust of wind, a splatter of raindrops – the night is growing blustery and bad-tempered. All over London people are heading home and bonfires are burning down. We cross the river and head south through Bermondsey. The glowing dome of St Paul's is visible between buildings and above the treetops.

Shawcroft is silent. I can see his face in the beams of passing headlights as I nurse my gun and he nurses his book. I should be frightened. Instead I feel a curious calmness. My only phone call has been to my home – checking to make sure that Samira made it safely.

The car pulls off the road into a driveway and stops in a rear courtyard. I step out and I see the driver's face for the first time across the vehicle's glistening roof. It's not Brendan Pearl. I didn't expect it to be. Shawcroft isn't foolish enough to be seen with a known killer.

A woman dressed in a French peasant skirt and oversized

sweater appears at Shawcroft's side. Her hair is pinned back so tightly it raises her eyebrows.

'This is Delia,' he says. 'She runs one of my charities.'

I shake a smooth dry hand.

Delia leads us through double doors and up a narrow staircase. There are posters on the walls with confronting images of hunger and neglect. Among them is a photograph of an African child with a distended stomach and begging-bowl eyes. In the bottom corner there is a logo, a clock with letters instead of numbers that spell out: O.R.P.H.A.N.W.A.T.C.H.

Reaching behind me, I slide the gun into its holster.

We arrive at an office with desks and filing cabinets. A computer screen, dark and asleep, is silhouetted against the window. Shawcroft turns to Delia. 'Is it open?'

She nods.

I follow him into a second room, which is fitted out as a small home theatre with a screen and a projector. There are more posters on the walls, along with newspaper clippings, some dog-eared, torn or frayed at the edges. A small girl in a dirty white dress peers at the camera; a young boy with his arms folded eyes me defiantly. There are other images, dozens of them, papering the walls beneath display lights that have turned them into tragic works of art.

'These are the ones we could save,' he says, his pale priestly hands clasped before him.

The wall panels are concertinaed. He expands them, revealing yet more photographs.

'Remember the orphans from the Asian tsunami? Nobody knows their true number but some estimates put it at twenty thousand. Homeless. Destitute. Traumatised. Families were queuing up to adopt them; governments were besieged with offers; but almost every one of them was refused.'

Shawcroft's gaze slides over me. 'Shall I tell you what happened to the tsunami orphans? In Sri Lanka the Tamil Tigers recruited them as soldiers, boys as young as seven. In India greedy relatives fought over the children because of the relief money being offered by the government – and abandoned them once the money was paid.

'In Indonesia the authorities refused adoption to any couple who weren't Muslim. Troops dragged three hundred orphans from a rescue flight because it was organised by a Christian charity. They were left with nowhere to go and nothing to eat. Even countries like Thailand and India that allow foreign adoptions suddenly closed their borders – spooked by unconfirmed stories of orphans being trafficked out of the country by gangs of paedophiles. It was ridiculous. If someone robs a bank you don't shut down the international banking system. You catch the robber. You prosecute them. Unfortunately, each time a child is trafficked they want to shut down the international adoption system, making things worse for millions of orphans.

'People don't understand the sheer scale of this problem. Two million children are forced into prostitution every year – a million of them in Asia. And more children are orphaned every *week* in Africa than were orphaned by the Asian tsunami. There are thirteen million in sub-Saharan Africa alone.

'The so-called experts say children shouldn't be treated as commodities. Why not? Isn't it better to be treated as a commodity than to be treated like a dog? Hungry. Cold. Living in squalor. Sold into slavery. Raped. They say it shouldn't be about money. What else is it going to be about? How else are we going to save them?'

'You think the end justifies the means.'

'I think it *should* be a factor.'

'You can't treat people like a resource.'

'Of course I can. Economists do it all the time. I'm a pragmatist.'

'You're a monster.'

'At least I give a damn. The world needs people like me. Realists. Men of action. What do you do? Sponsor a child in Burundi or pledge to *Comic Relief*. You try to save one, while ten thousand others starve.'

'And what's the alternative?'

'Sacrifice one and save ten thousand.'

'Who chooses?'

'Pardon?'

'Who chooses the one you're going to sacrifice?'

'*I* choose. I don't ask others to do it for me.'

I hate him then. For all his dark charm and elegant intensity, Shawcroft is a bully and a zealot. I prefer Brendan Pearl's motives. At least he doesn't try to justify his killings.

'What happens if the odds change?' I ask. 'Would you sacrifice five lives to save five hundred? What about ten lives to save eleven?'

'Let's ask the people, shall we?' he replies sarcastically. 'I get eleven votes. You only get ten. I win.'

Fleetingly, unnervingly, I understand what he's saying but cannot accept a world that is so brutally black and white. Murder, rape and torture are the apparatus of terrorists, not of civilised societies. If we become like them, what hope do we have?

433

Shawcroft thinks he's a moral man, a charitable man, a saintly man, but he's not. He's been corrupted. He has become part of the problem instead of the solution – trafficking women, selling babies, exploiting the vulnerable.

'Nothing gives you the right to choose,' I tell him.

'I accepted the role.'

'You think you're God!'

'Yes. And do you know why? Because *someone* has to be. Bleeding hearts like you only pay lip service to the poor and destitute. You wear coloured bands on your wrists and claim that you want to make poverty history. How?'

'This isn't about me.'

'Yes, it is.'

'Where are the twins?'

'Being loved.'

'Where?'

'Where they belong.'

The pistol is resting against the small of my back, warm as blood. My fingers close around it. In a single motion I swing it towards him, pressing the muzzle against his forehead.

I expect to see fear. Instead, he blinks at me sadly. 'This is like a war, Alisha. I know we use that term too readily, but sometimes it is justified – and some wars are just. The war on poverty. The war on hunger. Even pacifists cannot be opposed to wars such as these. Innocent people get hurt in conflict. Your friend was a casualty.'

'You sacrificed her.'

'To protect others.'

'Yourself.'

My finger tightens on the trigger. Another half-pound of

pressure and it's over. He is watching me along the barrel – still not frightened. For a brief moment I think he's prepared to die, having said his piece and made his peace.

He doesn't close his eyes. He *knows* I can't do it. Without him I might never find the twins.

8

A large portrait above the fireplace shows a patrician man in legal robes with a horsehair wig that looks surprisingly like a Shih Tzu resting on his forearm. He gazes sternly down at a polished table that is surrounded by high-backed chairs.

Felix's mother is dressed in a tweed jacket and black slacks, clutching her handbag as though someone might steal it. Beside her, another of her sons rattles his fingers on the table, already bored.

Barnaby is at the window, studying the small courtyard outside. I don't notice Jarrod as he crosses the room. He touches my shoulder.

'Is it true? Am I an uncle?'

His hair is brushed back from his temples and beginning to thin.

'I'm not sure what you are, technically.'

'My father says there are twins.'

'They don't belong to Cate. A girl was forced to have them.'

His eyes don't understand. 'Biologically they belong to Cate. That makes me an uncle.'

'Perhaps. I really don't know.'

The solicitor enters the conference room and takes a seat. In his mid-fifties, dressed in a three-piece pinstriped suit, he introduces himself as William Grove and stretches his face into a tight smile. His whole demeanour is one of contained speed. Time is money. Every fifteen minutes is billable.

Chairs scrape backwards. People are seated. Mr Grove glances at his instructions.

'Ladies and gentlemen, a codicil was added to this will six weeks ago and it appears to be predicated on the likelihood that the Beaumonts would become parents.'

A frisson disturbs the atmosphere, like a sudden change in the air pressure. The solicitor glances up, tugging at his shirt cuffs. 'Am I to understand this marriage produced children?'

Silence.

Finally, Barnaby clears his throat. 'It does seem likely.'

'What do you mean? Please explain.'

'We have reason to believe that Cate and Felix arranged a surrogacy. Twins were born eight days ago.'

The next minute is one of exclamation and disbelief. Felix's mother makes a choking noise at the back of her throat. Barnaby is looking at his hands, rubbing his fingertips. Jarrod hasn't taken his eyes off me.

Unsure of how to proceed, Mr Grove takes a moment to compose himself. He decides to continue. 'The estate consists of a heavily mortgaged family home in Willesden Green, North London, which was recently damaged in a fire. Insurance will cover the cost of rebuilding. Felix also had a life-insurance policy provided by his employer.

'If there is no objection, I shall read from the wills, which are each ostensibly the same.' He takes a sip of water.

'"This is the last Will and Testament of me, Cate Elizabeth Beaumont (née Elliot) made on the fourteenth day of September 2006. I hereby revoke all Wills heretofore made by me and declare this to be my last Will and Testament. I appoint William Grove of Sadler, Grove and Buffett to be Executor and Trustee of this, my Will. I give, devise and bequeath to my husband, Felix Beaumont (formerly known as Felix Buczkowski) the whole of my estate provided that he survives me by thirty days and, if not, then I give the whole of my estate to my child or children to be shared equally as tenants in common.

'I appoint Alisha Kaur Barba as guardian of my infant children and I direct her to love and care for them and to expend so much as is necessary from the estate of the children to raise, educate and advance their life.'

Barnaby is on his feet, his jaw flapping in protest. For a moment I think he might be having a heart attack.

'This is preposterous! I will not have my grandchildren raised by a bloody stranger.' He stabs a finger at me. 'You knew about this!'

'No.'

'You knew all along.'

'I didn't.'

Mr Grove tries to calm him down. 'I can assure you, sir, that everything has been properly signed and witnessed.'

438

'What sort of idiot do you take me for? This is bullshit! I won't let anyone take my grandchildren away.'

The outburst has silenced the room. The only sounds are from the air-conditioning and distant water pipes filling and disgorging. For a moment I think that Barnaby might actually strike me. Instead he kicks back his chair and storms out, followed by Jarrod. People turn to look at me. The back of my neck grows warm.

Mr Grove has a letter for me. As I take it from him, I have to keep my hand steady. Why would Cate do this? Why choose me? Already the sense of responsibility is pressing against my lungs.

The envelope is creased in my fist as I leave the conference room and cross the lobby, pushing through heavy glass doors. I have no idea where I'm going. Is this it? One poxy letter is supposed to explain things. Will it make up for eight years of silence?

Another notion suddenly haunts my confusion. Maybe I'm being given a chance to redeem myself. To account for my neglect, my failures, the things left unsaid, all those sins of omission and commission. I am being asked to safeguard Cate's most precious legacy and to do a better job than I managed with our friendship.

I stop in the doorway of an off-licence and slide my finger beneath the flap of the envelope.

Dear Ali,

It is a weird thing, writing a letter that will only be opened and read upon one's death. It's hard to get too sad about it, though. And if I am dead, it's a bit late to fret about spilling that particular pint of white.

My only real concern is you. You're my one regret. I wanted to be friends with you ever since we met at Oaklands and you fought Paul Donavon to defend my honour and lost your front tooth. You were the real thing, Ali, not one of the plastics.

I know you're sorry about what happened with my father. I know it was more his fault than yours. I forgave you a long time ago. I forgave him because, well, you know how it is with fathers. You weren't the first of his infidelities, by the way, but I guess you worked that out.

The reason I could never tell you this is because of a promise I made to my mother. It was the worst sort of promise. She found out about you and my father. He told her because he thought I would tell her.

My mother made me promise never to see you again; never to talk to you; never to invite you to the house; never to mention your name.

I know I should have ignored her. I should have called. Many times I almost did. I got as far as picking up the phone. Sometimes I even dialled your parents' number but then I wondered what I'd say to you. We had left it too long. How would we ever get around the silence, which was like an elephant sitting in the room?

I have never stopped thinking about you. I followed your career as best I could, picking up stories from other people. Poor old Felix has been bored silly listening to me talk about our exploits and adventures. He's heard so much about you that he probably feels like he's been married to both of us.

Six weeks from now, God willing, I will become a mother after six years of trying. If something happens to me and to Felix – if we die in a flaming plane crash or should suicide bombers ever target Tesco at Willesden Green – we want you to be the guardian of our children.

My mother is going to pass a cow when she learns this but I have kept my promise to her, which didn't include any clause covering posthumous contact with you.

There are no strings attached. I'm not going to write provisos or instructions. If you want the job it's yours. I know you'll love my children as much as I do. And I know you'll teach them to look after each other. You'll say the things I would have said to them and tell them about me and about Felix. The good stuff, naturally.

I don't know what else to tell you. I often think how different my life would have been – how much happier – if you'd been a part of it. One day.

Love, Cate.

It is just after five o'clock. The street lights are smudged with my tears. Faces drift past me. Heads turn away. Nobody asks after a crying woman any more – not in London. I'm just another of the crazies to be avoided.

On the cab ride to West Acton I catch my reflection in the window. I will be thirty years old on Thursday – closer to sixty than I am to birth. I still look young yet exhausted and feverish, like a child who has stayed up too late at an adult party.

There is a 'For Sale' sign outside 'New Boy' Dave's flat. He's serious about this; he's going to quit the force and start teaching kids how to sail.

I debate whether to go up. I walk up to the front door, stare at the bell and walk back to the road. I don't want to explain things. I just want to open a bottle of wine, order a pizza and curl up on the sofa with his legs beneath mine and his hands rubbing my toes – which are freezing.

I haven't seen Dave since Amsterdam. He used to phone me every day, sometimes twice. When I called him after the funerals he sounded hesitant, almost nervous.

The elephant in the room. It can't be talked about. It can't be ignored. My patched-up pelvis is like that. People suddenly want to give me children. Is that ironic? I'm never sure with irony: the term is so misused.

I go back to the door. It takes a long while for anyone to answer. It's a woman's voice on the intercom. Apologetic. She was in the shower.

'Dave's not here.'

'It's my fault. I should have phoned.'

'He's on his way home. Do you want to come in and wait?'

'No, that's OK.'

Who is she? What's she doing here?

'I'll tell him you dropped by.'

'OK.'

A pause.

'You need to give me your name.'

'Of course. Sorry. Don't worry about it. I'll call him.'

I walk back to the road, telling myself I don't care.

Shit! Shit! Shit!

The house is strangely quiet. The TV in the front room is turned down and lights are on upstairs. I slip along the side path and through the back door. Hari is in the kitchen.

'You have to stop her.'

'Who?'

442

'Samira. She's leaving. She's upstairs, packing.'

'Why? What did you do to her?'

'Nothing.'

'Did you leave her alone?'

'For twenty minutes, I swear. That's all. I had to drop off a mate's car.'

Samira is in my bedroom. Her clothes are folded on the bed – a few simple skirts, blouses, a frayed jumper . . . Hasan's biscuit tin sits on top of the pile.

'Where are you going?'

She seems to hold her breath. 'I am leaving. You do not want me here.'

'What makes you say that? Did Hari do something? Did he say something he shouldn't have said?'

She won't look at me, but I see the bruise forming on her cheek, a rough circle beneath her right eye.

'Who did this?'

She whispers, 'A man came.'

'What man?'

'The man who talked to you at the church.'

'Donavon?'

'No, the other man.'

She means Barnaby. He came here, spoiling for a fight.

'He was hitting the door – making so much noise. He said you lied to me and you lied to him.'

'I have never lied to you.'

'He said you wanted the babies for yourself and he would fight you and he would fight me.'

'Don't listen to him.'

'He said I wasn't welcome in this country. I should go back where I came from – among the terrorists.'

443

'No.'

I reach towards her. She pulls away.

'Did he hit you?'

'I tried to shut the door. He pushed it.' She touches her cheek.

'He had no right to say those things.'

'Is it true? *Do* you want the babies?'

'Cate wrote a will – a legal document. She nominated me as the guardian if she had children.'

'What does "guardian" mean? Do the twins belong to you now?'

'No. You gave birth to them. They might have Cate's eyes and Felix's nose, but they grew inside your body. And no matter what anyone says they belong to you.'

'What if I don't want them?'

My mouth opens but I don't answer. Something has lodged in my throat – a choking lump of desire and doubt. No matter what Cate wanted, they're not my babies. My motives are pure.

I put my arm around Samira's shoulders and pull her close to me. Her breath is warm against my neck and her first sob thuds like a spade hitting wet dirt. Something breaks inside her. She has found her tears.

9

The digital numbers of my alarm clock glow in the darkness. It has just gone four. I won't sleep again. Samira is curled up next to me, breathing softly.

I am a collector of elephants. Some are soft toys; others are figurines made from cut glass, porcelain, jade or crystal. My favourite is six inches high and made from heavy glass, inlaid with mirrors. Normally it sits beneath my reading light, throwing coloured stars on the walls. It's not there now. I wonder what could have happened to it.

Slipping out of bed quietly, I dress in my running gear and step outside into the darkness of Hanbury Street. There is an edge to the breeze. Seasons changing.

Cate used to help me train after school. She rode her bicycle alongside me, speeding up before we reached the hills because she knew I could outrun her on the climbs. When I ran at the national age championships in Cardiff she begged her parents to let her come. She was the only student from Oaklands to see me win. I ran like the wind that day. Fast enough to blur at the edges.

I couldn't see Cate in the stands but I could pick out my mother who wore a bright crimson sari like a splash of paint against the blue seats and grey spectators.

My father never saw me compete. He didn't approve.

'Running is not ladylike. It makes a woman sweat,' he told me.

'Mama sweats all the time in the kitchen.'

'It is a different sort of sweat.'

'I didn't know there were different kinds of sweat.'

'Yes, it is a well-known scientific fact. The sweat of hard work and of food preparation is sweeter than the sweat of vigorous exercise.'

I didn't laugh. A good daughter respects her father.

Later I heard my parents arguing.

'How is a boy supposed to catch her if she runs so fast?'

'I don't want boys catching her.'

'Have you seen her room? She has weights. My daughter is lifting barbells.'

'She's in training.'

'Weights are not feminine. And do you see what she wears? Those brief shorts are like underwear. She's running in her underwear.'

In darkness I run two circuits of Victoria Park, sticking to the tarmac paths, using the street lights to navigate.

My mother used to tell me a folk tale about a village donkey that was always mocked for being stupid and ugly. One day a guru took pity on the animal. If you had the roar of a tiger they would not laugh, he thought. So he took a tiger skin and laid it across the donkey's back. The donkey returned to the village and suddenly everything changed. Women and children ran screaming. Men cowered in corners. Soon the donkey was alone in the market and feasted on the lovely apples and carrots.

The villagers were terrified and had to be rid of the dangerous 'tiger'. A meeting was called and they decided to drive the tiger back to the forest. Drumbeats echoed through the market and the poor bewildered donkey turned this way and that. He ran into the forest but the hunters tracked him down.

'That's no tiger,' one of them shouted. 'Surely it's only the donkey from the market.'

The guru appeared and calmly lifted the tiger skin from the terrified beast. 'Remember this animal,' he said to the people. 'He has the skin of a tiger but the soul of a donkey.'

I feel like that now – a donkey not a tiger.

I am just passing Smithfield Market when a realisation washes over me. At first it is no more than an inkling. I wonder what prompts such a reaction. Maybe it's a pattern of footsteps or a sound that is out of place or a movement that triggers a thought. It comes to me now. I know how to find the twins!

Forbes has been concentrating on couples who have succeeded in obtaining a child through genetic surrogacy. They cannot give evidence against Shawcroft without incriminating themselves. Why would they? Science supports them. Nobody can prove they're not the birth parents.

But whoever has the twins doesn't have a genetic safety net. DNA tests will expose rather than sustain them. They haven't had time to fake a pregnancy or set up an elaborate deceit. Right now they must be feeling vulnerable.

At this hour of the morning it isn't difficult to find a parking spot in Kennington, close to Forbes's office. Most of the detectives start work at nine, which means the incident room is deserted except for a detective constable who has been working the graveyard shift. He's about my age and quite handsome in a sulky sort of way. Perhaps I woke him up.

'Forbes asked me to come,' I lie.

He looks at me doubtfully. 'The Boss has a meeting at the Home Office this morning. He won't be in the office until later.'

'He wants me to follow up a lead.'

'What sort of lead?'

'Just an idea, that's all.'

He doesn't believe me. I call Forbes to get approval.

'This better be fucking important,' he grumbles.

'Good morning, sir.'

'Who's this?'

'DC Barba.'

'Don't "good morning" me.'

'Sorry, sir.'

I can hear Mrs Forbes in the background, telling him to be quiet. Pillow talk.

'I need access to Shawcroft's phone records.'

'It's six in the morning.'

'Yes, sir.'

He's about to say no. He doesn't trust me. I'm bad news or bad luck. Everything I've touched has turned to shit. I sense another reason. A nervousness. Ever since he released

Shawcroft, the DI has backtracked and made excuses. He must have copped some heat but that goes with the territory.

'I want you to go home, DC Barba.'

'I have a lead.'

'Give it to the night detective. You're not part of this investigation.' His voice softens. 'Look after Samira.'

Why is he being so negative? And why the briefing at the Home Office? It must be about Shawcroft.

'How is your wife, sir?' I ask.

Forbes hesitates. She's lying next to him. What can he say?

There is a long pause. I whisper, 'We're on the same side, sir. You didn't screw me that night so don't screw me now.'

'Fine. Yes, I can't see a problem,' he answers. I hand the phone over to the night detective and listen to their yes-sir-no-sir exchange. The phone is handed back to me. Forbes wants a final word.

'Anything you find, you give to me.'

'Yes, sir.'

The call ends. The night detective looks at me and we smile in unison. Waking up a senior officer is one of life's small pleasures.

The DC's name is Rod Beckley but everyone calls him Becks. 'On account of me being crap at football,' he jokes.

After clearing a desk and finding me a chair, he delivers a dozen ring-bound folders. Every incoming and outgoing call from the New Life Adoption Centre is listed, including the numbers, the duration of each call, the time and the date they were made. There are six voice lines and two fax lines, as well as a direct-dial number into Shawcroft's office.

Further folders cover his mobile phone and home line. Text messages and e-mails have been printed out and stapled together in chronological order.

Taking a marker pen, I begin to group the calls.

Rather than concentrate on the phone numbers, I look at the times. The ferry arrived in Harwich at 3.36 a.m. on Sunday. We know that Pearl walked off the ferry just after four. At 10.25 a.m. he bought nappies and baby formula from a motorway service station on the M25 before stealing a car.

I look down the list of calls to Shawcroft's mobile. There was an incoming call at 10.18 a.m. that lasted less than thirty seconds. I check the number. It appears only once. It could be a wrong number.

DC Beckley is flicking at a keyboard across the office, trying to look busy. I sit on the edge of his desk until he looks up.

'Can we find out who this number belongs to?'

He accesses the Police National Computer and types in the digits. A map of Hertfordshire appears. The details are listed on a separate window. The phone number belongs to a public phone box at Potter's Bar – a motorway service area near Junction 24 on the M25. It's the same service area where Brendan Pearl was last sighted. He must have phoned Shawcroft for instructions about where to deliver the twins. It is the closest I've come to linking the two men, although it's not conclusive.

Going back to the folders, I strike a dead end. Shawcroft didn't use his mobile for the next three hours. Surely if his plan was coming apart he would have called someone.

I try to picture last Sunday morning. Shawcroft was on

the golf course. His foursome teed off at 10.05. One of his playing partners said something when Samira interrupted their game and Shawcroft tried to drag her off the course: 'Not again.'

It had happened before – a week earlier. After the phone call from Pearl, Shawcroft must have abandoned his round. Where did he go? He needed to let the buyer or buyers know that the twins had arrived. He had to bring the pick-up forward. It was too risky using his own mobile so he looked for another phone – one that he thought couldn't be traced.

I go back to Becks, 'Is it possible to find out if there is a public phone located at a golf club in Surrey?'

'Maybe. You got a name?'

'Yes. The Twin Bridges Country Club. It could be in a locker room or a lounge. Somewhere quiet. I'm interested in outgoing calls timed between nine-twenty a.m. and ten-thirty a.m. on Sunday, October the twenty-ninth.'

'Is that all?' he asks facetiously.

'No. Then we have to cross-check them with the adoption waiting list at the New Life Adoption Centre.'

He doesn't understand, but he begins the search anyway. 'You think we'll find a match?'

'If we're lucky.'

10

'New Boy' Dave hears my voice on the intercom and pauses for a moment before pressing the buzzer to unlock the front door.

When I reach his flat the door is propped open. He is in the kitchen, stirring paint.

'So you're definitely selling.'

'Yep.'

'Any offers?'

'Not yet.'

There are two cups in the drainer and two cold tea bags solidifying in the sink, alongside a paint roller and a couple of brushes. The ceilings are to be a stowe white. I helped him choose the colour. The walls are a misty green, cut back by fifty per cent, and the skirting boards and frames are full-strength.

I follow Dave into the living room. His few pieces of

furniture have been pushed to the centre and covered in old sheets.

'How is Samira?' he asks.

The question is unexpected. Dave has never met her, but he will have seen the TV bulletins and read the papers.

'I'm worried about her. I'm worried about the twins.'

He fills the roller from the tray.

'Will you help me?'

'It's not our case.'

'I might have found them. Please help me.'

Climbing the ladder he runs the roller across the ceiling, creating long ribbons of paint.

'What does it matter, Dave? You've resigned. You're leaving. My career is finished. It doesn't matter what toes we tread on or who we piss off. There's something wrong with this case. People are tiptoeing around it, playing softly-softly while the real culprits are shredding files and covering their tracks.'

The roller is gliding across the ceiling. I know he's listening.

'You're acting like these kids belong to *you*.'

I have to catch myself before my head snaps up. He looks down at me from the top of the ladder. Why do people keep questioning my motives? Eduardo de Souza, Barnaby, now Dave. Is it me who can't see the truth? No, they're wrong. I *don't* want the twins for myself.

'I'm doing this because a friend of mine – my best friend – entrusted to me what she loved most, the most precious thing she had. I couldn't save Cate and I couldn't save Zala but I *can* save the twins.'

There is a long silence. Only one of us feels uncomfortable. 'New Boy' has always been defined more by what he dislikes than by what he likes. He doesn't like cats, for instance, or hypocrites. He also loathes reality-TV shows, Welsh rugby fans and tattooed women who scream at their kids in supermarkets. I can live with a man like that. His silences are another matter. He seems comfortable with them but I want to know what he's thinking. Is he angry that I didn't leave Amsterdam with him? Is he upset at how we left things? We both have questions. I want to know who answered the intercom last night, fresh from his shower.

I turn towards his bedroom. The door is open. I notice a suitcase against the wall and a blouse hanging on the back of the open door. I don't realise I'm staring and I don't notice Dave climb down the ladder and take the roller to the kitchen. He wraps it carefully in cling film, leaving it on the sink. Peeling off his shirt, he tosses it in a corner.

'Give me five minutes. I need to shower.' He scratches his unshaven chin. 'Better make it ten.'

Two addresses: one just across the river in Barnes and the other in Finsbury Park, North London. The first address belongs to a couple whose names also appear on a waiting list at the New Life Adoption Centre. The Finsbury Park address doesn't appear on the files.

On Sunday, a week ago – just after ten o'clock – both addresses received a call from a public phone in the locker room of the Twin Bridges Country Club in Surrey. Shawcroft was there when those calls were made.

It's a hunch. It's too many things happening at the same time to be coincidental. It's worth a look.

Dave is dressed in light cords, a shirt and a leather jacket. 'What do you want to do?'

454

'Check them out.'

'What about Forbes?'

'He won't make this sort of leap. He might get there in the end by ticking off the boxes, methodically, mechanically – but what if we don't have time for that?'

I picture the smaller twin, struggling to breathe. My own throat closes. She should be in hospital. We should have found her by now.

'OK, so you have two addresses. I still don't know what you expect to do,' says Dave.

'Maybe I'm just going to knock on the front door and say, "Do you have twins that don't belong to you?" I can tell you what I *won't* do. I won't sit back and wait for them to disappear.'

Brown leaves swirl from a park onto the pavement and back to the grass, as if unwilling to cross the road. The temperature hasn't strayed above single figures and the wind is driving it lower.

We're parked in a typical street in Barnes: flanked by tall gabled houses and plane trees that have been so savagely pruned that they look almost deformed.

This is a stockbroker suburb, full of affluent middle-class families who move here for the schools and the parks and the proximity to the West End. Despite the cold, half a dozen mothers or nannies are in the playground, watching over pre-schoolers who are dressed in so many clothes that they look like junior Michelin Men.

Dave watches the yummy mummies, while I watch the house, No. 85. Robert and Noelene Gallagher drive a Volvo Estate, pay their TV licence fee on time and vote Liberal

Democrat. I'm guessing, of course, but it strikes me as that sort of area, that sort of house.

Dave rakes his fingers through his lopsided bramble of hair. 'Can I ask you something?'

'Sure.'

'Have you ever loved me?'

I didn't see this coming.

'What makes you think I don't love you now?'

'You've never said.'

'What do you mean?'

'You might have used the word, but not in a sentence with my name in it. You've never said, "I love you, Dave."'

I think back, wanting to deny it, but he seems so sure. The nights we lay together with his arms around me, I felt so safe, so happy. Didn't I ever tell him? I remember my philosophical debates and arguments about the nature of love and how debilitating it can be. Were they all internal? I was trying to talk myself *out of* loving him. I lost, but he had no way of knowing that.

I should tell him now. How? It's going to sound contrived or forced. It's too late. I can try to make excuses: I can blame my inability to have children but the truth is that I'm driving him away. There's another woman living in his flat.

He's doing it again – not saying anything. Waiting.

'You're seeing someone,' I blurt out, making it sound like an accusation.

'What makes you say that?'

'I met her.'

He turns his whole body in the driver's seat to face me, looking surprised rather than guilty.

'I came to see you yesterday. You weren't home. She answered the intercom.'

'Jacquie?'

'I didn't take down her name.' *(I sound so bloody jealous.)*

'My sister.'

'You don't have a sister.'

'My sister-in-law. My brother's wife, Jacquie.'

'They're in San Diego.'

'They're staying with me. Simon is my new business partner. I told you.'

Could this get any worse? 'You must think I'm such an idiot,' I say. 'I'm sorry. I mean, I'm not the jealous type, not usually. It's just that after what happened in Amsterdam, when you didn't call me and I didn't call you, I just thought – it's so stupid – that you'd found someone else who wasn't so crippled, or troublesome or such hard work. Please don't laugh at me.'

'I'm not laughing.'

'What are you doing?'

'I'm looking at that car.'

I follow his gaze. A Volvo Estate is parked near the front gate of No. 85. There is a sunshade on the nearside rear window and what looks like a baby seat.

Dave is giving me a way out. He's like a chivalrous gentleman spreading his coat over a muddy puddle.

'I should check it out,' I say, opening the car door. 'You stay here.'

Dave watches me leave. He knows I'm dodging the issue yet again. I have underestimated him. He's smarter than I am. Nicer, too.

Crossing the street, I walk along the pavement, pausing

457

at the Volvo and bending as if to tie my shoelaces. The windows are tinted but I can make out small handprints inside the glass and a Garfield sticker on the back window.

I glance across at Dave and make a knocking motion with my fist. He shakes his head. Ignoring the signal, I open the front gate and climb the steps to the house.

I press the buzzer. The front door opens a crack. A girl aged about five regards me very seriously. Her hands are stained with paint and a pink blot has dried on her forehead like a misplaced bindi.

'Hello – what's your name?'

'Molly.'

'That's a pretty name.'

'I know.'

'Is your Mummy home?'

'She's upstairs.'

I hear a yell from that direction. '*If that's the boiler man, the boiler is straight down the hall in the kitchen.*'

'It's not the boiler man,' I call back.

'It's an Indian lady,' says Molly.

Mrs Gallagher appears at the top of the stairs. In her early forties, she's wearing a corduroy skirt with a wide belt slung low on her hips.

'I'm sorry to trouble you. My husband and I are moving into the street and I was hoping to ask about local schools and doctors, that sort of thing.'

I can see her mentally deciding what to do. It's more than natural caution.

'What beautiful curls,' I say, stroking Molly's hair.

'That's what everyone says,' the youngster replies.

Why would someone who already has a child buy a baby?

'I'm rather busy at the moment,' says Mrs Gallagher, brushing back her fringe.

'I understand completely. I'm sorry.' I turn to leave.

'Which place are you buying?' she asks, not wanting to be impolite.

'Oh, we're not buying. Not yet. We're renting number sixty-eight.' I point down the street in the direction of a 'To Let' sign. 'We've moved from North London. My husband has a new job. We're both working. But we want to start a family soon.'

Mrs Gallagher is at the bottom of the stairs now. It's too cold to leave the front door open. She'll either invite me inside or tell me to go.

'Now's not the best time,' she says. 'Perhaps if I had a phone number I could call you later.'

'Thank you very much.' I fumble for a pen. 'Do you have a piece of paper?'

She looks on the radiator shelf. 'I'll get you one.'

Molly waits in the hallway, still holding the door. 'Do you want to see one of my paintings?'

'I'd love to.'

'I'll get one.' She dashes upstairs. Mrs Gallagher is in the kitchen. She finds an old envelope and returns, looking for Molly.

'She's gone upstairs to get one of her paintings,' I explain. 'A budding artist.'

'She gets more paint on her clothes than on the paper.'

'I have a boyfriend like that.'

'I thought you said you were married.' She fixes me with a stare. There's steel behind it.

459

'We're engaged. We've been together so long it feels like we're married.'

She doesn't believe me. Molly yells from the top of the stairs.

'Mummy, Jasper is crying.'

'Oh, you have another one.'

Mrs Gallagher reaches for the door. My foot is faster. My shoulder follows. I have no right to enter. I need a warrant or I need proper cause.

I'm at the bottom of the stairs. Mrs Gallagher yells at me to get out. She grabs my arm. I shrug it away. Above the noise, behind it, in spite of it, I hear a baby crying.

Taking the stairs two at a time, I follow the sound. The first door I come to is the main bedroom. The second door is Molly's room. She has set up a painting easel on an old sheet. I try a third door. Brightly coloured fish spin slowly above a white cot. Within it, swaddled tightly, a baby is expressing its unhappiness at creation.

Mrs Gallagher pushes past me, scooping up the boy. 'Get out of my house!'

'Is he yours, Mrs Gallagher?'

'Yes.'

'Did you give birth to him?'

'Get out! Get out! I'll call the police.'

'I *am* the police.'

Wordlessly, she shakes her head from side to side. The baby has gone quiet. Molly is tugging at her skirt.

Suddenly, her shoulders sag and she seems to deflate in front of me, folding from the knees and then the waist. Still cradling the baby, refusing to let go, she lands in my arms and I manoeuvre her to a chair.

'We adopted him,' she whispers. 'He's *ours*.'

'He was never available for adoption. You know that.'

Mrs Gallagher shakes her head. I look around the room. Where is she? The girl. My heart skips between beats. Slow, then fast.

'There was a baby girl. A twin.'

She looks towards the cot. 'He's the only one.'

Worst-case scenarios haunt me now. The baby girl was so small. She struggled to breathe. Please God, let her be safe!

Mrs Gallagher has found a tissue in the sleeve of her cardigan. She blows her nose and sniffles. 'We were told he wasn't wanted. I swear I didn't know – not about the missing twins. It wasn't until I saw the TV news. Then I began to wonder . . .'

'Who gave him to you?'

'A man brought him.'

'What did he look like?'

'Mid-fifties, short hair – he had an Irish accent.'

'When?'

'The Sunday before last.' She wipes her eyes. 'It came as a shock. We weren't expecting him for another fortnight.'

'Who arranged the adoption?'

'Mr Shawcroft said a teenage girl was pregnant with twins but couldn't afford to look after both of them. She wanted to put one of them up for adoption. We could jump the queue for fifty thousand pounds.'

'You knew it was against the law.'

'Mr Shawcroft said that twins couldn't legally be split. We had to do everything in secret.'

'You pretended to be pregnant.'

461

'There wasn't time.'

I look at Molly who is playing with a box of shells, arranging them in patterns.

'Is Molly . . . ?' I don't finish the question.

'She's mine,' she says fiercely. 'I couldn't have any more. There were complications. Medical problems. They told us we were too old to adopt. My husband is fifty-five, you see.' She wipes her eyes. 'I should phone him.'

I hear my name being called from downstairs. 'New Boy' must have witnessed the doorstep confrontation. He couldn't stay put.

'Up here.'

'Are you OK?'

'Yeah.'

Dave appears at the door, taking in the scene. Mrs Gallagher. Molly. The baby.

'It's one of the twins,' I say.

'One?'

'The boy.'

He peers into the cot. 'Are you sure?'

I follow his gaze. It's amazing how much a newborn can change in under ten days, but I'm sure.

'What about the girl?' he asks.

'She's not here.'

Shawcroft made *two* phone calls from the golf club. The second was to the Finsbury Park address of a Mrs Y. Moncrieffe, which doesn't cross-reference with any of the names from the New Life Adoption Centre files.

I can't leave. I have to stay and talk to Forbes (and no doubt peel him off the ceiling).

'Can you check out the other address?'

Dave weighs up the implications and ramifications. He's not worried about himself. I'm the one facing a disciplinary hearing. He kisses my cheek.

'You make it hard sometimes – you know that?'

'I know.'

11

DI Forbes storms through the house, his face hardened into a mask of fury and cold hatred. Ordering me into the rear garden, he ignores the muddy lawn and paces back and forth.

'You had no right!' he yells. 'It was an illegal search.'

'I had reason to believe—'

'What reason?'

'I was following a lead.'

'Which you should have told *me* about. This is *my* fucking investigation!'

His rectangular glasses bobble on his nose. I wonder if it annoys him.

'In my professional judgement I made a necessary choice, sir.'

'You don't even *know* if it's one of the twins. There are no birth records or adoption papers.'

'Mrs Gallagher has confirmed that she is not the biological mother. The baby was delivered to her by a man matching Brendan Pearl's description.'

'You should have waited.'

'With all due respect, sir, you were taking too long. Shawcroft is free. He's shredding files, covering his tracks. You don't *want* to prosecute him.'

I think Forbes might explode. His voice carries across the neighbourhood gardens and mud sucks at his shoes.

'I should have reported you to the PCA when you went to Amsterdam. You have harassed witnesses, abused your authority and disobeyed the orders of a senior officer. You have failed at almost every opportunity to conduct yourself in a professional manner . . .'

His foot lifts and his shoe remains behind. A sock squelches into the mud up to his ankle. We both pretend it hasn't happened.

'You're suspended from duty. Do you understand me? I'm going to personally ensure that your career is over.'

Social Services have been summoned – a big woman with a backside so large that she appears to be wearing a bustle. Mr and Mrs Gallagher are talking to her in the sitting room. They look almost relieved that it's over. The past few days must have been unbearable, wondering and waiting for a knock on the door. Being frightened of falling in love with a child that might never be truly theirs.

Molly is in her bedroom, showing a policewoman how she paints flowers and rests them on the radiator to dry. The baby is sleeping. They called him Jasper. He has a name now.

Forbes has peeled off his sock and thrown it into the rubbish bin. Sitting on the back step, he uses a screwdriver to scrape mud from his shoes.

'How did you know?' he asks once he's calmed down.

I explain about the phone calls from the golf club and cross-checking the numbers with the adoption files, looking for a match.

'That's how I found the Gallaghers.'

'Did he make any other calls?'

'One.'

Forbes waits. 'Have I got to *arrest* you to get any co-operation?'

Any remaining vestiges of comradeship have gone. We're no longer on the same team.

'I had an interesting conversation with a lawyer this morning,' he says. 'He was representing Barnaby Elliot and he alleged that you had a conflict of interest concerning this case.'

'There's no conflict, sir.'

'Mr Elliot is contesting his late daughter's will.'

'He has no legal claim over the twins.'

'And neither do you!'

'I know that, sir,' I whisper.

'If Samira Khan decides that she doesn't want the babies, they will be taken into care and placed with foster parents.'

'I know. I'm not doing this for me.'

'Are you sure of that?'

It's an accusation, not a question. My motives are under fire again. Perhaps I'm deluding myself. I can't afford to believe that. I won't.

My mobile phone is vibrating in my pocket. I flip it open.

'I might have found her,' says Dave. 'But there's a problem.'

12

The Neonatal Intensive Care Unit (NICU) at Queen Charlotte's Hospital is on the third floor above the delivery suites and maternity ward. Amid low lights, soft footsteps and the hum of machines there are fifteen high-domed incubators.

The unit manager is two paces ahead of me and Dave two paces behind. Our hands are washed with disinfectant and mobile phones have been turned off.

Passing the nearest crib, I look down. It appears to be empty except for a pink blanket and a teddy bear sitting in the corner. Then I notice an arm, no thicker than a fountain pen, emerge from beneath the blanket. Fingers curl and uncurl. Eyes remain shut. Tubes are squashed into a tiny nose, pushing rapid puffs of air into immature lungs.

The manager pauses and waits. Perhaps people do that

a lot – stop, stare and pray. It's only then that I notice the faces on the far side of the crib, distorted by the glass.

I look around. There are other parents sitting in the semi-darkness, watching and waiting; talking in whispers. I wonder what they say to each other. Do they look at other cribs and wonder if that baby is stronger or sicker or more premature? Not all of the newborns can possibly survive. Do their parents secretly pray, 'Save mine! Save mine!'

We have reached the far end of the ICU. Chairs beside the crib are empty. A nurse sits on a high stool at a control screen, monitoring the machines that monitor a child.

At the centre of a plain white sheet is a baby girl, wearing just a nappy. She is smaller than I remember, yet compared to some of the premature babies in the ICU she is twice their size. Small pads are stuck to her chest, picking up her heartbeat and her breathing.

'Claudia was brought in last night,' explains the ward manager. 'She has a serious lung infection. We're giving her antibiotics and feeding her intravenously. The device on her leg is a blood-gas monitor. It shines light through her skin to see how much oxygen is in her blood.'

'Is she going to be all right?'

The manager takes a moment to choose her words. The delay is enough to terrify me. 'She's stable. The next twenty-four hours are very important.'

'You called her Claudia.'

'That's the name we were given.'

'Who gave it to you?'

'The woman who came in with her in the ambulance.'

'I need to see the admission form.'

'Of course. If you come to the office I'll print you a copy.'

Dave is staring through the glass. I can almost see his lips moving, breathing as the baby breathes. Claudia has captured his attention, even though her eyes are fused shut by sleep.

'Do you mind if I stay for a while?' he asks, directing the question as much to me as to the ward manager. Every other patient in the unit has someone sitting alongside them. Claudia is alone. It doesn't seem right to him.

Retracing our steps, I follow the manager to her office.

'I called Social Services this morning,' she says. 'I didn't expect the police.'

'What made you call?'

'I wasn't happy with some of the answers we were getting. Claudia arrived just after midnight. At first the woman said she was the baby's nanny. She gave the mother's name as Cate Beaumont. Then she changed her story and said that Claudia had been adopted, but she couldn't give me any details of the adoption agency.'

She hands me the admission form. Claudia's date of birth is listed as Sunday, 29 October. The mother's name is written down as Cate Elizabeth Beaumont. The address is Cate's fire-damaged house.

Why give Cate's name? How did she even know about her?

'Where is this woman now?'

'One of our consultants wanted to talk to her. I guess she panicked.'

'She ran?'

'She made a phone call. Then she walked out.'

470

'What time was that?'

'About six a.m.'

'Do you know who she called?'

'No, but she used my phone.'

The manager points to her desk. The phone console is a command unit, with a memory of the most recently dialled numbers. A small LCD screen displays the call register. The ward manager identifies the number and I hit the redial button.

A woman answers.

'Hello?'

'This is Queen Charlotte's Hospital,' I say. 'Someone called your home from this number early this morning.'

She doesn't answer but in the silence I recognise a sound. I've heard it before – the squeak of wheels on parquetry floor.

I don't have Ruiz's photographic memory or his mother's gift for telling fortunes. I don't even know if I have a particular methodology. I put facts together randomly, sometimes leaping ahead or trying things out for size. It's not very efficient and it can't be taught, but it works for me.

The woman speaks again. Nervously. 'You must have the wrong number.'

It's an officious voice, precise, not quite public school. I have heard it often enough, albeit a decade ago, berating her husband for coming home late smelling of shampoo and shower gel.

The line has gone dead. Ruth Elliot has hung up. Simultaneously, there is a knock on the door. A nurse smiles apologetically and whispers something to the ward manager, who looks at me.

'You asked about the woman who brought in Claudia. She didn't run away. She's downstairs in the cafeteria.'

A pressure pad opens the doors automatically. The cafeteria is small and bright with white-flecked tables to hide the crumbs. Trays are stacked near the doors. Steam rises from the warming pans.

A handful of nurses are picking up sandwiches and cups of tea – healthy options in a menu where everything else comes with chips.

Yvonne is squeezed into a booth, with her head resting on her forearms. For a moment I think she might be asleep, but her head lifts and she blinks at me wetly. A low moan escapes her and she lowers her head. The pale brown of her scalp is visible where her grey hair has started to thin.

'What happened?'

'I did a foolish, foolish thing, cookie,' she says, talking into the crook of her arm. 'I thought I could make her better, but she kept getting sicker and sicker.'

A shuddering breath vibrates through her frame. 'I should have taken her to a doctor but Mr and Mrs Elliot said that nobody could ever know about Cate's baby. They said people wanted to take Claudia away and give her to someone she don't belong to. I don't know why people would do something like that. Mr and Mrs Elliot didn't explain it so good, not sufficient for me to understand, you know.'

She draws back, hoping that I might comprehend. Her eyes are wet and crumbs have stuck to her cheek.

'I knew Cate weren't having no baby,' she explains. 'She didn't have no baby inside her. I know when a woman is with child. I can see it in her eyes and on her skin. I can smell it. Sometimes I can even tell when a woman's having another man's baby, on account of the skin around her eyes, which is darker 'cos she's frightened her husband might find out.

'I tried to say something to Mrs Elliot but she called me crazy and laughed. She must have told young Cate 'cos she avoided me after that. She wouldn't come to the house if I was working.'

Details shiver and shift, finding their places. Events are no longer figments or mysteries, no longer part of my imagining. Barnaby *knew* I was in Amsterdam. And even before I mentioned Samira he *knew* she was having twins. He read Cate's e-mails and began covering her tracks.

At first he probably intended to protect his precious reputation. Later he and his wife came up with another plan. They would finish what Cate started. Barnaby contacted Shawcroft with a message: 'Cate and Felix are dead but the deal isn't.'

Why would Shawcroft agree? He had to. Barnaby had the e-mails. He could go to the police and expose the illegal adoptions and baby-broking. Blackmail is an ugly word. So is kidnapping.

At the funeral Barnaby told me he was going to fight for the twins. 'I want *both* of them,' he said. I didn't realise what he meant. He already had one – Claudia. He wanted the boy. And his tirade at the lawyer's office and the scene at my house weren't just for show. He was frightened that he might be denied, if not by Samira then by me.

The Elliots swore Yvonne to secrecy. They charged her with looking after Claudia and hopefully her brother if they could unite the twins. If the scandal unravelled and Shawcroft was exposed they could play the grieving parents, trying to protect their daughter's precious legacy, their grand-children.

Yvonne accepted the heaviest burden. She couldn't risk taking Claudia to a doctor. She tried her own remedies: running hot taps, filling the bathroom with steam, trying to help her breathe. She dosed her with droplets of para-cetamol, rubbed her with warm flannels, lay awake beside her through the night, listening to her lungs fill with fluid.

Barnaby came to see the baby, his thumbs hitched in his belt and his feet splayed. He peered over the cot with a fixed smile, looking vaguely disappointed. Perhaps he wanted the boy – the healthy twin.

Meanwhile, Claudia grew sicker and Yvonne more desperate.

'I couldn't take it any more,' she whispers, lifting her gaze to the ceiling. 'She was dying. Every time she coughed her body shook until she didn't have the strength to cough. That's when I called the ambulance.'

She blinks at me. 'She's going to die, isn't she?'

'We don't know that.'

'It's going to be my fault. Arrest me. Lock me up. I deserve it.'

I want to stop her talking about death. 'Who chose the name?'

'It's Mrs Elliot's name.'

'Her first name is Ruth.'

'Her middle name. I know you don't have much time for Mrs Elliot but she's harder on herself than she is on anyone else.'

What I feel most is resentment. Maybe that's part of the process of grieving. Cate doesn't feel as though she's gone. I keep thinking that she's just walked off in the middle of things and will come back presently and sort this mess out.

I have spent weeks delving into her life, investigating her movements and motives, and I still don't understand how she could have risked so much and endangered so many. I keep entertaining the hope that I'll stumble upon the answer in some cache of her papers or a dusty bundle of letters. But I know it's not going to happen. One half of the truth is lying upstairs, pinned like an insect to a glass display case. The other half is being looked after by Social Services.

It sounds preposterous but I'm still trying to justify Cate's actions, trying to conjure up a friendship from the afterlife. She was an inept thief, a childless wife and a foolish dreamer. I don't want to think about her any more. She has spoiled her own memory.

'The police are going to need a statement,' I say.

Yvonne nods, wiping her cheeks.

She doesn't stand as I leave. And although her face is turned to the window, I know she's watching me.

'New Boy' Dave is still beside Claudia in the NICU, sitting forward on a chair, peering through the glass. We sit together. He takes my hand. I don't know for how long. The clock on the wall doesn't seem to change. Not even for a second. Perhaps that's what happens in a place like this: time slows down. Every second is made to count.

You are a very lucky little girl, Claudia. Do you know why? You have *two* mothers. One of them you'll never meet but that's OK, I'll tell you about her. She made some mistakes but I'm sure you won't judge her too harshly. Your other mother is also very special. Young. Beautiful. Sad.

Sometimes life can turn on the length of an eyelash, even one as small as yours.

The ward manager touches my shoulder. A police officer wants to talk to me on the phone.

Forbes sounds far away. 'The Gallaghers have given a statement. I'm on my way to arrest Julian Shawcroft.'

'That's good. I found the girl. She's very sick.'

He doesn't rant this time. 'Who should we be talking to?'

'Barnaby Elliot and his wife, along with their house-keeper, Yvonne Moncrieffe.'

Behind me a door opens and I hear the sound of an electronic alarm. Through an observation window I notice curtains being drawn around Claudia's crib.

The phone is no longer in my hand. Like everyone else I seem to be moving. I push through the curtains. Someone tries to shepherd me away.

'What's wrong? What are they doing?'

A doctor is issuing instructions. A hand covers Claudia's face, holding a mask. A bag is squeezed and squeezed again. The mask is lifted briefly and a tube is slipped into her nose before being slowly fed into her lungs. White tape crosses her cheeks.

Dave has hold of my arm, trying to pull me away.

'What's happening?'

'We have to wait outside.'

'They're hurting her.'

'Let them do their job.'

This is my fault. My mistake. If I had been stronger, fitter, faster, I would have saved Claudia from Pearl. She would have gone straight to hospital instead of being smuggled off

476

the ferry. She would never have gone to Yvonne or caught a lung infection.

Thoughts like this plague me as I count down the minutes – fifteen of them, stretched and deformed by my imagination. The door swings open. A young doctor emerges.

'What happened?'

'The blood-gas monitor triggered the alarm. Her oxygen levels had fallen too low. She's too weak to breathe on her own so we've put her on a ventilator. We'll help her breathe for a while and see how strong she is tomorrow.'

The sense of relief saps what energy I have left and I feel suddenly dizzy. My eyes are sticky and I can't get rid of the coppery taste in my mouth. I still haven't told Samira and already my heart has been shredded.

13

Sometimes London is a parody of itself. Today is like that. The sky is fat and heavy and the wind is cold, although not cold enough to snow. Ladbrokes is offering 3–1 on a white Christmas in London. All it takes is a single snowflake to fall on the rooftop of the Met Office.

The bail hearing is today. I'm wearing my court clothes: a red pencil skirt, cream blouse and a short jacket that is cut well enough to have an expensive label but has no label at all.

Shawcroft has been charged with people trafficking, forced pregnancy and offences under the Child Protection Act. The penalty for trafficking alone is up to fourteen years. More charges are pending, as well as possible extradition to the Netherlands.

Samira is sitting on the bed, watching me apply my make-up. An overcoat lies across her lap. She has been dressed for hours, after waking early and praying. She won't have to give evidence until the trial, which could be a year away, but she wants to come along for today's hearing.

'Shawcroft is still only a suspect,' I say. 'Under our legal system a suspect is innocent until *proven* guilty.'

'But we know he *is* guilty.'

'Yes, but a jury has to decide that after hearing all the evidence.'

'What is bail?'

'A judge will sometimes let a defendant out of prison just until the trial if he or she promises not to run away or approach any of the witnesses. As a way of guaranteeing this, the judge will ask for a large amount of money, which the defendant won't get back if he breaks the law or doesn't show up for the trial.'

She looks astonished. 'He will pay the judge money?'

'The money is like a security deposit.'

'A bribe.'

'No, not a bribe.'

'So you are saying Brother could pay money and get out of jail?'

'Well, yes, but it's not what you think.'

The conversation keeps going round in circles. I'm not explaining it very well.

'I'm sure it won't happen,' I reassure her. 'He won't be able to hurt anyone again.'

It has been three weeks since Claudia left hospital. I still worry about her – she seems so small compared to her brother – but the infection has gone and she's putting on weight.

The twins have become tabloid celebrities, Baby X and

479

Baby Y, without first names or surnames. The judge who's deciding custody has ordered DNA tests on the twins and medical reports from Amsterdam. Samira will have to prove that she is their mother and then decide what she wants to do.

Despite being under investigation, Barnaby has maintained his campaign for custody, hiring and sacking lawyers on a weekly basis. During the first custody hearing, Judge Freyne threatened to jail him for contempt for continually interjecting and making accusations of bias.

I have had my own hearing to deal with – a disciplinary tribunal in front of three senior officers. I tendered my resignation on the first day. The chairman refused to accept it.

'I thought I was making it easier for them,' I told Ruiz.

'They can't sack you and they don't want to let you go,' he explained. 'Imagine the headlines.'

'So what *do* they want?'

'To lock you away in an office somewhere – where you can't cause any trouble.'

Samira adjusts her breast pads and buttons her blouse. Four times a day she expresses milk for the twins, which is couriered to the foster family. She gets to see them every afternoon for three hours under supervision. I have watched her carefully, looking for some sign that she is drawing closer to them. She feeds, bathes and nurses them, giving the impression that she is far more accomplished and comfortable with motherhood than I could ever imagine myself being. At the same time her movements are almost mechanical, as though she is doing what's expected of her rather than what she wants.

She has developed a strange affectation around the twins.

Whether expressing milk, changing nappies or dressing them, she uses only her right hand. When she picks one of them up, she slides the hand between their legs, along their spine and scoops them up in a single motion, supporting the head with the palm of her hand. And when she feeds them, she tucks a bottle under her chin or lays the baby along her thighs.

I thought for a while that it might be a Muslim thing, like only eating with the right hand. When I asked her, she raised her eyes dismissively. 'One hand is enough to sin. One hand is enough to save.'

'What does that mean?'

'What it says.'

Hari is downstairs. 'Are you sure you don't want me to come with you?'

'I'm sure.'

'I could hold up an umbrella.'

'It's not raining.'

'They do it for the film stars who don't want to be photographed – hold up umbrellas. Their bodyguards do it.'

'You're not a bodyguard.'

He's a lovesick puppy. University has broken up for Christmas and he's supposed to be helping his brothers at the garage but he keeps finding excuses to spend time with Samira. She'll even be alone with him, but only in the garden shed when they're working on some pyrotechnic project. The fireworks on Guy Fawkes night were supposed to have been a once-off but Hari has kept that particular fuse burning – for obvious reasons.

'New Boy' Dave is waiting outside for us.

'You're not wearing black?'

'Strange, isn't it?'

'You look good in red.'

I whisper, 'You should see my underwear.'

Samira pulls on her overcoat, which has toggles instead of buttons. It used to belong to Hari and the cuffs have to be folded twice because the sleeves are so long. Her hands find the pockets and hibernate there.

The day is growing brighter, climbing towards noon. Dave negotiates the traffic and parks a block away from Southwark Crown Court, ready to run the gauntlet. Ahead of us, on the pavement, TV cameras and photographers are waiting.

The charges against Julian Shawcroft are merely a sideshow to the main event – the custody battle for the twins – which has everything the tabloids crave: sex, a beautiful 'virgin' and stolen babies.

Flashguns fire around us. Samira lowers her head and keeps her hands in her pockets. Dave pushes a path through the scrum, not afraid to drop his shoulder into someone who won't move out of the way. These are tactics from the rugby field, not a sailing school.

Southwark Crown Court is a soulless modern precinct with less charm than the Old Bailey. We pass through the metal-detectors and make our way upstairs. I recognise some of the people holding meetings in the corridors, discussing last-minute tactics with counsel. Dr Sohan Banerjee has hired his own QC in expectation of being charged. He and Shawcroft still haven't turned on each other but the finger-pointing is only a matter of time, according to Forbes.

Shawcroft's barrister is a woman, five-ten in two-inch dagger heels, with white-blonde hair and drop pearl earrings that swing back and forth as she talks.

The prosecutor, Francis Hague QC, is older and greyer, with glasses perched on top of his head. He is talking to Forbes, making notes on a long pad. DS Softell has also turned up, perhaps hoping for some clue in the search for Brendan Pearl, who seems to have vanished completely. I wonder how many different identities he's stolen.

Samira is nervous. She knows that people are looking at her, court staff and reporters. I have tried to reassure her that the publicity will stop once the twins are home. Nobody will be allowed to identify them.

We take a seat in the public gallery at the rear of the courtroom with Samira in between us. She shrinks inside her overcoat, keeping her hands in the pockets. I spy Donavon slipping into the row behind us. His eyes scan the courtroom and rest on mine for a moment before moving on.

Soon the press box is full and there are no seats in the public gallery. The court clerk, an Asian woman of indeterminate age, enters and takes a seat, tapping at a keyboard.

Feet shuffle and everyone stands for the judge, who is surprisingly young and quite handsome in a stuffy sort of way. Within minutes, Shawcroft emerges via a stairway leading directly into the dock. Dressed in a neat suit, speckled tie and polished shoes, he turns and smiles at the gallery, soaking up the atmosphere as though this were a performance being laid on for his benefit.

'You wish to make an application for bail?' asks the judge.

Shawcroft's QC, Margaret Curillo, is already on her feet,

introducing herself in plummy obsequious tones. Francis Hague QC plants his hands on the table and raises his buttocks several inches from his chair, mumbling an introduction. Perhaps he feels that everyone knows him already – or at least should do.

The door of the court opens quietly and a man enters. Tall and thin, with an effeminate air, he nods distractedly at the Bench and barely raises his polished shoes from the carpet as he glides towards the bar table. Bending, he whispers something to Hague, who cocks his head.

Mrs Curillo has begun her submission, outlining the many 'outstanding achievements' of her client in a 'lifetime of service to the community'.

The prosecutor rises fully to his feet this time.

'Your Honour, I must apologise for interrupting my learned friend but I wish to request a short adjournment.'

'We've only just started.'

'I need to seek further instructions, your honour. Apparently, the Director of Public Prosecutions is reviewing details of the case.'

'With what aim?'

'I'm not in a position to say at this point.'

'How long do you require?'

'If it pleases, your honour, perhaps we could re-list this matter for three o'clock this afternoon.'

The judge stands abruptly, causing a chain reaction in the courtroom. Shawcroft is already being led back downstairs. I look at Dave, who shrugs. Samira is watching us, waiting for an explanation. Outside, in the corridor, I look for Forbes, who seems to have disappeared, along with Softell. What on earth is happening?

For the next two hours we wait. Cases are called for different courts. Lawyers have meetings. People come and go. Samira is sitting with her shoulders hunched, still wearing her overcoat.

'Do you believe in Heaven?' she asks.

It is such an unexpected question that I feel my mouth fall open. Consciously, I close it again. 'Why do you ask?'

'Do you think Hasan and Zala are in Heaven?'

'I don't know.'

'My father believed we should live our lives over and over, getting better each time. Only when we're completely happy should we get into Heaven.'

'I don't know whether I'd like to live the same life over and over.'

'Why?'

'It would diminish the consequences. I already put things off until another day. Imagine putting them off until another life.'

Samira wraps her arms around herself. 'Afghanistan is leaving me.'

'What do you mean?'

'I am forgetting things. I cannot remember what sort of flowers I planted on my father's grave. I once pressed the same flowers between the pages of his Koran and made him very angry. He said I was dishonouring Allah. I said I was praising Allah with flowers. He laughed at that. My father could never stay angry with me.'

We have afternoon tea in the cafeteria, avoiding the reporters whose ranks are starting to thin. Francis Hague and Shawcroft's barrister still haven't surfaced and neither has Forbes. Perhaps they've gone Christmas shopping?

Shortly before three, a Crown solicitor finds us. Counsel wants to talk to Samira. I should come too.

'I'll wait for you here,' says Dave.

We climb a flight of stairs and are shown through a door marked 'Court Staff Only'. A long corridor is flanked by offices. A lone potted palm sits at one end alongside a rather annoyed-looking woman waiting on a chair. Her black-stockinged legs are like burned matchsticks sticking out from beneath a fur coat.

The solicitor knocks gently on a door. It opens. The first person I see is Spijker, who looks depressingly sombre even by his standards. He takes my hand, kissing my cheeks three times, before bowing slightly to Samira.

Shawcroft's barrister is at the far end of the table, sitting opposite Francis Hague. Beside them is another man, who seems pressed for time. It could be his wife waiting outside, expecting to be somewhere else.

'My name is Adam Greenburg QC,' he says, standing and shaking Samira's hand. 'I am the Deputy Director of Public Prosecutions at the Crown Prosecution Service.'

He apologises for the stuffiness of the room and almost makes a running gag of his Jewishness, dabbing his forehead with a handkerchief.

'Let me explain my job to you, Miss Khan. When someone is arrested for a criminal offence, they don't automatically go to court and then to prison. The police first have to gather evidence and the job of the Crown Prosecution Service is to examine that evidence and to make sure that the right person is prosecuted for the right offence and that all relevant facts are given to the court. Do you understand?'

Samira looks at me and back to Greenburg. An elephant is sitting on my chest.

The only person who hasn't introduced himself is the man who entered the courtroom and interrupted the bail hearing. Standing by the window in a Savile Row suit, he has a raptor's profile and oddly inexpressive eyes, yet something about his attitude suggests that he knows a secret about everyone in the room.

Mr Greenburg continues: 'There are two stages in the decision to prosecute. The first stage is the evidential test. Crown Prosecutors must be satisfied there is enough evidence to provide a realistic prospect of conviction against each defendant on each charge.

'The second stage is the public-interest test. We must be satisfied there is a public interest to be served in prosecuting. The CPS will only start or continue a prosecution when a case has passed both these tests, no matter how important or serious it may be.'

Mr Greenburg is about to cut to the chase. Spijker won't look at me. Everyone's eyes are fixed on the table.

'The CPS has decided not to proceed with the prosecution of Mr Shawcroft because it does not pass the public interest test and because he has agreed to cooperate fully with the police and has given certain assurances about his future conduct.'

For a moment the shock takes my breath away and I can't respond. I look at Spijker, hoping for support. He stares at his hands.

'A case such as this raises serious moral and ethical issues,' explains Greenburg. 'Fourteen infants born as a result of illegal surrogacy have been identified. These children are now living with their biological parents in stable loving families.

'If we prosecute Mr Shawcroft these families will be torn apart. Parents will be charged as co-conspirators and their children will be taken into care, perhaps permanently. In prosecuting one individual, we risk destroying the lives of many, many more.

'The Dutch authorities face a similar dilemma involving six children from surrogate mothers. The German authorities have identified four births and the French could have as many as thirteen.

'I am as shocked and appalled by this evil trade as anyone else, but we have to make decisions here today that will decide what legacy remains afterwards.'

I find my voice. 'You don't have to charge the couples.'

'If we choose to proceed, Mr Shawcroft's counsel has indicated that she will subpoena all the couples involved who are – legally and ethically – raising children who belong to someone else.

'That is the situation we face. And the question we have to answer is this: do we draw a line beneath this, or do we proceed and upset the lives of innocent children?'

Samira sits passively in her overcoat. She hasn't stirred. Everything is done with such politeness and decorum that there is a sense of unreality about it all.

'He murdered innocent people.' My voice sounds hollow.

Mrs Curillo protests. 'My client denies all involvement in any such crimes and has not been charged in relation to any such event.'

'What about Cate and Felix Beaumont? What about Hasan Khan and Zala?'

Greenburg raises his hand, wanting me to be silent.

'In return for the dropping of all charges, Mr Shawcroft has provided police with the whereabouts of Brendan Pearl, an alleged people trafficker and wanted felon who is still on parole for offences committed in Northern Ireland. Mr Shawcroft has given a statement saying that he had no involvement in the deaths of the Beaumonts, alleging that Brendan Pearl acted alone. He also maintains that he played no part in the trafficking operation that led to the unfortunate deaths at Harwich International Port in October. A criminal gang took advantage of his naivety. He admits to commercial surrogacy, but says that Brendan Pearl and his associates took over the scheme and blackmailed him into participating.'

'This is ridiculous! He's the *architect*! He forced women to get pregnant! He took their babies!' I can't hear myself yelling, but no other voices are raised. Focusing my anger on Greenburg, I use words like 'justice' and 'fairness' while he counters with terms like 'common sense' and 'public interest'.

My language is disintegrating. I call Greenburg gutless and corrupt. Growing tired of my tantrum, he threatens to have me removed.

'Mr Pearl will be extradited to the Netherlands where he will face charges related to prostitution, people smuggling and murder,' he explains. 'In addition, Mr Shawcroft has agreed to relinquish all involvement in his charities including the New Life Adoption Centre – effective immediately. The Centre's licence to oversee adoptions has been revoked. The Charities Commission is drafting a press release. "Early retirement" seems to be the agreed terminology. The CPS will also make a statement saying that the charges are being dropped due to lack of evidence.'

There is a tone of finality to the sentence. Greenburg's job is done. Getting to his feet, he straightens his jacket. 'I promised my wife lunch. Now it will have to be dinner. Thank you for your cooperation.'

Samira shrugs me away, pushing past people, stumbling towards the lift.

'I'm sorry, Alisha,' says Spijker.

I can't answer him. He warned me about this when we were sitting in his office in Amsterdam and he talked about 'Pandora's Box'. Some lids are best kept closed, glued, nailed, screwed down and buried under six feet of earth.

'There is a logic to it, you know. There is no point punishing the guilty if we punish the innocent,' he says.

'Someone has to pay.'

'Someone will.'

I gaze across the paved courtyard where pigeons have coated the statues with mouse-grey excrement. The wind has sprung up again, driving needles of sleet against the glass.

I phone Forbes. Gusts of wind snag at his words.

'When did you know?'

'Midday.'

'Do you have Pearl?'

'Not my show any more.'

'Are you off the case?'

'I'm not a high enough grade of public servant to handle this one.'

Suddenly I picture the quiet man, standing by the

window, tugging at his cuff links. He was MI5. The security services want Pearl. Forbes has been told to take a back seat.

'Where are you now?'

'Armed-response teams have surrounded a boarding house in Southend-on-Sea.'

'Is Pearl inside?'

'Standing at the window, watching.'

'He's not going to run.'

'Too late for that.'

Another image comes to me. This one shows Brendan Pearl strolling out of the boarding house with a pistol tucked into the waistband of his trousers, ready to fight or to flee. Either way, he's not going back to prison.

Samira. What am I going to say to her? How can I possibly explain? She heard what Greenburg said. Her silence spoke volumes. It was as if she had known all along that it would come to this. Betrayal. Broken promises. Duplicity. She has been here before, visited this place. 'Some people are born to suffer' – that's what Lena Caspar said. 'It never stops for them, not for a second.'

I can see Samira now, smudged by the wet glass, standing by the statue, wearing Hari's overcoat. I want to teach her about the future. I want to show her the Christmas lights in Regent Street, tell her about the daffodils in spring, show her real things, true things, happiness.

A dark-coloured car has pulled up, waiting at the kerb. Photographers and cameramen spill out of the court building, walking backwards, jostling for space. Julian Shawcroft emerges, flanked by his barrister and Eddie Barrett. His silver hair shines in the TV lights.

He laughs with the reporters, relaxed, jovial, a master of the moment.

I spy Samira walking towards him in a zigzag pattern. Her hands are buried deep in the pockets of her coat.

I am moving now, swerving left and right past people in the corridor. I hammer the lift button and choose the stairs instead, swinging through each landing and out the double fire doors on the ground floor.

I'm on the wrong side of the building. Which way? Left.

Some track athletes are good at running bends. They lean into the corner, shifting their centre of balance rather than fighting the g-forces that want to fling them off. The trick is not to fight the force but to work with it by shortening your stride and hugging the inside line.

A Russian coach once told me that I was the best bend-runner he had ever seen. He even had a video of me that he used to train his young runners at the academy in Moscow.

Right now I don't have a cambered track and the paving stones are slick with rain, but I run this bend as if my life depends upon it. I tell myself to hold the turn, hold the turn and then explode out. Kick. Kick. Everything is burning, my legs and lungs, but I'm flying.

The two hundred metres was my trade-mark event. I don't have the lungs for middle-distance.

The media scrum is ahead of me. Samira stands on the outside, rocking from foot to foot like an anxious child. Finally, she burrows inside, pushing between shoulders. A reporter spies her and pulls back. Another follows. More people peel off, sensing a story.

Samira's overcoat is open. There is something in her

hand that catches the light – a glass elephant with tiny mirrors. *My* elephant.

Shawcroft is too busy talking to notice her. She embraces him from behind, wrapping her arms around his waist, pressing her left fist against his heart and her head against the middle of his back. He tries to shake her loose, but she won't let go. A wisp of smoke curls from her fingers.

Someone yells and people dive away. They're saying it's a bomb! How?

The sound of my scream disappears beneath the crack of an explosion that snaps at the air, making it shudder. Shawcroft spins slowly, until he faces me, looking puzzled. The hole in his chest is the size of a dinner plate. I can see right inside.

Samira falls in the opposite direction, with her knees splayed apart. Her face hits the ground first because her left arm can't break her fall. Her eyes are open. A hand reaches out to me. There are no fingers. There is no *hand*.

People are running and yelling, screaming like the damned; their faces peppered with shards of glass.

'She's a terrorist,' someone shouts. 'Be careful.'

'She's not a terrorist,' I reply.

'There could be more bombs.'

'There are *no* more bombs.'

Pieces of mirror and glass are embedded along Samira's arms, but her face and torso escaped the force of the blast, shielded behind Shawcroft.

I should have realised. I should have seen it coming. How long ago did she plan this? Weeks, maybe longer. She took my elephant from my bedside table. Hari unwittingly helped her by buying the model-rocket engines full of black powder.

The fuse must have been taped down her forearm, which is why she didn't take off her overcoat. The glass and mirrors of the elephant didn't trigger the metal detectors.

The frayed lining of her coat sleeve is still smouldering but there is surprisingly little blood. The exploding powder seems to have cauterised her flesh around a jagged section of bone. She turns her head. 'Is he dead?'

'Yes.'

Satisfied, she closes her eyes. Two paramedics gently take her from me, placing her on a stretcher. I try to stand but fall backwards. I want to keep falling.

I thought I knew everything about friendship and family: the happiness, simplicity and joy within them. But there is another side to devotion, a side which Samira understands. She is her father's daughter, after all.

One hand is enough to sin. One hand is enough to save.

Epilogue

I had a dream last night that I got married in a white dress, not a sari. My father came storming up the aisle, haranguing me, and the congregation burst into spontaneous applause, thinking it was some sort of Sikh floor show.

Samira was there, holding up Jasper, who kicked and giggled and waved his arms excitedly. Hari held Claudia above his head to watch. She was far more serious and looked ready to cry. My mother was shedding buckets, of course. She could cry for two countries.

I am having a lot of dreams like this lately. Perfect-life fantasies, full of ideal matches and soap-opera endings. See how wet I've become. I used to be a girl who didn't cry at sad endings or get mushy over babies. Nowadays I have to bite my lip to hold back the tears and I want to float through the ceiling, I love them so much.

Jasper is always happy and laughs for no apparent reason,

while Claudia watches the world with troubled eyes and sometimes, when you least expect it, she produces tears of abject sorrow and I know that she's crying for those who can't.

Their names have stayed. That happens sometimes: something is given a name and it just doesn't seem right to change it. I won't be changing mine when I get married, but other things are already different. It used to be *Me*; now it's *We* and *Us*.

Rolling over on my side, I run my fingers across the sheet until they touch Dave's chest. The duvet is wrapped around us and it feels safe. We're cocooned, shielded from the world.

He's letting his hair grow longer now. It suits his new lifestyle. I never thought I'd fall in love with a man who wears Aran sweaters and waterproof trousers. His hand is lying between us. There are calluses forming on his palms from working the sheets and raising sails.

There is a snuffled cry from the next room. After a pause, I hear it again.

'It's your turn,' I whisper, tickling Dave's ear.

'You're getting up anyway,' he mumbles.

'That makes no difference.'

'It's the girl.'

'How do you know?'

'She has a whiney cry.'

I jab him hard in the ribs. 'Girls do *not* whine. And since when has there been any demarcation?'

He rolls out of bed and looks for his boxer shorts.

'You just keep the bed warm.'

'Always.'

*   *   *

Although it was only three months ago, the events of those days have become a surreal blur. There was no custody battle. Barnaby Elliot withdrew gracelessly when faced with charges of withholding information from the police and being an accessory after the fact.

Judge Freyne found Samira to be the mother of the twins. However, the DNA test threw up another twist to the story. The twins were brother and sister and the eggs came from Cate, as expected, but they had been fertilised by some third party, someone other than Felix. More than a ripple went round the courtroom when *that* little piece of information became public.

How was it possible? Dr Banerjee had harvested twelve viable embryos and implanted ten of them in IVF procedures. Cate took the remaining pair to Amsterdam.

There could have been a mix-up, of course, and someone else's sperm may have contaminated the process. According to Dr Banerjee, the primary reason why Felix and Cate couldn't conceive was because her womb treated his sperm like cancerous cells and destroyed them. In another womb, with stronger sperm, who knows? But there was another issue: the recessive gene carried by Cate and Felix that caused a rare genetic disorder, a lethal form of dwarfism. Should she conceive, there was a twenty-five per cent chance that the foetus would be affected.

Cate would never have cheated on Felix in the bedroom or in her heart. But she desperately wanted a child and having waited for so long and taken such risks she couldn't afford to be disappointed again. Perhaps she found someone she trusted, someone Felix would never meet, someone who looked a lot like him, someone who *owed* her.

It is just a theory, of course. Nothing but speculation. It first occurred to me as I watched the twins sleeping and glanced at the dream catcher above their heads, letting my fingers brush the feathers and beads.

I doubt if Donavon had any idea what Cate planned. And, even if he is the father, he has kept his promise to her and never revealed the fact. It's better that way.

I slip out of bed, shivering as I pull on my track pants and a fleece-lined top. By the time I step outside the cottage, it is beginning to grow light over the Solent and the Isle of Wight. Taking Sea Road past The Smuggler's Inn, I turn left through the car park and arrive at a long shingle spit that reaches out into the Solent almost halfway to the island.

Wading birds lift off from the marshes as I pass and the beam from the lighthouse flashes every few seconds, growing fainter against the brightening sky. The sound of my shoes on the compacted shingle is reassuring as I cover the final mile to Hurst Castle, which guards the western approach to the Solent. Some days, when south-easters have whipped the sea into a foaming monster, I don't reach the castle. Great white-tipped rollers arc upwards and smash against the sea wall, exploding into a mist that blurs the air and turns it solid. I can barely walk against the wind, bent double, blinking away the salt.

The weather is kind today. There are skiffs on the water already and, to my left, a father and son are hunting for cockles in the shallows. The sailing school will reopen in May. The skiffs are ready and I've become a dab hand at repairing sails. (Those years of watching Mama at her sewing machine weren't entirely wasted.)

My life has changed so much in the past three months.

The twins don't let me sleep beyond six a.m. and some nights I bring them into bed, which all the experts say I shouldn't. They have pushed me around, robbed me of sleep, filled me up and made me laugh. I am besotted. Spellbound. My heart has doubled in size to make room for them.

As I near the coastal end of the spit, I notice a figure sitting on an upturned rowboat with his boots planted in the shingle and hands in his pockets. Beside him is a canvas fishing bag and a rod.

'I know you don't sleep, sir, but this is ridiculous.'

Ruiz raises his battered cap. 'You have to get up early to catch a fish, grasshopper.'

'So why aren't you fishing?'

'I've decided to give them a head start.'

He slings the bag over his shoulder and climbs the rocky slope, falling into step beside me.

'Have you ever actually caught a fish, sir?'

'You being cheeky?'

'You don't seem to use any bait.'

'Well, that means we start as equals. I don't believe in having an unfair advantage.'

We walk in silence, our breath steaming the air. Almost home, I stop opposite Milford Green and get a newspaper and muffins.

Samira is in the kitchen, wearing pyjamas and my old dressing gown with the owl stitched on the pocket. Jasper is nestled in the crook of her left arm, nuzzling her right breast. Claudia is in the bassinet by the stove, frowning slightly as if she disapproves of having to wait her turn.

'Good morning, Mr Ruiz.'

'Good morning, lass.' Ruiz takes off his cap and leans over the bassinet. Claudia gives him her most beatific smile.

Samira turns to me. 'How were they last night?'

'Angels.'

'You always say that. Even when they wake you five times.'

'Yes.'

She laughs. 'Thank you for letting me sleep.'

'What time is your exam?'

'Ten.'

Ruiz offers to drive her into Southampton where she's studying for her A levels at the City College. Her exams aren't until June and the big question is whether she'll sit them at Her Majesty's Pleasure or in a normal classroom with other students.

Her lawyers seem confident that they can argue a case of diminished responsibility or temporary insanity. Given what she's been through, nobody is very enthusiastic about sending her to prison, not even Mr Greenburg – who had to choke back his emotions when he told her that the CPS was pressing ahead with the murder charge.

'What about the public interest?' I demanded, acidly.

'The public saw it happen on the BBC, prime time. She killed a man. I have to let it go to a jury.'

Samira posted bail thanks to Ruiz and my parents. The DI has become like a grandfather to the twins, who seem enthralled by his craggy face and the low rumble of his voice. Perhaps it's his gypsy blood but he seems to understand what it's like to enter the world violently, clinging on to life.

My mother is the other one who is besotted. She phones

four times a day, wanting updates on how they're sleeping and feeding and growing.

I take Jasper from Samira and hold him over my shoulder, gently rubbing his back. She scoops up Claudia with her right hand and offers her a breast, which she nuzzles anxiously until her mouth finds the nipple.

Samira's missing hand doesn't even seem like a disability when you watch her with the twins, loving them completely; doing everyday chores like washing and feeding and changing nappies. She is a bright, pretty teenage mother of baby twins.

Samira doesn't talk about the future. She doesn't talk about the past. Today matters. The twins matter.

I don't know how long we're going to have them or what's going to happen next, but I've come to realise that we can never know something like that. There are no certainties in this life or in death. The end of one story is merely the beginning of the next.